One Wish

ROBYN CARR

One Wish

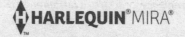

First Published in Great Britain 2016
By Harlequin Mira, an imprint of HarperCollins*Publishers*
1 London Bridge Street, London, SE1 9GF

© 2015 Robyn Carr

ISBN 978-1-848-45471-2

63-0716

Our policy is to use papers that are natural, renewable and recyclable products and made from wood grown in sustainable forests.The logging and manufacturing processes conform to the legal environmental regulations of the country of origin.

Printed and bound by
CPI group (UK) Ltd, Croydon, CR0 4YY

One Wish

One

Grace Dillon's flower shop was very quiet on the day after Christmas. She had no orders to fill, no deliveries to make, and she'd be very surprised if her shop phone rang at all. Most people were trying to recover from Christmas; many families were away for the holidays or had company to entertain.

Grace drove to North Bend to grab an early skate before the rink got busy. Figure skating classes were suspended over Christmas break and people, mostly kids who wanted to try out their new skates, would dominate the rink later in the day. Grace loved these secret early morning skates. She had a deal with Jake Galbraith, the rink owner. She could call him and if it was convenient, he'd let her skate for an hour or two while they were getting ready to open. He didn't want to charge her, but she paid him fifty dollars an hour anyway. It was a point of pride.

He smiled at her when she came in and told her to have a good skate.

She stretched and then stepped onto the deserted ice, closely following the Zamboni ice resurfacer that had just finished. She warmed up with forward and backward crossovers, backward half swizzle pumps, figure eights, scratch spins and axels. She noticed Jake was watching, leaning his forearms on the boards. She performed a forward spiral and a leaning tower spiral. She executed a perfect sit spin next. She circled the ice a few times, adding a jump here and there. She had been famous for her straddle split jump, touching her toes with her fingers. When she looked for Jake again, he had disappeared.

Suddenly, the music started, filling the rink with the strains of "Rhapsody in Blue." She glided into an arabesque, arms stretched, fingers pointed, wrists flexible. She saw that Jake had returned, was watching her every move. She went for a double axel and fell on her ass. She got up, laughing to herself. She glided around the rink a few times, tried the jump again and landed it, but it wasn't pretty. The music changed to another Gershwin tune. She'd practiced to this music as a little girl; it was familiar and comfortable. Her earliest memories of skating always filled her with nostalgia and comfort. That was before the competition got really fierce.

She'd been on the ice for an hour when the music segued into Alicia Keys's "Girl on Fire" and it lit her up. Her signature music. *She* was on fire! She skated like she was competing. When she was fifteen, stronger but lighter and more flexible, she could really catch the air. She noticed other people watching—a guy leaned on his broom and gazed at her, a couple of teenage girls who worked in the skate rental shop had stopped working to watch, the Zamboni driver leaned a shoulder against the rink glass, hands in his pockets. Two hours slid by effortlessly. She slowed and got off the ice when she heard the sounds of people arriving to skate.

"Beautiful," Jake said. "It's been a while since I've seen you."

"Holidays are busy at the shop," she said. She tried to get to the rink on Sunday mornings, but the past month had been frantic—wreaths, centerpieces, two weddings and increased day-to-day traffic in the shop.

"You should spend more time on the ice. I have a long list of people looking for a good coach."

She shook her head. "I don't think I'd be a good coach. I don't have time for one thing. And I'd never go back on the circuit, even with students. I left that world."

"I thought the day would come that you might be interested in going back, maybe not in competition for yourself, but coaching. I think on name alone you'd make a fortune."

"I left the name behind, too," she reminded him with a smile. "We have an agreement."

"I haven't said a word. People ask me, who is that girl, but I just say you're training and asked not to be identified. Some of them guess and would show up to watch you if they had any idea when you would be skating. The ice misses you. Watching you skate is like seeing music."

"Nice try. I don't train anymore. I spent as much time on my ass as on my blades. I look like crap."

"Your worst is better than a lot of bests I see. I've missed you. Maybe you'll have more time in the new year."

"We'll see."

She took off her skates and pulled on her Ugg boots. Sometimes she questioned her decision to leave it all behind, because being on the ice made her so happy. Then she'd remind herself that while a couple of hours felt great, the difficult routine of a competitive figure skater was grueling, exhausting. As a coach she'd never be able to push young girls the way she'd been pushed.

She pulled out a hundred dollars in cash for her two hours alone on the rink. Jake had told her he put the money in a special scholarship fund for young wannabe Olympians who couldn't otherwise afford lessons. She told him however he wanted to spend it was fine with her. As long as he didn't sell her out.

As she left the rink she reflected that her life in Thunder Point was so much more peaceful than it had been in competition and her freedom was hard-won. She had friends now, even if they didn't know who she had been before. At least no one thought of her as tragic or complicated or as one of the saddest yet most triumphant stories told on the competitive skating circuit. No one was threatened by her, hated her, feared or resented her. No one called her a rich bitch or a dirty liar.

Of course, the weight of her secrets sometimes wore on her. Jake Galbraith had recognized her at once. All she had to do was ask the cost of a private rink for a couple of hours and he knew immediately who she was. She hadn't confided in anyone in Thunder Point.

When she got into the van she saw that she had a message on her cell phone. She listened to it before leaving the parking lot. It was Mikhail, her old coach. He still kept tabs on her. They stayed in touch. Often, they left each other a series of brief messages because he could be anywhere in the world. "I am wishing you happy Christmas," the Russian said. "I think I am day late. If so, you will understand."

Grace waited until she was back in her tiny apartment above the flower shop before returning the call. "I thought you had forgotten all about me," she said to his voice mail. "It *was* a happy Christmas. I was a maid of honor for my friend Iris yesterday—that's how I spent the day. I've never been in a wedding before. It was small and intimate, a beautiful experience. And this morning I went skating. I fell three times." Then she mimicked his accent. "What can I say? I am clumsy oaf with no training." Then she laughed, wished him the best New Year ever and said goodbye.

Grace's beloved father and coach died rather suddenly when she was only fourteen and he was sixty. Her mother, once a competitive and professional figure skater, responded by hiring an even better coach, a very short Russian of huge reputation who could take Grace all the way. There was no time for grieving, they had work to do. Mikhail Petrov was a tough, brilliant coach and they were together for nine years. He had been very unhappy with her decision to leave competition and for a couple of years he pestered her to return to the sport. "Before you forget everything I taught you!"

Her mother, Winnie Dillon Banks, who had herself been a teenage skating wonder, was worse than devastated. She was furious. "If you quit now, after all I've invested in you, you are dead to me." After the 2010 Winter Games in Vancouver, Grace walked away from everything and everyone. All she'd ever wished for was to be like everyone else. To not be constantly judged every time she took a breath. She wanted to be normal.

In the afternoon, when Grace was just about to ruin her dinner with a big bowl of popcorn while looking through various online floral arrangements on her laptop, there was a light tapping at her back door. She pulled the curtain to peek out through the window in the door and was shocked to see Iris. She opened the door.

"Don't newlyweds lay around in bed for several days after the wedding? Doing it until their parts give out?" Grace asked, only half teasing.

"Maybe when one of the newlyweds isn't the town deputy," Iris said. "We did eat breakfast in bed and

Seth didn't go to the office until about one. I cleaned the house, thawed something for dinner and…" She paused. "I called Troy to tell him."

"You didn't tell him before, huh?" Grace asked.

Iris shook her head.

Troy Headly, high school history teacher and the fantasy of all the high school girls, had had a very big crush on Iris. They had dated for only a few months last spring when Iris told him theirs would have to be a friendship-only relationship. She was the high school guidance counselor and before getting involved with a teacher in the same school, she had to be powerfully sure. And she hadn't been. But Troy had pursued Iris right up until Seth was in the picture. Even then, it was pretty obvious he still had a serious thing for Iris and wouldn't mind if Seth fell off the face of the earth.

"How'd he take it?" Grace asked.

"Like a man," Iris said. "Is it too early for wine?"

"Certainly not!" Grace pulled a bottle of Napa Cellars sauvignon blanc from her little refrigerator and opened it. "Was it awful?"

"Nah, it was fine. Good, really. He was surprised we got married so soon, but then so was everyone. So were we, when you get down to it. He congratulated me and said he hoped I'd be very happy—all the right things. Then I asked him if he was going to be all right and he laughed, but he didn't sound amused. He said he was surprised to find himself disappointed an old girlfriend got married. It's hard for me to think of myself as his girlfriend—it was never that serious. Even Troy admits he's not looking for a wife! Not now. He likes the single life."

Grace poured the wine and put the bowl of popcorn between them. "A gourmet treat," she said. "Or maybe dinner. So, is it different? Being married?"

"Not yet," Iris said. "Ask me again when we merge bank accounts. We've been solitary, single adults for a long time. Right now we're each taking care of our own obligations until Seth either rents or sells his town house. There's plenty of closet space at my house, but we could have issues when his manly furniture looks for space among my decidedly female things."

"You're staying in your house," Grace said in relief.

"It's perfect for us. I like to ride my bike to work in good weather."

"I love your house," Grace said. "Aren't you ever going to have a honeymoon?"

"Eventually. We're looking for deals online right now. We're going to sneak away in a couple of months, hopefully somewhere warm and sunny, when Seth can get away from the town and I can escape my office at school. But what about you, Grace? Why aren't you seeing anyone?"

Grace burst out laughing. It wasn't the first time Iris had asked. "First of all, who? Second, when?"

"Don't you ever meet a groomsman at any of the weddings you do?"

"Never. They all come long after I'm gone and I'm not invited to the receptions. Besides, isn't that the kiss of death? Hooking up with someone in the wedding party at the reception? No thanks."

"We have to get you out more," Iris said.

"Right," Grace said doubtfully. "Maybe I could help you chaperone the prom and meet some very promising eighteen-year-old? Nah, I don't think so."

"We'll go clubbing or something."

"Clubbing?" Grace sputtered. "In Thunder Point?"

"Okay, we'll go up to North Bend. And graze."

"I'm sure Seth would appreciate that!"

"Well, I won't take any phone numbers or bring anyone home…"

"Iris," Grace said, lifting her wineglass. "Let it go. I'll handle my own love life. In my own time, in my own way."

"There's always Troy," Iris said, sipping.

"Nah, we're pals. There's no chemistry." *On his side.* "We had a beer together once, followed by grilled cheese and tomato soup. It was swell. Besides, I'm not interested in your sloppy seconds. I read, you know. Rebound boyfriends are not a good idea."

"You can't just work all the time," Iris said.

"No?" Grace asked. "I thought you could."

Growing up, everyone thought Grace was a spoiled rich kid, but she had been raised on hard, committed, constant work. If she took a day off she felt ashamed. Her program would suffer. But her work hadn't been the kind average people understood.

Her full name was Isabella Grace Dillon Banks. She'd given up most of her name and went by Grace

Dillon because Izzy Banks was very well-known in some circles. Probably not among her Thunder Point acquaintances, but for those who watched champion figure skating competitions around the world, Izzy Banks was known, both for her skating and for her involvement in dramas and scandals that rocked the skating world.

Grace's mother, Winnie Dillon Banks, was a wealthy heiress whose grandfather made money in tobacco. She was a well-known skater in her time, though never as successful as Grace in competitions. Winnie's best show as a competitive skater had been second place in Nationals. But she saw in her daughter her chance to win and became the ultimate stage mother.

Grace had a privileged, isolated childhood where skating was everything.

Grace was born to an ice-skating icon and her coach. Winnie Dillon began a love affair with her coach, Leon Banks, when she was twenty-two. Some cynical rivals and professional observers suggested she succumbed to marriage and motherhood when all signals pointed to her competing days being over.

Winnie and Leon had their daughter on skates before she was four years old. They pushed and trained her hard. In those early days, when skating was simply fun, when she yearned to be the best, Grace was happy. She begged to skate and hated her time off. She'd have been on the ice eight hours a day if her father had let her. She was coddled and loved and indulged. She had a few friends, other little girls who were training and taking lessons and part of a skating club, some of them Leon's other students.

Grace loved her parents very much and didn't quite understand until after her father's death that theirs had been a difficult marriage. Her father was much older than Winnie and more focused on his students than his wife. Her mother was a demanding diva and socialite; she dragged a reluctant Leon to charity events and parties. Her parents disagreed on almost everything, especially Grace's training and education. Grace never went to traditional school, public or private—she had tutors. Leon thought this might be a mistake, feared she wouldn't be a well-adjusted child.

At the age of twelve the level of competition turned serious. But Grace was winning everything in her age category and was quickly viewed as unbeatable. She trained on the ice several hours a day, took gymnastics, ballet and practiced yoga. The family moved from Atlanta to Chicago and finally settled in San Francisco, following the best opportunities for her training and education, as well as for Leon's coaching prospects. Her father was diagnosed with pancreatic cancer when Grace was fourteen. Winnie sought a tougher, stronger, more famous coach the moment Leon fell ill. It was almost as if she'd chosen Mikhail before he was needed. Then Leon passed away rather swiftly, within months of his diagnosis.

Winnie and Grace took a few days off, then it was back on the ice. "Your success meant everything to your father," Winnie kept saying. It was true that

Leon wanted the best for his daughter, but it was Winnie to whom winning was everything. No matter the personal cost. And skating became less for fun and more for life. Winnie blew a gasket whenever Grace didn't take first place.

Grace left the world of competitive skating when she was twenty-three, right after the Vancouver Games. She went to Portland to stay with a sweet older couple who had once worked for her mother. Ross and Mamie Jenkins had known Grace since birth. They'd been part of Winnie's staff, Ross a driver and Mamie in housekeeping. They had retired to open a flower shop a few years before Grace quit the circuit. When she needed them, they took her in.

She collapsed. She was exhausted and depressed and afraid of the future. Mamie pampered her and gave her time; it seemed as if she'd slept for a month. Then one evening Mamie spoke up. "If you lay around one more day, you won't be able to walk. You have to do something—it's your choice. Get a job, go to school, something."

Grace didn't want to be around people and she didn't believe she had any marketable skills. So she started helping in the flower shop, in the back, learning to make beautiful bouquets and arrangements. Portland was a funky, interesting, welcoming city— not too big, not too small, not uppity or flashy. Little by little, Grace came out of the back room to deal with customers, sometimes delivering flowers, even helping Mamie and Ross with weddings. No one made a fuss over her or asked her a lot of questions.

Every time a major skating competition was covered by the mainstream or sports networks, Grace was glued to the TV, watching every move. And invariably there'd be some short vignette about Izzy Banks, the girl who had it all and threw it all away. "Izzy Banks, the brat on the ice, the fiercest competitor in figure skating, obviously couldn't take the pressure," one sportscaster noted of her.

Brat. Boy, that stung.

Her mother would usually get in touch, proving that Winnie couldn't ignore the competitions any more than Grace could. She'd pressure Grace to return home, return to skating, and the few conversations they had would end in a fight and they wouldn't speak again for months.

A year before the 2014 Winter Games in Russia, when the dramatic story of her life might be publicly examined yet again, Grace went in search of a new place to settle and tackle life on her own. A little money had been set aside for her by her father and she found Pretty Petals, the shop Iris's mother had owned. She'd been in Thunder Point almost a year when the winter competition took place. When Grace couldn't watch it, she'd record it. There had been the usual newsy dish about the more stunning events of the life of Izzy Banks, but no one seemed to recognize Grace. There were, thankfully, more interesting sports scandals that year. And Thunder Point was more a football than figure skating town.

All she'd ever wanted was a life she could control. A life that didn't include backbreaking labor, cruel rivals, endless travel across too many time zones, the occasional crazed fan or terrible loneliness. She wanted to know what it felt like to have real friends, not a staff of coaches, therapists, a security detail and competitors. She'd never had a boyfriend.

She did, however, have more than one gold medal. She'd won every significant competition in the world.

It drizzled in the days following Christmas, typical Oregon Coast weather in winter. Grace's only part-time employee, a local married woman with a child in elementary school, came into the shop to resign. The woman's life had grown too busy and complex, she complained. Grace knew it was going to create a challenge, even though all the woman had done was manage the front of the store. Grace was going to be back to doing it all, just as she had when the shop was new. She'd had the doorbell installed so she could lock the front door and go upstairs. The doorbell would buzz in her loft. And she could always close the shop to make deliveries when necessary. She'd ask around for a delivery boy.

Business was typically down the week following a holiday and the days were much shorter so Grace closed the shop at four one afternoon and drove out to Cooper's for a beer. She wasn't surprised to see Troy was back from visiting his family in Morro Bay. She was also not surprised that there was no one around the bar. People didn't hang out on the beach in cold, wet weather like this. But she had to admit surprise at seeing a big pile of books and papers beside his laptop on the bar next to his cup of coffee. She jumped on a bar stool. "Welcome home. Did you have fun with the family?" she asked.

"More or less. My sister has three little undisciplined kids and I slept on her couch. It was brutal. What can I get you?"

"Beer?"

"Was that a question or order?" he asked.

"Beer, please." She glanced at the books. "Homework?"

"Lesson plans," he said, closing everything up, stacking it all and pushing it to one side. "We're caught up in a couple of my classes so we're going to have some fun. I'm going to offer them a chance for extra credit if they research the history of something that interests them—like a rock band or in-line skating or maybe a sport like kayaking. I'm writing up a few examples."

"That almost sounds fun, but not enough fun. Did you get in any skiing over the holiday?"

"Nope," he said, drawing her a draft. "We played some golf, but the weather wasn't great. I might make a drive up to Mount Hood before I get back to work, maybe for a day. If I had more time and money I'd check out Tahoe. So, you were the maid of honor."

"I was. Kind of short notice."

"I heard it wasn't exactly planned in advance…"

"That's how I heard it, too. Iris said they decided and just did it. They got a marriage license, called a judge Seth knew, told Seth's family and got it done.

I didn't even have time to order special flowers." She sipped a little of her beer. "How are you handling it?"

"Fine," he said.

"Good. That's good."

He leaned both hands on the bar. "I went out with my little brother and got roaring drunk. Then I bought a Jeep I can't really afford."

"Oh," she said. "Gosh, I hope you don't get your heart broken too often or you'll go broke."

"I'd wanted that Jeep anyway. And I deserved a good drunk."

"Is that what caused…" She reached out toward the remnants of what looked like a healing bruise on his forehead.

He ducked away from her fingers. "I forgot I was sleeping on the couch, fell off and hit the coffee table."

She couldn't help herself. She laughed.

"And my heart isn't broken," he insisted. "Just a little coronary bruise. Gimme a week or two and it'll be like nothing ever happened."

Bullshit, she thought. He looked completely miserable. "You're very resilient," she said. She sipped her beer.

"I guess we've all been there," he said.

"Where?"

"Heartbreak hotel."

"Hmm. Well, I don't think I have. I haven't had my heart broken. Not by a guy, at least."

Troy appeared to be momentarily frozen. "There's no polite way to ask this, but has your heart been broken by a *girl*?"

She giggled. There were times, and this was one of them, that it would feel so good to dump the story on someone, explain how a heart can be broken by ruthless competitors or the media. "No, Troy. I'm perfectly straight. I'm into guys, I just haven't been seriously involved. I guess it's not in my nature to be tied down to one guy."

"No boyfriend, then?"

"Are you fishing?" she asked. "I've had some terrific boyfriends, just nothing serious. No steadies, engagements or live-ins."

"Why haven't I ever met any of them?" he asked.

She shrugged. "I guess you weren't around at the same time one of them was. I have a date later tonight, as a matter of fact."

"Oh? What's he like?" Troy asked.

"He's kind of like a medieval knight, but has a gentle, sophisticated side. Big and brawny, very physical but disciplined. He's also clever. Wise."

"Fantastic," Troy said. "Where are you going?"

"We're staying in, actually. We might watch a movie."

Troy lifted an eyebrow. "If I popped over unannounced, would I meet him?"

"Very probably. He's a little possessive but I completely ignore that. Like I said, I'm not one to get serious. Let's talk about your girlfriends."

"I don't kiss and tell."

She straightened. "Humph. Yet you expect me to!"

"I think you were bragging and maybe stretching the truth. You're a little weird, Grace. The last time we hung out was Halloween and you were a witch, complete with missing teeth. And you put a hex on me."

She smiled, remembering. She'd told him she was going to shrink his thing. "How'd that work out?"

"Turns out you're not much of a witch. So when you say your heart was never broken…"

"Come on, I've had my share of disappointments like everyone else, just haven't had a romance end badly. We can moan about our various letdowns another time, when we're both drowning our sorrows and feeling sorry for ourselves. Let's not do that now, okay? I have a feeling if you get started…"

"Did Iris ask you to check on me?"

"Absolutely not. She said you were very grown-up and wished her every happiness. And I must say, buying a Jeep you can't afford is definitely mature." Then she grinned at him.

"It's a great Jeep. Maybe I'll take you off-road in it sometime. Besides, I only have one person to worry about so if I have trouble paying the bills, it's not like I'm taking milk out of the baby's mouth."

She leaned her head on her hand. "You're all about fun, aren't you, Troy?"

"I work two jobs, Grace. I like to think of myself as active."

"And your favorite activity is?"

"It's a toss-up between diving and white-water rafting or kayaking. One of the things that brought me to Oregon is the great river trips. I was torn between Colorado, Idaho and Oregon. Oregon had the job. In a town on the water."

"And you're a teacher for the time off?"

"And the high pay," he said, smiling.

"Iris says you're the most dedicated teacher she knows," Grace said.

"Iris should raise her standards."

"Okay, so you're still a little pissy."

"I said I'd need a week or two," he reminded her. He lifted his coffee cup to his lips. "What's your favorite thing to do with time off?"

She didn't answer right away. "I need more balance in my life," she finally said. "That shop gets too much of my time. But it's a good workout."

"Flower arranging?" he asked doubtfully.

"I beg your pardon! I stand all day, haul heavy buckets full of fresh-cut flowers in water, deliver hundreds of pounds of arrangements to weddings and other events, get in and out of the back of that van all day, lift heavy pots and props and that's before I have to clean up and do the books. It's not for sissies."

"And for fun?"

"I like to dance," she said. "I don't very often, but it's fun."

"I bet you were a cheerleader," he said.

"I was *never* a cheerleader. I think I could've been. But I wasn't interested."

"You are the first girl in the history of the world, then."

"I'm sure I'm not," she said. "When I was that

age I was into ballet, sort of. They are not the same moves at all. That, like flower arranging, takes strength. Plus, I have a bike."

He raised his eyebrows. "A Harley?"

"A mountain bike. Retired for the winter due to ice, rain, cold and slick roads." She drank the rest of her beer and put her money on the bar. "I'd love to stay and keep you company but I have a date." She started for the door and turned back to him. "I'm glad you're doing well, Troy. I'd like to see what that Jeep can do off-road. Maybe when the weather warms up. And dries up."

"It's a date," he said.

But Grace knew it wasn't a date. She went back to the shop but didn't go inside. She went upstairs to her apartment, put some leftover lasagna from Carrie's deli into the microwave, changed into her soft pajamas and turned on the TV. While her lasagna cooled on the plate she went through the channel guide and settled on some reruns until her favorite shows came on. With her dinner on a tray and her e-reader in her hand, she opened an old and beloved book—*The Wolf and the Dove*—and settled in with Wulfgar, her medieval knight.

She loved him. And she trusted him.

Two

When Cooper asked Troy about his plans for New Year's Eve, Troy agreed to work. He hadn't gone skiing and was getting a little bored—might as well make money. Even though the night was clear and cold, it was a party night and Cooper's wasn't where the party was. Cliff was packing a full house at his restaurant and would stay open past midnight to accommodate his revelers, but Cooper's on the beach didn't have patrons past eight o'clock.

At a little after eight Troy locked up and walked next door to Cooper's house and brought him the contents of the till. Cooper and his wife, Sarah, were bundled up and had been sitting on the deck where an outdoor hearth blazed under a star-studded black sky. "I hear Cliff is going to shoot off some fireworks over the bay if the wind stays down," Cooper said. "If we're awake, we'll have the best seats in town. The problem with having a house like this—you never want to leave it."

"You look pretty comfortable. The fireworks might wake you up," Troy said.

"We had invitations for New Year's Eve," he said.

"I'm sure," Troy said, grinning. "Getting old, Cooper?"

"Oh, yeah, I guess so. But look at you—working tonight and all washed up before nine…"

Troy was ready to move on. "I'm going to stop at the store, grab a six-pack and drop in on a friend."

"Let me save you a trip," Cooper said. He got up, went to the refrigerator and pulled out a six of Heineken bottles. "Will this cut it?"

"I wasn't going to spend that much," Troy said with a laugh. "What do I owe you?"

"Gimme a break," Cooper said, waving him off. "Just get outta here and happy New Year. I hope the friend is female."

"She's female, but just a friend. I hope she's home or I'll end up at my apartment alone with a six-pack like a loser," Troy replied.

"I guess calling ahead didn't cross your mind?"

"I didn't think about it," Troy said. "Like I said, nothing special. Just a friend."

But Troy *had* thought about it. He was completely prepared to find Grace not at home and he didn't really care. Or she could be entertaining, which he'd kind of like to interrupt. Since Grace never brought out these boyfriends, he figured the only way he was likely to get a glimpse of one was to surprise her. What he'd really like to know was if Grace was as lonely as he was. Because two lonely people could negotiate a deal that would get them through. Why not?

He'd been thinking about her for the past couple of days, ever since she stopped by Cooper's while he was working. Grace had been in Thunder Point a little longer than he had, but he was just discovering her. He'd run across her a few times with Iris; she made him laugh. She was cute. Pretty, actually, but not the kind of gorgeous or sexy that slapped him upside the head. If he was honest with himself, women like that made him nervous. Grace had a wholesome look about her, kind of freshly scrubbed and glowing. She was very small, like a woman in a girl's body. But when she started talking, all traces of the girl vanished—she was clever and had a sassy, cynical wit. There was a sharp edge to her, like she'd lived a lot. She was full of the devil.

He privately acknowledged he was looking for a woman to spend some time with. The truth was, he hadn't often been without one. This might be one of his longest stretches; he'd been too damn focused on a woman he couldn't have. He wasn't above brief liaisons but he preferred something a little steadier. For that, he had pretty rigid standards. First of all, appearance was important. Not the only criteria, but someone who made an effort, put her best foot forward, kept up her looks. Next, she had to like to play. Troy loved extreme sports and it was not required that a woman he was dating be into the extreme, but it was important she liked trying new things, liked being outside, enjoyed physical activity. Iris had fit those requirements. She appreciated the outdoors, liked hiking, biking, paddle boarding. And she'd liked watching his videos of his own more adventurous experiences. She'd covered her eyes sometimes, but she'd watched his white-water challenges, rock climbing, diving with sharks, whales, squid.

Troy wanted a woman who was a good sport, at least. Of course she had to be intelligent and have a sense of humor. And since he was on the rebound, it was probably a good idea if she wasn't the clingy, needy type. That made Grace, who didn't get serious, a contender. She seemed to be casually dating someone and that sort of thing was usually a turn-off, but not at the moment.

He knocked on her second-floor apartment door, not really expecting her to answer. He saw the curtain move and then the door opened. She was wearing yoga pants, heavy socks, an oversize, long-sleeved T-shirt and her hair was pulled back into a ponytail. He tilted his head and smiled at her. "You don't have a date tonight?"

"Well, not at the moment."

Troy tried looking past her. "Is the medieval knight here?"

She put a hand on her hip. "Did you want to come in, Troy?"

He lifted the six-pack. "If you're not too busy. I brought beer. Sorry, I should've called."

She held the door open for him. "I'm surprised *you* don't have a date."

"It's not like I'm desperate," he said, entering. He

held out a beer for her, took one for himself, then opened her little refrigerator to stow the rest. "Oh-oh," he said. It was stuffed. Small to begin with, there was no room for a six-pack.

"Here, I'll do it." Some maneuvering was involved in getting four bottles of beer into the little fridge and ditching the cardboard pack.

"You're sure I'm not interrupting anything?"

"Come in, Troy," she said, moving through the dinky kitchen to the couch.

There was a movie on Pause and a plate of something snacky on the coffee table. He peered at it.

"Pizza rolls. I was just watching a chick flick but it'll keep. Now what's up with you? And take off your shoes."

He did as he was told, then sat on the far end of the couch. "Really, nothing. I worked at Cooper's, which is why I don't have a date or anything. It was dead tonight, and it was still early. I had about three choices—Cliff's, Waylan's or your place."

"You could have taken that new Jeep up to North Bend or even Bandon. Found a lively bar. Party a little." She picked up the plate and offered him a pizza roll.

"Thanks." He chewed it and nodded. "Not bad. I didn't feel like dealing with a bunch of strangers," he said. "I just felt like some company before I go home." He grinned at her. "And I thought maybe I'd run into one of your boyfriends."

"Oh, so that's your ulterior motive and the reason you didn't call. I didn't want to go out tonight. I went for a run."

"A run? You don't get enough exercise?"

"Short hours in the shop today. The nice thing about being a one-person operation, I can close early or open late if I want as long as I have a cell number for the shop. That way I can take orders anytime. In fact, if I'm available and someone needs something, I can run downstairs and make up an arrangement. But I knew there wouldn't be any calls tonight and, God, it was beautiful on the beach. There were a few people out there—Sarah Cooper and her dog, a couple of teenagers, one older couple I've never met—maybe part-timers. And me. I like to work out, but there isn't a gym around here that matches my oddball hours."

"You work out?" he asked.

"Not regularly. Just a bike ride or jog. I don't lift anymore—my arms and legs get enough of a workout in the shop. My flower girl calisthenics are enough. I add cardio just so I can drink a beer and eat pizza rolls." She offered him the last one. After putting the empty plate back on the coffee table, she curled into her corner of the sofa, her knees under her chin. "Tell me about Christmas, tell me about your family. Are you close?"

"I guess. As long as we don't have too much to-getherness."

"What does that mean?"

He took a pull on his beer. "I love my family. I do. We don't all get together that often and when we're gearing up for a family thing, I get excited. Then on the third or fourth day I want to kill my sister and shove my brother in a hole."

She sat forward a little. "Really?"

"My sister can be a bossy bitch and my brother is a screwup. Jess was married at nineteen and they started trying to repopulate the world—my niece was born when Jess was twenty. Then came a nephew and another niece and she thinks she runs a tight ship but if you ask me, the ship is sinking. The kids are out of control, my brother-in-law, Rick, works as much overtime as he can—he's a firefighter— the house is upside down and I think Rick likes the firehouse because it's the only place there's enough quiet to watch a game. And my brother, Sam, can be such an idiot. He's twenty-one going on seven and my mother would cut his meat for him if she could. He's spoiled and irresponsible. He doesn't even walk his plate to the sink and he has to eat on the hour. He looks in the refrigerator and sees eight slices of leftover pizza, so does he ask if anyone wants some? Of course not—he eats them all."

Her eyes were large. "Should I be sorry I asked?"

Troy took a breath. "Nah, I'm just coming off another successful family gathering. I should've stayed in the motel with my folks—it gets a little tight at my sister's"

"Your parents stayed in a motel? Why?"

"Because they're smart! But take 'em one day at a time and they're great, they're really great. Jess's kids might be loud and messy and hyperactive, but they're also *happy*! Rick's such a great guy, I don't know how Jess captured him. And when I got moody and wouldn't tell anyone what was bothering me, Sam took me out on the town. Not that it's much of a town. We must've hit three whole bars. Of course Sam wasn't really trying to cheer me up as much as he was hoping to get laid, but then..." His voice trailed off.

"Then...?" she asked.

"When I was twenty-one, that was always foremost on my mind. No apologies."

She giggled. "And now?"

"Not *always* foremost."

"So you love your family, when you don't hate them?"

"I'm crazy about them all the time—we just get on each other's nerves. We're typical, I think. I'll say this—half the time I want to punch my brother and slap my sister, but if anyone ever laid a hand on either one of them, I'd take 'em out. Really, I don't know how my folks lived through us. What about your family?" he asked.

She didn't answer right away. Instead, she got up, took the plate and her bottle to the little kitchen area, retrieved two fresh beers and returned to her corner of the couch. "There's very little to tell. My father died when I was fourteen and I'm an only child. My grandparents are gone, one set before I was even born and the other set before I was eighteen. There are some very distant relatives, but if I met some of them even once, I don't remember. I did get a letter from someone who claimed to be a cousin or half cousin or something, but he only wanted a loan." She laughed. "He apparently didn't know anything about me."

"How did you respond?"

She smiled. "I wrote back that it was very kind of him to reach out, but I wasn't making loans at this time."

"No one, huh?" he asked. "Your mother?"

"Also gone," she lied, looking away. She just wasn't willing to get into all that. Plus, she'd told Iris that she was alone. "There are friends, but probably not as many as you have. The couple who owned the flower shop in Portland where I worked, we're close and stay in touch. I talk to them every week and visit now and then. They not only trained me in the shop but took me under their wing. Good people. They're in their sixties and never had children, which probably explains why they think of me as family, though we're not. And there are a couple of other friends who also stay in touch—Mikhail, to name one, but he travels all the time so I never see him. That might be one of the reasons I became good friends with Iris—we have that absence of family in common. And there's the fact that I bought her flower shop, of course. Sometimes I look at people like Iris…and…well, you—and I feel a little abnormal, like I should try harder…"

"Iris? And me?"

"You're both so connected to people. Iris doesn't have family, but she has more good friends than anyone I know. The whole town loves her. The school definitely leans on her. And your family isn't around here, but I bet you talk to them every week."

"Pretty much," he admitted.

"You're really involved with people, too. The school, Cooper's, even Waylan's. All over town, people yell hello! But the reality is, I was raised an only child, had a very solitary upbringing and I'm probably a little too comfortable being alone."

"People around here are pretty friendly to you, aren't they?"

"They are. That's what I love about this town. But I'm kind of a loner."

"But you've had a lot of boyfriends," he reminded her.

"This is true. And they've all been amazing. I spend time with a guy who actually owns a plantation in South Carolina, a guy with a British title of some kind—viscount I think. There's Malone—he owns a lobster boat on the East Coast, there's a bar owner, a guy in the ski patrol, a navy SEAL…very interesting, sexy guys. But I own a flower shop—my time is precious."

He tilted his head and peered at her. "I think you're bullshitting me, Grace."

She got off the couch and went to the wall unit, opening a cupboard under the TV and there, lined up neatly, was a tidy row of books—paperbacks and a few hardcovers. Below the books was a similar collection of DVDs. She left the doors standing open and went back to the couch. She gracefully extended a hand toward the bookcase. "My keeper shelves. From medieval knights to navy SEALs. And there's Wrath…I'm afraid he's a vampire, but a very nice and sexy vampire. They're all mine."

"Should we have a little talk about your medication, Gracie?"

She smiled. "I know they're pretend boyfriends, Troy. But they never cheat and I haven't had to get one single screening for an STD." Then she giggled. "I don't have space for a lot of storage and books so I do most of my reading on an e-reader, but I have a special collection there. I can't be without them. What would I do if my e-reader wasn't charged or I lost it?"

Troy felt a tug of some kind inside, somewhere in his chest. He knew it was a warning sign—it was too soon to feel affectionate toward her. In fact, he'd prefer to never feel anything but friendly. But he couldn't deny it felt good to know that Grace wasn't involved with anyone. Her claim to never having been very involved was unusual for a woman her age and beauty. And he liked it.

"How are you fixed for real dates?" he asked.

"I have a very demanding schedule. When you own your own business every day off is a day without pay. I don't have much help at the shop. I've had a couple of part-timers over the past couple of years, but right now I have no one—the last one had to quit. She wasn't that much help anyway, but at least she kept the shop open while I delivered flowers. I have to try to figure that out. Like I said, I need a more balanced life."

"Have you thought about a high school or college student? Or maybe two who could job share, putting together two part-time schedules that equal one full-time employee? There are so many at the high school who don't want to go to college or who do but have trouble affording tuition."

"Good idea, but when I advertise for help, hardly anyone answers."

"You need help advertising in the right place. There's a work-study program at school. If you can train your student-employee in a trade, they'll get a credit toward graduation and get a morning or afternoon off to work. Didn't Iris ever suggest this?"

Grace looked a little excited. "No! Should I ask her to help me with this?"

"Yes," he said. "Not tonight. Tonight we drink beer and eat something. What've you got? I could run out for something…"

"How hungry are you? Because I make some amazing nachos. And since I have some black olives, taco meat left over from taco salad and sour cream…"

"Oh, *yeah*," he said.

"Didn't you have any dinner?"

"I had a couple of Cooper's mini pizzas…"

"And you say it's the little brother who eats on the hour?" She went to her tiny kitchen.

"Are you sure you don't want me to run down

the street for something? I hate to ask you to feed me," he said.

"Don't go," she said. "It's not much trouble and it sounds good."

She bent over to dig around in her little refrigerator and Troy felt a fever coming on. Those yoga pants had a real nice fit. He had to look away, take a breath. Sometimes, he reminded himself, you don't notice what's right in front of you. He'd spent all that time thinking Iris was right for him. Even though she made it clear it was a no-go, he never bothered to get to know any other women and here was Grace, right under his nose. Making him hot.

She was complicated, he knew that. She said her life was boring, not much to tell, solitary…and he knew that was just a cover. And he didn't mind at all.

"Then let me help," he said, joining her.

They put together a fabulous plate of nachos, ran out of salsa very quickly since that little fridge couldn't hold much and cupboard space was at a premium. They spent the next hour talking about the town, the rivers Troy liked to run in the summer, the kids he taught. Every time he asked Grace a question about herself she gave him a brief answer and steered the conversation back to him.

"You know there are dorm rooms bigger than this loft," he said to her. "You live like a college student."

"I know. I'm keeping my life simple and my expenses down until the shop does better, and it's doing better all the time. There aren't that many weddings in Thunder Point, but I get a lot of weddings out of town. They're killers but they pay like mad. Where do you live?"

"In a small old apartment on the edge of town that's decorated with castoffs from my folks. You're saving for the flower shop and I'm saving for travel." He noticed her eyes widened and wondered where it came from. Envy? Longing? Surprise? Something else? He told her about the dive trips in summer, ski trips in winter, hunting trips with old Marine Corps buddies here and there.

"Marines?" she asked.

"I did a year of community college, enlisted, went to Iraq and got out. That's how I finished college— GI Bill. I was a lowly jarhead but I made some excellent friends. There's good hunting in the mountains not far from here. I'll take you sometime if you like."

"Oh, I've never touched a gun," she said. "I couldn't hunt."

"Then I'll take you for the scenery."

Just then, as they were talking about guns, something that sounded like gunshots punctuated the night. Almost as if choreographed, they both turned to open the shutters behind the couch. In the sky above the bay, fireworks blasted the dark sky, exploding into bright fireballs and falling in sparkling streamers.

"Fireworks," she said in a breath.

"The wind has been too high in the couple of years I've been here," Troy said. "I think Cliff hires someone to do it. Not bad, for a dumpy little town."

"This place surprises me all the time."

Troy turned to her and caught her chin in his finger and thumb. He leaned his forehead against hers. "Me, too."

"Listen, Troy," she said, and there was no mistaking nervousness in her voice. "I... There are things..."

He stopped her by kissing her gently. He slid his hand around her head to the nape of her neck under her ponytail. His kiss was soft, brief and gentle. Instinct told him he was dealing with a major unknown emotional situation and should go slowly, carefully. He moved over her lips very tenderly.

"What things?" he asked.

She took a breath. "I didn't exactly tell the whole story about my family, about growing up..."

"I know," he said.

"How? Do you know things about me? Is there something..."

"Shh," he said. "I'm a high school teacher. I can smell excuses and evasion a mile away. It's an acquired skill. So there's more to you? That's okay, Gracie. Don't panic. You'll tell me when you feel safe."

"Okay?" she said, more of a question than a reply.

He chuckled. "Okay. We're just friends. And we're getting to know each other. Take it easy."

Then he leaned in again, taking another taste of her lips as the popping, exploding sound of fireworks provided the background music. Again he was gentle and sweet because the last thing he wanted was to scare her off.

"I'm not experienced," she whispered when their lips parted.

"Well, except for the navy SEAL, knight and vampire?" he asked with a laugh in his voice.

She smiled against his lips. "Yes, except for them there aren't many experiences. I made out with a guy named Johnny when I was fifteen. For about ten hours I think. He was fantastic and turned out to be gay. Such has been my luck."

He gave her a little kiss. "I'm not."

"Yeah, I was afraid of that."

"Don't be afraid," he said. "It's all good."

"Should we be down on the dock, watching the fireworks?" she asked.

"Uh-uh," he said, shaking his head. "We should be right here." Then his arms tightened around her and he covered her mouth again with kisses that had become hot, demanding and promising.

Troy left at around one in the morning but Grace stayed on the couch. She grabbed a pillow and blanket and decided to spend the night right there, where it all happened, where the kissing and snuggling and whispering took place. She was still licking her lips, touching them with her fingertips, contemplating his skill, his taste. The last time she'd been kissed was in Portland by a nephew of Ross and Mamie's. That was over two years ago. His name was Gary, last name long forgotten. He'd attached himself to her mouth like a plunger and attempted a tonsillectomy with his tongue. He'd gotten away with that three times before she finally told him to stop.

There were some things for which she had very little training and one of them was romantic relationships. She hadn't been in a position to have boyfriends. And if she did have a crush, which happened rarely, her flirting felt conspicuous and clumsy. She'd had a crush on Troy, as it happened, but because she was Iris's friend and Troy had been trailing Iris for a year, she never let on. Growing up, she trained mostly alone, the only exception being her father's younger students—almost exclusively girls. There were men on the skating competition circuit and other athletes competing in some of the national and world competitions. Some of the figure skaters she competed against were so much more womanly—tall, with breasts, worldly, sexy, flirtatious. And they hated her. They had plenty of reasons—she was raised with money while many of them had parents who worked several jobs to pay for their training, not that that had anything much to do with one's ability to perform a perfect double axel. She often competed against older skaters because her talent meant she was a force to be reckoned with. But the other girls tended to act as if she could buy the medals.

Her biggest rival was a girl her age named Fiona Temple. Fiona beat her once and only once, but that was all it took for Fiona to believe the only thing that stood in the way of her stardom was Izzy Banks. Fiona hated her and spread rumors about her whenever she could. Fiona's parents leaked stories to the media. Grace would never forget the time, age twelve, when Fiona told other skaters Grace was a rich bitch and how everything was easier for her. Grace had cried and told Winnie all about it. "Never let them see you cry!" Winnie had said. "Never! Lift your chin and beat her instead! Beat the tights off her!"

That's what she wanted to do, but it was so hard not to feel hurt. So she lifted her nose in the air, ignored them, and they started calling her a stuck-up snot who had everything handed to her.

And then she did something that caused a world of trouble. Winnie had warned her to keep her mouth shut, but she couldn't stay silent. She accused a famous skating coach of sexual misconduct with one of his students, a minor. She quickly learned speaking out gets you treated like a leper, even if it's true. True or not, a smarter person would have proof to offer before opening her stupid mouth. When she asked her coach's advice Mikhail had been blunt. "He is piece of shit but it will get you nothing to say so."

That world-famous coach was not prosecuted and ultimately sued Izzy and Winnie. They settled, giving him money. A year after Grace retired from competitive skating the coach was arrested and eventually convicted of sexual misconduct with minors.

She'd been right. Vindicated. For what good it did her.

She hadn't been completely without friends growing up, but her few relationships had been superficial and strained. When the girls doubled up in hotel rooms to save money, Winnie rented spacious quarters for the two of them and Mikhail, removing Grace yet again from her contemporaries. The only skaters she didn't actually fear were on the men's team. And most of them *truly* wanted to be nothing more than friends.

She couldn't look to her parents as models for a healthy, strong love match. Her mother had married her father because she needed a keeper. Her father had married her mother as he had married a young skater before her, one who bore him a child twenty years before Grace came along. As much as she had always adored her father, she understood—he had a *type*. Young, vulnerable, needy, willing to do whatever he demanded because they were convinced he'd help them win.

She could, however, look to her parents to see what she *didn't* want in a relationship.

Her other advisors on romance were in the bookcase—the romances and some classic chick flicks. She and Iris had debated them often enough. Some were pure fantasy, some unreasonably coincidental, but some of her favorite contemporary romances revolved around very strong women and men with integrity. And then of course she studied their fictional presumptions, mistakes, missteps, blunders, and from them she learned. Or at least hoped she had.

She had been unprepared for Troy. She had wished for someone like Troy for a long time but assumed that kind of man would never happen into her life.

Troy had kissed with such amazing skill and tenderness. And there was passion—hot, deep, panting, groaning passion. Grace wanted to fall in love with him, something she attributed to her lack of experience. But she thought about what he'd said to her. "You aren't with anyone, I'm not with anyone and it seems like we might as well enjoy the moment. Right?"

So. He was just lonely and had finally accepted that Iris had moved on. She didn't care. She loved his mouth, his arms, his hands. She would try very hard not to fall in love with him.

Grace snuggled down into her blanket on the couch and thought it didn't matter at all. She never imagined she'd have this with anyone and certainly not the very guy she lusted after. They had kissed for an hour. He didn't rush her, didn't push her, didn't treat her like someone he was using to pass the time and it was *delicious*! She decided to close her eyes and dream about him, dream about them taking it to the next level. She was twenty-eight; she so wanted to know what that was like.

Instead she dreamed of Mikhail, the little Russian in his sixties with a cane he pounded for emphasis, shouting in half Russian and half English. It was so unfair, she thought, slowly rousing to the sound of knocking that was not Mikhail's cane.

She was suddenly afraid and her heart started racing. Who could be pounding after one in the morning? Then she saw that it was starting to grow light and at just that moment she heard Troy's voice. "Gracie? Gracie? It's me," he called softly.

She opened the door for him. He was holding a bag. "What in the world are you doing here at the crack of dawn?"

He looked at his watch. "It's nine, Grace."

"Nine? It looks like the sun isn't even awake!"

"It's a gloomy day. I brought breakfast and then I'm going to take you storm watching."

"Why?" she said, frowning.

"Because the swells are huge and I think you need me to show you how to have fun."

"I beg your pardon, I know how to have fun."

"Working all the time, then working out for diversion. Nah, you definitely need a coach. We'll start small—just a little sightseeing. There are big swells, the waves will be awesome."

"But it's cold."

He put his bag on the little table. "And it's kind of wet. You should dress warm, but first, breakfast." He pulled some fast-food breakfast burritos and potato pancakes out of the bag. Lots of them. On the bottom were two large coffees.

"Hungry, Troy?"

"Starving." He sat down and peeled the wrapper off one of the breakfast burritos. "Come on, Grace. Let's do it. This is going to get you all excited. Promise."

"I was going to catch up on some paperwork since the shop is closed today. Accounting and stuff."

He shook his head. "See what I mean? This is exactly why I came over. I don't know you that well but I already know you're working too much. I have two jobs and still manage to take some days off." He took a big bite. "It's New Year's Day. It's a *holiday*."

She sat opposite him and reached for one of the burritos. He was right. Not only was he right, she'd told him last night she needed to find more balance. "Do you have an aversion to making plans?"

"No," he said. "I'm usually much more polite—call ahead, make plans, all that stuff that girls like. I'll work on that. For now, I think we should have some fun. Especially today."

"There are lots of football games on TV."

"I'm recording them," he said. "I might not watch them all and I'm not going to sit around inside all day when there are things to do. You'll be glad you let me drag you out," he said.

"We'll see," she said, but she already was.

Three

"The outstanding question is why have you appointed yourself my fun coach?" Grace asked once they were in Troy's Jeep and driving.

"It's not complicated at all," he said. "I need someone to play with. I work a lot. I give a lot to the students. I have a second job at least ten days a month. Between school vacations and weekends, I manage some time off and Cooper is great about letting me put together days off from his place so I have time to pursue my interests. When I'm not working I look for fun things to do. Mostly skiing, diving or river trips, but since there's decent skiing and diving right here, I only take about one big trip every year. There are lots of places I need to see—Costa Rica, Barcelona, Paris, Montreal, China, to name just a few. My real passion is kayaking or rafting and, honey, there are some rivers in the tristate area that can keep me busy through spring and summer. Who knows? Maybe you'll try it sometime, maybe not. But this is a great place, Grace—there's a ton of stuff to do and see and experience."

"You need someone to play with," she repeated as if that was the only thing she got out of all that. But it wasn't what she was thinking. *I've been all over the world. I could almost work as a guide.* Except, Grace had never toured the countries she'd visited, never really taken in the sights. She'd been all over the world to compete. Usually with an entourage. And now, Troy needed someone to play with?

Her heart beat a little faster.

"Well, that's not the whole story," Troy continued. "I'm not shy about doing things on my own. I meet people all the time, great people who have like interests. But, Grace, you're kind of fun. Let's see if there's anything you like better than working all the damn time."

"You have a point," she agreed. "The problem is I have my own business. And every day off—"

"I know, every day off is a day without pay."

"You pay attention," she said.

"It's admirable, having your own business. But I think your business is a ball and chain. It's all about working out a schedule you can live with, Grace. People don't need flowers twenty-four/seven. And I bet you'll be a happier business owner if you get out a little more."

Of course he had no idea how much getting out she indulged in because she didn't talk about it much—her yoga, working out, secret skating. "So that's why you think you can kidnap me like this?"

"Really, Grace? Kidnap?"

"Hijack."

"Look at that coast," he said as he drove north. "Damn, not a day to go fishing, I don't think. Have you seen the coast up this far?"

"Of course," she lied. In fact, she'd driven down the coast from Portland one summer, barely took in the landscape, made a bid to buy the shop and went right back to Mamie and Ross, where she spent a week lost in a panic attack, terrified of being completely on her own. She was so nervous she nearly called her mother! In the end, she toughed it out and when her offer was accepted by Iris, she drove straight to Thunder Point, never really taking in the coastal beauty.

They passed through the outskirts of North Bend and then Coos Bay. It appeared very little was open for business, it being a holiday. There were a few bars and a Chinese restaurant that seemed to have customers. A souvenir shop on the highway had an Open light shining in the door. Gas stations were operational and a firehouse had the big rig doors spread wide. But the traffic was sparse. Everyone was probably home taking in the football games and recovering from New Year's Eve.

"Have you ever seen it on a day like today?" he asked as they drove toward the ocean. He pulled into a small lookout that faced the water. The clouds were dark and the wind was blowing wicked and wet. There were patches of rain over the ocean and the waves were huge. The air was frigid and the fun coach was grinning. "Yeah, this is gonna be *great*," he said.

"What in God's name have I let you get me into?" she asked. He laughed as if he found that extremely amusing.

He put a knit stocking cap on his head and jumped out of the Jeep. When she joined him, he grabbed her hand and pulled her along a path that she knew led to the edge of the lookout because she could hear the deafening sound of crashing waves. When the path crested she stepped back with sudden anxiety. The waves looked like mountains as they crashed against the rocks.

"God," she said, but only God could have heard her above that noise.

"Come on," he said. "They're about a hundred feet in some places, some of the biggest waves in the world. We can get closer. It's safe."

She shook her head. "I can see just fine!"

"What?"

She put her hands around her mouth and shouted in his ear. "I can see fine!"

He laughed. He put his mouth close to her ear. "It's safe. Look, there's a stone wall. Not like we'll slide off. I can see from here that it's dry. I want to get a couple of pictures with my phone."

It was a very low stone wall, about knee-high. She shook her head. A lot.

"Is it scary, Grace?" he asked, shouting.

She nodded.

"I'll go check," he yelled. He let go of her hand

and walked along the path closer to the edge. Waves rose above the level of the ground she stood on, but they crashed to the surf below. The path began to wind downward, which gave her no peace of mind and she hung back. She wasn't sure of herself on high cliffs over rocky shores facing off with hundred-foot waves. Troy continued on, of course.

The waves were magnificent, she had to admit. The power was *stunning*, no other word.

Troy leaned against the wall, his back to the ocean, and waved at her. She waved back. He jumped over the wall and walked a bit farther toward the edge and she felt her stomach clench. There was a sign, for God's sake! Don't Go Past This Point! But over the wall he went. He turned toward her and shouted something that she didn't have a prayer of hearing so she just shook her head. He spread his arms wide and high, as if in victory.

Probably the award-winning wave of the day came up behind him and her eyes grew as round as plates. Her mouth hung open and she watched in awe as the crest of the enormous wave came down on Troy. She screamed in terror, afraid he'd been washed out to sea. As it receded, there he stood, looking for all the world like a drowned rat. With gunk hanging from one shoulder.

Grace grabbed her heart in relief. He just stood there. Dripping. He plucked the gunk off his shoulder and began to climb back over the wall.

After a couple of relieved breaths, once she was sure the fun coach was all right, Grace hugged herself and sank to her knees in hysterical laughter. She could barely see him trudging toward her because her eyes were watering with tears. His jacket and pants were heavy from water, making his movements slow. She wanted to spring into action and tell him she was taking charge, except she couldn't talk. Instead, she rose slowly to her feet and by the time he reached her, she was upright again. She took his hand and pulled him back up the path toward the Jeep.

"Oh, my God," she rasped weakly, still hysterical with laughter. "Oh, Troy!"

"It's thirty-eight degrees," he said, shivering. "Get a grip! Stop laughing!"

"I'm sorry," she said, but she couldn't stop. "I had no idea you could be such a funny fun coach! Get in—I'm driving."

"It's m-m-my new Jeep!"

"You're shaking. I'll drive, crank up the heater and you can start peeling off wet clothes. I don't suppose you have a blanket in the car?"

"N-n-no. That was a f-f-freak wave!"

"There was a sign!" she said. "Did you want to go over Niagara Falls in a barrel, too?"

"Funny. You're so f-funny."

"Oh, God, I wish I'd gotten a picture. Here," she said, opening the passenger door. "In you g-g-go!" she said, mocking him. Then she doubled over in laughter again.

By the time she got into the driver's seat, he had already started the engine. "Take off that jacket and throw it in the back. And that stocking cap," she said, yanking it off his head and pitching it over her shoulder. It took him a minute to peel off the jacket and once he had, she started touching his shirt. "Not that bad, really, but still wet. That was probably forty gallons of water." Then she touched his pants, patting his thighs and knees. "Oh-oh. These are soaked. Hang in there, the heater will get going pretty quick." She put on her seat belt and made a big U-turn, taking off down the road. Hunching up against the steering wheel, she was still laughing. "That was seriously the funniest thing I've ever seen in my life," she said.

"Shut up, Grace."

That only made her laugh harder. "Relax, I'm going to fix this for you. I hope."

"How?"

"You'll see. Don't be so crabby—I'm going to get you dry."

Troy aimed all the vents at himself and turned up the fan. "Lucky I didn't get washed off the edge," he muttered, rubbing his hands together.

"I admit, that wouldn't have been as funny," she said.

"You have a very big laugh for a little girl."

"I know."

A few minutes later, she parked in front of the souvenir shop. "What are you doing?" he asked.

"You'll see." She grabbed her purse and jumped out, leaving the car running for him. She jogged inside and less than five minutes later came running back to the car with a roll of paper towels in one hand

and a shopping bag in the other. "These were donated by the cashier," she said, handing him the paper towels. "And these are for you!" Grinning widely, she pulled a sweatshirt out of the bag—it read My Heart Is in Coos Bay. "I got the largest one. And here are some shorts." She pulled out a pair of women's shorts with eyelet lace sewn around the legs. "They're actually from a pajama set, but they're XL. They didn't have any men's pants, just tops. This was all they had, but they're dry."

"You're kidding, right?"

"It's okay, you have nice narrow hips. If this place hadn't had clothes, I was going to take you to that fire station, but this is better. And you don't ever have to wear them again, just till we get you home." She craned her neck, looking around. They were alone in the parking lot. "Take off your shirt and dry your head and body…"

"In the car?"

"You're a guy! Guys strip on the street if they have to! Guys pee off boats!"

He ripped off his shirt and used paper towels to dry his hair, neck and his damp chest. He put on the sweatshirt. "Good. That's good."

"Pants. Come on."

"They're not that wet…"

"You're soaked. I won't look," she said, turning away.

"I'm okay, but thanks for the thought."

"Your pants are wet and it's cold. You already made the seat wet—get your pants off and sit on a bunch of paper towels. Even if we get it warm in here, you can't be sitting in cold, wet pants."

"It's New Year's Day and nothing is open. How'd you know about this place?"

"We passed it on the way up. I asked myself what would be open on a holiday—the souvenir shop was all I could think of." She smiled. "I almost grabbed you a couple of refrigerator magnets while I was in there." She touched his shoulder. "Put on the nice, dry shorts, Troy. I'll close my eyes. Besides, cold and wet as you are, there probably isn't that much to see."

He lifted one eyebrow. "Did it ever occur to you that's why I'm not undressing in front of you?"

"Fine," she said. "I'll go back inside the store. There's no one in the parking lot. Get it done."

And with that, she was out of the car. She chatted it up with the cashier for a minute, explaining Troy's shyness. She glanced at her watch, supposing enough time had passed. When she walked back outside, what she saw caused her to stop dead in her tracks.

A police car was parked next to the Jeep and an officer had Troy out of the car, standing in his wet stocking feet wearing his ladies' shorts, talking and shivering. *Oh, no!* she thought. He must have been changing when the officer pulled up. Of course he had to take off his shoes to get out of his pants. She could imagine what the officer thought! She took two steps toward them to help, to be a witness to Troy's explanation.

But she started to laugh again and was absolutely no help at all.

* * *

Troy insisted on taking over the driving. He was no longer chattering and shaking. He was, however, a little out of sorts. And he cast glances at Grace, who was looking out the window attempting not to laugh, the attempt causing her to snort now and then.

She turned toward him, her hand suspiciously covering her mouth. "So, how did the police become involved?"

"He snuck up on me as I was changing pants. I was at a disadvantage. My wet jeans were tossed over the seat and these pretty little shorts you so kindly bought me were around my ankles and I was drying off when I looked up and he was staring in the window. He told me to get out of the car. I had barely stopped explaining the situation when you came out of the store and laughed until you almost peed yourself. I'm writing a letter to the city council. I think it's unprofessional for a police officer to laugh until he farts."

Grace quickly looked out the window. She snorted again. She got the hiccups.

"Glad I could be so entertaining," he grumbled.

"Are you going to drop me off at the flower shop?" she asked.

"Oh-ho, no way, Gracie. I might've screwed up my first attempt at showing you how to have fun but I'm not giving up. And I'm not letting you do accounting on a holiday! I'll just clean up and we'll go at it again."

"Really, Troy, I think your work here is done. I

don't think I've ever had more fun in my life." She snickered a little and bit her lip. "Besides, I think you might be mad at me for laughing. And that doesn't sound like fun."

"I'm not mad," he snapped. "I'm *wet*!" He took a breath and said, "I'll be more fun when I'm dry and not wearing girl pants."

"I think you're fun right now," she said. Then she grinned at him.

He parked behind his apartment complex and led her up to the second floor, leaving all his wet clothing outside the door. He unlocked his dead bolt. Once inside, she looked around. "Wow. Nice."

He smiled to himself. It was a crappy old complex on the outside, but Troy had done a little work on the inside. He'd painted, for one thing, and bought a nice, deep and fluffy area rug to put over the old and worn carpeting in the living room. He had some nice shelving and a fifty-seven-inch flat screen. He'd made repairs and improvements here and there, like taking down the shower curtain and installing a glass shower door, sanding and refinishing the bathroom cabinets, scrubbing the place like he owned it. His parents' old leather sectional fit right in. The only things he had that were new were the butcher-block table and high chairs. His bedroom furniture was only a few years old and he had been collecting a few framed LeRoy Neiman prints for the walls. The frames were more valuable than the prints, but he liked Neiman's sports art.

"Make yourself at home. Help yourself to anything—eat, drink, whatever. There's the remote. I have to get a shower. I'll be quick."

He left her standing in the small living room. Once he was under the hot water, sudsing the smell of salt and seaweed from his hair and body, he smiled to himself. Grace was a free spirit. A little wild and uncontrolled with a deep-down joy and playfulness that turned him on. He might've acted a little insulted at her lusty humor directed at him but, to be honest, he wouldn't have it any other way. That was no prissy little laugh the girl had: she laughed down to her toes. There was passion in her.

He revisited his checklist in his mind and moved *She must be a happy person* to number one in his requirements. If that meant laughing at his foibles, he could live with that. Grace didn't come across as whiny, self-pitying, cloying or desperate. If he demanded a woman be a good sport, then he had to be, too. And who forced him to jump that wall? He'd been showing off. He loved showing off.

She might just prove to be a good little playmate.

When he got back to the living room to Grace, she was curled up in the corner of the sectional, holding a cup of something hot with both hands. Her boots were sitting at attention beside the couch and she was wearing bright pink socks. One of the many New Year's Day bowl games was on television. He stood looking down at her, smiling, with his hands on his hips.

"Do you feel better?" she asked a little sheepishly.

"I'm tempted to hold you down and give you

something to really laugh about. You ticklish, Gracie?"

She pulled back a little. "Don't even think about it," she said, holding up the cup. "I'm armed."

"What is that?"

"Hot chocolate. You had some envelopes of mix in the drawer by the refrigerator."

He wrinkled his brow. "That could be very old."

"I don't think dry powders spoil. Want to taste it?"

"Thanks," he said, reaching for the cup. She handed it to him and he put it behind him on the coffee table. Then he tackled her on the couch. While she shrieked and begged and laughed, he pinned her with his body and attempted to tickle her.

"I'm sorry, I'm sorry, I'm sorry," she squealed.

"What are you sorry for, Grace?" he asked, a devilish gleam in his eyes, pinning her to the sofa.

"I'm sorry I laughed and bruised your delicate little male ego," she said, smiling.

"Ooh," he growled, giving her a good rib-tickle.

"Ack! I'm sorry, I'm sorry, I'm sorry! Stop it, stop it!"

"What are you sorry for?"

"Okay, I lost it, I was out of control, I laughed at you when you were vulnerable and I'm sorry. No tickling!"

"A cop was threatening to arrest me for indecent exposure!" Troy said. "He thought I was a parking lot predator!"

A smile beamed across her face. "That was the best," she said. "I'm sorry, but that was the best part.

Although, that wave…I will never see anything like that again in my lifetime! You are an excellent fun coach."

"It wasn't my intention that you have fun at my expense," he said. But he was smiling when he said it. "I was going to show you how to have a good time."

"And so you did," she said, smiling into his eyes. "Think of how successful that might've been if you could *read*. I mean, there was a sign. Can I make you some stale hot chocolate?"

"I don't think so. I think my mother sent me that in one of her many boring care packages. What should we do today? Want to go out? Any ideas?"

She shook her head.

"Let's stay in," he said. "Let's make some game food. I have stuff in the freezer. I have tri-tip and buns for tri-tip sliders. Or we can go with wings or pizza. I have beer but no wine."

"I have wine in the flower cooler," she said. "I just feel like such a slouch, eating so much trash and bar food."

"I'll slice some onion and pickles for your sliders. I have some deli potato salad but I don't know…"

"Dangerous?" she asked.

"By this date, very likely. I don't expect you to be that much of a good sport."

"Oh, so that's your game? You want a good sport?"

He gave her a quick kiss. "I want to enjoy myself with someone who's enjoying herself. I have a feeling, a dark feeling, you don't need my help with that."

"Okay. I'll do one more day of carbs and fats. But the next time we eat together there will be green things."

"I love green things," he lied.

He told her to take the Jeep to her place to retrieve her wine and she brought back a Scrabble game. She also threw in a DVD of one of her favorite non-chick flicks, *Red*. He looked at it and said, "I love *Red*!"

"Just in case your brain goes numb from football," she said. "But I can do football as long as you can."

They had a rousing game of Scrabble, which Troy won by a stretch. They curled up on the couch together to watch *Red*. Every once in a while Troy invaded her space for a make-out session. In midafternoon they worked together in the kitchen to build some sliders, which they ate on big plates in front of the TV. Troy quizzed her about football teams and stats. "You're a big football fan," he said.

"I'm a small football fan," she corrected. "Or maybe medium. I enjoy the game but I don't live for it like some people do. And I have a good memory for football facts."

"And your favorite sport?" he asked.

"That's a tough question. I think I like watching everything competitive."

"I think I'll invite you to my Super Bowl party," he said while they rinsed the dishes.

"You're having a Super Bowl party?"

"Uh-huh," he said, directing her back to the couch, pulling her down and getting her back in his arms. He loved that there was no hesitation from her.

His arms went around her waist, hers went around his neck, lips on lips and bodies pressed together. It being the height of winter, the sun was lowering and the only light was that from the kitchen and the TV.

"Who's coming to your party?" she asked, lips pressed against his neck.

"I'm thinking of a very small party. It could be a private party." He caressed her back, her sides, ran a hand over her butt and down her thigh. "Maybe just us."

"I'm not sleeping with you," she said.

He backed off a little. "Ever?"

"I'm not ready," she told him. "I want to know you better."

"That's very reasonable," he said, kissing her again. "But really, Gracie, you taste so good…"

"That's sweet. I'm still not ready."

"Are you going to be unready for a real long time? Because, honey, you are a turn-on. And I risked my life for you on the cliffs of Coos Bay today. Just to make you happy."

She chuckled against his lips. "You are such a giving man. I'll be sure to let you know when I'm ready."

"Just out of curiosity, Grace, are you waiting for a sign?"

She nodded. "I am. Plus, I'd like to be sure you're all done pining over Iris. That just feels weird."

Troy immediately put a little space between them. He grew serious. "Iris is married, Grace."

"I know this. I was there."

"Listen, here's how it is. I'm crazy about Iris. She's an awesome person and great counselor for the kids. I consider her a good friend. It's true, for a long time I thought if she gave it a chance we might be more than friends, but we weren't on the same page. All right? We were *never* on the same page and even though she told me over and over, I thought she might reconsider. She didn't."

"I know all that, but you have to remember—Iris is my good friend, too. I don't want the situation to be awkward."

"I hope we're all good friends for a long, long time," he said. "When I kiss you, I'm not thinking about Iris. I'm not thinking about anyone but you."

She frowned slightly. "I'm pretty sure you didn't answer the question," she said.

"Iris married the love of her life, her one true and forever love. Even if I did still carry a torch for her, I'd never admit it. Especially to you. But I don't. She's moved on and so have I. Do you believe me?"

She smiled a little bit. Her expression said she didn't believe him at all, but how could she argue without calling him a liar. "Okay, I believe you," she said. "But there are also things about me… I want you to get to know me a little better."

"I'm ready whenever you are. But so far, you're the mystery. You have some pretty vague answers to questions about your life, your family, your friends…"

"I know, Troy. Since I was raised an only child,

isolated in some ways, I tend to be on the private side. If you're just patient…"

He leaned toward her. He kissed her again and she melted into him.

"How do you like me so far?" he asked against her lips.

She smiled without breaking her hold on him. "You're growing on me."

"You can trust me. When you're ready to tell me more, you can trust me. And you can ask me anything."

"Okay. One important question before we go any further. Are you sure I'm not just a booty call?"

Four

On January second, Grace did an inventory of her stock, updated her calendar, cleaned out the flower bin and made herself a to-do list. She had two couples coming in at the end of the month to get estimates for spring weddings. Valentine's Day would be her next major event and she wanted to begin decorating the shop right away. Soon it would be spring, when her stock would be more beautiful and plentiful than ever. The most important thing on her list was to find help for the shop! She really wanted to spend more time with the fun coach.

Being with Troy was intoxicating. They made out like teenagers, but she knew she was going to have to get ready for the next stage. Oh, so inviting! She was amazed he agreed not to rush her.

She heard the bell on the shop door tinkle and looked out of her workroom to see a familiar face as Al Michel stepped into the shop. He had the most handsome smile, a man who seemed perpetually happy. He was a big man, in his fifties with a powerful physique, who looked impervious to aging. He wore his blue work shirt, his name embroidered above the pocket.

"Hey there," she said, coming into the shop. "How was Christmas?"

"Excellent," he said.

"And what made it so special?" she asked.

"Well, my lady, for one thing, Ray Anne really went overboard to make sure it was nice for the boys. We had Christmas Eve at her house and she cooked most of the food, but I helped a little. She decorated and wrapped presents for everyone. Christmas Day was at our house, but she took care of most of the food. We brought the boys' mom from the nursing home for a few hours and it was great. Her MS is under control for the moment, and I could tell the boys were proud to have her home, if only for a little while. I think it was the nicest holiday any of us has had in years, especially the boys."

Grace leaned on her counter and tilted her head. "I don't have any idea how you got hooked up with those boys," she said.

"Simple," he said. "Justin, the oldest, worked with me at the service station. He's nineteen and real private. I found out he was taking care of his mother and two younger brothers, killing himself to hold it all together while his mom was just getting more and more infirm. So we teamed up—me and the boys. I'm their foster father. Their mom needed the nursing home and it made sense for me to move into their house.

The two younger boys are in school. They're good kids, but they still need supervision. Not constant, but regular. Know what I mean? But just to be sure things couldn't be simple or real easy, I found my lady, Ray Anne, right about the same time I found my family of boys."

He shook his head and chuckled. "Now, Ray Anne is a good woman and I think she loves those boys like they're her own, but she's..." He cleared his throat. "I don't know if Ray Anne even knows how old she is, but she's not as young as she looks. She's probably too set in her ways to live with a man like me and three teenage boys. She's particular and fussy. The way we got it worked out is good. I live with the boys, she lives in her own house. She visits, invites us over sometimes, and then there's the times those boys grant me leave and I visit my lady without them chaperoning. It verges on a perfect life."

"Wow. All that happened at once?"

"Pretty much," he said. "I didn't think I'd ever be this settled."

"In two houses," Grace said with a laugh.

"Aw, it won't be two houses forever. Justin passed his GED and we're looking into college courses. Scares him to death but the boy is smarter than he thinks. Danny's in high school, Kevin's almost done with middle school. Before I know it, I won't be that necessary to them."

"Oh, I bet you'll be the dad for a long time to come. Maybe even a grandpa."

"Hush now," he said, grinning. "We're in the

grandparent prevention program at my house. Those boys don't need any more complications. Now, Grace, I should take my lady some pretty flowers. She worked so hard over Christmas to make sure me and the crew had a great holiday. That woman is a dream come true. What've you got that's perfect for her?"

"I just cleaned out the bin," she said. "Would you like a bouquet or an arrangement?"

"I don't know," he said with a shrug. "What's the difference?"

"The last flowers I sold you in the square vase— that was a bouquet. A table arrangement is like a centerpiece for her table or bedroom dresser. I have some lavender and white roses, hydrangea, lilies— the pretty green and white ones. Next week I'll have a new crop of calla lilies."

He contemplated for a second and she was thinking what a good catch he must be—a man with tender feelings, strong enough to take on a brood of teenage boys and sensitive enough to think of his lady with flowers. "Just make something pretty, Grace. Fifty bucks or so?"

"Wow, you do love that lady."

"Every time I think of her I want to fill her house with flowers. Ray likes pretty things. I waited a long time to find someone like her."

"What's it like, asking three teenage boys if you can go out on a date?"

He laughed. "A lot of monkey business, kissing noises, that kind of thing. Especially the younger two—I can't wait till they have girlfriends. I'm planning to be relentless and obnoxious, they've earned it. So, how much time do you need on the flowers?"

"Thirty minutes, tops. Want to wait?"

"I think I'll go get lunch at the diner while you work, then come back. Can I bring you anything?"

"That's so sweet," she said, shaking her head. A couple of weeks ago she might've said, *Yeah, your younger brother*! But now there was Troy. "I'm good. I'll get right on this. And don't forget to put in your order for Valentine's Day roses early!"

Twenty minutes later the bouquet was finished— white, lavender, dark green and a little blue delphinium. She might've put extra love in the bouquet just thinking about Al and Ray Anne, finding each other a bit later in life. Here she'd been thinking that at twenty-eight she was long overdue.

When Al picked up the flowers they had a brief discussion about her need for help in the shop and he said Justin might be able to run some deliveries for her if he didn't have to pay for gas. Al promised to ask him.

When she was alone, her personal cell rang and she answered.

"Hey there, flower girl. What are you doing?" Troy asked.

"Ah, you do know how to use a phone. I'm doing flowers. Beautiful flowers. How about you? Wanna go see the waves?"

"You're adorable, you know that? I'm going to work for Cooper today and tomorrow, but Sunday is my day. And I go back to school on Monday. The flower shop is closed on Sundays. So—what should we do?"

"This implies you want to have an adventure? Is that it?"

"Let's take 101 south, check out the redwoods, drive into the Humboldt County mountains and maybe break bread with some illegal pot growers. We can have a picnic in the redwoods. We might have to have it in the car—it's going to be kind of cold but sunny. Except back in the trees, it's dark and cold."

"How do you know it's going to be chilly and sunny?"

"My phone says it's going to be sunny with a high of forty-five degrees."

"What did we do before smartphones?"

"Listened to the farm report. So, what do you say, flower girl? Date?"

In all the places she'd been, from China to Charlotte, North Carolina, she'd never been to the redwoods. "I think that could be fun. We should pack extra clothes this time in case you have to show off again."

"Yeah, I'll take that under advisement. So, that's Sunday. I'll be at Cooper's tonight. It's Friday night. A clear and cold Friday night so there will be people. There might be teenagers on the beach with their fires and shenanigans. If you're not tied up with the knight or the vampire or some loser Navy SEAL you could always come out."

"I could, but I should think about it. Ever since I've had a fun coach some of my boyfriends have felt neglected."

"I'll be here till nine or ten, depending on people. I'll follow you home to make sure you get in safely. Because I'm such a gentleman."

"I'm sure you would. Let me see what I have to do."

"You do that, Gracie."

No one had ever called her Gracie or flower girl. She loved it.

She went to Cooper's at almost eight, climbed up on a stool, her cheeks rosy and her fingers like icicles. It was a perfect night on the beach and there were three different fires surrounded by people, mostly young people.

"Hi," Troy said, smiling. He grabbed her hand. "Whew. Cold."

"I walked over," she said. "I might need a ride home."

He smiled wider. "Gotcha covered," he said, a twinkle in his eye.

Troy found lots of things he could do with Grace. She had never dated like this before. They drove down the coast to the redwoods, another day they went up the coast to Ecola Beach. They drove over to Eugene, and they drove up into the snowy Oregon mountains on a clear day. They went out to dinner twice and saw two movies. She went with him to a couple of high school basketball games and she closed the shop early one Saturday so they could drive to the university for a Ducks hockey game and they watched the Super Bowl together—just the two of them. They always ended the dates with more of that wonderful kissing. And with Troy always dangling the suggestion of an overnight. Grace kept pushing that idea back *for now*. But they made out every night. Every. Night. She really couldn't get enough.

She found herself watching one of her favorite comfort chick flicks a lot—*The Holiday*. It was sweet, warm and fuzzy and she thought Troy looked very like Jude Law, except for the dimple. Grace was falling in love.

Because Grace and Troy had been seen around with Iris so often, not much was made of the fact that Iris was now missing—she was a newlywed, after all. In fact, Troy and Grace ran into Iris and Seth at a high school basketball game and they seemed completely unsurprised to see Troy and Grace together.

Then Iris popped into the shop one day after school. She'd been doing that quite regularly since Grace bought the shop. Iris liked to make her own flower arrangements and Grace gave them to her cheap. But, since she'd been married, the visits had become rare. Grace already had the workroom cleaned up. "I haven't seen you in a while," Iris said. "Are you anxious to close?"

"I'm in no great hurry, but no one will be by now. People who want flowers after five call ahead—they know I'll stay open for them to pick up if I can. This married business—I don't see that much of you any-more!"

"Because now I go home and cook! If I don't, Seth's mom will try to feed us every night and we can't have that. And I run errands and do laundry and get caught up on my homework before Seth comes home."

"*You* cook? Oh, God, has he filed for an annul-ment yet?"

"Very funny. I'm getting better, but sometimes he cooks. Have any flowers you can spare? I could use something cheery in the house—this weather can be a downer."

"Oh, I know exactly how to perk you up," she said, going into the cooler. She brought out a bottle of nice sauvignon blanc and two icy glasses she kept in there for just such an occasion. "Ta-da! You can pick your flowers while I get the corkscrew out of my desk."

"You are a good person, Grace," Iris said, approv-ing of the wine and going into the cooler. Grace had the wine poured by the time Iris returned with a se-lection of flowers. Iris knew exactly where to get clippers, tape and a vase. She chose a very attrac-tive oval vase to hold the bouquet. "I'll return it, of course," Iris said.

Grace passed her a glass of wine and lifted her own. "To your new status, Mrs. Sileski."

"Thank you, Grace," she said. "And should we toast a new relationship for you? You seem to be spending a lot of time with Troy."

"You left him lonely," Grace said with laughter in her voice.

"Oh, please don't tell me he's complaining that I'm off the market! I thought we had that all taken care of!"

"He's not complaining, Iris," Grace said, taking a sip of her wine. "But we're just friends."

"Are you sure about that?"

"Oh, yes. I asked, as a matter of fact. He said he needs someone to play with. And so do I, since you decided to get married!"

"There's no question about it—Troy is fun."

"The fun coach," Grace said with a laugh, then she told Iris about the giant wave until both of them were laughing hysterically. Grace told Iris about some of their fun dates, but she didn't mention the more personal things, like all that wonderful kissing.

After a glass of wine and a very beautiful bouquet were both done, Iris said it was time to get home.

"I bet Troy's not just looking for fun," Iris said.

"Oh, I bet he is," Grace replied. "But so am I."

Grace locked the front door behind Iris, lost in thought. *Why can't I let myself lean on Iris, give her the whole story? She might know how I should guard my heart because I'm starting to fall in love and Troy isn't looking for love. Especially from me.*

She went back to the workroom, put the cork in the bottle and heard a light tapping at the back door. She looked up and smiled.

"Ah, I see you've been working hard," Troy said, pointing to the wine bottle.

"I was about to put this back in the cooler. Iris came by to make herself a bouquet," she said. "You just missed her," she added, watching his expression.

"I saw her earlier," he said, picking up the glasses. "I'll carry these up for you."

"You saw Iris?" she asked.

"I see her at school every day, Grace. Want to go out for Chinese?"

"I need a shower," she said.

He reached for her. With the wineglasses in one hand he lifted her chin with the other and put a sweet kiss on her lips. "Want to have a shower and I'll go get takeout? Or, if you need help with that shower…"

"I'll manage," she said. "So, you're hungry for Chinese?"

"I am. And I want to ask you something. Want takeout or should I wait for you to have a shower?"

"What do you want to ask me?"

"Hold on. I'm going to soften you up first. Is there a beer upstairs?"

"There are two," she said. "You go get dinner while I wash off the flowers. How long will it take you?"

"Forty minutes, tops," he said. "You okay to lock up?"

"I do it every day, Troy. Just get going."

This was what it was like to go steady, she thought. Just a couple of small things missing. Like, there was no future and he wasn't falling for her. Well, if nothing else, it was good dating practice. Troy was a great date, after all.

Troy's question was a simple but difficult one. The high school was having a Valentine's Day dance and he wanted her to be his date. He was going to chaperone. "Oh, God, that's almost the busiest day of the year for me!" she exclaimed.

"How late do you stay open?"

"Just till six, but I will be toast! I might be the worst date of your life."

"I can help you after work, help you clean up the shop and lock up. How about deliveries?"

"I have a little part-time help with that. Justin Russell, Al's boy, is running some flowers for me before he goes to work at the station and he's going to be sure to help that day—I already told him it's madness, but there could be good tips. Oh, Troy, what if I'm no fun? And it's a dance! I love to dance, but I might be knee-walking tired."

"The next day is Sunday. You can sleep all day," he begged. "Come on. I want to take the prettiest girl in Thunder Point to protect me from all the teenage girls."

"Really?"

"You are the prettiest girl in—"

"No," she said. "To protect you?"

"Okay, I can handle them," he said with a laugh. "Come with me, Gracie. We'll dance. Put a sign on the shop door. Closing promptly at six on Valentine's Day so make arrangements to get your flowers early or ask for delivery. The flower girl has a date."

Grace couldn't resist him. And while everything else felt casual, even the kissing part, this felt like the real deal. She asked if the right dress was going to be an issue.

"Not for you," he said. "All the high school girls are competing with each other and trying to impress their dates. But you already have me. You can wear a barrel if you want to." And that was exactly the right thing to say, but she warned herself not to get too excited. At least not until he said something that sounded like *we're more than friends*.

Valentine's Day met all of her expectations for craziness. Grace started early and made up as many bouquets as she could ahead of customers. The pre-ordered roses had been ready the day before and by the end of the day every rose in the shop was gone, along with many other arrangements. Justin started deliveries early and continued right up till five o'clock. Without him, she'd have been lost. She tried to stay ahead of the mess but in the end she left a lot of it—she could give the shop a good cleaning on Sunday.

She would have liked a little extra time to get dressed, but even rushed as she was she went to more trouble than usual with her hair and makeup. Grace wore her maid of honor dress, a sleek little black number and the only fancy dress in her arsenal. She usually pulled her hair back to keep it out of the way of the stalks and stems, but for this date she wore it down. It had grown long, past her shoulders. She even used the curling iron!

"Wow. You clean up good!" Troy said when he picked her up.

Grace expected to stand around a punch bowl with a bunch of teachers while the high school kids danced, but it was so much more than that. She was immediately enchanted. The high school gym was beautifully transformed with painted murals, twisted crepe paper streamers, snowy scenes, balloons, glitter balls, white and colored twinkle lights. The bleachers were pushed all the way back and the gym floor was circled with small round tables covered with long white tablecloths. Candles and little centerpieces decorated each table and there was a disc jockey at one end of the dance floor. To enter the gym the couples walked through a heart-shaped arch decorated with hearts, clouds and snowflakes and their pictures were taken as they appeared. The chaperones hung back and chatted among themselves; only a couple had brought dates or spouses. As the music played, almost everyone danced, and refreshments were being served by volunteers.

It was magical. Grace had never been to a high school dance. She'd never been to a high school!

Iris was at the dance, of course. "No date tonight?" Grace asked.

"My date is patrolling the parking lot and looking for trouble. I'm sure he'll cruise through the dance once in a while."

"Are police necessary?" Grace asked.

"Seth is a little overprotective. He likes to feel the kids are as safe as possible. And since I have to be here anyway..." Iris was pulled away by another chaperone with a question.

A young man approached Grace and Troy. "Is this your girlfriend, Mr. Headly?"

"Yes, this is Grace Dillon, Ms. Dillon to you."

He gave a short bow. "Would you like to dance, Ms. Dillon?" he asked politely.

"Ah, I…ah…"

"It's entirely up to you, Grace," Troy said. "Jerome here won't put any moves on you because he knows I'd have to kill him."

"Is it all right?" she whispered to him.

"No slow dancing. Those are mine," Troy whispered back.

Grace began what became a series of dances with a variety of young partners who were funny and charming and devilish. It was obvious they thought it was a real hoot to get Mr. Headly's girl on the dance floor. Whenever the music slowed Troy was instantly at her side, cutting in, holding her as closely as he dared at a high school function. It seemed as if all the slow dances were crooned by Michael Bublé, but she was surprised by the wide variety of music, from oldies to current rock. There was even a line dance performed to the strains of Aretha Franklin singing "Chain of Fools." It took Grace about two seconds to learn it and Troy joined in. "Am I dancing with students too much?" she asked.

"I love watching you," he said. "There's one small problem—I can't wait to get you alone."

"Are you dancing much?" she asked.

"Very judiciously and as little as possible. Giggly high school girls are just not my thing. Besides, I'm supposed to be keeping an eye on things, make sure the kids aren't getting into trouble."

"What kind of trouble?"

"Oh, you know, sneaking out to the parking lot to be too alone or to get a bottle or smoke a joint or get in a fight over something, like a girl. You know."

That was the point, she *didn't* know. "Really?"

"Been a while since you've been rockin' the high school dance?"

"You could say that," she said. "I thought this would be boring. I can't remember when I've had so much fun."

"Just remember, don't fall in love with anyone because you leave the dance with me." He grinned at her.

She noticed that Troy danced with Iris. Not a slow dance, but not so fast, either. He twirled her around and they laughed. She had no worries that Iris would invade her territory, none at all. But did Troy still wish that romance had worked? She forced herself to look away. When she looked back, Iris was talking to her husband. Troy was nowhere in sight.

He was right behind her, claiming a dance. It was an old tune with a good beat—"Knock On Wood"— and Troy improvised, moving her two beats left, two beats right, a little twirl. She'd been very impressed by his dancing tonight. And it was sexy! Then the tune segued into a bebop beat and she noticed a few kids getting together for another line dance, but Troy pulled her back from the crowd, gave her hands a little shove and made a jitterbug move. "Huh?" he asked, lifting his eyebrows.

She laughed at him. "As long as you don't slide me between your legs or toss me onto your hips and over your shoulder."

"Aw," he said, then led her into a really good jitterbug, so good that kids stopped what they were doing to watch. *This guy knows what he's doing,* she thought.

When the song ended, there were a few claps from the crowd. Grace heard a teenage girl say, "Oh, God, why can't he just *marry* me!"

Five

Four hours flew by and at almost midnight they were on their way to Grace's place in Troy's car. She was completely amazed by the variety of music, from oldies to current rock to hip-hop and even country. And now that she thought about it, Troy was up to speed on all of those dances, even picking up the line dance steps quickly. "Care to explain that dancing, Fred Astaire?" she asked.

He laughed. "Short story. I dated a dance instructor. Not like Arthur Murray—she taught little kids. Her sister was getting married and she wanted someone who could dance to go to the wedding with her, so she taught me a bunch of moves, including the tango. It was fun, to tell the truth. She broke up with me the day after the wedding."

"Aw, was your heart broken?"

"A little bit," he said. "I didn't think I'd ever have fun dancing again."

"Well, you wowed 'em tonight. I even heard a marriage proposal."

He laughed.

"Does that ever become…you know…difficult?"

"What?"

"The girls," she said. "They crush on you! And some of them are beautiful! And look older than me, by the way! Does that ever worry you?"

"Worry me in what way?" he asked, his brow crinkling.

"What if one of them got the wrong signals? Thought you were romantically interested or something?"

He chuckled. "They do all the time, but not because of anything I do—because of their imaginative, nubile young minds mixed with the irresponsibility of raging hormones. Grace, teachers have to play it real safe or find themselves in a bad place."

"What does that mean?"

He shrugged. "There are very specific guidelines. We don't touch the students, except maybe a hand on an arm or shoulder to say, 'Wait up a second.' We can never have private conversations with students with doors closed. We don't give them a lift home even in a nice little town like this. We don't make gestures that could be interpreted as seductive, and we don't respond to such gestures—the list is long. And it's not just for young male teachers but for all teachers—young women, old women, crusty old codgers, guys like me. Counselors like Iris. If she closes her office door, the door to the main hallway is closed to the passersby, but all the offices are internal cubicles that share a common hall between them so that a conversation can be private but if someone yelled or called out, it could be heard. Counselors, principals, nurses—they have to be afforded a degree of privacy to do their work. Students need to feel safe. I, however, am always seen in a crowd. During my private conversations with students, the door to the classroom is open. And we're on opposite sides of the desk."

"But has it happened, Troy? That some girl takes her crush too far?"

"You understand that I like women, but women my own age, right? I'm not tempted by children. High school students are minors. And our school system forbids fraternization with students even of legal age, like eighteen-year-olds. There is absolutely no compromise there."

"Of course," she said. "But..."

"To a certain degree, there are some normal feelings in the mix for the kids. Little girls sit on their daddy's laps and promise to marry them and the fact is, they probably will marry a man just like their father. Crushing on teachers is not unusual, but they're children and it's the adult teacher's job to keep that from escalating. You get to be good at recognizing the signs and creating appropriate distance and barriers before..." He stopped. He pulled up behind her building and parked. He turned to her. "Gracie, why are you asking me this?"

"I just thought it must sometimes be challenging."

He rubbed a knuckle along her cheek. "Honey,

were you molested? Assaulted? By an older man or teacher? Someone in a position of authority?"

"Me?" she asked, genuinely shocked. "No! No, of course not."

"Then you knew someone who was," he said matter-of-factly.

Boy, did she! Years ago, and it all ended so tragically it marked one of the most traumatic experiences of her life. But that was not the direction Grace wanted this conversation to go. Not tonight. So she smiled gently.

"You must either be a very wonderful teacher or so intuitive it's scary," she said. "Once, I thought someone I knew was a victim, a younger girl, but even though I had suspicions, I never had proof. She wasn't a good friend of mine, just a girl I knew. Seriously, I didn't bring it up to discuss that—that was so long ago. I really was curious about how you manage the situation with the students. I'd have asked Iris all the same questions if it had ever come up. It was the dance that brought it to mind. Some of those girls are gorgeous. And you do kind of make them giggle."

"The really scary part is I don't have to do much to make them giggle. There's a real dearth of young teachers in Thunder Point. Another one who gets their constant attention is Coach Lawson. But he doesn't have female students." He leaned toward her and put a small kiss on her lips. "You must be exhausted."

She gave him a little smile. "Would you like to come up?"

"If you think you can stay awake awhile…"

"Come on up," she said. She hummed under her breath all the way up the back stairs to her little loft, and right inside the door, she turned to him and, for once, she made the advance. She put her arms around his neck and kissed him like she really meant business.

"Whoa," he said.

"Would you like a glass of wine? I think we should have a little talk."

He paused for a moment. "Should I go down to the flower fridge for the wine?" he finally asked.

"No, tonight is this very special Shiraz. I hope you like it." She picked up a bottle from the counter and handed it to him so he could look at it.

But Troy frowned, as if he was worried about what was coming. "Let me open it for you so we can get to the talking part."

She turned to grab the corkscrew, then picked up the two glasses that she'd set out earlier.

"Where are we talking?" he asked as he shed his coat and tie.

"How about right in here?" she said, carrying the glasses to the little living room. She put the glasses on the coffee table, kicked off her shoes and got comfortable. "Why do you look worried?"

"Because this seems planned and I have no idea what's coming. I hope it's not bad news."

"I hope so, too. Open that wine and let it breathe." While he did that, she took a deep breath. "Troy, I've never been to a high school dance before tonight."

He stopped twisting the corkscrew for a second, then looked at her. He pulled the cork. "A lot of kids don't go to the dances, Gracie."

"I bet you did," she said.

"I did," he admitted. "But by now you know me—I'm a flirt. I get along with everyone. I'm the fun coach. I almost always had a girlfriend or at least a date. I didn't date just anyone, though—I'm no man whore. I'm not a screw around kind of guy."

"Troy, I never went to a high school dance because I never went to a high school."

He seemed to be momentarily confused. "Boarding school? Some private academy?"

She shook her head. "Homeschooled. With tutors."

"And some classes here and there?"

"Some," she said. "Small groups of tutored kids, now and then. Mostly independent study with guidance and lots of tests to track my progress."

"Wow. You'll have to share that study plan with me someday. It seems to have worked. You're very accomplished for someone who never went to high school."

"I didn't say they were lazy tutors," she said. "I learned things a lot of high school students wouldn't even get to. But there's a reason I'm telling you this, Troy. I've also never had a boyfriend."

He chuckled. "That's very hard to believe. You're beautiful."

"Oh, I had a couple of bad dates, but that's about all. I just wasn't in the mainstream of life like other young women. See, I said my parents were gone and that's true, sort of. My father died when I was only fourteen and my mother and I fell out five years ago. We had an argument about what I wanted to do with my life. She comes from money—she's very spoiled and demanding. She's a diva, that's the only way to describe her. The very thought of me in the back of a florist's shop, filthy, lifting big pots, driving to residences to deliver flowers, being *the help* at weddings and funerals..." Grace shrugged. "She was mortified. We had a standoff. She wanted me to live at home with her, follow in her footsteps, plan charity events, travel with her, let her... Well, she probably had some guy lined up for me from somewhere. We never got that far in a discussion. I wasn't interested. I wanted my own life and I wanted it simple. We haven't spoken in years. It's very sad. It's for the best, I think."

By his expression, he was stunned. He reached out and grabbed her shoulder. "Grace...I'm sorry."

"Thank you. Maybe someday it will sort itself out. What I really want you to know is..." She lifted her chin bravely. "Troy, I'm not like Iris. I'm not like other girls. I'm probably less experienced than some of your students. I've never had a guy I really liked before. I'm pretty lame at it."

"You're doing very well," he said with a smile. He poured them each a glass of wine.

She took a sip. Then a breath. "Well, even though you're probably going to figure it out anyway, I thought you should know—I don't know much about men. Just what my boyfriends in my romances told me. That's it."

He raised one eyebrow. "And how am I going to figure that out?"

"When you realize I don't have any idea what to do! You're going to guess, if we do decide to do it, that I've never done it before. You will be my first unless you run for your life right now." She grinned at him. "No pressure."

He grinned right back. "I'm not worried, Gracie. Are you?"

She nodded. "Maybe a little," she said.

"Want me to tell you how it's going to be?"

Again she nodded.

"The first time it's going to be very slow and safe. We're going to kiss until we're steamy. We're going to touch and get so close we can feel each other's heartbeat." He leaned over and gently kissed her cheek and her throat and she let her head drop back and closed her eyes. "We're going to lie down together and lose some clothes… We'll discover each other. I'm going to touch you in all your special places and you're going to touch me when you're ready. We'll ease into things slowly and carefully, but the most important thing is, you can say no or stop whenever you don't want to go any further. Even if we're naked and breathing hard, if you say stop, we stop."

Her eyes were still closed and she whispered into his cheek. "I don't use anything…"

"I do," he said.

"When is this going to happen?" she asked.

"In a hurry, Grace?"

She shrugged. "Well, when I make a decision…"

"We're going to enjoy a glass of wine. Then, if you're ready, you'll let me know."

Troy hadn't been prepared for this—a twenty-eight-year-old woman as beautiful and funny as Grace, a virgin. He would have expected her to have sexual history, like most women her age. Some had a lot of notches, some only a few, but he'd never encountered *none* before. Even his first girl, his first experience, wasn't a virgin. She'd had a serious boyfriend before him. Of course, just because he was a flirt and liked to have girlfriends didn't mean he'd been a sexual prodigy. He had sex for the first time at nearly the end of his first year of college. At eighteen, he was the last among his buddies, unless they were lying.

They were probably lying. Of course they were lying. At least mostly lying.

He took this very seriously, making love to Grace. It had to be a good experience for her and he was definitely eager to take on the challenge. He just hoped there wasn't some virgin consciousness that would have her leaning toward true love and marriage because of sex. He wasn't opposed to that in the long run, he just didn't want it all to happen in one night. He was crazy about her, couldn't wait to get inside her, didn't see any red flags that would warn him to get out of this relationship—he just needed time to get more serious. *This is how grown-ups court.* They have dates, they discover common interests, they examine their rapport, they go to bed together, they ask, *Does this have staying power?*

They kissed and whispered their way through a glass of wine, then Troy took hers out of her hand and put it on the coffee table. He stood and pulled her to her feet and led her toward the bedroom, which was only about ten feet away. When they stood beside the bed, he took her gently into his arms and kissed her some more, drawing deep sighs from her. Then she turned in his arms and presented her back, pulling her hair away, and he saw the zipper for her dress.

He drew it down slowly, taking a taste of her neck in the process. He pushed the dress off her shoulders and she let it fall, leaving her in a silky black slip. She stepped out of the dress and bent to pick it up, but he took it from her and turned to drape it across the only chair in the room. He got rid of his belt and shirt and when he turned back to her, she had removed her hose and kicked them aside. She was a determined little thing; he wasn't going to find going slowly an easy thing.

When she sat on the bed he withdrew a couple of condoms from his pocket.

"Do you have to put them out now?" she asked.

"Believe me, I do," he said. He let the pants drop, kicked them off and they joined the clothes on the chair. He sat beside her, embraced her, pulled her down beside him and rolled a little, adjusting till their bodies were flush and tight. "There," he said, feeling every curve of her against him. "Perfect."

And he was ready.

"I can feel your heart," he said. He ran his hands down her back and over her butt. She was so firm and solid. "The flower business must be good exercise," he said, chuckling softly.

Her hands were on his chest, caressing every inch of him, kissing his chest, his neck, his mouth and all the time wiggling up against him. He still wore his boxers, but they were doing nothing to keep his secrets. He pushed himself between her legs without really meaning to—he was on automatic pilot.

"Let's get rid of this," he said, pulling a strap of the slip down over her shoulder.

She sat up and drew the silky garment over her head and tossed it aside, leaving her in nothing but a tiny thong. And that, he thought, wouldn't get in his way for a second. But to level the playing field and give her a chance to get used to him, he shed his boxers. There they were. In all their basic glory. He pulled her hand, drawing it to him. She didn't hesitate; she put both hands on him and hummed softly as she figured him out. "Easy does it," he said.

There were so many things he wanted to do to her, but not the first time. He'd like to lick her whole body, make her come before she even knew what hit her. He'd like to lift her onto his lap and watch her ride; he'd like to take her against the shower wall. *Not this time*, he told himself. He had promised it would be slow and safe and he never broke a promise. He slid his hand under her thong. "Open for me, honey," he said, giving her thighs a nudge. He slid one finger into her silkiness. Then two fingers. *Wow*, she wasn't going to need much warming up. He massaged her for a few seconds and she was squirming against his hand, almost whimpering. He slid a finger inside.

"You okay?" he asked in a whisper.

"Okay," she whispered back.

"This has to go," he said, pulling her thong down. She kicked it away as he turned to the bedside table and retrieved a condom, quickly rolling it on. If he didn't suit up, she was going to climb all over him. She was straining toward him, making beautiful little noises. He turned her on her back, spread her legs with a knee and placed himself in the zone. Leaning down to her lips once more, he whispered against them. "Ready to see how this works?" he asked.

"Yes," she whispered back, her eyes closed.

"Look at me, Gracie." She opened her eyes. "I want you to go limp…relax everything. It's not going to hurt."

"Are you sure?"

"I'm sure." He pressed himself against her. "Nice and easy," he said. "It's okay. It's good." And he pressed into her very, very slowly. He kissed her deeply as he went all the way. She moaned. "Okay?" he asked.

"Mmm," she murmured. "Okay."

But damned if he was! This was the best place he'd been in a very long time. And she hugged him like a velvet vise. A quivering, soft, slick vise. He was dying. He started to move, slowly, looking for that sweet spot, pressing deeply into her, listening to the sounds she made, trying to judge them for the right spot, the right friction, the perfect stimulation for her. As for himself, if he unclenched his molars for one second, he was gone.

"Oh." She sighed. "Oh! Oh! *Oh!*"

"Oh, yeah," he said.

"Please," she said, gripping his shoulders. "More. Please!"

He moved a little harder, hanging on for dear life. He took her mouth again, kissing her deeply as he moved inside. "You're beautiful, baby," he whispered. "You're perfect."

"I think maybe you're perfect," she said.

"Only with you," he said. "With you I feel perfect." And he followed that with a kiss. And a thrust.

She came apart. She clenched him inside her body, drawing on him, leaving him to wonder if it was his expert moves or the words. Then thinking stopped. She closed her eyes, tilted her head back and her pelvis forward, upward, bit her lip and if he could see, he'd bet she curled her toes. So he did what came naturally, thrusting a couple more times and having the best orgasm of his life, right then, right there, with her. His eyes teared; his brain clouded over and he wondered if he lost consciousness for a second. He pulsed until there was nothing left in him. Even his brain was empty; her body was still holding him for so long he was amazed. She rode through it with him, the whole way.

He pressed his lips softly to hers, kissing her gently. She didn't move. He gave her another kiss. She still held him in a beautiful, delicious, unimaginable grip. "Gracie," he whispered. "Breathe."

She let out her breath in a slow *whoosh*. "Holy shit!" she said.

He smiled. "Nice?"

"Mmm," she said, her lips curving into a smile.

He chuckled. "Just when I was wondering what to get you for Valentine's Day…"

"Oh. My. God. Do it again."

He laughed. "Maybe in a little bit," he said, but there was really no maybe about it. "No regrets?"

"You're kidding, right?"

"I might not have figured it out," he admitted. "Except I also might not have tried so hard to go slowly and patiently. Because, really, Gracie, you had me in a real vulnerable spot there for a while."

"I did?"

"You did. We came together like old pros."

"If I hadn't told you, what would you have done?"

"I think I'd have just gone for it. I think first, to be sure you had everything you deserved, I'd have licked your whole body. Then I would have just gone for it."

"Okay. We'll do that next time!"

He couldn't help but laugh at her, she was so damn cute. "You like sex, don't you, sweetheart?"

"I like sex," she admitted, smiling. "Oh, God, is that a slutty thing to say?"

"No, Gracie." He brushed her rich brown hair back from her brow. "It's the perfect thing to say."

They made love again and again. Troy knew he was screwed, and not in the usual way. He had himself a beautiful young woman who thought he was pure magic, who would do anything he wanted to do, bring him greater satisfaction than he could remember having and…and he didn't know anything about her. Added to that, he wasn't sure what had caused it, but being the first man to ever get inside her like that really did something to his head. A kind of possessiveness consumed him; he couldn't even think about letting her go. But who was this young beauty who hadn't been properly loved until now? Who asked questions about whether it was difficult being a young male teacher surrounded by teenage girls with crushes? Who was this young woman who'd never been in a traditional classroom yet who seemed to be smarter and more worldly than other women her age? And did mothers and daughters really part ways over the choice to own a flower shop?

He was lying on his belly in her bed, thinking about how he was going to get the answers to these questions when he felt her small hand, slightly calloused from hard work, slide over his buttocks.

"You have the nicest guy booty I've ever seen."

"Roll me over and see what else I've got that's nice," he said.

"I'm afraid to," she said with a laugh. "I think you've had enough. And I've definitely had enough!"

"Feeling a little tender?"

She nodded and blushed.

He laughed. "After the gymnastics of last night, how can you blush?" he asked her.

"It's daylight," she said.

"Better yet," he said, rolling over to show off his rather impressive morning erection.

"Oh, my," she said. "Keep that thing away from me!"

He ignored her and pulled her into his arms. "Let's talk about how to have fun when we're feeling a little…delicate." And he began kissing his way down her body, over her belly, between her thighs. Just a few minutes later he had to say again, "Gracie. Breathe."

"Oh, God," she said weakly.

His pleasure couldn't have been greater.

"Is it my turn now?" she asked.

"Not this time, honey," he said, hoisting himself out of the bed. "Much as I'd like to lie around in bed all day, I have things to do. I have to get ready for classes tomorrow and I'm working at Cooper's all afternoon and evening. You should nap, rest up. If you want me to drop by later to make sure you're okay, just say the word."

"The word," she said with a smile.

"Would you like me to take you to breakfast at the diner before I start my chores?" he asked.

"Would you?"

"I definitely would. You make a man hungry, but I have to go home first and, you know…freshen up."

She laughed softly. "I guess it wouldn't do to go out to breakfast in last night's clothes. Not to mention…"

"Don't mention it," he suggested, knowing where that was going. The scent of sex was all over them. Even without that, anyone who saw her this morning was sure to know. She was wearing a very fetching whisker burn on her pink cheeks, her lips were bright and rosy from a night of kissing and that sleepy twinkle in her eye said everything. Here was a very happy, satisfied lady. "I'll be back in thirty minutes."

Six

An hour and a half later, breakfast done, Troy was back in his apartment, where he was not planning to do any school preparation. Instead, he got on the internet. He had a couple of hours before he had to be out at the beach bar. He didn't expect to find anything, unless perhaps there had been some kind of molestation and charges were filed, but if Grace had been a minor, her name wouldn't have been included. He typed her name into the search bar and the italicized question popped back:

Do you mean Isabella "Izzy" Grace Dillon Banks?

Just for grins, he clicked on the name, expecting to see the picture of a sixty-year-old opera singer.

"Are you shitting me?" he asked the empty room.

Figure Skating Gold Medalist walks out of the Vancouver arena and doesn't look back.

It was *her* in the picture. *Izzy Banks? Gold medalist? Retired at the age of twenty-three?* It just didn't compute. Was that something you didn't think to mention? Although Izzy apparently issued a statement, she refused all interviews. He read her statement.

"The figure skating community and competition has been very good to me and I'm tremendously grateful to my family, my mother, the intrepid Winnie Dillon Banks, my coach Mikhail Petrov, U.S. Figure Skating, and every friend and competitor I've known over the past twenty years, but this is my time to exit. There are so many wonderful athletes prepared to have their chance and, believe me, I won't be missed for long. I crave a quieter life."

Troy was stunned. He almost couldn't inhale. How was this possible?

There were a number of articles and much conjecture, comparing Izzy to other athletes who, exhausted and overloaded, perhaps depressed, crashed after a big win and retreated. She wasn't the only story, for sure.

There were a few differences that stood out to him, maybe because of their conversation just the night before. A grievance was filed against her with U.S. Figure Skating by figure skating coach Hal Nordstrom, a world-famous coach whose students had won many medals. He alleged slander and defamation of character. The direct quote seemed to be well-known but wasn't in the article. Apparently when a fifteen-year-old student of Nordstrom committed suicide Izzy Banks, then eighteen, commented that he mishandled his students and drove them to tragic ends with his sexual misconduct. No charges were filed against the coach, no corroborative complaints emerged, no other students stepped forward and there was no evidence against the man. The grievance was dismissed; Izzy had uttered an opinion in the presence of other skaters in training, their coaches and parents—it didn't say how many. There were comments from Nordstrom's other students that had nothing to do with sexual misconduct. They claimed he'd taken his student, Shannon Fields, out of his number-one slot and put another skater in it and some believed she was despondent with disappointment and jealousy after so many years of hard work. No one seemed sure why she took her own life.

But Troy knew. He knew Grace. If she said a younger skater had been molested, she thought she knew something. It didn't mean she was wrong just because she had no evidence.

Nordstrom sued Izzy and her mother in a civil court. There was an undisclosed settlement.

He read other articles. Grace had been trailed by not one but three stalkers. She was hardly the only internationally known athlete with this burden, but she was one of only a few who had actually been kidnapped. It wasn't for more than a few hours, but he couldn't imagine how terrifying it must have been. That particular stalker was captured, arrested, prosecuted and hospitalized. His name was Bruno Feldman and he was schizophrenic and delusional, which made him ill but no less frightening or dangerous because of his illness.

He typed her name into the search box again.

There were over five thousand hits. As far as he knew, no one in Thunder Point had any idea who she really was. His little flower girl had accomplished things most people never dared dream of and, apparently, the price had been high. He had an overwhelming urge to run to her, take her into his arms and tell her she was safe now. Instead, he took his laptop with him to work at Cooper's, where he planned to read more on the sly when he wasn't too busy.

He was at the bar by noon. There were ten people, all inside. Cooper and his young brother-in-law, Landon, were behind the bar. Troy was barely in the door when two patrons left. He hung up his coat and put his backpack under the bar.

"If the weatherman is right, it shouldn't be too busy today. Just the occasional Sunday driver," Cooper said.

Sunny Sundays were typically pretty busy. "What's the weatherman saying?"

"Guess? Wind and rain. The baby's trying to get a tooth so we're going to look at a couple of cars for Landon," Cooper said.

"Trucks," Landon corrected.

"*Maybe* trucks," Cooper clarified.

"I thought you had a truck," Troy said.

"It pretty much bit the dust and has been retired," Cooper said. "Landon needs some reliable wheels so I don't have to drive to Eugene every time he feels like a weekend at home."

"And this has what to do with a tooth?"

Both guys winced. "You have no idea how hard it

is to get a tooth," Cooper said. "Apparently she has to work on it twenty-four hours a day and it makes her very pissy."

"She's not happy about anything right now," Landon said. "We're getting out of there."

Troy laughed. "Poor Sarah."

"I did my shift last night," Cooper said. "If it's stormy and empty, close early. Six or so?"

"I'll stay as long as you want me," Troy said, but he knew if the weather was bad, the bar hardly ever saw business after sunset and sunset came early in February. In football season, there'd be people inside watching the game, but that was past.

"You decide," Cooper said. "Let's go, Landon. Have a good day. And thanks."

By midafternoon there was just one couple in the bar, drinking Bloody Marys and eating sandwiches at a table by the fire. Troy checked the kitchen and dishwasher, but as usual Cooper had left the place spotless and organized. In winter this was a one-man operation, but in summer it took a full crew—there were lots of people on the beach, renting paddle-boards and kayaks, eating and drinking, enjoying the bay and lighting fires on the beach at night, a constant flow of customers, sometimes until after ten.

He brought a stool behind the bar and opened his laptop. There was enough information about Grace to fill a book. She even had her own Wikipedia page, as did her wealthy mother, Winnie Dillon Banks, a champion figure skater before her. There was a half brother, twenty years her senior, a child of her father's by a previous marriage. One article explained the many ways people managed the expensive training without being wealthy, but such sponsors were difficult to come by before the athlete had at least come very close to winning major competitions. And to his surprise, the number of moneyed US and world medalists was quite small. Most of them, in fact the best known among them, had hardworking parents who got up at four in the morning to drive them long distances to rinks where the best coach could be found. Some moved to accommodate their young champions.

By late afternoon the rain hit the deck outside and the last couple left, and he could get back to his research. Grace and her parents moved a few times; her father was sought after and drew a handsome coaching salary. He did not train Grace's competitors, however. His income and notoriety, in addition to Winnie's old family wealth, was a huge advantage for her. She didn't make the cut for the 2006 Winter Games and there was some talk of moving her to another country. Obviously they hadn't moved.

Lord, who was this girl?

He looked up Winnie Dillon Banks. There were dozens of pictures and all Troy could surmise from them was that she looked rich and cold. Many pictures of her watching her daughter skate in competition had her with a frozen face, wearing furs and diamonds.

That's when he knew they hadn't exactly fallen out over a flower shop. His best guess was that Winnie disapproved of her daughter leaving competition while she was still young enough to train and win.

He looked up figure skating training. It was typical to be on skates by four years old. Six hours on the ice every day, endurance and weight training, ballet and gymnastics, school or, in Grace's case, tutors. Add in travel to every competition that would take her—first Nationals and then World Championships. He looked up international ice-skating championships. Jesus, she'd been to almost every country on the globe.

He watched a couple of YouTube videos of her skating, a long program and a short program, one when she was only sixteen and competing in Seoul. It was the most amazing thing he'd ever seen. She looked just the same. Did no one ever remark on her likeness to a women's figure skating champion? Her skill and beauty on the ice was nothing short of breathtaking.

Next on his list to research was sexual misconduct by coaches. He felt his heart race. It was everywhere. There were some horrifically wrong allegations. One female coach had her life nearly ruined by an accusation that never even went to court as her alibi was actually on film, placing her far from the alleged victim at the time; yet, years later she was still banned from certain gyms, even after the child finally recanted. It sent shudders through him. He thought a person had to be crazy to leave their child in the hands of a stranger even if he or she was a renowned coach.

To get a reality check, he searched the same subject with teachers and it was just as shocking, some cases getting national attention and being made into television movies.

I just thought it must sometimes be challenging...

He closed the laptop and turned on lights around the bar, though if anyone was out in this storm, he'd be amazed. He had a lot to process. It was almost five and the sun might just be on its downward path, but with the clouds it was already dark. He got himself a beer.

He'd known Grace for a year, maybe a little more. He only knew her superficially—he had gone into her shop to buy flowers for Iris twice and once to pick out an arrangement to be sent to his mother for Mother's Day. He'd seen her at Cooper's with Iris. He didn't even really think of her as a friend but rather as one of Iris's friends. He'd liked her but never thought about her—not before Christmas. He'd been looking right through her. He had no idea there was so much to Grace. She was amazing and complicated, part heroic, part tragic. And after last night, more woman than he ever imagined. Little virgin flower girl, a little shy, a little curious and cautious and, oh, God, so willing, trusting and sensual. So loving and innocent. She asked him to take her there, to sex and passion, then put herself in his hands. And man, what a ride.

"She's an athlete, you dope," he said to no one in the bar.

"Who's an athlete?" Sarah Cooper asked, just coming in the door. She shook off her slicker.

"Jesus, you scared me to death!" he said. "Where's the baby?"

"Finally sleeping. Ham's babysitting."

"Sarah, Ham's a dog."

"Best babysitter there is, trust me. He's barely left her side since the day she was born. Don't worry—she's in the crib and the bedroom door is closed, but I trust Ham more than most humans. And I only came over for a second. You should close the bar. You're wasting your time out here. This deluge isn't exactly welcoming customers. Is there anything you need before you go? Besides to finish your beer?"

"I'll just make a quick phone call, maybe take a couple of little pizzas from the cooler—I have a date tonight, I hope. Thanks, I think you're right. No one has come in since two."

She grinned at him, looking at the laptop. "Get your homework done?"

"I sure did," he said. "And it was a load, too."

"Thanks for helping out, Troy. Stay dry." She pulled the hood of her slicker over her head and went out the back door.

He picked up his phone. "Gracie," he said. "Thanks to the weather, I'm closing up early. Would you like me to bring you dinner?"

"I cooked! I cooked, hoping you would come here for dinner!"

"Your kitchen is the size of my closet. What did you cook?"

"Crock-Pot chili. A brick of cheddar and crackers. If I had a fireplace up here, it would be perfect."

It's already perfect, he thought. "I'll be there in a little while. It sounds great."

He wasn't going to tell her what he knew. He decided right then, he was going to wait for her. When she was comfortable, when she trusted him to know that part of her life, when she finally confided in him, he might tell her he'd known for a while. *Might*.

A week later, when Troy was just packing up his papers to take home, he caught a flash of color out of the corner of his eye and turned to see Iris leaning in his classroom doorway. She was wearing a sly grin. "I saw you and Grace at the basketball game last night," she said.

"We said hello," Troy said, frowning slightly, not understanding.

"I was too busy in the concession stand to chat, but not too busy to notice."

"Notice what?" he asked.

"You are officially completely over me."

He smiled and put his papers in his backpack. "I'm over you," he said. "I hope you're not offended. You are married, after all."

She walked toward him. "I saw the way you looked at Grace. I was glad you and Grace were hanging out, but it's a lot more than that. Troy, this makes me happy. Grace is wonderful and I love her. And you're one of my best friends." Then she laughed. "There's the final proof! You didn't wince when I called you a best friend!"

"There's a lot more to Grace than meets the eye," he said, zipping the backpack.

"I think you're falling in love, Troy."

"Easy, Iris. That's a powerful diagnosis. And I don't think you can make it." He picked up the backpack. "My complexion has cleared up, that's all."

She laughed at him. "I hear the hearts of dozens of sixteen-year-old girls breaking."

"Don't even joke about that," he said, suddenly very serious. "That could be a world of trouble a teacher doesn't need."

"Oh, Troy, you haven't had a problem in that area, have you? No one's making you nervous, I hope."

He didn't want to explain the situation with Grace, that her questions on this issue combined with what he thought he'd learned from his research brought the whole thing closer to the surface of his thinking. "No, not at all, it's just that it's a real slippery slope, that relationship. Sometimes I'm afraid to make even the most innocent joke. Know what I mean?"

"Listen, your behavior has always been above reproach, but if you're ever worried about the smallest gesture or comment, come to me immediately. Don't take a chance on seeing where it goes. We don't fool around with that stuff."

"Good. That's good to know because—" He ran a hand around the back of his neck. "I read an article over the weekend about a coach whose life was nearly destroyed by accusations of impropriety with a youngster and she wasn't even in the same city at the time. It filled me with cold dread. Made me think way too much."

"I understand. I get the willies about similar situations in counseling now and then. All I have to do is hear about a terrible counselor, one who does grave damage, and I don't sleep for a couple of nights. But if you're not facing any problems, try to relax and be yourself. The kids love you. And you've been consistently great with boundaries. And now you're in love on top of everything else."

"Don't get ahead of yourself, Iris," he said, but he smiled when he said it. "I've only been seeing Grace for a couple of months." He was suddenly aware that he'd dated Iris for months, thought they were a perfect couple and yet had never uttered those three important words. "When did you know you loved Seth?" he asked, suddenly curious.

"When I was about four, but he was busy playing the field all through high school. Since he never noticed me as anything more than a buddy, an outfielder or tutor, I hated him."

"You're married to him. I guess you got that straightened out."

"Yeah," she said a little wistfully. "Luckily." She collected herself. "Well. If you can be half as happy as I am, you won't know what to do with yourself. Want to go get a beer?"

"I can't," he said. "I'm going to mind the flower shop while Grace meets with some couple about their wedding flowers. Grace has Justin doing some deliveries but no steady part-time help yet. It's just Grace, sometimes closing the shop to deliver flowers, unless I can help her."

"She told me. We talked about student help for her, but it's kind of late in the year to start any kind of work-study situation. I posted an after-school help position on the bulletin board, but…"

"I hope something turns up for her. Hey, tomorrow I'll be out at Cooper's—come on out. I'll treat. Bring Prince Charming. I'll even buy him a beer."

"You're on," she said.

Troy drove to the flower shop, parked in the alley right behind the Pretty Petals van and went in the back door. Grace was finishing the creation of an arrangement at her big messy worktable, but he didn't care. He grabbed her around the waist and pulled her against him, kissing her hard.

"Troy, stop it, I'm filthy."

"I know. Filthy is good. We can get a little filthy later if you feel like it." He picked up her hand and looked at the green and brown fingers, ick under her nails. "Jeez, this is ugly work. Who knew? You'd think working with flowers would be more attractive. Are you sending me home after I help here?"

"Do I ever send you home?"

"What do you want to do for dinner?"

"I grabbed one of Carrie's meals from the deli— teriyaki chicken, rice, asparagus and cheesecake. Will that do it for you?"

He kissed her neck. "For my first meal. Then I'm having you."

She laughed, pushing him away. "I have to run

upstairs and scrub up a little bit," she said, taking off the green apron. She hung it on the hook by the door. "If the Jackson-Paulson couple comes in before I'm back, just put them in my office, will you? I'll be right back."

"Sure," he said. When she'd gone upstairs, he looked around at the mess. Miss Gracie had had a busy day at the flower shop. The big worktable and floor were covered with clippings, stems, florist's foam, tape, all manner of rocks and a couple of glue guns. He put her arrangement in the cooler, picked up the glue guns and swept off the debris on the table onto the floor. The second he'd done that, he realized he was an idiot. Now the rocks and in some cases what looked like flattened marbles pinged around the floor. If he wasn't pretty quick with a broom, someone could break a hip.

He immediately started sweeping a path away from her office door. It could be unpleasant if her customers fell and broke their backs. He was quick about it. He liked it when Gracie thought he was the perfect man and really didn't want to expose himself as just another stupid guy who didn't think.

It didn't take him long to have a nice pile of trash between the back door and the cooler. Just in time, too. The bell on the door tinkled and the couple came in.

"It's just bullshit, Janet. We don't need all this," a man's voice said.

"Maybe I need it," the woman said, her voice watery. "I haven't asked too much and I work for every dime."

"You want a house?" he asked meanly.

"Yes, but not a new truck!" she threw back.

"You want a baby?" he flung.

"When we can afford it, but I don't want to just skip the wedding! I know you don't care, but I care! My mother cares!"

"Then your mother should pay for it!"

"You know my mother has *nothing*!"

"And that's what we're going to have! Nothing!"

"I thought you wanted a wedding?" she said in a near sob.

"I thought so, too, until I saw the list of things we have to buy! I wanted a band, a keg and a good party! Now I'm buying a goddamned coronation!"

The back door opened and Grace stepped in looking completely refreshed in a crisp white blouse, a little shine on her lips and her hair brushed. He wanted to eat her alive, gobble her up. "They're fighting," he whispered.

"Happens all the time. Weddings are famous for it." She looked around. "Oh, Troy, you cleaned up." She took a closer look at the table and floor. "A little…"

"You want me to mop?" he asked.

"No, but thanks. Just mind the front of the store for me, and if someone comes in and needs something, please interrupt me. I can take two minutes while my clients look at pictures, run a sale, get back to them in no time."

"I work in a bar, Gracie. I can ring up a sale. If there are price tags."

"Everything is priced. Let any calls go to voice mail." She kissed him real quick on the lips. "Thank you."

"You are so hard to wait for," he muttered under his breath as she walked away. He watched as she approached the tortured couple.

"Mr. Jackson? Ms. Paulson? Hi, I'm Grace. Would you like to come back to my office and talk about your wedding flowers?"

"We're *fighting* about the wedding," Ms. Paulson said.

"Well, I'm here to lessen your wedding tension and help you find very practical and affordable options in the flower department. Don't worry— looking at pictures of bouquets and arrangements carries no obligation at all. I only want to help. Come with me. Would you like a cup of coffee? Tea? Bottled water?"

"How about a beer," the groom said testily.

"I had to stop stocking beer," Grace said with a laugh. "Too many stressed-out, drunk grooms left my flower shop! Come right in here, let me get a couple of waters." She put them in the chairs in front of her desk and when she walked through the workroom to her cooler, she rolled her eyes at Troy, smiling a little.

Troy went to the front of the store to stand sentry while Grace had her meeting with the bridal couple. She usually met with couples like this at six or later, after work for them, after closing for her. This particular couple had to schedule something a little earlier, so she'd invited them to come at four, which was how Troy got this babysitting job. He positioned himself behind the small counter. There by the computer lay two phones—her personal and her work phone. Everywhere she went, two phones. When the shop was closed and they were together, she rarely answered the work phone. And the personal phone rarely rang. She'd gotten calls twice since they'd been a couple and both times it was Iris.

He heard her tell the couple to "start with this album."

"There aren't any prices," the man said.

"Jake!" the woman said.

"That's a reasonable observation and question. Every bouquet and arrangement can be downsized or enlarged, depending on personal taste. For example, see this beautiful arrangement of roses, fern and calla lilies? I had a bride want a much smaller version of this with just the dusty miller and lilies plus a little baby's breath. I'll be glad to itemize everything with cost per stalk, stem and vase."

"I don't know why we're making it so fancy," Jake muttered.

"It needn't be," Grace said. "Small weddings can be elegant, classy and memorable. In your life together there are going to be many moments you're going to want to capture in pictures. You'll be amazed when you get to your thirtieth anniversary how many boxes or albums or disks of pictures you'll have—every camping trip, T-ball game, graduation, every family celebration. One of the first will be the day you marry. It doesn't have to be any certain kind of wedding, just the one you both want. And done the way you want to remember it."

"And there's the problem," Jake said. "Janet wants a big fancy wedding and I don't."

"I don't need a big fancy wedding," she argued. "I just want it to be beautiful!"

"Completely doable. When you talk it over, you'll find a reasonable compromise. I'll do whatever I can to help with that. I've had couples who ordered so many flower arrangements and bouquets I thought I was outfitting the Rose Bowl. There was a recent wedding where the bride and her attendants each carried a single calla lily. The good news is…for a spring wedding literally every flower will be available and the prices will be more reasonable than at other times of the year."

"This is beautiful," Janet said, looking at a photo. "Isn't this beautiful, Jake?"

"I bet it cost a fortune," he snorted.

"Hmm, if I remember, that wedding ran about twelve hundred dollars."

"Are you freaking kidding me?" Jake said.

"Flowers were very important to that couple, but they didn't have a fortune. Now, there are ways to bring the cost way down, to less than half of that, and still have a beautiful display. Bows instead of flowers on the ends of the pews, smaller altar arrangements or larger fluffier flowers and table centerpieces, less fussy bouquets for the attendants."

"That's still a lot of money," he grumbled.

"When is the happy day?" Grace asked.

"June twentieth."

"Perfect. A great month for flowers and flower prices. And do you have a budget?"

Just as Janet said six hundred dollars Jake said fifty. Troy made a noise as he tried to cover his burst of laughter.

"Let me start by asking you to select your favorite wedding photos from this book. It will help if you can come up with at least three you love and figure out why you love them. The particular blooms? The shapes? The arrangement of the flowers? The colors? Once you do that we can find the wiggle room in the ideas and the price, something that better fits your budget. You're going to buy a lot of flowers in your lifetime, Jake. These flowers are going to live on forever in your wedding pictures. I'm sure you and Janet will find exactly the right ones. I'll leave you to look through the pictures. Just call me if you have any questions. I'll be right out front, ten steps away."

Troy was smirking as she walked out of the back room to where he stood behind the counter. He put an arm around her waist and whispered in her ear. "That's not going to work," he said.

"You'd be surprised," she said. "I think I can handle things if you want to leave."

"Nah, I'm not leaving you with this. I think I'll go get my backpack and start on those papers I have to look through. Then tonight I don't have to spend all my time on homework."

"Let me wipe down the worktable for you."

For about twenty minutes the only sound in the shop was the soft murmuring of the bridal couple as they went through the albums. The loud and snappish remarks had stopped but when Troy glanced into the office, they really didn't appear happy. In a very short time they thought they had selected a few pictures and Grace sat at her desk once more.

"Very good choices," she said.

"I'm sure they're out of the question," Janet said. "They're just too beautiful to be affordable."

"Well, let's see," Grace said. She sat at her computer and, after looking at one of the selected photos, she went to work. She began to type in numbers. "And how many parents and attendants?"

"Four parents, six grandparents, two ushers and four bridesmaids and groomsmen. This has been so stressful," Janet said. "We can't afford a lot. The reception will kill us if we can't figure out a way to get our mothers to stop adding people to the guest list!"

"Happens at absolutely every wedding," Grace said. Then she turned the screen toward the couple. "Here's the package you like the best—it includes everything from bridal bouquets to altar arrangements to centerpieces for a reception that seats one hundred and forty. Even flowers for the mothers and boutonnieres for the men are included. The cost is steep—twenty-four hundred fifty dollars."

"Jesus," Jake said, running a hand over his head.

"Now, let's take a closer look. Tell me your favorite things about these flowers?"

Janet pointed to the screen. "I love this lavender color, this fullness is so beautiful, the lavender roses, oh, my! And this kind of faint green with the white. This altar arrangement is so rich looking and huge…"

"Watch this," Grace said.

Troy was too curious just sitting there. He wanted to see what she was doing and her back was to him. She was literally pulling flowers from the bottom of her computer screen and positioning them together. "For the altar arrangements, a different flower, same color, the hydrangea for color, take out the expensive orchids, three or four lilies with two to five blooms per stalk, baby's breath rather than fern and pale green dusty miller, some carnations for fullness and maybe accented with this white stephanotis. I can use a disposable paper pot that won't be visible under the draping flora instead of the square glass vase, or I can rent you the vases and you can return them reducing the cost. Voilà! The cost is cut in half. Now, look at the bridal bouquet—once again, take out the big orchids but look what I can do with cymbidium orchids, a few lavender roses and daisies. Less expensive flowers, but still very beautiful, very appropriate in a summer wedding. If you don't love the daisies, I can use carnations or even white tea roses. And the bouquet is a bit smaller. The one you liked was three hundred. This would be one hundred. I can add roses pretty inexpensively if you want it bigger."

Troy was astonished. Whatever program she was using—amazing. He had no idea this business could be so complicated or high-tech.

"Let me show you something I've used very successfully for table centerpieces." She clicked on a picture. "A clear glass cylinder vase, flowers, white rocks, greenery at the base—I can do this for forty dollars per table. Or, I can tell you where to buy these glass vases and rocks very inexpensively and you can put the girlfriends to work and make it happen for less than twenty per table."

"They're beautiful," Janet said.

"How'd you do that?" Jake asked.

"I buy in bulk, June prices should be good, I thinned the flowers and I know what everyone else charges. You can't do better and I'll make that a guarantee. I'm going to suggest you get your bridesmaids or mothers or both together to fashion big white or lavender tulle bows for the pews. Skip the flowers, though they are so pretty. You can buy the tulle at a fabric shop like Jo-Ann's and save at least a couple hundred dollars and still have the decor of a fashionable and classy wedding. If they don't show you how to make the tulle bows, I'll be happy to. Now, those pew stands with candles are pricey—they have to be rented and you can probably live without them if you're cutting costs. The things that really show in a wedding are the altar flowers, bouquets and table arrangements. I can work up an estimate for this package and email it to you if you like, but I'm guessing this selection will be in the neighborhood of six to eight hundred. Plus delivery, which I do myself. I want my flowers presented perfectly. And, of course, I guarantee everything."

"Can we look at the next one?" Janet asked, opening the album to another page.

Troy smiled to himself and moved away. An hour later the couple was leaving with a contract in their hands and an official estimate on the way via email. And they were *kissing*.

Grace turned the sign on the front door and locked it. She was closed. Her meeting with the bridal couple had lasted almost two hours.

"I don't know how you did that," Troy said, stacking up his papers.

"I was taught," she said. "The couple I worked for—they were so perfect at pleasing people."

"When I first met Jake and Janet I thought they were headed for divorce. When they left, I thought everything would be fine."

"This is so typical. They think they have a budget, but what they really have done is run out of money after the dress and reception and pictures, but they still want flowers."

"For fifty bucks," Troy said with a laugh.

"You have exceptional hearing."

"Yeah, it's a teacher thing."

"They'll probably argue about the expenses several times between now and the wedding and they'll spend more than they plan to because it's always more. But I use all the flowers I order so the bouquets and arrangements will be stunning, and that's a fact. I'm very good at this."

"Where'd you get the program that pulls the flowers together?"

"Mamie and Ross, the couple I worked for, daydreamed about something like that. We could make up sample arrangements and bouquets, photograph them and load them on the computer, but this is state-of-the-art. I worked on it with a nerdy girl I met in Portland. I admit she did most of the program work, but I designed the site and loaded the flowers and arrangements. Isn't it great? It's like creating an online greeting card. Mamie and Ross sold it to a couple of noncompeting florists. I think they got a good price."

"Did you get a good price?" he asked.

"More than that, I got my future."

Seven

For Ray Anne Dysart, life was more productive and satisfying than ever before, at least as far as she could remember. She had her real estate business, mostly property management, small but respectable. She owned her own home, something she had worked hard to make happen as a hedge against retirement, even though she had no intention of retiring until she had no other option. She had her best friends, Lou McCain Metcalf and Carrie James. And she had Al.

Dear Al. He was hardly her first steady man. She was a little afraid to think about what number he was in a long line of previous beaux and lovers; in fact, she had been married three times. All water over the dam. Al was the most special man she'd ever known and completely unlike her usual type. He was a mechanic for one thing—grease under the blunt nails on those big calloused, gentle hands. He was physical, rough and ready and the best-natured man she knew. Plus, he had those three foster sons. Yes, there was a time Ray Anne had wanted children but she'd gotten over that a long while back. The boys, Justin, Danny and Kevin, were nineteen, fifteen and thirteen respectively. Good boys and Al kept them in line, but Ray Anne didn't feel equipped to be a parent to boys, foster or otherwise. She was a girlie girl. Yet she couldn't help but admit she enjoyed them and got a kick out of the way Al was able to manage them.

She felt she was thriving with Al and his family of boys. Of course, most of the time it was just Al she was with. She saw him every day. She would swing by Lucky's, the service station where he worked. Or he would drop by her house before or after his shift, provided his boys were taken care of. Sometimes they met at the diner for a quick meal or Cliffhanger's for a drink. Cliff's was the only restaurant in town with tablecloths. Sometimes they managed a whole evening or day off together; sometimes she joined Al and the boys for dinner. And if they planned carefully, she and Al could get naked and have some real quality time. Once or twice a week.

Like now.

It was Sunday, early afternoon. Al had the day off. The boys had driven to the nursing home where their mother resided. They visited her at least once a week, such devoted sons. Ray Anne took complete advantage of the opportunity when the boys were otherwise occupied.

She stretched out in bed. She smiled. She could hear the shower running. Al had spent the morning in her garage, changing the oil in her car, checking her brakes and such. He wanted to clean up before joining her in bed. She wore one of her sheer lacy, seductive little nighties, waiting. Her cell phone chimed and she frowned. *It better not be important*, she thought. She'd been looking forward to a little time alone with her man.

It was her cousin, Dick. Ray Anne had very little family, but she and Dick had been close growing up and kept in touch. She picked up. "Dickie, let me call you back in a little while…"

"It's important, Ray," he said. "Call me back right away, okay? As soon as you can?"

"What's so important?"

"It's Ginger," he said. "She's just not doing well. I don't know what more to do. Me and Sue, we're out of ideas. She's had counseling, talked to the minister, her friends have tried to boost her up. We thought maybe if she went to stay with you for a little while…"

"Honey, I don't know what to do, either."

"Could you think about it? Even if it's only a few weeks? Because we worry about her and she just won't help herself. We thought maybe a change…"

"Do you have any idea how gloomy it is here in winter? I wouldn't expect it to lift her spirits any. And besides, I'm in a… Well, I'm in a relationship and it's hard enough finding time."

"Ray, it's almost spring and you always got a relationship, don't you? Girl, I think I need help this time. Could you just think about it? See if you get any ideas that could help us out? Because we don't want to lose her. Ain't we lost enough?"

She took a deep breath. "Sure. Of course. Let me think about this. Let me ask some of my close friends for ideas. They know a lot more about kids and family stuff. I love her, you know that." The shower stopped. "I just don't know anything about how to help in a situation like hers. And God, I'd hate myself forever if I just made it worse. You know I'm not much of a mommy kind of girl."

"You were her fairy godmother," he said. "Just the sight of you made her happy."

"Well, the sight of me is damn hard to fix up these days. I'm not young anymore."

"Neither am I," he said. "And she isn't that young, either."

"I'll call you later, okay?"

"Thanks. Anything you can do. Thanks."

She clicked off and sat on the edge of the bed. Thinking. Dickie had always been there for her. He was a hardworking trucker who'd ended up with his own company and any time Ray Anne had a problem—a man, a big bill she couldn't pay, a need to move, a co-signer, a shoulder—he never asked a single question, never hesitated. He was there. His wife, Sue, wasn't quite as warm and loving toward her, but she sure accepted her and never balked when Ray and Dickie got together or when Dickie helped Ray Anne out.

And they'd never asked much of her.

Al came out of the bathroom, towel wrapped

around his waist, rubbing a smaller towel over his short hair. His arms and shoulders were muscled, his belly flat, a body that usually filled her with all kinds of dirty expectations. But she was distracted.

"Did I hear you talking?" he asked.

She still gripped the phone. She lifted it and showed him. "My cousin, Dickie. Remember, his daughter was the one whose baby died—crib death."

"Yeah," he said, kind of wearily. He sat down beside her. "I wasn't likely to forget about that." In fact, way back in Al's youth when he was a young husband, he and his wife had lost their only child the very same way. Al had spent decades trying to run away from that sorrow. "Poor thing."

"Well, she's not good. She's not getting better. She's grief stricken and they've tried everything from medication to counseling and Dickie wants me to take her in for a while, even if it's only a few weeks."

"Why?" he asked.

"Because she was my little princess and always loved staying with me. But she's not a little princess now—she's a thirty-year-old woman whose baby died and I don't think I can help her get over it with facials and mani-pedis." She looked up at him. "I wouldn't have the first idea what to do. I might just make it worse."

Al shifted into the bed, stretching out his long legs as he leaned against the headboard. He pulled her back into his arms. "Ray Anne, just being you puts a smile on most faces. You're kind and sweet and funny—maybe that would lighten her spirits a little bit. You could let her talk about it."

"Ugh," she said before she could stop herself.

"I know, I know. But they know you're not a professional counselor. I mean, your cousin and his missus. They don't expect you to cure her or anything, right? They just want her to have a safe place to go, right?"

"I think so," she said. "The poor thing. Her marriage was breaking up when she was barely pregnant, so she was alone. Had the baby alone. She moved back with her parents so she could take three months off work and she never went back because... How do you get someone over something like that?"

"Honey, you don't," Al said, pulling her closer against him, holding her in the crook of his big arm. "You can't get someone over something. All you can do is give 'em a little love and space and pray. You pray, baby?"

She laughed in a short, sarcastic huff. "All my damn life, but my prayers weren't very holy. 'Please God, let that big stud buy me a drink.'"

He laughed at her. "I think you should let her come."

"You do? Like we don't have enough complications..."

"I think if you don't, you might not get over it later. Sometimes we have to do things like that just to keep from having too many regrets." He kissed her forehead. "Might have to get a room at the Coast Motel again." Then he laughed.

"She doesn't work," Ray Anne said. "What am I going to do with her?"

"You should talk to your girls—Lou and Carrie. They've been through some rough times. So have you, for that matter."

Indeed, she had. An abusive husband, a couple of acrimonious divorces, getting financially wiped out by at least one of them. That was just for starters. She'd learned a lot, been around the block a time or two.

She'd even lost a child, but hardly anyone knew about that. And her baby hadn't died the way Ginger's had. Hers was a secret teenage mishap that ended sadly and she'd never talked about until very recently.

"I'm not smart or wise enough," she said.

"You're the smartest woman I know. And you're so full of love I can't even hold all of you."

She turned her head to look up at him. "I've never had anyone like you in my life before. Really, I haven't. You're the best thing that ever happened to me."

"I feel the same," he said.

"We've got an awful lot on our plates," she said.

"Bounty," he said. "That's what we call a full plate. Bounty."

"Hope it doesn't kill us," Ray Anne said.

Al planned to take his two younger boys to the high school basketball game on Friday night. Lou's husband, Joe, was a trooper who worked the swing shift four nights a week and Carrie didn't open the deli early on Saturday mornings. Friday night was a perfect night to get together with her girlfriends, so Ray Anne reached out to see if they felt like a little hen party at her house—a little wine and whine.

"Come to my house, instead, and I'll put out some snacks. You bring the wine and I'll invite Gina," Carrie said, including her daughter, who was also Lou's niece-in-law. "If Mac is working or something, she'll just sit around at home. If that's okay with you."

Of course Gina was a welcome addition, anytime. For a woman under forty, she was very prudent in the ways of the world. When Ray Anne arrived at Carrie's, the others were already there and Rawley was just leaving. "You're not staying for the hen party?" she asked.

"I ain't no hen," he said, pulling down his cap. "Thought I explained that."

"Rawley is babysitting tonight," Carrie said from behind him. "Cooper and Sarah want to go out without the baby."

"Really?" Ray Anne asked. "How are you with babies?"

"Perfect," he said. "If they go to bed and stay there."

The women had gotten used to having Rawley in the background of their little gatherings, silently serving them, saying nothing unless specifically asked, hiding out in front of the TV when sports were playing while they gathered in the kitchen. "We'll miss you," Ray Anne told him. "Having you around at a girl's night is kind of like having a butler—there to serve, but not there at all."

"I reckon you'll have to get your own food and drink and do your own dishes tonight," he said. "Don't wear yourself out." And with that, he was gone.

The women were sitting around the kitchen table where Carrie had put out a selection of her best hors d'oeuvres. As Ray Anne moved toward the table, Gina held up an empty wineglass, more than ready for Ray Anne's contribution to the party. She quickly uncorked one chilled white and one red.

"Will Rawley come back?" Ray Anne asked Carrie. Carrie merely shrugged and reached for a crab ball from the platter in the center. "Does he stay over?"

"Sometimes," Carrie said. "If he doesn't want to drive all the way to Elmore, to his house."

Ray Anne put both bottles on the table and sat down. She lifted one of Carrie's amazing crab balls and raised her eyes heavenward. "I have such a hard time picturing you and Rawley together. Romantically, that is."

"Then don't," Carrie advised.

"But seriously, are you a couple now? I mean, I know he's been around for months, like your boyfriend and partner, but…"

"Not everyone is as comfortable talking about the personal side of things as you are," Carrie said.

"He has his own room," Gina pointed out. When everyone stared at her, including her mother, she added, "Well, he does! He has my old room. Which doesn't mean anything, just that it's the way they want it! But believe me, I knock before walking in now."

"Seriously?" Lou said. "His own room? Jesus, are you set in your ways or what."

"Very much so," Carrie said. "Rawley is, too. I've gotten so used to him, I don't know what I'd do without him. He loves to cook, clean up, shop and run errands."

"Very exciting," Lou said.

"That's all the excitement I can stand."

The women were incredibly different. Just a look at them would make anyone wonder what they could possibly have in common. Carrie was plump and grandmotherly; she had never colored her short, steel-gray hair. She nurtured with food that was lovingly and thoughtfully prepared. Lou was small, trim, fit, kept her shoulder length auburn hair free of gray and looked younger than her sixty-two years. Gina was lovely, blond, midthirties with an eighteen-year-old daughter and three stepchildren and had been working at the diner for years and years, yet she looked like a girl.

And then there was Ray Anne. She teased her blond hair, wore her clothes on the tight, short, sexy side, her heels as high as possible. Well, she was short. But that had nothing to do with it, really. She liked them. She'd always worn more makeup, long nails, fancier and, for lack of a better word, *spicier* clothing. Lou called her a Dolly Parton knockoff and Ray Anne was not offended.

The women weren't alike in many other ways, either. Lou was an educator who had raised her nephew Mac and then helped him raise his three children after his wife left him. Carrie had been a single mother and small business owner—the deli and catering. Gina had only married Mac a year ago or so and became the instant mother of a big crowd. Only Ray Anne had been this solitary, childless woman. But somehow they understood one another.

"Remember my cousin Dickie?" she asked, sipping her wine. "Remember his daughter, Ginger, whose baby died a while back?"

"Terrible," Lou said, shaking her head. "Was that almost a year ago?"

"Almost nine months. Last summer," Ray Anne said.

"Nothing could be harder than that," Carrie said.

"Poor thing," Gina said.

"She's coming to stay with me for a little while," Ray Anne said. "And I'm terrified."

"You?" Lou asked. "Terrified? I didn't know anything scared you."

"This does. Her daddy called me—he said she was still in a world of hurt. I knew she wasn't getting better. She's been so depressed she can't work and can hardly get out of bed, lost a ton of weight and is so pitiful she can't talk to anyone for five minutes before she just has to go someplace to be alone. She's still in terrible pain."

"How sad," Carrie said. "Are you going to try to cheer her up?"

"Oh, Lord, what do I know about that kind of grief?" Ray Anne said. "If her daddy hadn't asked me, begged me really, I never would've signed up for this. I have no idea what I'm supposed to do!"

"Has she had counseling?" Lou asked.

"Yes, they've tried that. She even took antidepressants for a while. And I know there was some grief group at the church or something. That didn't go well, either."

"We can look around here for a counselor or grief group. Wouldn't hurt to try again," Lou said.

"I thought she was your niece," Gina said.

"She's like a niece. Dickie's like a brother. He and Sue had two little boys then along came Gingersnap and I was in heaven! A pretty little thing who could have fun spending the night at my house—we'd curl our hair, paint our nails, cream our faces, shave our legs…we shaved when she was a little older. We watched musicals and Disney shows together, dressed up, went shopping. I drove to Portland to help her pick out a prom dress, and I helped her stage her wedding—I was the official bridal assistant. Got way under Sue's skin, I'll tell you that, but my little Gingersnap was so happy!"

"She's married?"

"No," Ray Anne said. "No, her marriage only lasted a couple of years and was falling apart right as she realized she was pregnant and her husband, the bastard, didn't even try to give it a chance to help raise his own baby. So Ginger did it on her own. At the end of her pregnancy she moved home with her mom and dad. They'd fixed up the upstairs for her so she and the baby had rooms of their own and she could save some money. She worked right up till she started labor. Four months later her little baby boy died in his sleep."

"What did your cousin ask you to do for her?" Gina asked.

"Nothing," Ray Anne said with a helpless shrug. "He said the change might help, but he didn't ask anything specific of me. I think they're worn-out, that's what I think. It was Dickie and Sue's loss, too. They have other grandchildren, but this little one lived with them—their baby's baby. And I suppose the others can't get any attention because everyone is busy grieving." She rested her head in her hand. "I'll be useless. I'll probably just sit around and cry with the poor thing."

"For an hour or so, maybe," Carrie said. "Then you'll be done with that."

"Listen, I don't have any natural parenting skills. None. God knew what he was doing when I didn't get to have children."

"You'd have been an ideal parent," Lou said. "God's mistake."

"Me? Oh, believe me, I know nothing about being a parent and even less about what I can do to help my poor little Ginger while she goes through this terrible time. This is the worst idea Dickie has ever had, and he's had some real stinkers."

"No, this is perfect," Lou said.

"She's right," Carrie agreed. "Won't be so easy on you, but then when our youngsters hurt, it's awful. Worse for us, I think. But of all the people I know... yes, you're the one to do it."

"How can you say that?" Ray Anne demanded.

"I know about some of your tough times," Carrie said. "I've seen you through a few of them since you came to Thunder Point. Money trouble, broken hearts, struggles... There were a couple of times that were pretty awful. You had a mean son-of-a-bitch husband stalk you and you had to run and hide. You had a good friend die—what was her name?"

"Marisa Dunaway," Ray Anne said, and tears instantly sparkled in her eyes. "She was a good friend for twenty years and the Big C took her, but not until it kicked her ass, made her so sick and weak she was begging to die. Horrible. Horrible."

"And your parents died when you were little more than a girl," Lou reminded her as if she needed reminding. She was twenty-two and her parents, both in their late fifties, died so close together, both of cancer. That had been forty years ago. Cancer treatment had come a long way since then, but still, it had taken her best friend ten years ago. "That was a dark time for you. We weren't friends then," she added. "I wasn't there for you."

"I didn't even know you then. You've been through a lot since I've known you," Carrie said. "But you never indulged self-pity. You grieved hard, but never felt sorry for yourself."

"Ginger has a right to feel sorry for herself," Ray Anne said.

"This isn't about rights," Lou chimed in. "You had a right to self-pity, too. But you're a survivor. And you're a damn good role model. Your cousin is doing a smart thing, sending his daughter to you."

Ray Anne looked at Lou in surprise. "I didn't think you liked me enough to say something like that," she said.

"It's those shoes I never understood," Lou said. "And you did steal all my boyfriends until I started keeping them secret from you. But I always admired your strength. You're a woman on your own, alone, except for a couple of girlfriends and your recent boyfriend, but we don't count on boyfriends. Women alone have to be smart, strong and durable. We don't bruise easy. And we can't waste time and energy feeling sorry for ourselves. We might want to collapse, but we don't. Probably no one would pick us up!"

"You, too," Ray Anne said. "When Mac's wife left him—"

"Ach!" Lou barked. "Alone with three little kids—the smallest nine months old! Practically no money, two low-paying jobs and his only relative was me. I was a full-time teacher. I don't know how we got through it. And he was a mess! A pathetic, broken mess. Talk about self-pity! Sometimes when you have someone to lead, it's easier to be strong."

"What am I going to do?" Ray Anne asked.

"Be yourself," Gina said, smiling. "Be your wonderful, loving, strong self. Let her talk, push her a little bit, like my mother pushed me when I was a sixteen-year-old mother with no one but her. Get her a little counseling help, bring her around your friends, prop her up with example. Let her see we don't give up, we work. Sure we cry, sometimes scream, but we take it one day at a time and make every day a little better than the one we just left behind. You're really one of the best people for the job, I know it."

"I had no idea you all thought that way about me."

"Pfft. The only thing I feel sorry for you about is that you just can't dress yourself properly. You should be in double knits and wedgies like the rest of us over-sixty broads," Lou said.

"Don't listen to her," Carrie said. "The best part about you is you're unique. As long as you don't make me dress like a cocktail waitress I won't make you dress like a gray-haired grandmother."

Ray Anne couldn't answer. She felt the emotion in her throat. She'd give anything to be a grandmother. "You really think I'll be able to help her?"

"If you have trouble…if you have frustrations, we'll get together and hash it out. We've all been through the bitter side of life. It comes with breathing. Giving up was never an option," Carrie said.

"I have a confession to make," Ray Anne said. "It's not like I didn't feel sorry for myself sometimes. I've cried my heart out. Sometimes I cried till I couldn't stand up straight. It's just that I never cried like that in front of anyone."

"I know," three voices replied together.

Carrie was having trouble falling asleep. She heard the front door open and close. Then she heard the soft drone of the TV and she rolled over and looked at the clock. Almost one in the morning. She got up and found her robe and opened her bedroom door.

"Did I wake you up?" Rawley asked.

She shook her head. "I was tossing around, not sleeping." She gave her neck a stretch, tilting her head from side to side, trying to touch her chin to each shoulder. "This is so late for you."

"That Cooper. He thinks he's a kid. They went to some party up in North Bend with some of Sarah's old Coast Guard pals. Sarah had to drive him home."

"He'll pay for that."

"I hope so. Why aren't you sleeping?"

"I think too much," she said.

"Come here, girl," he said. When she sat beside him on the couch, he turned her so he could rub her shoulders. "Kids okay?" he asked as he massaged.

"They're all fine. It's Ray Anne's kin that's having trouble." She told him about Ginger and her need for a change of scenery. "Brings to mind how I always complained so much about how hard my life was when I never lost anything that dear."

"You lost a husband," he reminded her.

"Exactly as I said. Nothing very dear."

He made a sound that was almost a laugh. "Now you got some old vet taking up space in your house."

"You fit in so well, too. You hardly ever visit that house in Elmore anymore," she said.

"I almost never go to that house. I keep it as insurance for you."

She looked over her shoulder at him. "What does that mean?"

"Means I don't want you to worry none if you start to feel crowded and need your space—there's a place I can go. But I ain't got hardly a shirt left over there anymore. I never thought I'd end up living in some woman's house. Who'd a thought there'd be a woman could put up with me?"

"You're the easiest man I've ever known."

"No one ever accused me of that before."

"Rawley, I've been happy." She patted one of the hands that massaged her tight shoulders. "You're a good man."

"I'll do my best never to be a burden."

"I'm the burden!" she said. "Bad knees, sore back and neck, a family that just seems to grow, friends who count on me, a demanding business!"

He leaned forward and kissed her cheek right below the ear. His lips were dry and his face whiskery, but she leaned back against him for a moment.

"We get along fine," he said. "And you just tell me when you need something. I'll help if I can and get out of the way if I can't. Since we don't have all that much time, might as well enjoy it."

"I hope there's plenty of time!" she said. "I might be getting creaky but I'm not ready to give up. Especially now that life's gotten so sweet."

"Maybe I should've said, there ain't likely to be enough time. I know what. Let's find the lotion and I'll give you a proper rubdown. Get some of those creaks out."

"That sounds lovely."

Carrie went to her bedroom; the lotion was on the bedside table. The television was turned off and Rawley padded into the bedroom in his stocking feet. Carrie lay down on her side and, after just a minute, Rawley lay down behind her, rubbing lotion between his leathery palms. She lifted her pajama top all the way up, almost over her shoulders, baring her back and most of her front.

"My hands are gonna be a little cold," he said.

"I think maybe you should consider renting that house in Elmore. You could let it bring you some income."

"You in need of money, girl?"

She sighed. "No, Rawley. For the first time in my life, I think I have everything I need."

"Then maybe we'll sell that house. Put the money against retirement." He put a hand on her shoulder and pulled a little, rolling her toward him. "How many houses we need?"

"Only one, as far as I can see," she said. "Think anyone really notices?"

"In this town they notice everything," he said. "Think I really care?"

She laughed with him for a minute, then she rolled back so he could rub her back. He had strong, kind hands, the sort of hands she'd never expected to feel on her bare back. "That's so nice," she murmured.

Eight

Troy parked his Jeep behind the flower shop and called Grace. "I'm done at Cooper's. Is it too late for me to come by?"

"I'm with one of my other boyfriends," she said.

He grinned at that. "Can you ask him to step aside for a little while?"

"Is this a booty call?"

"No, it's not, as a matter of fact. I wanted to tell you something, but if you turn it into a booty call, I probably won't fight you off."

She laughed. "When will you be here?"

"I'm parked in the alley. And it's not really so late."

"Come up!"

He was already standing at the top of the stairs when she opened the door.

"You didn't work very late tonight," she said, pulling him inside. She put her arms around his neck, kissing him. "You know what? I really like this boy-

friend stuff. It's very convenient. I was just thinking about a kiss."

He pulled her closer. "You were, were you?" He
nuzzled her neck and pressed against her. He fit so
well against her soft curves, even though she was
much shorter. He put his hands under her butt and
lifted her, lining them up even better. Then he kissed
her again.

"I thought you wanted to tell me something," she
whispered against his lips.

"Right," he said distractedly, kissing her again.
"No rush." Of course he began to grow against her
enticing form.

"If you keep this up, you'll forget what you wanted
to tell me," she warned him.

"No worries. It'll come back to me. You okay?"

"With you? Always okay."

He kept kissing, then touching, then gyrating.
"Aw, Gracie," he moaned. "Let's talk a little later,
all right?"

"All right."

"Bed? Sofa? Table? Floor?" He swallowed. "Wall?"
She giggled.

"I could rip your clothes off right here," he said.

"Oh? And do you sew?" She pulled his hand from
her breast and led him to the bed. "It will be more
practical if we just undress. Ripping and tearing
could be fun, but problematic."

"What if I'm feeling a little wild?" he asked, smiling into her pretty eyes.

"You can get a little wild when we're naked," she

said, dropping her jeans and shedding her denim shirt.

"I can do that," he said, getting rid of his clothes even faster. She was down to her tiny panties, so sheer and small they almost weren't there. He followed her onto the bed and reached for those panties with one big hand. "Oops," he said, ripping a short seam.

"You're very hard on my underwear."

"I'm surprised you have any left," he said.

"I love my panties."

"Not as much as I do! God, Gracie, I think you were expecting me," he said, covering her mouth with his and separating her knees with one of his. "You have no idea what you do to me."

"Just as long as I can do it to you again," she whispered. "And again…"

Even with all the romances Grace had read, just dreaming about true love, nothing had prepared her for what it would really feel like. As she lay naked in Troy's arms, enjoying postcoital bliss, catching her breath, ready for sleep, she sighed his name.

"Right here, baby," he said, pulling her tighter against him.

"I think you spoil me."

"That's my intention. You feel good?"

"I'm ruined for other men."

"Good. I can't think about you ever being with another man."

They were quiet for a few seconds. "You said *ever*," she said.

He rolled her over until she was on top of him, her hair a mussed canopy around their faces. "I did. You bring out some feelings in me that I don't recognize. I don't want to think about you ever being with anyone else. I don't want to be with anyone else." He brushed back her hair. "I should slow down, right? Because you're not ready for talk like that. Your other boyfriends never try to hold you down like that."

She shook her head. Pretend boyfriends rarely did—they were both all too aware of that. Here was the first flesh-and-blood boyfriend to hold her, love her, possess her. She didn't want anything to change.

"We both know what's missing from this perfect relationship," he said.

"Missing?" she asked.

"What you've told me about yourself, about growing up, wouldn't fill a chapter in one of your romances, Grace. Even your paper boyfriends would have questions."

"But you haven't asked me any questions," she said.

He shook his head. "I told you, you can trust me. And when you feel safe you'll tell me."

"You think I'm hiding something." It wasn't a question.

He nodded. "It's all right. I'm hiding a few things, too. Just things I don't talk about a lot. Iraq. I hate talking about Iraq, except sometimes with my boys—we laugh about terrible things that aren't really funny. There were youthful scrapes here and there. Trouble in high school, but nothing worse than the kids I teach now run into. We have years. We have plenty of time to learn everything about each other. I hope we don't take too long."

"But what if I say something that changes everything?" she asked him.

"See, that's the other thing missing—you know me, Gracie. You think I'm that kind of guy? That I'd measure you? Judge you by something in your past? You're an amazing, beautiful, kind, wonderful woman. I dare you to try to change my opinion."

She chewed her bottom lip. *Do it*, she told herself. *Do it* now.

But she couldn't. Not naked!

"Is that what you wanted to talk to me about? Is that why you came over tonight?"

He looked startled for a moment, then he started to laugh. He rolled with her again so that she was beneath him. "No, no. Gracie, the second you put your lips on me, you empty my brain! Don't you understand—I can't stay away from you? If I'm alone with you, I can't think of anything but getting busy. Then I want to do it again. Then I want to eat."

"Does everyone make love this much?"

"I don't know. They should. I think we're getting better, don't you?"

She nodded and smiled.

"I wanted to come over and tell you—a friend

of mine is coming to visit in a couple of weeks, if it works out. And I have to ask a favor—can I stay with you while he's here? I don't have an extra room or bed. If it was just Denny, I'd take the couch, but he's bringing his wife and she's pregnant. I think they could use a decent place to sleep and a little privacy."

"You stay here half the time anyway," she said.

"Will you check your calendar, because if you have a wedding or something, we'll change dates. He's a farmer, see, and he either comes before the planting gets serious or he has to wait till after harvest."

"A farmer?" she asked. "You never mentioned a friend who's a farmer."

"He's a buddy from the Marines and he stumbled on this organic farm down in California. He was just helping out while he was looking for a better job and it turned out he liked it. His wife is a teacher like me, that means it's weekends or nothing."

"A farmer and a teacher?" she asked. "Wow, that's so...*normal*!" With normal childhoods, no medals or stalkers, going to school every day, going to the prom, getting speeding tickets or into fights or falling in love like normal kids...

"Wait till Denny tells you about his farm—it's pretty far-out. So—can you check for weddings? Because I know you have to keep the shop open, at least a little bit, but I was hoping we could have some fun with them."

"If I don't have any big events I can post a notice that I'll close early on that Saturday."

"That would be great, Gracie. If you wouldn't mind too much, if it doesn't cost too much. Because we could have fun. And with Becca pregnant, it won't be anything too adventurous."

"So, you're not going to risk your life this time?" she asked.

He snuggled closer. "Gracie, sweetheart, wiggle up against me…yeah, just like that. Move those perfect little hips, aah. You're a witch, aren't you?"

"Tell me about Denny's farm," she said.

"No, we're not talking about him anymore. He's a buzzkill." He grabbed her legs at the backs of her knees, lifting them, tilting her upward. "God, you're magic. I'm glad I taught you how to do this."

She couldn't help but laugh at him. "Don't you think I'd have caught on eventually? Are you really going to take credit?"

"It makes me feel manly," he said. Then his breath caught. "God," he said when he felt her hand on him, gently stroking. "Gracie, Gracie, you're a witch… You're going to kill me, that's what you're going to do. Please, kill me."

She directed him into her, felt him fill her, dug her heels in and pushed against him. Then she wrapped her legs around him and rode with him, stroke for delicious stroke, just like they'd been doing it for years. She came first. When she felt him let go, she held on. He liked it when she did that. And when he was coming down she whispered, so softly he might not have heard, "I love you."

He didn't say *I love you, too.*

* * *

Troy was in a daze when he went into the bathroom in Grace's loft. He was thinking about her beautiful smile, her perfect laugh, the body that welcomed him so naturally, as if they were experienced lovers when they were really new. His fulfillment was always complete, leaving him weak and grateful. And she'd said she loved him. His heart was so full he was tempted to push the issue then and there, tell her what he knew, force her to come clean with him so they could get on with their lives. But it would be better if she came to him with the truth, trusted him.

He went back to bed, crawled in beside her and pulled her into his arms. He pulled her hair aside and kissed the back of her neck.

"Hmm. I thought you were hungry."

"Honey, we have to get you on the pill. Soon."

She rolled onto her back and looked at him. "Huh?"

"I think it's time for us to stop messing around with just a condom. They're not a hundred percent."

"So, what are you getting at?" she asked.

"We should be better protected. Is there any reason you're not on the pill?"

"It never occurred to me before. Before you."

"Yeah, of course. You should see the doctor. Or Peyton—Peyton could take care of you if you prefer a woman. We don't want to have to deal with complications like pregnancy."

She gasped. "You mean I could be pregnant?"

"You shouldn't be—we've been careful. But it's not worth the gamble. It would be a bummer to get pregnant—that's not the plan. That could put a serious damper on our fun."

"Our fun?" she asked softly. "You can say pregnant and fun in the same sentence?"

"Well, I'm not in the market for a baby, are you?" he asked. He grabbed her small waist. "At least it would be a few months before your belly got in the way of our good times." Then he laughed at his own joke.

"Did you just say that? Really? That it would get in the way of our good times?"

"Sorry. I shouldn't joke about it. Listen, can you do it? Check with the doctor and see if you can take the pill?"

"Sure," she said.

Then she rolled away from him and closed her eyes and her mouth before she screamed.

Grace didn't stir when Troy got up early. She feigned sleep while he dressed, kissed her cheek and left to go back to his apartment to get ready for work. When her loft was quiet, she rolled over on her back and blinked. She wasn't sure why she felt so emotional. He was right, after all. This was no time to get caught. But she was a hopeless romantic—she wanted love, marriage, children, happily ever after. Weddings were a big part of her job, after all.

It was just that when a guy you'd whispered love words to talked about the possibility of an accidental pregnancy, shouldn't he say something tender? Something like *Please don't worry—I'd never leave you to deal with it alone.* Or maybe, *You know how much I care about you.* Or how about a real stretch? *It'll be okay, Grace, because I love you.*

Then she asked herself, was she expecting him to do it all when she still hadn't been completely honest with him? After all, the secret of who she was wasn't shameful. It was just weird and complicated. She had no idea how he'd react. Would he let it out? Would Grace Dillon vanish as she became Izzy Banks all over again?

She opened the shop a little early, tidied up and made herself a list, and the top of the list was a visit to the clinic. She refreshed the water in the flowers in the cooler. She'd go see Peyton as soon as the clinic opened to get it over with. When she heard the bell to the shop's front door jingle, she peeked out and almost had a heart attack. There stood Peyton! She had a sudden irrational fear that Troy had called her, told her to go take care of Grace.

"Are you all right?" Peyton asked. "Did I startle you or something?"

"I just… I mean, I was just going to walk down to the clinic to see if you were available. What a co-incidence!"

"I'm totally available," Peyton said, smiling. "Scott's covering for me. What's up? You feeling okay?"

"I'm fine," Grace said. "But why are you here?" she asked.

"Well, Scott and I plan to get married on my folks' farm in late April. Everything will be blooming and there will be a lot of fruit blossoms involved. Is there enough time to talk about some other wedding flowers?"

"I'll have to check my book—I have a couple of weddings in April. But there's plenty of time to order and make up arrangements and bouquets," she said happily. This was her comfort zone. While she talked flowers, she'd work on her confidence. After an hour of flower talk, she'd be ready. "What have you got there?" she asked, indicating a flat box Peyton held under one arm.

"Some pictures. I know—usually the florist shows the bride-to-be flowers. But a wedding on the farm is unlike anything you've ever seen before. The pear trees will be in full bloom. If it's a warm winter they'll start early and if it's a late spring they'll just be starting. My mother's gardens will be blooming and so will my aunts' and cousins'. When a Basque girl gets married, everyone brings flowers and food." She laughed a little. "Even when the *girl* is thirty-five!"

"It doesn't sound like you need me," Grace said.

"But yes, I do. Let me show you."

"Come on back," Grace invited. The worktable was still clean because it was early. Grace only had a couple of orders to make up later, to be delivered tomorrow.

They sat at a corner of the large table and Peyton leafed slowly through a lot of loose pictures, describing them as her brother's wedding, her oldest sister's wedding, her youngest sister's wedding. "She got married quickly—no pear blossoms for her. We had to order from the flower growers. I thought my mother would have a stroke over that—her baby, getting married off the farm. To add to the insult, she married a chef and he insisted his restaurant cater. The fact that I'm finally getting married, in late spring, on the farm—it goes a long way to helping her get over it."

"These pictures are gorgeous. They should be published," Grace said. The trellises were adorned with blossoms, and the women wore flowers in their hair. The tables sitting outside for the reception had arrangements on each one. The women carried beautiful bouquets and the buffet table that held enough food for an army also displayed roses, gardenias, cherry and pear blossoms, hydrangea, roses, baby's breath and rich, dark fern. It was a fortune in flowers, and a great deal of work. More than Grace could possibly manage alone. "You're right, I've never seen anything like it. Who did the flowers?"

"My family," she said. "I'd like to do a few things differently."

"I can't imagine why," Grace said, flipping through picture after picture.

"Well, I certainly can't find any fault with it, except for two things—my mother works too hard and every wedding in our family looks the same. Everyone contributes so much. I know they love it, but it becomes almost a competition." She shook her head. "Not almost. It *is* a competition—in the kitchen, in the garden, everywhere you look. We're going to change a few things. For starters, we're going to get married in a very old church in Mount Angel in an ecumenical service, not outside with the orchard as backdrop. The Catholic Basque relatives will be a little put out, but they won't boycott. There are too many of them anyway. There are so many of them, we're thinking of renting actors to play the parts of Scott's family—his family is so small by comparison. But our friends from Thunder Point will make up the difference. I want to supply some flowers, the bouquets, altar arrangements, boutonnieres and corsages. My mother and aunts can decorate the tent..."

"Tent?"

"My father likes the men to dance under the stars. I want to rent a tent, a dance floor and a bandstand. I'm hiring a Basque band from San Francisco. I'm sure they'll step aside long enough for my father, my brothers and uncles and others to have a turn, but I want my parents to celebrate with me. If it rains, and rain in spring is not at all unusual in north Oregon, we'll be covered. And I want Scott's mothers to have a good time. If possible."

"Mothers?" Grace asked.

"His mother and his late wife's mother. The grandmothers. If you pay attention, you'll hear him complain about them, but I have a mother, grandmother, a million aunts and cousins all over the place, all the way to Spain and France. The Basque people are the only ethnic group to come from two countries, Spain and France, and the tradition and ritual in the old country, even though there is no old country anymore, is rigid and colorful and often troublesome as they argue over control. His mothers can't hold a candle to that!"

"So there will still be pear and cherry blossoms?" Grace asked almost weakly.

"Thousands," Peyton said. "I grew up on that farm. I'm committed to a zillion flowers and fruit blossoms and bees!" she said, laughing. "The sheep are not invited!"

"Oh, God, it sounds amazing! I hate bees," Grace added.

"I'm sure Scott will be packing an EpiPen if you have a reaction. Because, of course, the reason I'm asking you for flowers is because I'd like you to attend if you can. I'm kind of hoping you'll bring some of the flowers. I realize it's a very long trip for a delivery."

"Invited? Me?"

"Of course! I love the flowers my mother and aunts bring, but I'd like a few different blooms this time. Day lilies, calla lilies, hybrid roses, maybe some more tropical blossoms, an orchid or two. If you don't count my younger brother who is divorced, I'm officially the last Lacoumette to marry. I've already talked to my mother about the flowers and the food…"

"The food?" Grace asked.

"She'll be cooking and freezing for weeks, but I'm holding her back. I wouldn't celebrate without her more famous dishes but my brother-in-law, the chef, owns a five-star restaurant! I want him to participate. He's gifted and he's honored to be asked. If you want to really compliment a Basque, praise their cooking, dancing, music making or children raising. My mother is being very stoic about this, that Lucas would provide some of the food. At least he's family." She laughed and shook her head. "They won't share recipes with each other, it's hilarious."

"Peyton, this sounds huge. Maybe bigger than I am. I don't want to buck tradition."

"We *have* to buck tradition," she said. "I'm Basque but my fiancé isn't. He's getting married, too! Although…he can't get enough of them, of that farm. He's so happy when he's there. I can't take him there too often or he'll grow big as a bull! No one loves to eat like Scott."

That made Grace smile. "Troy could probably give him a run for his money."

Peyton's dark eyes twinkled. She was silent for a moment. "How's that going? You and Troy?"

"Nice," Grace said. "Tell me about your family. About how you met Scott. About the farm and the culture and the traditional Basque wedding."

Peyton explained that she was the oldest of eight and, no, she hadn't been dreaming of a big family! She had been determined to be single for a long while but now that she'd found Scott and his two kids, she was very anxious to have one, maybe two, to add to the pack. She described her parents, her siblings, nieces and nephews, talked about Scott and how he was the last thing she ever expected. She explained the Basque people as best she could, how she worked in a Basque clinic in the south of France for a while after graduating from college, getting to know the old country. Grace couldn't wait to do a little online research about the culture. Almost two hours had passed before they got around to blooms and stalks, number of guests and colors.

"It's spring. I'm dressing my bridesmaids in all the spring colors—lavender, pink, baby blue and yellow. I want a colorful wedding! I want their bouquets to match their dresses and mine to represent all of them. I want spring colors in the altar arrangements, then we'll take them to the farm for the reception. The groom's dinner is Scott's responsibility and he's chosen a hotel in Portland that can cater in a banquet hall and I offered flowers, which his mother snapped up immediately. There will be at least thirty people at the dinner.

"There will be about two hundred people, all arriving in cars, RVs, trucks with camper shells and fifth wheels. My mother thinks the tent for the reception is uppity, and my father complains it will block the sky, but he already contacted cousins in the old country to send him crates of their best wine. We always have to rent tables so at least no one is complaining about that. But I want a waitstaff and bartenders for this event, if only to help with the cleanup. My family should celebrate and enjoy the fruits of their labors."

"It sounds positively wonderful," Grace said somewhat dreamily. "I can't imagine having that many family members around to celebrate."

"Oh, there will be arguing, too," she said. "Fights,

even. Big families—big control issues. They're very opinionated, very strong, very nosy. There is always lots of laughter, lots of yelling."

"I'd love to do this," Grace said. "But I'll be honest, I've never done a wedding this big or this far away. The people I worked for before coming here to open the shop are in Portland. I know they could do it…"

"Get them to help you, if you want," Peyton said. "I only want two things from you—flowers and to see you dance at my wedding. I hope a lot of people from Thunder Point will be there."

Grace gave the situation some thought. There were many different ways this could be accomplished. She could order the flowers and even make the bouquets and arrangements and drive up with them—the van was refrigerated in back. Or, she could transport the flowers and make them into bouquets and arrangements once there. Or, she could have Ross and Mamie order the flowers and she could go up a day early, visit with them and make up the flowers in their shop. They'd be thrilled. She ran over all these possibilities with Peyton and Peyton left the final decision in her hands.

"And now, what can I do for you?" Peyton asked.

"Oh. That." Grace cleared her throat. "A checkup, I guess. I haven't had one in a while, like too long. Oh, don't make that face—it's only been a few years!"

Peyton's black eyes grew huge. "A few *years*?"

Grace leaned toward her a little. "I've had lots of

physicals over the years, all with good results, but only a couple of *those* exams. But now it seems I need to be on the pill."

"Ah," Peyton said. "Gotcha."

"Your first thirty-year-old virgin?" Grace asked with a smirk, though she was not thirty yet.

"No," Peyton said, laughing. "I'm very happy to oblige." She glanced at her watch. "Can you come down to the clinic this afternoon at around two? That's a really slow time. Scott will be at the hospital and I can arrange with Devon to get you in right away so we don't take too much of your time. But I'm going to want to do a blood panel to make sure everything is in order."

Grace hadn't been exaggerating—she'd had a ton of physicals. A competitive skater had to be in peak condition, couldn't risk anemia or vitamin deficiency or, God forbid, some lurking condition like a heart or kidney problem. But this was different.

"I can do that. Two o'clock."

Nine

Although they didn't talk about it, Grace realized that she and Troy were having a standoff. She wanted to hear some words of love before she told him the whole story of her life and he wanted the story of her life before there could be words of love. She might be very vulnerable to the promise of first love, but she wasn't an idiot.

She had kept her appointment with Peyton.

When Grace had visited Peyton and asked her about birth control pills, she told her they'd only been using condoms for protection. "I'm not worried about it," she said. "But Troy is getting a little nervous about depending only on that when the pill is safer."

"Perfectly understandable. Are your periods regular?" Peyton asked.

"No, unfortunately. I'm pretty sure I'm due any day now. Seems like it's been a while."

"Well, let's do a physical exam and blood work and then I'll give you a prescription for birth control pills. You can start taking them the first day of your period, but stick with your other protection until two weeks on the pill. I'll also give you a pregnancy test to take home just in case that cycle doesn't arrive—you can check to be sure you're not pregnant."

Troy hadn't even asked her about it. She decided she was going to tell him everything about her past before his friends visited on the weekend. If there was anything about her he no longer liked, he could just sleep on his own couch while they were in town.

She put the morning mail on her desk, went about her work, put together a few floral arrangements for Justin to deliver later. She went upstairs to fix a sandwich for lunch, then cleaned up the shop, made a list of flower orders for the week and visited with customers. It was late afternoon and Justin had already picked up his deliveries before she went through the mail. She leafed through the usual ads and bills, then came across a letter. Her name and address were typed on the envelope and she expected an offer of cheap insurance or something similar. But inside was one folded slip of paper. She opened it and read what was typed across the page.

"I dream of you every night. B."

She stared at it, mouth open. Her hands began to shake. She looked over her shoulder left, then right. Her breath came in short gasps. She locked the back door. She wanted to go upstairs and lock her loft, but she was afraid to go outside. She grabbed her cell phone and then spoke aloud, to calm herself. "Stop. Stop. You're alone here. He's not here."

But she checked every nook and cranny, in the cooler, the office, even under the desk. She looked into the alley and saw nothing unusual. She didn't know who to call. Not her mother, who would only say *I told you so*. Not Mamie and Ross in Portland—what could they do? She finally speed-dialed Mikhail's cell phone. She had no idea where he might be; he could be anywhere in the world. She usually got his voice mail and was constructing the message she'd leave him when he answered in Russian.

"Mikhail, he found me! I just got a letter. It says what he used to say, that he dreams of me every night. It's Bruno! Oh, God."

"Sons of bitches!" he barked into the phone.

"It's not addressed to Izzy. It's addressed to Grace Dillon. Here at the shop. Where I *live*."

"But he is in hospital," Mikhail said. "I will call them now. Then I call you. Stay where you are," he instructed as though she'd leave the phone if she left the room.

"Thank you. I couldn't make myself call them."

The first note had come when she was twelve, just a little girl, but her parents hadn't shared it with her. At twelve she was already a skater with enormous promise and a winner in her age category. Her parents screened everything that came near her, but she saw one of the notes lying on her father's desk a year later. She got a little excited at first—someone loved her? Dreamed of her? But her mother said, "Don't be ridiculous! It's another nutcase! We reported him to the police."

She didn't think another thing about it. Then, not long after her father's death, after an early morning practice with Mikhail, her new coach, she took off her skates in the arena where she'd been skating and walked toward the exit where the chauffeured town car waited. A man she didn't know and couldn't remember ever seeing before stepped out of a dark hallway, grabbed her, put his hand over her mouth and ran down that dark hallway with her. She struggled and fought and he babbled that he was going to take care of her, rescue her from the people who were exploiting her.

He held her in a maintenance closet with a broken lock on the door. She huddled in the corner, sitting on the cold floor, while he paced and babbled about foreign countries using children to spy for them, that the beautiful children should be freed, on and on with nonsense that had no meaning. He hadn't been armed that she could see, but he was a large man. His hair was thinning on top but long on the sides and back; she found out later that he was twenty-four. She tried to get up and run for the door of that small space but he smacked her right down and threatened her, told her he'd have to hurt her to protect her if she didn't follow his rules.

It took a little over two hours for the police to open the unlocked door, wrestle him to the ground and remove her. It was much later that she learned he was delusional and had to be hospitalized.

After that incident there were a couple of other stalkers that were handled quickly, efficiently and with restraining orders. Those two later perpetrators were not delusional but appeared to be aficionados of the young female sporting scene and seemed to move on with little argument. Who knew who they bothered after her?

Once Grace understood exactly what had been going on she also understood there were predators out there, people who preyed on pretty young athletes, male and female. They usually began by giving small gifts or flowers and praising their talent, but too soon they'd be seen at every practice and competition, always trying to get closer, to chat it up with the coaches or athletes.

It was very likely a combination of her own close calls and the tearful words from that young skater, Shannon Fields, that caused Grace to fire such rash and destructive accusations at the coach, Hal Nordstrom, suggesting he'd been inappropriate. Poor little Shannon had said to Grace, "You don't understand! I gave him *everything* he asked for. *Everything*, even if it was horrible!" Grace believed, in her gut, that Shannon had been talking about something other than, *more than*, practice. She had no evidence. But he did have a sleazy, lecherous look in his eye and he did way too much fondling and butt patting.

What did she know about it? She had Mikhail Petrov, that cold, angry, often silent little Russian who never touched her, not in anger, not in praise. Since his compliments came in the harsh, brittle Russian tongue, she had no way of knowing, for years, that he was sentimental on the inside. Looking back, she could see that Mikhail had almost become the man of her small family; both Winnie and Grace had depended on him. He was always present, completely devoted.

Mikhail also had strong opinions about Hal Nordstrom. He used one phrase whenever he referred to that particular coach. "He is piece of shit."

Winnie had told her to keep her mouth shut and when she hadn't, Nordstrom sued them for defamation and Winnie had settled with an undisclosed sum. When, a few years later, Nordstrom was arrested for molesting several young skaters, Grace felt vindicated. But did Winnie apologize? Just the opposite. "You could have saved me considerable money if you'd just kept your mouth shut. And he would've eventually been found guilty anyway."

It was a long couple of hours before Mikhail called her back. "He is out, *moya radost*," he said, his Russian for *my happiness*. "But he is with family in Florida. They swear on bibles he is safe and taking medicine. I'll get this verified to my satisfaction."

"Oh, Mikhail, what if they're lying? Making excuses?"

"I have called police. I want they should answer me. We shall see. Are you safe?"

"I think so," she said weakly, looking around again. "Why would he even want me now? I'm not on the ice or in the news! He shouldn't even want me anymore!"

"Ach, I can't know the head of a crazy man! If there is doubts, you must take steps. Call police. Or," he said, hesitating briefly, "call Winnie. She will not abandon you."

A nervous laugh that was almost a sob escaped her. The last thing she wanted was to be controlled by her mother again. She talked to Mikhail while she walked to the front door, put up the closed sign and locked it. They talked for just a few minutes. She learned he was in Chicago for some exhibition skating and then would be heading to Southern California, which had become his home base.

Mikhail was over sixty. He was once a competitive skater but gave that up in his early twenties, knowing he was not good enough to be great. But he had the potential to build champions and had been coaching ever since. He'd had only one brief marriage because, *Is not the life for family man.* Grace wasn't quite sure how much or how little that influenced her decision to get out. *What do I care?* Mikhail would say. *I make winners, that is what I do.*

Grace wanted more. Or less, as the case may be.

"I would like to see you sometime," she told him before hanging up.

"You have to find me," he told her. "We would have good meal, laughs, old times. Maybe you skate for me once!"

"Maybe," she said. "For old times only."

"I was better making rules, telling you when you will skate and what you will do. I don't follow so good."

"I know this," she said, laughing through nostalgic tears.

After they hung up, she dimmed the lights in the shop. *When you're closed, you're closed.* She didn't have the courage to go upstairs to her loft. She had an irrational fear that he was waiting for her up there. He was really a kind of tragic, pathetic man who was completely out of reality, left in the care of an older sister who wasn't married and promised to always guard him closely, a woman who really cared about him and was traumatized by the reality that he could possibly hurt someone.

She heard from Troy every day. If he didn't call her after school, she called him. She'd give him till six or so, then she'd text him and ask him what he was doing after work.

In the meantime, she thought about Mikhail and she cried. The truth was, she missed skating for him. She even missed competition and the raw nerves of it. She had no regrets about leaving it—she'd accomplished everything she could and the strain was sometimes debilitating.

It was funny that the girl who was her fiercest rival, who hated her more than anyone on the circuit, an American named Fiona Temple, hadn't ever made her mark. Fiona, who had her own posse of mean girls, spread more dirt about Grace than anyone else, making sure everyone knew that while most hardworking parents got up at four to take their kids to training and borrowed against the mortgage to pay for it, Rich Bitch Izzy's mother put her in a town car at dawn to be delivered to the rink. Fiona, who celebrated the most when Grace walked away, hadn't done anything significant since. She had believed the only thing that stood in the way of gold medals was Grace, yet with Grace gone China and Russia wrapped up the medals.

The pressure to stay in the competition had been fierce from all quarters, from Winnie, from her team, from her country. "You do what you have to do, but until the day comes, say *nothing*!" Mikhail had warned her. "Telling is losing."

Any other coach would've dumped her. In her circles, winning was everything. World-famous coaches don't waste their time on competitors who want to quit. But he stuck with her, gave her everything he had and she worked her ass off for him. Mikhail wasn't warm and fuzzy, but he loved her like a daughter, protected her and challenged her and to this day had not abandoned her.

So she went to her last competition, the biggest in the world, angry and determined to strike one final blow for everyone who depended on her. And she took it. Took it *all*. She took it home by a mile. Winnie had her gold medal. Fiona hadn't even made the cut.

The back door to the shop rattled as someone tried to get in. She nearly jumped out of her skin. She had to take a couple of deep breaths and wipe her eyes before creeping to the door to see who it was.

"Gracie, what's wrong?" Troy said. "You're crying."

"Don't ask me why, just please go upstairs and

make sure no one is up there, ready to jump on us and kill us," she said.

"What?" he asked, aghast.

"When it's safe, we'll talk up there. I'm not sure if I locked the door, but some days I don't. I've gotten so relaxed…"

"Grace, what the hell?"

"Please," she begged. "You'll understand as soon as I can talk about it. I was going to explain some things anyway. Before your friends came to visit, I was going to tell you so it wouldn't be vague anymore…but for right now, can you please check? And be very careful!"

Troy shook his head and went upstairs. He looked around her loft thoroughly, but nothing seemed out of place. He was back down in less than two minutes. "It's okay."

"Did you look everywhere?"

He nodded. "Even in the kitchen trash and the refrigerator. Come on."

She clutched an envelope in her hand. When they were sitting across from each other in her tiny kitchen she started to explain. "My real name is—"

"I know," he said.

"You *know*?"

"Sorry. I wasn't going to tell you, but I can't fake surprise. You're all over the fucking internet, Gracie. I don't know how you felt, how you feel, but I know who you are. And that you won it all and walked away."

"Do you know about the rumors? That I accused a

coach of inappropriate sexual behavior with a minor? That I was *sued*? That there were stalkers? That everyone hated me?"

He shrugged. "I got most of the facts. I don't know how anyone could hate you. Most of all, I don't know why it's a secret."

So she started at the beginning, born into figure skating, the daughter of a champion and coach, the bullying from jealous girls, pranks aimed at hurting her skating, the exhausting training and travel and no friends.

"The coaches demanded everyone behave nicely toward each other, but when the coaches weren't looking... The rest of them were all so close," she said. "They shared hotel rooms to save costs and I stayed alone. My mother would rent big town houses that came with domestic help and everyone thought because of that, I had it so easy, why wouldn't I do well? It came up in every interview and article—as if all we had to do was write a check and first place was mine. All I wanted, the whole time I was growing up, was to be like everyone else."

"Nothing nastier than jealous teenage girls," he said. He gave her cheek a little stroke.

"If I cried or pouted they called me poor little rich girl."

"And yet there were millions of girls all over the country who watched you skate with envy and adoration."

"But I never met them. The happiest day of my

life wasn't winning the gold—it was handing it to my mother and walking away."

"Where did you go?"

"To Mamie and Ross. They were a couple without children who had worked for my mother since she was a girl—over thirty years. He was a driver and she was a housekeeper. They were always so good to me and when they left my mother's employment they opened a flower shop in Portland. They trained me in the business."

"Is there no other family?"

"Remember I told you about a cousin who wrote me asking for a loan?" He nodded. "That wasn't a cousin and it wasn't a loan. That's a half brother, Barry, who is twenty years older than me. My father and his first wife divorced years and years before my mother knew him. He supported his ex-wife and Barry until Barry was twenty-one. He's forty-eight now and has been asking for money his whole life, but I don't remember even three times he visited. My dad gave him money sometimes—my parents fought about it. When my father died, he didn't leave Barry anything. I don't know where he is. Last I heard from him, when I told him there was no money, he was in Texas."

Troy immediately smelled an ill wind. "Maybe Barry is still butt sore about that," he said, tapping the envelope in her hand.

She handed it to him. "I never had a relationship of any kind with him—he was grown when I was born. No, this is just like the note I remember from years ago. The only one I saw before I was snatched."

"Could he know exactly what was in it?" Troy asked, opening it up and looking at the typed sentence. *I dream of you every night. B.* "It's signed 'B.'"

She shook her head. "That's Bruno. Bruno Feldman. The man who held me in a supply closet until the police came. He's been in a psychiatric hospital and I'm told he's out and with family somewhere in Florida. Barry doesn't know that's what the notes looked like. No one knows—just me, my mother, Mikhail…"

"Mikhail?"

"My coach. One of my coaches. We keep in touch a little bit. Of course he was there at the time. Things got pretty crazy because the first notes came while my father was sick, then he snatched me after my father had died. So much happened at once."

"*One* of your coaches?"

She nodded. "There was a team and several different coaches and instructors and trainers. Endurance training, ballet, ice work. For me there was also yoga, sports therapy, and then the tutors and homework."

"How many hours a day was that?" he asked.

"I don't know. Every one of them, I think. It started early, ended late. That's not even counting fittings for costumes, choreography, music…and did I mention homework? How about the number of nights I went to bed with bags of ice wrapped to my ass or calves?"

He smiled at her. "You earned those medals, Gracie. It was a lot to give up. But are you happy now?"

"I was," she said, her eyes glistening again. "Until that came." She sighed. "What kind of jollies does a person get out of just scaring me to death?"

He shook his head. "It's not normal, you know. It's sick and twisted. And from what you tell me, not entirely his fault."

"I don't know what to do," she said. "I feel like I should run and hide."

"That's because you're scared and upset. But it's going to be all right. You'll have to think things through a little, ask yourself some questions…" He got up and opened the little fridge. He didn't find what he wanted, so he looked in the small wine rack on top and pulled out a bottle of Merlot. He opened it and poured a small glass for her. "Have a little of this and take a few deep breaths. I'm not going to let anything happen to you."

"I really don't expect you to—"

"You don't expect me to help protect the girl I love?" he asked.

She stared at him. "You love me?"

"Of course I do, Gracie. Couldn't you tell?"

"You never said anything about love…"

"I was waiting for you to trust me, to be honest with me. Look, I understand how you could want to escape that old life, as difficult as—"

"No, Troy, you don't! I don't want to be that person anymore! That friendless person so many people talked about and hated! Do you have any idea how painful it is to be the constant object of everyone's jealousy? As if I had something that belonged to them? As if my mother's money could buy anything—well, it can't buy safety or a family or love!"

"And so many people admired you, also," he said. "But, no matter what name you decide to use, I'm always going to think of you as Gracie. Everyone loves you. You're not an overworked, abused, over-exposed teenage girl anymore. And the first thing you have to let go of is all the secrecy. Your friends can't watch out for you if they don't know anything. When you let the cat out of the bag, people are going to wonder why in the world you'd keep an accomplishment like that a secret."

"Because they don't understand how hard it is to be in that life!"

"You're not in it anymore, honey." He laughed a little and grabbed the last cold beer out of her fridge. "I have to admit, I had trouble understanding why you'd hide that. Gracie, I get that a lot of it was hard, worse than hard, but it's also an achievement. No one's going to hate you for it."

She sipped her wine. "We don't know that for sure."

"Yes, I know it. First thing we're going to do is get you a couple of things for protection. I think we can find 'em online real easy and get them sent overnight. Maybe some pepper spray. How about a stun gun? A Taser."

"I have to admit, there are a few people I'd like to zap…"

"That's my girl. Only bad guys, okay, baby? Then

we're going over to see Seth. He needs to know there's been this contact. I don't know if you'd call it a threat, exactly, but it's creepy and he's the law around here. Besides that's a good time for you to unload all this on your best friend. You know you can trust Iris to accept you as exactly who you are, no kidding."

"I guess," she said.

Ten

Iris's house was the scene of quiet domesticity. It almost brought tears to Grace's eyes, she was that envious. It wasn't quite seven and apparently they were just getting around to dinner. Seth had changed out of his deputy's uniform into a pair of jeans and a sweater. Since Troy had called and asked if he and Grace could stop by to have a word with them, Iris had added two plates to their dinner table.

"Oh, you shouldn't have," Grace said.

"But of course I should have! And I apologize—it isn't much. I was just about to put in a frozen pizza and since you wanted to stop by, I pulled out a second. To my embarrassment, I have a good supply of frozen pizzas! I doctor them a little—extra pepperoni, cheese and mushrooms."

"That's almost like cooking, right?" Seth said. "Come in. Let's toast whatever you have on your mind."

"I don't think this is toastable, but it's definitely

drinkable. Grace has something to tell you. Then we could use a little help," Troy said.

"Absolutely," Seth said. "Let's sit in the kitchen."

"I hope nothing's wrong," Iris said, pulling out a chair for Grace.

"Something's wrong," Grace said. "I'll try to give you the short version. I haven't been entirely honest with you about my past. My life. I'm not exactly who you think I am. I'm sorry—it's not that I didn't trust you."

By now it was getting a little easier to talk, since telling Troy was the hard part. She got the whole story out without *all* the details about daily life as a competitor, in about fifteen minutes. Iris, stunned by this new information, punctuated the story with *Seriously? You're kidding me!* and *Holy crap!*

"My God, you're famous," she finally said. "I thought you looked familiar but couldn't place the resemblance."

"Only famous at certain times and in certain places, but I'm not that competitor anymore. Which is why I didn't say anything. And it's also why this freaked me out. This guy was obsessed with me." She slid the envelope toward Iris while she explained what had happened with Bruno.

Iris passed the note to Seth, who frowned when he read it. "Is this the only contact?" he asked.

"There hasn't been anything since he was put in the hospital. And only my parents and the police knew about the way the note was written—that one typed line and the initial *B*. Could he still be obsessed with me?"

"Anything is possible," Seth said.

"Can you find out if he's still secure with his family in Florida?" Troy asked.

"I'll make some calls. I'll get in touch with the police department there. Do you know the name of the psychiatric facility?"

She gave it to him. "When my old coach checked, he was told he wasn't a patient any longer, that he lived with his family."

"Grace," Iris said. "This envelope has no postal stamp on it."

"Huh?"

She gave the envelope to Seth. "It wasn't postmarked," she repeated. "It must have been slipped into your mailbox."

"Oh, God," Grace said weakly. "He's *here*?"

"Let's not make assumptions," Seth said, reexamining the envelope and then slipping the note inside. The envelope went in his pocket. "I'm going to look into this. Iris, get those pizzas in, okay?" He immediately turned his attention back to Grace. "Let me tell you something, Grace. If there's an odd stranger lurking around Thunder Point, he's going to stand out like a wart on my nose and even without telling anyone I'm looking, someone's going to tell me. Especially on the main street that runs through town, past all the businesses. Gina never misses a thing, I miss less. Waylan was robbed about ten years ago and he's still talking about it, still checking every face on the street. In fact, this whole mystery will be easier to solve if some stranger came around and slipped the note into your mail slot."

Iris put a glass of wine at her place and Grace's and asked Troy what he'd like. Then a couple of beers appeared in front of Troy and Seth. After sliding the pizzas into the oven, Iris sat down again.

"But," Seth went on, "I'm going to tell my staff and the business neighbors that a suspicious note was left in your mail slot and I'm looking for who could have done that to be sure you're safe. In the meantime, put a note on the door to ring the bell and lock the front and back doors. I'll find out about your former stalker, but I may not hear back from anyone until the morning. Listen, I don't know if you'll take this as good news or bad, but I would be very surprised to find some mentally ill patient from fourteen years ago is still obsessed with you and made it across an entire continent, made himself invisible and shook you up with a copy of an old note. I think this is something else altogether."

"But no one knows about this," she said.

"That's seldom the case, especially after so long. I have no idea what the motive could be, but I doubt this is still a closely held secret."

"But who would do this? Who could possibly care?" she asked.

Seth shook his head. "I don't know. Yet. But I'll be looking for a reason. And you have to think about it, too. Maybe an enemy? Someone who thinks you have money? Have you ever been followed by reporters? A jealous family member?"

"Your mother?" Troy asked. "She's not happy with your decision to leave competition and you said she's really controlling."

"I can't imagine," Grace said. "She's been impossible and demanding but, to her credit, she's never been underhanded."

"Maybe you should contact her," Seth said. "Try to get a read on her."

"I'd hate to do that. We've been estranged since I left competition."

"Well, give it serious thought," Seth said. "And keep the doors locked."

"I won't leave Grace alone," Troy said. "I'll make sure she's safe in her shop before I go to school tomorrow. And we're going to get some self-defense things. You know—pepper spray and a Taser."

Seth groaned. "God, I hate when people do that. People get hurt. Waylan got himself a Taser—the kind that shoots out the prongs. He accidentally Tasered his cat."

"I have guns," Troy said.

Seth groaned again, louder. "I assume Grace is not trained in firearms."

"I am," Troy said. "But they're for hunting. And you're right, she's so small I'd be afraid it would only put a shotgun or rifle in the hands of someone who shouldn't have it."

"Hey," Grace interrupted. "Am I a part of this discussion? Because I kind of like the idea of having some kind of weapon! The bigger and scarier, the better!"

"Are those guns in a safe place?" Seth asked Troy.

"They're in my apartment and there's a great lock on the door. I replaced the apartment lock with a couple of good dead bolts because I have some expensive equipment in there. They're not loaded. Like I said, I do a little hunting."

"Make sure they stay unloaded," Seth said.

"I can keep her safe until you're back on duty tomorrow," Troy said.

"Yeah, I've seen you in action," Seth said with a chuckle. "That takedown at the high school a few months ago, that was dramatic. You were showing off, but it was helpful."

"Helpful," Troy said sarcastically, speaking of the day Iris was threatened by a very big, very angry and abusive student and Troy happened to be there at the right time. Seth was there *second*.

The men talked about that incident while Iris took the pizzas out of the oven, let them sit on the counter for a few minutes to cool. Then Grace and Iris stood at the counter, cutting up the pizzas.

"Iris, I can't eat. I'm sorry," Grace said.

"I know it's not chicken soup, but you should have something. A bite or two. Don't be afraid now—Troy and Seth are on this."

"He didn't say anything about staying with me until we came over here."

"Grace, don't you know how he feels about you?

He's crazy about you! And I can't believe you were this famous person and were afraid to tell me!" Iris said.

"I wasn't afraid. I just wanted you to like me for who I am—a flower girl."

"How could you doubt that? You're the best flower girl this town has ever seen."

"Oh, jeez, what am I going to do?" Grace said. "I have weddings in April! I can't shut down! I can't run! You know brides—they're all on such a weak string to start with. Every small thing that goes wrong turns them insane. Their flowers have to be on time and perfect."

"You don't have to shut down. I can't explain how this would be possible but I bet this note is some kind of ugly prank. Seth will find out. He's not only very good at this sort of thing, he's committed. He's a good cop."

Grace and Troy took a swing by his apartment so he could gather up some clothes, his backpack and laptop so he wouldn't have to go home in the morning before work. Grace was restless through the night, even with Troy beside her. She tossed and slept little and had one terrible dream, but it was not about Bruno. She was skating but her costume wasn't covering her body and her legs wouldn't move. She couldn't see the audience but she could hear them laughing. There was one face—her biggest rival, Fiona, laughing at her, pointing, howling.

In the dream, Grace worked harder. She tried relaxing and focusing and her legs began to move, but something about what she was doing was horribly difficult. She realized she was trying to skate uphill; the ice was slanted sharply upward. Her heart was pounding and her stomach ached, but she strove for poise. She looked down at her feet and the skates were gone, replaced by her Ugg boots. All the pressure of performance crippled her; all the fear of failure brought that lump back to her throat and she knew she couldn't do it, that it would be a disaster. Worse than that, she looked like a fool. She tried to skate in boots while covering her breasts where the costume had fallen away. And what costume was that? Some purple tulle thing that looked ridiculous!

Her heart raced and she woke up with a sob, gasping.

"Hey now," Troy whispered. "You're okay. You're safe."

She curled into him and tried to slow her pulse. She wanted to tell him she hadn't been afraid—she'd been back in that stressed place, the weight of performance anxiety bearing down on her.

Troy's arms were around her and she came back to her senses—it was just a silly dream. Nothing like that had ever happened to her. But she had felt those feelings before—the fear that she'd biff it and go slamming into the ice. Her mother would harp on it for ages, pointing out every flaw. In fact, even her best skating seemed not to be good enough.

She had so loved skating, yet every day of her life had been filled with the burden of anxiety and desperation.

Troy's lips were on her neck and she turned in his arms to meet his mouth with a kiss so hungry she all but consumed him. He growled deep in his throat and his hands were urgently moving. She parted her legs for him and with a deep groan he rolled her onto her back. He reached for a condom and then he reached for her. His fingers massaged her roughly; she was slick with desire. She pulled him to her, her hands on his butt. He was quickly inside her, pumping expertly. She couldn't be quiet. Her sighs turned to soft moans as she met him thrust for thrust.

This is the only place I want to be, she thought with a mixture of gratitude and despair. Her orgasm was so tight and hard Troy stopped breathing for a second. Then he slammed into her and pulsed with incredible power, making her come all over again.

They lay panting, clinging to each other. They were silent for a long time before Troy spoke. "That should help you sleep."

"I don't want to sleep," she said, gently stroking his back. "I just want this."

"Do you now?" he asked with a chuckle. He brushed her hair back from her face and kissed her again. "Sometimes you make me wonder if I have any control at all."

"It seemed like you had plenty."

"No, sweetheart. I definitely lost my head. Gracie, if we're going to get ahead of this thing with the note, you're going to have to be very brave. You're going to have to get back some of that feisty girl. Like the little witch I met on Halloween night—full of attitude. You're going to have to trust some people to help you."

She was quiet for a moment. He had no idea how strong she'd had to be! Since she was just a little girl.

But then she remembered she had won the gold by being pissed off and single-minded. She had decided to give it everything she had. "You really haven't seen me in action yet," she finally said.

In the morning, they proceeded as planned. After showering and eating a light breakfast, Troy made sure she was secure in the shop behind locked doors. At midmorning, Seth rang the bell and she let him in.

"Well?" she asked.

"I hope you consider this good news because I do. Your stalker, Bruno, is safely monitored in a group home in Hillsboro County, Florida. He takes his meds and visits his sister regularly and has not been out of contact with his sponsors for even twenty-four hours since entering the group home. According to his sister, he has not had delusions about you for over a dozen years, thanks to his medication."

"And that's good news?" she asked. "Then who's trying to drive me insane?"

"Easy, Grace. It's a mean prank. But there was no threat."

"What are you going to do about it?" she asked.

Seth frowned, she couldn't miss it. "I'm going to be vigilant. I'm going to tell Gina, Carrie, Waylan and Dr. Grant that someone left an anonymous note that frightened you and we don't know who or why.

I'm going to ask them to watch for strange or suspicious persons. That's about all I can do."

"Can't you do something more? Like check it for fingerprints or something?"

"No, Grace," he said. "I know you feel vulnerable and I'm going to keep my eyes open for this joker, but there hasn't been a crime. Your shop or residence hasn't been broken into, no one has threatened you. I have no reason to think you're in danger. I think you should be cautious and alert—definitely let me know if there's further contact—but even though it's suspicious and suggests a link to an old, resolved crime, at this point it's nothing more than an innocuous note. In itself, the note isn't even malicious. In fact, it could be a coincidence that the wording is the same."

"It's not a coincidence," she said.

"Stick with the locked doors for the time being, all right?"

"And look over my shoulder a lot?" she asked.

"Look, Grace, when those notes were originally sent by your stalker he had a plan that put you in jeopardy. He hasn't delivered this note. Do you have any reason to believe anyone means you harm?"

She thought for a moment before she shook her head.

"I think it's mean, doing that to you. I'll keep my eyes open. I'll watch the shop when I'm in town. I'll tell the other deputies to watch. But it just doesn't follow that whoever did this wants to hurt you."

"Of course you're right," she said. "But someone did do it to scare me. I can't imagine why."

"That's the mystery, isn't it?" he said. "You going to be all right?"

She shrugged. "I guess. I'm not going to let something like this beat me. It really pisses me off."

"Good. It should. Call me if anything happens that worries you. Anything at all."

"Thanks, Seth. I understand there's nothing much more that can be done. I appreciate the time you put into this."

He touched his forehead in a salute. "We'll be on duty, Grace."

When he left, she stepped out onto the sidewalk behind him. It was a sunny early April day, but the front of the shop wasn't as exciting as usual. She hadn't put out her sidewalk displays because some asshole had forced her in behind locked doors with a stupid little note. She turned, stomped back into the shop and dragged out her big wooden bunny for Easter. She cranked out her awning. Next, she pulled out a wicker basket filled with plastic daffodils and a sign that read Spring Sale! Then she unpacked her yellow, pink, mint-green and pale blue banner that read Easter Flowers! Order Now! She fixed it over the door. And finally she tore off the note over the doorbell.

Seth was right, she thought. It's mean and creepy but it's not an open threat. She would be cautious and safe. She refused to be insanely paranoid. If anyone crazy came at her, she'd beat him over the head with her ceramic tulip sculpture.

However, she did keep the back door locked, just to be sure.

* * *

Ray Anne painted her second bedroom, bought new linens for the bed and reupholstered the window cornices with matching fabric. She did it all herself, as she always had. Although she knew every handyman within a hundred-mile radius, she was also adept at home repairs and decorating. She knew how to hang wallpaper, install crown molding, replace wallboard and a dozen other things. In preparation for Ginger's arrival, she removed all her clothes, shoes and purses from the closet in the guest room— she had used it for her overflow wardrobe.

There was a small bath and shower in her bedroom and a larger bathroom with tub and shower beside the guest room. She cleaned under the sink and stocked it with bath gels, bubble bath, scented soaps, lotions and sponges. She put candles on the back of the commode and on the side of the tub.

She was nervous as a cat, waiting for her Gingersnap. She didn't know how she could help her get beyond this dark patch. *How does anyone get past it?* Poor Al had spent over thirty years trying to move beyond the death of his own baby son.

"I must have held on to that pain as stubbornly as an old bull," Al told her.

Ginger was driving down from Portland on Monday. At noon she still hadn't arrived and Ray Anne started to worry. She called her cousin and Dickie said she'd gotten an early start and should be there. Ginger didn't answer her cell phone when her father called or when Ray Anne called. At two, just

about the time Ray Anne was thinking of asking
Seth to check with the state troopers to see if there'd
been any accidents, Ginger pulled up in front of Ray
Anne's little house.

Ray Anne had seen Ginger four times in the months
since the baby died. She hadn't been looking good
then. She wasn't looking any better now. As Ray Anne
walked toward Ginger, who was pulling her suitcase
out of the trunk, she thought perhaps the girl was
steadily deteriorating. She was far too thin, that was
obvious even while she wore her coat. She was pale
under her freckled complexion and her expression had
become permanently downcast. Her hair was pulled
back in a ponytail; the beautiful strawberry blonde
locks had gone dull and dark. She obviously hadn't
done a thing to it in months.

"There you are!" Ray Anne said cheerily. "I was
starting to get worried!"

"I stopped to look at the ocean," Ginger said.

"Well, of course! I should have thought of that!
But now you're here, let's get your things inside."

"I've got it," Ginger said, snapping up the pull
handle.

"Is that all you've got? One bag?"

"It's all I need," she said.

"Well, I guess you'll be doing laundry then. Come
on, let's get you settled." Ray Anne took the handle
of the suitcase and pulled it up the walk and into the
house. "I cleaned out the guest room and the bathroom, so it's all yours. I put some pampering things

in there for you—soaps, lotions, candles. Did you bring a hair dryer?"

"I don't need one."

No wonder her hair was so flat and thin looking. She must be washing it and letting it dry any which way. And she wasn't using any product! "We can share mine. Or maybe we'll get you a new one."

"Really. I'm fine."

"Right in here," Ray Anne said briskly, pulling the suitcase into the newly painted and decorated bedroom. "Voilà!" she said, throwing an arm wide to showcase her decorating.

"Thanks," Ginger said, not noticing how pretty it was. "I'll just lay down for a while."

"No, ma'am," Ray Anne said, lifting the suitcase onto the bed. "We're going to unpack, hang and put away your clothes." She unzipped the suitcase and found the items inside had shifted because it wasn't even full. Or maybe they hadn't and Ginger had just haphazardly tossed them inside. She lifted out the first pair of wrinkled jeans. Then a second. Then a long-sleeved T-shirt. Then an old sweatshirt that she might have used when she painted something…years ago. And her underwear—pathetic.

"Oh, brother," Ray Anne muttered.

Ginger just sat on the bed. She didn't respond.

"Are we even related?" Ray Anne asked her. She lifted a dingy pair of granny panties and let them dangle from one finger. "Do we share any DNA at all?"

Ginger shrugged. "Just wasn't a priority, Ray. Why bother?"

Ray Anne sat on the edge of the bed and took one of Ginger's hands. "I'll tell you why we bother. Because there are things you can do to try to get beyond devastating pain. They might be small, stupid things, but they actually help a little. Things like fixing yourself up so you look better than you feel. Getting out helps—you have to live in this world. Work helps. Meaningful work, if possible, and that's something different for everyone, but keeping busy instead of lying in bed and making constant love to the hurt—that can help. Tell me something—are you taking anything?"

"Like what?"

"Like tranquilizers or antidepressants or anything?"

"Not anymore," she said. "They weren't working. And I kept thinking about swallowing the whole bottle."

Ray Anne gasped. "Jesus," she muttered. She wondered if she should hide all pills from Aspirin to hormones. And sharp objects. She stiffened her spine resolutely. "All right, I have to run a quick errand I put off while waiting for you to get here so you wouldn't find me gone when you arrived. I want you to put away your clothes in this chest and the closet. Then put the empty suitcase in the closet. Do that before you lie down. From what your daddy tells me, you've perfected napping and I'm willing to bet you're all caught up on sleep. I'll be back in fifteen or twenty minutes."

"All right," Ginger said, standing.

When Ginger hung her coat in the closet, Ray Anne noticed her jeans were sagging off her flat butt and her tennis shoes were beat-up. The girl was a complete mess. Her attire and body language were such a put off, holding back any well-intentioned person, it was as if she longed to go it alone and wallow in grief.

"Do you have my cell number?" Ray Anne asked.

"Probably," she said.

"Where's your phone?"

"I don't know. Probably in my purse. It's turned off."

"Why is it turned off?"

Ginger flashed her an angry look. "Because no one's going to call me! And there's no one I want to talk to!"

"Is that so?" Ray Anne asked without flinching. "Well, your father and I were trying to reach you to see if you'd had a problem on your drive and we went straight to voice mail, worrying us even more. Now, I can understand if you're avoiding calls, but is it either fair or kind to ignore people who love you and are concerned about you? If you want to do this to yourself forever, I don't suppose anyone can convince you otherwise, but your parents suffered a painful loss, as well, and I don't think they can deal with another one. I'm going to call them and tell them you arrived safely. Meanwhile, please turn on your phone. Charge it. Whatever. I'll be back in twenty."

Ray Anne, who never walked anywhere and was always seen in her little BMW, walked down the street, down the hill and into Carrie's deli. Carrie and Rawley appeared to be cleaning up. Customer traffic was usually at its lowest in midafternoon, heaviest for lunch and dinner. When Ray Anne walked in, Rawley automatically disappeared into the kitchen in the back of the deli.

"Well, hello," Carrie said.

"Call Lou and cancel dinner. Ginger just arrived and she's not fit to go out."

"Is she sick?" Carrie asked.

"She's horribly depressed. She can barely speak. The only thing more depressing than her personality right now is her wardrobe. Apparently it feels better to dress in poorly fitting rags. It's like sackcloth and ashes." She shook her head in misery. "I should have listened to myself. I can't help with this. She is way outside of my experience. I don't know what to do with her." She took a breath. "Can I please have a to-go dinner? Since we're not able to go out?"

"Sure. Now tell me what happened."

Ray Anne explained about Ginger's gaunt appearance, horrible clothing, turned-off phone and so on. "I was already very sad for her and about the baby. Of course I held that baby—he was a perfect baby! But it's been months and one look at her and you'd think it happened this morning. She's in terrible pain. Just terrible."

"She'll have to work through it, Ray. Everyone's grief time is different. Maybe you can get her into some kind of counseling or something."

"We'll look at that," she said. "First, I have to clean her up and feed her."

Carrie stood back from the deli case. Feeding people was her specialty. "What's your pleasure?"

"Something with carbs. And a big salad for me. God knows, I don't need fattening up. If my ass gets any bigger I won't be able to stay up on these heels."

Carrie laughed. "The chicken enchiladas are pretty irresistible. And I have some chips, salsa and guacamole."

"Perfect. And a salad. I can eat a little Mexican food and plenty of salad and she can eat a lot of chips and enchiladas and a little salad. And listen. Would you ask Lou about counselors?"

"I can do better," Carrie said. "When Ashley was on that downward spiral a couple of years ago, Lou found Gina a great counselor for Ashley. She specialized in young adults, but she might know someone to recommend for Ginger. Would you like me to ask Gina to give her a call?"

"Please," Ray Anne said. "I don't know if I'll be able to convince Ginger to go, but really—something has to be done to move forward. I don't know what else to do. And her daddy is right—she hasn't gotten any better."

"What have you done so far?" Carrie asked as she dished dinner into containers.

"Not much. I told her she couldn't take a nap until

her clothes were unpacked and she'd better turn on her phone or else. And..." She looked down somewhat shyly.

"I bought some lotions and stuff for her bathroom. I always feel better if I'm a little nice to myself. Baby steps," Ray Anne said.

Carrie smiled. "Just do what comes naturally to you, Ray. You're not a professional grief counselor but you know a lot about managing your own grief. And you're very sympathetic."

"Thank you," she said. "I'm trying not to mother Ginger, but I'm thirty years older than she is and even though I haven't been a mother, it kind of comes naturally."

Carrie passed the food across the deli counter. "Be yourself. You're a good woman and you love her."

"I do love her. She was my little angel." She dug around in her purse for money.

"Ah, on the house, Ray Anne. Tell her I'm sorry we're not going out tonight, but this is my contribution."

Eleven

Grace had always been capable of focus and discipline. She had amazing willpower and she thought with a clear head about what Seth had said. She reminded herself it was a note and not from the person who had threatened her fourteen years ago. She would be careful. Perhaps she'd be overly cautious for a while, but that was all right. She was not going to melt into a sniveling little girl.

In years past, when she was a teenager and the exhaustion or the other competitors or even her mother got the best of her, when she broke down, it got her nowhere. When that happened, when she *cried*, the abuse was even worse. The only thing that had ever worked for her was strength and grit. So she relied on that again. She focused on her abilities. She was small but very strong.

Troy was at the shop as soon as he was done with work. He had to knock on the back door because, feisty or not, she wasn't an idiot.

"I called Coop and told him I couldn't help at the bar this week because there's stuff going on."

"Let's not do that," she said. "Let's not panic and run scared."

He frowned. "You shook and had nightmares all night."

"Yeah, I hope I don't do that anymore. I'm much stronger and more sensible than that. Go help at the bar—I know how much you enjoy it. I think I'll get something from Carrie to warm up for dinner. If it'll make you feel better, I'll text or call you when I've closed the shop and gone upstairs. If you want to come by later, that's okay, but really, you don't have to. I think I'll be fine. I'll lock the back door and even slide a chair against it."

"This is a pretty sudden shift. What did Seth say to you?"

"Nothing so much—just that Bruno is not a threat and it was only a note, not a crime."

"Are you sure you're not in shock?"

She took a deep breath and leaned one hip against the worktable. "Sometimes I forget about my greatest accomplishments growing up because they weren't medals or ribbons or plaques. Do you know what one of the ESPN commenters said about me when I was fifteen? He said, 'That little girl is one hell of a fighter. Don't mess with her.'"

That made Troy smile. "You must regret leaving it sometimes."

"Never. I was done with that life. I did everything I could do. You can't imagine what it was like—I don't even expect you to try. No," she said, sliding her arms around his waist. "I like this life. And if I ever figure out who would try to screw it up with a scary little note, I'm going to make his life miserable."

"When I said I wanted you to be brave, I didn't mean that you should take any chances. I'll watch the shop while you go get some dinner for later. I want you to call me tonight. Then I'll come over when I'm off work."

"I love it when you come over. But you don't have to babysit me. You had a life before all this, a busy life. We can talk on the phone later, if you want to go home."

"I think I'll come over, if it's all the same to you. At least tonight."

"Then go home and change, bring your work clothes and laptop...you know the drill."

"Are you faking brave? Because of what I said last night?"

"No," she said with a laugh. "I'm faking brave because I just remembered it's how I get control. It's how I begin to feel brave. Now stay put—it shouldn't take me ten minutes to walk down to Carrie's."

Two days later, Troy decided to stop by the deputy's office after school before going to the flower shop. As luck would have it, Seth was there, sitting behind his desk, one foot propped casually on the desk while he talked on the phone. Another deputy, Charlie, seemed to be working at the computer on the desk behind Seth's. When Seth saw Troy he made excuses into the phone and disconnected.

"Hey," Seth said. "Everything all right?"

"Fine. I just thought I should tell you—that stuff I ordered came today. Grace texted me that she got it at the flower shop. Pepper spray and a Taser."

"Really," he said, standing up. "Mind if I look at it?"

"No, of course not. But it's completely legal."

"Sure. But I'd like to know what you could buy so easily and have delivered in just a couple of days. If you can, anyone can. I'd just like to know."

Troy shrugged. "Come on, then. There's a DVD with the package. Should be instructions and safety measures. I'll feel a lot more comfortable knowing Grace has something handy she can use to protect herself if…well, you know. She had that scare years ago."

"I don't think we're dealing with the same set of circumstances, Troy."

"I get that, but wouldn't you feel better, if it was Iris, knowing she had some kind of self-protection?"

Seth laughed. "Have you met Iris's left hook?" he asked. "I'm not sure I'd arm her on top of that."

"Grace needs a little something, if only for her confidence."

"Yeah? Well, be careful. Don't sneak up on her," Seth advised. "I wouldn't mind having a look at the DVD after you've seen it. If you don't mind."

"Not at all." He opened the shop's front door and yelled, "Gracie?"

"Troy! Come and see! You're not going to believe how cool this is! It even comes with a *holster*!"

He walked into the workroom and the box stood open on the table. Scattered about was packing material, extra Taser cartridges, two small pepper spray cartridges, a DVD and a catalog.

"Look at this!" she said, turning to one side so he could see the Taser affixed to a leather belt that was far too large. She took a gunfighter's stance, arms out at her sides. Then she did a fast draw, popped the Taser off the belt, pointed and...

Shot him.

She screamed and dropped the Taser while Troy felt the jolt go through him. He stiffened, trembled and down he went. His hearing was fine, even if he couldn't move his body. In fact, his hearing was a little too good—Grace wouldn't stop screaming.

"Troy! Troy! Troy! Oh, my God, Troy!"

All he could do was twitch on the floor.

Suddenly she stopped.

He heard her talking into her phone. "It's Grace at the flower shop! Send the doctor and hurry! I shot Troy! I electrocuted him! He might be dead!"

As the stinging shock passed, he lay still and pain free, except for the back of his head, which had hit the floor pretty hard. And his right thigh, where the Taser prongs hit. A few more inches and he'd have been a eunuch.

Seth crouched beside Troy, grinning. "Well. That works pretty good."

"Shut up."

"Great idea, Troy. Get a figure skater a stun gun."

"I said, shut up."

"Good thing it wasn't a Magnum." He chuckled. "I don't think she watched the DVD. What do you think?"

Troy groaned and struggled into a sitting position. There was a small amount of blood, very small, where one of the prongs stuck into his jeans, his flesh. He reached for it and Seth grabbed his wrist.

"Leave it, since Grace called for a doctor. Or I could take it out for you."

Then she was there, kneeling on his other side. "Oh, my God, Troy! It just fired itself!"

"Because you had your finger on the trigger! Don't you know you can't put your finger on the trigger?"

"I didn't! I mean, I didn't think I did. Oh, Troy, I'm so sorry! Scott's coming."

"Do you see where this is? I'm lucky he isn't going to pull it out of my dick! Didn't I tell you not to open the box? You could have neutered me!"

Seth smothered a chuckle as he stood. "I guess you turned it on, right, Grace?"

"The instructions said it wouldn't fire just because it was armed. You have to turn it on because it runs on batteries, but… Oh, never mind. I didn't mean to, I promise." Grace added some tears to her apology, hovering and begging for his forgiveness.

"All right, all right," he said. "I think you're perfectly safe from any potential attackers. Might want to work on your aim so you don't kill the poor bastard."

"Troy, really, I thought it would take a little pressure to make it fire! I can't believe I shot you! Oh, God, I'm so sorry. I would never hurt you!"

The shop door crashed open and Scott Grant, breathless, ran in carrying his medical bag.

"Take it easy," Seth said in a calm voice. "It was just a Taser. He's fine."

"*Just* a Taser?" Troy said. "It came a little close to the next generation of schoolteachers! Grace obviously has a shaky trigger finger."

Right behind Scott was Peyton and their office manager, Devon. Behind them was Carrie, who shouldn't be able to move that fast with her bad knees. Then crowding into the little shop was Waylan from the bar across the street and at least two of his customers and, in addition, every person who happened to be outside or even driving by when Scott Grant was seen running down the street with his medical bag.

Scott, panting, stopped in the workroom doorway to catch his breath. "Jesus, you took ten years off my life. I thought you shot him!"

"I did, but I shot him with this," Grace said, reaching for the Taser that lay on the floor where she had dropped it.

"No!" at least four people shouted at once.

Troy grabbed her and pulled her toward him. "Gracie, it's still got voltage. If you accidentally pulled the trigger again, you'd give me another blast."

"Oh, God! Troy, this isn't going to work. I can't be trusted with one of those things. I'm going to kill someone. I'd be better off with a road flare."

"Ever hear of the great Chicago fire?" Seth muttered to Scott.

"Shh, I forgive you already," Troy said. "Just don't touch it again until we figure it out."

Scott Grant crouched next to Troy, his open bag beside him. "Why didn't you take these prongs out?"

"Seth told me not to."

"We usually have to call medical for that," Seth said. "Not that I think it's necessary, but I figured…"

"Not complicated," Scott said, moving one slightly so it slid right out. They were shaped like small apostrophes and pulling it straight out could make it bleed a little, but wasn't likely to even require stitches. He then removed the second prong. "There. Feel better?"

"I'm fine," Troy said.

"I'm not," Grace said. "I'm not fine. I almost killed my boyfriend."

"Nah, not even close," Scott said, standing. "Want a Band-Aid for that, Troy?"

"Funny," Troy said, standing. "Let's joke around after you've taken your hit."

"I don't know how much physical damage was caused, but your mood is definitely affected," Scott said, smiling.

That's when Troy heard all the voices from the shop. *She shot him with the Taser. Worried about that note, so he bought her a Taser. It's just a Taser. Yeah? You ever been hit by a Taser? Damn near killed my cat with one of those! At least something interesting finally happened. Let's have a beer on that, should we?* And there was laughter all around as the shop emptied of everyone but Seth.

"Damn," Troy said, giving his leg a shake as if to bring the feeling back into it. "That sucker packs a punch!"

"I'm going to leave now if you think you can manage the situation without further injuries," Seth said.

"You're going to tell Iris, aren't you?" Grace asked.

Seth nodded. "I'm thinking of quitting early. I can't wait to get home."

"I'm never going to hear the end of this," she said. "I guess everyone knows about my note."

"They don't all know what it said or how it was written out. Just that it upset you and we're looking for a prankster. If gossip works like usual around here, I think you're probably safe." Then he smiled. "Have a nice evening."

Seth was home by five o'clock and Iris walked in right behind him. Iris laughed so hard at Seth's tale that she could hardly stay upright. "Oh, she's right, she's never going to hear the end of it. Poor Grace. How does that thing work? Let me see yours, Seth."

"Ah, no thanks, Iris. You never touch my weapons, right? Because that wouldn't be good. You don't know anything about them."

"Maybe you should train me," she suggested, then giggled again.

"You're doing just fine not touching."

"Aw, come on," she said, moving closer to him, sliding her arms around his neck.

Instead of arguing with her, he kissed her. Then he kissed her more seriously, sliding his hands over her butt and pulling her close. After a little more kissing, he said, "I have an idea…"

"Before supper on a Wednesday afternoon? Why, Deputy…"

"Are you expecting company?"

"Only your mother," she said. "But ever since she caught you in your boxers, she calls ahead if your car is home."

"Good. Troy said something interesting. He told Grace that a few inches to the left and she could have wiped out the next generation of schoolteachers and I thought, don't we have work to do?"

"I wouldn't call it work, exactly."

"Wouldn't it be easier to do naked?"

"Absolutely," she agreed. "But then we have to stay in bed for a while."

"I can do that. I'm very good at staying in bed with you. Are we making any progress on the next generation of deputies and school counselors?"

"I don't know, Seth. We've only stopped using protection for a few months and Peyton said to check with her if we have no results in six months. I'm doing my best. And you are definitely doing your best."

He kissed her again. "I love when you talk dirty."

She laughed. "I haven't started talking dirty yet. I just said you were doing your best…"

"I can do better," he said, and his voice had grown husky.

A half hour later, as they lay tangled in the sheets, Iris said, "That *was* better."

"That had to make a baby. That was good," Seth said. "Maybe two babies."

"I only want one at a time, if it's all the same to you."

"Are you hungry?" he asked.

"Yes, but I'm staying in bed for thirty minutes to give those little guys time to swim. Then we can get up and eat."

"We don't have to get up. I'll be right back." He found his boxers and disappeared.

Iris snuggled into the sheets, her head against the pillow. There were so many times, like now, that she couldn't believe her life had worked out the way it had. She'd loved Seth since she was just a girl, but they'd been estranged for seventeen years while they took different journeys. Hers took her to university and a postgrad program in counseling to bring her back to Thunder Point as the high school counselor. Seth had gone from the football field to a long recovery from injuries he sustained in a terrible car accident, but in the end his choice of law enforcement brought him home. And now he was hers again. All hers.

It wasn't very long before he was back. Iris had actually dozed a little. Seth held a tray with one plate that held two grilled cheese, bacon and tomato sandwiches, pickles, a glass of wine and a bottled beer, a bag of chips held tenderly under one arm.

"Here we go," he said. "It's not much, but it was fast and I bet it's good. Scoot over," he said. He put the tray between them and sat on the bed. He passed the wine to her hand and lifted his beer. "To us."

Iris brought the wine to her lips and to Seth's dismay, she sniffed. He took a big swallow of beer and when he looked at her again, tears were running down her cheeks. "Iris?"

Her nose turned a little pink. "This is all I've ever wished for," she said. A small sob followed.

"Grilled cheese?" he asked.

"You. You and me, together, in love, trying to make a baby. I didn't even hope for a baby. I thought that was impossible. Just you and me, that's all I ever wished for. I love you so much."

He frowned. Then he took her glass of wine from her. "Congratulations. I bet anything you're pregnant."

"What do you mean? You don't know anything."

"I do so. I listen to men talk about their wives. I don't want to—I hate all that talk—but it happens all around me. First their wives cry, then they throw up, then they get grumpy, then they nest, then they whelp." He put the wine on the bedside table. "Bet you anything," he said.

"Whelp?" she asked with a sniff.

"You know," he said, taking a big bite of grilled cheese. He chewed and swallowed. Then he grinned at her. "Bet I nailed you last week. I was *outstanding*."

"You're an arrogant know-it-all," she said, reaching for a tissue.

"And you're pregnant." He pushed the tray toward her. "Have a sandwich, honey. And if you're still hungry, I'll make you another one."

Scott was working late so Peyton got the kids ready for bed and settled them with their tablets and movies in their beds. Then she collected the tablets and turned them off and kissed the kids. She cleaned up the tent the kids had made with blankets over the dining room table. She'd been in the tent with them for a little story time earlier.

She had her shower, put on soft lounging pajamas that were nice and warm. She lit a couple of candles in the darkened living room. She put wineglasses out next to a bottle chilling in an ice bucket. But she turned on the lamp beside her on the couch to read for a while before Scott finished up in Bandon. It wasn't very late when he texted her. On my way. Need anything?

Just you, big boy.

Fifteen minutes later he came in from the garage and left his bag in the kitchen. When he took in the darkened room, the ice bucket, glasses and candles, he smiled at her. "Are you planning to seduce me?"

"Could be. Are you covered with blood and guts?"

"Nah. I washed up. Let's get on with the seduction!"

"No one ever accused you of being shy, did they?" Peyton said. She lifted the bottle out of the ice bucket, poured and handed him a glass. "I do have something to tell you. You know how we decided that I'd go off the pill but we'd use protection for a couple of months until my body got used to the idea?"

"Uh-huh. I might've gotten carried away once," he said.

"Actually, five times. At least. So, cheers," she said, clinking his glass. "I really don't mind when you get carried away. It's kind of fun."

He sipped. "Peyton, I think this wine is bad. It tastes sour."

"It's sparkling cider," she said. "You did it, you brute. You knocked me up before the wedding."

He grinned stupidly. "Peyton! That's wonderful!" Then he was stunned silent for a moment. "Crap," he finally said. "Your father is going to kill me. I'm a little terrified of your father, did I mention that?"

"Paco? He's all bluster. But, I think we won't tell him. Or Mama either, for that matter. Do you think you can keep your mouth shut around the grandmothers?"

"Oh, sure. I don't tell them anything. They're a pain in my ass. But it's going to be hard not to tell some of the guys. You know—Spencer, Coop, Seth."

"Try. Because at least two of those three have big mouths and they're coming to the wedding. It would be just like one of them to toast the bride and groom and baby. However, when I don't drink, someone's bound to ask."

"They know we're together. You can tell them you're five minutes pregnant. Just how pregnant are you?"

"Five minutes. I haven't missed a period yet but I peed on a stick."

"You did?"

"Uh-huh. Iris came in to set up a prenatal appointment. She's five minutes pregnant and it made me just wonder."

"Good for Iris! They want a baby! And by the way, we want a baby. This isn't going to screw up your plans, is it? I mean, the big wedding, the dress, the flowers, all that stuff? You're not going to get morning sickness at the altar or anything, are you?"

"No."

"And you're still planning to seduce me tonight?"

"Yes, Scott. I put your children to bed and when you've lost your mind on the sparkling cider I'm going to strip and make you crazy."

He leaned toward her, slid a hand under her sheet of black hair and pulled her closer. "I do love that. If you haven't folded up the tent, we could do it in there."

"I'd rather do it in bed."

He touched her lips with his. "I love you. Have I told you that lately?"

"Several times a day. And I love you, but apparently you have a real talent for procreation. I'm going to keep my eye on you."

"Thank you, Peyton. I really want children with you. At least a few."

"I agreed to one so far. Let's see how it goes."

"It's going to be great. Your family specializes in big herds. Your grandmother had the last child at forty-six."

"In your dreams, doctor hottie," she said, kissing him.

"Hmm. Do I have to drink this," he said, holding his glass up. "It tastes like shit."

She laughed. "If I have to be off wine for nine months, then shouldn't you? As a sign of solidarity?"

"Absolutely, I'll swear off wine if it makes you happy. Thank God, I'm a beer man. Now come on, enough talk about dietary restrictions—let's get you naked."

Troy asked Grace several times if it would be best to cancel his friend Denny's weekend visit. "No," she said. "In fact, it might be better to have things to do, people around. But, Troy, do you have to tell them I shot you?"

"No, I don't have to, but if we introduce them to anyone in town, they're going to find out."

"Oh, God," she moaned. "Things were so quiet, then…"

"All of a sudden," he agreed. "Well, it still isn't bigger than we are, babe."

The early April weather cooperated. Every day was sunny and bright except when those afternoon showers came in over the Pacific. The days had grown longer and Grace could keep the shop open until six and still close in daylight. The downside was that after Denny and Becca's visit, Troy was going to be needed more at the beach bar—people would start migrating to Cooper's for sunset. The weather was warmer, and more people were seen outside, walking rather than driving.

While it gnawed at Grace that someone could send her a note identical to the ones Bruno sent before capturing her, knowing he was under wraps brought her some peace of mind. And while she was loath to admit it, seeing that Taser take down her boyfriend gave her a little confidence. Aside from the confusion about a motive, she was quickly feeling calmer. She did not, however, wear the Taser on her belt. She handled it very carefully. She carried it in her purse and it was turned *off*!

On Friday afternoon at around five o'clock, Troy brought a lovely young couple to the flower shop to meet Grace. Denny was a tall, handsome man in his late twenties and his wife was a pretty blonde with the sweetest little baby bump. They introduced themselves, looked around the shop appreciatively and thanked her for welcoming them so nicely. And then Becca froze. Her mouth stood open slightly and she covered it with her hand. She stared at Grace, wide-eyed. "Oh, my God!" she said. "You're her! You're Izzy Banks!"

Twelve

It turned out that Becca Cutler had been hooked on figure skating and kept up with all the competitions. She loved it all, pairs, ice dancing, long programs, short programs. When it wasn't Winter Games, she watched national and world championships on ESPN. Becca and Grace were the same age. They literally grew up together. Grace admitted who she was.

After closing up the flower shop, they drove out to Cooper's so Troy could show his friends his other place of employment. "Not too different from your little bar in Virgin River," Troy said. "Just a different landscape."

Cooper and Denny shook hands like old friends. "Jack sends his best. Said to call him if you need anything."

"I need his cook if I'm going to get rich. Tell him to send Preacher," Cooper said.

"Like that'll ever happen," Denny said.

"Take a table, the weather's great. Beer on the

house for my friends. What can I get the little lady with that expectant look in her eye?"

"Just a noncaffeine cola, if you have it."

"Sorry, darlin', but everything here is high-test except the light beer."

"There's green tea in the cooler," Troy said. "I'll get you one."

"Can I have one, too?" Grace asked. "I'll drink along with the preggers, here."

Grace was greeted by a number of people as she and Becca went out on the deck, where it was still cool enough that they had to stay wrapped in their sweaters. The men stayed inside. Cooper brought the women some chips. He leaned down to whisper in Grace's ear.

"You doing okay, Gracie?"

"I'm fine, Coop. Thanks."

"If you need Troy next week, all you have to do is say so. We back each other up out here on the water."

"Thanks," she said. "I forget sometimes how great people are here."

"Never forget," he said, giving her hand a pat.

When he left, Becca was smiling. "This reminds me a little of Virgin River," she said. "Everyone is so bonded. I can see they all love you, Grace."

"I think I took that for granted. But tell me how you knew who I was?"

"Seriously? You were always my favorite. I watched you compete in all the big events!"

"How could I be your favorite?" Grace asked. "I didn't think I was anyone's favorite!"

"You were *everyone's* favorite!"

"No," she said, shaking her head. "I had the worst reputation in the business. People called me rich and snotty. My scores always suffered most because of my facial expressions! I never smiled enough for the judges."

"Really?"

"I thought everyone was rooting for Fiona Temple."

"She was the underdog. Underdogs always get attention, in all sports. But you? You were gifted, people said so all the time. A natural on the ice. And scared. You were just a scared kid. But in the Vancouver Games, you nailed it. You owned that competition—there was no contest. There hasn't been a competition like that since. Every newcomer is compared to you. Fiona was a good skater, but a total poser. They caught shots of her cursing or scowling all the time, showing she wasn't the sweet darling she pretended to be for interviews. I bet she was mean."

Grace was stunned. "As a snake," she said. "People knew?"

Becca shrugged. "I bet they did. Don't you remember what people said about you? Your reviews? Kiddo, you stole the show."

She had to shake herself. She only remembered the very critical comments.

"Why did you quit?" Becca asked.

"It's a long story, but it boils down to this—I couldn't take the pressure anymore. I'd gone as high as I could go and I was exhausted. I like my life better now, hard as that might be to understand."

"Not hard at all," she said with a laugh. "A good life, a good man like Troy? That's more than a lot of people have."

"Tell me about you and Denny," Grace said.

"Talk about a long story!" she said. She launched happily into her tale of on-again, off-again romance that finally stuck after she chased Denny to Virgin River and captured him with a broken ankle. She was getting to the wedding and her decision to stay in the mountains with the love of her life when Denny and Troy joined them on the deck, adding bits and pieces to her story. The sun was sinking in the sky when Troy announced that he'd made reservations at Cliffhanger's for dinner.

"Think about what you'd like to see and do while you're here," Troy said. "The weather is supposed to be good all weekend and the coast is beautiful."

"I can think of one thing I'd absolutely die to do," Becca said. "I'd so love to see you skate, Izzy…I mean Grace!"

Troy put an arm around Grace's shoulders. "Gracie doesn't skate anymore," he said.

"Actually, I do," Grace said. "There's a rink in North Bend where the owner lets me skate before they open in the morning. It's early, though."

"Oh, my God, that would be so awesome," Becca said excitedly.

Troy put a thumb and finger on Grace's chin, turning her face toward him. "You're skating again?"

"Now and then. Secretly. Just because, you know…"

"I *don't* know."

"Because I've been skating my whole life, but for the past five years not for an audience. Except the owner of the rink."

"Why didn't you tell me?" he whispered.

"Because I don't want to coach or compete and I wanted you to believe that."

"Gracie, I believe everything you tell me. So, you'll skate for me now?"

"Would you like that?"

"Only if it feels right to you."

"I think I'd like to. If you promise you can love a flower girl."

He just smiled at her.

That Friday night was more fun than Grace had had in years. Seth and Iris were at Cliff's, sitting up at the bar eating crab cakes, so they picked up their plates and joined them. Cliff teasingly asked Grace if she was packing tonight and the story of the Taser came out to the hysterical laughter of everyone but Grace. After Denny and Becca were dropped back at Troy's apartment, Grace and Troy went to her loft, to bed. But there was no sleeping. They cuddled close and talked late into the night.

Grace was enchanted by Troy's friends; she loved what they seemed to have together. "Do we have anything close to that?" she asked him.

"Close," he said. "If I'm not kidding myself, I think we're building something that could be solid."

"You don't talk about the future with me," she said. "Do you want something like what your friends have? A marriage? Children?"

"Of course I do. But, Gracie, we've been together three months and change. That's not long enough. There are a few things we still have to sort out."

"Like what?"

"Well, let's start with how many more secrets you're keeping."

"Troy, I'm not keeping secrets!"

"I didn't know you were skating. Couldn't you trust me with that?"

"Oh, Troy, that's not a secret. I've only been on the ice a few times since right after Christmas. There hasn't been time! You've kept me too busy. And besides, I only do a little skating now and then to keep in shape."

"But why didn't you mention it? That's something I would have told you."

"I don't know. I guess because I don't want anyone to say I shouldn't give it up. I know it's something I'm good at, but everything that goes with it…"

"Grace, you could have told me that."

"I'm sure there are plenty of things you haven't told me," she said hopefully.

He shook his head. "I can't think of anything. Nothing that has an impact on us. I'm just glad Becca brought it out of you because I can't wait to see you perform. And I think if we're just patient, as we get closer, you'll realize you don't have to be afraid of how I'll react."

She wasn't so sure about that.

* * *

Spending time with pregnant Becca brought Grace back to reality. She was sidetracked, busy, and she realized she still hadn't gotten her period and couldn't start the pills yet. She suddenly realized it must be late. She hadn't thought about it—life had been too crazy. First the note came, then she almost killed Troy with the Taser and then his friends came for a weekend visit...

And now she lay in his arms listening to him whisper his love, as well as his concern that she kept things from him.

Grace dug out her tights and skates before first light. She had a flouncy little blue skirt and pulled her hair back into a ponytail. There was a time she had as many pairs of skates as other girls had shoes, with one pair she loved best. One that brought her luck. That was the only pair she had kept.

Troy, Becca and Denny drove to the rink in North Bend at seven on Saturday morning. Grace took the flower van so she could work for a while after the skating. The rink would officially open at ten. Becca was wriggling with excitement. Grace explained that she had to stretch and warm up before she could do any real skating. "And please remember, I haven't trained in years. I'm not on top of my game. Just a few tricks, that's all I have."

Jake Galbraith met them at the door. "Well, an audience? That holds promise."

"It's just a favor for a friend," she said. "It's still private."

"And I still hope you'll train the younger girls one day. It would be a dream come true for them."

"I wouldn't make a good coach," she said.

"You'd make a phenomenal coach," he said. "You want some music?"

"If it's not too much trouble."

Grace took her time warming up. She stretched out on a mat in the girl's locker room, then laced up her skates and raced around the rink a few times, doing front and back crossovers, a few jumps. The music came on, her Gershwin training music, and she started with a few easy moves, working up to the more difficult jumps and spins. She took a spill but got herself up and carried on. She didn't look at her audience but sprayed the ice in their direction a couple of times. She was lost in back crosses, front crosses, figure eights, spins and axels.

Then Alicia Keys blasted into the arena and Grace put on a show. She didn't think about anything but skating. She could lose herself so easily. She didn't try anything fancy, all she wanted to do was make it pretty for Becca. And for Troy. If she were up to speed there would be triple axels and risky jumps, but she was smart enough to know she'd only hurt herself by taking ridiculous chances.

The reason she kept skating was simple. When there was no competition, she felt free, beautiful and fearless. She loved what she could do on the ice.

She'd been on the ice about a half hour, but steady

and hard. She skated around the rink to cool down, then she made her way back to her audience, smooth and sleek, hands on her hips.

"Not much, but that's all I have without training," she said.

"That was awesome," Becca said. "I would give anything to be able to skate, even a little bit."

"Tell you what—when you're not carrying around a little bump, we'll get you on skates. It would take about fifteen years of hard training to do some of those moves, but there are some easy things I can show you."

"I would love that so much."

Grace looked at Troy and he was smiling. "I guess I understand why people try to get you to skate professionally again. Or coach."

"I think that was a compliment, so thanks. But I really like what I'm doing now. And I have to be a drudge now—you guys go play. I'm going to have to open the shop for at least a few hours today. I can catch up with you later. You're in good hands—Troy is the fun coach."

"Thank you, Grace," Becca said. "I know you wouldn't have done that for just anyone."

"It was time to share that part of me with Troy," she said. "And now I have to get into the flower business."

"Do you need me?" Troy asked.

"Nah. It's a sunny Saturday morning. I'll let you walk me to my van, though."

"We're going to see some more of the coast since

we're this far north. Then tonight I'm cooking for us," Becca said. "Get your flower chores done and this evening you're going to relax and let me pamper you."

"Just a word of warning. When Troy tries to talk you into getting closer to the really big waves, don't do it."

"Enough," he said.

When Grace had her boots on, she left her usual hundred dollars with Jake for his scholarship fund. At the van, Troy gave her a kiss that he didn't seem to want to stop. She liked that so much.

Thirteen

Grace prepared a special order of four expensive centerpieces for a customer. An exclusive golf resort in Bandon had a guest who was throwing a party in one of the spacious cottages and wanted a delivery on Sunday afternoon. She could have told them she was closed on Sunday, but the resort was a regular customer, had an account with her and it was an easy five hundred dollars. She made up the arrangements on Saturday and put them in the cooler, then enjoyed dinner with Troy and his friends at his apartment. After dinner they played poker, and she cleaned house. She told Troy she was going to be closed on Sunday as usual but would make a delivery to the resort in Bandon in the afternoon.

"Becca and Denny are leaving around noon and spring break is next week—I'm off. I'll go with you. I love that place. Someday I might even be able to afford to play golf there. Once, though. I'll only be able to afford it once."

They set out at about one o'clock on Sunday. The resort was a beautiful place with lodges, cabins and rooms, not to mention fine dining and gorgeous facilities that could be reserved for everything from weddings to business meetings. There were three golf courses and it was expensive. People traveled from all over the country to stay there. And they liked Grace's flowers. They didn't use her all the time, but when a guest had a special function that required flowers, they recommended her. She billed the resort and they paid promptly.

She had the unit number for the cottage where the flowers were to be delivered and she knew her way around the country club. As they drove through the property, she had to slow for a couple of deer crossing the road.

"Cottage?" Troy asked.

"I know," she said, laughing. "I looked it up online. Living room, four bedrooms, galley kitchen, fireplaces in every room, plus four bathrooms. And a view."

"I'd kill to live in a house that big," he said.

She backed up to the unit. "You take one, I'll take one and we'll go back for the other two. Try not to gawk too much."

"It'll be hard."

She was proud of the flowers she'd put together— lilies, orchids, bird of paradise, roses, baby's breath and greenery. She balanced her arrangement on one hand and rang the bell. Troy waited right behind her with his flowers. In a moment the door opened.

Grace looked into the blue eyes of Winnie Dillon Banks and dropped her floral arrangement. The ceramic dish shattered and water splashed on her jeans, but the flowers stayed in a lump because she had fastened them into the base with tape.

"Mother!"

"Izzy," she said smoothly.

"Holy shitballs," Troy said.

There stood the indomitable Winnie, small like Grace, ivory skin, black hair and red lips. She could double for Snow White. Except for the expression, which was not sweet. No, he couldn't see Winnie singing to the birdies in the forest. But she was so beautiful. And she radiated power.

Troy noticed that Grace began to tremble a little. She must feel so vulnerable in front of her mother.

"Please come inside, Izzy," she said. "I'll arrange for that to be cleaned up."

"What are you doing here? Why?"

"I need to see you. Talk to you. You can send your helper away. I'll make sure you have transportation."

"He's not my helper! He's my *boyfriend*! What the hell is this? Why didn't you call me, tell me you were in the area?"

"Because you wouldn't have seen me," she said.

"Precisely. Because I am dead to you, remember?"

"Look, I take it back. I take it all back. Izzy, you have to give this a chance. I only want to help you!"

"Fine. You'd be helping by acting like a normal mother. That means you communicate. You call and ask if I'm available to visit with you. And if this is about returning to professional skating, there's no need to waste your time."

"I only want what's best for you. I want you settled! Let me help."

"I am settled!"

"Working in a flower shop!"

"*My* flower shop, my business, that I built on my own!"

Grace stooped and began to pick up the flowers, sans ceramic dish. She stood, holding most of the arrangement, and kicked the broken pieces off the walk and into the bushes. "Where do you want this?"

"The patio?" Winnie said, standing aside.

Grace walked in and Troy followed her. Winnie tried to stop him by holding out her hands for the flowers he carried. "I'll take that," she said.

He ignored her and put them down on the first available surface, the small breakfast table.

A woman stood near the patio doors. She was around fifty, very short reddish-brown hair, casually dressed in slacks and a sweater.

"Thank you, Virginia, you can go back to what you were doing. And you can leave us, young man. This business is between me and my daughter."

"I'm not leaving," he said.

"Just tell me what you want, Mother," Grace said when she came back from the patio.

"I'm not comfortable talking in front of a stranger."

"Oh, forgive me, Winnie," Grace said. "This is my boyfriend, Troy Headly. He came with me to help me deliver these bogus flowers. You might as well spit it out because I'm going to tell him everything we say to each other anyway."

Winnie sank into the nearest chair. "I thought we could have a conversation." She appeared to be near tears. "You're all I have left."

"That isn't my fault. I'm done skating, I haven't changed my mind about that."

"There are other options. I get emails and calls all the time. You could report on the competitions. CBS or ESPN would take you to the Games! You could coach! You could consult! Hell, the committee would be thrilled to have you! There are so many things…"

"No," she said. "No, no, no. I'm done. I don't want to coach, don't want to push young girls the way I was pushed! I don't want to report on the sport, critique and label figure skaters the way I was labeled. I don't want to consult or serve on any related committees."

"But you still skate!"

Grace was stunned. *How did she know?* "For pleasure, to keep in shape, and that's all. I don't want to skate professionally or work in the industry."

"But why? It's what you know!" Winnie said pleadingly. "It was our life!"

"Because I don't love it enough to give so much of myself. I'm very grateful that I had such wonderful opportunities, but it's time to move on. I'm retired from that life. I have a new life."

Winnie stood. "You'll have children," she said, her voice shaking a little bit. "A daughter. She'll be born with it, like you were. Will you forbid her?"

"If I'm lucky enough to have a daughter someday, I'll support her, but I'm not going to ride herd on her twenty-four hours a day. I'm not going to expect her to live out *my* dream. I'm going to tell you for the hundredth time, the only way we can communicate is if you give this up!"

"Are you really happier, Izzy? Living in a tiny room over a flower shop, toiling seven days a week to make centerpieces for people you don't even know? You have a legacy. Your time is nearly up—if you wait many more years, these opportunities will dry up and you'll be forgotten!"

"Only if there's a God," Grace said. She whirled around and left the house.

Troy just watched her go, not knowing what to do. When Grace came back with another floral arrangement, he caught on. Of course, even though this was a ruse, she would leave the flowers and the resort would pay her and bill Winnie. She put her large and beautiful arrangement on the coffee table and went back to the van.

It was as if his feet were glued to the floor. He was mesmerized by Winnie, dressed in a silk pantsuit in a rose color, complete with jewelry that was daunting. Diamonds on her fingers, gold on her wrists. When Grace said her mother was rich, he really couldn't make a mental picture of it, but he was getting there now. It wasn't just the clothing or the classy digs she could easily afford, it was the power she thought she had. Winnie speaks and the world comes to heel.

He had no experience with the wealthy. At least

not that he was aware of. There were business owners in town who must be doing well. Cooper was
building houses on the hill, so he must be pretty set.
Cliff owned the restaurant and a goodly share of the
marina, so he had heard.

Grace looked very much like her mother, but he
couldn't imagine her becoming this person. Grace
was soft and loving; she wasn't controlling or ma-
nipulative. Not his Gracie.

Grace came back with the final floral arrangement. Tears were running down her cheeks. She put
it down on the coffee table beside the last one. Then
she looked at her mother. "I know what you've done,
you know." Winnie stiffened as if slapped. She was
clearly stunned by this statement, or maybe by the
tears. "You placed an order for flowers that you knew
I wouldn't be able to resist and asked for them to
be delivered on Sunday, when the shop was closed,
when I had no delivery help so I would be forced to
come to you. Why, Mother? Why couldn't you just
love me for myself? Why did you only love me for
the gold medals?"

"Izzy, why do you act like it was a curse? We
conquered the *world*!" Winnie said. Her expression
was pleading. No, it was *yearning*. "Because of your
skill, the training the other athletes couldn't afford,
because of the dedication, the commitment I made
to training, travel, everything you needed to get to
the top, we had the dream. My parents didn't care.
They paid the bills but never believed in me the way
I believed in you. But together, we did it! We were

the most powerful mother and daughter in women's figure skating in the world! It meant everything to me. I couldn't do it, but with my help you could."

Grace shook her head sadly. "I'm so sorry for you, Mama," she said quietly. "I love you, but I'm never going to change my mind."

"All right, then!" Winnie shouted. "Stay. Send him away, stay awhile and let's just talk."

Grace shook her head. "Maybe some other time. Sometime when you haven't tried to trick me or back me into a corner."

Grace turned and went back to the van. Troy followed, slowly closing the door as he left the cottage. *My God*, he thought. *No wonder Grace couldn't trust anyone. The people who should be most protective and devoted, like her mother, used her.* He caught up with her just as she was getting in the driver's side.

"Let me drive for you, babe," he said, reaching for the keys.

She wiped at her eyes. "No. Thank you, but no. I'm fine."

He hurried around to his side, buckling in. "Well, that was pretty terrifying," he said. "I think I understand now."

She gave a little hiccup and had to wipe her eyes again. She started slowly driving away from the cottage. "Poor little rich girl?" she asked.

"I think Winnie is the impoverished one. She has no idea all she lost."

"If you win gold medals in the end, you're not allowed to complain about how hard life is. It's self-pitying. Winning is hard and the cost is high. Even if you throw in a bad reputation, a lawsuit, constant pressure, a couple of stalkers, a kidnapping and—" She stopped talking. Then she slammed on the brakes. Troy braced a hand on the dash just before hitting his head. She turned wild eyes toward him. "Shit!" she said. Then she threw the car into Park, unbuckled, got out and ran down the street, back to the cottage.

Troy was too shocked to move for a moment. Then he jumped out and followed her, leaving the van abandoned in the middle of the road, still running. He chased her right to the cottage. Grace barged in without knocking. Her mother sat in the chair.

"My God," Grace said. "How could you do that to me? Are you really that selfish?"

"Grace, what's going on?" Troy asked.

"The note," she said, but she looked at Winnie, not Troy. "She sent it. To scare me so I'd come home."

Winnie didn't respond. She raised her chin defiantly.

"Are you really crazy? As in, need-medication crazy? Or have you absolutely no shame? Your only child? The child who gave you what you wanted, you would do this to me? I was terrified!"

"Nothing happened, did it?" Winnie said.

Grace shook her head. "I think it might take me a lifetime to recover from you."

"I gave you everything! I gave you my whole life!"

"Well, I'm giving it back to you. Leave me alone."

Grace turned and marched back to the van. Troy had to jog to catch up.

"Okay, I am driving," he said, pushing her around to the passenger side of the van. "You're really in no shape."

She didn't argue with him. She silently stared through her window while he navigated the winding road out of the resort, past woods, oceanfront, golf courses and three large clubhouses. He didn't say anything and heard the occasional sniff coming from her side of the van.

"All right, look, lots of people have crazy families," he finally said. She didn't respond. "Most, I think," he added. "In fact, as dysfunctional goes, most families have bigger and tougher issues than a rich mother who pushed you to win gold medals. So, your heart is a little broken, but you're an adult and can decide for yourself how you want to live your life. Think about what some people deal with—death, divorce, abuse, addiction, all kinds of dark secrets. Your mother pushed you and had her own agenda but she never physically hurt you, right? It's emotional abuse, I get that, but, Gracie, honey, you're okay. You're better than okay. You have your head on straight, you're a good, kind person, you know what's really important in life. So she's a pain in the ass. You don't have to deal with her if you don't want to. And if you do want to, demand your boundaries. You know?"

She turned to look at him. "Do you?" she asked. "Do you have dysfunction in your family?"

He laughed. "My immediate family seems reasonably sane. Or maybe we're just used to each other. We lived on a shoestring. Paycheck to paycheck. We got by. It turned my mom into a really good money manager. But in the extended family we have some real interesting characters. My dad's dad was married five times. If you knew him, you'd find that hard to believe—there's nothing all that special about him. My dad has twelve siblings, none of them full siblings, all halfs and steps. Some of them are real losers—money issues, chronically unemployed. One's a scam man—we give him a wide berth. They're always looking for handouts—makes my dad crazy. One of my mother's aunts is a hoarder and the other one keeps cats. Like twenty or thirty cats. We visited them both exactly once. I think there are some serious mental health issues at work there. There's one of those 'funny uncles' somewhere in the family tree—he was not allowed to visit. I'm told my maternal grandfather smacked around my grandmother—my mother said it could get pretty nightmarish when she was a kid. She said if my dad ever raised a hand to her she'd just shoot him. I take it he never did. My dad is kind of a big, handsome, sweetheart of a guy—I guess he inherited the side of my grandfather women fell in love with, but he's managed to be married only once. My mom, though, was married for a very short time when she was real young. Married for a year or something. She divorced her first husband. She never liked to talk about it. I don't think I even knew until my sister, Jess, got married at nineteen and my mother lost her mind, terrified that Jess was headed down the same path. Jess is fine. My mom didn't marry my dad until she was thirty."

"But you had a normal childhood," she said.

"Well, I guess. I don't appear to be scarred. I don't have any medals, either. And I've never been to Russia or China."

"It wasn't what you think. It was work."

"I know. I'd love to see your passports sometime. You're going to think about this for a while and you're going to realize you can deal with her now. She didn't love you enough and she was selfish. She neglected you in ways that still hurt, but you're whole and strong. You're all right. You won't be like that. Because of that experience, you'll be a completely different kind of mother."

"You sure about that?"

"I'm confident. But I want to suggest one thing. It'll be hard because right now you're bruised. I suggest you think about all the things you *had*. You've been putting a lot of focus on what you *didn't* have. Your mother doesn't love you the right way, but she loves you." He reached across the console for her hand. "You have a chance to write the script here, Gracie. You write the life you want. In fact, I don't really get it—you're completely sane. How'd that happen with that prima donna of a mother?"

"Years of therapy," she said. "It was sports therapy, but you can't dump the phobias and anxieties and neuroses without some good old-fashioned counseling. And there was Mamie—sweet, loving Mamie. She worked for my mother and she coddled me."

"That explains a lot," he said.

"I don't want to do all the things that I, on the receiving end, couldn't bear."

"I understand completely," he said.

"I want an ordinary, happy life," she said. "I am not lazy."

"I like your life," he said. "I like the life you envision."

When they finally got back to town, Troy drove the van into the alley behind the shop. No need to park in the front of the store anymore—there was no danger from the mystery man of the note. His Jeep was back there anyway.

"Troy, I think I need some time alone," she said. "I hope you understand. I feel pretty pathetic right now."

He leaned toward her and gave her a small kiss. "Don't work this too long, honey. Lots of people have superannoying mothers."

"I know. But I need a little time. And there's no need to worry that anyone is threatening me."

"Let's at least talk later," he said. "I'll call you."

Troy didn't have to think about it long. He went back to his apartment, cleaned up and changed clothes and drove back to Bandon. He entered the resort property on a guest pass at about six o'clock. There was no answer at Winnie's cottage and he asked himself where she might be. He drove around a little bit, thinking. There were five restaurants on the property—a couple of clubhouse restaurants and then fine dining. He went to the one with the view of the ocean.

The maître d' greeted him. "I'm here to meet Mrs. Dillon Banks," Troy said smoothly as if this visit was planned.

"I wasn't aware she was expecting a guest. This way, sir."

She had a table near the window and she was alone. Her table was a bit secluded from the other diners. She wasn't eating. She had her fingers wrapped around a drink and she looked pensively out the window.

"Mrs. Banks," he said.

She looked up at him.

"May I join you for a few minutes?"

"I suppose this has something to do with my daughter. Yes, Mr. Headly. Have a seat. Have a drink."

"Thank you," he said, pulling out the chair opposite her. The waiter was instantly beside him. "Bring me whatever Mrs. Banks is having."

"So, is Izzy all right?"

"She's a little rattled, but she's resilient. You'll have to forgive me, Mrs. Banks—it's hard for me to think of her as Izzy. She's Grace to me."

"Grace. Yes," she said, sipping her drink. "What do you do for a living, Mr. Headly?"

"I'm a high school teacher. And a part-time bartender at a local beach bar. Not exactly a high-profile profession, but I find teaching rewarding."

"And your relationship with Izz...Grace? Is it serious?"

"Yes," he said. "I'm very serious about her, though we don't have marriage plans. I'm not rushing into anything. That doesn't mean I'm hesitant. It just means we deserve time. Tincture of time, my grandmother used to say."

"Are you hoping for a big inheritance?" she asked forthrightly.

"Until very recently, I didn't know anything about Grace's family. Until this very moment, inheritance never crossed my mind." He laughed uncomfortably. "By the looks of you, such an event is a very long way off."

She didn't make eye contact. She lifted her drink and took a sip. Her hand trembled and she used her other hand to help stabilize it.

His drink arrived quickly. He took a sip. He made a face. "What is this?"

She actually smiled. "A Manhattan. With bitters."

"Delicious," he said, putting it down.

She chuckled in spite of herself. "Well, let's have it, shall we? Why are you here? What do you expect me to say?"

"I've never seen two women more adept at button pushing, and I have a sister and mother. They've had their share of standoffs. But what I saw a couple of hours ago was brutal. So, here's my question. What's it going to take, Mrs. Banks? Is it possible for you to have some kind of decent relationship with Grace?"

She thought for a moment. "I should be having this conversation with my daughter."

"Of course you should, but you haven't. Grace is unhappy and if I'm not mistaken, you're unhappy. There must be a way."

"Look, I don't expect you to understand."

"That there's baggage? That you have a history of conflict? That finding a compromise is difficult? Try me. I've mediated some legendary arguments in my time. Right now, I have at least fifty teenage girls in my classes. Go ahead, lay it on me."

She took another sip. "I've made mistakes with my daughter, but this time I can't afford to make another mistake."

"Sending her that note…"

"It was wrong. I shouldn't have done that. I want my daughter to come home, Mr. Headly. It's imperative that she come home. But I don't want her to come out of pity."

"For a visit?" he asked.

"For a very long visit. In a rash moment I thought if she felt unsafe on her own she would let me help her. I made a mistake."

"She's safe. And I don't think she needs help. She was pretty clear—she doesn't like the career choices you suggested. She's really good at what she does. And she's happy."

"Mr. Headly—"

"Mrs. Banks," he said, leaning toward her. "My name is Troy. For just a minute, let's pretend we're friends and that we trust each other. At the least, let's assume we both have Grace's happiness and safety as our shared priority."

She took another bolstering drink. Her hand continued to shake a little. "Troy. I have money. Family money. Taking care of it is complicated. With money comes predators. With old money there is responsibility. When that money is Izz—Grace's, I frankly don't care if she spends it, gives it away, puts it to work or does what I've been doing—preserve it and grow it. But I don't want her to be robbed or to lose it because of her inexperience. It's time for Grace to trust me. To let me show her how to manage. She has absolutely no experience in the management of wealth."

"She managed to buy a business and operate it at a profit," he said.

"Please. Don't be naive. Her father left her a trust. She used it to buy that flower shop."

Troy sat back in his chair. "What has that got to do with skating or broadcasting or coaching?"

"I thought it would be best if she chose a career path with some longevity in a field she loved. But she's adamant…"

"You're not going to win that one," he said. "I don't know why you can't open a dialogue about what it will one day take to manage your old money. She doesn't have to coach or work for the media for that to happen. And, for God's sake, this is not urgent."

Winnie Banks pierced him with her cold blue stare. "Mr. Headly. Troy. I wanted Grace to come to

me out of loyalty and love. I had planned to tell her
once we were talking again—there isn't much time.
I'm ill, Mr. Headly. I have ALS. The symptoms are
getting stronger every day."

He was speechless. She was a young woman, early
fifties, he guessed. She appeared strong, except for
the tremor. She was beautiful and willful, but with
ALS, the mind would be strong until the body finally gave out.

"You have to tell her," he finally said.

"Of course," she said. "At once. I've written a letter. I wrote it before we had our altercation today. I
was going to have my driver take it to her tomorrow
but if you're willing, you can give it to her."

A bellman came to their table pushing a wheelchair. "If you're not ready, I can come back anytime
you like," he said.

"It's fine, Bruce. I'm ready." She transferred herself into the chair. "Will you? Take my daughter a
letter?"

He nodded, numb from the news. "Mrs. Banks,
I'm sorry."

"The letter is in my room. Can you pick it up?"

A few minutes later, Winnie was resettled in her
cottage. Virginia, who was a maid or assistant or
keeper of some kind, was there to assist her, some
fresh fruit and cheese put out on her small breakfast
table. The letter was on the coffee table, addressed
but not stamped. She put it in his hand.

"Are you sure this is ready?" he asked her.

"It begins with an apology," she said, reassuring him. "That's something easier to do in a letter, I've found. Easier than while facing her anger."

Fourteen

Troy hadn't liked the Manhattan that he'd had with Winnie but he could really use a drink. In fact, a drink in a dark bar sounded like just the thing. He didn't feel like running into friends so that eliminated Cliff's and Cooper's. He parked in front of Waylan's and went inside.

"How about a Crown. Neat," he told Waylan. "And then another one."

The letter to Grace was in the center console in the Jeep. There was only one dim light shining in Grace's loft. She needed time alone but he was going to have to go to her. There was no way he could have that conversation with Winnie and not tell her; no way he could be in possession of that letter and not give it to her right away. But he thought it was reasonable that he have a couple of belts for both his nerves and need of courage.

So he sipped slowly, dreading what had to be done.

What a complicated mess. There was a lot of rage

between Grace and Winnie, and now they were going to throw heartbreak into the mix. Heartbreak and impending death. And an inheritance? This was quickly getting bigger than he was. He was beginning to wish he hadn't made that drive up to the resort to confront Winnie. It might be easier not knowing. But he had thought he could help; he had thought he could be the voice of reason. The way he saw it, Grace shouldn't have such a hot button at the mere suggestion she think about a career in the figure skating industry. And Winnie should drop the subject after being told about fifty times it was out of the question.

Here were two stubborn, pigheaded women.

It was nine-thirty when Troy called her. Grace answered sleepily.

"I miss you. Are you calmer now?" he asked.

"I am. I stomped around and cried for a while, then I think I nodded off. I'm exhausted."

"Let me come over and hold you. I don't know how to sleep alone anymore," he said.

"Okay, but you have to be quiet and sleepy. I don't want to talk," she said.

"I don't blame you."

He drove around to the alley access and parked behind the Pretty Petals van. He used his own key to get in and found the loft was dark. There was an empty wineglass on the coffee table. He took the envelope from his jacket pocket and left it on the small table in her galley kitchen, left his jacket over a chair and went to the bedroom. She stirred and sat up.

"Hi," she said. "Can't stay away from me, can you?"

"I sure can't," he said, taking off his shoes. His pants and shirt quickly followed and he slid into bed. She rolled right into his arms and kissed him.

"Wow. Whatever that is on your breath, it's powerful."

"I needed a stiff drink," he admitted.

"Winnie can have that effect on people. Tell me the truth. Did she make you want to run for your life?"

"No." He pulled her into his arms. "I can see the challenge, however. Close your eyes. You don't want to talk, remember?"

"I'm wiped out," she said with a yawn, snuggling against him. "You are such a good pillow. I don't think I know how to sleep alone anymore, either."

"Just rest, baby. I'm right here."

Troy didn't sleep all that well, but it felt good to know that Grace did. She snored, a sure sign she was deep into sleep. He woke at five-thirty, just like most mornings, and after lying quietly for a while, he got up. He brewed coffee and waited for her to wake up. It was almost an hour.

"Why are you up?" she asked, stretching. "You don't have work today!"

"Grace, I have something to tell you," he said, sitting up straighter. "I went back to the resort after I dropped you off yesterday. To see your mother."

"You what? Why would you do that?"

"Get a cup of coffee, honey, and let me tell you." She was back in just seconds, sitting beside him. "I went because I was really disturbed by the way you

two went after each other. Not that it was unique—
my mom and sister have had a couple of good rows.
But they always patched things up, even if it took a
few days or even a couple of weeks. It looked like
this conflict with your mom has been going on for
years."

"True," she said.

"I went back to see her, to ask her what it would
take to have a civilized relationship with you. You
don't have to like each other, but you're mother and
daughter. But that conversation didn't really happen.
She knows she's made mistakes, Gracie. Big ones.
And she has issues." He tapped the letter. "She wrote
you a letter. She was going to have it delivered to you
if that flower delivery she trumped up didn't result
in a conversation. She asked me to give it to you."

She put down her coffee and snatched it. "Do you
really think that was your place? Going to see my
mother?"

"I don't know," he said honestly. "It looked like
you were both in pain. And it also looked perfectly
ridiculous. I couldn't imagine why on earth you
two had to have such a blowup over your future in
the skating industry. It made no sense to me." He
watched her rip open the envelope. "I get it now."

She started reading. She frowned angrily and
made a grunt of disapproval. But then she read to
the bottom of the page and looked at him with a
shocked expression. She put down that page and read
further. Her eyes glistened and her lips moved as

she read. She lifted her gaze from the page to look at Troy. "Is this true?"

"Does she lie? Because she was taken from the restaurant where I found her back to her cottage in a wheelchair."

Grace shook her head. "She's bossy and controlling and uppity. She doesn't lie. That I know of. Well, except for that note, but when confronted, she admitted it."

"Read it," he said, nodding to the pages.

She read on, getting to the third page. She gave a huff of laughter but had to wipe her eyes at the same time. "This is so Winnie. She thinks I'm completely incompetent. If I don't go to San Francisco and live with her for at least six months and learn everything there is to know about her finances I will bungle it and be completely wiped out in six months after she's gone." She looked at Troy. A couple of tears ran down her cheeks. She gave her head a little forlorn shake. "She really cares about me. In a completely insulting way. If she's so worried, why doesn't she just leave it all to a cat or something?"

"She loves you. She's just used to telling people what to do. It would get on my nerves, too."

"She's a pain in the ass," Grace said with a hiccup of emotion.

"But she wants to make it right with you. Before… you know."

Grace put down the letter. Without explaining what she was doing, she grabbed her personal cell and dialed a number. As he watched, she was pursing her lips. They'd become red around the edges and her nose grew pink and wet. She wiped at her face. Then she spoke into the phone. "Mikhail. Winnie finally found a way to break me. She's dying."

Ray Anne had given it a lot of thought. She couldn't make Ginger less sad; she couldn't help her get beyond her grief and there was no way to replace the life that had been taken from her. But it had been nine months since the baby died and she could get her moving.

When Ginger got up in the morning, she stumbled into the kitchen in her shapeless T-shirt and Capri-length leggings, her hair all lank and flat and ratty. She'd barely gotten down three swallows of her first cup of coffee when Ray Anne challenged her. "Well, buttercup, I'm taking you on an outing. We're going to Eugene for the day. We're going to shop and have a nice lunch and go to the beauty shop."

"Thanks, Ray, but I'd rather just stay here, if you don't mind."

"But I do mind, honey, because we've gotta do something. What you've been doing isn't working. You need a fresher-upper." She smoothed her hand over Ginger's hair and resisted the urge to say *Ack*. "A cut, some color, some new clothes. I'm going to get in the shower while you have your coffee. Make yourself some cereal or toast or both. You'll need your strength."

"Ray, really…I'm just not interested."

"Believe me, it's necessary."

"Look, I don't have money to spend on clothes that don't matter, that I won't wear."

"I'm taking care of that for now, but we have to do something about your money situation, too. Once you're fixed up a little bit, we're going to find you a job."

"I'm not sure I can…"

"I want you to try. It doesn't have to be a fancy job. We can go out to the beach and see if Cooper and Sarah need help in the bar. Spring is here, summer is on the way and the beach gets real busy. Maybe Cliff needs a waitress or one of the businesses in town needs clerical help. But you can't look like a vagrant if you mean to work with the public. Ginger, you have to do something with your time. You can't sit around and think all the time. It's not helping."

"But I'm not staying here!"

"As far as I can tell, you have no idea what you're going to do or where you're going to do it. So we should just act like you need to get your life moving forward and part of that is work. Even if you leave in a few weeks."

"Look, I'll just call my mom, have her pack up a couple of boxes of clothes I left there and—"

"Ginger, honey, I'm sure those clothes you left behind don't fit you any better than the ones you brought. Now, you keep an open mind and come along with me. I promise I won't force anything on you that you don't like. I'm not going to make you dress like me," she added, then laughed.

"I don't want you to do this," Ginger said. "I'm not your problem. I just want to be left alone."

"I know, baby," she said softly. "I know you just want to sink in a hole and die. Want to know how I know? Because I've sort of been where you are. Not as bad, but still… I don't usually talk about this, but when I was real young, way younger than you, I had a baby that didn't live. She was stillborn, so I didn't get to know her, didn't get used to her. Because I was so young my folks sent me to Portland to stay with your daddy and his family until she was born. I wasn't married, still in high school, no reason everyone had to know, right? Way back then, we worried a lot more about reputations. And I wasn't real sure who the daddy was, so… Well, there've been times in my life when I made some hasty choices."

Ginger just stared at her, eyes wide, mouth open.

"I held her for a long time before I let her go and the nurses didn't rush me. I wasn't even going to keep her—I figured she could do a lot better than me! I didn't have much going for myself back in the day. Oh, that was so long ago. But for the longest time after that I just wanted to die, myself. Then my mom and dad both died a few years later and I was so alone. And then I really did want to sink in a hole and die. I didn't know what to do. I still don't know what to do. So you know what I do when there's a tragedy? When my life is falling apart? I try really hard to do the best I can. I wake up in the morning, put my feet on the floor, walk. I put on clean clothes every day. I fix myself to look like I'm getting through life even if everything inside me says I won't make it another day. I mostly pretend, have a good hour here and there, then I collapse and cry because I just can't do it, then I put my feet on the floor again and take another step."

Ginger didn't say anything, but a tear ran down her cheek.

"When you came along, I kind of felt like an auntie. You were a gift to me. We had so much fun playing, dressing up, watching movies, going on little trips together, having sleepovers. We can do this."

Ginger shook her head, another tear sliding down her cheek.

"Now, you don't have to tell me what I already know—getting a haircut and a pair of jeans that actually fit—that won't help much. It's just a shallow remedy. My friend Lou says I invented shallow.". Ray Anne smiled. "I think she's secretly jealous I can still walk in those spike heels."

"Ray…"

Ray Anne held up a hand. "I know, I get a little melodramatic. A little pushy, too. I can't fix what you feel, Gingersnap. I know I can't. But I can get you a good haircut, put you in a decent pair of jeans and get you some underwear that's not shameful just in case you ever have to be taken to an emergency room. And don't you worry about the money because if I can look at my pretty Ginger again, it's worth my life savings. And if it makes you feel one inch better, it's the right thing to do. Now eat something for breakfast—you're wasting away. I'll be ready to go in forty-five minutes. And it's going to be a busy day."

If Ginger went along with this refresher idea, she thought it was merely because Ray Anne, who she had loved so much since she was just a little girl, had revealed herself and her own losses. Ginger couldn't imagine being a pregnant teenager and giving birth to a dead baby. Of course, she also couldn't imagine giving one away—that notion was impossible to comprehend. But then she was thirty now, and had waited so long to get married and have her baby. And the right husband had clearly been a delusion.

So, to make an effort and to be kind, Ginger went with Ray Anne. Their first stop was the beauty salon. While Ray Anne had a manicure, Ginger sat in the beautician's chair. The woman, Char, took the rubber tie out of her hair and combed it out. "So, what are we doing today?" she asked.

Ginger stared at herself. Her hair, which had always been one of her assets, looked like it had gotten thin. It was straight, lank, the color of dirty water, and lying against her too-thin face. She thought she resembled an Afghan hound. "I don't care," she said.

"I care," Ray Anne said, jumping up from the manicurist's table. "She needs some highlights, a couple of shades. Maybe throw in some lowlights. Bring out the bright in that strawberry blonde. And for the love of God, let's get some kind of shape in there! Layer it. And when you're ready to blow it out, don't save money on the mousse. Women in our family need a little body in our locks."

Char met eyes with Ginger in the mirror. She raised one brow. "That okay with you?"

"Sure," she said, listless.

Ginger couldn't deny that it felt good to have someone's hands in her hair, massaging her scalp. It had probably been a year since she'd had a color and cut. But she paid no attention whatsoever; she was doing this for Ray Anne. If it made Ray feel that she was doing something to help, fine.

But an hour and a half later her mouth dropped open at the sight of her own reflection. Her hair was shaped along her jawline, a little shorter in the back, and it looked full and thick. The highlights made her look sun kissed and healthy. It was an easy style to maintain—a circular brush, a blow-dryer and some styling mousse. Not that she'd bother.

"Now we're getting somewhere," Ray Anne said, satisfied. "Now, wax her brows back into shape."

From there they went to Macy's to the makeup counters and Ray Anne went straight to MAC. It had not missed Ray's attention that Ginger hadn't packed cosmetics. Nor did she wear any. And every woman, Ray Anne said, can use a little help now and then. "My God, this stuff costs a fortune!" Ginger said. "I just buy my stuff at the grocery store!"

"Yes, I know, precious. I've been meaning to have a word with you about that. That stuff turns you orange. Now, we don't need to buy the full monty at the expensive counters, but there are some things you can't do without. Your moisturizer, base, powder, lip color and mascara. That cheap mascara clumps. You need the right colors for your skin and hair. We can get things like blusher, eye shadow and lip gloss at the grocery store." Ray Anne sat her down in a chair and gave orders to the saleswoman in her black smock. "Do her up."

It was transforming. Ginger didn't exactly feel happier in her heart, but when she looked at herself she didn't feel like a walking corpse. "Amazing," she said to her own face in the mirror.

The image that came to mind was when she was getting ready for the baby's funeral and her mother sat her on the closed toilet lid and put a little color in her cheeks and on her lips, saying, "This is nothing more than a little superficial frosting, but it makes you look a little less like you died with the baby." And Ginger had cried so hard, she couldn't sit still for her mother's ministrations. She had wanted to die with her baby, it was that raw in her chest.

But this was somehow different. All Ray Anne wanted from her was a little attempt to reenter the world of the living. It was so easy to lie in bed, to never leave the house, when every time she looked at herself she saw a dead woman.

Ray Anne's phone rang a few times while they were out and she briskly answered that she was spending a day with her "niece" but would look through her listings when she got home and follow up.

While they were at Macy's, Ray Anne whisked Ginger through lingerie.

"Do you have a preference in bras and panties?" she asked. Ginger merely shook her head and Ray Anne sighed. "I don't want you trying on clothes until you have the right underthings and those baggy granny panties aren't going to lay right under a nice pair of pants." She poked through some brands and types—bikini, high cut, boy shorts. She handed three pairs to Ginger. "Try these on while I have a look through the bras."

Ginger did as she was told. She was a little startled by the difference in her body with silky, colorful panties that fit. By the time Ray Anne arrived in the fitting room with bra samples she was able to say something positive. "I like them all."

"Well, that was easy." Ray Anne handed Ginger four bras to try. Then she took all of the underwear with them to the women's wear department next door. Ray Anne didn't even bother selecting but went straight to the saleslady, who she apparently knew. She asked to see a few things in Ginger's size.

"I'd take that to be about a four," the saleslady said. "Is that right, dear?"

She had been a ten or twelve. Her hips had been wide, her booty a little on the big and round side and she'd always had this issue with her thighs. And that was before she'd been pregnant. She had no idea what size she was now. "Sure," she said.

Ray Anne made her put on new underwear, giving the saleslady the price tags for purchase. Then she took Ginger's old underwear away and Ginger had the feeling she was never going to see them again.

The saleswoman put Ginger in a pair of slim jeans with a plain white silky tee and, over that, a pink denim bomber jacket with silver buttons. She had to stand up on her toes to be tall enough for the hem of the jeans but the effect was, well, shocking.

"You look eighteen," Ray Anne said.

In fact, she did.

Next, another pair of jeans, different brand, a black blouse, a white V-necked sweater. Not a heavy sweater—lightweight for spring and summer. Again, amazing. Then came black pants with a tunic-style long-sleeved top. Sleeves pushed up, it was so pretty. It was something a person could wear out to dinner, if a person ever went out to dinner again in her life. A few more slacks, a few more tops, a few more jackets or sweaters.

Then the saleslady held up a dress. "I wish you'd try this on," she said. "I've been dying to see it on someone with your figure. It's so streamlined." It was dark purple with yellow piping across the shoulders to the edge of capped sleeves and down the side seams. There was a gold, slightly glittery pattern embossed on part of the front. It was diamond shaped and in an abstract design, from right below the mandarin collar to right below the waist. It was the most beautiful thing.

"Oh, I don't need a dress. Plus," she said, looking at the tag, "it's much too expensive."

"Put it on, Ginger," Ray Anne commanded.

It was stunning. Ginger felt a little like a princess.

Then she reminded herself that she couldn't be a princess or feel that beautiful. She was in mourning.

"It's irresistible," Ray Anne said. "Now just don't bring us any more clothes. Ginger, put on those jeans with the white tee and pink jacket. You're wearing it to lunch and then home."

"Ray, don't throw out my jeans."

"Of course not, darling. You might need them for the next time you paint a house. We'll stop in the shoe department and then we'll have a lovely lunch together." She looked at her watch. "Good, the lunch crowd will have passed and not only will it be quiet, it's late enough in the day that we can manage with something light for dinner much later." She examined her phone. "Looks like I'm going to be on the phone and computer after we get back to Thunder Point. For a Realtor and property manager a day with a lot of phone calls is a good day."

They were alone in the dressing room and in a whisper she hoped wouldn't be overheard, Ginger spoke. "Ray Anne, I appreciate all this so much, I do. But you can't rescue me from grief with a few new outfits and a haircut."

Ray Anne gave her a pitying look. "No one knows that better than I do, Gingersnap. But the other thing I know is that you have two choices—you can grieve that useless ex-husband and your precious lost baby forever or you can do what you must to move on and make life bearable. Because, honey, we're stuck with life."

Ginger positioned her arms as though cradling a

baby in her arms. "When I put my arms like this, I can still feel the weight of his tiny head right there, in the crook."

"Sugar, that's not ever going away. You're not going to forget. You're just going to carry on. It's not easy. It's all you can do." She blinked. "Now I think we need some shoes and some guacamole. You get dressed. I'm going to deal with the receipts."

Fifteen

When Grace called Mikhail, he asked for the details of this dying. So she read the letter, though she stumbled from time to time.

My Dear Izzy,
First of all, I'm very sorry about my harsh words when you retired from skating. I didn't mean it, you know I didn't. Shock and disappointment got the best of me. And I apologize about the mysterious note. I knew it would frighten you. I actually hoped it would. I think I must have had a stroke of some kind, that something like that would make perfect sense to me. Then you would come to me and I would pull all the right strings—you would feel safe again with my protection.

A fool's game. I apologize. I wanted you to come home but not because you pitied me.

I am sorry about the years of arguments

about skating and, if not skating, coaching or consulting or reporting or judging. Every time we get through with one of those conversations, with one of those power struggles, I am filled with hate for myself and anger with you. It's the worst feeling and I always pledge never to allow myself to do that again. And yet I have.

There is a reason. Not an excuse, but a reason. I learned a couple of years ago that I have ALS. For a while the symptoms were manageable and it was easy to imagine it would be years before it would matter. And I resolved to use those years to lure you back to your roots. It wasn't so much that I wanted you to compete. It was that I wanted you to be secure. I have always known I wouldn't be alive forever, but never panicked that my time was short.

You are the only heir to this old Dillon money. Your half brother is not a part of my family and your father settled with him generously before and after his death. There is no one else, Izzy. It's only you. And to my embarrassment, I've never acquainted you with the complications and responsibilities associated with this legacy. I've been managing since my parents died, before you were even a teenager. The work is immense. The threat of cons and predators and incompetent advisors is constant. People will take advantage of you. Steal from you if you even blink. Even charities will use you. Frankly, I don't care if you spend it all on something that makes you happy, but I worry that if I don't do my job you could lose it or be swindled.

That's why I want your undivided attention for a few months. It is complex and you'll find there are decisions to be made.

This ALS is hard. The symptoms are coming faster now. I'm an athlete at the core and even when I stopped competing, my body never betrayed me before. I was always competent and confident and now I don't dare cross the street alone. The jitters and weakness and trembling and unbelievable fatigue are getting the best of me. I don't know how much time there is. We should get this thing between us settled once and for all.

It's not important that one of us wins, Izzy. It's very important that we forgive each other. Before it's too late. Before we can't go back.
Love,
Mother

When she was finished, still wiping away the occasional tear as she read, she heard Mikhail curse. She had noticed that Troy wandered into the kitchen for more coffee, lingering at the coffeepot with his back turned to her as if it was painful to listen.

Mikhail said something she didn't understand. "Sheet of the gods. I will come. Where do I come?"

She laughed through her tears. *Shit of the gods?*

When he was himself, when he wasn't pushing her to do more, do better, he could make her laugh and love him. "Why come, Mikhail?" she asked. "There's nothing you can do."

"I can see her one time. She made my life when she gave me you. I am now best coach. I was not best coach before you." He grunted. "But is Winifred. Will be hard. Where do I come?"

"Well, I live in one-and-a-half rooms, but Winnie is in a nice house at a resort in Bandon, close by. She has bedrooms."

"She will not have me," he said. "She is diva. Where is this Brandon?"

"It's Bandon. Oregon."

"Oregon? Did we skate in this Oregon?"

Grace smiled. Mikhail was a Russian immigrant; his US geography wasn't great. They used to study the map before every competition. He was much better with Europe and Asia than the US. "We did not. It's about an eight-hour drive north of San Francisco. She brought her car and driver. Before you buy a ticket, let me be sure Winnie goes for this idea."

"Just make me a place to stay. Some dirty hotel will do. I just need empty room. Bed would be nice."

"How can you get away so suddenly?"

"Did you say someone is dying? Ah, is good time. Best matches are coming in fall. Right now I can be spared. For a little while, not forever. I have only terrible athletes now. Maybe they get nervous and work harder if I ignore them, eh? I can throw a little pout so they think I quit, yes? Then we see what we see! Don't tell Winifred. She hates me."

"She loves you," Grace said.

"That is love? She has the hardest love in my experience."

"Yeah. I know." She sighed. "I think you can fly into Eugene. That could be closest. But really, you don't have to—"

"In Russia, is important to pay gratitude. Otherwise, there might not be a place for me when my time comes."

When she disconnected, Troy came back to sit beside her on the couch. "You okay?" he asked.

She nodded. "I'm going to have to see her. Will you come with me?"

"I'll take you," he said. "But I'm not going to sit with you while you talk to your mother. I think she feels this is personal family business."

"What am I going to do? I'm not going to San Francisco to live with her!"

"You can do whatever you have to do, Gracie. No matter what you decide to do, the sad reality is that it's not forever. Be sure that in the end you don't have any regrets. That's all."

Grace hung a sign on the flower shop door. Closed for the Day. Open Tomorrow 9:00 a.m. She put her work cell number at the bottom for phone orders.

Troy was determined not to be involved, at least not at this point. He dropped her at the cottage Winnie occupied and he left. He said he wouldn't be far away and she could call him. He'd come back when she needed him.

Winnie was comfortably settled on a chaise longue in her bedroom, a soft throw around her shoulders and a pillow under her knees. She had a book in her lap, but it was closed. Virginia let Grace into the room.

"You look very comfortable," Grace said, kissing her mother's cheek.

She lifted the book. "The one thing I thought I'd do with all this godforsaken leisure time was read, but do you suppose I can concentrate?"

Grace laughed and sat on the upholstered bench at the end of the bed. "Skating wasn't the only gift you gave me, you know. I love to read and I suppose a lot of that is because of you. On all those long trips we took, you always had a book going. You packed books. You read during practice and in the car on long rides."

"And now I can't seem to focus."

"You will once we get a few details organized. I wanted to bring you flowers but since I brought you five hundred dollars' worth yesterday, it seemed ridiculous."

"I kept the smashed arrangement and sent the other three to hospitals and nursing homes," she said, having the grace to blush slightly. "They're beautiful, Izz—is it really Grace now?"

"It is. And thank you." She took a breath, shaking her head. "Oh, Mother. The drama. You could have just told me the moment you knew. Instead of fighting we could have planned how we'd manage the time. I didn't quit skating because of you. I competed as long as I did because of you. And I don't hate skating—I love it. But I was done with so many aspects of the trials. They were right—Izzy Banks couldn't take the pressure."

Winnie sighed. "They say the mind is not affected by ALS. They're wrong. I've made some foolish decisions in the past couple of years. I've snapped at you in anger and lived to regret it. But that's not all. I've flown as far as Switzerland for a miracle cure when my specialist assured me all along the research hasn't caught up with the power of this disease."

"Well, I guess you're lucky you had that option to fly to Switzerland. Does your specialist do anything for you?"

"I've been taking a drug to slow the progression, but it's not going to cure me and there comes a time… Grace, you'll need genetic testing. You should be prepared."

Grace nodded. "What is Virginia's role? Nurse?"

"She's an assistant. She's been with me for three years and now she does far more for me than she bargained for. I hired her as a secretary but she exceeded my expectations. She's a genius with the computer."

Grace tilted her head and smiled. "Is that so?"

"She's amazing. And she knows she'll be looking for work before long."

Grace knew that anyone who worked closely with Winnie or inside the house went through complete background checks and came with high recommen-

dations. Winnie was a genius at hiring the best people. Just look at what Mikhail was able to accomplish
for her. "When you say *before long...*"

"How long will I live? I have no idea. Six months?
A year? If I live a year, it won't be a good year.
I've already had more time than eighty percent of
ALS patients. But Virginia knows her way around
files and names and accounts. She can help you with
that—she's managed all of my correspondence for a
couple of years now. And she will be replaced with
a nurse sometime soon."

"In San Francisco?" Grace asked.

"It's where I've lived since you were twelve years
old," she said.

"Isn't that big house getting a little overwhelming?"

"What do you mean?" Winnie asked.

"It's just that—doesn't it take quite an army to
keep that place going?"

"Indeed," Winnie said with a curl of the lip.

"Mother...Mama...I called Mikhail and he's coming. He wants to see you."

She stiffened in shock. "Why?"

"Well, aside from the fact that he's fond of you?
He also believes he owes his reputation to you. It
was because you hired him that he had such success.
Now, here's what I need to know—how long are you
staying here? In Bandon?"

"I can have this cottage for another week, but I
was going to go home as soon as possible. Hopefully,
you will be coming with me."

Grace shook her head. "I have commitments. For this week, I have lots of orders. After that there's a wedding out of town—one that I've been looking forward to. If I had an emergency, there are several florists who would be happy to take my orders. In fact, for the out-of-town wedding, Mamie and Ross could do the job—they trained me."

"I'm aware," Winnie said, and not happily.

"I want to tell you about my business, Mama," she said. "Let me make us some tea."

Grace started with an idea right after reading her mother's letter and that idea grew as she thought about it. She understood that many people would think running a small flower shop could be a little boutique business, a small-scale and simple operation. And that was true, it could be. But it could be more, depending on who operated the business. Iris had told her that when her mother operated that little shop, they could barely squeak by financially—Rose had done little more than create floral arrangements for the locals who were familiar with her.

Grace had grown the shop significantly, hiring a marketing firm to assist in PR with computer marketing, coupons, specials, advertising in bridal catalogs and in bridal stores, not to mention a website. She'd implemented a creative and complicated computer program to minimize the time spent on demonstrating what was available along with pricing. She was an expert in buying the finest and most cost effective flora and her designs were definitely among the most beautiful. Why else would brides come from towns surrounding Thunder Point rather than going to their own neighborhood florists?

All of her accounting was computerized and she had not run through the trust her father had left. After buying the store and renovating the loft to live in, she had some modest investments that were managed by a wealth-management firm. She hoped the work she was doing would keep her quite nicely for the rest of her life, but it was possible she could actually expand if the notion suited her lifestyle.

"And what about this boyfriend?" Winnie asked.

"Troy? He's the most wonderful man, but I thought we'd talk about my business, Mama. It's really important to me that you know I'm not dabbling to pass the time. I love it, I'm serious about it, I'm good at it. I'm one of the best, Mama. I realize it's not the career you would choose for me, but it's not a waste of time. And depending on how I run it, it can be very successful. Will you come to see it? This week?"

"Of course, Grace," she said. "I'd like to see your store. Now tell me about this man. Does he know you're very wealthy?"

Grace sighed. Well, Rome wasn't built in a day. "Until yesterday neither of us knew I even had the potential to be wealthy. Apparently Troy found out first. I read your letter this morning."

"You must have known that I—"

"Number one, you and I have barely spoken in five years and when we did, it didn't go well and, number two, I have always thought of you as…" Her voice trailed off and, unexpectedly, tears gathered in her eyes.

"Thought of me as what, Grace?" Winnie asked.

"I'm twenty-eight. You're fifty-one. I thought you'd live forever. To at least ninety-five."

"I thought I'd live through at least two face-lifts," Winnie said sourly. "I haven't even had my first yet!"

Grace let go a huff of laughter, but she had to wipe her eyes.

"I was planning to be the best preserved ninety-year-old in the city," Winnie said. "Just tell me about your young man, Grace."

Grace took a deep breath, wiped her eyes and carried on. "The woman I bought the shop from became my best friend—Iris. She's a high school counselor and she's married to the sheriff's deputy in charge of the substation in our little town. I met Troy through Iris—he's a high school history teacher. He makes light of it, as if it's just something he does to fill the days and finance his adventures—he loves everything from river rafting to skiing to rock climbing. I think he's into every sport but figure skating and surfing. But when Iris talks about Troy's teaching she describes him as the most dedicated teacher she knows. He doesn't just teach them history, he keeps an eye on them, paying close attention to any issues that need intervention. He watches for signs of abuse, bullying, drug and alcohol use, any problems teenagers might have. Iris says Troy would make an outstanding guidance counselor—his instincts are right on. There are students whose lives are changed because of Troy's skills as an educator."

"You had good teachers," Winnie said defensively.

"Probably, but it's not the teachers I think about when I look back and examine the choices I've made, when I think about the opportunities and accomplishments. It's the coaches. I've had two of the best."

Grace called Troy's cell and asked him if he'd join her and her mother for lunch at one of the resort restaurants. He was pleased to do that and he showed up at the cottage to push Winnie's wheelchair.

Winnie might not be ready to admit it, but Troy charmed her. He made her laugh and her eyes twinkled. If there was a sweeter, kinder and funnier man, Grace had never met him. And he was completely sincere, Grace felt that in her heart.

On the way back to Thunder Point, she asked him what he would do if money were no object. "Grace, that is such a remote possibility for me, I've never even thought about it. I have no idea. Probably something fun and irresponsible."

"But you're the most responsible person I know. You work hard, you save, you measure every penny."

"That's because in my life, money has always been hard to come by. I learned to be careful at an early age."

Grace and Troy were back in Thunder Point by three, but Grace didn't open the shop. Instead, she made and returned a few phone calls, and then she went upstairs to her apartment and got on the laptop, researching ALS. At six, Troy showed up with crab cakes and salad from Cliff's and a bottle of wine. They talked about all she'd learned in just a few hours of research, how much more she should know, including the need for genetic testing.

"I'm going to do a little more reading tonight," Grace said.

"Would this be a good night for me to spend at my place?" he asked.

"Can you stay? I'm not going to read all night. And tomorrow I'm going to work in the shop in the morning and in the afternoon I'm going to close the shop and drive over to Eugene to pick up Mikhail. He's going to stay at the resort with my mother for two or three days."

"And what will you be doing? Will you spend the evening with them?"

"Maybe part of the evening, but I think it would be best if I let them catch up. Would you like to join us?"

"I don't think so. But I hope I'll meet him before he leaves. Why don't you let me keep the shop open till five or so. I can sell what you have on hand, then I'm due to help Cooper for the next couple of nights."

"Troy, did you plan to go somewhere? Is my sudden crisis keeping you from doing something fun with your spring break?"

"You think I'd run out on you now? Gracie, I think the way you handle this is one of the most important things you'll ever do."

"Because?" she asked, but she knew. She just wanted him to put it into words for her.

"Because you have this one chance to get things right between the two of you. And you should take it."

"Right," she agreed. "I hope I don't really screw it up. And I hope I don't mess things up with you, because you're pretty important to me."

"I'm a big boy, Gracie. Don't worry about me. I'll stick with you while you go through this."

"And after I'm through it?" she asked.

"After? You might be living an entirely different life. Let's see what all this means. I gather there's a fortune involved. And not a small one."

"Troy, that doesn't matter. You can't imagine that it would matter."

"You can't say that yet. That's one of those questions that will have to be answered when it's not just talk, when it's real. But for now, while you try to sort all this out, you can count on me."

That had such an ominous sound, Grace was a little nervous. Concerned enough that she didn't sleep all that well.

When he took her in his arms, everything felt the same—easy and delicious and perfect. But she suspected that Troy, like just about anyone would be, was a bit intimidated by Winnie and her money. Money that she wished to confer on Grace but only after Grace jumped through all the right hoops. What

Troy didn't understand and couldn't until it was, as he said, *real* was that Grace had been happier since she'd been on her own than ever before. And she'd been happier with Troy than she thought possible.

Once she was alone in her shop, when Troy was off doing his own thing, she placed a call to Ray Anne Dysart. Everyone knew Ray Anne was the person to contact for real estate needs. She wasn't sure how to phrase her request exactly. She asked Ray Anne if she had time to stop by Pretty Petals this morning. She wanted to talk about property for rent or sale.

Ray Anne walked in not too long after, and with her was a pretty blonde woman. "Hi," Grace said with a smile.

"Grace, meet my niece, Ginger. Not really my niece, but almost. My cousin Dickie is like a brother to me and this is his daughter. Ginger is staying with me for a while." After the brief introductions, Ray Anne was all business. "How can I help you? Ready for a little more space than your darling loft?"

"Not exactly. I love my little loft. My mother lives in San Francisco and she's up here for a visit. She's staying at the Dunes in one of their beautiful little cottages. And she's handicapped. She's not getting around well and the San Francisco house isn't the best for her disability. She can barely manage the stairs and it's only going to get worse, and soon. Of course I'd like her to be closer. I'm afraid she has a progressive degenerative disease, and we don't know how much time there is."

"Oh, Grace," Ray Anne said, hand to her heart.

"We're doing as well as we can with the diagnosis," she said, making it sound almost as if she'd known as long as her mother had. "Now, when I'd like her nearby, when she's getting worse, I want a house for her. A one-level house. A beautiful flat house. She's certainly not up to looking at houses, but everyone knows you're the best there is. Fortunately, my father took care of my mother—he passed a long time ago. That San Francisco house will bring a nice price and she has a healthy pension. She can afford to spend her last months in comfort."

"Almost anything in San Francisco can fetch a good price. Do you know what kind of house you're looking for besides one level?"

She shook her head. "I don't. It has to be ready. We don't have weeks or months to decorate. Even though my mother isn't getting around much, it should be spacious."

"And will you be staying with her?"

"I'm sure I'll be spending my share of nights there, but let's think of her. I want her to have something to look at—"

"Oceanfront?"

"That would be wonderful, but anything that doesn't feel like a hospital room. She has ALS. The symptoms are coming faster now. I think she'll be bedridden in a few months."

"And your price range?"

"I don't have one. I don't know how much my mother has socked away, but there's plenty. She has old family money and, Ray Anne, I don't want any of it. I want her nearby or else I'll have to close the shop and go to San Francisco until…" She cleared her throat. "If you find something wonderful, I'll look at it and if it's perfect, I'll find a way. My mother has always lived well."

"I assume you want to rent?"

"I'm flexible," Grace said. "If there's nothing stunning for rent but there's a listing that's perfect, I can always sell it…" She looked down. "Later," she finally said.

Ray Anne reached out and touched her arm. "There are some nice properties around. Have you looked online?"

"I haven't. But I could—"

"Don't worry about it. Write your email address on the back of this card," she said, helping herself to one of Grace's flower shop business cards and flipping it over. "I'll get right to work on this. I can see why you're in a hurry. I'll send you some links."

"Is this possible, Ray Anne?" Grace asked. "Because I have to convince my mother that this is a better idea than me moving to San Francisco for a year."

"If it's possible, darling, I can do it. It'll give me a chance to show Ginger a few things about real estate and hunting property in case… Well, my darling girl is with me for at least a few weeks, maybe longer, and we're visiting local businesses to see if anyone needs help. Ginger wants to work while she's here."

"Are you serious? What kind of work?" Grace asked.

Ginger flushed and looked down. "My experience is mostly in retail. I worked in women's clothing, housewares, a little bit in an office. I've done a lot of things."

"Did you work in decorating at all, while you worked in housewares?"

"I wouldn't call it decorating, no. But I did things like bridal registries."

"I'm desperate for help. Especially now, with my mother and all. Do you have any interest in flower design? This is a small boutique, but it's busy. Not crowded, but busy. There are a lot of phone orders and arrangements to design. I spend a lot of time in the workroom, putting them together. Most of them are not originals but created from pictures I have and they're pretty easy to learn. I try new things from time to time."

"I don't know," she said with a shrug. "I could try."

"Would you like to spend a morning with me? Just to see how it feels? It's very messy work."

"Could I? The idea of a small shop appeals to me a lot more than a restaurant or—" she glanced at Ray Anne "—real estate."

"It's okay, babe," Ray Anne said. "Not everyone is cut out for my job, even though they think they are."

"Can you come tomorrow morning? Early? Eight o'clock?"

"I can do that," she said.

"Wonderful! Ray Anne, thank you. Send me pictures, please."

Sixteen

Mikhail Petrov's flight arrived promptly at three in the afternoon and he walked into the baggage-claim area with a duffel over his shoulder. He was sixty-six and his face was whiskery and lined with age, but his hair was reddish brown. *Bad color*, Grace thought. He'd had bad hair color for so many years. But for a man his age, he was fit and strong. Small but built like an ox with his big shoulders and short legs. She held up her tablet upon which she had typed, in very large letters, PETROV. He didn't smile, but she did. He was accustomed to limos or at least town car service. It wasn't as if he wouldn't recognize the best figure skater he'd ever coached.

"I see," he said. "You think you're funny."

"I do," she said, grinning. "Do you have luggage?"

He held out his duffel. "Only this. Two days, maybe three, that is all I have for you."

"Not for me, Mikhail. You came for Winnie, remember?"

"Right," he said. "Lead the way."

Grace directed him to the parking area and opened the back of the van. It was custom painted in pink, yellow, purple, blue with lime-green lettering in script. *Pretty Petals.* "Your luggage, sir."

"What is this?" he said, handing over the duffel.

"The flower mobile," she said. "Jump in front. We have a long drive."

He did as he was told "We'll make one stop, *golubushka*. The grocer, please," he said.

"You won't need food," she said, buckling in.

"Is just for some fruit, if you don't mind so much. You drive this thing?"

"Remember Mamie and Ross Jenkins? Ross taught me to drive. I love driving! Love the control. Tell me, Mikhail, have you been well? You look exactly the same."

"They call it preserved," he said. "I have been six months traveling and now we train in Chicago. There are three assistants and twelve US contenders, from which the US will take a few to the finals, maybe not mine. There is time, but this will be my last Winter Games, if any of my girls are selected. From the look of it, I say there is no a chance in hell. But there is time. And sheet of gods, they need it!" He turned in his seat and looked at her. "Tell me how is Winifred?"

"I spent the day with her yesterday. The first day I've spent with her in five years. She looks very beautiful, but she's thinner and has aged. I think it's the stress of knowing she's battling ALS and is losing. The tremors and weakness are obvious and she said this is just within the past few months. She has no idea how much time she has. She's taking a drug to slow the progression but she's cynical—she doesn't see how it matters. She said, 'What good is three more months?' All she wants to do is clean house, so to speak. Settle her affairs. Get the end of her life in order, but this would mean in order to her satisfaction. It's not as though she can control it from the grave." She bit her lips against the threat of tears.

"If anyone can do that, is Winifred," he grumbled. "I am afraid she has contract with God."

That brought a laugh from Grace. Spurts of laughter through tears had become common the past few days. "We never communicated, Mikhail. She instructed, criticized, praised, but we never talked about our feelings. I talked with my therapist or Mamie. Now I understand that Winnie wasn't ready to retire when I was. It destroyed her."

"There is the thing with athletes and their mothers." He peered at her. "The mother is not doing skating. She can't make decisions like that. She is there for cheering, no more. It is not about Winifred. Unless she wants to take on the ice, then it is not about her. Is about you."

"I wish I'd understood," Grace said.

"You understood," he said. "You knew. You did the right thing. Is time to have life for yourself." He looked around the van. "In flower mobile."

Grace pulled into a grocery store lot not far from the resort in Bandon. It occurred to her that since

Mikhail wanted some fruit, she could pick up a couple of things for later. Troy would probably come over after his evening at Cooper's. They walked into the grocery store and Grace went immediately to the deli and bakery while Mikhail presumably went to the produce section. When she went looking for him he was holding a bottle of vodka and looking a little lost.

"Have you found your fruit?" she asked.

"Where is raisins?"

"Raisins? Let's see," she said, walking down an aisle and around a central counter. "Ah. Raisins."

He selected a big box of plump golden raisins. "Wow. You like your raisins," she said.

"Fruit of the gods," he told her.

"Would you like some apples? Oranges? Bananas?"

"Good to go," he said, heading for the checkout.

"Are raisins your favorite snack?" she asked.

"Put raisins in the vodka, let sit overnight, perfect."

"Ah," she said, laughing at his pronunciation. "And then you eat the raisins?"

"*Nyet!* Drink the vodka!"

She was a little shocked, even though she had remembered that Mikhail liked his *wodka*, especially after the trials or competitions were done. She laughed softly. "Right," she said.

Virginia let them into the cottage and then discreetly left the room. Winnie was standing beside the sofa. There was a tray of hors d'oeuvres on a small table, a couple of wineglasses sitting out and an ice bucket.

Mikhail dropped his duffel and put his grocery bag on the short counter in the little galley kitchen before entering and going to Winnie. "Winifred, this is lie I am told, that you are sick." He put his hands on her face and kissed her cheeks. In high society they stuck to air-kissing, but Mikhail always gave the real thing in loud smacks. "You are beautiful."

"It's all fading," she said.

"Sit down, my dove. You are tired? Weak?"

"Things don't work like they once did but I'm getting by fine. Can we get you something? Food? Drink?"

"Ice," he said. "A glass and ice." He brought his grocery bag to the chair adjacent to her and pulled out his bottle of vodka, putting it on the coffee table. Grace quickly fixed his glass for him.

"As refined as ever," Winnie quipped.

Grace took one of the chairs near them. It had the feel of a reunion, the way these two poked at each other, but the affection between them was so obvious.

"Is perfect," he said. "What do we give you?"

"I'm fine, Mikhail. After you've had a drink, we can order some dinner. Grace," she said. "Will you have dinner? A glass of wine?"

"Nothing for me. I have a drive ahead."

"And your young man?" Winnie asked.

Mikhail peered at her.

"He's working tonight, his part-time job. I'll see him later."

"Grace is in love with a schoolteacher," Winnie said.

"You could not find her a prince or dictator?" Mikhail asked with a smirk.

"I choose my own men," Grace said. "If you don't mind, I think I'll go home now so you can visit. I have to open the shop in the morning, Mother. I have a new employee coming early to train. If you're feeling well, maybe you'll come and look at my little town?"

"Let's see what the morning brings, Grace." Then she shook her head. "This new name. It just doesn't fit you."

"You'll get used to it." She gave her mother a kiss on the forehead. "We'll talk in the morning."

Left alone, Mikhail fetched the tray of snacks and placed it on the coffee table, within reach. He sampled a small toast square with tapenade and hummed his approval. He sipped his drink. "What is your plan, Winnie?" he asked.

"Plan?"

"Do not do this coy with me, it is Mikhail you talk to. You have plan. Like always."

"I want to take Izzy to San Francisco. Home. But she doesn't want to go."

"Then why? Leave the child to have her life. She will visit."

"There's an estate to settle. A complicated estate.

Furnishings, jewelry, art, investments. I can't wave my wand and have it done. It's hers. She has decisions to make. I don't know what she wants to do with all of it. I can't just leave it behind."

"Ah, you will take it with you?" He chuckled and sipped his vodka. "If anyone can, is you."

"I just want to make sure it's all properly dealt with. All the possessions."

"She looks better than I've ever seen her," Mikhail said. "I think it is because the weight of all the world is not on her back. All the burdens of the world— gone. The need to win for her mother, for her team, her country, is done now. Behind her. And she thrives. That is your legacy, Winnie—Izzy. She is your estate. Think on this."

"I have a responsibility..."

"She has had hard life, working to bring home gold when she is only a child. You gave birth to champion, Winnie, and she spent her life to give you what you could not get for yourself. You want her to miss you when you are gone? Set her free. She doesn't work for us any longer."

"That's cruel."

"Is truth."

When Grace was back in Thunder Point, she texted Troy to tell him she was home with food and wine. If there wasn't so much going on, she'd be out at the beach, keeping him company while he served. Instead, she poured herself a glass of wine, got out her laptop and checked messages. Ray Anne had sent her a dozen listings to look at and she breezed through them with disappointment. There was one with a Pacific view that was spacious and beautiful, but the kitchen was dated and the bedrooms were all upstairs. Just like the San Francisco house.

Did her mother really want to die in that house? That small mansion? The thought made her shudder. Was that a conversation that had to take place? Two days after she learned about Winnie's degenerative disease? She was up to the task of saying, *I think you should live near me, where we can be close to each other.* But the subtext of that discussion would be, *Come to Oregon where I can be available when the end is near.* That's what this was really about, wasn't it?

From all she read, she wasn't sure what was involved in taking care of someone with ALS. They could hire nurses. Hospice seemed to be the end-stage necessity. But were specialists required? Because Winnie would have to have the best, she'd demand it. It seemed many ALS patients needed feeding tubes. IVs. Respirators.

She'd have to see Scott Grant, talk to him. Maybe he could tell her what she'd need and whether it was all available here.

She started to cry. It came at the most unexpected moments and she told herself it was because she was so tired. She hadn't been sleeping well and the pressure was back, that pressure to do the right thing, to please. And this time she had to get it right because her mother was terminal. As soon as she managed to get her crying jag under control, she went back to her internet research.

Finally a text came in from Troy. Nice night on the beach. Won't get there till around ten.

Then she started to cry again, for no reason and every reason.

Ginger got up earlier than she had in months. She showered, blew out her hair, applied a little light makeup and put on one of her new outfits. Just to be safe, she put a pair of her old jeans and a T-shirt in a little bag—Grace had said it was dirty work. She'd ask Grace if she should change before doing anything that might wreck her new clothes.

When she looked in the mirror she admitted to herself that Ray Anne had been right—she needed to be presentable. It didn't make that ache in her heart disappear, but it made her feel slightly less pathetic. Her father had given her some money, just walking-around money he called it, but if she earned a little something she might run over to Target in the next town and buy herself some less expensive jeans and shirts that fit, that she could afford to go to work in.

Ray Anne was in the kitchen, sitting at the table with her laptop open, glasses perched on the end of her nose, clicking through listings. "Well, don't you look pretty," she said.

"I feel kind of guilty," she said. "My mom has been asking me for months to try to do something about my appearance and I blew her off. But I'm here two days and you have me cleaned up and in new clothes."

"I'm very bossy that way," Ray Anne said. "Plus, we have a lot of shopping history, you and me. Are you excited about your new job?"

"Nervous," she said. "What if I just don't have the...energy?"

"Then you'll tell Grace you need a break. Get a soda or cup of coffee. Eat a little something. I think you're going to like it. It's such pretty work—making up beautiful bouquets."

"I've never done anything like this before."

"You helped people pick out their household accessories, linens, dishes, table accoutrements. You have good taste. And if it doesn't prove to be right for you, you'll get a different kind of job. I don't think Grace is going to expect you to take on weddings. She'll probably hand you a broom."

"Probably," Ginger agreed. "I think I'll get going."

"Ginger!" Ray Anne snapped. "Choke down a cup of coffee and a piece of toast! Don't go to your first day without any fuel!"

"Right," she said, going to the coffeepot. "Are you finding anything for Grace? I mean, for her mother?"

"It's pretty tough. I have absolutely no idea what the woman's expectations are. I mean the mother's— would she be grateful just to be near Grace or is she very particular? There are a couple of little duplexes with good views for rent. They're small. I sent pictures to Grace yesterday and last night she emailed back that she was looking for something larger and more *custom*. Something more like the resort facilities but with a full kitchen and deck and view and one level, at least three thousand square feet. And don't worry about the price, she says. When people say that, they mean anything from two hundred thousand or seven-hundred-a-month rent. They don't know how pricey their wishes and dreams can get."

"Are you going to ask those things?"

"Sure. Finding the right house usually takes many conversations, never all at once. Asking again and again, dribbling it out, so it isn't so overwhelming. And I find the answers change over time. Unfortunately, Grace is in a hurry. But lucky for her, I'm good." Then she smiled. "How did you sleep?"

"Very well, as a matter of fact. This house is so quiet. And small—it feels cozy. Plus, I think I'm still recovering from shopping with you."

"I don't have time to screw around," Ray Anne said. "We'll see how you survive the day and if you get through it all right, I'll plan a dinner with my girlfriends for the end of the week. They're dying to get a look at you."

"Oh, Ray, I'm no fun," she complained.

"You don't have to be fun, but I bet you accidentally have a good time." She snapped her computer shut. "I better get on it. I have properties to preview."

Grace was in the workroom of the shop, working on her designs for centerpieces on order. If she got them done this morning Justin could deliver them all this afternoon. She had three orders for church flowers—two in Bandon and one in Coquille—that she really couldn't do before Saturday morning.

The shop wasn't open yet. She was wearing her yoga pants and a long-sleeved T-shirt—the mornings on the ocean were pretty nippy in April. Troy was still upstairs in her bed. Leaving him there hadn't been easy—he'd been facedown, arms stretched over his head, beautiful round booty sticking out of the sheets. She knew if she kissed his shoulder or stroked his handsome butt he would roll over and—

There was a knock at the back door. It was Iris, peeking in the window.

"What are you doing here?" Grace asked, opening the door.

"Grace, why didn't you call me? I can help you!"

"Call you?"

"Seth and I went for a walk on the beach last night and stopped by the bar for a beer. Troy told us about your mother—that she's here in Oregon and she's sick. I mean, very sick. As in trying-to-settle-her-affairs sick."

"ALS," Grace said somberly. "I see her after five years and apparently our reconciliation has an expiration date on it."

"Oh, Grace, I'm so sorry."

"Thank you. But look, try not to worry. I just have to find a way to make sure our last year together is… My relationship with my mother wasn't like the one you had with your mother. It was… God," she said. Then she started to cry again. "I'm sorry. I am out of control. My mother and I had a very difficult relationship, but we loved each other. I thought being estranged was for the best, our time together was so frustrating. But I didn't want this. I thought she'd live to be a hundred and ten. In fact," she said, brushing away a tear. "I thought she'd be a giant pain till a very old age. She's really much too controlling to succumb to this."

Iris stroked her upper arm. "Listen, I can help you. I'm off this week. I'm back to school next week, but I can work after school. And I'm off all weekend, of course. I can help with big jobs. I can clean up and take orders. Whatever you need."

"Can you help train a new employee? I gave Ray Anne's niece a job and she'll be here at eight."

Iris puffed up. "Yes. I can!"

"I don't want to take advantage of you."

"Let me help you get on your feet."

"My mother wants me to go to San Francisco. She wants to get her house in order."

Iris made a sad face. "She probably has no one else to ask."

"Oh, she has an army of people to ask. But she wants me involved. Iris, my mother is wealthy. She has expensive things and complicated finances and I think she believes I'm not up to the job of taking care of her things."

Iris was shaking her head, but she had a kind smile on her face. "It's peace of mind, Grace. Ten years before my mother died she started asking me questions like, 'Before I take this old sewing cabinet to the thrift shop, is it something you might want someday?' and 'Iris, I have all these old Christmas cards—years of them. Do you want to save them so you know the names of all our acquaintances?' I was surprised that it even mattered to her because it didn't matter to me. But it was important to her. And she was the opposite of wealthy."

"Well, when things lighten up a little, I'm going to go for a few days. I'll listen to her tell me what she's worried about, look at her inventory and talk to her lawyers, who I actually already know. I lived in that house for thirteen years. Then she can lock up the house. I'm trying to find her something up here so I can see her often. When it's all over and done, I can go back, take a couple of things to remember her and have her lawyers arrange an estate sale."

"Wow," Iris said. "The difference between rich and poor. Garage sale versus estate sale. You don't want to live in that house?"

"And do what?"

"I don't know. Have a kitchen and a large bathroom?" She rolled her eyes upward, indicating the loft.

At that moment, Troy came in the back door. His hair was errant from sleep and he wore a set of sweats that had somehow found a home in Grace's loft. Hands in his pockets, he shuffled in wearing his docksiders and no socks. He nodded at Iris and went straight to Grace, kissing her cheek.

"I'd rather have this," Grace said, putting her arms around his waist.

Iris, Troy and Grace had a completely unplanned and very productive brainstorming session and it was Iris who provided a solution, if Winnie would go along with it. "Go now," she said. "Go now, while I'm on spring break. Take a few days. Make sure you leave me with your flower orders. Knowing you, you have everything you need for Peyton and Scott's wedding written down somewhere so I can place the order. If your new assistant is good, she'll be available to open the shop next week if you're still gone. If not," she said with a shrug, "I'll post a sign. Closed For Family Business. Leave me your work cell and I'll fill phone orders after school."

"I can help," Troy said.

Grace bit her lip. "I was kind of hoping you'd come with me," she said.

"Me? I don't want to get in the way."

"Even if it's just for a couple of days..."

"You should, Troy," Iris agreed. "All this—Grace's mother, the business of Grace dealing with her will and property—this could affect you."

"She's right, Troy. If you can. If you don't want to, I understand. I know my mother can be hard to take."

"Winnie doesn't get to me like she gets to you," he said. "But you better open this discussion about her relocation right away. She doesn't strike me as the kind of woman who gives in to someone else's ideas easily. And moving out of her home when she's sick and feeling vulnerable—that might be too much to ask of her."

"Moving is hard, but Winnie won't have to actually do any moving. She's been directing traffic her whole life. She'll have other people do it all. She'll board a plane. Her assistant will handle everything from the luggage to the flight. She's the gatekeeper of the records and BlackBerry. When I was young, before I left Mother's house, there was a different assistant in charge and my mother showed me a cataloged inventory of her possessions that was as thick as a big-city phone book."

"Must be nice," Iris said.

"It's how she chooses to live, the same way her parents lived. It's not that it's easy—a lot of energy goes into everything she does. And she does good things. She's a socialite—she's raised millions for charities. But she can't drive a car. I prefer a different kind of life, a much lighter load. I don't want my life to be that complicated." She thought for a second. "This could work except for one thing—the Lacoumette-Grant wedding. I have to be back for that. I *want* to be back for that wedding. It's a big job but I really want to see a Basque wedding in a pear grove! It could be so good for my résumé!"

"Grace, you have a week. And I can keep the shop open for you on that weekend, if you want me to. We're not going. Half the town is going and my deputy is going to guard the town," Iris said.

Grace sank onto the stool at her worktable. "Do you think there's any chance Winnie will go for this idea?"

"What's the alternative?" Iris asked.

"I guess I could fly down to San Francisco a lot."

Seventeen

Ginger started her day at eight that morning and at five she went back to Ray Anne's. To her surprise, Ray Anne was there as if waiting for her. She was sitting on the sofa with her laptop open. Ray Anne had stopped by the flower shop in the afternoon to talk with Grace, but Ginger was too busy to say more than a quick hello. She suspected Ray was watching her, making sure she wasn't going to pieces or running to hide.

"How was your day?" Ray Anne asked.

"Oh, God, it was unbelievable!" Tears suddenly ran down Ginger's cheeks. "The second I walked in, Grace and her friend Iris explained all the complications of the week and how important it was that I get the feel of the shop because they were desperate for help. Iris's mother used to own that shop and Iris started showing me how to make centerpieces and bouquets. She had me watching videos of floral construction right away. Then she helped me do my own—following a picture—and my first two weren't so good, but my third was pretty good and she could fix them. A shipment of flowers came in the afternoon. And Grace's mother and some man came to see her. I had to constantly clean up, run the register, take orders—but I could never get them right the first time so I needed help. I had so much trouble pricing them at first." She sniffed. "Grace's boyfriend brought us lunch that we had to eat in shifts. Iris's husband stopped by three times to see if she needed anything, and Peyton who's marrying the doctor came to check in with Grace about her wedding up near Portland on her family's farm, and I had to learn to write up flower purchase orders, and I think I swept that shop floor more than I've ever swept in my life."

"Oh, honey," Ray Anne said sympathetically. "Was it just horrible?"

"Huh?" she said, and grabbed a tissue to blow her nose. "It was *wonderful*!"

"Wonderful?" Ray Anne asked carefully.

"It's just a little flower shop but it felt like the hub of a big city! I guess word has gotten out that Grace's mother is sick, but she didn't look very sick. She's beautiful and is being chauffeured around with some Russian man who is her escort or something. But people were dropping in all day to check on Grace, ask if there's any way they can help, offering anything she might need and they were so *nice* to me!" And then she broke down and sobbed into her tissue.

Ray Anne moved closer to Ginger. She put a hand

on her back. "Is this normal? To be sobbing because it went well?"

"I don't know," Ginger murmured. She blew her nose again. "Now that I'm home and sitting down, I'm exhausted. And I want my baby, Ray! I want my baby so much."

"Oh, angel."

"But I only thought about him a couple of times today because I was so busy. Maybe it was a few times, but I didn't dwell. I usually think about him from the second my eyes open till I close them again at night."

"I know it seems like such a little thing, but sometimes being busy helps us persevere. Especially if the work feels meaningful. Did it feel meaningful?"

"To the people who chose flowers for special occasions, it means the world to them. Thankfully we didn't make up any funeral flowers. Grace told me if I wanted to go to the wedding to help her, she'd be so happy. And I can visit my parents. I can spend a night with them."

"Do you want to do that, Ginger?" Ray Anne asked her.

Ginger grabbed Ray Anne and hugged her hard, crying on her shoulder while Ray Anne stroked her back.

"Will you do me a favor, Ray?"

"If I can," she said.

"Will you call my mom and ask her to take down the crib? And put away some of those baby things?"

Ray Anne held her away, looking at her in shock.

"Ginger, have you had the crib and all those baby things sitting out all this time? For nine months?"

She nodded and wiped her eyes. "I couldn't let go. I don't know if I'll ever be able to get rid of everything. But I'm afraid if I go to my folks, even for one night, with all his little stuff sitting around like it's ready for him to come back and use it, I'll just spiral downward. I'm afraid I'll crawl right back into the bed and stay there forever."

"Listen to me," Ray Anne said. "You will have bad days. You will get emotional and sad and long for little Josh. And you'll get through it and move on to the next hour, the next day, the next week. And if I hear you're in bed and can't get up, I will drive up there and get you." She gave her hair a stroke. "Don't make me do that. I'm very busy right now."

"I have to get a grip," Ginger said, sniffing. "I think maybe I need a shower. And on Sunday I'm going to run over to Target and get some nice clothes that aren't so expensive for work. I just couldn't make myself change into those baggy old jeans."

"That's my girl."

"I think I fell apart a little bit."

"Ya think?" Ray Anne asked. She gave her a fond pat on the shoulder. "I think I better have a glass of wine. You take a shower."

Troy and Grace were on their way to Bandon to have dinner with Winnie and Mikhail. They were both extremely quiet for the first fifteen minutes. Then Grace reached for his hand and gave it a squeeze. "I know you didn't sign on for this. I really appreciate all your support, but I know how stressful and crazy it is. When you've had enough…I understand. It's too much to ask of anyone."

He squeezed back. "I'm not going to bail out on you in the middle of this."

"We were just dating, seeing where it would go, then the world seemed to explode. Listen, I can do this. I can. I can go with my mother for a few days, get things a little organized, plan how it will go after her… Enough for her to have some peace of mind. Hopefully Ray Anne will find a suitable house and—"

"And if Winnie rejects that idea?" he asked.

"Then I guess I'll be making some trips to San Francisco to visit her, but my life is here. I'm not moving. Not even for six months. The only way we'll live near each other is if she's willing to move here."

"She said you have a trust from your father. Are you actually rich?"

"Nah. I have enough to ensure I won't be homeless or hungry. I could've spent it in one weekend, but I've taken very good care of it."

"Could you live off it?"

"The way I live? In one room? For a few years. But I love working. Listen, I'm never going to live the way Winnie lives. Do you think I'm just saying that? That's one of the two main reasons we barely spoke for five years. I wouldn't compete anymore and I wouldn't come home to step into that life."

"Was it hard?"

"I gave it a lot of thought. I'm not the first person to disagree with her parents or to reject their lifestyle for my own choice. But what was hard was disappointing my mother, letting her down like that. It made her so angry. I might have made a different decision had I known she only had five years. But as Mikhail would say, *die is cast*! I'm sorry this has landed on your shoulders."

"Just do what you have to do and when I can help, I will."

"Thank you," she said quietly. "This isn't what I envision my life to be—one crisis after another."

"Gracie, sometimes that's how it is. We can't plan everything."

"I try. I really try. I like to stay ahead of things, but this…jeez, it's insane, that's what it is."

Winnie had chosen the same restaurant Troy had met her in last Sunday evening. This time when he approached the maître d' he *was* expected. Mikhail stood when they approached the table. He grabbed Grace's face and kissed her on each cheek in his way. Then they sat and ordered drinks while looking at the menu.

"Your flower shop is very cute, Grace," Winnie said. "You must be proud of it."

"Is perfect!" Mikhail said loudly.

Grace looked over the top of her menu. "All right, who are you and what have you done with my mother?"

"If I understood you, it's exactly what you want. Yes?"

"Yes," Grace said. "Why are you being so nice to me?"

Troy grabbed her hand. "Gracie, let your mother be nice."

"Right. Thank you. Troy says we're button-pushing maniacs."

"He would be correct," Mikhail said sharply. "Where is waiter? We should toast something. I don't know what, but something. We are together. Is good enough."

"I have an idea, Mother. Why don't I go to San Francisco with you for a few days. You can tell me all the things you're concerned about. We can make decisions about how you want things to be handled, and you can give me the names of agents and lawyers if you feel like it. Then I'll come home. I already have someone looking for a house for you in Coos County so we can be closer to each other."

"What?"

"I asked a Realtor to look for something nicer than the cottage you're staying in here at the resort, one level with a full kitchen, and I asked for an ocean view. The ocean is beautiful in summer. It's beautiful all year, but we have six months of mild weather ahead. I'll be nearby and can see you all the time."

"What about my house? My things?"

"We'll have Virginia and the housekeeper pack and ship what you want with you. I think I can find a place and have it ready quickly. Let's close up the house. I'll deal with it later. With your instructions and Virginia's help, I'll take care of everything, down to the last crystal ashtray. Right now, I want you nearby. I want to spend more time with you if possible."

"Then come to San Francisco!"

She calmly shook her head. "I don't live there. In fact, with all the traveling you do, you don't even spend six months a year there. I'm willing to do anything you say—dictate your instructions to whomever you like. If I know you, you've already done so. If you don't like this idea then I'll visit you as often as I can. But I'm not going to move to San Francisco. My home is here. But I can move you. I can find you a lovely place and excellent home care professionals if that becomes necessary."

"Is excellent notion!" Mikhail bellowed. "We will toast it."

Heads turned in the restaurant.

"Excellent notion?" Winnie said. "Leave my home for a strange place during the last months of my life? How is this excellent?"

Grace reached for her hand. "Because I don't think I can keep you comfortable in that big drafty urban mini-mansion. It's full of stairs, even in your bedroom and bath. The kitchen is a mile from the master bedroom and when you need assistance with things like getting around, bathing, eating…believe me, you're going to want a little less space and no stairs. Remember that little house you rented in Cabo? One story, nice accessible patio, view of the sea from the window? Hardly a prison, Mama. But I think you'll be miserable stuck in an upstairs bedroom in San Francisco, tended by servants."

She sensed rather than saw Troy's head turn to look at her.

"I don't know…"

"Mama, I want you to be comfortable. I want to be around to be sure…"

"Do you even know anything about this condition?"

"Oh, yes," she said. "I've been up till all hours reading about it every night. I talked to our local doctor about what you might need and if it would all be readily available." She got a little teary. "I think this can work," she said softly.

"Is excellent notion!" Mikhail bellowed again. The drinks arrived right as he shouted. "We go at once! This can happen."

"Don't you have a team to coach?" Grace asked.

"I have family emergency. Excuse me—I will have lovely Virginia make arrangements," he said, standing.

"I'd like Troy to come, if that's all right."

"Certainly," Winnie said, leaning her head into her hand. "But, Izzy…Grace, I meant Grace, we'll be busy with family matters."

"No problem," Mikhail said. "I will teach him poker."

"I know poker," Troy said.

"Ha. You think you know poker. Is too early to tell!"

Before dinner was over, Virginia had flight arrangements for all of them. They were to meet at the regional airport in North Bend for a two-o'clock departure the next afternoon.

Troy took Grace home and stayed the night. He was holding her after loving her. "Are you sure, Troy? You feel okay about going with me? Even though you'll miss a couple of days of work?"

He stroked her hair away from her eyes. "I don't know how we can go forward until you try to fix this thing with your mother. She's not easy, I can see that. But she's your family. And I think if you and your mother's roles were reversed, she'd be there for you. As best she could. And maybe not in the exact way you want her to be—just like you—but she'd do her best."

"Probably..."

"And if you were relying on her, you'd go to her."

"Probably."

"I get real put out with my family sometimes. We have our issues, our fights and standoffs. Then we pull it together. My folks are in their early sixties now, thinking about retirement, and I can't even imagine losing them." He gave her a little kiss on her temple. "When we get through some of this craziness, I want you to meet them."

"I bet they're very nice people."

"You're very nice people, Gracie."

"I know you must ask yourself how you got into this situation."

"Oh, I think it was New Year's Eve." He chuckled. "I'm sure you can't come up with any more surprises now."

"God, I hope not," she said emphatically, then curled up against him and went to sleep.

Grace was a little frantic in the morning, trying to figure out how to get everything ready. She wanted to leave the shop in good shape for Iris and Ginger, her loft cleaned up for her return, and she wanted to pack, shower, look presentable when it was time to go. She threw on her jeans from the day before and dashed down to the shop, leaving Troy in her bed once again. To her surprised delight, Iris and Ginger were already in the shop and Ginger had before her a beautiful white centerpiece.

"Look at *you*!" Grace said.

"I'm getting a little better, but my instructor is right beside me, moving things around, pointing, shaking her head when I choose the wrong stem or stalk, cutting off ends to the right length. I didn't exactly do this alone."

"But she's catching on," Iris said. "In a couple of weeks, she'll be re-creating some of your stock pieces on her own."

"Also, I'm extremely slow and careful," Ginger said. "Iris whips 'em out in twenty minutes."

"Iris grew up in this shop."

"I was helping to make centerpieces and wreaths and bouquets when I was ten. I guess you could say I've had a little practice."

"I'm leaving at around noon today for a two-o'clock flight," Grace said. "Let's go over the schedule and what you need from me before I leave. Iris, there will be a flower delivery today. The vendor will get here at about two and I'll be gone."

"I've done it before, Grace," Iris said.

"Be sure to give him the order for next Thursday, which includes the flowers for the Lacoumette-Grant wedding, and tell him I'll need it before noon. Post a sign that the shop will be closed Monday and Tuesday. I'll be back Tuesday night, open Wednesday."

"I can open Monday and Tuesday," Ginger said. "Don't worry, I won't attempt any extravagant arrangements. If you think it will be slow, I might not even have orders to fill."

"Ginger and I can make up a few stock arrangements so she has some on hand in the cooler to sell if anyone wanders in. And I'll check in after school on Monday to see if we should make anything up for Tuesday."

"You guys," she said. "You're so fantastic."

"We can figure out how to put a sign on the door. When are you headed to Portland for the wedding?"

"Friday morning, first thing. You still want to go, Ginger?"

She nodded enthusiastically. "Are you sure it's okay? Are you sure I won't be deadweight?"

"I'd love for you to come. I'm going to make up a few centerpieces early Friday morning for their Friday-night party but I'll transport the rest of my flowers in the back of the van, which is refrigerated. I'll make up the wedding flowers at my old shop in Portland early Saturday. That way if I'm missing anything Mamie and Ross can probably help me fill in. We're closing the shop for the wedding. That's how it rolls for a big out-of-town affair."

"I'll be around if you want someone in the shop that Saturday," Iris reminded her.

"Nah," Grace said. "When I took this wedding I made a decision—I'd close for a couple of days. What I could earn keeping the shop open is more than offset by Peyton's wedding. Let's not drive ourselves crazy. I can recommend other florists in the area or take orders for Monday pickup or delivery."

"Excellent," Iris said. "In that case, hand over the store cell phone. I'll take it until you're back."

Grace took it off her belt, looked at it and gave it to her. "The charger is on my desk. I think I'm having separation anxiety already."

"Just make sure your desk and computer are just as you want them—I might have to share them until you're back. Then get out of here, get ready to go."

"Right," she said, heading for her office. A half hour later she was hauling some of her spring sidewalk displays outside. When she turned, Iris was standing there, tapping her foot, arms crossed over her chest.

"All right," Iris said. "Ginger and I have this. Go."

"You're sure? I still have time…"

"Go. If I have a question, which I probably won't, I know your number."

"Okay." She looked at her watch. "I'll be upstairs till noon. I'll stop in to say goodbye."

"Great. We'll be fine."

Grace dashed up the stairs and into her loft. Troy

was just tugging up and zipping his pants and she grinned. "Looks like I'm seconds too late."

He pulled the zipper down. "I have a little time to spare."

"I should have learned by now, we don't joke around about sex, since you're a sex maniac. Zip those britches, mister—I have a lot to do. I want to clean up around here and pack. I'm sure you have things to do, too."

He tilted his head. "I'm a guy. My cleaning up and packing will take about fifteen minutes."

"That's great, just don't show up here until noon. It takes me longer."

"Yes, ma'am," he said, grabbing her around the waist and pulling her close to kiss her. "Thanks for last night." Then he let her go and shot out the door.

Grace took just a second to savor the moment. It was so nice having a real live boyfriend wanting her and letting her know it. She never in her wildest dreams imagined this could happen to her, especially not with someone as wonderful as Troy. She thought it only happened in novels.

She shook herself and got busy. It wouldn't take long—this was like living in an RV and she loved it. She changed her sheets and smoothed the comforter over her bed. Then she opened the suitcase on top of the bed but before she packed her clothes, she scrambled around the little loft. She ran the vacuum she kept in the small broom closet, dusted off her wood furniture, wiped off the table, counters, microwave, fridge and left the cleaner in the bathroom for the sink and mirror. She checked the fridge for food that should be thrown out, packed her charged laptop in her briefcase, and then she started on her clothes.

She wasn't taking anything dressy. She folded and packed underwear, a couple of pairs of nice pants, jeans, coordinated tops and a blazer. Shoes were added. She glanced at her watch, proud—there was plenty of time. She'd take a shower, clean the bathroom behind herself and be ready with time to spare. She stepped out of the shower after a nice scrub and shave, dried and moisturized, wrapped herself in a towel and reached under the sink for her makeup. She'd leave her makeup bag, hair dryer, brush and comb, lotion out on the counter so they could go right in her suitcase and—

There it was. Her box of tampons. That hadn't been touched in she wasn't sure how long. And right beside it in a little plastic bag was that pregnancy test Peyton had given her. Just in case… "Oh, dear baby Jesus," she said aloud. She sank onto the closed toilet lid.

What had happened?

Okay, Peyton had suggested the test if her period didn't come.

But instead of getting a period, she'd gotten a scary note that appeared to be from her stalker. The world tipped. She had been consumed with fear, with protection plans that included using a Taser on her boyfriend. She had been filled with frightening memories of being a fourteen-year-old girl held captive in a maintenance closet until police could come. Denny and Becca came for a weekend, and Grace skated for them. Her mother made a surprise appearance and...

Somewhere in there, with one crisis after another, she'd completely forgotten about everything else. She tried counting the weeks since she'd had a period and couldn't figure out the exact number.

The best thing that could happen would be a negative test result now. She unwrapped the test, read the directions quickly and got ready.

And nothing came.

"Come on, come on, come on," she chanted.

She sat and sat and finally, she felt the urge and wet the stick. Then she had to let it sit for a few minutes. She just stared at it. Gradually, after the first minute and a half, a pink shadow began to appear on the yes side. But she stared at it without blinking, because surely it would go away.

But no. It was two lines. A red button appeared and the word *yes* popped up.

Grace felt as if she was going to throw up. She sat weakly on the toilet lid. *Pregnant*, she thought. "Crap."

Eighteen

When Troy arrived back at Grace's place with his packed bag, he saw that hers was sitting at the foot of the stairs to the loft. Sure enough, he found her in the shop, going over last-minute details with Iris and Ginger.

"If Peyton should come in to check on things, tell her we're right on schedule and not to worry about a thing. I think she plans on going to Portland with her sister, Scott to follow with his kids. Even though I won't be here, tell her we're good to go, her flowers have been ordered, rest easy. She might not have my personal cell number so you can give it to her if she needs reassurance."

"Peyton's not the jittery sort," Iris said. "And I didn't think you were, but you seem to be wound up. Is taking the boyfriend home a little nerve-racking?"

She shook her head. "My mother has met Troy, so that's not it. I haven't been home in years. In fact, my last four years in competition I was rarely home.

I was wherever my coach or the competition was and that was everywhere but home. I seemed to be training in LA or Chicago, only visiting San Francisco when my mother happened to be there. I have no reason to be nervous."

"Well, if leaving the shop worries you, relax. Even if I really screw up the next four days, your shop will be here when you get home," Iris said. "And I promise you, I can keep the place standing."

"You will never know how much I appreciate this," Grace said. "I'll make this up to you somehow."

"Just go. Try to enjoy it a little even though it's a heavy burden you're dealing with."

"We'll be fine," Troy said. "I'm anxious to see Grace's home. Come on, Gracie, relax. Iris will take good care of things. Let's go—our flight leaves in a little less than two hours and we have a drive."

Grace gave Iris and Ginger hugs and let herself be drawn away. Troy picked up her suitcase. "Anything else?"

"That's it."

"I hope there's a little time to go into the city," he said. "If you can't, I understand." He hefted the suitcase into the back of the Jeep. "I love the city," he said as he got in the car. He drove out of the alley and reached for her hand. "Are you really jittery?"

"Oh, maybe a little overwhelmed at all there is to deal with. But I'll be fine once we get there."

"It's all good," he said. "Pays to have friends like Iris. Not only is she taking care of the flower shop, she's lining up a substitute for me for Monday and

Tuesday. As much as I enjoy the kids, I'm looking forward to summer." And he proceeded to talk about things he hoped to do over the summer. He realized she might be pretty busy this summer, but he hoped there would be time for a couple of short camping trips along one of his favorite rivers in Idaho. He talked a little bit about some of his favorite river trips in the five-state area. Although Grace nodded a lot, he could tell she was barely paying attention to him. But he thought he was doing her a service by regaling her with stories to take her mind off four days with her mother.

When they got to the regional airport he looked around. "I've never flown out of here. And get this— it appears parking in this lot is free."

She gave him a strange look.

He pulled the suitcases out of the back and Grace took control of hers, extending the handle and pulling it.

"What airline is this?" he asked her.

"Oh, Troy," she said, walking ahead. "I haven't prepared you for this. I'm sorry."

He held the door for her and they entered a small reception area banked by a counter behind which people worked on one side, offices and refreshment machines on the other. A sign pointed to the restaurant. A double door led right onto the runway. There were a few people waiting, and Winnie, Virginia and Mikhail were seated by the door. Mikhail stood up and greeted them. "Good, you are here. We can go."

Mikhail took Winnie's left arm while Virginia

took her right and they carefully guided her out the door and onto the tarmac. They passed through what appeared to be a metal detector but nothing like the usual airport security.

"Where are we going?" Troy asked.

"Air Winnie," Grace said, indicating the small jet straight ahead. There were air stairs, but a uniformed man waited at the bottom with a chair-like contraption for Winnie. The plane was not a little six-seater: it was a private jet.

"Shits of the gods," Troy muttered.

Troy could not believe he was flying on a private jet. Like most people, just affording coach fares was a challenge. And when he thought about rich people, he thought they were very different, not people just like he was. "Did you always travel like this?" he asked Grace.

"No, not very often. We took a chartered jet on occasion. Now, I think my mother indulges this because of her condition. Her days of traveling are numbered."

The jet was midsize, generously spaced with seating for ten, a large galley, large restroom, tables and closet space. The cabin was beautiful, the seats wide and comfortable. And Grace could tell from the glitter in Troy's eyes that he was loving it. "This is shit-hot," he whispered to her.

Hmm. He isn't put off, she thought. Well, that was a good sign.

She wanted to tell Troy about the pregnancy test,

but she didn't dare. Not now, not at the onset of four days with her mother. The second they had this visit behind them, the moment they had some time alone that wouldn't be interrupted by her mother's needs, she would tell him. But the last thing she wanted was for Winnie to find out before she settled things with Troy. She had to know how he wanted to deal with this situation. What if he didn't want it? What if he didn't want *her* anymore? What if everything collapsed because she had screwed up the plan?

The captain came into the cabin and introduced himself to Winnie, saying a brisk hello to the others. "We're ready if you are," he said.

"By all means," Winnie said.

"Our flight time should be just slightly over an hour," he told her. "If you need anything at all, press your call button."

"Thank you," she said.

Once they were airborne, Winnie and Virginia had a little meeting. Virginia had her notebook out and made a list from Winnie's comments. There were many details. Alex, Winnie's driver, had left them at the airport and was driving the car back to San Francisco. A car service had been arranged to pick them up when they landed. Dinner at the house was being prepared and the guest rooms were freshened. There were people Winnie wanted called, household maintenance she wanted done, bills paid. Mikhail pulled out a deck of cards and started playing solitaire. And before long Winnie stopped dictating and nodded off.

"Are you all right?" Troy asked her.

"Sure. Fine. I just have very mixed feelings about going home. A part of me wants to see the place once more but..." She shook her head. "A part of me is afraid I won't be able to leave."

"Because you love it?"

"No, because I'll be trapped somehow."

"Don't be irrational, Gracie. You can do what you want."

"That's always been hard," she said. "Doing what I want instead of what my mother wants."

"Yes, but now you've had some practice."

Just over two hours later a black Cadillac SUV was passing through the iron gates into a Nob Hill neighborhood filled with large old houses fronted by manicured lawns and beautiful landscaping. Their driver pulled into a circular drive and right up to the front entrance of a rich-looking manor house. The driver parked and raced around to help Winnie get out. He was quickly replaced by Virginia on one arm and Mikhail on the other while Troy assisted the driver with the luggage.

"If you'll help me get it inside, I can manage it from there," Troy said.

"Be happy to, sir."

When he passed through the big double doors Troy found himself not in a house but in an impressive courtyard with durable outdoor furniture scattered around, an outdoor sofa and two overstuffed chairs in front of a beautiful hearth. There were two sets of tables and chairs, vines climbing along the walls, small trees, flower beds lining the courtyard, hanging and standing pots filled with plants and a couple of decorative statues.

He brought a couple of suitcases into the court-yard, Grace brought his and her own inside, the driver assisted him with the rest, most of which must have belonged to Winnie. She traveled well, but she didn't travel light. "This is fine," Troy said. "I can get it from here."

"Thank you, sir."

He walked with Grace through the next door, into the house, and he stopped inside the massive foyer with marble mosaic floor, wide curving staircase and huge formal sitting room opposite the staircase. He looked around in awe.

Winnie was four steps up the stairs, grasping the rail on one side, Virginia on the other, Mikhail close behind her. Then she stumbled back a step and Mikhail steadied her. Troy gasped and whispered, "Jesus." He left the suitcases where they sat and went to them.

"Winnie, here," he said, brushing Virginia out of the way. "Let's do this, it's safer." He swept her up in his arms and told Virginia to lead the way.

"Leave those bags, Gracie. I'll come back for them."

But she followed him, pulling her own bag up the stairs. It made her so proud, the way he stepped up to the plate and carried Winnie to her bedroom. He asked her where she'd like him to put her down and she pointed to the chair beside the veranda. He even bent over and moved the footstool for her feet.

"Thank you, dear boy," she said.

He glanced around the room briefly, and his eyes settled on the big four-poster bed. "Winnie, you're not going to be able to get in and out of that bed by yourself."

"Don't worry, I'll stay in the adjoining room," Virginia said. "I'll be able to help her."

"It was where I stayed when my husband was ill," Winnie said. "Grace?" she called, looking past Troy to where Grace stood in the doorway. "Grace, I'm so tired. I might have to miss dinner. I hope you won't be offended."

"Of course not. Let me put my suitcase away and I'll come and help you undress and get into bed."

"Virginia can help me—"

"Let me, Mama. I'll be right back. Troy, let me show you where we're going to be."

"I'll bring up your luggage, Winnie," he said. "It'll just be a couple of minutes."

Grace led the way down the hall to the room that was hers when she lived in this house. She was a little surprised—not a thing had been changed. It looked the same as the day she left. Out of curiosity she opened the walk-in closet and everything was there. She'd even left a comb and brush on the dressing table in the attached bathroom. She hadn't exactly expected Winnie to turn it into a sewing room or anything, but this was almost a shrine. There was a special case for her trophies, medals and ribbons. And there were many.

"Will you be comfortable in here with me?" she asked Troy.

"Will it upset your mother?" he asked. "Us sharing a bed?"

"I hope not, because I can't have it any other way. Seriously? I think she knows I'm no longer a child. She's not a prude."

"If you're sure…"

She left her suitcase standing by the closet door. "I'm sure. I'm going to go help her get comfortable and into that bed. Thanks for offering to bring up her bags. Then you can poke around."

"I might get lost. Grace, I've never seen anything like this in my life. At least not since I toured Hearst Castle."

"Come on, it's not that big. I think it's under ten thousand square feet."

"Right. Four houses. I should take a whistle in case I need to be rescued."

"Don't tease me about it, okay? I know it's a lot of house."

"I can see how something this big can be overpowering," he said, looking around her bedroom. "I think it's hilarious that you live in that little loft."

"And love it," she said. She got up on her toes and kissed his cheek. "Thanks for carrying Winnie up the stairs. That was very gallant."

"I saw a broken hip in her future if I didn't. I'll go get her luggage."

"When the driver is here, he handles things like that. But he probably hasn't even hit Eureka yet."

"Well, you've got me. Maybe I'll come in handy."

* * *

Grace and Troy had their dinner in the kitchen. A caterer delivered and served gumbo, linguini, bread, tomatoes with buffalo mozzarella. Virginia took Winnie a tray and Mikhail joined her, leaving Troy and Grace alone.

They ate in silence while the caterer closed up containers and left them on the work island in the big kitchen to be placed in the refrigerator after they'd cooled. When she left, Grace put down her spoon. "This place isn't going to work for my mother," she said. "I admit, I was being a little selfish when I said we should find her a place near Thunder Point—I didn't want to leave my shop, you, my friends...I knew this house was too big, the furniture and stairs difficult for an invalid, but until now I didn't realize how right I was. This isn't a good place for her now." She shook her head. "If she doesn't fall getting in or out of that bed..."

"You can't leave her here without nursing help," Troy said.

"I won't. Virginia knows everyone. She's like a personal concierge. That's part of her job, knowing where to look, who to call."

"Tell me what you'd like me to do while I'm here," he said.

"I don't know. I'll spend tomorrow with Virginia and my mother. We have to pull together a plan. I better call Ray Anne and see if she's making progress. This is more urgent than I realized."

"Gracie, this is all going to be yours," he said. "What are you going to do with it?"

"I'm going to figure that out. And then I'm going home, where there's a life that's not bigger than life."

"Really, I don't know how you can leave this."

"Do you want it, Troy? All this house, all the upkeep, maintenance, work? All the space? All the responsibility? All the *people*?"

"I don't think so," he said. "But, Gracie, it's damned intimidating."

"In what way?" she asked.

He was quiet for a second. "If you have all this, what more could you possibly need? What could I ever give you that you don't already have ten of?"

"Do you really have to ask?"

Grace had to take on a house she'd never known, not really. It had never been her burden to make sure it was cared for or staffed—that had been something women like Winnie were bred and raised to do. And Winnie was dying.

No matter how much Winnie might want to be in charge, it was no longer practical. Virginia called Winnie's neurologist, the man who initially diagnosed her almost four years earlier. Dr. Halstead came to the house in the late afternoon the very next day. Grace understood that house calls were not typical for him, but he'd known Winnie long before she needed his medical expertise—they had served together on several charity boards over the years. He confirmed that Winnie had hobbled along with her disease for longer than was typical; now it was a matter of finding a team who could help manage her quality of life. When asked how long that life might last, his prognosis wasn't positive. It could be as short as a few months, as long as a year but more likely something in between. Now it was down to staying comfortable and taking advantage of her mental acuity, which would probably be the last to fail.

"I live up the coast in a very small quiet town," Grace told him. "I have someone looking for a place for Mother so I can be on hand, where I can see her every day. I don't want her to have to go to a hospital."

"That's the best way. Most end-stage ALS patients require a great deal of support, but there's no way to reverse the disease."

The first order of business was moving a smaller bed into Winnie's room. Virginia contacted a home health care service and since Winnie didn't go through insurance or require approval, she arranged to pay top dollar for a couple of experienced nurse's aides who would start helping out immediately, taking the burden of her personal care off Grace and Virginia.

And Mikhail.

"You're still here," Grace observed. "When do you plan to return to your team?"

"I think, much later. They're in good hands. If they choose other coach, so be it."

"I'm taking her to Thunder Point as soon as I can," she reminded him.

"Thunder Point," he said with a shrug. "Not so bad."

"Are you planning to stay with her, then?"

"I have nothing so important right now."

He was the perfect distraction for Winnie. He wasn't ready to retire, but he wasn't a young man at sixty-six. "I had no idea Mother meant so much to you," she said. "All the years you coached me, you ran interference between Mother and me. You're the one that kept me working and her in line. I didn't know you loved her."

"Love? Not the love you know, *pupsik*. We understand each other. It could be my life closing, not hers. She would not turn me out. Is family. There should be one person who doesn't hate me on the other side. I'm not long behind her."

But he was long behind her—he was strong, his health good, and this was a sacrifice for him. He was in demand as a coach, his business was still thriving. She knew he would be missed. She also knew that he could stay a few weeks and go back to his team, currently managed by coaching assistants, and pick up right where he left off. "I'm glad you're staying awhile. Don't get underfoot, now. Maybe teach Troy poker or something."

There was a housekeeper who came in weekdays from eight to five. She was fifty-five, of German descent—the woman who had replaced Mamie. She wasn't as warm and motherly as Mamie, but that might've had more to do with the fact that they didn't really know each other. She seemed to have a wonderful rapport with Virginia, who was younger by only a few years.

Gretchen didn't do much housework and only a little cooking. She was the manager of a big house— she hired and supervised a cleaning service, ordered groceries to be delivered and called local restaurants to bring in meals customized to Winnie's needs. Virginia and Grace met with her in the kitchen and Gretchen was more than happy to stay on after Winnie was moved. After all, it was great pay for far less work.

Meeting her mother's two lawyers was emotionally exhausting, but not because it was hard work. Just as Grace had suspected, Winnie had been prepared. She'd known for years that this was coming. Everything in the house had been cataloged, photographed and appraised, including jewelry. As for Winnie's accounts and net worth, it had all been managed and audited—after all, the money was old. It wasn't as though it was a new job.

Grace met briefly with a Realtor. She wouldn't make a commitment and even suggested she wasn't sure what she would do with this property, but she knew exactly what would happen. Whispered feelers would go out and when the time came to sell, there would be an auction. The house was a prime property.

It was all so huge to her. Even flying first-class, going to skate practices in a chauffeured car and owning her own business hadn't really prepared her for the magnitude of her imminent inheritance.

But as Grace began to understand the full weight of it, she felt Winnie's stress. It had been a life's work. "Please don't worry," she told her mother. "I won't let it be abused, stolen or ignored. I promise."

"But what will you do with it?" Winnie asked.

"Just as you did, Mama. I'll take very good care of it."

"And the house and all these possessions?" she asked.

"I want you to be at peace about that. It's all being guarded and cared for. And later, when you don't need it anymore, I'll go through it, claim those things that have sentimental value to both of us and then... Then there will be an estate sale managed by the company you suggested. If it will give you peace of mind, I can meet with them before I go home."

"Grace, do you have to go home?"

"I have to get a place ready for us," she said.

She wanted enough space so that when necessary she could stay the night with her mother, but she wasn't planning to live in the house with her.

"You'll need money. Virginia has some banking cards for you to sign for your checking account. And when you find that house, I want my bedroom rug, the Aubusson. And the antique dressing table. And the china. Not the expensive china, the Audun Fleur. And there's silver that was my mother's—if you don't want to use it, I understand, but if there's a granddaughter someday..."

Grace touched her hand. "I might not use some of my grandmother's and great-grandmother's treasures, but I promise to keep them in case… There could be daughters one day."

"Wouldn't it be wonderful if there were daughters for you?" she said. "You will do so much better with them than I did."

"I hope there are daughters and I hope I can love them as much," she said, even though for so many years she had found fault with her mother's form of affection.

"We got to the top, Izzy," she said.

"Yes, Mother. Thank you for all you did."

"No, Izzy. Thank you for doing it for me."

Grace never thought she'd hear that! "We were a good team when it came to winning," she said. She made a vow. When she had children, she wasn't going to put the burden of her desires on them.

Every day exhausted her. She would see Troy on and off through the days. He poked around the house and neighborhood, went down to the wharf a couple of times and kept himself busy. He made friends with the maintenance men, pestered Gretchen in the kitchen, got lost in the library and spent some time on his laptop. She'd have dinner with him in the kitchen, fall into bed with him at night and sometimes she cried. She was losing the mother she had always loved, tried so hard to please and never really known.

Finally Tuesday came and it was time to go back to Thunder Point. She was so relieved, but frantic at the leaving. Virginia would stay, help get her mother to Thunder Point when the time came. Mikhail was planning on coming to Thunder Point, as well. Then Virginia would return to San Francisco. The housekeeper would remain to keep the house in order and in good repair until it was time to close it up. All the account information and household data was uploaded to accessible accounts so they were easy for Grace to oversee. She could call the accounting firm or lawyers whenever there was a question or request. The neighborhood and the house had private security; the contents had been inventoried, and her mother was in good hands with Virginia running herd on her health care providers.

The plane that Virginia arranged for Troy and Grace wasn't a large plush jet, but rather a small Lear that returned them to Thunder Point in no time at all.

Grace wanted to tell him about the baby. Funny, in her mind it had gone from a positive pregnancy test to a baby. Oh, she was falling in love with the baby already.

But she was so tired after four days of getting things settled, she just fell asleep on the plane. They had a quick bite to eat on the way home from the airport then Troy helped her get her suitcase up to her little apartment. "I have to go home, babe," he said. "I need to get ready for work in the morning. You going to be all right?"

"I'll be fine," she said. "Thank you for coming with me. Thank you for everything you did."

"I didn't do much. You handled it all. I'll talk to you after work tomorrow."

Nineteen

Troy couldn't count the number of times Grace had said "You don't understand" when she was telling him about her childhood, her life as a competitive figure skater, her parents. Likewise, he couldn't imagine how many times he had replied, "Of course I do, Grace." Now, he realized, he really hadn't. Grace had come from a world so alien to him he wondered if he would ever understand it.

Troy had never been around people with the kind of money it took to rent a jet or live in a mansion with a complete staff to take care of it. But of course there had to be a staff—no one could take care of something that big alone. The closest he'd ever come to that kind of wealth was knowing a guy who had a cousin who was a pro football player and bought himself a three-million-dollar house and a fast car. He couldn't even remember what kind of car because of course he'd never seen it. Troy didn't even read about rich people. He read about rafting, climbing, diving. He was scrimping to make his Jeep payments. Grace could probably pay it off out of her allowance.

Did Grace get an allowance?

He left Grace at her place and went home to his apartment, which was very quiet. It was also very lonely. He had only rarely spent a night alone since he started sleeping with Grace and he wasn't thrilled about being alone tonight, either. Troy had never lived with a woman and he still didn't, not officially at any rate. He and Grace each had their own place. Except he checked in with Grace at least three times a day and saw her when they were both off work. And stayed the night more often than not.

But right now he needed a little space and time to think. He thought he knew her inside and out, but after four days in San Francisco he wondered if he knew her at all. He was more than a little intimidated by the magnitude of her wealth. It made him feel like a failure by comparison. Intellectually he knew that wasn't the case, but somewhere inside, he had that sinking feeling of not being good enough.

The next day, during his free period, he went looking for Iris, whom he considered his closest friend. She was a counselor and he needed counseling. There was a part of him that hoped she'd be busy with a student, because he wasn't sure how he was going to put into words what he was thinking.

"Got a minute?" he asked, standing in her doorway.

"Sure," she said with a smile. "Want to sit?"

"Thanks," he said, sitting in front of her desk. But then he didn't say anything.

"Troy? Problems with a student?"

He shook his head. "Listen, I don't know how to say this, how to explain this, so if I sound like an idiot…"

"Just spit it out. We can rake through the idiocy afterward."

"Can this be confidential?" he asked.

"Of course!"

"It's about Grace. We've gotten pretty close."

Iris smiled. "You two seem great together."

"You know we're not alike, right?"

She made a doubtful face. "You seem a lot alike. You laugh at the same things, you appear to be insep-arable, she's an athlete and you're a pretty physical guy. I bet you finally found someone to play with."

"But we come from completely different back-grounds. *Completely.* Did you know Grace is—" He struggled. "She's well-to-do."

Iris leaned back. "I heard that. I mean, she told me. It was pretty recently, when she was telling me about growing up on the ice-skating circuit. She said she had tutors and traveled the world to compete and I asked how expensive things like skating lessons were. Lessons for kids can be as much as ninety dol-lars an hour but coaching for world champions? It can be any amount, depending on the coach, maybe four hundred a day! Plus expenses. So I asked…"

"Her mother is rich," he said. "*Old* money. Ap-parently there's a difference," he added.

"She didn't make it on a dot-com," Iris said with a grin. "I assume there's enough so that it keeps growing itself. Not only was Grace born into it, apparently her mother was, as was her grandmother."

"It might be billions," Troy said.

"Billions? Come on!"

"I don't know. How would I know? But here's what I know after spending a few days at her childhood home. The house is bigger than four normal houses, and it takes a full staff to run it so just one person can live in it. There's a full-time driver, even if he's not driving much. I think her mother might have other houses—she likes to spend time in Cabo, in New York, in London. There's art and jewelry and her mother can rent private jets anytime she wants to. I mean, she stinks with it. I'm serious."

"Wow. Incredible. Sounds like the Gettys. You should look and see if they're on the Forbes List."

"I'm afraid to," Troy said.

"Why?" she asked with a laugh. "She'll still be your friend."

"Iris, we've been more than friends. And I can't relate to that kind of money."

"Just as well," she said, laughing. "It's not yours. It's hers."

"Iris, could you please stop laughing. It makes me feel like a poor relation with his hand out."

"You have your *hand* out?"

"Of course not! But that's how I feel! Do you know anyone that rich?"

"I'm not sure," she said. "Peyton comes from a pretty rich family."

"She does?" he asked, shocked.

"Uh-huh. Her parents own one of the biggest farms in Oregon. Huge. They grow pears for Harry & David, potatoes for grocers, have a ton of sheep for the wool and now she says her father and brothers are into Christmas trees. Scott says it's a huge family, almost all of them in the business, and her father has holes in his jeans and drives an old pickup with no shocks. He probably doesn't have a twenty in his pocket, but his net worth is astronomical."

"I didn't know that," he said. "Do they live in a big house?"

"Yes. With one bathroom. Eight kids, one bathroom. Try to imagine."

"Okay, we're not talking about the same thing at all. Grace has money to burn. I think if she started spending it now she couldn't go through it all. Unfortunately for her mother, it's in Grace's near future."

Iris sat back in her chair and chewed on her pen. "Troy, what about this is a problem?"

He shrugged and looked down.

"Spit it out before I start guessing."

"I don't feel good enough."

"Ridiculous," she scoffed. "Your individual incomes have nothing at all to do with your worth. After all, Grace didn't earn hers, did she? She was born to it—that's nothing but luck. You should start playing the lottery, maybe you'll get lucky."

"Tell me how to get past this," he said. "My brain is

telling me it makes no sense to feel this way and I don't know why I can't shake it. I'm a smart person. I don't discriminate against anyone. What the hell is this?"

"I think it's testosterone," she said. "Really!" she said, her tone indicating some disgust.

"Where'd you come up with that?"

"It sounds like just another version of 'let's get 'em out and measure 'em, boys.' Men have this competitive thing, this need for mastery. You have a hard time if you think you're not in control, especially in control of your woman. Something about Grace's family money makes you feel vulnerable and awkward. And yet the girl lives in a tiny loft! She drives a flower delivery van!"

"I've never been like that," he said. "I've never been controlling toward women. If you knew my mother or sister, you wouldn't even suggest that."

"Then what is it?" she asked.

"I don't know. It's just...I wonder what I could ever get her if she has everything. What can I do for her if she can pick up the phone and hire it done?"

Iris stared at him in wonder. She leaned toward him and her voice was disarmingly soft. "Troy, I want you to think about those questions—what could you give her, what could you do for her? When you come up with the answers, you will have solved the problem. I'm not going to be able to answer for you. But can I just tell you one thing?"

"Please."

"The important things Seth gives me never come out of his pocket."

* * *

Grace didn't sleep as well without Troy as she had with him, but after all he'd done for her the past week, she'd never complain. She was up early, not because she was ambitious but because she didn't want to struggle again and again to fall back to sleep. The look it left on her was less than gorgeous. After the past week, including her four days in San Francisco, she had dark circles under her eyes. She used a little cosmetic concealer and hoped she wouldn't yawn all day.

She got into the shop early and found it was as clean as an ICU, her flowers all well cared for and chilling, her desk clear and the front of the store sparkling. Even the scarred, stained worktable had been scrubbed and if she wasn't mistaken, the floor had been thoroughly mopped, something she didn't bother with more than once a week. That workroom saw a lot of action and keeping it pristine was a never-ending task.

Ginger wasn't due until nine but she came in at eight, using her own key. She was clearly surprised to see Grace and her face lit up with a happy smile. "Welcome home! How was the trip?"

"Productive," she said. "And very tiring. I'm going to want to speak to Ray Anne at her earliest convenience. Is she awake?"

"Awake, already left the house and said to tell you she's planning to come down to talk with you today, probably before noon."

"Outstanding," Grace said. "The place looks

great, Ginger. It looks like you were scrubbing all night."

"No, not at all. There wasn't much business. I only tried my hand at one arrangement, which didn't turn out too well, then I stopped. I didn't want to waste flowers on practice."

"Well, we get a new shipment tomorrow and since they're mostly for the wedding, I'll order yet another for Monday. Later today you can feel free to practice. Flowers that have reached their life expectancy have to be disposed of anyway."

"It must kill you to throw away flowers," Ginger said.

"It kills me more to get a phone call from a customer saying their centerpiece lasted two days! Fresh is beautiful, remember that."

"Can I make you some coffee?" Ginger asked, going to the workroom.

Grace thought about it, then lied. "I've already had coffee, thanks. Go ahead, make yourself a pot. The minute we have time, I'll show you how to use the designing computer programs I have."

While they were in San Francisco, Grace had stayed away from wine and caffeine, though she could have used a full tank of each. She'd let Troy pour her a glass of wine, then nurse it. She'd take a sip and complain of being too tired to enjoy it and once she tipped it into a potted plant when he wasn't looking. She poured coffee down the drain. No one seemed to notice. She wasn't sure Troy would question it but since she wasn't ready to confront it, she kept silent.

Tonight, however. Tonight it had to be done. She was afraid, of course. She hoped he wouldn't suggest they terminate to give themselves more time, because in the days since she'd peed on the stick she'd been seeing a real, beautiful baby in her mind. Now there was no direction for her other than to have it, to hold it and love it.

It was late morning when Ray Anne came into the shop.

"I'm so glad you're here," Grace said. "I'm afraid I have to do everything I can to find a place for my mother and quickly. I knew that old house in the Bay Area wasn't going to work for her—everything is a challenge, from the bed to the stairs to the bath. We practically have to have her doctor flown in and she's pretty much captive in that bedroom with no fresh air or—"

Ray Anne was smiling. "We've got the solution. Everything you need, everything you asked for."

"Really? How'd you find it?"

"I'd love to take credit, but Cooper will rat me out eventually. He has three spec houses that can be occupied in three months or less and he's given me the contracts."

Her face fell. "Ray Anne, we don't have three months."

"Not to worry. The exteriors are nearly finished on all three and one of them only needs a little... Oh, listen, come with me, come and see. Ginger can stay here, can't she?"

"She sure can," Grace said. "She left the place better than I leave it!"

Grace jumped in Ray Anne's car and they drove along the beach by the high road that wound behind the houses right down to Cooper's bar. Stairs led from the bar and houses down to the beach, the structures being safely perched on the hill. Ray Anne parked in the drive of the house nearest Cooper's, next door to Spencer and Devon Lawson's home. There were a lot of trucks and construction equipment everywhere and Grace was immediately disappointed. "These houses look far from ready," she said. "And, Ray Anne, they're three levels! Stairs!"

"Oh, they're not completely ready, but Cooper's hoping to get contracts on them before the interior is finished so new owners can choose their flooring, paint, appliances, decorator items like wallpaper. Come inside, you'll see." She led the way and held the door open.

They stepped into a wide foyer that opened right to a large living room and dining room. Very large. "Twenty by twenty," Ray Anne confirmed. Behind the great room was a nice-sized kitchen with plenty of cupboard space, once the cupboards were installed, that is. A breakfast bar divided it from the dining room and there was an island with a small sink. Straight ahead, a triple sliding door led to a wide deck. There was a fireplace on one wall, mantel unfinished. There were no countertops or appliances; the floors were plywood and still littered with construction trash. To the right of the kitchen were matching up and down staircases with crude railings in want of the finished decorator banisters. There was a door into the kitchen from the garage.

"This way," Ray Anne said. She walked to the left down a wide hall. The master bedroom was in front, beach side, with a large en suite bath. French doors led onto the deck. A second bedroom was across the hall. There was a generous bathroom down the hall for the use of anyone on that floor. "Now listen," Ray Anne said. "What do you hear?"

"Hammers and saws," Grace said, again disappointed.

"But not as loud. And I have a solution for that. But consider this. We can get the flooring, appliances and bathroom fixtures in very quickly. Countertops would have to be rushed. You have your choice of cupboards—once you make up your mind about the wood type. They're constructed off-site and installed in a day. Paint on this level would take two days."

"Ray Anne, it's not finished! It's noisy! My mother isn't well!"

"Your mother is quickly becoming wheelchair-bound but she's not feeling ill or in pain—isn't that what you told me? And there won't be any more noise in this property once we get this level finished. And as far as the neighboring houses are concerned— once the exteriors are finished, all the construction noise will be indoors. A good pair of soft noise-canceling headphones can solve that problem easily.

Come back this way." Ray Anne clacked down the hall to the great room in her heels. She stood in the center of the room. "The slab is poured and doors and windows installed on the lower level. The walls for two bedrooms, game room and large bathroom aren't finished, but it's closed up, airtight. There are two rooms and a small bath in the loft. The bedrooms have ocean views. The garage has unfinished walls but it's completely functional. Now use your imagination…" And with that, Ray Anne closed her eyes as if dreaming.

"I'm trying," Grace said. "I've got to get my mother out of that San Francisco house soon, before she goes stir-crazy in that big old bedroom of hers. Before she breaks a hip falling down the three stairs into the bathroom or slips trying to get into the pedestal tub…"

"Grace, if we concentrate on this floor and leave the lower floor and loft until last, we can get you in here in a month at the very longest, but I bet I can do better, lots better, if it doesn't take you long to make your decorating selections. I recommend hardwood floors, shutters for the ocean-side doors and windows—that setting sun can be brutal. I can place all the orders and call in favors—people all over Coos County owe me. And once they start, I know how to motivate. That gives you a finished main level with access to the bath, kitchen, two bedrooms, great room and deck. The other two levels can be left until…" She swallowed and cleared her throat. "Until it's more practical. Devon and Spence moved in when all they had finished was this level.

Spencer worked over the summer and finished the lower floor and loft himself to save money."

Grace was beginning to see it in her mind. She'd been in Cooper's house once when she delivered Mother's Day flowers for Sarah and it was spacious and beautiful. The deck with the fireplace was to die for. She pointed to the deck. "Awning and fireplace?"

"Anything you want. The awning and some comfortable outdoor deck furniture is easy, the fireplace much more complicated, but you're not going to crave an outdoor fireplace for six months. At least."

Anytime she heard six months, it caused her eyes to water, but she'd been very emotional lately. Her mother could be gone in six months. Then again, she could live another year. She could live long enough to meet her grandchild.

"You're close to town. You're close to Dr. Grant and Peyton if you need medical attention for your mother."

"Yes," she said. There was that second bedroom for health care workers who stayed full-time. "Washer and dryer?" she asked.

"In the hall," Ray Anne said, pointing to the two spaces. "Washer and dryer on one side, linen closet on the other. No laundry room, I'm afraid. There is room for one downstairs if a laundry room with a sink is important, but there are a lot of stairs involved in that idea."

Grace walked back down the hall. The master had two walk-in closets and it was, in itself, a spacious room. The bathroom, very roomy. "Could we put a glass block wall in here for the shower? No sliding glass door?"

"I think so!" Ray Anne said. "Not only handicap accessible but very up-to-date decor!"

Grace looked at her. "All right, how much?"

"Brace yourself," Ray Anne said. "It's oceanfront, even though it's a good twenty feet above the beach. One-point-two."

That wasn't thousands, Grace knew that.

"Cooper said because it's you, he'd rent it to you for up to a year, but the rent would be pricey, too."

"How in the world does Spencer do it on a coach's salary?"

"I'm sure he got a great deal. He and Cooper share a son and it was important to everyone that Austin live close to them both. You said not to worry about the money. I know it's a lot, but for what you want..."

"I know. I want my mother to be comfortable and near beauty. And near me, and my shop is walking distance. But I need that loft finished as soon as possible—how complicated is that?"

"Well, there are only floors and paint needed up there, no cupboards or countertops, so that should be quick. But you're going to have to add light fixtures. Light fixtures are simple if it doesn't take you six weeks to decide what you want. Even I know how to install light fixtures."

"Is that fireplace ready?"

"Except for the glass and ceramic logs—accessories. But you won't be cold for..."

"Just thinking about what has to be done to make it ready."

"Take a little time to think about it, Grace. But don't think long if you want to get started. You won't be able to close on it for about thirty days if all goes well, but this is Cooper's property and, given your circumstances, he's willing to start the interior work and even let you in before closing. He didn't ask for a contract for that, but I will. I want him protected in case you change your mind or…" She blinked and made a face. "Or in case something unexpected happens and you don't need the house anymore."

"In case she dies before I get her here? Well, that's not going to happen—she's in pretty good shape for the shape she's in. And we have to move ahead before she gets worse. Where do I have to go to make selections?"

"You want it?"

"Let's do it. Will twenty percent down for a cash sale convince Cooper to take a chance on me?"

"I believe so," Ray Anne said, smiling. "Even better, it'll convince him he made the right choice giving me the listings." She laughed merrily. "I can get this in shape for you, kiddo. You won't believe how good I am at that. If Ginger can watch the shop, I can take you to a couple of places. You should choose countertops, appliances and flooring first. Cupboards and banisters should be next. I can bring you catalogs for fixtures, blinds, shades and shutters, ceramic logs and paint. Given the openness here, you're going to want to match your cabinetry with floors and banisters." She stuck out her hand. "Let's shake on it and go over to Cooper's bar and sign papers."

* * *

Grace had to call Ginger and ask her if she felt confident enough to manage the shop another day and, bless her, she was good with that. She then spent four hours with Ray Anne, first signing the contracts for the house and then heading to Bandon and North Bend to make decorating selections. She didn't screw around pondering her choices, but Ray Anne enthusiastically endorsed every one.

About two hours into the project, Grace suddenly felt very faint and woozy with a touch of nausea. "Oh, damn, I forgot to eat," she said to her Realtor.

"I have an energy drink in my purse," Ray Anne offered.

"Oh, so that's what keeps you going," she joked, but a bit weakly. She used to live on those! But with a bun in the oven, she wasn't sure what was safe. "Pull into the next grocery or deli. All I need is a half sandwich or something and I'll be fine." But it reminded her that she had other important business at hand.

She was just getting back to the flower shop a little after three when she finally texted Troy. Am I going to see you tonight?

He texted back that he was working at Cooper's from four till whenever and if she wanted him to, he could stop by afterward.

If I want you to?

It was usually hard to keep him away.

Please, she responded. I really have to talk to you about a couple of things.

From that point until nine-thirty she wondered what she was going to say. How she was going to say it. When he finally arrived and used his own key to get in, she leaped to her feet and ran to him, throwing her arms around him. Even twenty-four hours away from him was too much.

But he didn't embrace her as wildly. His hands rested on her hips. This was where Troy usually wondered how fast he could get into her. *Counter, table, floor, wall?* And yet there was a sudden distance she couldn't understand.

"Why are you different?" she asked.

"Different how?"

"I don't know," she said. "There's something different. You're not clutching me. You're not trying to get under my clothes. It's like you don't want to be here!"

"No, no, I want to be here. Gracie, we should talk about a few things."

"Yes," she said, drawing him into her little space. "Yes, we have to talk. You first. What's bothering you?"

They sat on the couch together. He held her hands. He gazed into her eyes—all the gestures of impending bad news. "Grace, I'm not proud of this, okay. I have to be honest with you. The money. *Your* money. It was ten times greater than I imagined. A hundred times greater. It kind of blew me away. Intimidated me. Filled me with doubts."

"Doubts?"

"About us, Gracie. I don't feel like we have as much in common as I thought we did. It worries me a little. I'm wondering…what do we do if we find out we don't fit? If we're just too different?"

She was stunned. "Are you breaking up with me?" she asked.

"No. *No*, of course not. I'm just a little…I'm worried about us. I need time to figure out how we go forward together. I don't have anything, Grace. You're as rich as the Gettys. I don't want to live off you. You can't live off me. We have to figure this out."

"Oh, for pity's sake," she said. "Do I look like I'm rich?" she said, throwing an arm wide, indicating her little loft. "I have an idea—how about if I earn a living, you earn a living and neither of us *lives off* the other?"

"And that fortune you're sitting on?"

"I'll do exactly as I promised my mother—I'll take care of it. Troy, I'm not going to live in a big cold stone manor house with a full-time staff. I do need more space than this someday, but…I bought my mother a house today. On the beach. One of Cooper's new houses. Something that would be perfect for her—the warm sun on the deck, the sound of the ocean. I think it could be comforting for her, much more so than the big house in the city. And I—"

"See? See? That was just so easy. You just went

out and bought a house that must have cost, I don't know, a million dollars or—"

"One-point-two," she said, lifting her chin a notch.

"Holy Jesus…" He leaned an elbow on his knee and put his head in his hand.

"Close to my shop, close to the doctor, close to the sound of kids having fun, dogs barking as they play fetch or chase birds along the beach, nice neighbors…"

"Do you have any idea how weird that is? That you can just plunk down over a million dollars and—"

"So much for *You don't have to be afraid to tell me anything, Grace*, and *You don't have to worry about how I'll react, Grace*. It's who I am!" she shouted. "I'm sorry I couldn't be broke and up to my eyeballs in student loans for you, but this is who I am and I'm not a bad person!"

"I never meant to suggest you were—"

"And I'm pregnant!"

All sound and motion stopped. She could tell that Troy didn't breathe. He just held his breath and looked at her. Finally he said, "Whoa." And that was all. After actual minutes had passed, he asked, "How pregnant?"

"I don't know. Not very."

"I thought you were going to see Peyton. I thought you were going to—"

"Take care of it?" she asked tartly. "I went to Peyton. She said I had a few days to see if my period would just come on its own so I could start on the pill. I was supposed to follow up with her."

"And you didn't?"

"A few things happened! I got that note, I tried to electrocute my boyfriend, your friends came for the weekend, my mother showed up with ALS...I forgot. It just slipped my mind. When I realized my period was really late, I used a test and peed on the stick. I wanted to tell you that second, but we were literally on our way to the airport and things were complicated enough. This is the first chance we've had to talk."

"Oh, God," he said.

"You didn't remember, either! You never asked!"

"Grace, I take responsibility and you're right, I didn't follow up, either. But let's not panic. It's early. We don't have to make any decisions tonight. We can process this."

"I don't have any decisions to make, Troy. I have a baby in me. It's just a little seed, but it's there and I'm not making it go away just because it's inconvenient."

"Okay, fine, right. But we don't have to make any irrevocable decisions tonight. There's time to think this through."

"All right. You go think this through. When you know what you want, you know where to find me."

"You want me to *leave*?"

"Yes," she said. "You have a lot of issues. Whether we're right for each other, whether we have enough in common, whether the fact that I come from a family with money is going to be a problem for you, what you want to do about a baby. I have no issues. I have nothing I have to *process*."

"Okay, now you're getting mad," he said. "Be fair, Grace—what can I ever give you if you have everything? If all you have to do is point and it's yours?"

Right, she wanted to say. *The same way I bought the gold medals.* Her hand slid over her flat tummy. "I want you to go," she said evenly. "I want you to process. When you know how you feel about me, about us, about this little seed, you let me know. You'll get more thinking done on your own. Besides, I'm not lying naked in bed with someone who isn't sure. That's too much to ask."

"Gracie, I love you," he said.

"Great. Thanks. Doesn't sound like that's going to do me much good right now. So let's take a break while you decide whether this is all too complicated for you. I have to take care of myself, my little seed, my mother, my shop. I don't have any extra energy to take care of you right now."

"Are you sure that's the way you want it?"

"I'm sure," she said.

Twenty

Early Thursday morning, Peyton stood in the doorway locked in a passionate kiss with Scott while her sister, Adele, waited in the car. When the kiss wouldn't stop, Adele tooted the horn. Peyton laughed against Scott's lips. "I'll see you tomorrow night," she promised. "And you'll bring my honeymoon suitcase."

"And you have your wedding dress and will pick up my tux."

"And you'll take the kids to the grandmothers."

"They want to stay at the farm, which is going to hurt the grandmothers' feelings."

"Talk to them about that on your drive up, okay? They'll get plenty of time at the farm, but they do have to visit all the grandparents and take turns and be fair. They know how to share and be fair."

"I'll talk to them," he promised. "But I want to stay at the farm, too. With you."

"Starting Saturday night we will always stay together and I won't have to sleep in your mother's craft room anymore," she said.

"I never understood that," Scott said. "She doesn't do crafts. Not really."

"I love you, Scott. I'm going to marry you."

"I can't believe it. Are you sure?"

"I'm sure. Are you?"

"I was sure the day you walked into my office. The only reason I didn't make a pass right away was because I thought you were a lesbian. Lesbian hearts are breaking all over the world and I got you."

She laughed. "You got me all right. My breasts are actually getting sore already."

He grinned at her. "Then they're going to get big."

Adele gave the horn another toot.

"Think I'd better hit the road?" she asked.

"Call me when you reach the farm. I'll get to my mom's tomorrow. I'll help her with the groom's dinner if she needs it."

"Grace is bringing the centerpieces."

Another quick kiss and Peyton was in the car with her sister. Adele's baby girl was in the car seat in the back. "Are you absolutely sure you don't want to go back in there and maybe have a little more sex before you leave?" Adele asked.

"I've had all the sex I can take for a while."

"Ah. Spoken like a wife!"

"And a mother?" Peyton asked.

"Oh, my God, you're pregnant?"

"Just a little," she said. "I wasn't going to tell anyone, but you're not just anyone."

"This is fabulous! I'll be counting the days! Our kids will be so close to the same age! Have a girl, will you?"

"I'll see what I can do. Now don't tell anyone, all right? Because we should concentrate on the wedding, not the pregnancy."

"Everyone will know the second you say no thank you to a glass of wine."

"It's not like I drink that much wine," Peyton said. "You didn't notice last night."

"You appeared to have wine!"

"No, that was citrus green tea in a wineglass." She grinned. "I can fake my way through this."

"Oh, this is going to be so fun! Thank you for getting rid of that ass Ted and finding adorable Scott. I love him. What ever happened to Ted?"

"Last time I talked to his daughter, she said they had a very nice housekeeper and he was playing grandfather. Apparently he's better with her little one than he ever was with his kids. A transformation, it sounds like. Good for him."

"No regrets?"

"Are you kidding me?" she asked. "Scott is my dream man."

The drive to the farm, near Portland, was four hours from Thunder Point. Adele lived in San Francisco and had arrived two days ago; her husband would be driving up on Friday morning in a catering truck stocked with prepared dishes—he was a restaurateur and would be catering much of the reception, but not all—Peyton's mother, sisters, aunts, grandmother and cousins would not be held back from sharing their special Basque dishes. But Lucas was an amazing chef and wanted to do this for Peyton. He would follow Adele back to the city on Sunday.

Peyton and her youngest sister were best friends. It was odd in a large family how the siblings paired up and there was no formula to it. Peyton was always there for Adele and vice versa. They talked all the way to the farm—about their men, their jobs, the wedding, the other siblings, their parents.

When they arrived, all was as expected. There were vans, RVs, trailers and trucks with camper shells everywhere. The kitchen was full of women, talking, laughing, some arguing here and there. Adele walked in ahead of Peyton, carrying baby Rose, named for her great-grandmother and at least three women on Lucas's side of the family. Peyton followed with her wedding dress hidden by a garment bag so that Scott wouldn't see it.

"We're here," Adele said. "Peyton's pregnant."

Peyton gasped but the women shrieked and came running, fussing over her, hugging her, laughing and shouting, "Way to go, Adele," Peyton said when the din died down.

"It's an icebreaker. They're going to find out within twenty-four hours anyway. It's not like you're a virgin bride. And besides, they're Basque women. They have a couple of pregnant brides every year. We have the passion," she added with a heavy accent.

"Now I'll have to call Scott so he can tell the grandmothers. I'm never telling you another secret."

"Yes, you will," Adele said with a grin. "I'm very responsible. Most of the time."

Grace and Ginger were under way with the flowers by seven on Friday morning. Grace was so glad to be leaving town.

Troy had texted her once in the past twenty-four hours— Are you okay? She texted back one word. Fine. Was she angry? Damn straight. This was all so familiar. Her mother had furs and jewelry, so that made her life simple? Easy? The reverse was also not true—there was family money and that made her tragic, evil and doomed? No. It made her an individual. *We're all very different with our own challenges and joys.*

What could Troy give her since she had everything? Well, she didn't have a father for her baby. *My mistake*, she mused. *I thought he could love me no matter what.*

She didn't betray her feelings, something she'd become an expert at. She'd done it for years, starting when she was a young girl. She could be terrified and her heart breaking, but she could smile for the judges like she had the world on a string. She knew how to cope. Or cover.

She used the time to get Ginger's story. When she gave her the job in the shop, she had no idea what Ginger had been through, the selfish husband, the baby's death. "I think the job at the flower shop has saved me," she told Grace. "It's like a brand-new chapter for me. I haven't been happy in so long, but I get excited to go to work every day. I hope you'll need me for a while."

"Are you kidding? You're doing wonderfully. And my mother will be moving here in a month or so and you know all about that. I want to be able to see about her if she needs me or wants me. It's so nice to know there's someone who can take care of the flowers. I might have had to go to part-time hours, but with you in the shop and Justin to deliver, I'm in great shape. I can give my mother some time. When you get down to it, that's the one thing you can't buy or trade or borrow."

"And you're close to your mother?" Ginger asked.

"Yes and no. My mother was always so proud of me and my father died when I was young, so it was just the two of us, no siblings. But she was also demanding and impatient and sometimes she angered too easily. But now her life is slowly ending and all she wants is to be comfortable and near me. This is our chance to close on a good note."

"A second chance. We should never take that for granted."

"Your husband," Grace said. "You said you should've known. Why did you marry him if you should've known?"

"Oh, it's a long story, but the truth is, I loved the wrong man. I wanted him so much and put up with so much to have him. And in the end he wasn't worth it. Listen, it was very nice of Peyton to invite us to the wedding, but do you think she'd be offended if I didn't go? I'm completely over my ex, but a wedding might just make me very sad. I could go to the reception for a little while, just to see the wedding party with their flowers, but not the wedding ceremony. Would it hurt Peyton's feelings?"

"Not at all. I'm going—she's a friend of mine. But the way we usually service a wedding is to deliver the flowers early, arrange and stage them in the church and make sure the bride and her wedding party have theirs, leave the centerpieces and any other decorations either with the catering staff or if the tables are ready, put them out, then leave. Just that much takes quite a while. When we've done our work and are ready to go clean up, I can drop you anywhere you like."

"And on Sunday morning, you want me to drive the van back to Thunder Point?" she asked.

"I might be going back in the van, also. I don't know if Troy will make it. He has stuff going on. He'd like to, I'm sure, but it's iffy. I can stay with my friends, Mamie and Ross. I'll know for sure about Troy on Saturday night. That okay?"

"Sure. Anything you want."

On Friday afternoon, Troy leaned in the doorway of Iris's office, arms crossed over his chest. She looked up and raised an eyebrow. "What now?" she asked.

"Are men born stupid or does it come over time?" he asked.

"Sadly, I think you're born with it."

"That's what I was afraid of. Think I can still make it right with Grace?"

"I don't know, Troy. How badly did you screw it up?"

"I carefully explained all my doubts and feelings," he said. "I was very articulate. I listed them and suggested there was plenty of time for me to *process* them. I was eloquent! She told me to go away and process. She showed me the door. I thought I had been extremely sensible and sensitive."

"Is that so?" Iris said.

"Turns out Grace is a little bit pregnant. I didn't panic, not me. I said we didn't have to make any decisions about what to do right away. I got the distinct impression that wasn't the best response."

Iris rolled her eyes. "Wow. What an idiot. You're lucky she didn't fire up that Taser."

"I think I'm figuring that part out. I bet you know exactly what I should have said instead. Why don't you tell me and I'll tell you if you're right."

"No, I don't think so, Troy," Iris said. "I think you should puzzle this out for yourself. I don't want to mix you up with my words. You've been whispering in Grace's ear for months now. You know what makes her happy and what doesn't. Get your head out of your butt and think like a hero instead of an escaped convict who's trying to dodge the law. You're not going to be put in prison, you know. If you're smart and lucky, you'll get to share lives."

"Right," he said. "Good advice. I'll let you know how it turns out."

"You do that, Troy."

He left and she looked back at her paperwork. She smiled. Peyton had confessed she was a little pregnant when Iris confessed she was a little pregnant. And now Grace was, too. "I guess we know what everyone was doing the first week in April," she said softly.

Grace was looking forward to seeing Peyton and Scott's wedding reception in the orchard but on Friday night, after putting out her table arrangements at the restaurant where the groom's dinner was held, Grace was so happy for a quiet evening with Mamie and Ross. Although she talked to them almost every week, she had held the news of her mother's health until she could tell them in person. Mamie and Ross had spent twenty years in Winnie's employ. They felt much closer to Grace than to Winnie, but they immediately promised they would be visiting Winnie when she was relocated in Thunder Point.

"I'm so happy you two have reconciled," Mamie said. "For both your sakes."

"We are, too, Mamie. The sad truth is, if Winnie weren't ill I don't know if we'd have this relationship. But I'll do my best to be sure she's comfortable and well cared for. Winnie is making it surprisingly easy and I think Mikhail has a lot to do with it. He came immediately and is in no hurry to leave her."

"Like your mother, he has very few people he's

tied to. For many years they kept each other close. Your mother always listened to Mikhail."

On Saturday, Ginger borrowed her mother's car and drove to Mamie's shop and all of them worked together on the flowers for the wedding. They had the altar arrangements and bouquets at the church by noon and the rest were delivered to the Lacoumette farm. Then Grace went back to Mamie's house to clean up for the four-o'clock wedding. She wore a peach dress and nude sandals she loved and wore her hair down because Troy loved it that way.

But she had not heard from Troy.

Their plan had been that he would meet her at the wedding. They would spend the night in one of the coastal inns and let Ginger take the van back to Thunder Point on Sunday while they rode together in the Jeep, but she had a sense of foreboding. Maybe in the course of all his processing he had decided that getting involved with someone like Grace had been a mistake. Grace came from a different world, a world he wasn't comfortable even thinking about.

It could be worse, she thought. He could try to marry her for her money.

It just felt so hopeless. What could she do? Nothing. It was on him now.

When she got to the church, she was distracted for a while, chuckling to herself when she saw the parking lot. It was full of trucks, RVs, SUVs—all big vehicles, some that family members would be staying in while attending the Lacoumette wedding and reception. If they didn't look like a band of Gypsies, she didn't know what did. There was Peyton's car, parked in front. She knew that Peyton had ridden to the farm with her sister and Scott was driving up here in that fancy Lexus. There were only a couple of late-model cars. These farmers and fishermen and vintners were hardworking country folks and although Grace had heard it was a very successful family, you'd never know it by looking at them. They just weren't showy.

There was no Jeep anywhere and her heart sank.

She turned her phone to Silent, but, ever the optimist, she sat near the back of the packed church and on the aisle. If he came, he would find her.

The church was so beautiful. She hoped someone would mention the flowers, the aisle drapes, the bridal bouquets—she was so proud of them. Peyton had such good taste and when she finally walked down the aisle and all heads turned to her, she was stunning in her strapless gown. But Grace watched Scott. Even from a great distance she could see the glow in his eyes. He adored Peyton. He worshipped her. This was what every woman should have on her wedding day.

The ceremony was not long. It was an ecumenical service performed by both a Catholic priest and a protestant minister. Grace silently chuckled as she noticed some of the Basque family members whispering and she remembered that Peyton had said some would be disgruntled by her not having a mass but they wouldn't boycott. The family disagreed often and heartily, but at the end of the day they were one for all.

A large family, Grace thought. Maybe that's the answer to all these issues. A huge family, like the Lacoumette family, so many of them they were like countries tied together by treaties and pacts. *Oh, hell*, she thought. She had a hard enough time functioning in a family of two.

Peyton and Scott spoke vows they had created themselves. They were blessed by both the priest and the minister and then, after less than a half hour, they embraced passionately and cheers erupted inside the church. Down the aisle they fled, followed by their wedding party, then family and friends, out the door, where a receiving line formed and someone from the family released white doves. By Peyton's surprised expression, she had not expected it.

No Jeep. No Troy. She would not cry.

While there were a few pictures taken in the church, most of the caravan headed back to the farm, and it was not a short drive. It was nearly an hour away from this ornate, historical church. Grace was happy to see that Ginger had decided to come to the reception.

By five they were serving wine and tapas in the reception tent and the flowers looked beautiful, as did the plentiful fruit blossoms everywhere. The band was playing and Grace noticed that some of the Basque men had changed into their native dress— trading their suits and tuxes for white pants and shirts, red vests and caps. They were getting ready to party.

By six the bride and groom had arrived, and another cheer erupted. The music picked up its pace, the champagne flowed, all glasses were filled and the noise was wonderfully happy. Caterers brought plates to the wedding party. The rest of the guests, mostly the Basque population of the Pacific Northwest, fell on the buffet like locusts. But the food was never ending, as was the wine, it seemed. And the dancing, even during dinner while others ate, was extraordinary. Paco Lacoumette took the floor and was joined one at a time by his brothers, his sons, nephews, even his klutzy son-in-law, and showed them all what this clan could do. It was like a flash mob, so much fun. The cheers were enough to almost bring the tent down.

Grace sat with a few of the people from Thunder Point: Spencer and Devon and their kids, Cooper and Sarah and little Summer. They asked if Troy was coming and she said she had hoped so, but he wasn't sure. "He had something going on today."

"Well, it wasn't work. Rawley's holding down the fort. I could do that," Cooper said of the men dancing.

"A couple more glasses of wine and I'm sure you will," Sarah agreed.

"Why didn't I come from a clan like this?" Spencer asked. "These people know how to have fun."

"From the looks of this place, they know how to work, too," Cooper added.

Grace took her plate as if she'd be going back for more, but she put it in the bussing cart and wandered out of the tent. The sun was setting, the party was going strong and she walked toward the orchard. She wanted a good look at it before it was dark. The house and garden stood between the big party tent and row after row of blossoming pear trees. She looked at Mrs. Lacoumette's garden with envy and crouched down—vegetables, flowers, herbs. Everything was just coming in—the vegetables weren't even showing their faces yet, but she longed for this. That's what she would do next—get a house with room for a garden and teach her child how to grow things.

"Grace?" a voice called.

She looked up and saw Troy. He looked like he'd slept in his suit—his tie was crooked and there was a smear of dirt on his face. His duffel was sitting on the path behind him. "I thought that was you."

She stood. "Troy. You came? Why weren't you here for the wedding?"

He waved over his shoulder and a noisy tow truck pulling his Jeep edged away from the party, leaving Troy behind. "The car broke down. The tow driver dropped me here. In all the calls I had to make to get service, my phone went dead."

"What happened? You have grease on your—"

"What didn't happen?" he said, pulling out a handkerchief. "I was running late to start with, then the damn thing just crashed. Transmission. It wasn't going anywhere. I bet a million dollars the jerk who sold me that Jeep put a rebuilt transmission in it. I have to go to the guy's garage in the morning before we head home to see what's up. I might have to tow it home, get Eric at the service station to look at it. Jesus, I'm sorry."

"I didn't think you were coming," she said. "I didn't hear from you. In fact, you've been pretty quiet."

"Did you know that when men are in love there's a kind of atrophy of the brain that causes them to do stupid things? Even when they know better?"

"I didn't know that."

"I'm living proof," he said, taking her hand and walking with her along the path to the orchard. "Gracie, can you forgive me?"

"For having doubts?" she asked.

"For not grabbing you and kissing you and begging you to marry me the second you told me there's a baby."

"Oh. That. Well, yes, I guess so. You want to get married? Because you don't have to. I'm going to have it no matter what you say or do."

"Grace, I want to marry you even if there is no baby! I love you. I can't sleep unless you're next to me. And I may not be rich but I have important things. There are a million things I can give you that nobody else can. It appears I can give you children, without hardly trying."

That made her smile. "In fact, trying not to," she said.

"Did I mention I'm good with kids?" he asked her.

"I'm not a teacher for the time off. I love what I do. I get a kick out of the kids. I'd like a few of my own."

"A few?" she asked.

"I get that I'm slightly less than fifty percent of the vote, but I think we'll be good parents. As a matter of fact, I think we have a lot in common."

"A couple of days ago you were worried that it wasn't enough."

"Yeah, I got hung up on things that had nothing to do with us. We have fun together. Really, I've never had this much fun with a girlfriend before, and we don't even have to do anything to laugh a lot. Who would've guessed a picnic in the Jeep would get you excited? Good thing, too, since it looks like that's about all that Jeep's going to be good for. I spend half my time off in that little dorm room you live in and it's not too crowded—that means something. Every day when I wake up if you're not right next to me, I start thinking about when I'm going to see you."

"You've had a lot of girlfriends, Troy. What makes this different?"

He stopped walking and turned her toward him. "You do, Gracie. I've dated a lot, but I've never been this serious about a woman. I've always known I'd settle down when the right woman came into my life and a couple of times I asked myself, *Is this her? Is this the right one?* I never asked with you. I knew. I knew right away. But we had to learn about each other. You had to learn to trust me."

"Yes, and the minute I did…"

"Brain atrophy," he explained. "At least it's not permanent."

"And if you get it again?"

"Try a club," he suggested. And then he pulled her against him and kissed her stupid, a kiss that seemed to last forever. His hands roamed up and down her back. and her arms went around his neck. Their bodies were flush together so that only an earthquake could distract them. "And then there's this," he whispered against her lips. "The way we fit together. The way you can't breathe for a minute after you come. The way I can't stop after once and almost can't after twice. We were made for each other, that's the truth. Sometimes I can taste you in my dreams."

"And what if I want six kids?" she asked very softly.

"Bring 'em on."

"You're the only man I've ever been with. Except for the knight, the Navy SEAL and the vampire."

"You're not going to need those boys anymore, Gracie. I'm going to keep you busy." He kissed her again. "I bought you a ring. It's not flashy. Or big."

"You bought me a ring?"

"You can't have it unless you promise to marry me and get old with me."

"I don't know…let me think…"

"I can promise you hand-holding and picnics and laughter. I can give you children and loyalty and love. I will stick by you through hard times and beside you through good. And I will never again doubt you, I swear. I'll trust you and you can always trust me. I'll be a good husband and a strong father for our kids. Do it, Grace. Forgive me, trust me, marry me. I can't make it without you."

"Okay. But only because I love you so much in spite of your flaws."

He sighed in relief and pulled a ring box out of his pocket. Without letting an inch separate them, he slipped it on her ring finger. It was a lovely solitaire, certainly not too little on her small hand. She thought it was the most beautiful thing she'd ever seen. But it could have been a cigar band and she would have been filled with love for him. "Be my life, be my love, be my wife."

"Yes," she said.

* * * * *

Turn the page for a sneak peek at
A NEW HOPE,
the next book in Robyn Carr's
#1 New York Times *bestselling*
THUNDER POINT *series.*

The Basque really know how to get married, Ginger Dysart thought. She hadn't attended the wedding ceremony and had had doubts about attending this reception, given all the sadness she'd suffered over the past year. Her own marriage had barely begun when it ended in divorce. But she was so glad she'd come to the reception. It was an ethnic extravaganza—the Basque food, the music, the dancing. The bride and groom, Peyton and Scott Grant, had whirled around the dance floor a few times, then parted so Scott could dance with his mother and Peyton could dance with her father. And then there were a series of handsome dark-haired men who claimed the bride—brothers, cousins, uncles.

Paco Lacoumette presided over the party with all the aplomb of a king and was clearly in his element. The couples dancing would cease and the Basque men in their traditional white outfits with red vests and caps would take the floor and put on a show to the wild applause of the guests. Then more couples dancing. Even Ginger was dragged from her chair and pulled out to dance, despite her efforts to decline. She danced with men she knew—Cooper, Spencer, Mac, Scott—and men she didn't know, those good looking Lacoumette relatives. At one point she spied Troy, Grace's boyfriend, who must have just arrived. Grace, Ginger's boss and owner of the flower shop in Thunder Point, had believed he wasn't going to make it and was so disappointed; yet there he was, twirling Grace around with almost professional skill. And by the glowing look on Grace's face, she was completely thrilled.

Wine flowed, food was constantly replenished, dancing and laughter filled the night. Ginger felt pretty for the first time in so long. She wore a new dress, cut to her slim figure. She'd lost a lot of weight in the past several months; men were looking at her in a way they hadn't before, and she actually enjoyed the feel of their eyes on her. Those lusty, dark-haired Basque men did nothing to conceal their appreciative gazes.

The whole atmosphere was magical—teenagers were dancing or dashing about the grounds and orchard, sneaking behind trees for stolen kisses; children were riding on the shoulders of fathers, grandfathers and uncles; women were clapping in time to the music, laughing, singing, gossiping. Peyton and Scott were in much demand on the dance floor, and in between songs many toasts were made.

There were far too many Lacoumettes to remember all their names, but they made Ginger feel welcome and appreciated.

There was one darkly handsome man she'd noticed right away because he was the only one who seemed sulky and unhappy, and he was the one approaching her now as she stood beside her table. He had the swarthy good looks and fierce eyes of a pirate or maybe serial killer. And with such precision timing, he had singled her out when everyone else from her table was dancing.

"Hey, pretty lady," he said, attempting a smile that was off-kilter. His words were slurred. That would at least partially account for the half-mast eyes and pouting expression—he was obviously drunk. Well, this happened at weddings with great regularity, she thought, especially weddings where the wine flowed so liberally.

"Time for a dance!" he said.

"Thank you, but I'm going to sit this one out," she replied.

"Hmm," he said, stroking his chin. "Then we should go straight to the hayloft!"

She was appalled. But she remained composed and confident. "I'm sitting that out as well."

"No, come with me," he said. "You and me—let's do this." And then he reached for her. And grabbed her right breast.

She shrieked, shoved him away. His feet got tangled, he fell backward over a chair and went down, hitting his head on the way. And there he lay, motionless and unconscious.

"Help," she said. Then louder. "*Help!*"

She got far more attention than she wanted or expected. And of course, there were the questions. *What happened? Are you hurt? Did he pass out? Is he dead?*

"He grabbed at me," she said, waving a hand over the area of her breast without pointing or saying it. "I shoved him away and he fell and I think he might've hit his head on the table."

There he lay in a heap, on his back, his legs twisted awkwardly.

In just seconds Peyton and Scott were there, Scott crouching and lifting the man's eyelids, looking at his eyes. "Well, they're equal, but damn…they're big. Does he take anything?" he asked his bride.

"Yes, wine," Peyton said. "He killed a full skin before the dancing."

Then Paco was pushing his way through the crowd, looking down. "I knew it would come to this," he said. "There was no slowing him down."

"I think we call 9-1-1, get a head CT, make sure he didn't crack his skull," Scott said.

"His head is made of wood," Paco said. "It would serve him right, to be carried out of his sister's wedding on one of those back board things and spend the night in a hospital." Paco reached for the ice bucket on the table. Everyone scooted back immediately, as if they knew what was coming. Peyton pulled Scott away while Paco took a bottle of white wine out of the bucket and put it on the table, then doused the man with the ice water.

He sputtered and coughed and sat up.

"See what I'm telling you?" Paco said. "Wood. George! Sal! Mikie! Get Matthew from your sister's wedding! Hide his keys!" Three men moved to action immediately. Paco looked at Ginger and said, "There's always one. I apologize." Then he took in the gathering crowd and clapped. "I think it's time I dance with my wife!"

Grace arrived, pushing her way through the crowd. "Ginger! Is everything all right?"

"I'm not sure," she said, watching as the men were leaving—three of them walking steadily and one weaving dangerously.

"My brother, Matt," Peyton said. "He has issues. Divorce issues. He was divorced a little over a year ago but it appears he's still very bitter. Weddings don't seem to bring out the best in him. He didn't hurt you, did he?"

"He didn't quite connect," Ginger said. "I was about to say good night anyway. I'm going back to my folks' house in Portland for the night."

"I might kill Matt," Peyton said.

"Just enjoy the rest of your party," Ginger said. "No harm done. To me, anyway. God, I hope I didn't hurt him."

"You heard my father—his head is made of wood."

"I'll call you in the morning," Grace said. "Troy had some car trouble on the way up here and we'll have to see where that stands in the morning and figure out how we're all getting home. I've got the van. You take your father's car back to him."

Ginger turned to Peyton. "It was a wonderful reception. You look ravishing. And I was just thinking, the Basque people really know how to get married."

Ginger's parents, Dick and Sue, had waited up. That was definite evidence as to how concerned they were about her—they'd stayed up past ten when their usual bedtime was before nine. And when she walked in the front door, looking perfectly alive, they both stood from their recliners. They looked at her expectantly.

"Did you have a good time?" Sue asked hesitantly.

"I had a lovely time," Ginger said. "The flowers were beautiful, the wedding party was gorgeous and the party was like one out of a fairy tale. You wouldn't believe the fun of Basque dancing and music! And the food? Oh my God, the food was just amazing. And I'm exhausted—I'm going straight to bed."

"Are you…comfortable in your room, Ginger?" Sue asked.

"Yes, of course. And thank you for making it so nice for me."

She kissed them both on their cheeks and went upstairs. Upstairs to the large bedroom and adjacent room that had been renovated especially for her when she'd come home to her parents, pregnant and alone; to the room where she had cared for her little son for the four short months of his life.

Ginger had been staying with her cousin Ray Anne in Thunder Point for the past month. It was through Ray Anne that she'd gotten the job in Grace's flower shop, a job that was really saving her life, hour by hour. Before she came back to Portland with Grace for this wedding and weekend visit, Ray Anne had called Sue and asked her to pack up all the baby things that Ginger had been looking at since his death over nine months ago. The crib and mobile had been taken down, the clothes removed from the drawers, boxed up and stored, the necessary accoutrements like car seat, bouncy chair, bath items and changing table were all gone. She didn't think her parents had given them away, but they were out of sight. Probably stored in the attic or garage. There was only one framed picture of Ginger and Josh, which she found in the top drawer.

She took it out, put it on the bedside table, and changed into her pajamas.

When her father had suggested, rather emotionally, that Ginger go to Thunder Point and stay with Ray Anne for at least a few weeks, she had not wanted any part of it. But it was plain to see her parents needed a break from her grief. Now she was so glad she had gone. When she was in Thunder Point, she at least had the illusion of getting on with her life. She had a new, improved appearance, at Ray Anne's insistence. She had that lovely little job in the flower shop. She had slept well and had an appetite again. Oh, she'd longed for little Josh, like always. But she was marching on.

She crawled in the bed at her parents' house, turned the picture of herself and her baby toward her, left the light on so she could see it, and sobbed.

Shall we dance?

After a humiliating divorce and watching her former rock star husband leave her for a model live on reality TV, Pippa is determined to disappear. So she returns to the small Kent village where she grew up to make a fresh start.

Little did she know that would mean saving her beloved childhood dance school or falling for her old school crush Tom too!

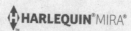

40 years of marriage
8 golden charms
One man's journey of discovery

On the anniversary of his wife's death, 69 year-old
Arthur Pepper finally musters the courage to go
through her possessions, and happens upon a charm
bracelet that he has never seen before.

What follows is a surprising adventure that takes
Arthur from London to Paris and India in an epic
quest to find out the truth about his wife's secret
life before they met, a journey that leads him to
find healing, self-discovery, and love in the most
unexpected of places.

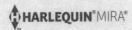

A fast-paced, fun-packed rummage
through the ultimate dressing up box.

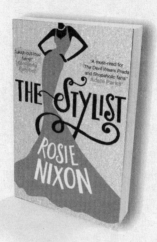

When fashion boutique worker Amber Green is
mistakenly offered a job as assistant to infamous,
jet-setting 'stylist to the stars' Mona Armstrong,
she hits the ground running, helping to style some
of Hollywood's hottest (and craziest) starlets. As
awards season spins into action Mona is in hot
demand and Amber's life turned upside down.
How will Amber keep her head?

And what the hell will everyone wear?

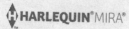
M439_TS

Praise   HANDSOME BRUTE

'In this fine, balanced book, which spares no details but avoids any hint of salacity, O'Connor has written something more valuable than a whydunnit. A fascinating portrait of a dreary, uncertain post-war world of drinking dens, cruddy hotels and hopes unfulfilled.'
Ben McIntyre, *THE TIMES*

'An astute study … Sean O'Connor's keenly intelligent book is essentially an attempt to fit these two Neville Heaths together … O'Connor restores its human dimension, using evidence and witness statements from previously restricted Home Office and police files.'
John Carey, *SUNDAY TIMES*

'Sean O'Connor's brilliance is to sustain the horrific dramatic tension of these murders while providing a rich and detailed context of place and period. His tone is careful and dispassionate, his research painstaking and extensive.'
THE INDEPENDENT

'The story of how this weak-willed conman and small-time fraudster turned from a former RAF playboy into a savagely sadistic sex killer makes fascinating reading in Sean O'Connor's meticulously researched book.'
DAILY EXPRESS

'O'Connor tells the whole story beautifully. It's the best true crime book I've read for ages. His short description of Heath's execution at the hands of Albert Pierrepoint is superb.'
EVENING

SEAN O'CONNOR is a writer, director and producer and works in theatre, radio, television and film.

He produced the feature film version of Terence Rattigan's *The Deep Blue Sea*, directed by Terence Davies and starring Rachel Weisz and Tom Hiddleston. He edited the BBC's long-running radio drama *The Archers* and also worked as executive producer of the BBC's *EastEnders*. His Shakespeare adaptation *Juliet and Her Romeo* played to great acclaim at the Bristol Old Vic, directed by Tom Morris. His adaptation of John Osborne's *The Entertainer* toured the UK in 2019. His latest book, *The Fatal Passion of Alma Rattenbury*, was published by Simon & Schuster in 2019.

HANDSOME BRUTE

The TRUE STORY of a LADYKILLER

SEAN O'CONNOR

**SIMON &
SCHUSTER**

London · New York · Sydney · Toronto · New Delhi

A CBS COMPANY

First published in Great Britain by Simon & Schuster UK Ltd, 2013
This paperback edition published by Simon & Schuster UK Ltd, 2019
A CBS COMPANY

1 3 5 7 9 10 8 6 4 2

Simon & Schuster UK Ltd
1st Floor
222 Gray's Inn Road
London WC1X 8HB

www.simonandschuster.co.uk
www.simonandschuster.co.au
www.simonandschuster.co.in

Simon & Schuster Australia, Sydney
Simon & Schuster India, New Delhi

A CIP catalogue record for this book is available from the British Library

Paperback ISBN: 978-1-4711-8700-1
eBook ISBN: 978-1-4711-0135-9

Typeset by Hewer Text UK Limited, Edinburgh
Printed and bound by CPI Group (UK) Ltd, Croydon, CR0 4YY

MIX
Paper from
responsible sources
FSC® C020471
FSC
www.fsc.org

This is an astonishing case, is it not? The probability is, of course, that Heath knows no more about the state of his mind than any of us do about our own minds. It is something that is part of his nature; it is natural; to him it would not appear extraordinary.

J. D. Casswell KC

Is there any cause in nature that makes these hard hearts?
Shakespeare, *King Lear* (III, vi)

For Jo O'Keefe
1969–2010

CONTENTS

FOREWORD   ix

CHARACTERS   xxi

PROLOGUE: Mrs Brees   1

PART ONE: London

 1   Summer 1946   11
 2   Miss Symonds   21
 3   Mrs Gardner   43
 4   Thursday 20 June 1946   66
 5   Detective Inspector Spooner   79
 6   The Pembridge Court Hotel   90

PART TWO: Neville George Clevely Heath

 7   Rake's Progress   103
 8   Borstal Boy   149
 9   Lt. James Robert Cadogan Armstrong 173
10   Out of South Africa   200
11   Thursday 20 June 1946   217
12   Rogue Male   235

PART THREE: Group Captain Rupert Robert Brook

13	Bournemouth	251
14	Miss Waring	258
15	Miss Marshall	270
16	The Tollard Royal Hotel	287
17	Detective Constable Suter	297
18	Branksome Dene Chine	313

PART FOUR: The Twisting of Another Rope

19	3923	327
20	Mrs Armstrong	340
21	The Old Bailey	344
22	Wednesday 16 October 1946	361
23	Mrs Heath	383

AFTERWORD	388
APPENDIX	396
ACKNOWLEDGEMENTS	401
FURTHER READING	405
ENDNOTES	413
INDEX	456

FOREWORD

So much for Raffles. Now for a header into the cesspool.
George Orwell, 'Raffles and Miss Blandish', 1944

Heath's story is not a pretty one ... it will be remembered as
a sort of sadistic bloodbath not untypical of an age of crime
where sadism and bloodbaths are, if anything, coming to be
the rule rather than exceptions.
Nigel Morland, *Hangman's Clutch*, 1954

With the passing of the Second World War generation into history, the story of Neville George Clevely Heath, once regarded as 'the most dangerous criminal modern Britain has known'[1] and 'the most atrocious murderer in modern times',[2] has dwindled in our collective memory in the sixty-eight years between 1946 and today.

Heath's reputation – once a byword for sadistic perversion and psychopathic violence – has not held the popular imagination as Christie's or the Moors Murderers' have. This is despite the fact that the case caused a media furore at the time, providing gruesome (and titillating) copy in newspapers dominated by the grey realities of austerity Britain: the national debt, the initiation of bread rationing and the painfully slow process of demobilization. The case was a gift for the tabloids with its sensational ingredients of aberrant sex and violent death, set in a world undergoing a process of radical change. The blond, handsome Heath, still tanned from his time abroad, was a great distraction for a nation in flux, exhausted by six years of wartime privation and looking towards an uncertain future. All the elements of the case came together to make a classic English narrative: a charming but vicious protagonist ridden with class anxiety, an ambitious detective, a national manhunt for a killer on the loose.

From a twenty-first-century perspective, the background to the murders – the pubs, bars and nightclubs of west London and the genteel hotels of south-coast seaside resorts – conjure a lost, very English world. It's the socially and sexually anxious environment of Agatha Christie and Terence Rattigan, filtered through the prism of Patrick Hamilton's drink-sodden novel, *Hangover Square*. But despite the classic and comfortable mid-twentieth-century English setting, the savagery of the crimes and Heath's at once charming, yet pathological, personality anticipate an American style of slaughter much more akin to Bret Easton Ellis's *American Psycho* or Jim Thompson's *The Killer Inside Me*. And despite the period details – the Royal Air Force slang, the pipe clenched in the teeth and the old school tie – Heath's laconic attitude both to his crimes and to the prospect of his own extinction is redolent of the casual cruelty of contemporary murderers like John Maden, who killed his niece Tia Rigg in Manchester in 2010, 'because I felt like it'. When he was finally arrested, Heath responded in a similarly offhand manner: 'Oh, all right.'[3]

Such was the appetite for news of the case at the time, that in the summer of 1946 when newspapers were generally restricted to four skimpy pages because of newsprint rationing, the Heath case received enormous coverage. In reporting the trial, journalists took licence to report – in surprising detail – the most graphic revelations of the murders as well as the more salacious details of Heath's sex life. The trial offered an opportunity to examine the darker avenues of sexuality in modern Britain – and this was all available over the breakfast table with the post and the toast. Heath's friends even negotiated a newspaper deal for him in order to give his exclusive side of the story.

Curiously, given the nature of his crimes, the audience for Heath's story was primarily female. Some women, it was reported, queued for fourteen hours outside the Old Bailey in the hope of getting just a glimpse of this most notorious of ladykillers. 'Rarely', noted the *People,* 'have women been so strangely fascinated by a murder trial.'[4]

For a society struggling to negotiate its place in the new world order, Heath's story articulated an alarming new postwar anxiety. With millions of soldiers, sailors and airmen returning to Britain – many of them trained killers – the Heath trial exposed the tension created by re-integrating servicemen *en masse* into the hugely changed communities and families they had left years earlier. Newspapers of the time are filled with tragic stories of servicemen returning home and killing their estranged wives, unable to settle into the brave new, post-war world. Commenting on the case of one former soldier who had done just that, which resulted in the conviction being commuted to manslaughter, Mr Justice Charles warned that 'the law of the jungle'[5] was creeping into

English courtrooms. The *News Chronicle* worried that 'it would seem from some recent murder trials that the unfaithful wife of a serviceman is an outlaw with no benefit of law whatsoever. She may be murdered with impunity.'[6]

Heath's career encapsulated the civilian population's particularly ambivalent attitude towards pilots from Bomber Command. Taking their lead from Winston Churchill, the public had lauded 'the Few', the brave boys in Spitfires who defended the nation from invasion in 1940, dog-fighting the Luftwaffe across the skies above the South Downs. But Bomber Command had flown into Europe causing devastation on an unprecedented scale, wiping out civilian and military targets alike with a seeming disregard for human life. They were at once glamorous but deadly – the creators of those iconic symbols of wartime destruction, Berlin, Hamburg and Dresden.[7] In his study of the RAF during World War II, *The Flyer*, Martin Francis observes 'a broader ambivalence among the public and the men of the RAF themselves, as to whether they were chivalric knights of the air or merciless agents of violent destruction'.[8] Neville Heath – the charmer turned killer – absolutely embodies this disorientating anxiety, and this may well be a key to the extraordinary interest the public took in the case; for Heath's story dramatized one of the unspoken fears of the age.

As early as 1947, only a year after the murders, a serial killer with remarkable similarities to Heath appears in Ken Annakin's ostensibly upbeat film, *Holiday Camp*.[9] Dennis Price plays Squadron Leader Hardwick, a suave ex-RAF pilot, charming lonely women with tales of his wartime exploits, whilst hiding his true nature as the 'mannequin murderer'. The references to Heath would have been very clear to cinema-goers at the time. The film attempts to examine the new democracy ushered in by the Welfare State. All strata of society get to take a holiday – even if that only means a chilly week at Butlins in Bognor. But despite the optimism for the new Albion inherent in the film, it's clear that the murderous Squadron Leader Hardwick – and Heath himself – articulated the unease in British society at welcoming home a whole generation of men, many of whom had killed during the war. Having fuelled and channelled these violent instincts on behalf of the state, where were they to be directed now? And, indeed, could they be channelled at all? Or were these dark instincts to become a reality of the post-war world?[10]

The fascination with Heath continued after his trial and began to fill more than just newspaper copy. Two sensational monographs about the case were published with indelicate haste after Heath's trial, both by journalists who claimed to have known Heath personally. Gerald Byrne's *Borstal Boy: The Uncensored Life of Neville Heath* was published in 1946, printed to economy standards and bearing a suitably sombre black and white cover. Full of salacious (and often unsubstantiated) detail, it is a paperback shocker masquerading as a morality tale, 'of a man ... who stopped at nothing to satisfy his own craving for position, money and power'.[11]

Sydney Brock's *The Life and Death of Neville Heath* followed swiftly in 1947. Though the text attempts a serious examination of Heath's life and crimes from a first-hand point of view, it has a Mills & Boon-style subtitle: *The Man No Woman Could Resist*. The cover of this railway bookstore paperback depicts a sexy young woman in a saucy short skirt – a whip to her side, hanging sinisterly in mid-air. The cover promises a 'Sensational-Sadistic-Romantic-True Story'.[12] This uncomfortable tone – exploiting the case as soft pornography – came to dominate non-fiction writing about Heath. James Hodge, who published the much-admired *Notable British Trials* series, had hesitated about covering the Heath trial at all, precisely because the facts of the case could too easily result in something of dubious value, bordering on exploitative porn.

Eventually Macdonald Critchley successfully edited the case in 1951, winning resounding praise from Hodge:

> Heath could very well have deteriorated into a wretched book in less capable hands and that is why I did not want to include it in our series before, in view of the less savoury angle some might have taken.[13]

Heath's story continued to fascinate the public and resonated throughout popular culture in the years following the trial. In 1949, the writer, Elizabeth Taylor, reinvented Heath's story as a dark romance in her novel, *A Wreath of Roses*.[14] Shortly afterwards, Patrick Hamilton wrote a trilogy of novels focusing on an amoral con man, Ralph Gorse, in his *Gorse Trilogy* (1951–55). Even if Gorse's career as a petty criminal doesn't actually lead to murder (though there's a clear sense that he's capable of it), it's apparent that in his depiction of this satanic womanizer, Hamilton had drawn heavily on details from Heath's biography, including incidences of cruelty in childhood and the manipulation of women as an art form, both with a strong undercurrent of sadomasochism.[15] All these facts were readily available in the popular press at the time of Heath's arrest and trial.

In 1954, the criminologist and novelist Nigel Morland remarked on the dramatic qualities inherent in the Heath case, 'in that it unfolds almost like a film story, with backgrounds slightly out of focus'.[16] It's no surprise then that Alfred Hitchcock, renowned especially in his later works for his explorations of sex and psychopathy – particularly after the success of *Psycho* in 1960 – was drawn to Heath's personality and spent several years developing a film inspired by the events of the case. The script, originally written by Benn Levy, was called *Frenzy* (latterly *Kaleidoscope*).[17] By 1967 Hitchcock was already making camera tests for the film and had shot an hour of silent footage. This was to be Hitchcock as he'd never been seen before – informed by the European New Wave with a particular emphasis on realism, graphic sex and violence.[18] But this new Hitch proved too radical for the studio executives at MCA. They rejected the script and the Heath project was shelved. Howard Fast, who also worked on the script, claimed that the studio told Hitchcock that they'd never allow him to shoot it as 'his pictures were known for elegant villains and here was an impossibly ugly one'.[19] The title was eventually recycled for Hitchcock's more accessible 1971 British come-back featuring Barry Foster as Rusk, the 'necktie murderer'.[20] But the essence of the film *Frenzy* – a charming but ultimately terrifying sex killer – shares much in common with the char-acter of Heath, Rusk's fetish for neckties echoing Heath's widely reported fetish for handkerchiefs.

Though the facts of the case created an international media sensation, reported in newspapers and magazines across the globe, the trial was very English in tone; low-key and devoid of histrionics. The dramatic focus of the three-day hearing was a debate about Heath's sanity. This was assessed by a stat-ute over 100 years old – the M'Naghten Rules of 1843 – which posed the question: 'Did the Defendant know what he was doing – and, if so, did he know what he was doing was wrong?' This made no concessions for the developments in psychology and psychiatry since the turn of the twentieth century. The plea of diminished responsibility was not to reach the British statute books for another decade with the passing of the Homicide Act in 1957. This was to state that:

> Where a person kills or is party to a killing of another, he shall not be convicted of murder if he was suffering from such abnormality of mind ... as substantially impaired his mental responsibility for his acts and omissions in doing or being a party to the killing.[21]

No such plea was available to Heath's defence in 1946.

Key witnesses, who may have been able to offer crucial evidence in relation to Heath's past behaviour, his service career and his psychological state in the months leading up to the murders, were never called to the trial. With the lack of such evidence the issue of Heath's sanity (or insanity) was never fully debated. Beyond the categorization of Heath as a malevolent killer and sexual sadist, there was little curiosity, from either the prosecution or the defence, in examining Heath's character or background. Heath didn't deny committing the murders once he'd been arrested – consequently, there was no attempt at the trial to try and explain them. What provoked Heath to do what he did remains a mystery. Though he later gave a version of events to the press, this may have been motivated by his wish to leave money to his family and pay off his debts, rather than any desire to leave behind his version of the 'Truth'. And, with regard to *any* story Heath told, it's important to bear in mind that he was a sophisticated and practised liar, having talked his way into and out of dramatic situations since his schooldays.

In his essay, *Decline of the English Murder*, published in the same year as the trial, George Orwell observed a sea change in the culture of murder in Britain and firmly pointed to the Second World War as the tipping point.[22] He lamented the passing of the 'Elizabethan age' of English murder which, he suggested, spanned from 1850 to 1925 and included classic cases like Crippen, Seddon, Mrs Maybrick, Thompson and Bywaters – all domestic crimes motivated by money, sex or respectability. He contrasted these with the 'Cleft Chin Murder' of 1944, committed by Elizabeth Marina Jones and Karl Hulten, a meaningless killing set against 'the anonymous life of dance-halls and the false values of the American film'. In effect, he suggested that the average reader of the *News of the World* or the *Sunday Pictorial*[23] enjoyed the brutality of this new American style of murder because, as a culture, Britain had been brutalized by the effects of the war.

Orwell had first outlined this theory in 'Raffles and Miss Blandish', comparing the author E. W. Hornung's popular character, Raffles – the gentleman thief – with James Hadley Chase's hard-boiled American tale *No Orchids for Miss Blandish*, a novel of murder, torture, sadistic violence and rape. Significantly this became one of the most popular novels of the war years and Orwell was clear in what he felt lay at the heart of its huge success – it articulated the sublimated anxieties of the age:

> In his imagined world of gangsters Chase is presenting, as it were, a distilled version of the modern political scene, in which such things as mass bombing of civilians, the use of hostages, torture to obtain confessions, secret prisons, execution without trial, floggings with rubber truncheons, drownings in cesspools, systematic falsification of records and statistics, treachery, bribery, and quislingism are normal and morally neutral, even admirable when they are done in a large and bold way. *The average man is not directly interested in politics, and when he reads, he wants the current struggles of the world to be translated into a simple story about individuals* [my italics].[24]

This may well be another reason why Heath's story touched such a popular nerve at the time, articulating as it did a brutal and violent strain in modern culture, unnervingly close to the surface, through the story of a once-heroic individual turned bad.

For the first time, this book examines evidence and witness statements that have been held in previously restricted files from the Home Office and the Metropolitan Police. Some evidence relating to third parties remains restricted in the National Archives until 2045 as do the scene of crime and post-mortem photographs, which were described at the time as 'grotesque'. The post-mortem reports themselves are sufficiently graphic to make it clear the appalling nature of these images.

My intention is to examine the tragic events of 1946 in the fuller context of what we now know about the period and the case, as well as examining issues unexplored at the time concerning Heath's life leading up to the killings, which might have some bearing on his subsequent actions. What was the combination of circumstances that brought the crisis in Heath's life to a head that summer? And how far is Heath's case emblematic or indeed symptomatic of the age in which he lived? For in a country battered and exhausted by six years of war, a culture in a moment of change, and the sense of a new morality around the corner, Heath was regarded as 'the incarnation of war-time and post-war vices'.[25]

Throughout 1946, the major international news stories were the increasing violence in Palestine and the trials of the Nazi war criminals at Nuremberg. With the revelation of the horrors of the death camps, there's a sense that mankind was capable of a depth of cruelty, a lack of humanity barely imaginable in the relative innocence of the pre-war period. Certainly with Gordon Cummins, the 'blackout ripper', who mutilated the sexual organs of his victims with a can-opener, followed soon after by Heath, then the acid-bath murderer Haigh and the necrophiliac Christie, there does seem a real sense of extremity – a ferocity and violence extremely rare in British crime since the Whitechapel murders at the end of the nineteenth century.

Early in the investigation, Detective Superintendent Lovell of the Dorset Constabulary first articulated the intriguing power of Heath's complex nature: 'Certainly his personality is an extremely puzzling one, and capable of more than one single interpretation.'[26] Heath's solicitor, Isaac Near, later commented that 'whatever the facts of the case, Heath had certainly a remarkable personality – a personality that made one like him'.[27] As well as a startling lack of remorse, the persona Heath reveals in his letters from prison show real tenderness and self-awareness. He was capable of inspiring genuine affection in many of the people he knew, yet it's impossible not to be repelled by the atrocities he committed. What continues to fascinate is his elusive, contradictory character. How do we reconcile the suburban confidence trickster, the charismatic and articulate ladies' man with the savage and pitiless murderer who had the capacity not just to kill, but to violate the bodies of his victims with such ferocity that war-hardened police officers vomited on seeing them?

At times it's uncomfortable to examine the records of this case and find the lives of both killer and his victims described in such forensic detail, a knowledge denied to even their closest friends and family; not just a list of dates and places, but the most intimate details of their lives – the money they had (or more often didn't have), the dates of their menstrual cycle, their sexual predilections, their innermost secrets. But it's this sometimes invasive detail that diminishes the passage of time and brings home the fact that they may not be 'fools in old-style hats and coats' at all; that perhaps we share more with the wartime generation than we thought, and their ambitions and anxieties – despite the years between us – remain constant and universal, urgent and real.

William Bixley served for fifty years in Court No. 1 as supervising officer at the Old Bailey. He had held a uniquely privileged position, attendant at the most distressing and dramatic of trials. Yet, in his memoir of 1957, Bixley reflected that, of all the trials he had witnessed throughout his half-century of service, Heath's case was 'the most upsetting'.

The reason for the feeling of revulsion and dread which, I think, permeated the minds of everyone in that Court was that Heath seemed ostensibly so normal, and one had deep forebodings that only by a hair's breadth did other seemingly decent and pleasant young men escape from the awful sexual sadism which, at times, makes man lower than any animal that walks or crawls on the face of the earth.[28]

It's that hair's breadth that separates us from Heath that continues to chill us, too. How could this 'seemingly decent and pleasant' young man also be capable of some of the most brutal acts in British criminal history?

CHARACTERS

21 MERTON HALL ROAD, WIMBLEDON

Neville George Clevely Heath, 29	*ex-RAF pilot*
William Heath, 56	*his father*
Bessie Heath, 55	*his mother*
Michael (Mick) Heath, 17	*his brother*

'STRATHMORE', WARREN ROAD, WORTHING

Yvonne Marie Symonds, 21	*ex-WRNS*
Major John Charters Symonds, 55	*her father*
Gertrude Symonds	*her mother*

24 OAKHOLME ROAD, SHEFFIELD

Margery Aimee Brownell Gardner, 32	*artist*
Peter Gardner, 32	*her husband*
Melody Gardner, 2	*her daughter*
Elizabeth Wheat, 67	*her mother*
Gilbert Wheat, 30	*her brother, a schoolteacher*
Ralph Macro Wilson, 43	*family solicitor*

19 WOODHALL DRIVE, PINNER

Doreen Margaret Marshall, 21	*ex-WRNS*
Charles Marshall, 59	*her father*
Grace Marshall, 53	*her mother*
Joan Grace Cruickshanks, 25	*her married sister*

LONDON

Strand Palace Hotel
Leonard William Luff, 58   *assistant manager*
Thomas Paul, 59   *head porter*
Pauline Miriam Brees, 21   *model*

Pembridge Court Hotel
Elizabeth Wyatt, 65   *manageress*
Alice Wyatt, 40   *her daughter-in-law*
Rhoda Spooner, 26   *waitress*
Barbara Osborne, 32   *chambermaid*

Panama Club
Solomon Josephs, 56   *receptionist*
Harold Harter, 40   *taxi driver*

Associates of Neville Heath
Leslie Terry, 43   *restaurant owner*
Harry Ashbrook, 38   *journalist*
Ralph Fisher   *commercial pilot*
Zita Williams, 23   *shorthand typist*
Jill Harris, 20   *shorthand typist*
William Spurrett
Fielding–Johnson, 54   *squadron leader, RAF*

Associates of Margery Gardner
Peter Tilley Bailey, 29   *gentleman thief*
Trevethan Frampton, 26   *student*
Iris Humphrey, 29   *civil servant*
John Le Mee Power, 33   *building firm accountant*
Joyce Frost, 33   *friend of Margery Gardner*

Metropolitan Police
Reginald Spooner, 43   *divisional detective inspector*

Shelley Symes, 41   *detective inspector*
Thomas Barratt, 48   *superintendent, Scotland Yard*

JOHANNESBURG

Elizabeth Armstrong, 26   *Armstrong's wife*
Robert Michael Armstrong, 2   *their son*
Moira Lister, 23   *actress*

BOURNEMOUTH

Tollard Royal Hotel
Ivor Relf, 35   *manager*
Arthur White, 38   *head night porter*
Frederick Charles Wilkinson, 33   *night porter*
Alice Hemmingway, 47   *chambermaid*
Peter Rylatt, 31   *demobbed lawyer*
Gladys Davy Phillips, 62   *married woman*
Winifred Parfitt, 40   *married woman*
Heinz Abisch, 30   *designer, wire company*
Peggy Waring, 37   *student*

Bournemouth Police
George Gates, 45   *detective inspector*
George Suter, 40   *detective constable*
Leslie Johnson, 38   *detective sergeant*
Francis Bishop, 46   *detective sergeant, Dorset*

THE OLD BAILEY

Isaac Elliston Near, 45	*Heath's solicitor*
Mr Justice Morris, 50	*judge*
Anthony Hawke, 51	*counsel for the Crown*
J. D. Casswell, KC, 60	*counsel for the defence*
Dr Keith Simpson, 39	*pathologist*
Dr Crichton McGaffey, 43	*pathologist*
Dr Hugh Grierson, 60	*psychiatrist*
Dr William Hubert, 42	*psychiatrist*
Dr Hubert Young, 57	*psychiatrist*

PROLOGUE
Mrs Brees

23 FEBRUARY 1946

In the early hours of Saturday morning on 23 February 1946, a guest on the fourth floor of the Strand Palace Hotel was disturbed by violent noises from the room directly above. Something fell on the floor, a woman screamed for help. The guest reported the commotion to the head porter, Thomas Paul. Paul was accustomed to the realities of hotel life during wartime and was used to turning a blind eye to the excesses of alcohol and sex, so he discreetly went up to the fifth floor to see if there was a problem. When he got to Room 506, he listened at the locked door and heard a woman screaming from inside.

'Stop! Stop! For God's sake, stop!'

Concerned by the severity of her cries, Paul ran down the stairs to get his colleague, Leonard William Luff, the assistant manager.[1]

The Strand Palace was (and remains) a large building on the north side of the Strand, parallel to the Thames. Its exterior was built in the grand Empire style in 1909, but the hotel had been expanded and refurbished during the 1920s and by the Second World War boasted 980 bedrooms. The famous foyer of the hotel was remodelled in 1930. Claridges, the Savoy and the newly constructed Dorchester all had sumptuous Art Deco foyers, but Oliver P. Bernard's designs for the Strand Palace had made his creation one of the most celebrated hotel interiors in London.[2] The foyer combined traditional and contemporary marbles and made innovative use of glass and lighting. The walls were clad in pink marble and the floor with limestone. The balustrades, columns and door surrounds were made of mirror, chromed steel and translucent moulded glass. The foyer became regarded as an iconic Art Deco masterpiece and, indeed, is now preserved at the Victoria and Albert Museum after its removal from the hotel in 1969. Back in 1946, the hotel seemed to represent the epitome of pre-war elegance, bringing a touch of Hollywood glamour to war-torn London.[3]

Conveniently located amongst the pubs, bars, nightclubs and restaurants of London's West End, the Strand Palace had been popular with American forces during the war and had only recently been decommissioned as an official rest and recuperation residence for US servicemen. Now, with thousands of American troops awaiting shipment back home and huge numbers of British officers and service personnel newly repatriated to the UK, London was teeming with servicemen and the hotel was fully booked.

Ten months earlier, on VE Day, nearly 5 million Britons had been in uniform across the globe. The process of repatriation and demobilization was to take months, and in some cases, even years.[4] The large West End hotels provided discreet but accessible havens of transition between the past dangers and thrills of service life and the post-war world of spouses, families and responsibility. For many, such hotels represented the last opportunity for illicit liaisons, as well as offering the possibility of sensual indulgence amongst the legion of prostitutes in central London – a profession that had boomed during the war years.

The occupant of Room 506 at the Strand Palace was known to be Captain James Robert Cadogan Armstrong of the South African Air Force. Armstrong had checked into the Strand Palace on the previous Saturday, 16 February. On his uniform he wore the ribbons of the Africa Star and the DFC (Distinguished Flying Cross). He seemed to be a regular hero.

In response to the woman's screams, Thomas Paul and Leonard Luff headed upstairs to deal with the matter. When Luff opened the door with his pass-key, the two men were met by a shocking sight; a young woman lay face down on the bed, stripped naked and rendered helpless, with her hands tied behind her back. Standing over her, also naked, was Armstrong – tall, tanned, blue-eyed and handsome.[5] The woman twisted her face to the intruders, exclaiming, 'Thank God you came in.'

Armstrong turned to Paul and Luff in a fury.[6]

'What the hell are you doing, breaking in here?'

Mr Luff explained who they were, but Armstrong made no answer. Luff asked what had been going on, but the girl asked to be untied first. Luff told Armstrong to do so and the girl was freed. He then adopted a nonchalant attitude and tried to bluster the matter out, demanding what right the staff had to enter his room, but when Luff mentioned that he would call the police, Armstrong became more reasonable.

Luff asked the woman, Pauline Brees, if she knew the man and she said she did. She claimed that he had knocked her out and then undressed her. She turned to Armstrong and asked if he had raped her. This question he avoided at first, but finally denied. Asked by Luff if they should call the police, Pauline insisted that they shouldn't. She just wanted to leave the hotel and didn't want any publicity.

Despite Pauline's story, Luff didn't believe her. There were no marks of violence on her, her clothing was on a chair by the bed – undamaged – and there were no signs of a struggle having taken place. Luff thought that Pauline 'looked to me like a prostitute'.[7] He told Pauline and Armstrong to collect their things and leave. They got dressed and Armstrong took Pauline home in a taxi to her lodgings. He then checked out of the hotel himself that Sunday morning. Though the incident had raised alarm, it was regarded as embarrassing rather than serious.

Pauline, who had been widowed just six months earlier, had been introduced to Armstrong about a week before by a mutual friend at Oddenino's – a restaurant in Regent Street much frequented by RAF officers. When they met, Armstrong was wearing the khaki uniform of a lieutenant colonel in the South African Air Force. On the following Wednesday (20 February), Armstrong telephoned Pauline at her home in Maida Vale and invited her to lunch the next day. So, on Thursday, they lunched together at the Berkeley Restaurant in Knightsbridge. Afterwards they parted company in good spirits.[8]

On Friday, Pauline and Armstrong met again by appointment at Oddenino's and from there went to the Berkeley again for a drink. This initiated something of an all-day pub-crawl that took them from the Falstaff in Fleet Street where they had lunch and then to Shepherd's pub in Shepherd Market followed by the Brevet Club in Mayfair, which were both popular drinking venues with the Royal Air Force. They left the Brevet Club at about 10 p.m. as the club had run out of beer. This was a common occurrence throughout London at the time as publicans dealt with reduced supplies of beer as well as the increased demand for it since the outbreak of war.

Armstrong suggested that they go back to his room for a nightcap. Pauline agreed to accompany him to the Strand Palace where she knew he was staying but told him that she had to be home by 11.30 p.m. as she had an awkward landlady. The pair went up to the fifth floor to a double room overlooking the Strand and opposite the Art Deco entrance to the Savoy Hotel and the Savoy Theatre.[9]

In Room 506, Pauline sat on the bed while Armstrong poured himself a drink. Pauline refused to join him as she didn't like whisky. He went over to the bed and kissed her. As he became more persistent, Pauline told him that she had to be going.

'Oh no, you're not,' said Armstrong. 'You're staying the night with me.'[10]

At this point, events took a darker turn. Pauline got up, telling him not to be ridiculous as she headed for the door. But he had locked it. Grabbing her, he seized her arm and twisted it behind her back. Though she realized that she was in some danger, she claimed she didn't scream because she didn't want to embarrass him by getting him turned out of the hotel.

'Why are you doing this?' she asked him.

'I hate women,' said Armstrong.

He pulled off her coat and ordered her to strip. When she refused, they started to struggle. At 5 feet 11 inches, powerfully built and an accomplished rugby player, Armstrong threw her against the wall with such force that she lost consciousness. When she came to, Pauline realized that she had been stripped naked. Half conscious, she rushed for the door, but Armstrong grabbed her again.

'Oh, no you don't,' he said. 'We'll soon fix this.'

He took a handkerchief and tied her hands behind her

back, pushing her on to the bed. He then took off his own clothes. At this point, Pauline claimed that she didn't scream because she was 'only half conscious and paralysed with fright'. Armstrong then tried to turn her over, so that her face was in the pillow. But Pauline couldn't breathe and struggled to free herself again. He now threatened her.

'I'll make you do exactly what I want you to do.'

Forcing himself on to her prostrate body, he attempted to rape her 'in an un-natural way' but she struggled so intensely that they fell off the bed. He then put his hands around her throat. Now terrified for her life, Pauline screamed.

'Stop! Stop! For God's sake. Stop!'

Armstrong punched Pauline in the face with his fist, rendering her unconscious again. The next thing she was aware of was the arrival in the room of the assistant manager and the head porter. 'I was lying on the bed but I don't know how I got there,' she said later. Mr Luff told Armstrong and Pauline to get out, but he was, she remembered, 'quite nice to [her]'.

Some months later, it was established that James Robert Cadogan Armstrong was actually Neville George Clevely Heath, by then standing trial for murder. Reginald Spooner of the Metropolitan Police questioned Pauline Brees and was clear in his interpretation of the incident at the Strand Palace Hotel; she did not want to prosecute Heath because she admitted she had gone knowingly with him to the bedroom to be stripped and beaten.

The matter was forgotten, at least for several months. It seemed to be an illicit liaison, a sexual adventure that had got out of hand – typical in this period of transition. Many people were tasting their last moments of freedom before settling down to post-war life. Maybe too much alcohol was consumed in the various pubs, clubs and restaurants that the couple had visited; both Heath and Pauline had drunk consistently throughout their time together. Perhaps both parties misinterpreted the desires of the other? Or Pauline hadn't quite anticipated the intensity of 'Armstrong's' intentions? But this incident – referred to only obliquely as 'that incident at the London hotel' or 'a certain case not mentioned here'[11] – was to take on a much darker significance at Heath's trial. Had Pauline Brees chosen to prosecute Heath at the time, or had the hotel staff alerted the police to his behaviour, the whole series of tragic events that followed over the next six months might well have been prevented.

As it stood, by the end of the year, three young people would be dead, their families devastated and the nation appalled by the events of the summer of 1946.

PART ONE

London

CHAPTER ONE

Summer 1946

This is your victory! It is the victory of the cause of freedom in every land. In all our long history we have never seen a greater day than this. Everyone, man or woman, has done their best. Everyone has tried. Neither the long years, nor the dangers, nor the fierce attacks of the enemy have in any way weakened the independent resolve of the British nation. God bless you all.

Winston Churchill, VE Day, 8 May 1945

As the number of turkeys available this Christmas will not be sufficient to meet the demand, the Food Minister asks turkey retailers to spread the limited supplies among the largest number of families by cutting birds into two parts for sale. Half a turkey, he believes, will supply a good meal for most families.

The Times, 15 December 1945

The summer of 1946 was one of extremes.
A national sigh of relief had punctuated the end of the war and a concerted effort was made to move on from the conflict and look towards the future. After the popular rejection of Churchill's Conservative party in the 1945 election, Attlee's reforming Labour government had put social welfare at the heart of their agenda. These new social policies – particularly those regarding health, housing, education and pensions – seemed to embody the hopes for a new era for Britain, with Attlee declaring, 'We are on the eve of a great advance in the human race.'[1] But not everybody was so optimistic. The ultra-conservative Noël Coward observed, 'I always felt that England would be bloody uncomfortable during the immediate post-war period, and now it is almost a certainty that it will be so.'[2]

Balancing the government's progressive new initiatives, from the beginning of 1946 there was a reassuring effort to re-establish the pre-war patterns of British life. The Grand National and the Derby ran for the first time since 1940 and both the Cup Final and the Boat Race reappeared in the sports calendar. Even tennis was played at Wimbledon, despite bomb damage to Centre Court. In February, it was announced that London would host the Olympic Games in 1948.

The focus for June was the Victory Day (or 'V' Day) Celebration held in London over the Whit weekend, which was to formally mark the end of the Second World War. This was an opportunity to salute the people who had helped win the war and to showcase victorious Britain to the world – and the great survivor, London. The occasion was also to mark the first major outing for television broadcasting – a service still in its infancy when it had been curtailed by the outbreak of hostilities. 'Remember me?' asked announcer Jasmine Bligh as she introduced the same Mickey Mouse cartoon that had been playing when television stopped in September 1939. The message was clear; normal service had been resumed.[3]

On Saturday 8 June the Victory parade left Regent's Park heading towards Tower Hill, culminating in a royal salute on the Mall. As many as 10 million Londoners – as well as visitors from out of town – came to celebrate. Some had taken up their positions in the Mall on Thursday and Friday to secure the best view, bringing with them 'food, blankets and radios'. Many arrived on one of the seventy-five special 'Victory Express' trains that brought in sightseers from all over the country.[4] Typically, despite the weather reports optimistically forecasting 'ideal weather – plenty of sunshine, but not too hot',[5] after a promisingly sunny morning heavy rain fell throughout the rest of the day, drowning the city. But despite the weather, the crowd that braved it was determined to celebrate.

The parade was more than four miles long and consisted of over 500 vehicles from the navy, the RAF, British Civilian Services and the army. This was followed by a marching column of 20,000 troops and eighteen marching bands, which went from Marble Arch to Whitehall then along the Mall and up to Hyde Park Corner. The marching column was headed by the flags of the Allies, each with a guard of honour (apart, controversially, from Poland). Next came units representing the services of the British Empire and these were followed by units from all the British services. It took forty-five minutes for the whole marching column to pass any given point. The pageant, a spectacle 'never surpassed in Britain' marched in front of the royal family who stood for an hour and forty-eight minutes – much of it in the pouring rain – on the saluting base in the Mall, honouring the procession. Finally, 'under a weeping sky' came 'the most enthralling spectacle of all', as 307 RAF and Royal Navy planes roared over Trafalgar Square. This was followed by dancing, community singing, orchestral concerts and Punch and Judy shows in the various parks of central London as well as a free performance of *As You Like It* at the Regent's Park Open-Air Theatre. As one newspaper reporter observed, 'this beats everything – the coronation, the Jubilee and any of the cup finals'. At sunset, after years of blackout, the iconic buildings of London were lit by floodlights for the first time – the Houses of Parliament, Buckingham Palace, the National Gallery, St James's Palace, the Tower of London, Westminster Abbey, Horse Guards' Parade, Nelson's Column, the War Office and, most poignantly of all, St Paul's Cathedral – still standing indomitably, but surrounded by the devastation wreaked by the Blitz of 1940–41. Despite the sense of celebration, it was clear that recent wounds were barely healed.

The royal family appeared on the balcony at Buckingham Palace before travelling to Chelsea where the King and Queen embarked on the royal barge, accompanied by the young princesses, Elizabeth and Margaret Rose. The barge proceeded down the Thames to Westminster, with crowds packed on both banks of the river, as well as on the six bridges left open to the public that day. Ticker tape was dropped from Westminster Bridge as the King disembarked at the Houses of Parliament.

> Perhaps the most impressive moment in a day of memories came when, after the King had landed, the packed crowds thronging the bridges, streets, windows and roofs high above the river joined in singing 'God Save The King' to music relayed over 500 speakers.

The festivities continued at 11 p.m. with a firework display over central London, concentrated on the Thames. Fireworks and coloured water displays were accompanied by cascades of fire from temporary bridges across the river and bonfires burned along the Mall. The *News of the World* noted that 'in visual effect it was the Blitz all over again and floodlit buildings gave the impression of the aftermath of an enemy incendiary raid'.[6] Traffic came to a standstill and motorists and pedestrians 'talked to each other freely as they waited to move on'. After a year of peace, the whole event was a reminder of the spirit and camaraderie that had helped the nation through six arduous years of war. A second RAF fly-past at 11.15 p.m. helped reinforce this feeling. Responding to the still enormous crowds outside Buckingham Palace, the royal family made a final appearance on the balcony at 12.25 a.m. before retiring to bed, though parties continued across the city well into the night.

The colour newsreel that recorded the celebrations for posterity ended with images of the fireworks on the Thames – the 'most brilliant firework display in London's history', accompanied by strains of 'Land of Hope and Glory'. Stanley Maxted, the distinguished Canadian war correspondent, brought his feelings about the day to a suitably patriotic close, echoing one of Churchill's best-remembered wartime speeches:

> And this ends a great day, a day belonging to the little man of the free peoples. Tomorrow, with this day's glory in his heart, he – and the woman beside him – will return to the business of carving out the future of the nation. While behind him in his memory will rest this Victory Day to which he passed through his finest hour.[7]

Despite some grumbling ('We haven't got much to celebrate about'; 'People have had enough of it'),[8] 'V' Day was a great success, but it was a momentary highlight of celebration in what was to be a year of great anxiety and privation for the majority of the population. Britain was exhausted, bankrupt and bereft of basic commodities, not the least of these being food. The housing shortage had reached crisis point. During the war years, 116,000 houses had been destroyed across Greater London. Another 1,300,000 were in need of repair. Bombed-out families had nowhere to live and returning servicemen were exacerbating the problem. Building materials were scarce and many skilled tradesmen were yet to be demobilized. Desperate families became illegal squatters in empty houses and offices in Mayfair and Piccadilly, many of them garnering popular support from the general public. Just a few days after 'V' Day, on 19 June, Tom Williams, the Minister for Agriculture, observed that Britain faced 'a grim and melancholy situation' that was 'worse than the hardest days of the war'.[9]

In 1939, 70 per cent of Britain's food had been imported – including 50 per cent of meat and 70 per cent of cereals and fats. One of the main strategies of the Axis powers during the war had been to attack imports to Britain, thereby undermining British industry and potentially starving the nation into submission. The government had responded with an immediate programme of rationing in order to equitably feed and clothe the population.[10] Rationing had quickly become a way of life and continued to dominate conversation and headlines throughout the war and well into the next decade, only to fully cease in 1954; the whole period of rationing in Britain lasting fifteen years. Petrol rationing had begun immediately the war broke out and this had been swiftly followed by the rationing of foodstuffs. Bacon, butter and sugar were rationed first, soon followed by meat, tea, jam, biscuits, cereals, cheese, eggs, lard, milk and tinned fruit. Some imported fruits all but vanished – 80 per cent had been imported in 1939 – hence the iconic disappearance of bananas. By 1946 many basic foods and clothing had been rationed for years. Restrictions continued to affect almost every consumer product from basics like sheets and blankets to luxury items like nail varnish and nylons. Books continued to be printed to 'Wartime Economy Standard', with thin paper, narrow margins and cheap bindings. Newspapers were also still restricted, often to four pages – effectively just a single folded sheet. If the general populace had hoped that the end of the war was to bring an end to the misery of rationing, they were bitterly disappointed.

Clothing was rationed on a 'points' system. Initially the allowance had been for approximately one new outfit per year but as the war had progressed, points were reduced to such an extent that the purchase of a coat constituted almost an entire year's ration. By 1946 pre-war wardrobes had been 'cannibalized to destruction' as everybody attempted to 'make do and mend'. All demobilized servicemen, though, were fitted out with a 'demob suit': a complete civilian outfit from cufflinks to shoes. But 'it was strange to walk around a lot of young men your age wearing virtually the same suit', observed one young recently demobbed soldier. The demob suit was simply 'one uniform in exchange for another'.[11] To make matters worse, the quality of these suits was very poor, held in low esteem by the men who had to wear them; variously dismissed as 'foul', 'gaudy' and 'like walking around in a pair of pyjamas'.[12]

The food crisis was not only affecting Britain – it was global. As well as attempting to feed the nation fairly, the government, rather altruistically, was also trying to stave off famine abroad following poor harvests in Europe and Asia. In the summer of 1946, a 15 per cent cut in malting barley for brewers was made. The British public was told that it was being processed into animal feed, but in reality, the bulk of the barley was being sent abroad, 'particularly', noted an indignant *Daily Express*, 'to Germany'. This resulted in a 50 per cent cut in supplies of beer in many pubs and clubs. The situation was exacerbated by a change in British drinking habits. By June 1946, the average man (and now woman) was drinking 25 per cent more beer than they had done before the war started. Beer was cheaper than spirits, which were extremely expensive now that the duty on them was so high. Added to this, men who had generally favoured spirits before the war had changed their drinking habits after spending years in the army, where beer had been the most popular, accessible and affordable tipple for the majority of conscripts. Women were also drinking more beer as drinks like sherry had become expensive or unobtainable during the war years. Harvey's famous Bristol Cream Sherry was still unobtainable in 1946.

Consequently many venues regularly ran out of supplies of beer and had to close intermittently. Pubs in some areas were only able to open for three 'priority' hours a day: lunchtime, after work and for one hour in the evening. A chalked-up sign saying 'Sorry, Closed: No Beer' became a common sight in London to such an extent that the *Daily Express* suggested that beer should come under state control, much as the nationalized Coal Board was to supervise the provision of coal.

But the most emotive issue was the peacetime rationing of bread, which had never been restricted during the war. This was to prove very hard for the general populace, but particularly to housewives, who were already making do with the 'National Loaf' – the smallest and darkest that had been produced since the First World War ('We have stood everything else, but this is the last straw,' one housewife complained to her local newspaper). The issue was fiercely debated in parliament, with Winston Churchill commenting that the prospect of bread rationing was 'one of the gravest announcements I have ever heard in time of peace'. If Britain couldn't supply herself with her own daily bread, what hope was there for her future? When bread was finally rationed to an average 9 oz a day on 21 July 1946, it was front-page news both in

Britain and America. In practice, however, the bread ration proved to be adequate for most families' needs, but as David Kynaston notes in *Austerity Britain*, 'the very fact of peace-time bread rationing would remain a symbolic sore as long as it remained in force'.[13]

As well as adding more stress to the life of the average housewife, scarcity had also given birth to a new sort of crime wave, and it was around this time that the black-market 'spiv' began to emerge as a recognizable type – the opportunistic patter, the wide lapels, the gaudy tie, the pencil moustache. Many perfectly respectable citizens both condemned *and* used the black market. Some organized gangs stole basics – hundreds of thousands of poultry and millions of eggs were illegally traded. Others specialized in the luxury market for cars, furs and jewellery. These crimes were severely dealt with by the courts. One licensee, Gertrude Bryan of Epsom, was fined £1,236 (the cost of a semi-detached house at the time) for charges of receiving clothing coupons and stealing corned beef. Her accomplice, Frederick Gilbert, was sentenced to nine months in prison. The magistrate gave real weight to their sentences:

> When the whole of Europe is tightening its belt we have before us these offences connected with the abuse of ration-ing. It might be that people would go short because of these cases. The whole fair distribution of food might break down if these offences became widespread.[14]

Throughout the summer, the economist John Maynard Keynes attempted to negotiate a grant or financial gift from the United States that might help alleviate Britain's perilous situation (he referred to it later as a 'financial Dunkirk'). But despite his high hopes, all he could arrange was a reluctant loan. The Americans were very loathe to make the loan and the British equally loathe to need it so desperately. Ultimately, the Anglo-American loan of £1.1 billion was finally negotiated on 15 July 1946. It was only paid off sixty years later, in 2006.

Buffeted between severity and celebration, Britain in 1946 was suffused with a mixture of relief and uncertainty, hope and exhaustion. Even the weather, as if to reflect the confusions of the period, was unseasonably changeable. At the end of May, after a transatlantic depression lost its way, Britain was drenched by twenty-eight days of rain while Iceland basked in a typical British summer. The weather that followed in June was a mixture of sunshine and showers, so that nobody was sure whether to prepare themselves with headscarves or sunglasses. An artist and occasional film extra, Margery Gardner, unsure what to expect from day to day, carried both in her handbag: a pair of white sunglasses and a headscarf given to her by a boyfriend who had been in the RAF.

On Midsummer Day, Monday 24 June, the temperature reached 75 degrees in London – the highest of that summer – but was followed by violent thunderstorms. Houses were flooded, crops damaged and roads turned into rivers. In some areas, fields were white with hailstones as big as marbles. It was 'the worst June weather for nearly forty years'.[15]

The summer of 1946 was one of extremes.

CHAPTER TWO

Miss Symonds

15–23 JUNE 1946

Tall and slim, 21-year-old Yvonne Symonds was an attractive brunette, with blue eyes, olive skin and a 'Grecian nose'.[1] She had been demobbed from the WRNS in January 1946 and had since been living with her parents at their family home in a respectable suburb of Worthing, a seaside resort on the south coast.

Yvonne was one of many young women who had joined the services since 1941, when on 18 December the National Service Act had introduced the conscription of women. Every 'mobile' woman in the country between the ages of eighteen and fifty had been conscripted on behalf of the war effort – some to factory work, others to one of the three female services: the ATS (Auxiliary Territorial Service), the WAAF (Women's Auxiliary Air Force) and the WRNS

(Women's Royal Naval Service). As it became clear that the idea of merely volunteering for war work or to join the services would soon be abandoned, many women had joined up quickly before decisions were made for them. At the time, few women had any idea what the different services had to offer and for many the decision was made lightly – some going on instinct while others went for the uniform that appealed the most. Christian Oldham, the convent-educated daughter of an admiral, joined the WRNS in 1940 and was very taken with the 'flattering double-breasted jacket, svelte skirt and pert tricorne hat' that made up a Wren officer's uniform.[2] In 1942, Queen Elizabeth gave the royal blessing to the distinctive Wren hats. She had tried one in front of one of the mirrors at Buckingham Palace and declared that 'the children loved it!'[3] Certainly the WRNS was thought to be the most fashionable of the services,[4] the uniform having been designed by the couturier Molyneux, who had created Gertrude Lawrence's costumes for the original production of *Private Lives* in 1930 and the wedding dress of Princess Marina of Greece in 1934. In 1939 there had been only 3,000 serving WRNS personnel; by 1944 the number had reached a peak of 74,620.[5]

In the early part of the war, Wrens had only been allocated to five categories covering office or domestic work, but by the time Yvonne had joined the service, women were working in twenty-five categories covering a broad range of roles from mechanics to boat crew, from signallers to 'torpedomen'.[6] She had joined the WRNS at the age of eighteen in 1943 and had been stationed at various stone frigates – land-based naval depots – including HMS *Shrapnel*, which was actually the Great Western Hotel in Southampton, and HMS *Grasshopper*, which was the naval name for Weymouth Harbour where combined operations were focused on Operation Neptune, the D-Day landings. Yvonne had also

worked in Portsmouth on HMS *Marshal Soult*, a disarmed
World War One warship that was used as a depot ship to
supply clothing and food stores to the ships that were to take
part in the invasion of Normandy.

On Saturday 15 June, Yvonne attended a WRNS reunion
dinner dance at a pub in Chelsea. She'd arranged to stay
overnight at the Overseas Club just behind the Ritz in St
James's so she wouldn't have to travel back to Worthing late
on the Saturday night. Whilst at the reunion, Yvonne was
struck by a tall, tanned, handsome man – blond, well-built,
with eyes a peculiar shining blue. From his uniform she
could see that he was a decorated officer in the South African
Air Force. He had a plain gold ring on the little finger of his
left hand and also wore a gold watch with a leather strap. He
was extremely attractive, good company and full of stories
about his wartime exploits. There was the occasion when he
flew a plane under a bridge – much to the chagrin of his
commanding officer – and the time he baled out of a burning bomber over Holland – hence the caterpillar badge that
he wore proudly on his lapel. These were worn exclusively
by members of the Caterpillar Club – flyers who had baled
out of their aircraft and survived. Referring to the silk from
which parachutes were made, the club's motto was 'Life
depends on a silken thread': fragile, precious and fraught
with danger. Handsome, heroic and charming, the airman
fascinated Yvonne. He introduced himself as Lieutenant
Colonel 'Jimmy' Heath.[7]

Yvonne was not alone in succumbing to the glamour and
romance of air force flyers like Heath. Many observers of the
period noted the particular effect that airmen's uniforms had
on women. Joan Wyndham, who left a bohemian background in Chelsea to join the WAAF, recalls a dance she
attended shortly after joining the service. Hopeful of romance
with a glamorous young airman, she was distressed to find no

pilots present and that she would have to make do with 'pint-sized Romeos' and other 'wingless wonders'. An airman's wings were a badge of heroism and the uniform had a particular sexual allure ('I can't describe the effect wings have on a WAAF!').[8] In *The Naked Civil Servant*, Quentin Crisp makes a keen distinction between the sort of servicemen his gay friends fancied (young, lower-ranking sailors) and those his female friends were attracted to: '[Women] prefer airmen, by which they always mean the higher ranks.'[9] Romantic novels of the period were keen to exploit the iconography of these new 'Knights of the Air' in titles such as *Flying Wild*, *A Flying Visit*, *Winged Love*, *Air Force Girl* and *Wellington Wendy*.[10] One airman, William Simpson, summed up the appeal of his uniform to women; in a nutshell, it was 'redolent of glamour and courage'.[11]

Having charmed Yvonne with his wartime tales, Heath suggested that she join him at the Panama Club in South Kensington, where he was a member. They'd be able to have an after-hours drink. For a guileless young woman like Yvonne, this must have seemed to be the epitome of metropolitan sophistication. The Panama Club was only a short taxi ride away from Chelsea, situated near the Natural History Museum and just round the corner from South Kensington underground station. The club had been set up here at 23-24 Cromwell Place in August 1945 after its former premises had been destroyed by enemy action. Open from 3 p.m. to midnight, the club provided drinks, food and entertainment for members only. After drinking in public houses, many non-members tried to get into the club when the pubs closed, so the staff, led by receptionist Solomon Joseph, supervised admission to the club very strictly. He had been in trouble with the law before for licensing and betting offences and was determined not to have any more brushes with the police.[12]

At the reception area of the club, Heath signed himself in

with Yvonne as his guest on the yellow visitors' form. Solomon Joseph unbolted the door and ushered them into the club. For Yvonne this was an adventure into a glamorous night-time society, escorted by the most dashing of men – a world away from the cosseted life she lived with her parents in Worthing. Heath led her through the reception area and up the short flight of stairs to the first floor where there was a small bar. They carried on up to the club room on the second floor.

The club room at the Panama was partitioned into two sections – the area to the right was a dining room about 16 feet wide and 37 feet long with a dozen tables lining the longer walls, with sofas behind them and some small chairs. At the far end of the room was an area for the band, which played every night from 8 p.m. The dance floor dominated the centre of the room and was in full swing when Heath and Yvonne arrived.[13] The Perry Como hits 'Surrender' and 'Prisoner of Love', The Ink Spots' 'To Each His Own' and Margaret Whiting's version of the old Al Bowlly classic 'Guilty' were all popular tunes with dance bands that summer.

The left-hand section of the second floor was a lounge and bar where members had drinks served to them by two wait-resses, Joyce and Phyllis, who had worked there since the club had moved premises. It was in the club room while the band played dance music that Heath first suggested that Yvonne should sleep with him that night. Yvonne, despite her time in the WRNS, was a polite and well-brought-up young woman. She was also a virgin. She refused. After their evening together, Heath hailed a taxi and dropped Yvonne off at the Overseas Club in Park Place. He took her rejection of his advances with good grace. So she had no concerns about arranging to meet him again the next day. He seemed the perfect gentleman.

On Sunday morning, Heath rang Yvonne at the Overseas Club and suggested that they spend the day together. Yvonne met Heath at the club dressed in a blue and white print dress with a full-length light summer coat.[14] They took a taxi to Knightsbridge to one of Heath's regular haunts, the Nag's Head, a mews pub in Kinnerton Street, where they stayed until about 2.30 p.m. From there they went for tea to an hotel, most probably the Normandie, another favourite haunt of Heath's, which overlooked Knightsbridge Green. At tea, he again pressurized Yvonne to sleep with him, 'over-persuading' her. As was clear from many of his relations with women, Heath was deeply charismatic, very convincing and had a winning way with words. He was confident in his looks and took great care with his appearance. He was very aware of the seductive power of both his uniform and his tales of wartime heroism, and extremely confident in his physical allure. After the trial, an officer friend of Heath's who had known him a number of years stated that 'women were fascinated by him. Such was his magnetism that it was invariably embarrassing to be in his company when the girls were about'.[15]

Yvonne, trusting, inexperienced and swept along with the force of this apparently whirlwind romance, was conflicted. She was hugely attracted to this handsome, charming man. He told her that he loved her; why didn't they get married? If they were 'unofficially engaged', surely that would make it acceptable for them to sleep with each other? With wartime brief encounters still very recent history, there was nothing unusual in the swift trajectory of this courtship. The war had encouraged young people particularly to live for the moment and, as Virginia Nicholson observes in *Millions Like Us*, her study of women's lives in the 1940s, 'sex was a way to challenge extinction'.[16] This sense of impetuous desire with little-known bedfellows continued into the early post-war period and Heath was expert at exploiting it.

There's a sense too that he was well aware that women's attitude to sex had evolved since the 1930s. Since the outbreak of war, more women were having sex before marriage – or with men other than their husbands – more women were using contraceptives and more were contracting sexually transmitted diseases. The diarist Joan Wyndham confessed to the intimacy of her journal that she was aware at the time she was writing that pre-war mores were breaking down: 'Inside me I could feel every moral code I had ever believed in since childhood begin to crumble away.'[17]

For Yvonne, the speed and illicit nature of her romance with Heath intensified the experience, like one of the films she'd seen at the pictures. And here she was, living it herself – two young people desperately in love, wanting to be together. Now that marriage had been proposed, the engagement felt tangible; Yvonne agreed to sleep with him.

The couple took a taxi to Victoria to pick up Heath's luggage and then on to the Overseas Club to pick up Yvonne's small, cream overnight bag. Around 7 p.m., Heath telephoned ahead to an hotel he knew in Notting Hill to tell the manageress that they were coming. He told her that he was calling from a telephone box at Euston. Half an hour later, they arrived at the Pembridge Court Hotel, just off Notting Hill Gate.[18]

The Pembridge Court was a private hotel known for its 'good class clientele'. Elizabeth Wyatt ran the business with her husband Henry and her daughter-in-law, Alice. It was a typical mid-nineteenth-century double-fronted, stuccoed building with a pillared front porch entrance. It stood (as it still does) on Pembridge Gardens, nestled just off the south-west corner of Pembridge Square. It consisted of a ground, first and second floors with a basement beneath. On the first floor were three bedrooms, numbers 1, 3 and 4, as well as two private rooms. On the second floor were bedrooms 5 to

10 and a bathroom. On the intermediate landing between the two floors were a communal bathroom and lavatory.

Yvonne followed Heath through the outside gate and up the five stone steps to the entrance hall. He signed the register as Lieutenant Colonel and Mrs N. G. C. Heath of Black Hill Cottages, Romsey. Mrs Wyatt asked Heath how long they would want the room for? He said that he would like to book it for three or four nights, possibly five. He told her that he had stayed at the hotel a couple of years earlier when he was in the South African Air Force. Mrs Wyatt felt sure that she recognized him and that he had been a guest at the hotel on a couple of previous occasions.

Lieutenant Colonel Heath was offered Room 4 on the first floor. He was given a key to the room and another to open the front door, which was locked at 10 p.m. every night. Mrs Wyatt accompanied the couple up the stairs to show them their room. This was situated at the back of the building, at the top of the flight of stairs. The room was typical of the price range and period – 19 feet by 15 feet with a window overlooking the back garden. Opening the door, the wardrobe was against the left-hand wall. Behind the door, to the right, were twin beds, a couple of feet apart. On the wall opposite the foot of the beds was a fireplace with a gas fire and a small gas ring. The gas fire was to prove crucial later on. As there was no open fire in the grate, there was no necessity for a poker. Mrs Wyatt later confirmed that there had never been a poker in the room.

Between the fireplace and the foot of the beds were two armchairs, positioned side-on to the fireplace, facing into the centre of the room. To the left of the chimneybreast was a chest of drawers and to the right a dressing table at an angle. Another table sat beneath the window in the right-hand wall. To the right of the window, in the corner, was a washbasin. After explaining about breakfast and guiding them through the facilities, Mrs Wyatt left Heath and his 'wife' to settle in.

That night, in Room 4 of the Pembridge Court Hotel, Yvonne surrendered her virginity to Heath. They had intercourse twice, which brought about some bloodstaining on the sheets of the bed nearest the door. Throughout their night together, according to her testimony, Heath was very gentle with Yvonne and treated her with nothing but kindness and sensitivity.

The next morning, Monday 17 June, Mrs Wyatt sent Rhoda Spooner, the hotel waitress, up to Room 4 with tea and toast. Rhoda didn't usually serve meals in any of the guest rooms, but Mrs Wyatt had made an exception for the charming lieutenant colonel and his pretty young wife. When Rhoda entered the room with the tea, Heath and Yvonne were both in the bed nearest to the door. Rhoda went to open the curtains and left the tea tray. She noticed Heath's large brown suitcase on the table near the window and a flying helmet with large goggles hanging on one of the chairs. At about 11 a.m. that morning, there was a knock on the door from Barbara Osborne, the chambermaid.[19] Barbara generally cleaned and changed the beds between guest occupancies. By now, Yvonne was standing by the chest of drawers in her sky-blue dressing gown. Heath was sitting up in the bed nearest the window, wearing his red dressing gown.

'Will you be long?' asked Barbara, 'I'm keen to get on with my work.'

'I was just going to get up and come back later,' said Heath.

He suggested to Yvonne that she should stay with him at the hotel for another day or two, but she'd promised her parents that she would return to Worthing that day. They had sex again that afternoon, then Heath saw her off on the 9.28 p.m. train from Victoria to Worthing. He promised to phone her and that he would come and see her later in the week. Yvonne gave Heath her address in Warren Road and her telephone number, Swandean 906.

Yvonne arrived home that evening after 11 p.m., full of her romantic weekend with her handsome pilot. She was engaged to Jimmy and couldn't wait for her parents to meet him. He had said that he was coming down to Worthing that week anyway to attend the opening of the Shoreham Airport that was re-opening the following weekend. As he had promised, Heath telephoned Yvonne on the Tuesday, the Wednesday and then again on Thursday 20 June, like any ordinary, infatuated boyfriend who couldn't keep himself from chatting to his fiancée every day. Such excitement had rarely intruded into Yvonne's life before whilst growing up in one of the most archetypal of English seaside resorts.

In an age before foreign travel, Worthing was a hugely popular – if polite – holiday destination with none of the excesses and vulgarity of Blackpool, Margate or the 'somewhat overgrown' Brighton.[20] The town styled itself very much as a middle-class resort. Only eighty-six minutes from Victoria by the electric train, it was also popular with businessmen who worked in the City of London and commuted home at night. Increasingly Worthing had promoted itself as a winter resort and it appealed – as it still does today – to an older clientele of the well-heeled retired. The *Ward Lock Guide* of the time observed that:

> [...] perhaps the best evidence of a genial all-the-year climate is the large number of residences built in recent years at West Worthing and elsewhere in the borough by Anglo-Indians and others to whom sunshine is almost a necessity.[21]

In 1941 the threatened German invasion ('Operation Sealion') had seen a dramatic transformation along the beaches of the south coast from Lyme Regis in the west to Ramsgate in the east. Barbed wire and landmines took the place of buckets and spades as coastal defence had become a priority – especially during 1940–42 when the invasion of Britain seemed imminent. Consequently Worthing's famous pier, one of the principle attractions of the resort that had stood since 1862, was partially demolished and closed in 1940. Six years on, it remained a prominent and silent scar at the centre of the town.

At Whitsuntide of 1946, the weekend of 'V' Day, the local council had hoped that they could draw holidaymakers back to the resort, but a planned Victory parade through the town had been aborted due to lack of interest. As a focus to reinvigorate the tourist trade, the council had organized the reopening of the pavilion and bandstand on the parade. The opening was hugely anticipated as a matter of local pride. But despite their best-laid plans, the opening was, literally, a wash-out, cursed like the rest of that summer by bad weather. The *Worthing Herald* reported that 'June 1946 was the DULLEST for twenty-three years; the COLDEST for eighteen years; the WETTEST for thirteen years'.[22]

Inside from the pelting rain, Worthing's repertory company offered a weekly changing programme at the Connaught Theatre. That week the Overture Repertory Players presented *Fear Walks Behind* by Sydney Horler and Norman Lee. The town's four cinemas were packed. With such terrible weather and television still a novelty, 1946 was the peak of cinema attendance in Britain with some 1.6 billion attendances – 3 million cinema-goers a day. The cinema offerings at Worthing that summer were a mixture of long-forgotten titles and the occasional classic, the majority from Hollywood. The Rivoli played *She Wouldn't Say Yes* and *Cornered*. At the Odeon, Alan Ladd and Veronica Lake starred in *The Blue Dahlia*. Lana Turner smouldered in a risqué two-piece swimsuit in the screen version of James M. Cain's amoral murder story, *The Postman Always Rings Twice* and Ingrid Bergman

suffered beautifully in *Spellbound*, the poster asking boldly,
'Will he kiss me or kill me?'[23]

On Friday 21 June, Yvonne was surprised but delighted
when Jimmy telephoned her at about midday, telling her
that he was actually in Worthing and couldn't wait to see
her. Yvonne quickly changed into her most flattering green
dress and met Heath in the centre of town. When they met,
he told her that he was planning to stay for about ten days
so that he could see more of her and meet her parents. He
was smartly dressed, out of uniform this time in a grey pin-
striped suit, collar and tie, but no hat. He'd left his luggage
at the railway station until he'd decided on a place to stay.
But finding an hotel at the start of the most anticipated
holiday season since the beginning of the war would be no
easy feat.

That weekend, Worthing was to be overrun with holidaymakers, many taking their first holiday since 1939.
Two thirds of the population were to take a holiday that
summer and the south-coast seaside resorts braced themselves for the enormous demand. Trains, stations, hotels
and boarding houses were packed with thousands of
people. Mile-long queues formed at daybreak at London
stations when the railways handled the biggest crowds they
had seen for years. Some luggage-laden travellers waited
throughout the night to catch early trains. At Paddington
a 'crocodile' of people wound its way into the side streets
as there was no more standing space in the station itself.
Everybody, it seems, was in holiday mood and aiming for
the seaside.

Yvonne and Heath had lunch and with her local knowledge she advised him about places to stay. In Heath's *Daily
Telegraph* for that day there was a prominent advertisement
for the Ocean Hotel, right on the seafront.

WORTHING OCEAN HOTEL
'A Sun Trap on the Sea Front'
Unrivalled Position.
45 Bedrooms ~ World-famous Cuisine
Completely Redecorated ~ Central Heating
Dancing to Bob Crowder and his band.[24]

That afternoon, Heath and Yvonne called at the hotel on Marine Parade, opposite the beach. At the reception, the couple met George Girdwood, the hotel manager. Heath said that he was looking for accommodation for himself for the next ten days.[25] The hotel being full at the time, Girdwood suggested that Heath could be accommodated for a couple of days in the hotel annexe, round the corner at 11 West Buildings, after which they could accommodate him in the main hotel. Heath readily agreed to this. He said his name was Lieutenant Colonel Heath and signed the register accordingly. He gave his address – this time – as South Africa House in Trafalgar Square and his nationality as South African, but Yvonne didn't seem to notice. She and her new fiancé then left together to pick up his luggage from Worthing Railway Station. They returned to the hotel shortly afterwards with one of Heath's large brown suitcases. He went alone to the annexe to his room, but then returned to have tea with Yvonne in the hotel lounge.

At this point, Heath asked Yvonne what time the evening papers came from London. She told him that they were already out, so he bought two. Throughout tea he glanced through the pages of the newspapers and was reading them intently. Yvonne remarked to him about this, but he didn't reply. After he had finished with the papers, Yvonne flicked through them herself, but saw nothing to interest her. She thought that Heath was rather quiet and that something might be worrying him. Was it something she'd done? Or said? Perhaps he was cooling towards her? Now that she had allowed him to sleep with her, perhaps he had lost interest? But Yvonne kept her insecurities to herself. Whatever Heath's feelings, he too was unwilling to give voice to them. He said he would be all right tomorrow, and that he had been 'up all Thursday night'. He then jokingly mentioned some shirts that needed washing. Yvonne, eager to please her new lover, was only too happy to say that she'd wash them through for him at home and would collect them from him later. After tea, they went out together, but returned to the hotel for dinner at about 7 p.m. They were not seen together again that night, but they could easily have gone back directly to the hotel annexe without being seen. They certainly had sex again at the hotel and this may well be the occasion on which it occurred.

The next day was Saturday 22 June. Before she left her parents' house, Yvonne washed the shirts that she had taken from Heath the night before. As she was washing them, she noticed that one of the shirts had a number of small brown stains on the tail, but she wasn't quite sure what they were. Once washed, she put them out to dry, intending to iron them the next day. She then headed into Worthing to meet her fiancé.

At about 12.15 p.m., Heath and Yvonne went to the Ship Hotel in South Street, which was a quirky character pub modelled on an old galleon.[26] Again, Heath was wearing his 'civvies'. He was delighted to bump into an old friend, Angus Bruce, and introduced him to Yvonne. Bruce was drinking there with his friend, Dick Hollis, and the foursome had a drink together. Bruce asked what his friend was doing in Worthing?[27] Heath told him that he was staying ten days at the Ocean Hotel. He'd been demobbed and was about to start a business buying planes in England to sell abroad.

Bruce had known Heath for about two years. He had been

manager of the South Western Hotel in Wimbledon where Heath had been a regular. They'd once had a night out on the town drinking at Oddenino's and the Haymarket Club in Shaftesbury Avenue. But at that time, which wasn't too long ago, Heath had been known as 'Captain Armstrong' of the South African Air Force. Heath explained that he had been demobbed with the rank of lieutenant colonel and had received a letter of pardon from the King for a previous indiscretion in the RAF. He was no longer known as 'Armstrong' but as 'Heath'. This must have elicited some curiosity from Yvonne, who was witness to the conversation, but, as Jimmy had explained, he'd had a letter of pardon and besides, it was all in the past now.

Before they left the Ship, to celebrate their engagement, Bruce invited Heath and Yvonne to be his guests that evening to a dinner dance that was being held at the Blue Peter Club. The club was owned by his drinking companion Dick Hollis, who was Bruce's boss, as he was now working there as catering manager. The club was in Angmering-on-Sea near Littlehampton, just a short drive from Worthing. The young couple said they'd be delighted.

Yvonne and Heath went back to eat at the Ocean Hotel. Over lunch, he wondered if Yvonne had heard anything about an incident that had taken place in the hotel they had stayed in the previous Sunday? Yvonne had heard nothing about it, but was curious to hear more. Heath went on. A woman, he said, had been killed – murdered – there during the week. But before Yvonne could ask any more, Heath reminded her that they had an appointment to get to. They were to meet her parents at Worthing Golf Club, just near the Symonds' family home. He said that he would tell her all about the murder later on.

Arriving at the golf club, 'Jimmy' Heath was introduced to his future parents-in-law, John and Gertrude.[28] John Charters

Symonds (always known as Jack) was a civil engineer and had
been a major in the RASC during the First World War.
Either during or just after the end of the war, he had met and
married Gertrude Werther in Belgium before bringing her
back with him to England.[29] Yvonne, their only child, had
been born in 1925.

Heath explained that he was South African, though educated
in England. Whilst at Cambridge, he had joined the University
Flying Club, from which he obtained a commission in the
South African Air Force. He told Major Symonds about his
wartime experiences with the SAAF where he had seen active
service in North Africa and El Alamein. He also claimed to be
related to Lady Heath, the Irish aviatrix, who had been one of
the most famous women in the world during the 1920s. Flying,
Heath explained, was something of a family obsession – both
his parents also being flyers themselves. His present job was
buying and selling aircraft and he proposed to continue in this
line for the next five years after which his father wanted him to
give up flying and return to South Africa to join the family
stockbroking business. The meeting went very well, with
Heath expounding on life in South Africa and his time during
the war. Finally, Major Symonds delightedly accepted Heath's
suit for his daughter's hand in marriage.

Now properly engaged, the young couple left the golf
club at about 1.30 p.m. to spend the afternoon together.
Yvonne returned to her parents' house at 6 p.m. to change
for dinner. At 7 p.m., Heath arrived to take them to the
dinner dance at Angmering. While Yvonne finished dressing, Major Symonds chatted with Heath downstairs. A
military man himself, he noted that Heath was in British
khaki battledress with a lieutenant colonel's insignia with
two rows of decorations, led by the DFC and Bar. He also
wore pilot's wings and had red ribbons on his epaulettes,
denoting the SAAF.

Yvonne was finally ready, a taxi was ordered and the smart young couple were driven off to Angmering. To Jack and Gertrude Symonds, Yvonne's fiancé seemed the ideal son-in-law – an educated gentleman; charming, well connected and a war hero to boot.

The Blue Peter Club was situated right on the pebble beach at Angmering, twenty minutes' drive from Worthing.[30] Heath and Yvonne arrived at about 8.15 p.m. The day had gone well and Yvonne's parents had been impressed with her new beau. But one thing had been troubling Yvonne ever since Jimmy had mentioned it – the story of the murder at the Pembridge Court Hotel. At dinner, she took the opportunity to remind him that he was going to tell her about it. As the band played on in the background, Jimmy seemed only too keen to tell her everything, in all its shocking, graphic detail.

'Jimmy, you were going to tell me about the murder? At the hotel?' said Yvonne.[31]

'Yes. So I was. Well, after you left for Worthing on Monday, I stayed on at the Pembridge Court. On Thursday, I was at an hotel with a journalist friend and we got into conversation with a couple near us, so we all had a drink together. The girl was pretty well known as a prostitute. The man said he wanted to spend the night with her, but had nowhere to take her. So I said, why don't you use my room?'

For the young girl from Worthing, this tale of Heath offering up his hotel room (indeed *their* hotel room where they had spent such a romantic weekend) for an acquaintance to spend the night with a prostitute must have seemed distasteful enough – certainly outside Yvonne's experience. But having only recently lost her virginity to her fiancé, maybe this was another rite of passage, a swift education in the ways of the adult world where things were different and which she felt too inexperienced to question.

'What about the landlady?' she asked.

'I told her that if anyone called for me, they could contact me in Hendon where I was going to stay the night. So I gave my room key to the man – in front of my reporter chum.'

'I see,' said Yvonne.

'The next day,' Heath continued, 'on Friday morning, I was at Hendon and had a telephone call from an Inspector Barratt of the Metropolitan Police.[32] He said he wanted to talk to me as soon as possible, so he'd send a car to bring me back to the hotel. He was keen to establish that I hadn't slept in my hotel room, as a murder had been committed there. And he wanted me to identify the body. Obviously this was the woman I'd met in company with my friend the night before. So Barratt took me to Room 4 at the Pembridge Court.'

'And?'

'I saw the body of the woman. It was a gruesome sight. She'd been tied by her legs and thighs. Her body was very bruised. I've never seen so much blood in my life.'

'What had happened to her?'

'Inspector Barratt said that a poker had been stuck up her. That it was the poker that killed her. I'm not so sure. I think it's more likely that she'd been suffocated. He asked me to stay in town so that I could assist in trying to identify the man I gave the key to.'

'Who would do such a terrible thing?'

'It can only have been done by a sexual maniac.'

'Yes.'

'And, of course, you know it wasn't me.'

Here was Yvonne's fiancé, sitting before her and telling her the truth. Of course it couldn't have been him.

'No.'

'I've treated you kindly whenever we've been alone together, haven't I?'

Whatever she felt about this extraordinary tale, Yvonne said nothing. Jimmy bumped into some RAF friends and as the evening wore on, it receded in her mind. She and Heath met Angus Bruce again, as he was working that night at the club. Heath wondered if they might pop in once more in the morning and Bruce said he'd be delighted to see them. The couple stayed at the club until midnight and Yvonne clearly felt safe enough with Heath to share a taxi with him to her parents' house in Warren Road, where he dropped her off before going on to his hotel. It was the end of an eventful engagement day that Yvonne would never forget.

Back at home, Yvonne began to puzzle over the shocking story that Jimmy had told her. The more she turned it over in her mind, the more questions it raised. Jimmy had said at some point that he knew the woman had no money, but didn't say how he knew this. He didn't once mention the name of the mysterious man he had lent his key to and that the police were now looking for, nor the name of the woman who had been killed. And who was the journalist who had witnessed the transaction? Crucially, why had Jimmy come to Worthing? Hadn't the police specifically asked him to stay in London?

The next morning – Sunday – Yvonne woke early and started ironing the shirts that Jimmy had asked her to launder, ready to return to him later in the day. Then, a weekly ritual: the Sunday newspapers arrived before breakfast. Glancing at the headlines, Yvonne's parents were stunned; her fiancé was front-page news.

6ft MAN SOUGHT IN HOTEL CRIME

Scotland Yard detectives seeking a clue to the murder of Mrs. Margery Gardner, 33-year-old film extra, in an hotel in

Pembridge Gardens, Notting Hill issued a description yesterday of a man they wish to interview. They appealed to anyone who sees a man answering this description to go at once to a police station. The man is described as Neville George Clevely Heath, aged 29.

He is 5 feet 11½ inches tall of medium build, fresh complexion, fair hair and eyebrows, blue eyes, broad nose, firm chin, square face with good teeth and he is probably wearing a double-breasted light grey suit with a thin stripe and a cream-coloured shirt with collar attached or a check sports jacket, flannel trousers, dark brown trilby and dark brown suede shoes. He walks with a military gait and is known to frequent good-class hotels and guest-houses.

Mrs. Gardner's unclothed, bruised body was found in a first floor bedroom of the hotel on Friday afternoon with her legs and ankles bound. She is believed to have been suffocated.[33]

Major and Mrs Symonds were stunned. But when they showed her the paper, Yvonne did not seem at all surprised. She told her parents all about the conversation she had had with her fiancé the night before, outlining the details of the murder in Notting Hill. Yvonne's father told her that she should telephone Jimmy at once. At 9.30 a.m., Yvonne phoned the Ocean Hotel, but was told by the receptionist that Jimmy couldn't reply as he was sleeping in the annexe. Yvonne left her parents' telephone number – even though she knew he had it – and a message for him to call her urgently on Swandean 906.[34]

Twenty minutes later, Heath telephoned her. Yvonne explained that she and her parents had read the newspapers and that they were very worried. 'Yes,' said Heath with extraordinary understatement, 'I thought they would be.'[35] He told her not to worry. He had a car and was going to drive up to Scotland Yard right away. He would return to Worthing that evening and would ring her later on. Yvonne felt calmer. He was going to sort everything out. It must be some sort of mistake.

All Sunday evening Yvonne waited for a call from Jimmy. But he didn't ring her that evening. She hoped he might ring the next morning; he did not. She was never to speak to him again. The next time she would see him, she would be in the witness box and he would be in the dock in a police court. The story of her whirlwind romance and the intimate details of the loss of her virginity were to be crucial evidence in one of the most sensational murder trials of the century.

That Sunday night, Yvonne was left with her thoughts, stunned by the speed with which her romantic dream had mutated into a nightmare; her heroic pilot seemingly a devil; the fiancé she had fallen for, a sadistic killer. She was learning that the cinema-style romance she had imagined she was living was actually a very different sort of film. Like the picture where Ingrid Bergman seems to be losing her mind or the one where she falls in love with a man she suspects is a murderer ('Will he kiss me or kill me?').

Heath did not drive up to London that Sunday. He left Worthing in a hurry on Monday morning, leaving many of his possessions behind at the Ocean Hotel: his brown suede shoes, copies of the magazines *Flight*, *Aeroplane* and *Men Only*. Amongst the possessions he left were five newspapers: the *Daily Telegraph*, *Daily Mail*, *Daily Herald*, *Daily Mirror* and *Daily Express*. All were dated Saturday 22 June.[36] Clearly, Heath had a very specific interest in the news of that particular day. Each newspaper contained an account of the murder of Margery Gardner and the news that the police were attempting to trace a man 'Wanted for Interview': Neville George Clevely Heath.

After the trial, Yvonne Symonds was thought to be the luckiest girl in England because of her narrow escape. Though Heath may have taken her virginity, he had not taken her life. Margery Gardner had not been so fortunate.

CHAPTER THREE
Mrs Gardner

Mrs. Elizabeth Wheat   24 Bramham Gardens
24 Oakholme Road   S.W.5
Sheffield

16th June 1946

My Darling Mum,
Please excuse this paper, but I seem to have mislaid mine – and am
too late to get any more. Very many thanks for the £3, it has been
terribly acceptable as all this trouble has come back again – and I
have to see Dr Kelly again on Monday.

I get so tired, so quickly that I still have to lie down every
afternoon – but perhaps its just because I'm expecting the 'curse'
this week-end, according to my reckoning – since it started on the
21st. 'Iris Products' have closed temporarily, [because] Charles

has to be away so much but hope to re-open again — however I couldn't go back to their work at present, as I think I tried to explain before, they have no work there which doesn't require standing. I still have hopes of the toys, but have at the moment lost my only contact with the men as the boyfriend[1] has gone away, but in any case don't worry as I shall contact him and write again next week.

The grey suit has cleaned OK except that the skirt is lighter than the coat, it isn't too good. Please send the black and blue dress as soon as possible.

Now must go to catch the post, all my love,

Margy

P.S. I would like very much to go home for a bit, but feel that it would be a mistake, as my nerves have gone to hell.

24 Bramham Gardens
S.W.5

20th June 1946

My Darling Mum,

Many thanks for your letter and enclosure — I'm always kept on tenterhooks until the last minute, in case it doesn't arrive and today was a bit of a close shave. I have just 'phoned Dr Kelly again and hope to see her at the end of the week to get some more of a tonic she gave me which seems to have done me a lot of good.

The boy friend came back on Sunday and is seeing the man about the toys at the end of the week. Unfortunately I can't be there myself. No you don't have to be trained to make these toys apparently — all I would have to do would be to sew the skin together, which sounds very simple. As regards Iris Products there was nothing creative about the work there and even the nursery

[lamp] *shades, which I had looked forward to designing, were done by stencil, which is purely mechanical.*

I may have to go into the hospital again, but I sincerely hope not, because it wouldn't really be much of a rest, as I should be worrying the whole time. If only I had a tiny private income, no matter how small, with which I could buy myself a few necessary clothes and therefore gain confidence in myself, one of the first steps to a good job. Both our minds, I feel sure, would be easier, but as it is we have to make do with things that are really completely worn out, and which even the second hand dress shops wont take. Please send me the blue and black dress before you go away.

The weather here has been appalling, rained day after day but even the plastic macs are £5 upwards and cost 9 coupons.

Will you let me know if this letter is entirely readable or no, but the pen seems to be getting very bad,

All my love,

Margery[2]

Margery Gardner's letter of 20 June was the last communication her mother would have from her daughter. Within twenty-four hours, she would be dead, her body beaten and savaged. She was thirty-two years old.

Married, but estranged from her husband, Margery lived an insecure existence, moving between various bedsits and furnished flats in the Chelsea and Earls Court areas of west London. A middle-class woman by birth, from a distinguished Sheffield family, her life had been destabilized as much by her own ambitions as by the seductive but disorientating opportunities of the war years.

The journey of her life was a movement away from suburban security towards the attractions and dangers of a metropolitan, bohemian world in the midst of war. Though a trained and talented artist, by 1946 she had no regular income and lack of funds was the constant, exhausting issue in her life. She earned a little money from a series of unskilled jobs – turning her hand to anything including the odd session as a film extra. Though she sold some of her artwork to friends and was privately commissioned to paint murals, this never amounted to enough to make ends meet. Her husband provided no maintenance for her or their baby daughter, leaving it to Margery's mother and brother to help her out. This hand-to-mouth existence made Margery very dependent on the goodwill of her friends and the various men she had relationships with. Happy for them to stand her drinks and buy her dinners, she was sometimes similarly happy to sleep with them. She was promiscuous, certainly, but not (as was claimed by Heath after her death) a prostitute. Indeed, Detective Inspector Spooner observed that she was a woman of 'good breeding and education as well as good looks'.[3] A memorable figure on the drinking scene in Chelsea, she was popular and well liked, often seen in the neighbourhood wearing her signature coat – made of ocelot or 'leopardette' – a highly patterned leopardskin fur.

Margery lived a 'bohemian kind of life'[4] amongst a milieu of outsiders: artists, homosexuals (she was friends with Quentin Crisp) and petty criminals. When the war against Fascism had come to an end, the war against crime in London began. In 1946, the Metropolitan Police had 7 million people within its jurisdiction. Thousands of police officers had joined the armed forces; hundreds had been killed or wounded and recruitment had been stopped during hostilities. The Met was 4,000 men below strength – just as a new wave of crime exploded.

Against the depleted ranks of the police force was ranged a new type of criminal – cunning, ruthless and well informed. Many had served in the armed forces, some with distinction, and many more were deserters. They were younger, fitter, harder, more resourceful and more energetic than their pre-war equivalent. Crucially they also operated in a world with a new, post-war morality. Many commodities were scarce or rationed. Cigarettes and liquor carried heavy duties which had increased their prices to four times their pre-war costs. Years of hardship and scarcity had bred a public hungry for the comforting extras of life. Even the most honest citizen couldn't resist the temptation to buy 'something on the side'. The black market was booming and the new style of post-war crook took advantage of it. Housebreaking, robbery, shoplifting, even kidnapping became more common as the police struggled to control increasingly powerful criminal gangs.

In September 1945, Margery was questioned by the police herself. She was riding as one of five passengers in a car driven by a friend she'd known for about two years, Peter Tilley Bailey.[5] Tilley Bailey was a small-time gentleman crook with several convictions for stealing cars and burglary. He had been drinking and had stolen the car, driving eastwards at fifty miles an hour along Knightsbridge on the wrong side of the road, ignoring the traffic lights. The stolen vehicle was recognized by a police patrol car, which soon gave chase. One of the police officers jumped on the running board of the stolen car, but missed his footing and fell off. A member of the public driving a high-powered vehicle then joined in the car chase, ramming Bailey's car but failing to stop him. Tilley Bailey accelerated, but the police car continued to pursue him, following him twice around Hyde Park at great speed. Bailey then abandoned the car at Hyde Park Corner and tried to run away. Shortly afterwards, when he was caught by the police, he said, 'Well, I gave you a good run for it.'[6] Tilley Bailey was arrested and charged at West London Magistrates' Court for dangerous driving and carrying housebreaking implements (these were actually rubber gloves). In his defence, he said that he had been drinking and that it was only a prank. The magistrate, Sir Gervais Rentoul, took a very dim view of the case.

> I cannot conceive anything much worse than the lives and limbs of citizens being at the mercy of a drunken fellow driving round the West End at fifty miles an hour chased by the police.[7]

Tilley Bailey was jailed for six months and disqualified from driving for five years.[8] Margery, claiming she had no idea that the car was stolen, was released without charge. This fringe of small-scale criminality amongst Mayfair crooks and Chelsea opportunists was the world that Margery Gardner inhabited.

Like many of her generation, Margery's short life was bookended by cataclysmic world conflict. She had been born Margery Aimee Brownell Wheat on 21 May 1914, just a month before the assassination of Archduke Ferdinand and his wife plunged the world into the Great War. She was the eldest daughter of John and Elizabeth Wheat, a respectable couple from Sheffield. Her parents had married in 1912 when John Bristowe Wheat had reached the age of fifty-three, claiming that he could not afford to marry until his own father retired from the family business, a venerable firm of solicitors that had been in the family since 1763. His wife, Elizabeth Brownell, was twenty years his junior and also from an old Sheffield family. The couple rented 24 Oakholme Road in Sheffield shortly after their marriage and the family would remain there for the next forty-seven years.

The house remains – now a hall of residence for Sheffield University. It is a spacious semi-detached property built of

local yellow sandstone and sits on a quiet road of similar properties in a leafy suburb of the city near the botanical gardens.
With large rooms, but a small garden, it was a comfortable and
manageable home for the Wheats to bring up their family.
After Margery was born, a boy, Robin, followed in 1915,
then Gilbert in 1916. Two hand-tinted studio photographs
survive of Betty Wheat and her three children, showing a
close and happy family. However, soon after the photograph
was taken, the family was shaken by the loss of young Robin
who died from a constricted bowel before he had reached his
fourth birthday.

Margery attended a local kindergarten in Sheffield, before
going to live with an aunt in Chippenham where she shared
a governess with her cousin.[9] At the age of fifteen, she was
sent to a private school, the Manor House, in Brondesbury,
north-west London, where she stayed until she was eighteen.
Here her interests developed in the arts, which were to
continue throughout her life – singing, acting and painting.
She spent most of her time drawing and was particularly
skilled at drawing horses, but always in motion: battles, bull-
fights and scenes from the Wild West. From an early age,
Margery was impelled by a sense of adventure.

Her drawing abilities led to a Bronze Medal awarded by
the Royal Drawing Society and her headmistress thought the
young Margery precociously talented, 'more than half a
genius'.[10] It was no surprise to her family that, having left
school, Margery wanted to continue her art studies in
London. Her father, however, wouldn't allow her to do so
until she had reached the age of twenty-one, so she returned
to the north and attended the Sheffield School of Art. It was
while studying here that Margery began the first of her ill-
starred relationships with men. According to Mrs Wheat,
Margery fell in love with a man named Moseley whom she
had met in London. But Margery's mother very much

disapproved of the relationship – not thinking it 'a suitable association' – and, in order to affect an end to it, she encouraged Margery to return to London to continue her studies at the Chelsea School of Art.

Mrs Wheat had her way and succeeded in splitting up Moseley and her daughter. But her plans to protect Margery were to have unforeseen and far-reaching consequences. This was 1935 and the 21-year-old Margery Wheat was now a rebellious young woman curious about the world around her. Dark-haired, fashion-conscious and extremely good-looking, she was also as headstrong and single-minded as the horses that she loved to draw. London offered glamour, excitement and freedom, in contrast to the safe but parochial life of her family. Both temperamentally and generationally, Margery was alien to her parents, her father being seventy-five when she was only twenty, very much an eminent Victorian in contrast to his daughter, who was yearning for the new, the extraordinary, the modern.[11]

The temptations and freedoms of metropolitan life enthralled Margery and the idea of London as somewhere to finish her education or pursue a career took second place to her pursuit of adventure. She was distracted from her studies at Chelsea and started socializing with what her mother considered 'undesirable company'. Soon, Mrs Wheat suspected that her daughter's interest in the study of art was little more than a pretext for living an increasingly bohemian life in London. In 1936, she still held sufficient sway with Margery to prevent her making a trip to France with her Chelsea friends, but her influence on her daughter's life was already beginning to wane as Margery established her life – and her independence – in London.

In March 1936, Margery was living in an hotel for single middle-class ladies in South Kensington and was embracing life at the heart of the Chelsea art scene during one of its most

colourful periods. Tutors at Chelsea at the time included
Henry Moore, William Roberts and Ceri Richards. But it
was the social life surrounding the world of Chelsea artists
and students that Margery was most enamoured with. Her
brother Gilbert later commented:

> [It was] the night life of the capital, and the unusual and uncon-
> ventional ways of the Chelsea art world that appealed to her.
> More and more she became involved in a world as far removed
> from the home she had left as it is possible to imagine.[12]

Margery's letters home during this period are a detailed catalogue of gallery visits, exhibition openings, parties, romances,
'very jolly evenings at the flicks'[13] with drinks and debate at
Chelsea's famous Blue Cockatoo restaurant. At one of the
parties she attended in 1936, Margery met 22-year-old Peter
Gardner. He was the son of a brigadier in the regular army
and had been born in Cairo in 1914. Peter's mother had died
of malaria when he was only fourteen and from then on he
proved a troublesome son. He had been expelled from school
and though he trained as an officer at Sandhurst, he had been
dismissed before completing the course in 1933. He was
estranged from his father, who had married again since the
death of his wife and started a new family. In October 1936,
Margery's father died at the age of seventy-eight. Soon after,
she and Peter Gardner became lovers.

With the political crisis in Europe looming, Margery
married Peter at Chelsea Old Church on Cheyne Walk in
the spring of 1939. In their wedding photograph, Margery
and Peter make a stylish couple and according to Margery's
mother, 'she seemed very much in love with him'. But for
Margery the reality of married life with Peter was to prove
frustrating. With him seemingly unable to hold down a regular job ('he tried several jobs but could never keep a position

very long'),[14] the couple moved from rented flat to rented bedsit at various addresses in Chelsea; they never had a secure home of their own. When war was finally declared in September, Gardner took a position with the Air Ministry. Towards the end of 1940, he was called up for service with the RAF as Aircraftsman 1st Class, but never advanced any further, despite his officer-class background and credentials.

Margery accompanied her husband, living with him near each of the RAF camps where he was stationed. When he was based in Blackpool, eager to work, she took an apprentice position at a hairdressing and beauty salon where she had to pay £1 a week 'for the privilege of learning the trade'.[15] It was a far cry from her romantic dream of bohemian, metropolitan life.

In Sheffield too, Mrs Wheat was also facing a difficult war. With Margery now married and Gilbert away fighting in France, she was left alone to face the bombings that targeted the steelworks for which Sheffield was world-famous as well as the armaments factories that had been set up to bolster the war effort. On the 12 and 15 December 1940, Sheffield suffered the hardest night of the Blitz. Opposite Paradise Square, the home of the Wheat family business, the cathedral was damaged and Marples Hotel took a direct hit. Six hundred and eighty people were killed and 1,500 injured. Forty thousand people were made homeless.[16]

Margery and Peter's itinerant married life was soon to feel both internal and external pressure. In the summer of 1941 Margery gave birth prematurely to a stillborn child. But there was little time to mourn. For its size, Chelsea was one of the most heavily blitzed boroughs in London, due to its position on the river, situated close to two power stations and near the centre of government. The worst night of bombing was 16 April 1941 when 450 German bombers attacked south and central London for eight hours. The loss of life and property was considerable. Though the population of Chelsea had dwindled from 58,000 in 1939 to only 16,000 people, 1,000 civilians were killed in the attack, with twice as many seriously injured. Nowhere seemed safe – even the Royal Hospital Infirmary was hit, as were eighteen hospitals and thirteen churches. Chelsea Old Church where Peter and Margery had been married only three years earlier suffered a direct hit, leaving the church a devastated wreck.[17] With the familiar landmarks of London and Chelsea obliterated overnight and the knowledge that home in Sheffield was just as vulnerable to attack, Margery must have been under constant strain. Nothing was secure, nothing was certain and the world around her was in chaos. At the same time, her marriage began to fracture, with Peter revealing himself to be a troubled and needy man – alcoholic and highly strung.

Whilst based with the RAF in Grantham, Peter was hospitalized with a nervous condition. But he still managed to leave hospital every afternoon to go on illicit pub-crawls. Having little money, he began stealing cash from pubs in order to fund his drinking. On 13 October 1941 he stole £10 13s. 11d. from the Red Lion Hotel in Grantham and was duly arrested and charged. When he appeared before Grantham Quarter Sessions on 15 January 1942, he pleaded guilty to a string of offences. The recorder at Grantham thought the case 'a very painful one':

> I have a duty to the public to perform. If you go to prison you will be looked after by the doctor and, if necessary, be treated for your mental weakness, and perhaps your moral weakness, but your long list of serious offences are such that I cannot overlook them. You have been cunning enough at any rate to go on what you call 'pub-crawls' and steal money and commit other larcenies. You have mentality enough for that.[18]

He went on to say that he felt that Gardner was a danger to himself and others and was amazed that a man with his mental-health issues should have been allowed to join the RAF. He was sentenced to two years' hard labour, 'such as [he] could perform'.[19] Hearing the sentence, Margery left the court in tears. She returned home to stay with her mother in Sheffield, where she worked for a time in a factory making parts for aeroplanes. But relations between Margery and her family were strained at this point with regard to Peter; she was still keen to support her husband but her brother Gilbert was very critical of him. After only six months, she decided that she would return to London, find herself a job and fix up a home for Peter on his release from prison. She would need to help him find a job as well, as he had also been discharged from the RAF after his conviction.

But the return to London was not the success that either Margery – or her mother – had hoped for. As she had promised, Margery provided a home for Peter when he was discharged from prison, but after staying with him for several months, she returned to Sheffield again – and this time her feelings towards him seem to have changed. According to her mother, she claimed that he was 'mad and that he had maltreated her and had behaved dreadfully'.[20] Despite this, she returned to him a couple of weeks later. The relationship was by now dysfunctional, with both parties changeable, inconsistent and unreliable.

Margery found herself pregnant again in 1943 and perhaps she felt that this might be the opportunity for a fresh start. She gave birth at St Mary Abbot's hospital in Kensington. The baby, a girl named Melody Ann, was born prematurely on Wednesday 24 May 1944 weighing only 3 lb 2 oz. Since the war had started, St Mary Abbot's was one of the very few London hospitals that would still take maternity cases and it may be Melody's premature arrival that prevented Margery from travelling to Sheffield to have her baby there. Margery proudly sent a postcard to her brother Gilbert in Burma telling him that Melody was adored by the nursing staff and prospering on oxygen and brandy.[21]

Margery was still recuperating at the hospital when, on the morning of 6 June, the Allies began the invasion of Normandy by land, sea and air led by Eisenhower and Montgomery – the greatest combined operation in history.[22] By the end of the day, 150,000 Allied troops had landed in northern France and began their march into occupied Europe. For Londoners like Margery following the Allied advance on the wireless, this was a huge relief. However, exactly a week later, the Germans retaliated and once again Hitler targeted London. He was convinced that the 'secret weapon' he'd been developing would bring the country to its knees. On 13 June the first pilotless planes were sighted in Kent – the deadly V1s.[23]

These weapons caused indiscriminate destruction as they terrorized the city. They gripped the population in constant fear and anxiety as they fell relentlessly at all hours of the day and night. As they left no craters when they fell, their blast power was much greater than conventional bombs. Within three days of the arrival of the first V1, 137,000 buildings were damaged or destroyed, 499 people were killed and 2,000 injured.[24] The flying bombs were soon popularly christened 'doodlebugs' or 'buzz bombs'.

As the doodling or buzzing grew louder, those below waited tensely in case the engine cut out. When the V1 ran out of fuel it crashed to earth with a deep-throated roar followed by a blinding flash and a tall, sooty plume of smoke. If the noise seemed to stop directly above them, people flung themselves on the floor, under the table or into doorways.[25]

The artist, Frances Faviell, visited St Mary Abbot's hospital at this time and observed several heavily pregnant and terrified women begging the nurses to be put under their beds for safety. Faviell asked the nurses how the patients coped with the growing intensity of the doodlebugs. 'They're not too bad ... sometimes we get one who panics – that's dangerous – they all panic then.'[26]

At 4.05 a.m. on 17 June, the hospital was devastated when a V1 scored a direct hit. The bomb struck the nurses' home and the children's ward. One of the nurses, asleep in the nurses' home, had been wakened by the sound of the approaching rocket. 'It looked like a ball of fire in the sky,' she recalled. 'In a matter of seconds, there was a terrific explosion and the whole place seemed to blow up.'[27]

Nurses, patients and children were trapped under the debris of the building. Five nurses, six children and seven adult patients were killed. Thirty-three casualties were taken to St George's Hospital and the remaining patients, including Margery and her daughter, were evacuated. With London once again a target for destruction from increasingly sophisticated German weapons and the Gardners' marriage under immense strain, Melody was sent to be cared for at the Wellgarth Nursery, a nurses' training college which had evacuated from Hampstead to Bourton House in Shrivenham near Swindon. The fees were paid by Margery's mother from her limited widow's income. Children as young as ten days old up to the age of five were looked after at the nursery which tutored trainee nurses in the care of infants. Melody was one of forty children who lived there. The matron, Miss Talbot, fondly remembered their times at Bourton House, with bicycle rides over the hills, village socials and Christmas Days together with the children. The nursery relocated back to Hampstead in January of 1946, Melody returning with them.

In her correspondence Margery makes frequent reference

to the state of her health and the weekly medication that she was taking. It's possibly due to this that she was not called up by one of the women's services for war work. Her constant worries were about money and work. The only options that seemed open to her were unskilled jobs 'drudging' as a waitress or a cinema usherette, which would only bring in £2 a week. This she wasn't prepared to do. Writing to her mother, she despaired: 'I could do it for someone I loved, I suppose, in order to keep a home together, but I just haven't the heart to do it for myself.'[28]

She had been working as an artists' model but for a two-hour session she'd only earned 7s., so she resolved to join the Film Guild to see if she could get work as a film extra. However, she feared it would be 'a dog's life' of getting up early, with long hours and lots of hanging around doing nothing. The greatest frustration for Margery was that she couldn't find a way of making her art work pay a sufficient income, but with the city in the midst of war, art was not a priority for many. At this point in her life, Margery seemed paralysed by a sense of helplessness and possibly depression, when even the benefit of her former pleasures seemed to elude her. As she wrote in a letter to her mother on 27 July 1945, 'I feel altogether too worried and unhappy to want to draw.'

It was presumably due to this malaise, her deteriorating marriage, her worries about money and her ill-health that she decided against looking after her daughter herself, though she visited Melody frequently and exchanged regular letters with Miss Talbot at the Wellgarth Nursery.

Despite the birth of their daughter, as the war came to an end, the relationship between Margery and Peter seems to have deteriorated. Though Mrs Wheat thought that her daughter and son-in-law had stopped living together by the November of 1945, she suspected that they continued a casual sexual relationship. Peter claimed that he and Margery had got on very well together for four years, but that the relationship then began to fall apart. In his statement after Margery's death, he said that she was drinking heavily and spending too much time in pubs and clubs. Though it is certainly true that Margery lived at the heart of the Chelsea drinking scene, many witnesses challenged this, several saying that they had never seen Margery drunk.

The Gardners' unstable relationship was typical of many of the fractured marriages that floundered in this period. As the war had progressed and ended, the number of divorces had reached record numbers. In 1944 divorces had risen sharply to 12,314 (almost twice the number in 1939) and by 1947 they would reach a peak of 60,190.[29] The war had confronted ordinary men and women with the realities of conflict and the fragility of mortality – and in this war, death, destruction, injury and loss were not the sole preserve of foreign battlefields, but experienced as never before, close-up, first-hand in the streets of Chelsea and the suburbs of Sheffield. Such experiences led many couples to reassess their relationships in an attempt to redefine their post-war lives.

By VE Day on 8 May 1945, Margery and her family had come through the conflict alive, if not intact, and she now faced a precarious future with no income and a marital relationship that was at best draining and at worst, violent. With the war over, Margery attempted to at least resolve this latter issue by getting a divorce. She arranged to meet the family solicitor, Ralph Macro Wilson, who was also godfather to her daughter. He had known Margery for ten years, having started to look after the family's interests when her father had died. On 2 July, he travelled down from Sheffield to discuss the state of her marriage. Margery met him at Waterloo Station where they discussed the options for divorcing or arranging a legal separation from Peter on grounds of 'venereal disease, desertion and ill treatment'.[30] However, no action was subsequently taken and Margery and Peter remained legally married.

In the last year of her life, relations between Margery and Peter were unresolved, though he had left her in order to live with a woman called 'Tiddles'. In a letter to her mother on the 27 July 1945, Margery was exhausted by emotional and financial problems, but her prevailing worry was now her husband.

The biggest burden of all is Peter and I'll try to make you understand just how I feel about him and what a spot he has put me in. I met him the other day – he saw me coming along the road, dodged into a doorway and then popped out so that I almost ran into his arms – almost at once he started begging me to come back to him and told me a lot of lies about his home life with 'T[iddles]' etc. I knew he was lying but he persisted and finally flew into a rage when he tried to find out if I'd seen anything of Tony or anyone else and when I said I wanted a separation he dashed off, having first tried to get back the 10/- he'd just given me. He told me that he wasn't making any money at Car Driving – he's not working at Max's – so couldn't give me any. In reality, he's keeping Tiddles and the child (by her former husband) in a ghastly place miles from here, as she told me the next day. She was nearly crying as she told me what a hell he's making of her life – apparently he talks of me and Melody every night and is terrified of a divorce. The awful thing is that she tells me that she 'would crawl on her knees for him' which is just what he's making her do – they both get dead drunk every night and from what she told me it's pretty plain that Peter is rapidly getting worse – and I feel that I can only thank God for sparing me (if he has) from some awful end.

Now what can I do? I can't go and tell the police – they've got enough on him as it is and his one great boast is that I never will – if I do he'll go inside for failing to pay for my maintenance and *what would happen to that little bunch of misery and her child? By this he means the woman he is living with now. At the same time it's not fair that he should be supporting her instead of me – his lawful wife. <u>Now</u>, can you understand why I seem to be doing nothing? I just can't bring myself to administer the death blow – which is what it would amount to. Everyone else says I must do so and have no pity for him and only feel very sorry for me – but I understand Peter better than anyone – and I <u>know</u> he's not responsible for what he does. However, as I realize it can't go on like this – I'm being pressed on all sides – I will see my lawyer friend, with Michael and discuss with him the possibility of writing to P[eter] and telling him what I intend to do.*

I must stop now – I shall be very grateful for what you can spare, tho' everyone's been very sweet in helping me out – but I will pay you back over and over some day, I hope.

All my love,

Margy[31]

In August 1945, Margery met a man named Daniel Hamilton Shields at one of her local pubs, the Lord Nelson in the King's Road. At the time Shields was serving as a private in the 13th Holding Battalion based in Herne Bay. They were immediately attracted to each other. Margery told Shields about her unstable married life and that her husband had been in prison. As she was apparently penniless at the time he met her, Shields suggested that Margery should come and live with him in Herne Bay. He had a friend there called Ruth Wright who could offer her a room for a while at her home in Tankerton, near Whitstable. With little to keep her in London and no other options, Margery followed Shields to Herne Bay.[32]

Shields was on the permanent staff of the regiment and had a sleeping out pass. With Margery now settled in lodgings with Shields' friend Ruth, a young widow, he spent the next two weeks – or the nights at least – with Margery, returning to camp every day. Ruth found Margery not very talkative, but she did glean that she was separated from her husband and had been working as a film extra. She felt that Shields and Margery were very much attracted to one another. She was also aware that Margery had no money and when they left, it was Shields who paid the bill.[33]

After a couple of weeks, Shields tired of the daily journey from Tankerton to Herne Bay, so he arranged more convenient lodgings for himself and Margery with a Mrs Hambrook in Herne Bay itself. They were to stay here from early October to December of 1945. Shields and Margery signed in as 'Mr and Mrs Hamilton', but after a few weeks, Mrs Hambrook discovered that they weren't married and challenged Margery, living out of wedlock not being considered respectable at the time. Desperate not to be turned out of their lodgings, Margery explained that she had separated from her husband because of his drinking. He'd been pestering her to get back together again, but she had refused. She confided in Mrs Hambrook that when she had first met Daniel Shields, she had been destitute and that he had been extremely kind to her ever since. Margery may well have been overstating her financial peril to both Shields and Mrs Hambrook, as Mrs Wheat was sending her money via the Post Office at Herne Bay throughout this period. Mrs Hambrook allowed them both to stay. But, as ever in Margery's life, this moment of security was not to last for long.

At the beginning of November 1945, Shields was posted to Folkestone pending discharge from the army, but Margery wanted to stay on in Herne Bay. He continued to believe that his relationship with Margery was ongoing and was surprised when he returned one weekend to find her with a pilot who had been working on the jet plane record attempt at Herne Bay. The relationship with Shields deteriorated into recriminations about Margery's flirtations with other men. After a terrible row in Folkestone, Margery returned to London.

In the New Year of 1946, Margery bumped into Shields again in the Lord Nelson in Chelsea, where they had met the year before. Shields was anxious to have a suitcase returned to him that she had borrowed. Margery told him that she had lent it to her husband but would get it back from him. She also said that she had left some of her clothes at their lodgings in Herne Bay and wondered if he might collect them for her. Shields obligingly did so, collecting her belongings and even paying some money she owed to Mrs Hambrook. He met Margery at the Lord Nelson to give her her things. They then spent the night together in Notting Hill at the Connaught Hotel, Pembridge Square, booking in as 'Mr and Mrs Shields'. This was yards away from the Pembridge Court Hotel where she was to die six months later.

Margery's brother Gilbert was now twenty-nine and had recently been demobilized. Gilbert had joined the Territorial Army in 1939 and as a 2nd lieutenant had been sent to France with the British Expeditionary Force in April 1940. He survived the evacuation of Dunkirk and after two years of anti-invasion duties he had been sent to India. He later fought in the Burma campaign of 1944 as a platoon commander. He was then promoted to company commander and subsequently to intelligence officer at Divisional H.Q. after the capture of Mandalay.[34] It was while he was in Burma that Gilbert decided that he would not be returning to take up his position in the family firm as a solicitor. His father now deceased, the future of the business had fallen to him. But Gilbert's wartime experiences had led him to discover his true vocation as a teacher and in 1946 his old headmaster offered him a position at a prep school in

Derbyshire. In contrast to his sister, Gilbert Wheat was very much his parents' son, and even as a young man displayed a reserved and dignified character with a great sense of moral responsibility. Though very aware of his sister's frailties and temperament he was both supportive and kind to her and began to supplement her income with an allowance of £4 a week whilst she looked for the steady job that continued to elude her.

In the New Year, Gilbert travelled down from Derbyshire and visited Margery in her flat at 59 Earls Court Square. He found that she had only recently been discharged from St Mary Abbot's hospital and was recuperating from a miscarriage. Margery had previously told her mother that she was pregnant with Peter's child. Fortunately, Peter and his new girlfriend, Tiddles, had been present when Margery started to miscarry and had succeeded in getting her to the hospital.

After the miscarriage, Margery recovered and moved to Bramham Gardens, her final address, where her mother visited several times. At around this time, Margery confided to Mrs Wheat that she had a new boyfriend, but never revealed his name. She said that he was a 'nice quiet man who used to turn up for breakfast and bring her something to cook and he would sit with her in the evenings'.[35] In all probability, this was Peter Tilley Bailey, who had known Margery for about two years, but had only known her well since the beginning of that year. In January, they had bumped into each other at the Lord Nelson shortly after he had been released from prison having served his sentence for driving a stolen car along Knightsbridge. By June, Tilley Bailey was spending two or three nights a week with Margery at her flat in Earls Court Square and then at Bramham Gardens. He held a key to Margery's flat, where he was known by the landlady as 'Peter Gardner', but he was to offer a very fragile stability.[36] Though the relationship was exclusive on Margery's

side, whether she was aware of it or not, Tilley Bailey continued to have relationships with other women.

Like many women in this period, Margery Gardner
clutched at the sexual freedom that the war had offered, but
then struggled with the harsh consequences – a hand-to-
mouth existence with no security and little consistency in a
period already fraught with hardship. Her last letters to her
mother also suggest some sort of recurring gynaecological
problem as well as an overwhelming sense of exhaustion and
depression ('my nerves have gone to hell'). One of her friends,
Iris Humphrey, observed that in the seven or eight years she
had known her, she felt that Margery had 'changed':

> When I knew Margery some years ago she was a nice girl and
> I could not help noticing how she had changed in every way.
> She seemed to have become cheap and acted as if she would
> not have minded who she was with.[37]

Another close friend, Joyce Frost, offered a more compas-
sionate understanding of her character:

> [Margery] was a very straightforward sort of girl with no
> harm in her at all, and very quiet, who never made male
> acquaintanceships for money. She was content to spend the
> night with a man after a few drinks for company.[38]

And perhaps this was at the heart of her erratic emotional
life. She wanted company or, as her mother had said, 'a nice
quiet man ... to sit with her in the evenings'. Instead of
which she crawled from pub to pub, night after night, living
on hand-outs, cadging cigarettes and comfort from a series
of feckless men.

From the perspective of the early twenty-first century,
Margery Gardner seems very much a woman formed and

defined by the times in which she lived. But she was also a woman ahead of her time. Like Tennessee Williams' Blanche Dubois,[39] she is revealed, in various witness statements and her own letters, to be a highly creative woman in challenging circumstances, emotionally needy, trying to locate a haven for herself in a broken, half-familiar world where she resorted – of necessity – to some pretty desperate choices; dependent if not on the kindness, then on the indulgence of strangers.

CHAPTER FOUR

Thursday 20 June 1946

Joyce Frost had been friends with Margery Gardner since the late 1930s, but had lost contact with her for a couple of years during the war. They had bumped into each other again at a Victory Celebration Party on the rain-sodden 'V' Day, 8 June, which had been organized by Peter Gardner in Kensington.[1] A few days later, they had seen each other again at the Trevor Arms in Knightsbridge. From thereon they had picked up their friendship, meeting at the Nag's Head in Kinnerton Street, a pub much frequented by guardsmen from the nearby Knightsbridge Barracks. When they met for drinks, Joyce noticed that Margery always drank beer, but she was almost always broke. Joyce was thirty-three, had been married, but was separated from her husband. She lived in a flat at 51 Ennismore Gardens near

Hyde Park. A lodger, Desmond O'Dowd, shared the flat with her.[2]

On Wednesday night, 19 June, Joyce was drinking in the Nag's Head at about eight o'clock with her lodger. She caught sight of Margery in the back bar of the pub, just inside the door. Margery was with two men at the time whom she introduced to Joyce as 'Ken' and 'Jimmy'.[3] The latter was undoubtedly Heath, fitting his description perfectly: '[Joyce] distinctly remember[ed] he had a caterpillar badge in the left lapel buttonhole of his jacket.'[4] As the group chatted, Heath told Joyce that he was attached to the South African Air Force and had his own plane. She commented on Heath's caterpillar badge and he was only too delighted to tell her, 'That's for baling out.'[5] It seemed that Margery had been introduced to Heath a few weeks before. He had only recently made the Nag's Head one of his locals as he had previously been stationed abroad.

That night, Margery left the pub at about 10 p.m., but not before sitting down with Joyce and her lodger again, with Heath standing near them. Margery excitedly told Joyce that 'Jimmy is going to fly me to Brussels or Paris'. The two women arranged to meet for lunch the next day.

Thursday 20 June was the last day of Margery Gardner's life.

Peter Tilley Bailey called round to see Margery for about ten minutes at about 11 a.m. in the morning, finding her still in bed. He had stayed over at Bramham Gardens on the previous Sunday evening, as well as another night that week. Margery told him that she had met somebody that she hadn't seen for some time. She didn't say who it was or when she was going to meet him – and she may well have been testing Peter, trying to provoke a reaction from him.[6] The status of the relationship between Margery and Tilley Bailey is hard to read. He retained his own flat in Coliseum Terrace in

Regent's Park, yet spent two or three nights of the week at Bramham Gardens. They were sufficiently close for him to leave his identity card with Margery,[7] but though she was in dire need of money, he doesn't seem to have offered to help her out financially.

Just before lunch, Margery met Joyce and her lodger for a drink at the Packenham Pub on Knightsbridge Green. From there, they headed to the Lido Café which was opposite another of their locals, the Paxton's Head. Joyce paid for Margery's lunch, as she was broke again. After eating they went over the road to the Paxton's Head for another drink. O'Dowd left, leaving the two women alone together. They each had a glass of beer and Joyce subbed Margery some cigarettes. Margery was dressed in the same clothes she had worn the night before – her pale grey two-piece suit, a greyish brown cape made of possum fur, 'very dark nail varnish' and an unusual pair of earrings made from flowery fabric. Margery complained of a stain on her right-hand skirt pocket and went to buy a bottle of 'Thawpit' from Barnes' the chemist next door. She told Joyce that the shilling she had just spent on the cleaning fluid was her last, but it'd be worth it as she wanted to look her best that night.

'Why do you want to look your best tonight? Are you meeting somebody particular?' asked Joyce.

'An old boyfriend. Haven't seen him in a while.'

'Anyone I know?'

'No.'

'And this mystery man – is he on a promise?'

'Absolutely.'

According to Peter Tilley Bailey, Margery had been faithful to him throughout their relationship, but perhaps she was beginning to realize that this was not reciprocated. Despite her fidelity, her relationship with Tilley Bailey had not resulted in any tangible support from him. If Margery was contemplating being wined, dined and romanced by her date that evening, it would be the first time she had done so since she had started her relationship with Tilley Bailey.

Margery and Joyce carried on from the Paxton's Head to Cooper's Stores on the Brompton Road where Joyce bought some food. They then walked on to Joyce's flat in Ennismore Gardens. On the way to the flat, it started to rain. Margery took her headscarf from her handbag – an RAF scarf – and covered her head from the shower. When they got back to the flat, they continued chatting for about a quarter of an hour. Margery remembered that she was supposed to see her lady doctor (the Dr Kelly that she mentions in her letters to her mother), but she'd have to put it off until the next day. Whilst at the flat, Margery asked if Joyce would mind if she drew her picture? Joyce thought Margery a very good artist and readily agreed. While she was drawing, they continued their conversation.[8]

'Will you be in the Nag's Head tonight?' asked Joyce. 'Desmond and I are going.'

'I might do,' said Margery, then asked, 'Do you know Jimmy's surname?'

'How could I? I only met him last night.'

'Flying abroad. Exciting, isn't it? His own plane as well.'

'Margy. Do you have any money for this date tonight? How about I lend you £1?'

'I'll be fine.'

'Take it. You said you spent your last shilling on the "Thawpit".'

'I'll be all right once I meet my date tonight.'

Margery's date was never identified, but she was very clear that he was nobody Joyce knew. In no way did she suggest that she would be meeting either Jimmy Heath or Peter Tilley Bailey. About a quarter past three, Margery stopped her drawing as time was getting on.

'I want to get back to the flat. I have washing and ironing to do before tonight.' Margery paused. 'Joyce ...'

'Yes?'

'I don't suppose I *could* borrow a few pennies, could I?'

'Of course you can.'

'Just for my fare home.'

'How much do you need?'

'Fivepence?'

Joyce gave Margery the 5d. for her tube fare home to Bramham Gardens. She would never see her friend alive again.

The physical geography of the Earls Court and South Kensington areas that Margery lived and socialized in would have been very familiar to her today: terraces of tall, stuccoed buildings, graced with entrance pillars, and Edwardian red-brick town houses with leaded windows, all crouched in the shadow of the great cultural edifices on the Cromwell Road – the Victoria and Albert Museum and the Museum of Natural History. But the inhabitants of the area have changed dramatically since the mid-forties. Gone are the bedsits, boarding houses and bomb sites that Margery would have known, replaced by duplex apartments and day nurseries with clipped box hedging. Bramham Gardens itself is a shady garden square in Earls Court. The flat, at number 24, was in a slim, five-storey red-brick terrace. It is now part of a retirement home and retains an air of down-at-heel gentility; the brickwork dulled by years of soot and traffic, yellowing net curtains draped at windows permanently fastened by decades of paint.

Margery successfully managed to clean the stain from her skirt pocket with the 'Thawpit', as she wore the same outfit that evening. Leaving the flat, she put her door key in her brown leather handbag and walked out past the derelict house next door, uninhabitable since the Blitz, and made her way to the Nag's Head.

Often hurriedly grabbed at the first sound of an air raid, Margery's handbag offers a revealing and intimate snapshot of her life.[9] Amongst some pencils and a notebook bearing her name was a pair of imitation suede gloves. Her cigarette case contained eight cigarettes. Margery – not vain, but always trying to make the best of her appearance – wore glasses occasionally and in their red case, together with her spectacles, there was a cheque for £4, payable to her husband. She also had a pair of white-framed sunglasses for the sunny weather that June promised but never delivered that summer. As well as a powder compact, a powder puff, a box of eyeliner, two broken combs and a hair clip, Margery had another small make-up purse containing lipstick, cream and rouge. Knowing she was expecting her period soon she carried three Tampax sanitary towels just in case, as well as a tube of Gynomin tablets ('the scientifically balanced, Antiseptic and Deodorant Contraceptive Tablet').[10] In a black leather wallet, she kept a large volume of letters from her family and a variety of male friends as well as some personal photographs, including one of her young daughter, Melody, now two years old. In her bag, she also kept her identity card, which would later help the police to identify her body – as well as an application for the replacement of some clothing coupons to buy the new clothes that she so desperately wanted.

Three pawn tickets spoke of the unstable fortunes that Margery had suffered in the preceding months. She had pawned an overcoat in February of 1945, one of the coldest months of that year, a possum fur cape in April of 1946 (which she must have redeemed as she was wearing it that night), and a typewriter. At the bottom of the bag was a single pink handkerchief, clean and folded – perhaps even washed and ironed by her that afternoon – and bearing the initials 'M. A. B. Gardner'. In her purse Margery had a single silver sixpence and two coppers, a total of 8d. (a pint of Guinness cost 11d. at the time). Even as she stepped out of her door and into the streets of Earls Court, Margery's options on the night of 20 June were extremely limited.

By 6.30 that evening, Margery was in the Nag's Head, where she chatted to the landlady, Eva Cole.[11] She told Mrs Cole that she was waiting for a telephone call, which finally came after she had been there about three-quarters of an hour. A few moments after she put the phone down she walked out of the pub, saying 'Goodnight' to Mrs Cole. She didn't indicate who the call was from, but it may well have been her friend Trevethan Frampton, whom she then went on to meet. She walked to the nearby Trevor Arms, across the road from Knightsbridge tube station where she met Frampton, an art student with whom she had been friendly since the beginning of the year. They stayed together for about an hour and during this time were joined by a number of men, two or three of whom Margery had met before. One of these was Jimmy Heath.

Heath asked Margery if she would have dinner with him later that evening, but she told him that she had already arranged to have dinner with an army captain who was in the bar. Margery's friend Frampton left at 8.30 p.m. to go back to his hotel for dinner. He told Margery that if she was free later, he would meet her at the Renaissance Club in Harrington Road. He would aim to get there himself for about 9.30 p.m. Margery said she'd most likely join him later, after she'd had dinner with her date.

However, the army captain that Margery had arranged to meet that night had met an old school friend at the bar and left the Trevor Arms with him, leaving her alone. All that Margery had in her purse was small change – not enough to buy a drink and certainly not enough to buy herself a proper meal. Catching sight of her alone, Heath went to the bar and brought her over to some of his RAF friends, introducing her as a 'great little scout'. The four men and Margery drank on for a couple of hours during which some half-dozen further rounds were ordered. Seeing that Heath was apparently flush with cash, Margery saw an opportunity to salvage her evening – and her chances of dinner at somebody else's expense. She wondered if she *could* take Heath up on his earlier offer? She would love to have dinner with him. Heath by now was spending his way through the £30 (an average month's wages at the time) he had acquired earlier that day and seemed like he had money to burn. So it was that Margery, not wanting to be alone at the bar and not having enough money to buy her own drinks or dinner, effectively sealed her fate.

Heath and Margery then left the Trevor Arms and went to the Normandie Hotel for dinner. They left between 9.30 and 10 p.m. and popped in to the nearby Torch Club for a drink. They then decided to go to the Panama Club, which had a late licence, where Heath had entertained Yvonne Symonds only the weekend before. Heath signed the yellow Visitors' Form 'Lt. Col. Heath and friends'.

Heath and Margery went up to the main bar on the second floor, with Margery carrying her opossum coat over her arm. Almost immediately they bumped into Peter Tilley Bailey accompanied by 25-year-old Catherine Hardie, a nurse at Battersea General Hospital. Given that Peter had spent two of the previous four nights at her flat, Margery may well have been surprised to meet him so blatantly dating another woman. Margery and Peter curtly acknowledged each other, without introducing their companions. Margery said nothing, but there was certainly a frostiness at this meeting. When Catherine Hardie was later questioned about Margery's movements that evening, she claimed that she deliberately ignored her: 'When I am with a party of men, I don't look around, especially as Peter Bailey had passed the time of day with her.'[12]

Another of Tilley Bailey's party that evening, Ronald Birch, was also a casual acquaintance of Margery's. At one point, he noticed her in company with Heath at the bar. They were holding hands and though she seemed very attentive to Heath, he appeared 'slightly indifferent' to her. Birch later recalled: 'All the time she stood at the bar she appeared to be trying to promote [Heath's] interest, so rather obviously that I thought that she did it deliberately to annoy Peter Bailey.'[13]

Margery then ran into another friend of hers, Iris Humphrey, a civil servant who lived in Earls Court Square. She had known Margery for about eight or nine years.[14] They had been very friendly before the war, but had lost touch during it when Iris had been evacuated to Bath. Since Iris had moved back to London in April 1946, the two women had met in various pubs around Earls Court. Iris was sitting in the club room by the dance floor with her friend John Le Mee Power when Margery entered with Heath. Margery called 'hallo' over to their table. When Iris and Le Mee Power got up to dance, Iris went over to the table that Margery had sat down at with her handsome companion.

'Would you mind looking after my things whilst we have a dance?'

'Of course,' said Margery.

She took Iris' handbag and copy of *Vogue* and put it on the table in front of her. Iris and Le Mee Power went off to the dance floor before Margery could introduce them to Heath. After a short while, Heath and Margery got up to dance themselves. Iris and Le Mee Power left the dance floor and went to collect her bag and magazine. For the next hour, Iris observed Margery and Heath sitting at their table, holding each other's hands, smoking and drinking – with Heath rubbing his hand against Margery's leg. At the time, Iris commented to Le Mee Power that she thought that Margery's companion looked 'dissipated', with big bags under his eyes. She remarked, with terrible prescience, that 'Margery was in for a bad time' that night.[15]

Phyllis, the waitress, first noticed Heath and Margery at about 11 p.m. when she checked to see that nobody was drinking alcohol without a meal, in accordance with their licence. Phyllis had seen both Heath and Margery at the club before, hanging around with what she called the 'Chelsea Crowd', led by Peter Tilley Bailey. Heath pulled at Phyllis' apron string, which caused her apron to fall loose. Phyllis turned round and he said 'Repeat the order', so she went to get them some more drinks. When Phyllis arrived with the drinks, the couple were getting up to dance again and this time Margery told her 'Repeat the order'. When Phyllis came back for the money (6s.), Heath said, 'I owe you for the last one. Aren't I honest?'[16] According to Phyllis, the couple sat on their own table all night and didn't speak to anyone else. Iris Humphrey and Le Mee Power left about 11.30, leaving Margery at the club with Heath. The band stopped playing at midnight but members had twenty minutes drinking-up time. Peter Tilley Bailey and Catherine Hardie left the club about ten minutes after midnight, but couldn't see Margery to say 'goodbye'. Perhaps smarting from Peter's date with a younger woman, at some point during the evening, Margery consented to go back to Heath's hotel – possibly for a nightcap – just as he had suggested to Pauline Brees in February.

Outside the Panama Club, Harold Harter was driving his taxi eastwards along Old Brompton Road in the direction of South Kensington tube station.[17] About 12.20 a.m., Heath was leaving the entrance to the Panama Club, talking with Margery. He saw Harter's cab and started to walk along the pavement to the corner of Thurloe Street, with his hand up, hailing it. Harter stopped on the opposite side of the obelisk in the middle of the road. The couple walked across the road, Heath holding Margery's hand as she dragged slightly behind him.[18]

According to Harter, Heath asked Margery where a particular address was, but she didn't seem to know. She was currently living in Bramham Gardens in Earls Court, less than ten minutes' walk away from the Panama Club down Old Brompton Road. Given the convenience of her flat they would have to be travelling for something specific to justify a taxi ride. Heath's suitcase, of course, was at the Pembridge Court Hotel with everything it contained. Heath then directed Harter to Pembridge Gardens in Notting Hill, which was just under two miles away. Harter observed that Margery 'seemed to be in a drunken stupor' and when Heath opened the door of the cab for her to get in, she had walked to the other side of him 'as if she didn't know where she was'. Heath looked around for her asking, 'Where the hell are you?' Once they were safely in the cab, Harter noticed that Margery was lying back and Heath had his arm around her.

According to Peter Tilley Bailey, Margery had never spent a night away from her flat since they had been together, so this was the first time she was to do so. It was also the first time she had been observed in an extremely drunken state – this perhaps exacerbated by her feelings towards Tilley Bailey as well as the large amount of cash that Heath had been spending at the bar.

After about ten minutes, they arrived in Notting Hill and Harter turned his cab into Pembridge Gardens.

'Whereabouts do you want?'

Heath told Harter, 'This will do.'

Margery said nothing and 'appeared not to notice what was going on and she did not seem to hear me'. Harter pulled up about fifty yards short of the Pembridge Court Hotel on the left-hand side. Heath got out of the cab first – his face illuminated by the light of the meter. He went to help Margery out of the cab. After about a minute, he got her out on the pavement where she stood 'as though in a stupor and had no interest in anything'. Heath left her and turned to Harter.

'How much is that?'

'One shilling and ninepence.'

With the precision of a very drunk man trying not to appear so, Heath slowly counted out 2s. and 2d. (a small tip), fumbling with his change under the meter light. Once he had paid the cab, Heath put his arm around Margery's waist and the couple walked the fifty yards ahead towards the Pembridge Court Hotel, effectively holding each other up. Harter watched from his cab as they disappeared through the gate outside the hotel and up the steps to the porticoed entrance. This was the last time that Margery Gardner was seen alive by anyone other than the man who killed her.

Earlier that evening, back at her flat in Bramham Gardens, surrounded by her own artwork, Margery had left an exercise book in which she had been writing (in pencil – she had pawned her typewriter) the first few chapters of a novel about a girl called 'Julie', not unlike herself – or at least, Margery's own vision of herself. Autobiographical in tone, the story poignantly articulated Margery's hopes and disappointments.

> Julie had not been with us more than a couple of weeks before she knew all the bars, all the cafes, all the clubs. She had green eyes and dark hair that fell on her neck and shoulders like a hood . . .
>
> People really liked her to talk to. She was fresh and vital

– different, amusing too, and she was innocent. She had girl friends, although she got on better with men. She was bold and reckless in those days, finding her feet and her own values – and her mistakes.

Always new places, new faces, for Julie was out to conquer the world. And she did conquer the world. At least she conquered one bitter bit of London. It was that bit of London by the river.

'What are you doing with your life?' She would open her eyes and say, 'Enjoying yourself for the first time. Finding a dream that is real.'[19]

But Margery Gardner's dream wasn't real. As with much in her life, the story was never finished and like her existence itself, brought to a tragic, abrupt end.

CHAPTER FIVE

Detective Inspector Spooner

At 3.15 p.m. on the afternoon of Friday 21 June, Divisional Detective Inspector Reginald Spooner was in his office at Hammersmith Police Station when he received a telephone call from one of his inspectors at Notting Hill, Shelley Symes. As soon as Spooner answered the telephone, the gravity of Symes' voice made it clear they had a serious case on their hands.

'Guvnor,' said Symes quietly, 'we've got one.'[1]

This call was to be the first step of a manhunt that was to extend the length and breadth of the country – even to ports and airfields – and which was to involve as many as 40,000 officers. Spooner's character and his skill as a police investigator were to be tested in an emotionally gruelling and intellectually demanding investigation, the success of which was to rely on thousands of man-hours, but would also pivot on the most extraordinary coincidences that would seem the preserve of fiction. Ironically, the case would also result in both pursued and pursuer becoming famous, indeed infamous – Heath as one of the most vilified criminals of the twentieth century and Spooner as the most celebrated detective of his generation. Spooner's superintendent, Nick Carter, later regarded him as 'the greatest detective this force has ever known'.[2] Years later, when Spooner wrote his memoirs, he started by writing about Heath, the case that defined his career.

Though they came from similar backgrounds – the respectable but financially anxious middle class – Heath and Spooner couldn't have been more different. The charismatic and seductive Heath was the antithesis of the cautious Spooner. Neville Heath was flamboyant and extravagant – a honey-tongued playboy spending his time and money in bars and nightclubs in the pursuit of pleasure and sex. Reginald Spooner (always 'Reg' to friends and colleagues) was a modest, precise workaholic who was extremely careful with money. In stark contrast to the womanizing Heath, Spooner dated only one other girl before becoming engaged to his future wife, Myra Newman, at the age of twenty-one.

Reg Spooner was a Londoner born in 1903 into the comfortable middle-class suburb of Upper Norwood and raised in Wood Green. He regarded himself very much as a cockney. His wife was 'my old woman', his boss always 'Guv'nor'. He prided himself on his in-depth knowledge of London, its dark hidden places and its people.

Spooner's early years were dominated by a series of personal crises that were to shape his attitudes in later life – particularly regarding money and security. These would preoccupy him throughout his working life and would ultimately guide him in his choice of career. His father, Jabez Spooner, worked for the family firm, a business transfer agency dealing with stocks and shares based in the Smithfield region of London. But Spooner's grandfather Alfred, who headed the family business, was known for his 'extravagant way of living'. Though successful in business, he had very little cash saved for emergencies. He never thought of the future. When he ran into a spell of bad luck on the markets, he realized he had nothing to keep the business or his family afloat; the business collapsed. In March 1904, Alfred was summoned to court over his mounting debts. He never turned up. Unable to cope with the shame of financial ruin, and the dire position into which he had placed both the family's business and their homes, Alfred Spooner shot himself in the head. The coroner recorded that he had taken his own life whilst temporarily insane.

Alfred's suicide left the family business – and Spooner's parents, Jabez and Blanche – in a financial crisis that initiated a domestic one. The family home in Upper Norwood, south of the river, had to be sold and the Spooners moved to a smaller, more modest home in Hornsey, north London. But the family hadn't seen the last of their worries. In 1911, at the age of thirty-four, Jabez became paralysed after having been involved in a fight. He died shortly afterwards, leaving his widow and her two young sons, Reg (8) and Rodney (6), without savings, insurance or security of any kind. As the widow of a professional man, Blanche didn't qualify for a widow's pension. Having neither skills nor training, and no means of income, Blanche was forced to sell the house in Hornsey and most of their possessions. Together with her sons, she moved to her parents' house in Elmar Road in Wood Green. At the age of thirty-five, Blanche Spooner, once a comfortable suburban housewife, became an apprentice embroideress. It was a humiliating fall. She would never let her young sons forget the value of money and the sheer struggle of life without it.

The Spooner brothers were educated at the local Lordship Lane School in Ellenborough Road, just a half-hour walk from their home. Class sizes were large (often of forty or more) and each class contained three age groups, as was the norm during this period. In 1917 in the midst of the First World War, too young to be called up for active service, fourteen-year-old Reg left school without qualifications. His priority was to bring in some money to help the household so his working life began as an office boy for the Hearts of Oak Assurance Company, based on the Holborn Viaduct. His pay, though only a few shillings to start with, eased the financial burden on his mother. Every week he would hand her his pay packet – unopened – and she gave him back a shilling to spend for himself. By application and study, Spooner rose to the position of clerk by 1923.

In 1924, Spooner applied to become a police officer. Though his maternal grandfather had been a police sergeant in the nineteenth century, it appears that his desire to join the police force was inspired by a need for security, rather than a desire to follow in his grandfather's footsteps. Even as a probationer, he would earn £3 10s. a week – 10s. more than he had been earning at the Assurance Company. But most importantly it offered a career with a regular income and a pension. Knowing that he would have to care for his future wife and family as well as his mother at some point in the future was critical in Spooner choosing the police as a career.

By the time he was twenty-one, Spooner was an athletic man, 6 feet 1 inch tall, with strong, handsome features and dark, thick, wavy hair. He was perfect force material. On 19 February 1924, he was summoned to Scotland Yard with sixty other candidates. Competition was fierce, with many ex-servicemen and guardsmen at the time also keen for the security of a police career and pension. By the end of the medical and academic tests, only nine candidates remained; Spooner was one of them. PC 475 'J' started on probation in Victoria Park, east London, on 7 March 1924.

From the start, Spooner set his sights on joining the Criminal

Investigations Department (CID) as a detective. After serving his time as a uniformed officer, which he disliked intensely (his girlfriend Myra never saw him in uniform once), he joined the CID in 1928, where he excelled. At the same time, Myra was training to be a Norland Nanny based at the Norland Training Centre in Hyde Park Gate. They were engaged on 9 March 1927 – Myra's twenty-first birthday. A two-year engagement followed whilst Spooner saved enough money for the wedding. He wrote to Myra explaining the reasons for his caution:

> It will be up to us during our engagement to save all we can so that we can meet all the initial expenses of our prospective home as soon as we get married. This will be much better than following the example of most other married couples who buy their homes a bit at a time.[3]

He was not prepared to borrow money, nor to buy on HP (hire purchase). Going into debt was anathema to him – a clear indication of the ghosts that haunted him from his family's past.

As a young detective, Spooner prospered and soon attracted the attention of his superior officers. He found that he had an amazing facility for remembering names, incidents and places; he became renowned for his 'card index' memory. He was a master of detail and took meticulous notes of everything, never throwing anything away. As his career continued he kept notebooks with newspaper clippings of every case he had been involved in. He was hugely industrious, putting in hours on the job beyond the call of duty (and these were already long – 9 a.m. to 2 p.m., 6 p.m. to 10 p.m.), much to the chagrin of his long-suffering wife. He had married Myra in 1929 and she had given birth to their daughter, Jean, a year later. With Spooner volunteering to work well into the night with only one day off, it was clear to Myra from the beginning of their marriage that family life would always come second. The landlady of his favourite pub in Limehouse, the Hole in the Wall, noted that Spooner 'never seemed to go home. I thought if I were his wife I wouldn't put up with a life like that.' Essentially, Spooner was married to the job. He continued to impress his superiors and received several commendations, including one for his part in the investigation of the 'Bow Cinema Murder', his first murder case that resulted in a conviction.

In the early morning of Tuesday 7 August 1934, 35-year-old Dudley Hoard, the manager of the Palace Cinema in Bow Road, had answered the doorbell to his staff flat above the picture house. On opening the door, he was attacked by an assailant armed with an axe. The two men fought in the entrance to the cinema balcony and after fourteen blows to the head, Hoard was left for dead and the takings cleared from the previous bank holiday weekend. The police investigating the crime couldn't work out how the intruder had gained entry to the cinema itself as it was protected by a locked iron grille. Despite the fact that the grille appeared to be securely locked, Spooner was convinced that this was the method of entry. He shook the grille until it came loose. It took a knack to open it. This, thought Spooner, together with the knowledge that the bank holiday takings remained on the premises, would only have been known to somebody who worked in the cinema. Spooner was led to nineteen-year-old John Frederick Stockwell, a cinema usher. Despite trying to cover his tracks with a suicide note, Stockwell was traced to Yarmouth where he was arrested. Despite an appeal, Stockwell was hanged, the first man Spooner was to send to the gallows. He would not be the last.

In November 1935 at the age of thirty-two, Spooner had been promoted as first class sergeant to 'Central One', commonly known as the 'Murder Squad', and transferred to Scotland Yard. Central One dealt not only with murders but crimes that involved several police divisions and government departments. Consequently Spooner gained a huge breadth of experience in a wealth of criminal activities including fraud, murder and assault. In 1938 he was appointed as Central One's officer in charge of pornography and in November of that year, he was promoted to detective inspector at Marylebone Police Station.

A considered, careful man, Spooner was also a heavy drinker and chain-smoker.[4] Even in this period when drinking and smoking 'on the job' was both common and universally tolerated in the force, Spooner's habits seem to have been extreme. Albert Pierrepoint, the public executioner during this period, became a friend of Spooner's and remembered that he always had a cigarette in his mouth, both on duty and off. 'There was always cigarette ash falling onto his waistcoat which he did not bother to brush off,' he recalled. Even in the 1930s Spooner was renowned for his smoker's cough.

When war broke out in 1939, Spooner and his family were on holiday on the Isle of Wight. They had barely settled in when a telegram arrived ordering his immediate return to London; all police leave had been cancelled. Spooner originally insisted that Myra and their nine-year-old daughter Jean should evacuate to the country, but Myra was reluctant for them to live apart for the duration, so they eventually settled in a house in Palmer's Green, also offering a room to Spooner's mother, Blanche, who was to remain with them for the next twenty-two years. Throughout the war, the correspondence between Spooner and his wife continued to be dominated by his anxieties about money, despite the fact that he was now earning a very healthy £11 a week. With a curious reticence, even up to his death in 1963, Spooner never told his wife how much money he earned.

He was not to see active combatant service during the war, but in June 1940 was seconded from the police force to MI5, the British Secret Service. He was appointed as Deputy Head of B57, a special anti-espionage and anti-sabotage unit that had been set up by Leonard Burt, a former boss of his.[5] The unit was based in a cell at Wormwood Scrubs Prison. Due to their top-secret nature, few of Spooner's investigations during the war were reported by the press, but it is recorded that he investigated a broad range of espionage crimes including sabotage in Barrow-in-Furness in March 1940, an attempt to sabotage the *Queen Elizabeth* in March 1941 and an attempt to sabotage warships in Scapa Flow later the same year.

After one trip to Stockholm during hostilities, Spooner returned home with a large paper parcel for his wife. He told Myra not to tell anyone that he had brought it back with him as, officially, he wasn't supposed to bring back gifts from abroad. Myra was thrilled at the prospect of some perfume or maybe a dress-length of material. She unwrapped the package excitedly, but was soon disappointed to find that he had bought her a vegetable colander.[6] Undoubtedly, with the privations of wartime, colanders were hard to come by, but Myra had hoped for something more personal, more romantic. But Spooner was nothing if not consistent. In his letters he always signed off 'Yrs Affect. Reg'. Myra later recalled that she longed for him to write something more loving, how he missed her, 'the sort of thing a woman wants to hear, but he never did'. Myra kept every letter Reg wrote to her, filing them in bundles according to the year.[7]

In 1945, as the war reached an end, and the Allies moved remorselessly through Germany, the search for spies and saboteurs changed to a hunt for traitors, both civilian and military. On 22 April 1945, Spooner was commissioned in the Intelligence Corps with the rank of captain and a week later flew to Paris. Though he admired the city, he missed English food and lamented the shortage of cigarettes, asking Myra to send him over a regular supply of 300 a week.

After the allied victory in May, Spooner travelled by car

further into mainland Europe in pursuit of traitors and deserters. Nothing could have prepared him for his first-hand sight
of the devastation the Allies had visited on the enemy. In
three days, he felt, he had 'lived a lifetime'.

> I always thought that people in London and other English
> towns knew what war was, but I have changed my mind.
> Nothing the people of London have experienced comes
> anywhere near what the people of Germany have undergone.
> The country – certainly the Western aspect – is literally
> devastated, and one wonders how it is all ever going to be put
> right. Aachen and Hamm for instance, are literally a sham-
> bles, *not one* single building remaining habitable, yet one sees
> a few – very few – people wandering aimlessly around, living
> goodness knows where and on Lord knows what ... The
> more we drive East the more of the debacle of the German
> Reich we have witnessed.[8]

British Intelligence had provided Spooner with a list of many
of the traitors he was seeking. The most important traitor that
MI5 were keen to capture was William Joyce, commonly
known as 'Lord Haw Haw'. Joyce had broadcast from
Germany throughout the war to Britain and encouraged the
British people to surrender. Though listening to these broadcasts was not illegal in Britain, it was officially discouraged. In
1940, Joyce had estimated that he had 6 million regular
listeners in Britain and 18 million occasional listeners. Many
ordinary people were keen to hear what the enemy was
saying and how they were justifying their attempts to dominate Europe. Since wartime information in Britain was strictly
censored, it was frequently possible for German broadcasts to
be more informative than those of the BBC.[9]

The investigation into Joyce's crimes was led by Captain
William Skardon of MI5, another former police officer.

Spooner helped Skardon build up the dossier of evidence about Joyce's life in Germany and his activities as Lord Haw Haw. When Spooner searched Radio Hamburg, he discovered a recording of what was intended to be Joyce's last broadcast. Joyce had made the recording whilst drunk, when British troops were less than twenty miles away from the city. In it he lamented the fact that Britain and Germany had not made the natural alliance that they should have done and warned of the looming power and influence of the Soviet Union. The recording was never transmitted.

Though he generally despised the wartime traitors he was pursuing, Spooner had some sympathy for Norman Baillie-Stewart, the 'Officer in the Tower' who had already, curiously, attracted the admiration of the young Neville Heath. 'I quite like him,' Spooner told his wife. 'He is not like the others.'[10] Baillie-Stewart was an ex-Sandhurst officer who had been court-martialled under the Official Secrets Act in 1933 for selling military secrets to foreign powers. Though not in danger of the death penalty at the time (as Britain was not at war), the ten crimes he was found guilty of carried a maximum sentence of 140 years in prison. However, Baillie-Stewart served only four, and when he was released from prison in 1937, he immediately applied for Austrian citizenship. When this was refused, he applied for German citizenship the next year, but because of complex red tape and the beginnings of the Anschluss, his application was not accepted until 1940. Baillie-Stewart had, however, been making pro-Nazi broadcasts from 1939 onwards – in fact he had begun reading Nazi-biased 'news' on the 'Germany Calling' English language service the week before the declaration of war. When he did so, he was still technically a British citizen and was therefore (again technically) guilty of treason, the penalty for which was execution, as was the case with Baillie-Stewart's more renowned successor, William Joyce. In 1945, Spooner arrested Baillie-Stewart on the charge of high treason. A very fair man, Spooner set out to actively save Baillie-Stewart from the gallows by interviewing all of his friends and acquaintances from the time he arrived in Austria and also uncovering the clerical delay in the approval of his citizenship. Due to Spooner's diligence, Baillie-Stewart avoided execution and served only five years in prison.

Spooner was demobilized from the Intelligence Corps with the rank of major on 4 March 1946. Much to the exasperation of his wife, who was keen to take the holiday that had been truncated by the outbreak of war, Spooner rejoined the police force the same day. With the current dearth of police officers and the booming post-war crime wave, his commissioner had told him how urgently they needed the return of qualified senior detectives like him. Spooner replied that he could start straight away; 'If you need me, here I am.'[11] Officially Spooner had already been a divisional detective inspector for two years but he had never actually worked in that rank. His promotion had come through in June 1944 while he was on loan to the Secret Service, so it was based on seniority rather than merit. Now forty-three, Spooner felt, like thousands of men his age, that the war had held back his career and he was now to be faced with competition from a wave of ambitious young men keen to prove themselves in the force once they had been demobilized.

But Spooner needn't have worried about being eclipsed by up-and-coming younger men – for his defining moment was just ahead. His experiences as a London-based police inspector before the war and his more recent achievements in the pursuit of the most agile and deceptive of traitors and saboteurs, together with his extraordinary memory and inherent tenacity, were to be the ideal qualifications for him to lead the most celebrated murder investigation of his career for which he would be remembered as 'Britain's greatest detective'.[12]

CHAPTER SIX

The Pembridge Court Hotel

21 JUNE 1946

At 9.10 a.m. on the morning of Friday 21 June, Elizabeth Wyatt, the manageress of the Pembridge Court Hotel, told her waitress, Rhoda Spooner, to go up to Room 4 and give Lieutenant Colonel and Mrs Heath a knock. Neither of them had come down to breakfast that morning.

Twenty-six-year-old Rhoda's duties were to serve breakfast to guests at the hotel from 7.30 a.m. until 11 a.m. seven days a week.[1] Though she never normally served meals to guests in their rooms, she had been instructed to make an exception by Mrs Wyatt on the previous Monday morning, when she had served tea and toast to Heath and his 'wife'. Rhoda had also chatted with the lieutenant colonel over the preceding few days. She had seen him in the hotel lounge on Wednesday morning where she had been serving. He'd asked her for a cup of tea and during the conversation he had mentioned that he was going away on Friday with his wife to Copenhagen and that 'Mrs Heath' had just left the WRNS.

So, on Friday morning, Rhoda went up to the first floor and knocked on the door of Room 4 as instructed. There was no answer. The door was closed, but not locked. Rhoda opened it and looked into the room. The curtains were drawn but there was sufficient daylight for her to see a woman asleep in the bed behind the door. This she assumed to be Mrs Heath (Yvonne Symonds) whom she'd last seen on Monday morning in bed with her husband when she'd taken up the tea and toast. The woman in the bed was covered up to her shoulders by the bedclothes. The other bed by the window was empty and didn't appear to have been slept in. Rhoda assumed that Heath had gone out and left his wife to have a lie-in.

'Will you be coming down to breakfast?' Rhoda asked.

There was no reply. She quietly closed the door, leaving the woman to sleep on. Downstairs she told Mrs Wyatt that she'd asked if Mrs Heath was coming down to breakfast, but had received no answer.

Later that morning, Barbara Osborne was attending to her morning cleaning rounds and knocked on the door of Room 4 at about 11.20 a.m. She received no answer either.

My duties as chambermaid are making the beds in all the guest rooms, sweeping the rooms, dusting the furniture and cleaning the wash hand-basins and generally to make each room clean and tidy. I start work at 9 a.m. and finish at 12 noon. And if I have attended to every room I just leave the house and go home, but should any of my work remain unfinished and I could not get access to the rooms, then I report it to Mrs Wyatt and the matter is left with her.[2]

Barbara entered the room. The curtains were still closed and the room in semi-darkness. She saw a woman whom she presumed to be Mrs Heath asleep in the bed nearest the door and noticed that her head was turned towards the window. The lady didn't stir when Barbara came into the room so presuming she was still asleep, Barbara left without speaking. She decided to come back later and went on about her business cleaning the other rooms. At midday, Barbara knocked on the door of Room 4 again. Receiving no reply, she opened the door and spoke to the lady lying in bed.

'Would you mind making the beds as I am going off duty?'

Again, Mrs Heath did not answer, so Barbara reported to Mrs Wyatt that she had been unable to clean the room. She finished her shift and went home, thinking nothing out of the ordinary.

By 2 p.m. that afternoon, Mrs Wyatt's daughter-in-law, Alice, who worked as assistant manageress at the hotel, went upstairs to Room 4. Mrs Heath may well have had a heavy night, but she surely wouldn't want to sleep on into the afternoon. Alice entered the room and drew back the curtains. Turning into the body of the room, she saw that there was no response from Mrs Heath to the daylight flooding in from the window. She approached the bed by the door, pulled back the bedclothes from the woman's neck and saw that she was dead. Alice replaced the bedclothes and hurried downstairs to find her mother-in-law. 'Come quick!' she called, 'I think this woman is dead.'[3] Mrs Wyatt accompanied her daughter-in-law back up to the room. The woman was clearly dead. Alice immediately telephoned the police.[4]

Sergeant Frederick Averill of 'F' Division, Notting Hill, arrived at the hotel at about 2.40 p.m. He was met by Alice Wyatt and shown up to Room 4. He noticed that the key was in the door on the inside but had not been locked. The bedclothes on the bed by the window had been roughly laid over the bed. The bedclothes on the bed near the door were pulled up to the woman's shoulders. He noticed that she had bruises to the left-hand side of her face. When Averill pulled back the bedclothes, the condition of the woman's body began to reveal the extraordinarily violent ordeal that she had suffered before she died. Averill then pulled back the bedclothes from the other bed and found the sheets beneath saturated with blood, with large clots in the centre of the bed. Averill called in the murder team.[5]

He was joined shortly afterwards by Dr Henegan, the deputy divisional surgeon, Detective Inspector Shelley Symes and Sergeant Frederick Anning of the CID. Henegan, a junior doctor, established that the woman had been dead for some time, but did not at this point look for the cause of death.

Reg Spooner arrived at the hotel at 3.30 p.m.[6] He alerted the pathologist, 39-year-old Dr Keith Simpson, whose reputation during the war had begun to eclipse that of the leading forensic pathologist of the pre-war period, Sir Bernard Spilsbury. Simpson had been lecturing that afternoon at the Police Training College in Hendon when he had a call from his assistant Jean Scott-Dunn to go to Notting Hill as soon as possible.[7] District Superintendent Tom Barratt also arrived at the hotel as well as the fingerprint division who carried out their tests and took the scene-of-crime photographs. The washbasin in the corner of the room bore traces of blood. It was evident that somebody had been attempting to wash something away after the murder. The side of the washbasin revealed one single bloody fingerprint.[8]

Spooner and Symes now took a closer look at the body of the woman on the bed near the door. She was completely naked, lying on her back. Her head was lying to the right-hand side of the pillow, turned towards the window, much as if she had been deliberately placed that way to look as if she were asleep. Her feet were tied tightly one over the other with a knotted handkerchief. Her right arm was pinned diagonally behind her back and her left wrist and left hand lay under the left side of the small of her back. The extraordinary position of the arms and hands, together with bruising on the wrists seemed to indicate that her wrists had been tied behind her back and the ligature later removed. There was a considerable amount of blood on the bedding, but the front of the body and the face were strangely free of it, as if she had been washed after her ordeal.

The cause of death was not immediately apparent. Spooner then tilted the body to see if there were any injuries to the woman's back. Across her back were several marks. The woman had been thrashed or lashed with a cane or a whip. There was also a trickle of blood from the woman's vagina, indicating some sort of injury there, but as her ankles were bound with the knotted handkerchief, it was impossible to establish what sort of injury this might be. Spooner and Symes noted that the bedding of the bed nearest the window was soaked with blood. This suggested that the woman had suffered her injuries on the bed nearest the window and had then been transferred to the bed by the door.[9]

Looking around the room, it seemed as if nothing had been disturbed. There was no sign of a struggle. On the mantleshelf was a white metal bracelet and on the dressing table were a pair of flowery earrings made of fabric. A large ornamental ring and two other rings were still on the dead woman's fingers. Her fingernails – varnished a very dark colour – were unbroken, although there were traces of blood beneath them. On a pillow on the bed nearest the window was a long, patterned, elongated mark in blood that suggested that a stick, a riding crop or whip had been struck or wiped across it. Keith Simpson arrived and examined the body at 6.30 p.m. and found it to be still warm. He estimated the death to have taken place at about midnight or in the very early hours of that morning.

A brown leather ladies' handbag lay on one of the armchairs. It contained all the personal elements of the woman's life including an identity card, which, together with several letters, confirmed that the woman was not 'Mrs Heath' at all. The dead woman was a Mrs Margery Gardner of Bramham Gardens, SW5.

Spooner interviewed the hotel staff and was informed that the room had been booked on the previous Sunday in the name of Lieutenant Colonel Heath. Mrs Wyatt was sure that she recognized the man's face and believed that he had stayed at the hotel before. When she later checked the register, she discovered that he had stayed there in November 1944 with a woman called Zita Williams. At the time he had been wearing a South African Air Force uniform and registered under the name of Armstrong. He had actually registered at the hotel twice before under that name.[10]

When interviewed, both Barbara Osborne and Rhoda Spooner were certain that the dead woman was 'Mrs Heath' because she had dark hair, but they had mistaken Margery for the dark-haired Yvonne Symonds whom they had both seen on the previous Monday morning. Importantly, Barbara also informed the police that she had thoroughly cleaned the washbasin as usual on Thursday morning, stating, 'I cleaned the washbasin and did so with a wet rag and Vim powder all around the inside of the basin and the edges. I have no doubt of that.'[11]

Curiously, despite the obvious violence of the attack, nothing untoward was heard during the night despite the fact that there were three other rooms off the first-floor landing. Alice Wyatt slept in the room directly opposite Room 4[12] and she had heard nothing after she retired to bed at 10.30 p.m. Of the residents in the hotel only a Mrs Thomas in Room 5 said that she had been woken in the early hours of Friday morning. She had heard creaking followed by the sound of the tap running in the bathroom on the landing. A little later on she heard the front door bang.[13]

When Spooner telephoned the Criminal Records Office at New Scotland Yard, he was informed that Lieutenant Colonel Heath was the name used by Neville George Clevely Heath who had a substantial criminal record and was said to be living with his parents at an address in Wimbledon. Spooner left Symes at the scene of the crime to supervise the examination of the body and made his way to Heath's parents' house in south-west London. After Simpson's examination at the hotel, Margery's body was removed in a cardboard coffin and taken to Hammersmith mortuary in Fulham Palace Road.

As the afternoon turned to evening, a *Daily Mail* journalist, Harry Procter, walked home past Pembridge Gardens and saw a 'small army of reporters' outside the hotel. Procter ran into a colleague of his, Sydney Brock, who said 'it looked like a murder, but it turns out to be an abortion'. Later that night, Procter met a police officer friend in his local pub, who presumed Procter was working on this latest murder case in Notting Hill. Procter had been told it was an abortion gone wrong. His police friend said, 'Then it's the queerest abortion I ever heard of', and told him that the dead woman had been tied up and beaten. Sensing a sensational story, Procter left immediately and headed for Hammersmith mortuary where he joined a growing crowd of reporters who had all been tipped off that an extraordinary investigation was under way.[14]

Across London, Spooner arrived at a comfortable, red-brick house in suburban Wimbledon. The house, standing proudly on the corner of Merton Hall Road, was a substantial three-storey semi-detached residence in a very respectable area, surrounded by avenues of trees and backing on to open playing fields. Spooner introduced himself to Mr and Mrs Heath, who were apparently a very decent couple in their fifties. William Heath was the manager of the Waterloo Station branch of Faulkner's, a chain of hairdressing shops, and his wife was a housewife. Bessie Heath told Spooner that her son had always been secretive, and was prone to being excitable which sometimes overcame him and made him sick. Heath's father told Spooner that Neville drank rather heavily, usually beer, but alcohol didn't seem to affect him. Neither of his parents had any information about their son's association with women, who he appeared to shun.[15] Though he was not unduly conceited, he was very particular about his appearance and bathed most mornings.[16]

After interviewing Mr and Mrs Heath, Spooner searched Heath's bedroom and took away some of his personal possessions including books, papers – and four whips.

He also took Heath's address book. This contained the names, addresses and telephone numbers of over 300 women.[17]

The post-mortem on Margery Gardner took place that night at 10 p.m., attended by both Spooner and Symes, where Simpson was able to make a more thorough examination of the body.[18]

Margery's breasts had been so savagely bitten that one nipple was hanging loose; the other was found, bitten off, under her body. Turning the body over, Simpson counted seventeen lash marks, many of them so severe that the diamond weave pattern of the whip and its ferrule-like metallic tip were imprinted on her flesh. Nine of the lashes were on her back and buttocks, six were on the right side of the body injuring the breast, chest and abdomen and the remaining two were on the head over the left and right brow. The lashes were so clearly defined that Simpson was able to measure them with mathematical precision. The left-hand side of Margery's face had been bruised by two blows or punches. There was also a group of bruises under the chin consistent with someone gripping it to prevent her head from moving.

The wound from which the blood had seeped when Spooner tilted the body was a seven-inch long tear of the vagina running four inches up the right wall and a further three inches across the back. It had been caused by a 'tearing instrument such as a whip or cane' being thrust into her and savagely rotated. The actual cause of death was asphyxia due to suffocation, though there was no indication of strangulation. Speculating about the order in which the injuries might have occurred, Simpson felt that the whip lashes took place first, followed by the blows to the face. The assailant then gripped Margery's jaw with his hand and then her arms. After this he savaged her nipples with his teeth, then penetrated her vagina with the haft of the whip. Finally he forced her face into the bedding, ending her appalling ordeal by suffocating her. Simpson also confirmed the telling detail that Margery's face had been washed after her death.

Though the injuries had taken place before she died it was not possible to ascertain whether or not Margery was conscious during the attack. She may have been rendered unconscious by the two blows to the head. She was certainly made helpless by the knotted handkerchiefs around her legs and wrists. She could also have been gagged, which may have contributed to her suffocation. This would also account for the fact that none of the nearby guests heard any screams from the room, despite the excruciating pain Margery must have suffered.

Simpson concluded that the injuries were the consequence of 'a most violent and sadistic sexual assault'.[19] Having investigated the lash marks and the internal injuries to the vagina,

Simpson was convinced that these injuries had all been executed with the diamond weave whip. 'If you find that whip,' he told Spooner, 'you've found your man.'[20]

Another clue that the post-mortem yielded was the handkerchief that had bound Margery's feet together. This bore the name 'L. Kearns' handwritten in black ink and also had an embroidered 'K' in blue silk cotton in one corner. This clearly didn't belong to Margery as it was a man's handkerchief and she had a clean and pressed one bearing her name in her handbag. So, who was this man Kearns and how was he involved in Margery's death? At the time it seemed to Reg Spooner that the hunt was on for *two* men, both potential killers, both on the loose – and judging by the brutality of the attack on Margery Gardner – both extremely dangerous.

Given how clear the case against Neville Heath looked, Spooner issued a memo to the *Police Gazette* and to the press with a description and photograph of him as well as a request for information regarding the owner of the handkerchief. This memo was dispatched to every newspaper editor in the country and arrived on their desks on Saturday morning. But by Monday morning, Spooner had a change of heart. Though he needed the press to help trace Heath as swiftly as possible, he worried that the photograph might compromise a future court case. The taxi driver's identification of Heath as the last person to be seen with Margery alive would be crucial. If the defence could prove that the driver had already seen a photograph of Heath in the newspapers, his evidence would be compromised and it might make it impossible to prove his guilt.

Another memo was hastily issued by Scotland Yard, withdrawing the photograph from all newspaper publication. Any deviation from the police's directive would be followed by the full force of the law. Consequently, though written

descriptions of Heath appeared in all newspapers, the photograph was completely withdrawn from circulation.

> In connection with the death of Margery Gardner at
> Pembridge Gardens on the night of 20/21 June the
> Commissioner of Police of the metropolis requests editors to
> kindly refrain from publishing any photograph of Neville
> George Clevely Heath as publication will seriously prejudice
> any subsequent court proceedings.[21]

In the months to come, this controversial memo was to lead
to questions in the House of Commons. Within days it was
to have a tragic, indeed fatal, impact.

PART TWO

Neville George Clevely Heath

CHAPTER SEVEN
Rake's Progress

6 JUNE 1917 – 12 JULY 1938

It is a difficult question, my friends, for any young man ...
whether to follow uncritically the track he finds himself in,
without considering his aptness for it, or to consider what
his aptness or bent may be, and re-shape his course accordingly. I tried to do the latter, and I failed ... However it
was my poverty and not my will that consented to be
beaten. It takes two or three generations to do what I tried
to do in one; and my impulses – affections – vices perhaps
they should be called – were too strong not to hamper a
man without advantages.

Thomas Hardy, *Jude the Obscure*, 1895

Neville George Clevely Heath was born at home in a
Victorian bay-fronted terraced house at Dudley Road,
Ilford on 6 June 1917. The world he was born into was

dominated by war, violence and loss – themes that for him, and for many of his generation, would characterize and define their lives.

The newspapers that day headlined a further offensive in Belgium where the British army was still fighting for control of the city of Ypres.[1] Unseasonally wet weather had turned the battlefields into a sea of mud and by October that year, British casualties would mount to over 159,000. This, the 'most gigantic, grim, futile and bloody fight ever waged',[2] became known to history as the Battle of Passchendale. At home, southern England was also being terrorized by German raids. By this point in the Great War, Zeppelin airships had largely been replaced by a newer and much more powerful aircraft – the sinister Gotha Bomber. On the evening of 5 June a great battle took place over the Thames between the Imperial German Air Force and the Royal Flying Corps; bombs dropped across the south and east coasts and the inland south-eastern counties. The *Evening Standard* noted that picturedromes and tearooms quickly emptied as crowds sought to find a vantage point to watch the extraordinary air battle.

> Our gunners smashed their formation almost at a volley, scattered them like fluttering birds, sent cones of bursting shells over them, around them, straight at them. The Huns had the gaping six miles of estuary below them. They pelted bombs down. Many hit the water. Great columns of water surged up and the din was terrific.[3]

The German planes were driven away by Royal Naval Air Service pilots resulting in the loss of ten 'Hun' aircraft. German air raids continued throughout the month and 300,000 Londoners sought nightly shelter in tube stations, just as they would do a generation later.

Heath's parents later claimed that their son had been born in an air raid and that this ill-starred beginning must in some way have contributed to his complex personality. As early as 1938, when Heath was sent to borstal, his father was citing the air raid as the reason for his son's excitable and highly strung nature.[4] Reg Spooner, thorough as ever, examined records of enemy action and found that no air raids were recorded in Ilford on 6 June itself. But there is no reason to doubt the Heaths' testimony, as they are generally reliable and honest. It may be that Bessie Heath's labour started on the evening before – the day of the raid over the south-eastern counties. This is the first of the many confusions that occur throughout Heath's life and story. Three doctors and two nurses attended the labour and Heath's head was 'badly damaged by instruments at [his] birth',[5] suggesting a forceps delivery. This would have been necessary if Mrs Heath was exhausted or if the baby was becoming distressed. Air raid or not, Heath's birth was clearly traumatic.

After his trial, Heath's parents were at pains to search their memories for incidents from their son's childhood that might have affected his emotional or psychological development. Their well-intentioned attempts to uncover a forgotten clue or some inherent pattern that could justify his later actions might seem a little unscientific. Was there a genetic root to his aberrant behaviour? Bessie Heath revealed that her uncle, William Clevely, had been confined to a mental home for most of his life and had died, institutionalized, in 1938. 'He was quite small when he set his bedclothes alight and bedroom on fire – and the shock was so great that his brain never grew on normal lines again,' she stated.[6] She observed that her son had 'always been susceptible to shock' and her husband concurred in a letter to Heath whilst in prison, reassuring his son that 'any kind of shock has always been the thing to upset you most'.[7] As well as reiterating the damaging psychological effects of being born into a world at war, they searched for concrete physical reasons to justify their son's acts – a broken wrist or a fractured elbow in childhood, maybe? For surely, to commit such horrific acts, to cause such pain and suffering – there must *be* a reason? But perhaps these are the desperate questions that any parent in the Heaths' circumstances would ask themselves. Where did we go wrong? Are we, as parents, in some way responsible?

Heath's father, William, was born in 1890 into a respectable, hard-working, lower-middle-class family from Highbury, north London. William's father had trained as a copperplate engraver of maps and charts, but then set up his own business, running an hotel.[8] William himself worked as an assistant clerk with the civil service. Bessie Clevely was the daughter of a printer and had also been born in London, a little further north than William in Stoke Newington. In 1899, the Clevely family had moved some distance away to Ilford in Essex. This could be because the Clevelys had relatives there, as the whole Heath family, after the traumatic events of 1946, moved back to the area in the 1950s.

In April 1913, 23-year-old William Heath married Bessie Clevely at St Alban's, Ilford – a classic pressed red-brick church – just around the corner from Bessie's parents' house at 35 Dudley Road. This was to be William and Bessie Heath's first married home and where they would live with their extended family for the duration of the First World War. William Heath had been registered as a 'warehouseman' at the time of his marriage and as a 'soft goods traveller' at the time of Heath's birth, but it's very likely that he saw active service at some point during the war. The Military Service Act in January 1916 made conscription compulsory for single men between eighteen and forty-one. Married men like William were only exempt until May 1916. By the end of the war, 25 per cent of the total male population had joined the army, a total of 5 million men.

Of the many English towns that are the backdrop to Heath's story, Ilford seems to have changed the most – not only because of wartime bombing and 1960s urban planning – but because of post-war immigration. A large Asian community of Hindus, Muslims and Sikhs now resides in the quiet and ordered streets around the Heaths' first home in Dudley Road. Hindu temples have replaced Anglican churches, front gardens concreted over to accommodate people carriers. Only half an hour from London by train, it's not the first time in its history that Ilford has undergone a dramatic cultural change. For over 1,200 years, Ilford had been a small village in Essex, part of the parish of Barking. But after the first rail link from Liverpool Street was constructed in the 1870s, the entire character of Ilford changed, and the town evolved with great speed into a dormitory suburb. With the advent of the railway, it was a comfortable commuting distance from central London and would house the clerks, assistant managers, teachers and shop workers – like the Clevelys and the Heaths – who served the booming city of London at the zenith of its imperial potency. Developers bought up large areas of land specifically for housing developments with the intention of attracting the new breed of owner-occupiers. Thousands of homes were built to suit the budgets of blue- and white-collar workers, from domestic staff to managing directors. In many cases even the deposit was the subject of a short-term loan provided by the builders. Shops, swimming pools, theatres, cinemas and libraries all followed as Ilford developed into a sedate and self-sufficient satellite of the metropolis. The expansion of the area was extraordinary; in 1881 Ilford had a population of 7,645 – by 1911, it had rocketed over tenfold to 78,188.[9]

By the 1920s, Ilford was established as a mature and fashionable suburb, but in 1922 the town was shaken by a story of sex and violence that took place on a politely ordered avenue and within an archetypal family that had come to define the comfortable but aspiring middle class that typified the area. This story – which was to wreck the lives of several local families – would anticipate the fate of the Heaths as well as touching their lives with an extraordinary, chilling coincidence.

Good-looking and sophisticated, Edith Thompson and her husband Percy were typical of the commuter families that had settled in Ilford. Edith was a professional woman who managed a hat shop in central London. Having married the dull and occasionally violent Percy Thompson, her head had been turned by a young man serving in the merchant navy, Frederick Bywaters, whom she had been introduced to by her younger sister, Avis. Looking for a room in the area when home from sea, Bywaters became the Thompsons' lodger. Nine years Edith's junior, he was handsome, virile and full of stories about his exotic travels abroad. Soon after he moved into the Thompsons' house at 41 Kensington Gardens, Bywaters and Mrs Thompson began an affair. When he was away at sea, Edith fuelled the relationship with a series of letters, heavily influenced by the romantic fiction she voraciously consumed, but also chronicling the journey of their own sexual relationship in intimate detail. She poured out her love for Bywaters and her desperate desire to be rid of her husband. She even suggested that she had dosed Thompson's food with poison and ground glass from an electric light bulb. This became the tabloid image of Edith Thompson – a 'Messalina of the Suburbs'[10] who used her age and experience first to seduce the naïve Bywaters and then to entice him to kill her husband. But this image proved to be a fantasy – a melodramatic attempt on Edith's behalf to keep Bywaters excited by the relationship during his time away at sea, whilst she remained at home, submitting uncomfortably to her husband in the bedroom. When Bywaters returned to England, Percy Thompson became aware of his wife's adultery and confronted the lovers, telling Bywaters to leave the house immediately. Bywaters did so, but insisted at the same time that Thompson should give his wife a divorce.[11]

On 3 October 1922, the Thompsons were returning home from the Criterion Theatre at Piccadilly Circus, having caught the 11.30 p.m. train from Liverpool Street, arriving at Ilford Station around midnight. Whilst they were walking along a part of Belgrave Road that was unlit by streetlamps, an assailant rushed past the couple and attacked Percy Thompson with a knife, pushing Edith aside. She cried out, 'Oh, don't, oh don't!' in 'a most piteous manner'. Percy collapsed against the wall. The Thompsons were only 54 yards from home.

Bessie Heath's older brother, Percy Clevely, was then living with his wife at 62 Mayfair Avenue, a few minutes' walk from the Thompsons' house. On the night of the murder, Percy had also been walking home from Ilford Station with a friend, Dora Pittard. Suddenly, Edith Thompson 'seemed to come out of the darkness', running towards them, hysterical and incoherent. She said that her husband had fallen down and was ill and that she desperately needed help. She wanted to know if they knew of a doctor? Percy Clevely and Dora took Mrs Thompson to a Dr Maudsley at 62 Courtland Avenue who said he would come and help. Mrs Thompson ran ahead and when Clevely and Dr Maudsley arrived, they found Percy Thompson propped up against a wall with his wife kneeling over him. Dr Maudsley struck a match and examined Thompson, but he was by then already dead. Percy Clevely asked Mrs

Thompson what had happened and she said that she couldn't say. Something had 'brushed' or 'flew' past them and then Percy had collapsed. When Dr Maudsley told Edith that her husband was dead, she asked, 'Why did you not come sooner and save him?'

Percy Thompson had died of stab wounds and both his wife and Bywaters were arrested and charged with murder. Percy Clevely was called as a prosecution witness to the Old Bailey on 6 December 1922.[12] He was cross-examined by Travers Humphreys who had appeared for the Crown in the trials of Oscar Wilde, Dr. Crippen and George Joseph Smith, the 'Brides in the Bath' killer.

Despite a lack of convincing evidence that Edith Thompson had in any way instigated the murder, both she and Bywaters were executed in January 1923 – with Mrs Thompson dragged, drugged and unconscious, to the gallows, causing mass protestations of her innocence and a strong lobby against the death penalty. This controversial case, essentially a miscarriage of justice, was to continue to fuel the debate for the abolition of the death penalty through-out the rest of the century. Such was the public fascination with the case, that later, when the contents of the Thompsons' home were put up for auction, the hedge in the front garden was completely stripped of its leaves by people wanting a souvenir.[13]

Edith Thompson's beautifully decorated, double-fronted Edwardian house – her pride and joy – was minutes away from the more modest Clevely family home in Dudley Road. But for the young Heaths and their little son, Neville, it must have seemed extraordinary that a murder could have taken place in the streets of Ilford – on their own doorstep. Bessie's brother Percy was in the papers – and not just in the *Ilford Recorder* and the *East Ham Echo*, but in the national press, too. This sort of scandal just didn't involve ordinary people like

William and Bessie Heath. But wouldn't it be a fascinating tale to tell their grandchildren by the fireside one day – the time when Uncle Percy was a witness in the most sensational trial of the age?

After Edith Thompson's execution, there was much local sympathy for her family who continued to live in the area. In the wake of such traumatic events, how did they find the resolve to face the world with such quiet dignity?

A generation later, William and Bessie Heath were to find out for themselves.

In about 1918 the Heaths had some studio photographs taken of their young son. Dressed in white, with long, golden curls, he looks girlish, as was the fashion of the day. His eyes are bright and lively and we know them to be a dazzling blue. In one photograph, he leans against his mother's head, his left arm resting on her shoulder, his baby teeth just visible as he and Bessie smile into the camera. His mother is an attractive woman, not yet thirty, with even features and dark hair. There's trust and love in the photograph. A proud and contented mother, an adored and beautiful child.

Possibly motivated by William's work as a manufacturer's agent in the textile industry, the young family left Ilford in the spring of 1920 and moved across London to Merton in south-west London. At the same time, Bessie had announced that she was pregnant again. The Heaths set up home in a corner property in a street of smart Edwardian houses at 1 Bathurst Avenue where, on 5 September, Bessie gave birth to another son, Carol William Clevely Heath – a younger brother and companion for little Neville. But tragedy was soon to cloud their lives.

Tubercular meningitis, popularly known as consumption, was an epidemic in the early twentieth century with no known cure. Feared by the entire population, it was known to be infectious and deadly. Children under four were most vulnerable as their immune systems were not sufficiently developed to fight the ravages of the disease which affected the lungs and resulted in lethargy, fever, weight loss and coughing – sometimes, distressingly, bringing up blood. Tragically for his family, Carol Heath soon began to exhibit symptoms. The disease was hugely contagious and both Bessie and William would have been vulnerable to it, but the family member at the highest risk of infection would have been Neville, who was six at the time. Many adults who developed the illness would be treated in sanatoria, effectively removed from society in order to prevent the spread of their disease, but Carol, being still a child, was cared for at home. Both parents would have been aware that his prognosis would be very bleak; in this period, the vast majority of individuals who contracted the disease did not survive. At the beginning of February 1923, Carol's condition deteriorated and he fell into a coma. He never recovered and died at home on 24 February 1923, his mother at his bedside. He was just two.

The Heaths were devastated by the loss of their son, but were particularly concerned about how it would affect his older brother, who was now 'grief-stricken'.[14] For the six-year-old Neville, without other siblings to console or distract him, Carol's death was deeply traumatic. His later relationship with his brother Mick gives an indication of how much Heath valued this fraternal bond. Heath's sole concern whilst in prison was to try to secure his brother's future. For Mick, too, this affection was reciprocal, even following his brother into the RAF when he was old enough, attempting to live out his brother's dreams.

After Carol's death, Heath had the upbringing of an only child. Mick would not be born until 1928 and it's very likely that Bessie Heath may have become pregnant in the interim, but not succeeded in bringing more children to term. The relationship between Heath and his parents was very loving – as his letters from prison testify. He felt them well suited to each other, with neither dominating the other – always kind and possibly, he admitted, indulgent towards him.[15] It's not surprising that the Heaths should have adored their golden-haired boy given their loss, but even so, Heath didn't think his mother was unusually possessive or emotional. Though he never shared any personal difficulties with his parents, he felt that if he were ever to do so, it would have been with his mother.

As a young boy, Neville began to reveal an acquisitive streak as well as a pronounced slyness. Though his mother later dismissed his childhood misdemeanours as 'stupid and unnecessary',[16] he was developing habits that he was to continue to practise as an adult. On one occasion he had been caught taking cakes from a confectioner and putting them on somebody else's bill. When he was found out, his first instinct was to run away. Tellingly, Bessie Heath noted that 'there was no need to [steal] as he always had plenty at home'. On another occasion, his parents found some cheap things in Neville's pocket which he admitted he had stolen, but were of 'no use to him'. None of young Neville's petty thefts were driven by need; they were driven by desire. Subsequently, Bessie Heath said that 'he was told how seriously wrong it was but [he] was not harshly treated'. Even as a child, Neville Heath had a growing awareness that he had a knack for getting away with things unpunished. Certainly Spooner felt that Bessie Heath had been an over-indulgent mother and that she had possibly, in sparing the rod, spoiled her child.[17]

Though his parents were Church of England by faith, young Neville was sent to Holy Cross Convent, a local Roman Catholic school in Wimbledon. This, the Heaths felt, was the only decent school in the neighbourhood and it's clear that from an early age his parents were ambitious for their son and wanted to give him the best start in life. Although kindly treated at the convent, he felt isolated with the other Church of England children, but he bore no lasting ill will towards the nuns who taught him in the three years he attended. He then proceeded to a local council school until he was old enough to go to a secondary school.

Significantly, even when he was discussing his past with a psychiatrist after his arrest, Heath insisted that he had actually spent this period at a private prep school. This suggests that Heath felt embarrassment or at least some anxiety about his background and education and, certainly, for the rest of his life he was to conjure a much more upmarket CV for himself than the modest reality.

By 1928, William Heath was still working in the textile trade, though now specifically as an underwear manufacturer. In the spring of that year, Bessie Heath found herself pregnant again and, perhaps wanting more space for two growing children, the family moved to 1 Melrose Road, a semi-detached cottage in a leafy, almost rural, garden estate. The house itself was around the corner from St Mary's in Merton – an ancient parish church where Lord Nelson used to worship. At Melrose Road, Bessie gave birth to another son, Michael Robert Clevely Heath, always known as 'Mick'. Despite the difference in their ages, the two boys were very close. Unable, at first, to pronounce Neville's name, Mick took to calling him 'Nen', a family nickname that stuck for the rest of Heath's life.

In 1932, the family moved house again, this time rising considerably up the property scale which presumably also increased their social standing. The Heaths' new home was a solid red-brick Edwardian villa, situated on the corner of Merton Hall Road, just outside Wimbledon town centre and in the same road that would house, from 1940, the Wimbledon School of Art. The house remains today – a five-bedroom property, typical of suburban London, with a garden looking on to playing fields at the back. It was a house of some comfort – certainly of no privation. Immediately the family moved in, Bessie took advantage of the extra rooms and offered them to paying guests, renting out rooms to as many as four lodgers at a time. At its most crowded in 1939, the house was home to seven adults plus the eleven-year-old Mick Heath. Several of these lodgers became long-term tenants including Lavinia Scoley who stayed with the Heaths from 1932 to 1938. There would continue to be lodgers at Merton Hall Road throughout the 1930s and for the duration of the war. The Heaths were never to live there alone and even in 1946 they had a single lodger.[18]

One of the reasons for taking in paying guests would have been that the Heaths had hopes of securing their sons places at the local grammar school, where the fees were £3 10s. per term.[19] Rutlish School was situated at the junction of Kingston Road and Station Road in Merton Park – a ten-minute walk from Merton Hall Road. Neville Heath's time there from 1929 to 1934 was typical of the period – a conservative haven of safe (if prosaic) middle-class values; a world of cricket teas, rugby XVs, Gilbert and Sullivan operettas, sports days and prize-givings.[20]

Rutlish, a typical suburban grammar school, had been set up in 1895. In 1921 an ambitious new headmaster, Edward Varnish, had taken over with an agenda for radical change. One teacher who had joined the school in the 1920s, remembered that he found the school 'undergoing a revolution':

[It was] filled with community spirit that I have never seen surpassed elsewhere and seldom equalled. It was clear from the first that Mr Varnish had in some way captured the imagination of boys and staff and made them believe that all belonged to a place that was unique and bound to succeed.[21]

Varnish promoted his ambitions, however, at the expense of the fabric and upkeep of the actual school buildings. In 1933, a school inspector recorded that the school was in an appalling state of squalor:

> The old premises are dark and dingy ... There is no library, no changing accommodation, no waiting room. The hall is inadequate. No gymnasium. Several forms are not adequately housed. No manual room. No geography room. The cadet corps headquarters were makeshift. There was no dining room. Cloakrooms wretched.[22]

But Varnish wasn't interested in the physical aspects of the school – he wanted to change its ethos. His agenda in the 1920s and 1930s was very much focused on reforming the school along the lines of one of the great English public schools. The foundation of Varnish's plan was a House system to instil in the boys a sense of competition and belonging. On entering the school each boy was allocated to one of eight houses named after an ancient warrior race: Argonauts, Crusaders, Kelts, Parthians, Romans, Spartans, Trojans and Vikings, the house that Heath joined. Each of the houses was made up of about sixty boys with a housemaster and a captain. Over the school year, points would be awarded to each individual boy for sporting and academic achievements and these would be added to a house score at the end of the year. The winning house would be known as Cock House.[23] This fostered a sense of camaraderie within each house as well as a sporting sense of competition between them.

The ethos 'For King and Country' married to driving

ambition was firmly established at the heart of Rutlish tradition – even enshrined in the school song:

> *We are arming for the fight,*
> *Pressing on with all our might,*
> *Pluming wings for higher flight.*
> *Up! – and On!*[24]

Several of the younger masters had seen active service in the First World War and ninety-eight Rutlish Old Boys were remembered on the War Memorial at the back of the school hall.[25] This environment was to engender a martial spirit in the generation of boys like Heath who were educated at the school in the period leading up to the Second World War. In 1922, Varnish had initiated a Cadet Corps, which was affiliated to the 5th Battalion of the East Surrey Regiment Territorial Army. Though this was an attempt by the headmaster to follow an established public school tradition, it was also very much a sign of the times, as the thirties progressed and Germany's international ambitions were becoming clearer. In the year that Hitler was appointed chancellor, the Rutlish Cadet Corps – including Heath – were the proud recipients of the inaugural 'Nation Cup', which was established to acknowledge the most outstanding Cadet Corps in Britain. The trophy was presented to the Corps by the Prince of Wales in the garden of St James's Palace in June 1933.

Varnish introduced a series of other innovations in order to ape the public school system. They began to play rugby rather than soccer and by the early 1930s Heath was playing for the First XV. He was also appointed as a prefect, this system also initiated by Varnish. As well as keeping order, prefects were authorized to give canings as punishment. These were always carried out in the presence of a witness and entered into the Punishments Book.[26] By this period, such beatings were ubiquitous in British public and grammar schools to the extent that in France the act of flagellation had famously been dubbed 'the English vice'. Though there's no reason to suspect Heath of overindulging his authority as a prefect, in all probability his time at Rutlish will have been his introduction either as a witness or a participant to corporal punishment.

In *The English Vice*, Ian Gibson notes that for many flagellants, very often the first excitement in connection with beating takes place in early childhood when a whipping inflicted by an adult has been witnessed, undergone or read about. Freud and the German sexual psychologist Krafft-Ebing observed that several of their patients had remarkably similar case histories, dating their first awareness of sexual arousal from reading flogging scenes in *Uncle Tom's Cabin*.[27] There was also a very strong tradition of school stories in boys' fiction published throughout the Victorian period and many of these described canings, whippings and thrashings as a matter of course. This was carried on into the twentieth century in twopenny weeklies like *The Gem* and *The Magnet* as well as in annuals such as *Boy's Own* and *Chums*. A typical scene from the period Heath would have been reading appears in *Chums Annual* (1927–8):

[Chummy] was wondering how many strokes it would be, whether it would draw blood, whether he would cry in front of all the form!

Mr London picked up the ground-ash and pointed to a vacant desk in front.

'Bend over there,' he commanded.

Chummy put himself in position and put his handkerchief into his mouth.

Mr London brought the stick down with all his force, four

times, four deliberate, even strokes, and each stroke raised a purple weal under Chummy's shorts ... and that is how Chummy came to worship Mr London with all his heart and soul.[28]

There's little difference, it would seem, between these stories aimed at children and the seamier reaches of 'adult' fiction.

But it is not only the casual sadism that these boys' weeklies depicted that might have influenced the adolescent Heath. George Orwell made a study of the culture surrounding these comics, often (inaccurately) described as 'penny dreadfuls' in his 1940 essay 'Boys' Weeklies'. He observed that 'nearly every boy who reads at all'[29] went through a stage of reading one or other of them. The most celebrated and the oldest were *The Gem* and *The Magnet*, each of which promoted an idealized view of life in public schools: St Jim's in *The Gem*, Greyfriars in *The Magnet*. These are represented as ancient institutions much like Eton or Winchester. The boys in the stories never aged and remained perpetually about fourteen. The stories were endlessly repetitive, focusing on horseplay, practical jokes, ragging, fights, canings, football, cricket and food.[30]

Orwell notes that boys who did actually go to public schools read the comics, but nearly always stopped reading them at about the age of twelve. But boys at cheaper private schools, like Rutlish, 'that are designed for people who can't afford a public school but consider the council schools "common"',[31] carried on reading them until they were fifteen or sixteen. Orwell's point was very much about class. These weeklies promoted a dated and conservative ethos that was consumed by vast numbers of schoolboys, like Heath, who felt excluded from some sort of paradisal boyhood promoted in their pages.

One Rutlish old boy from this period remembered that

from his first day, two specific objectives were outlined: 'By the time you leave Rutlish School you will be able to swim and to speak the King's English.'[32] Another pupil felt the Varnish agenda was extremely simple: 'Get educated, talk proper and you will succeed in life.'[33] Elocution was pivotal to a Rutlish education and was drilled into the boys by Herbert Cave, an English master who had written a book on the subject in 1930, *Practical Exercises in Spoken English*.[34] The Governors' Report of 1933 particularly commended this – 'a successful attempt had been made to turn out boys with power to speak correct Standard English'[35] – by which they meant Received Pronunciation. This was to prove invaluable to Heath who was to use his accent and the assumption of a patrician manner to masquerade as a member of the upper-middle class throughout his life and career.

Given how frequently he was to attempt to pass himself off as a product of Eton and Oxbridge, it's clear that something of Varnish's social ambitions for his boys rubbed off on the young Neville Heath; his yearning for upward social mobility, his self-aggrandizement and snobbery was ignited by Varnish's public-school ambitions for his grammar-school boys.[36] J. D. Casswell, Heath's defence counsel, was later to identify this key element of Heath's character. He was, he said, 'a man never satisfied to remain in the station to which he had been called and for which he was qualified'.[37]

Far from accepting the rigid class divisions of pre-war Britain, Heath was to study them, learn the manners and language of his social superiors – ape them – then ruthlessly exploit them.

In the various books and articles written about Heath over the past six decades, several cite uncorroborated incidents from his school days that identify embryonic sadistic behaviour. Gerald Byrne in *Borstal Boy* reports the instance of a girl in Heath's class at school being beaten by him so hard with a ruler that she had to be sent home in a taxi. If true, this must have taken place before the age of twelve, as Rutlish was a school for boys only. Certainly, Bessie Heath denied that this incident ever took place: 'I do not know of this incident [and] neither does his headmaster, who has nothing but good to say of him. Surely I, his mother, would have heard of this, if it had happened?'[38]

This may well be the opinion of a mother blind to the faults of a much-loved son. But, in the wake of the huge publicity surrounding Heath at the time of his arrest, many of the tales about him may well be apocryphal. Like this story, none are verifiable by any sources. *Borstal Boy* was published immediately after the trial in 1946, written in great haste and with a tabloid audience in mind. Its author, Gerald Byrne, was a journalist with the Sunday newspaper, *Empire News*. He had met Heath casually in various pubs and during the trial had talked to many of Heath's associates. Though he doesn't cite any sources, some of the incidents he describes do have the ring of truth. He quotes one young woman, a friend from Heath's schooldays:

Even at the age of fifteen Neville Heath started to show his sway over girls. The girls at the local school I attended used to take turns arranging regular little parties at their various homes and we wouldn't have dreamt of having a party without Neville – it wouldn't have been complete. He was an unmitigated liar, show-off swank-pot and all the things that usually go to make an unpopular character, yet although all the girls knew his faults, he somehow managed to blend them into an unusual and charming personality, and we all liked him.[39]

Heath was to develop this persona as the likeable rogue, the young dandy, throughout his adolescence to such an extent that by the time he reached borstal, he was a self-confessed 'Raffles'.

Byrne cites another incident, uncorroborated at the time, but verified a decade later by Giles Playfair and Derrick Sington in their study of psychopathy, *The Offenders*. Having read of the incident in Byrne's book and uneasy about quoting unverifiable sources, they had tracked down many of the individuals involved.

One winter night, when he was about fifteen, the young Heath and a boy called 'Howard' attended a party at the home of a mutual friend, Elizabeth, in Wimbledon High Street. The two boys, who were in the habit of drinking quarts of beer together in the garage behind Howard's house, had purchased a considerable amount of alcohol from the off-licence in Sutton High Street. As well as the boys, Elizabeth had invited five of her female friends. Her parents were out for the evening and the young people were left to their own devices. After a while, it was suggested that they play 'Murders' and the group dispersed to various parts of the house. They successfully played the game twice. The third time, Heath and Howard persuaded a girl called 'Jeanette' to accompany them in their search for clues. The three young people climbed to the top of the house and entered a bedroom. Suddenly, Heath grabbed Jeanette and threw her on the bed, calling to Howard to help him.

'Come on Howard, let's make real love to her!' Neville held Jeanette down as she violently kicked and struggled. The two boys first tried to kiss her face but she moved her head from side to side to avoid their lips. Then – 'We'll soon show her what love really is!' said Neville.

Jeanette screamed, alerting the other girls in the house. She returned home, deeply shocked, 'with deep blue finger marks on both sides of her throat'.[40]

Gerald Byrne interviewed both Jeanette's father and Howard in 1946. Then, in 1956, Playfair and Sington attempted to have the assault verified by Jeanette's father, a former MP.[41] He confirmed that the story was true. After the incident, he had gone off in search of the two boys and caught up with them outside Howard's house. He reprimanded Heath and warned him that not only might he be expelled from school for such behaviour, but he might also be reported to the authorities. This, after all, was a violent attempted sexual assault and not merely adolescent 'horseplay' as Byrne has Heath refer to it. Heath was 'disarmingly apologetic, courteous and contrite' and managed to persuade Jeanette's father not to report him to Varnish or the police. This was to become a well-rehearsed strategy in Heath's life. Having committed offences, he would rely on his innate charm and good manners to side-step difficult situations. Together with the appearance of sincere contrition this usually led to Heath being let off the hook. Not only did this allow him to refine his skill in petty offences, but it also began to cement his attitude to those in authority.[42]

This incident is the first evidence of violence in Heath's life, and it's worth bearing in mind that he stated to a prison psychiatrist in 1946 that he had no knowledge of sex until the age of eighteen,[43] some years *after* this attack. But it's also significant that Heath had been drinking before the assault – the marriage of sexual aggression and alcohol already fused, even before he had lost his virginity.

Though adept at sport – especially at rugby, cricket and athletics – Heath did not excel at school, mathematics being the only subject he felt confident in. He sat the matriculation exam but failed. He refused to take it again, despite appeals from his mother and Mr Varnish. Without matriculating, neither university nor a commission as an officer in the services were options for him. At the age of sixteen, on 9 March 1934, he started work as a warehouseman in the silk department of Pawson and Leaf, an established textile importer at St Paul's Churchyard in the City of London, which had been trading since the eighteenth century.[44] The building still remains situated directly opposite the cathedral. This job had probably been arranged for Heath through his father's connections in the textile business and William Heath may well have worked for Pawson and Leaf at some point himself. Heath earned 25s. a week for general menial duties and though the job was dull, he was buoyed by the social life.[45] In the City, he made friends with several other young men who were in the Territorial Army, specifically the Artists Rifles whose ranks were generally filled with young businessmen and public schoolboys. On 30 October, Heath enlisted as a rifleman 'terrier' in the 28th London Regiment Territorial Army at the Drill Hall, Duke's Road, just off the Euston Road. By now, Heath had specifically set his sights on a uniformed service career, commenting to a friend at the time that 'it is the uniform I want'.[46]

The appeal of the uniform was fundamental to Heath's psychology. For him it became a complex symbol which accumulated power and significance as his career progressed from peacetime to war – at once a signifier of status and class as well as an indicator of bravery and heroism. From the mid-1930s onwards, Heath would adopt various uniforms, only some of which he was entitled to wear. When he was on active service in Palestine in 1940, he lamented the fact that his division did *not* wear uniform and were allowed to wear 'civvies'.[47] By a conspiracy of historical events, Heath would reach his maturity when the world would be suddenly – and rapidly – flooded with uniforms as it launched headlong into the Second World War.

Heath's ultimate aim was to be a Royal Air Force pilot. His tenure with the RAF was the apotheosis of his life – the fulfilment of a *Boy's Own* dream. His relationship with flight and flying was intense and he was later to state: 'I have always been crazy on flying. All my successes, and all my failures, are bound up with my history as a flyer.'[48]

The RAF had only been a force independent of the army or the navy as recently as 1918 and throughout the 1930s, with Germany re-arming and investing in her defences, they launched an extensive campaign to expand the service. From 1935, forty-five new air stations were ordered to be built throughout the British Isles, most of which were operational by 1939.[49] This was accompanied by huge investment in new aircraft designs with up-to-the-minute technology and a mass recruitment drive. The RAF increased in strength from 31,000 personnel in 1934 to 118,000 in 1939, backed by 45,000 reserves; an increase in manpower of 500 per cent in five years.[50] With extraordinary speed, the RAF had transformed from a small and exclusive elite into an ultra-modern combat service with the manpower and technology to lead the Allies in the new frontier of warfare; the air.[51]

Throughout the 1930s, the priority for the RAF was to publicize their fledgling service and to find a way of engaging a generation of boys who would become the core of the force during the Second World War. It was essential for them to explain to the public who they were, what they did and what they stood for, *per ardua ad astra* ('through adversity to the stars') – a suitably aspirational motto for the boy from suburban Wimbledon. From 1920 to 1937, an air pageant was held every summer at Hendon Aerodrome, which included races, mock battles and aerobatics. These events

– later named the Royal Air Force Air Display – attracted huge crowds and were reported throughout the media. At the same time there was huge popular interest in the Schneider Trophy, an international air race that encouraged advances in aerodynamics. The 1930s became very much the age of the plane – fast, glamorous and modern. Aviators like Charles Lindbergh and Amy Johnson were as famous as film stars and stories of their record-breaking achievements filled the newspapers. Consequently a whole generation of boys became fascinated with the mystery, romance and power of flight. As Patrick Bishop points out in his study of Fighter Command, *Fighter Boys*, many of these boys' first encounters with aeroplanes and airmen took on a dream-like or mythic aura and many of those that are recorded have a sense of a meeting with Destiny.[52]

This generation had been brought up on illustrated papers like *The Magnet*, *The Gem* and *The Modern Boy*, which celebrated the heroism of the fighter aces from the First World War like Captain W. E. Johns. In 1932 Johns himself made a huge impact when he published the first of his Biggles stories. Captain James Bigglesworth was both a figure fit to hero-worship as well as a role model that a generation of schoolboys – including 'Dam Buster' Guy Gibson – would follow into the air in less than a decade. Crucially, Johns didn't depict a hardened and experienced flyer – but a boy, just like them.

> [Biggles was a] slight, fair-haired good-looking lad still in his teens but [already] an acting flight commander ... his deep-set eyes were never still and held a glint of yellow fire that somehow seemed out of place in a pale face upon which the strain of war, and the sight of sudden death, had already graven little lines ... he had killed six men during the past month – or was it a year? What did it matter anyway? He

knew he had to die some time and had long ago ceased to worry about it.[53]

The Air Ministry even appealed directly to schools for recruits and advertised in flying magazines and newspapers. One front-page advertisement from the *Daily Express* stated that though the basic educational qualification was a school certificate, 'an actual certificate is not necessary'. What the service required was not qualifications but a particular sort of character, as the RAF, even in its embryonic stage, had begun to establish its own identity, attracting a very specific type of recruit distinctly different from the other services. They tended to be louche and eccentric about their dress, hence the iconic look of pencil moustache, flying jacket and silk scarf, now the stuff of easy parody but at the time very much regarded as a fashion of dissent. RAF officers treated the army and navy (the 'senior' services) and their traditions flippantly, priding themselves, for instance, on their lack of knowledge of horses.

As well as dress, pilots adopted, by army and navy standards, an extremely casual attitude towards drill and saluting as well as a tendency to hard drinking and prank-playing. This carefree culture was more reminiscent of a private flying club than a focused fighting service. Many of these young men, were, like Heath, barely out of school or university; immature, high-spirited and literally, care-less. They brought with them in-jokes and slang from English public schools and American movies which was soon to develop into a specific language of understatement, bravura and cheek, all of which contributed to a great sense of camaraderie and belonging. Cecil Beaton, who was hugely impressed by the 'matchless team spirit' he found within the RAF, attributed this to the service being 'surprisingly free from conventions'.[54] Junior officers addressed their squadron superiors as 'sir' on the initial meeting of the day, after which they always used first names.

Something about this ambience, the culture, the uniform, this sense of belonging to a new type of defence force based on up-to-the-minute technology completely entranced the young Neville Heath.

On 25 November 1935, Heath attended the RAF Training School at Desford in Leicestershire where he was given *ab initio* training – the very first stage of flying instruction. For many young pilots, first flights left an indelible impression, akin, as some would remember, to their first encounter with sex. And it is perhaps significant that Heath lost his virginity in the same year that he started to fly. One young pilot from this period, remembering his first flight years later, was still moved by the intensity of the experience:

> I still find it hard to find the words to describe my sheer delight and sense of freedom as the little biplane, seeming to strain every nerve, accelerated across the grass and suddenly became airborne.[55]

Heath was taught to fly by George E. Lowell and Sergeant Bulman in a De Havilland D.H. 82, a 'Tiger Moth' – the RAF's primary training aircraft at the time. Now that he had completed his flying training and with a very strong recommendation from his superior officers in the Territorial Army, Heath left his job at Pawson and Leaf on 10 February 1936 and was granted a short service commission for four years in the General Duties branch of the RAF. He had had to pass a written test and a strict medical and was questioned by a panel of officers who were looking for technical knowledge as well as some evidence of enthusiasm. An aptitude for sports was usually taken as a strong indication of the latter and Heath had distinguished himself as an athlete at school, if nothing else. On 22 March he started at No. 11 Flying Training School at RAF Wittering in Northamptonshire as an acting pilot officer.

At Wittering, Heath spent three months flying biplanes – the Hawker Hart and Hawker Audax – followed by three months in the Advanced Training Squadron flying Hawker Furies. Trainee pilots went through twenty-two exercises, beginning with 'air experience' – the first flip – through to aerobatics. These were actively encouraged by flying instructors in order to increase the young pilots' confidence – but also to prepare them for the realities and unexpected dangers of aerial combat.[56] Heath was then sent to the RAF Depot at Uxbridge for two weeks of drilling, training and familiarization with mess protocol. The young recruits would be measured for their uniforms and mess kit and given £50 to cover everything – not enough if, like Neville Heath, they preferred the better outfitters. Student pilots would live in the mess and dress for dinner every night except on Saturdays, a 'dress-down' day when blazer, flannels and tie were permitted.[57]

After successfully completing the first half of the course, pilots received their 'wings' – a badge sewn over their tunic pocket, 'the most momentous occasion in any young pilot's career'.[58] The chief instructor would then assess each trainee pilot's qualities and abilities and whether he should go on to train as a fighter or bomber pilot.[59] Heath was assessed as 'above average', displaying the necessary discipline and audacity to become one of the most glamorous figures in the mid-1930s – a modern-day hero at the helm of a Rolls-Royce engine; a fighter pilot.[60]

On 24 August 1936, Heath was posted to 19 Squadron at RAF Duxford, near Cambridge. He was sent on parachute and armaments courses as well as given instruction in night flying. He was paid 14s. a day, from which 6s. went on mess costs covering food, lodging, laundry and a personal batman. The rest went on cars and alcohol, the two being inextricably linked in the social lives of young pilots on air bases. Cars were often bought collectively by a squadron and groups of young pilots would club together the £10 to £25 needed to buy one. These would be used to get to local country pubs or occasionally on trips to London where they would call in at Shepherd's in Shepherd Market – a favoured haunt for RAF servicemen, also popular with high-class prostitutes. But drink and petrol were both expensive, with fuel costing 1s. a gallon and a pint of beer costing 8d.[61]

19 Squadron was the first to be equipped with the fighter plane, the Gloster Gauntlet, the fastest aircraft in the RAF from 1935 to 1937. They were also the first to fly the Supermarine Spitfire, which was to play a pivotal role in the Battle of Britain and thereafter became the backbone of Fighter Command. Heath was training at an extraordinary time in a force at the forefront of modern technology. He was promoted to pilot officer on 25 November 1936, the lowest commissioned rank in the RAF. At this time, he genuinely seemed to prosper – his commanding officer remarking that 'this man has the makings of a first-class pilot and should prove himself an officer of outstanding abilities'.[62] Technology, history, opportunity – Heath was in exactly the right place at the right time, one of the young men of the moment with huge possibilities, as well as challenges, ahead of him.

Around this time Heath got engaged to Arlene Blakely, a Wimbledon girl who lived with her parents Alan and Grace at 15 Manor Gardens, just off the southern end of Merton Hall Road. At last his life and career seemed to be fulfilling his great promise – and yet this is when his RAF career started to go awry.

The source of his problem was not his ability in the air, but his issues with money. Though he had become an RAF officer by gaining a short service commission, he had not come from one of the major public schools or universities like many of his brother officers, nor, crucially, was he cosseted by their private incomes. Having succeeded in entering the well-to-do world of RAF mess dinners with their class-ridden rituals and parties, Neville Heath, the grammar-school boy from Wimbledon, was challenged with the task of keeping up with his peers without the money to do so. His father estimated that Heath's service wage was £250 to £300 a year, which was clearly insufficient (for Heath anyway) to support the lavish officer lifestyle to which he aspired. Like Pip in *Great Expectations*, despite the veneer of gentility and his accumulation of upper-class manners and tastes, Heath was not and would never be 'the real thing'.

Whilst at RAF Duxford, Heath was frequently to be found in the various pubs around Cambridge and became acquainted with students from the university. One of them, Allen Dyson Perrins, was introduced to Heath around this time.

> He joined my circle of friends and I saw him frequently for about three weeks. He was never more than a mere acquaintance. He appeared to be fond of the company of women and frequented public houses. He mentioned that he had been to Eton and Oxford and I had no reason to doubt this. On occasions he visited me to my lodgings ... I missed three cheques from my cheque book which I had left on my desk and I suspected Heath of taking them. I later received a telegram from my bank regarding one of the cheques. It transpired that it had been presented for payment, and as a result he advised me to communicate with the Cambridge Police.[63]

Already, at the age of nineteen, Heath was lying about his background and stealing money from friends. But it is within the RAF that he was to find himself in more serious trouble. On 15 March 1937, Pilot Officer Heath was transferred to Mildenhall to join 73 Squadron. He was already living beyond his means and was worried about money. He had arranged a loan from Lloyds Bank in Pall Mall and even had an appointment to go and discuss his financial issues with them on 16 March, arranging to do this by telegram the day before. But despite this, two cheques of his were returned; one for £1 10s. paid to the mess secretary at Duxford and another for £3 to the Aviation Club. Investigating Heath's recently released court martial files, it's interesting to note the sequence of events here, as the outcome of this incident was to have a profound effect on the rest of his life. Most significantly, the whole scenario could have been avoided if Heath had simply come clean and told the truth.

He didn't.

RAF Mildenhall had played a celebrated role in aviation history in the 1930s, famously hosting the Royal Aero Club's MacRobertson Air Race from London to Melbourne in 1934. At the time, the air race stood as the longest race ever devised and attracted over 70,000 spectators to Mildenhall, including George V and Queen Mary. For young flyers brought up on *Flight* magazine and tales of the pioneering aviators of their time, a transfer to Mildenhall must have felt like an extraordinary privilege. With no warning, Heath's squadron were transferred to Mildenhall overnight.

On his arrival, Heath had a telephone call from his commanding officer at Duxford, Squadron Leader J. W. Turton Jones, who had an 'official and serious' conversation with him about cheques he had written to pay his mess bill and the Aviation Club. The bank had returned them. After the telephone call, rather than thinking the matter through rationally, Heath panicked. Needlessly so, as is indicated by the records of the RAF, who investigated the matter with his bank, and discovered that he had indeed arranged a loan to cover the cheques.

> In view of the fact that the accused officer had on a previous occasion been granted by the Bank an overdraft to an amount greater than that which would have resulted from the honouring of either of these cheques, I am of opinion that the circumstances are insufficient to support charges under the Air Force Act in respect of these transactions.[64]

But next morning, when the squadron assembled on their first day at Mildenhall, Pilot Officer Heath had disappeared.

For Heath, this became his favoured response to difficult circumstances. Rather than attempting to explain, his instinctive reaction was to run away. He didn't want to have a discussion about his behaviour – but he did want to make a statement about it, so would frequently send a letter. Again, this became a recurrent tactic in his life – flight followed by explanation – but only on his own terms, in his own time and with the sole objective of justifying his actions. Before leaving Duxford, Heath had left a letter for Turton Jones, promising to honour the cheques. In another he tendered his resignation. 'I think it will be the easiest way out to save dragging the name of a decent squadron in the mud,' he wrote. 'I consider I have been a disgrace to the service which will be well rid of me.'[65]

He added that he was going to Scotland, but intended to go abroad in a fortnight. He wanted to keep the affair from his parents as his father was unwell, but he would settle all outstanding bills within the month. He gave no indication how he would be able to honour this. A postscript added that he could be contacted through the personal column of the

Morning Post (again, this detail of offering contact through the personal column of a daily newspaper became a regular tactic). If he had stayed at Mildenhall and the RAF authorities had confirmed the loan with Lloyd's Bank, everything could have been resolved. As it was, Heath compounded the problem by absconding, starting a whole series of complicated events from which it would be impossible for him to extract himself.

After leaving Mildenhall, Heath didn't go abroad – he didn't even make it to Scotland – but instead he went home to Wimbledon where he stayed for the next three months, living openly in Merton Hall Road with his parents. There was no sense that he was in any way on the run or in hiding. He even wore his RAF tie.

It wasn't until 22 June that the RAF service police arrived to arrest him on charges of desertion. Flying Officer Kerby went to Merton Hall Road and saw Heath running towards him.

'Are you Pilot Officer Heath?'

Heath initially denied it. He was surprised to see Kerby – confused even, but soon collected himself.

'All right. I won't run away.'[66]

Heath was taken to Debden Aerodrome near Saffron Walden to await court martial for desertion and fraud. He was kept under open arrest and allowed the freedom of the aerodrome, the RAF taking his word as an officer and a gentleman that he wouldn't abscond. Ian Scoular, who was stationed at Debden at the time, remembered Heath's time under arrest there: 'Twice a day he had to be escorted around the aerodrome for exercise, and if any members of 73 [Squadron] were airborne they would see how close they could land to him, sending him on his face in the grass.'[67]

For Heath had not been well liked by all quarters. Johnny Kent, the Canadian Flying Ace, met Heath in this period and thought him a 'strange and rather unpleasant young man,' finding Heath very moody.[68] But this may well be because of the pressures Heath was trying to manage at the time, knowing that the life and career he'd striven for was under threat.

Heath's word as a gentleman proved to be worth very little and in the early hours of 22 July, he further exacerbated his situation by running away again. He stuffed some pillows on top of his bed under a blanket, stole a car belonging to another officer and drove to London, abandoning the car in Waterloo Road. He had decided on a 'party in London' – threatening his whole career with the RAF for a night on the town. He was later arrested and on 20 August 1937 attended his court martial hearing at Debden. He was defended by H. L. B. Milmo, a civilian barrister who argued that Heath was guilty of escaping and stealing the car but not desertion. Heath made a rather disingenuous statement:

> Having sent in my resignation, I expected an answer, but I received no intimation that the resignation had not been accepted. Had I been notified, I would have returned to the squadron or communicated with the Air Ministry.[69]

Milmo reminded the court that this was Heath's first offence and that he should be treated leniently. His reasons for leaving RAF Mildenhall were 'due to a sudden impulse after experiencing financial difficulties'. He was a decent young man who had got into a scrape simply because of inexperience. He had admitted his mistakes and was both sorry and ashamed, as was indicated by his chivalrous letter sent to his squadron leader. As to the charge of desertion, Milmo was appalled at the thought. 'The charge is repulsive to an officer and a soldier. This "mere boy" has been a foolish fellow, but did not intend to desert,'[70] he claimed.

Heath was acquitted on the charge of desertion but was found guilty of the lesser offence of going absent without leave. He was also found guilty of escaping whilst under arrest and of stealing a superior officer's car without permission. The charges of fraud regarding the mess funds were dismissed when Heath's bank confirmed their loan. The court martial marked his first appearance in the pages of both the London and the national press: 'RAF Officer Not Guilty of Desertion' (*Evening Standard*),[71] 'Officer of 20 Did Not Desert from RAF' (*Daily Mirror*).[72]

Heath was dismissed from the service with effect from 20 September 1937. He had been an officer in the RAF for less than a year.

In 1946, when recalling this period 'when [he] really began to go astray', Heath remembered the events rather differently. He claimed that he had been arrested for 'a flying offence'. This incident he mentioned throughout his career and even to his defence counsel during his trial – that he had flown an aircraft, without permission, under a bridge, threatening his own life, public property and an expensive aircraft. There is no evidence that this incident took place. It might well be an early example of Heath's boastful and flamboyant deceit. But it's also exactly the kind of needlessly dangerous, devil-may-care prank that was typical of him. It's also true that young pilots were encouraged to take out planes on jaunts, as it gave them extra flying practice. Certainly, being arrested and dismissed from the RAF for such an act of daring makes a much better story than being arrested for signing a dodgy cheque. Already, Heath was altering the facts, heightening reality, embroidering his own myth.

After his dismissal from the RAF, Heath returned home to Wimbledon. He hired a car from a local garage and on

5 October he travelled by road to the Midlands, looking for a job. He also borrowed £18 from his fiancée, Arlene. This was the last time she would actually see him – or her money. On hearing that he had been dismissed from the RAF and with his name all over the papers, she broke off the engagement and despite his attempts to phone her, refused to take his calls.[73]

He first went to Cambridge, well known to him from his time at Duxford, and stayed at the Lion Hotel. He then travelled on to Nottingham and booked into the Victoria Station Hotel. On both occasions he left without paying the bill. From 15 October to 6 November, he continued to tender worthless cheques to shopkeepers and bought expensive clothes costing £47 8s. He then tried to buy a car worth £175 from the landlord of the Sherwood Inn, Nottingham, promising that he'd send a cheque in the post. Throughout this spree in the Midlands, the identity Heath used most frequently was that of 'Lord Dudley'.

Heath's adoption of this aristocratic identity is one of the more audacious fictions that he was to present. The Earl of Dudley had been a friend and confidante of the Duke of Windsor when he was Prince of Wales, so his name would certainly have had currency with the people that Heath met at this time, the abdication having only taken place in December of the preceding year. But there may be a more prosaic reason for Heath using Dudley as a pseudonym. Throughout his career he would use genuine names and addresses that would quickly come to mind, in order to give his stories a sense of authenticity. These names and addresses frequently did exist, as if he was keen to stay as close to the truth as possible; Dudley Road was the name of the street where Heath was born.

But local police soon tracked Heath down to an hotel. Detective Inspector Hickman of Nottingham CID approached him at the bar, where Heath was drinking, pipe in hand.

'Are you Lord Dudley?'

'Yes I am, old man.'

'Well, I am Detective Inspector Hickman of the CID.'

'Then, in that case, I am *not* Lord Dudley.'[74]

Heath was arrested and appeared at Nottingham Petty Sessions on 11 November 1937.

As well as attempting to obtain the car and money by false pretences, he was charged with eight other offences in Cambridge, Stafford and Peterborough. All these petty crimes had taken place in the three months since he had been dismissed from the RAF. He justified his actions at Nottingham by saying that he had been on a mad spree after the disgrace of his dismissal from the RAF. They were boyish pranks for which he was heartily sorry, particularly for the shame that it would bring on his family. Effectively he adopted the defence that he was to use throughout the rest of his life – that he was a good lad, high-spirited and foolish but not a felon: 'My parents want me home. I have learned my lesson.'[75] This tactic certainly worked at Nottingham; Heath was placed on probation – bound over on remand for two years and placed under the supervision of Mr F. V. Dale, a probation officer in Wimbledon. Again, Heath's misdemeanours were reported in the national press ('Ex RAF Man:"I'm Lord Dudley" – But Not If You're A Detective, Old Man'). Bessie Heath, interviewed by the *Daily Mirror*, was supportive, but weary of her son's behaviour:

I am afraid that Neville has been spoiled. By his last escapade he has ruined his father's business.[76] He is not a criminal. He is a really clean-living decent young fellow – a good sportsman. This will be a severe lesson to him and now he will have to find a job. His father and I are waiting for him to come back so that we can do our utmost to help him.[77]

He was lucky; this time he had got away with it. This sense of inviolability was to develop over the years – and with good reason – as Heath became more adept at side-stepping his way out of trouble. Despite his record of persistent offending, various authorities seduced by his 'hail fellow, well met' manner would continue to give this charming young man the benefit of the doubt, which can only have fuelled his confidence that he could get away with anything.

As he observed Heath's progress over the Christmas of 1937 and the New Year of 1938, Heath's probation officer noted the good relations he had with his parents, but was also concerned that Bessie Heath seemed to shield her son and excuse his conduct when he misbehaved. Mr Dale felt that this sort of indulgence was exactly the wrong way to force Heath to face his responsibilities.[78] Even by the beginning of 1938, Dale felt that young Heath was drifting into a 'slack and irresponsible mode of living'.[79] He reported regularly to the Court House in Queens Road in Wimbledon and he certainly gave Mr Dale the impression that he was settling down and making an effort to find work. He was always full of wonderful offers and opportunities that had come his way, but none of these ever materialized. And in February, Heath suddenly stopped reporting to Mr Dale and began a spree of petty theft and swindling, unprecedented in his career to date.

On 24 February, Mrs Maud Archdall of Woburn Sands, Buckinghamshire was rushing for the 4.10 p.m. train from Euston to Bletchley. Thinking she might miss her train, she flagged down a taxi to take her to the station. She made the train, but soon realized that she had left her handbag in the cab. In the bag were many personal items, some money and seven blank cheques. The next person to pick up the cab was Neville Heath. Broke, unemployed and desperate – this was too good an opportunity for him to pass up. He spent Mrs Archdall's cash and when that was all gone, he used the cheques to fund a swindling holiday across the country – from Sussex to Somerset, from Leicestershire to London.[80]

From 22 February, Heath had been lodging at 15 Oxford Terrace in Paddington under the name A. J. Banham. The day he moved in, he paid a visit to the gentleman's outfitters, Moss Bros in Covent Garden, announcing himself as Pilot Officer Banham. He walked out of the shop with £27 1s. 8d.–worth of new clothes; if he was really going to succeed in his latter-day Rake's Progress, he would need to dress the part. The real Officer Banham was later traced and the forgery detected. But by now Heath's deceptions had developed into an easy skill and, as well as his way with women, he was now practised at exploiting the deferential trust that lower-class shop workers placed in the officer class to which he confidently appeared to belong.

When he left Oxford Terrace on 7 March, he paid the landlady Mrs Bayley with one of the cheques that he had stolen from Mrs Archdall's handbag. On 18 March, he bought a wireless at Deaford in Leicestershire with another of the cheques. The rest were cashed under a variety of pseudonyms: J. Donaldson, J. R. Denvers, Richard C. Jeffries and James R. Bulmar.

Out of the blue, on 22 March, Heath's former fiancée Arlene Blakely received a letter from him with no address, enclosing a cheque for £20. She had never believed that she would see her money again. Surprised, but delighted, she paid the cheque into her account at Chancery Lane Post Office two days later. The cheque bounced. Given that she lived so close to his parents, it is understandable that Heath should want to repay the debt. But to make the grand gesture of sending a letter and cheque to dispatch it, knowing that it would bounce, seems perverse – particularly knowing how it would further embarrass his parents. But Heath seemed blind to the consequences.

At Deaford where he bought the wireless, Heath had accidentally left behind a sheet of paper with several names and addresses scribbled on it. These seemed to be leads that he was following up in pursuit of various jobs. One of the addresses was for the Hoover shop in Regent Street which trained vacuum-cleaner salesmen, hardly the obvious choice for this swaggering young man about town. Other names at Wardour Street and Gainsborough Studios suggested that he might have been looking for work much more suited to him as a film extra.[81] He does seem to have considered some sort of film work, as when he arrived at borstal later that year, his father wrote that his son was 'awaiting the results of these proceedings before signing a film contract'.[82] This, of course, wasn't true.

Another of the contacts from the Deaford list was particularly curious. Mrs Horace Ferguson of 31 Dover Street was the proprietress of the 'SOS Agency'. The nature of her business was to 'provide Guide Escorts to ladies who wish to have the company of a gentleman for dancing, dining, theatres, racing, motoring, etc. The guide escorts are men of title, ex-officers, public school and varsity men'.[83] When later questioned, Mrs Ferguson was sure that Heath never actually contacted her about employment with the agency. But it is apparent that at this time he had decided to exploit, or at least explore, his greatest asset – his looks.

A photograph from 1935 shows a smart and fashion-conscious eighteen-year-old, pale-skinned, perhaps pretty rather than handsome, but it's easy to see why magistrates were convinced by this respectable-looking young man and why women were also seduced by his sensitive features. His good looks in conjunction with his charm were a winning combination. Sydney Brock, one of Heath's early biographers, felt that Heath's growing awareness of these advantages resulted in a confidence that bordered on conceit: 'He felt confident that his personality was so winning that he would be able to go on indefinitely making a mockery of the law.'[84]

Brock was clear what he felt was at the heart of this confidence and people's willingness to be taken in by him. 'If Neville Heath had been an ugly, unprepossessing fellow, would he have been treated so leniently? I think not.'

Having now evolved into a modern-day Macheath, the charming, audacious (but always gentlemanly) thief had developed a simple formula for personal advancement – robbing from the rich to give to himself. But at this point, with several constabularies on his tail, he made an effort to get back on the straight and narrow. He seems to have been encouraged by Mr Dale, his probation officer, 'who helped him in every possible way to get a job'.

Consequently, Neville Heath – wanted man, fraudster and swindler – secured employment as a lowly assistant at the John Lewis department store in Oxford Street. In doing so, he realized that he would need to deal with the long list of petty offences he had been committing since he had appeared at Nottingham. Again, he relied on the strategy he had utilized in the RAF when faced with a situation that was threatening to spiral out of control – he wrote a letter to the chief superintendent of the CID at Scotland Yard.

8th April 1938

Dear Sir,

Before you read this letter I would like to make it quite clear that not in any way do I mean it to be taken as either being frivolous or impertinent. In view of this I beg that you submit my request for the consideration of the proper authority.

During the last few months I have been living a criminal

existence. I fully realize the serious view taken of the crimes I have committed and will, for the rest of my years, do the utmost to make full reparation. I was practically forced into this life of crime by financial circumstances and the inability to secure employment. You, who know my history will surely understand the reflex action upon the mind after once having ruined a decent career. I most sincerely ask you to believe and understand that I am not by nature a criminal, nor do I enjoy leading the life it entails.

Today I have been fortunate enough to secure employment of a legitimate nature with a reputable firm and this is the reason I am asking you for leniency and understanding and a chance to make good. I am going to make a most unusual request but I am convinced that if there is a human side to justice and any truth in the saying that the police are to prevent crime and prevent the making of criminals, I am convinced you will grant my request.

I am going to request that you withhold the warrants which are issued for my arrest, until you see that I am serious and telling the truth.

I want to start work on Monday and from my salary I shall make payments to all hotels, etc. from whom I have secured credit and money by false pretences. I shall keep these payments up until all my debts are cleared.

I further promise that from this time of writing I shall undertake nothing dishonest ever again. In the event of your granting my request and in the event of my failing to keep my promise, I ask that this letter be produced and that my normal sentence when convicted be doubled.

Once again, sir, I ask you for human understanding, and in helping me to take this chance which may never come again, you will very effectively rid the world of one more criminal.

I have the honour, to be, sir
Your Obedient Servant,

Neville GC Heath

> *In the event of your granting my requests I should be obliged if an insertion could be made in the personal column of the 'Daily Telegraph', in which case I shall be only too pleased to refund the expense incurred.*[85]

The notion of Heath being 'practically forced into [a] life of crime' is laughable – his protestations, of course, always pointing the blame elsewhere or on circumstances beyond *his* control. And offers that he will never be able to keep ('I shall undertake nothing dishonest ever again') are both childlike and childish in their naiveté.

Heath was employed as an assistant in the fabric department at John Lewis on a wage of £2 per week, half what he had been earning with the RAF. But this sojourn as a respectable wage earner was not to last for long – thirteen days in all. It was soon apparent that his references were not bona fide, and nor was he. Heath was sacked – a substantial blow to his confidence; he couldn't even hold down a job as a shop assistant. Despite his recent claims that he was not 'by nature a criminal' and did not enjoy the life it entailed, he now embraced his former life with a renewed alacrity and an increased audacity.

In June, Heath was staying at the Royal Sussex Hotel in Brighton and ran into a friend of his, Percy Masters, who was spending a few days by the sea. Masters was a bank manager and lived comfortably in Edgware. Knowing that his house was now vacant, Heath couldn't resist. On 7 June he travelled up to Masters' house, 42 Penshurst Gardens, and smashed a window at the back. He opened the catch and let himself in. Whilst he was there, he entertained a girlfriend, wearing Masters' pyjamas and even sleeping in his bed. The intruders ate a meal of sardines and beer in the kitchen, the table laid with fish knives – a precocious touch. A newspaper dated 7 June was later found in one of the rooms. Heath had made himself very much at home, effectively taking a holiday in his friend's house. When he left he took with him a selection of 'playboy' booty – a revolver, golf clubs, binoculars, a camera and some jewellery. At the same time he stole various clothes: a dinner suit, two lounge suits and an overcoat. He even took some of Masters' favourite cigars.

When Masters reported the break-in to Detective Sergeant Driscoll of Edgware Police, Driscoll felt certain that this was the work of somebody who knew the house and its owner. He asked Masters if he suspected anyone who might be involved. Masters mentioned Heath's name and it didn't take long for Driscoll to check the Criminal Records Office where he noted Heath's appearance at Nottingham the previous November. Heath seemed a very likely suspect indeed.

On 13 June, the golf clubs and binoculars were traced to a pawnbroker in Tottenham Court Road and Masters went to identify them. The pawnbroker described the man who had surrendered the goods and identified him as a James Bulman.[86] 'Bulman' was traced to the Royal Sussex Hotel in Brighton. The Metropolitan Police called their colleagues in Brighton to arrest the suspect. Bulman, a.k.a. Neville Heath, was taken to London where he was charged with housebreaking and stealing property worth £51 11s. 6d. He was further charged with his fraud at Moss Bros in February. A total of ten other offences at Pevensey, Weston-Super-Mare, Leicestershire and London were taken into consideration covering a period from 19 February to 28 May 1938.

In addition to these crimes, Heath had also defrauded his own family. His uncle, Walter Barker, worked as a market gardener at Laleham. Heath had offered him a cheque for £55, saying that he had won a bet on a horse. But Barker had loaned money to his nephew before and Heath still owed him £50, so he only gave Heath £5. Needless to say, Heath's cheque bounced. At Weston-Super-Mare Heath had also taken £5 from an aunt, again offering her a dud cheque.

Heath had no scruples, and strangers, friends and family were all fair game in his desire for personal gain. Neither his uncle nor his aunt pressed charges, but cumulatively the other crimes amounted to a career of wrongdoing. Heath was to be tried at the Old Bailey.

The two murders apart, all of Heath's crimes followed a similar pattern, usually stealing money or property (frequently clothes) or pretending to be somebody else. None of the crimes he was actually convicted of before 1946 involved violence or threatening behaviour. He was a small-time crook, a con man with a relentless, acquisitive instinct for money and status. The gilded lifestyle he aspired to was in some contrast to the reality of his modest background – his father a hairdresser, his mother a landlady.

Whilst awaiting trial, Heath was held in Wormwood Scrubs Boys' Prison in west London. The court commissioned a series of reports to assess what to do with him and how to plan for his future. Having failed to meet his probation commitments, could he be trusted again? Did he require a custodial sentence, or was that overly harsh? How could they rehabilitate this obviously intelligent young man and direct him towards a useful and law-abiding future? One thing was clear – despite his obvious charm and steady upbringing, the boy was patently dishonest, a liar and a thief. The court assessment was wide-ranging and included contributions from the prison governor, his probation officer, his old headmaster Mr Varnish, his parents and even his old employers at Pawson and Leaf. Generally, Heath seemed to have succeeded in convincing the various authorities that he was a good lad at heart who had gone off the rails: 'A boy who has got himself into a hopeless mess owing to his own irresponsibility and bad management and needs a lot of help and guidance.'[87]

But amongst the general chorus of support, there was one dissenting voice in the assessment of the incorrigible but charming boy gone astray. The chaplain at Wormwood Scrubs saw right through the veneer of Heath's bonhomie. 'He says he was so completely in debt that he has become a "Raffles",' he wrote. 'He is as crafty as they make 'em and I wouldn't give much for his future.'[88]

But even whilst awaiting trial at Wormwood Scrubs, Heath was keen to turn the situation to his advantage. With extraordinary resourcefulness, he contacted the editor of the *Daily Mirror*.

Wormwood Scrubs Prison

15th June 1938

Dear Sir,

No doubt you are astounded to hear from me, but perhaps it will help to clarify the matter if I mention two articles concerning myself which appeared in headlines in your paper. Firstly the court martial of Pilot Officer NGC Heath RAF which took place somewhere around last August and the more recent impersonation of Lord Dudley last November. Now I am on remand at the above prison, awaiting trial on yet another charge.

After my trial and sentence is over, I am going to make known the most sensational story since the Baillie-Stewart Affair.

I am communicating with you because you may be interested in having the sole rights of the story. I have however definitely made up my mind not to say a word until after my trial and sentence. If you are interested perhaps you would like to send your reporter or come yourself to interview me at this address. I am allowed to receive visitors on any weekday so I'll expect your representative one day this week. I'll give you a rough outline of the situation and afterwards you will be able to please yourself. I should, of course, expect you to respect my confidence.

By the way, if your reporter would care to bring with him any fruit, chocolate or magazines they will be most acceptable.[89]

But though his misdemeanours had indeed been reported in the press, the stories appeared on page four and beyond. Even as a criminal he couldn't make the front page. Not yet, anyway.

Heath appeared for the first time at the Old Bailey on 12 July 1938 before Sir Gerald Donaldson. In his defence he said, 'I have no excuse for what I have done.' Donaldson despaired of all the opportunities that the youth before him had been offered and yet had wasted so shamefully.

This is a tragic record. There were such bright prospects but now you have spoilt it all. There is only one chance for you and that is your instincts to do right. I cannot believe that you have lost all of them at your early age.[90]

Even at this juncture, Donaldson had highlighted a fundamental issue – perhaps *the* fundamental issue – at the heart of Heath's personality. Did he have an instinct to do right? Or had he indeed lost all sense of moral compass?

He was given a custodial sentence of three years. At the age of just twenty-one, it seemed that the golden boy's luck had finally run out.

CHAPTER EIGHT
Borstal Boy

JULY 1938 – DECEMBER 1941

I shall always remember that year at Hollesley Bay Colony and (I think you know it too) I was really happy there. It's a great pity I did not remember the many lessons I learned there, but unfortunately my memory had always been abominably short, and I've usually paid dearly for it . . .

Letter from Heath to C. A. Joyce, 8 October 1946[1]

Within a fortnight of his sentence at the Old Bailey, Heath was transferred from the grim surroundings of Wormwood Scrubs to a newly opened borstal institution near Woodbridge in Suffolk, Hollesley Bay.

Hollesley Bay is perhaps most renowned today for being the open prison that Jeffrey Archer was sent to for perverting the course of justice in 2002. The press dubbed it 'Holiday Bay'[2] at the time, but even in the early months of its opening in the 1930s it had garnered a reputation as a soft option, with critics feeling it was more like a rural public school than an institution for young offenders. Heath had landed on his feet.

The Irish writer Brendan Behan happened to arrive at Hollesley Bay shortly after Heath. At the age of sixteen, Behan had been arrested in Liverpool for agitating on behalf of the IRA, who had initiated a wave of terrorist attacks throughout 1939 in Manchester, Birmingham and London including bombings at King's Cross, Tottenham Court Road and Leicester Square tube stations. Behan recalled his time at Hollesley Bay in the period leading up to the outbreak of war in his memoir, *Borstal Boy* (1958), a title that had been used by Gerald Byrne for his biography of Heath published twelve years earlier.

The borstal colony, as it was called, was set in beautiful countryside, within sight of the Suffolk coast – Aldeburgh to the northeast and Felixstowe to the southwest. Much of the colony was given over to market gardens and orchards growing a rich variety of fruit and vegetables – plums, apples, cucumbers, tomatoes, greengages and even grapes and peaches, the coastal climate being favourable for more exotic fruits. There were also hives for collecting honey and grazing land for the flocks of sheep that were reared by the inmates – all the produce being later taken to market. The colony had only opened the previous May and Heath was one of the first boys to be sent there.[3]

Built at the end of the nineteenth century, the main buildings at Hollesley Bay were large and rambling, complete with dormer windows and a clock tower, all designed to resemble a great Tudor manor house. On arrival, the borstal boys, having travelled in chains, were unshackled and issued with a kit of blue jacket, shirt, shoes and shorts, finished with thick stockings and a woollen tie. Unexpectedly, they were also

given half an ounce of Ringers A1 Shag tobacco and a packet
of cigarette papers.[4] This welcoming touch was very much
the tone of the institution which had been established by
Hollesley Bay's enlightened governor, C. A. ('Jack') Joyce, a
man of great integrity who was convinced in the ability of
the borstal system to redirect the lives of young men who had
gone off the rails, empowering them by teaching them self-
respect as well as respect for others: 'While you are here, the
first thing I ask of you is courtesy to each other, to the staff
and to myself.'[5] Joyce stayed in touch with many of his former
borstal boys, including Behan and Heath. Both found their
experience at Hollesley Bay formative. From prison, Heath
later remembered the profound effect that Joyce's regime had
on him. 'You and ... your ideals which we all worked so
hard for once, occupy a very special corner in my long list of
pleasant memories.'[6]

Much of the daily routine at Hollesley Bay aped the structure of a public school timetable. Four houses – St Patrick's,
St Andrew's, St George's and St David's – accommodated
about 100 boys, each with prefects and a housemaster. Most
of the boys were between sixteen and eighteen but the colony
would admit young men up to the age of twenty-three. Most
were single, but some were married with children. The boys
were regarded very much as delinquents rather than criminals, deserving of rehabilitation, rather than punishment.
None of them were thought of as high risk and much of the
time they were unsupervised and able to abscond. Few did
though, so responsive were they to Joyce's methodology.

Though the manual work could be hard – sometimes
nine-hour days harvesting fruit and vegetables in all seasons
– the facilities at Hollesley Bay were very comfortable.
Though the dormitories in which the boys slept were basic
and unheated, there were several public rooms offering a
variety of leisure activities: a games room to play table tennis,

darts and billiards, a radio room to listen to the wireless, a gym, a library, as well as playing fields for football and rugby. There were frequent treats – Brendan Behan nostalgically remembered teas of bread and jam, treacle duff and sweet cake and Heath was regularly able to buy the *Daily Mirror,* the *Observer,* or his beloved *Daily Telegraph.* The centrally heated dining room was furnished not with refectory tables, but with sociable tables for four, each decorated with bowls of flowers from the Hollesley Bay gardens. The walls were hung with colourful prints of the colonies – a subliminal sugges- tion, perhaps, to the delinquents that in the future they could make a fresh start in one of the British dominions.[7]

The colony promoted a healthy, outdoor lifestyle that suited Heath and he certainly prospered there. Food was fresh and plentiful and the coastal breeze invigorating. At Wormwood Scrubs Heath had measured 5 ft 10 ¼ and weighed 152 lb. By the time he left Hollesley Bay he was 15 lb heavier and had grown half an inch.[8] His strategy whilst at borstal seems to have been to keep his head low and behave, in the hope of securing an early release. He did carting, crop- ping and general farm labouring as well as working with horses. He was most keen, though, to tend the colony's show sheep, regarded as a light job for a man of his athletic build and developing strength. This he did with Fred Sams, Hollesley Bay's shepherd.

> His sole job for months was to be my assistant and all he had to do was make sure the sheep did not fall into the sea. He would laze there, mostly lying on the bank of the saltings at the edge of the North Sea, dreaming and scheming and never working but to shoo the odd sheep back from danger.[9]

The colony provided Heath with a sufficiently easy life with the sort of public school or military structure in which he thrived.

But in the outside world, political events were conspiring to impact even on this sleepy corner of the Suffolk coast. On 30 September, Neville Chamberlain landed at Heston aerodrome and announced that war had been averted by the signing of the Munich Agreement. The increasingly acquisitive Nazi Germany had been appeased, with Britain, France and Italy agreeing to the annexation of Czechoslovakia's Sudetenland – an issue that had been causing international anxiety since Germany had annexed Austria in March of that year.

> We regard the agreement signed last night and the Anglo-German Naval Agreement as symbolic of the desire of our two peoples never to go to war with one another again.[10]

Arriving at Downing Street later that day Chamberlain (in)famously announced that he believed that this was 'peace for our time'.

Heath's housemaster, Mr Macfarlane, hadn't, at first, been impressed by his new charge. In the autumn of 1938, he worried that Heath was too conceited, showing off his superior education and culture to the scorn of the other boys who dismissed him as an affected snob. But by the following spring, McFarlane had completely revised his opinion and commented that Heath had settled into the colony's routine extremely well.[11] He was taking an active part in the community and was even appointed as captain of his house. On arriving at Hollesley Bay, the precocious Brendan Behan was introduced to Heath, noting how 'strongly built' he was, as well as the silver star he wore on his jacket – a badge of seniority and authority.

'My name is Behan,' said I.

[Heath] smiled and said in a mock Irish accent, 'An' it's aisy to say where you're from, Paddy.'

I smiled too, because it seemed to be meant as a kindness.

'Phwart paart of Tipperary, Paddy?'

'I'm not from Tipperary,' said I.

'Are you not, now?' said Heath.[12]

Heath advised Behan and the new 'receptions' to keep their heads down and to commit themselves to scrupulous, almost military self-discipline. Violence, boisterousness, even swearing was out of order.

'Look here, cock,' said Heath, 'as long as I'm here, you keep that kind of talk to yourself. I won't wear it, and if I get you or any other filthy bloody swine talking like that he'll know all about it.'[13]

It seems, as far as Behan and his contemporaries were concerned, that Heath was, if not one of the lads, certainly respected by the other borstal boys.

In February 1939, the first Anderson shelter[14] was built in London. By April the WRNS had been re-established, followed in June by the creation of the WAAF (Women's Auxiliary Air Force). The Military Training Act was introduced in April,[15] initiating conscription for men of twenty and twenty-one to take six months' military training. As the country watched the international situation darken and realized that Chamberlain's promise of peace looked more and more like naïve wishful thinking, Britain prepared for war. In May, eleven months into his sentence, Heath wondered if he might be eligible for discharge for military training, given his background in the services and his spotless behaviour since he had arrived at Hollesley Bay. He had already made it clear to Mr McFarlane that his ultimate ambition was to rejoin the RAF. McFarlane told Heath he must be patient. By now he genuinely admired Heath's 'persistent good humour and common-sense adjustments' that had enabled him to fit in with the other boys like Brendan Behan, 'without lowering his own standards'.[16] More and more, Heath seemed like the model borstal boy, his time at Hollesley Bay having moulded a mature and responsible young man.

During his time at borstal, Heath acquired some very useful friends in high places. As well as gaining McFarlane's admiration and support, he managed to catch the interest of Jack Joyce, the governor. Through him, Heath secured a meeting with Mr Scott, the Head of the Borstal Association, to discuss his future. These two friendships were to develop throughout the rest of Heath's life with Scott and Joyce as unofficial mentors, taking a genuine interest in Heath's progress. When he first met Mr Scott in June 1939, Heath's 'consuming anxiety' was to find out if there was any hope of his being accepted by the RAF on his discharge from borstal. He argued that he had held commissioned rank as a pilot and already had 200 flying hours under his belt. Surely he'd be ideally placed to rejoin the service in a time of national emergency, even if it meant starting again in the ranks?

Scott was impressed by Heath's passion, his excellent physique and superior intelligence and promised to help. In Mr Scott, Heath had secured a very influential champion. Later that month, Heath's father also visited Scott at the Borstal Association offices in Victoria Street to discuss his son's future. Again, the two men became very friendly, united in their desire to try and help young Neville fulfil his potential. Like the Heaths, Scott also lived in Wimbledon, so he began visiting them socially in Merton Hall Road, always curious to know how their son was getting on.

True to his word, throughout the summer, Mr Scott made a series of enquiries at the Air Ministry on Heath's behalf to see if there might be some chance of his rejoining the RAF. These appeals were all rejected. This can't have been surprising as Heath had been dismissed from the service only two years previously and since then had been in court twice, thereafter spending most of his time in borstal. There was also a rush by hundreds of thousands of young men to enlist. The RAF neither wanted nor needed him back.

From the end of the summer, Britain galvanized herself for war. On 23 August, the Soviets and the Germans signed their mutual treaty of non-aggression, the Molotov–Ribbentrop Pact. A week later, the Royal Navy manned their war stations and the evacuation began to remove children from major British cities to the countryside. On 1 September, the Germans invaded Poland. The British army was then mobilized and a blackout imposed across the British Isles. The international crisis had an impact even at Hollesley Bay; on 2 September, Heath was discharged under emergency regulations and sent home to Wimbledon. This wasn't special treatment, though, as approximately 1,750 borstal boys were similarly discharged on the same day. And though Heath had been released, he would remain on licence for another three years.

The day after Heath was released from borstal, the National Service Act was passed, introducing mass conscription for all men between the ages of eighteen and forty-one. The following day, Heath called to see Mr Scott at the Borstal Association offices in a frenzy of excitement. He burst into Scott's office with his arms waving and his eyes blazing, shouting, 'My God, sir, they're up and I'm not with them.' Knowing the boy and his history, Scott could understand Heath's passion, but he felt at the time that 'Heath's manner, appearance and expression disclosed lack of control and an excitability far from normal'.

Making full allowance for the excitement prevailing through-out the country on that day and for this ex-pilot's feelings of frustration and impatience, he displayed unnatural excite-ment and loss of self-control. His eyes were wild, his whole body shook with emotion and he could not sit down.[17]

For Heath the outbreak of war was both an opportunity to put the past behind him, but also a fulfilment of his destiny. There was no sense that he wanted to fight for King and Country with the old Rutlish rallying cry, 'arming for the fight, pressing on with all our might'. His objective seems to have been a personal one – to embark on a great adven-ture which at this point he felt was being blocked by vari-ous authority figures for mistakes he had made in his youth. He seems to have had no anxieties about actively pursuing a role in a war in which he might forfeit his life. This is very much the *Boy's Own* attitude to mortality enshrined in *Biggles*: 'He knew he had to die sometime and had long ago ceased to worry about it.' This became Heath's maxim for life.

Heath trudged from one RAF recruiting office to another, but was rejected by all of them. In a letter to Mr Scott, his sense of frustration is palpable.

Life is full of disappointments. I was ready, packed and preparing to depart yesterday morning when I received a letter from the Recruiting Centre at Croydon telling me not to go. Apparently Uxbridge is so full (5000 over number) that yesterday's and today's draft of recruits had to be stopped.

However, in spite of the letter, I went to Croydon complete with case, just in case there was an off chance of getting away. The Recruiting Officer was awfully sympathetic but said there was noth-ing he could possibly do.[18]

Despite his efforts and his obvious commitment, the RAF would not take him. He was 'horribly disappointed', but, with some tenacity, refused to be defeated. With his favoured options closed to him, he enlisted as a private in the army, volunteering for the Royal Army Service Corps. His admission to the RASC was in stark contrast to his former status as an RAF pilot – glamorous, heroic, daring, modern. The RASC was a much more mundane facilitating corps providing services and support staff. Heath joined them as a driver. This role could not have underlined more clearly the downward trajectory he had been on since being dismissed from the air force. A modern Icarus, his was a literal as well as figurative grounding; from flying a fighter to driving a truck.

Based at Buller Barracks in Aldershot, Heath's strategy at this stage – and it certainly seems like a careful and deliberate plan – was to join up as a lower-status private and then to pursue his goals from within the service. He may well have been starting at the bottom again but he was determined not to stay there.

By December of 1939, though there had been attacks at sea, there had been no significant offensives by the major powers in the war. Heath was at home in Wimbledon, visiting his parents for Christmas. While at a dance at the Dog and Fox on Wimbledon Hill, he bumped into Peggy Dixon, a 24-year-old girl from Loxley Road in nearby Wandsworth. They had been introduced some years before at a twenty-first birthday party. Peggy remembered that Heath had been in the RAF at the time, or was just about to join. Heath told her that he was an army cadet now and Peggy told him about her work as a civil servant. The pair got on well, arranging to meet again. Peggy visited Merton Hall Road and was introduced to William and Bessie Heath and Heath was introduced to Peggy's parents, too. The couple had a lot in common and it seemed a very sensible match. Given Heath's recent history, his parents must have been relieved that their son was settling down at last, with a job, a girlfriend – a future. Everything was looking up for him.[19]

Early in 1940, Heath joined the Officer Cadet Training Unit, passing out on 23 March as a 2nd Lieutenant. He visited Mr Scott and proudly showed off his uniform. He had passed ninth out of thirty-four cadets. He told Scott that he had discussed his past history with his company commander who was 'awfully understanding and terribly nice about everything'. Neville Heath the rakish playboy seemed to have turned prodigal. Not only was he prospering in the RASC, but he was confronting his past mistakes, being upfront and honest about them. His commanding officer had approached the RAF on his behalf and had arranged for a transfer. He was to be drafted to the Middle East soon as a reconnaissance pilot attached to the Mediterranean Expeditionary Force on a 'special job'.

Mr Scott was hugely impressed by the extraordinary turnaround in Heath's fortunes. But little of the information he gave Scott was actually true. Though he was certainly scheduled to travel out to Palestine and might have *hoped* for some sort of flying role, there is no indication from Heath's War Office records that he was offered one.[20]

Like many romances of the time, the overseas posting intensified Heath's relationship with Peggy. He asked her to marry him and she accepted. On Saturday 13 April 1940, Heath and Peggy celebrated their engagement with a family party at her parents' home in Wandsworth.

The heroic young subaltern was waved off to war on the 18 April, leaving his sweetheart and his family at home, all bursting with pride.

On 10 June 1940, just as Heath arrived in Palestine, Italy declared war on Britain and France.

Mussolini had designs on the French and British colonies in North Africa with the intention of expanding Italian territories in the area, seizing the Arabian oil fields and controlling the Suez Canal. Italian forces would first have to drive through Egypt, which, though officially neutral, had agreed by treaty to allow British occupation forces if the Suez Canal was threatened. Almost immediately, the Italian air forces started bombing the strategic port of Tel Aviv and the oil terminal and refinery at Haifa.

Heath was stationed at Sarafand in Palestine and in July of 1940, he sent letters to Mr Scott saying that he was now with the Mediterranean Expeditionary Force, 'longing to have a crack at the Italians'.[21] He had also written to his parents indicating that he had been promoted to the rank of captain, but there's no mention of this appointment in his service records. These advancements and his tales of the war from the centre of the action were all fantasy. The reality was rather different. Despite the entry of Italy into the war, if Heath had been expecting to be thrown right into a *Biggles*-style adventure, he was to be extremely disappointed. As he wrote later in his life story in the press:

> I was very bored of the enforced inactivity [at Sarafand]. We would wear civvies and everything was just like peacetime. When Italy entered the war I applied dozens of times for a posting to the Western Desert but this was consistently refused.[22]

Norbert Gaffrey, an orderly room clerk with the RASC, noted that when Heath first arrived at Sarafand he had carried out his duties well. Working in the office, Gaffrey was also aware that Heath had applied for a transfer to the RAF. Gaffrey typed a copy of Heath's application and dispatched it with a letter from the commanding officer to the Supplies and Transport Force Headquarters in Jerusalem. According to Gaffrey, the application was refused and this had a marked effect on Heath's behaviour. He now became 'unmindful and careless'.[23]

On 13 September, Italian forces crossed into Egypt from their base in Cyrenaica in Libya, outnumbering British forces four to one. But the Italians only made it as far as Siddi Barrani, a town near the Mediterranean. By the end of the year, the Western Desert Force under General Wavell had launched a counter-attack, Operation Compass. This resulted in the defeat of the Italian Tenth Army and the repossession of all the Italian gains in Egypt and most of Cyrenaica. British forces took 130,000 Italian prisoners of war. Frustratingly for Heath, all the action seemed to be happening nearby, but beyond his reach. Despite this, he wrote letters home telling a very different story – placing himself at the centre of the action, 'giving the Italians hell and it's just too easy'. In reality, he was more likely to have been playing football on the beach at Sarafand.

On 20 February 1941 he wrote to Mr Scott claiming that his transfer to the RAF had been approved and that he would soon be with a fighter squadron. Again, this is a fantasy, Heath's application having been rejected. But he does seem to have seen some action in the Middle East, during the little-remembered Anglo-Iraqi war.

Rashid Ali, the former anti-British prime minister of Iraq, launched a coup d'etat against the Iraqi Regent. Once in power, he threatened two British air bases in Iraq, much to Churchill's chagrin. But after British forces launched a pre-emptive strike against the Iraqis, Rashid Ali fled to Persia and the pro-British monarchy was restored.

Heath claimed to have played a subsidiary role in this war, which lasted for twenty-nine days in 1941. He was stationed away from the fighting at H4, the pumping station on the Haifa-Baghdad road that was a potential target for sabotage. But during the ongoing conflict, Fort Rutbah near to H4 had been seized by the Iraqis. Heath heard of a British raiding party that was to attempt to re-take the fort – and, like a *Beau Geste* fantasy, he was determined to be part of it. It's certainly true that Blenheim Bombers from Squadron 203 did attack the Iraqis at Rutbah on 9 May and they did fly from H4. But, as ever, it's difficult to know with Heath what is true and what isn't. But he was certainly not the sort of man to hang around when there was action to be had in the immediate vicinity. It's also true that many servicemen keen to see active service did join in raids without the permission of their commanding officer.[24]

Heath claimed that after the raid on Fort Rutbah, when he returned to H4, his commanding officer had noted his absence and ordered him back to Sarafand for deserting his post. Shortly afterwards he claimed that he had more trouble with his superior officers when he was working on convoy duty. He had sent 200 trucks to Syria, but by the time they reached Beirut, there were two trucks missing. A furious superior officer upbraided Heath. An argument ensued between the two men and Heath was again sent back to Sarafand – this time, under arrest. Heath's stories about his time in Palestine conform to a particular pattern: headstrong young man seeks adventure. Though there's probably some truth in his stories of insubordination in Palestine, records from the War Office give a much more prosaic reason for his arrest.

Heath had been in financial difficulties for some time – to such an extent that in April his commanding officer devised a scheme for the supervision of his financial affairs. Heath agreed not to cash any cheques without the consent of his commanding officer or adjutant until all his debts were repaid. But despite this, he carried on writing cheques that continued to bounce. However, all the time, he had been drawing money from the field cashier with a *second* Advance Pay Book that he had stolen – which effectively enabled him to cash twice as much money as any officer of his rank. Certainly, off duty, Heath would have enjoyed a luxurious lifestyle – sumptuous dinners in smart hotels and free-flowing alcohol. But given that he was living in a war zone, with most of his needs provided by the army, how had he got into debt so quickly and what was he spending his money on?

Paull Hill's *Portrait of a Sadist* was published in 1960, some fourteen years after Heath's trial.[25] Significantly, Hill was a lawyer and would have known that the material that he discussed in the book would not be publishable until the passing of the Obscene Publications Act in 1959.

During the war, Hill had been an adjutant on a troop carrier, SS *Mooltan*, where he had first met Neville Heath. How much of the story Heath told Hill is true is unclear. But it would certainly account for Heath's increasing issues with money during his time in Palestine, as well as anticipating his later sexual predilections. During off-duty periods, Heath left the tedium of Sarafand and spent much of his time (and most of his money) in Jerusalem and particularly, Cairo.

In the Middle East at the time, Cairo was the focus for the entertainment of Allied troops on leave or for those passing through to the various desert theatres of war. By 1941, Cairo's population of half a million was increased by 35,000 troops from Britain and the Empire. It offered a pre-war, colonial lifestyle of indulgent luxury. Noël Coward, who made a journey throughout the Middle East at this time, was stunned and slightly sickened by the sybaritic existence lived out in the foyers and restaurants of the Continental and Shepheard's Hotel – where, famously, stocks of champagne didn't run out until 1943.

The restrictions of wartime are unknown; people sat there sipping Gin-Slings and cocktails and chatting and gossiping, waiters glided about wearing Fezzes ... There were uniforms everywhere of all ranks and nationalities ... [indicating] that perhaps somewhere in the vague outside world there might be a war of some sort going on. This place is the last refuge of the soi-disant 'International Set'. All the fripperies of pre-war luxury living are still in existence here; rich people, idle people, cocktail-parties, dinner parties, jewels and evening dress. Rolls-Royces come purring up to the terrace ... it [all] felt rather old fashioned and lacking in taste.[26]

The large department stores Cicurel's, Chemla's and Le Salon Vert carried on business as usual and Groppi's, the most famous café in Cairo, continued to serve its famous coffee accompanied by pastries rich in clarified butter. Even the corner shops of Cairo were packed with goods that had long since been rationed in England; butter, sugar and eggs as well as exotic local produce like oranges, dates, beans, maize and the huge cabbages and cauliflowers that thrived in the Nile Delta. Luxury goods like French wine, grapes, melons, steaks, cigarettes, beer and whisky were all easily obtainable. This abundance was an extraordinary vision of plenty for troops fresh from the desert and used to tinned British Army rations of M&V (meat and veg), fatty bacon, cheese, marmalade and bully beef.[27]

The Gezira Sporting Club was the focus for many of the social events for officers in wartime Cairo. Given to the British Army by the Pasha of Egypt, the club covered the entire southern end of Gezira Island and boasted gardens, polo fields, a golf course, a race course, cricket pitches, squash and tennis courts, croquet lawns and a lido. At the same time, the Turf Club swarmed with officers and a dozen open-air cinemas showed films every night throughout the city. But the entertainment for which Cairo became infamous during the Second World War was the sex trade.

The brothels in the red-light district of wartime Cairo have become legendary – dens of vice and iniquity providing an extraordinary variety of services for the most diverse taste, from pornographic films and cabarets to peep shows, prostitutes, rent boys and orgies. The majority of brothels were situated along the Wagh el Birket or 'the Berka' as it was known – opposite Shepheard's and the Continental Hotel. Prostitutes called down from hundreds of New Orleans-style balconies that overlooked the long, narrow street, touting for business from below. The incidence of murders and rapes in the area at the time caused such concern that British military police attempted to make the worst districts of the city 'Out of Bounds to All Ranks' by putting up circular white signs with a black 'X' across them. But with 90,000 clients a month,[28] it proved impossible to police the warren of backstreets and alleyways that stretched across the ancient city, and the legend of extraordinary sexual practices – including the spectacle of women copulating with a variety of animals, among them a donkey – continued to lure troops on leave in search of relief, or adventure. Graham Tylee, an army private during this period, offers a first-hand account of Cairo's vice trade in his memoirs, held in the Imperial War Museum.

Each brothel had a number, some were better patronized than others. Each had a 'Madame' in charge of the girls – usually a prostitute who had moved from the bed to the cash desk … whoever you went with you still ran the risk of 'copping a packet' despite the fact that army doctors regularly inspected the girls. To really lessen the risk of venereal disease it was advisable to visit the PAC (Prophylactic Ablution Centre) and take the necessary precautions, which consisted of squirting a solution of permanganate potash crystals up the penis. After this performance the customer collected a blue ticket on the way out which guaranteed him no loss of pay if he contacted gonorrhea or syphilis. [At the brothel] You went up the stairs and sat down in company with dozens of other customers and sightseers. Each girl had her own gimmick to attract custom. But the best gimmick was youth and beauty. Some girls resorted to particularly perverted practices: others would stand in front of you clad only in transparent nighties and the tiniest bikini briefs which they would pull down a shade to reveal pubic regions completely denuded of hair. [The Berka] was recognized officially by the army authorities but there was another area definitely off limits and this was known as the Black Berka. Once you got off the main streets of Cairo you found yourself in a rabbit warren of narrow streets and dark alleyways where vice in all shapes and forms reigned supreme. The only way into this labyrinth of evil alleyways was with a guide, usually a ragged youngster who furtively tugged at your shirt or pullover, whispering, 'You want to see exhibish?' If you were on your own and you had any sense you shook the youngster off or if he was still persistent, you belted him round the ear. For once in the quarter by yourself you stood a very good chance of being robbed and murdered.[29]

At the Continental Hotel, Heath became friendly with the barman and told him that he'd heard rumours that a certain house in the red-light district – most probably in the 'Black Berka' – provided not only graphic sexual 'exhibitions', as described by Graham Tylee, but also provided an exclusive place known as the 'Amazon Room' where 'you could do what you like and no questions asked'. The barman told Heath that the Amazon Room could provide him with girls who liked to be beaten – and boys too, if that was to Heath's taste.

According to *Portrait of a Sadist*, Heath was shown into a house deep in the red-light district. The place was decorated in the Arab style, with no tables and chairs, but carpets, cushions and low sofas arranged on the floor. Coffee and cigarettes were offered by the brothel keeper, as Heath negotiated what he wanted and how much it was going to cost. He was offered two Greek girls by the brothel keeper – one sixteen years of age, and the other, her fifteen-year-old sister. A night with both sisters ('do anything you like, but no blood')[30] would cost £50. This is at a time when a London prostitute would charge £1 for her services.

The room that Heath was shown into had no windows and was padded. The floor, walls and ceiling were all painted red, as were the electric light bulbs. A collection of whips, canes, woven thongs and paddles were arranged in a rack against one wall. Against another were some low sofas and some horizontal bars. From the ceiling dangled a variety of ropes.

The sixteen-year-old was sent to Heath first – in tears and shaking with fright. He tied her to one of the horizontal bars and chose a whip to beat her with. Shortly afterwards, her younger sister was sent into the room, half-naked. Her ankles were then tied with one of the ropes dangling from the ceiling. She was then pulled up, upside down, until she was about two or three feet above the floor – just able to touch it with her hands. She was then beaten with a whip. Hill goes on to say that Heath witnessed further sex acts, including rape, but that 'this sort of thing didn't appeal to [him]'.[31] Hill's story is extreme and reads like pornography but it's clear that whatever Heath did at the Amazon Rooms, it was no more extreme than any of the other customers – fetishistic rather than sadistic violence.

Whether these stories of the Amazon Room are true or not is open to question. Veteran crime writer Donald Thomas feels that Hill is a reliable source (a lawyer with a good memory for what Heath might have told him). But it might be Heath himself who inflated the tale, turning various brothel visits into a sexual epic, casting himself as an outrageous Don Juan. It's also unclear how developed Heath's sexual tastes were at this time. It seems unlikely that he would have been able to practise fetishistic sex at borstal or in the English county towns around the RAF and army bases where he had been stationed. What is certainly true is that sexual practices of this type did go on in Cairo during the time Heath was stationed in the Middle East and perhaps it is here that he first witnessed extreme sexual behaviour.

It was not long before Heath's financial misconduct and various other offences in Palestine were exposed. Taken individually, each of the issues could have been dealt with by his commanding officer, but it is clear that Heath had repeatedly flouted authority, his wrongdoing now habitual.

As well as his issues relating to money, Heath was also found to be absenting himself from his unit without permission. He had told his commanding officer that he was having an operation on 2 June 1941 at the military hospital in Jerusalem because he had tonsilitis. He then claimed that he needed further follow-up appointments. But he was lying. He had only been required to attend the hospital once. His service records indicate that he had also been admitted to hospital twice in September of 1940 and once more in January 1941. These medical troubles may well have been valid, but it seems that he was exploiting them as excuses to be absent from his unit so that he could indulge himself in bars, brothels, restaurants and nightclubs. In mitigation, Heath later said that he was a fully qualified flying officer and was anxious to take a more active part in the fighting. He had applied for a transfer to the parachutists and the RAF, to no avail. His absences suggest his frustration at not being at the heart of the action; he'd rather spend a few illicit days 'on a party' in

Jerusalem or in the Berka in Cairo than guard a static oil-pipeline in the middle of a desert.

Heath was arrested on a number of charges – for lying about his absences from his unit, for using the second advance pay book and for five bounced cheques. For the second time in his career, he appeared before a General Court Martial at Jerusalem on 17 and 18 July 1941. Found guilty, he was to be stripped of his rank and commission and ignominiously repatriated back to England. On 8 August, Heath wrote to his parents that he would be returning home soon, 'on leave'. Given the circumstances of his dismissal, how would he face his parents? What would he tell his fiancée?

He was held under close arrest from 15 August and was to be repatriated to Britain in October. Since Italy had entered the war, the passage home across the Mediterranean was closed, so he would be sailing by the much longer Cape Route via South Africa.

SS *Mooltan* was docked at Port Tewfik on the Suez Canal, loaded with troops, guns, tanks and stores. A former P&O Liner, she had been requisitioned by the RAF and was now painted a uniform grey as troop ship *W7*. Even at a speed of 17 knots, the voyage back to Glasgow – the final port of disembarkation – would take the best part of two months.

The *Mooltan* crew were repatriating 420 wounded British Army personnel from Crete, supervised by twenty-one VAD Nurses. Also travelling were 200 civilian refugees comprising friendly diplomats and their families as well as oil company representatives from the Balkans. Locked in the lower decks were thousands of Italian POWs. Sixteen officers who had been court-martialled were also on board. Some had been under close arrest for weeks – some, like Heath, for months.

Paull Hill was adjutant on the *Mooltan*. With the ship still docked, he called the sixteen cashiered officers together and told them that their sentences would now be officially promulgated. Heath was sixth or seventh in line in this process of sanctioned humiliation. First, he was sent to the Orderly Room to remove all decorations and insignia of rank from his uniform. Returning with them in his hands, he was told to place these insignia on the table in front of him, thereby reverting to civilian status.

Heath made quite an impression on Hill. Nearly six feet tall, with broad shoulders and slim hips, he seemed the least likely person to commit the offences he had been charged with. '[He was] a perfect specimen of young manhood – he was only twenty-four then – with blue eyes, fair curly hair and a carefree expression on his handsome face,'[32] Hill wrote in *Portrait of a Sadist*.

Hill took a keen interest in Heath throughout the voyage and on several occasions had to talk to him about various romances that he was having on board, particularly those with civilian passengers. It is during these discussions that Heath apparently revealed to Hill his adventures in the brothels of Cairo.

The *Mooltan* sailed south towards the Cape and docked into Durban's large lagoon harbour. Whilst taking on supplies for the rest of the voyage, it became apparent that the engines needed immediate attention. Essential spares would have to be found locally – or even flown in from England. The ship would be docked at Durban for at least a fortnight, possibly longer. Plans were made to transfer the POWs to a camp just outside Durban. The rest of the passengers would remain living on the ship, but would be allowed ashore during the day. Heath and the other court-martialled officers were subject to military law until the point of disembarkation, but having caused no trouble on the voyage so far, they were also permitted shore leave, on the condition that they were back aboard by 00.01 a.m. each night.

South Africa's ports and harbours, particularly Cape Town

and Durban, had become of global strategic importance since Italy had joined the war, making the route around the Cape of Good Hope a crucial artery in the Allied campaign. During the war years 45,000 ships would call at South Africa's ports – 400 convoys carrying a total of 6 million men. More than half of these ships would pass through Durban.

South Africa's geographical position meant that the war still felt distant. As in Singapore and Cairo, it was possible to live the classic colonial lifestyle of sundowners on the Durban Club terrace and polo at the Inanda Club. Even the currency reassuringly remained sterling, a legacy of the British Empire continuing to dominate the South African economy.[33] For clubbable (apparently), public-school men like Neville Heath, South Africa was a home from home, with few of the wartime disadvantages and much better weather.

Durban itself was a city of contrasts, an exotic combination of European and African cultures. A line of luxurious hotels and Art Deco buildings sat along the harbour rather like Miami in Florida.[34] There were handsome shops and elegant houses, impressive public buildings, cinemas, and an art gallery with fine English and Dutch paintings. Bernard Shaw's wife had claimed that Durban was the one city outside England that she could live in as it was 'so very English', but it was also very multicultural, with mosques and Hindu temples situated just off the main streets which were populated with Indians, Zulus, Muslims and Europeans. It was the perfect melting pot for Heath to be absorbed within and for him to indulge his hotel and bar-room lifestyle. It was also, for a young officer from dusty Palestine, a city of refreshing greenery with wide avenues and roads shady with flowering trees, flamboyants, jacarandas and bougainvillea,[35] that gave Durban a tropical air.[36] Alongside the tramcars and motor buses, the famous Zulu rickshaw boys ran barefoot along the tarmac, wearing head-dresses of bull's horns and feathers, coloured beads dangling from their neck and wrists. On the pavements, witch doctors sold the fat of the hippopotamus as a love charm, not fifty yards from the local chemist. Even in the suburbs, Durban exhibited an exotic fusion of modernity and elemental Africa as hundreds of monkeys played within sight of the newest apartment buildings.[37]

After a fortnight docked in the harbour at Durban, her engines now fixed, the *Mooltan* was ready to proceed on her voyage. But when Paull Hill tried to track him down, 2nd Lieutenant Heath was nowhere to be found. Returning to bombed-out Britain and facing an awkward and humiliating homecoming in Wimbledon, South Africa, with its colour and opportunities, must have seemed to Heath like an extremely tempting place to start a new life. When the *Mooltan* finally set sail for Glasgow, it left without him.

CHAPTER NINE
Lt. James Robert Cadogan Armstrong

DECEMBER 1941 – OCTOBER 1944

You don't know what it's like to feel frightened. You get a beastly, bitter taste in your mouth, and your tongue goes dry and you feel sick, and all the time you're saying – this isn't happening to me – it can't be happening – I'll wake up. But you know you won't wake up. You know it's happening and the sea is below you, and you're responsible for the lives of six people. And you have to pretend you're not afraid, that's what's so awful. Oh God, I was afraid tonight, when we took off and saw that [plane] on fire, I didn't think: There are friends of mine in that. I thought: That might happen to us.

Terence Rattigan, *Flare Path*, 1942

The Union of South Africa had joined the Allies in 1939 but only after a narrow vote when the nationalist and anti-British prime minister, James Hertzog, had been deposed following his attempt to promote South African neutrality in the war. Hertzog lost the debate by only thirteen votes and was replaced by his coalition deputy, the Boer War veteran, Jan Smuts. Smuts was very much pro-British and went on to acquire senior status within the Allied Commanders.[1] Given that his majority to commit South Africa to the Allied cause was small, there was to be no enforced conscription – the Union Defence Forces were to be bolstered by volunteers alone. At the outbreak of war there had been only 3,353 troops in the regular army with 14,631 territorials, so a vigorous recruiting drive was launched with posters encouraging prospective volunteers. 'Don't miss the greatest adventure of all time!'[2]

However, because of South Africa's race policies, there was a restricted pool of eligible whites from which to form a volunteer army. Black, coloured and Asian South Africans were, on the whole, committed to the Allied cause. They appreciated the dangers of Nazism and were well aware that supporters of the German cause in South Africa – led by the political opposition – were also the most vociferous advocates of segregation. A number of support corps providing cooks, drivers, stretcher-bearers and labourers were formed of black, coloured and Asian South Africans in order to release whites for active combat. Despite their much larger numbers, non-white South Africans were not allowed to fight because, in the convoluted logic of the prevailing ideology, they were not allowed to take arms against Europeans. At the end of the war 20,000 South Africans – of all races and creeds – celebrated a 'People's Day of Victory' in Johannesburg. At the same time, the government published cash and clothing allowances for discharged servicemen. Whites received £5 in cash and a £25 clothing allowance. Blacks were given £2 and a khaki suit.[3]

One of South Africa's greatest resources was labour. Before the war, industry in the Union was focused on the mining of diamonds and gold. In 1939 there was only one munitions factory in the entire Union. But within months of joining the Allies, South Africa converted much of her manufacturing power to wartime production, making shells, mortars, guns and a huge variety of equipment, including 32,000 armoured vehicles, 12 million pairs of boots, 5.5 million blankets and 2,435 million cigarettes. As a consequence, the number of South Africans in manufacturing, many of them women, rose by 60 per cent. Urbanization increased with great rapidity and by the end of the war many towns had doubled in size. In 1946, for the first time, there were more black Africans living in South Africa's towns than whites. Many settled in makeshift communities outside the major cities and though they had provided the essential workforce demanded by the war effort, this contradicted the segregationist principle that blacks should not become permanent urban residents. This legacy of the war was to play a direct part in the initiation of apartheid under the re-elected National Party in 1948.

In 1939, daily life in the Cape was barely affected by what seemed a distant European War. But shortages and restrictions did begin to appear in 1942 and towards the end of the war there were meatless days, a national loaf was introduced and petrol rationed, but the shortage of food and basic commodities was insignificant compared to the deprivations in Britain. Luxury goods like pins, toilet paper and cosmetics were frequently hard to come by – women finding lipstick frustratingly scarce. But the shortage most painful to many men was whisky. This was still being imported, but many freight ships had been torpedoed, driving up the price of remaining supplies. Before the war, branded whisky had been sold at a controlled price of 14s. a bottle (equivalent to £24 in today's money). After a black market for spirits developed, a bottle of whisky could cost anything up to £5 (£172 today).[4] Except for certain regions in the Cape, South Africa had always been a whisky-drinking country. Wine appeared only on formal occasions and it was common to drink several whiskies before dinner. A strange piece of legislation was introduced just before Christmas 1940, in order to curb excessive drinking amongst servicemen. This forbade anybody from buying a drink for anybody else in public. This ill-considered directive became known as the 'no-treating law'. Barmen, however, were quick to point out that it was impossible to enforce and the law soon fell into disuse.[5]

On 7 December 1941, the Japanese attacked Pearl Harbor, forcing America into the war. Two days later, South Africa declared war on Japan and immediately her long coastline and harbours felt vulnerable to attack. At the time, South Africa had only eight anti-aircraft guns and six searchlights throughout the entire Union. The Union Defence Force itself consisted of just 334,000 troops. In contrast, the Japanese had 1.4 million troops and 2,400 aircraft supported by a navy with 350,000 personnel. Like the south coast of England, attempts were swiftly made to fortify coastal areas from German and Japanese attack and to protect the Cape Route, the Allies' lifeline. Durban's south beach was cut off with barbed-wire fences, submarine nets were spanned across the harbour entrance and armed sentries patrolled the harbour gates.

Having jumped ship, Heath was now an illegal alien in a foreign country with few prospects and no money. But, ever resourceful, he posed as a Captain Selway of the Argyll and Sutherland Highlanders, awarding himself the Military Cross, one of the highest decorations for exemplary gallantry. As Captain Selway he procured £85 from Barclays Bank in Durban. Leaving the city, he went on to stay at a series of hotels in Maritzburg and Johannesburg – under different names – always moving on without paying the bill. From Johannesburg, he next travelled the thirty-five miles to Pretoria to the air base at Voortrekkerhoogte. On 22 December, he volunteered for the South African Air Force (SAAF).

Unlike the RAF, the SAAF had been little prepared for the outbreak of war with only 160 permanent officers and 1,400 ranks in 1939. Despite this, the Air Ministry would not recruit black or coloured volunteers. A concerted effort was made to dramatically increase training for the RAF, SAAF and other Allied flight services with the Joint Air Training Scheme (JATS). By 1941, there were thirty-eight Air Schools throughout South Africa and the SAAF had grown to a strength of 31,204 aircrew including 956 pilots.

Heath joined the SAAF as James Robert Cadogan Armstrong. The 'Cadogan' related him by implication to one of the wealthiest aristocratic families in Britain who were known for owning much of Chelsea. On his application form, he embellished his history with half-truths, fantasies and lies. Though he claimed he was born in Cape Town, he wrote that his family home was in England – Melton Hall, in Woodbridge, Suffolk – hence his English accent. Even in deceit, vestiges of Heath's real biography remained, 'Melton Hall' being a corruption of Merton Hall Road, the rather more modest home of his parents in Wimbledon. Woodbridge is indeed in Suffolk – the closest village to Hollesley Bay, the borstal colony that Heath had joined in 1938.[6]

Heath stated that he had been educated at Harrow and Trinity College Cambridge and that he had joined the Officers' Training Corps in both. He also claimed to have resigned his commission in the RAF in 1937 – lying again about his dismissal – and that he was a journalist by profession. He may have suggested that he had been a war correspondent and that this accounted for the fact that he had not joined the services before, given his useful training with the

RAF. In all official documents relating to his identity as Armstrong throughout his time in South Africa, Heath gave his date of birth as 6 June 1915, adding another couple of years to his real age.[7] This confusion might have been a simple ruse to cover his tracks if ever his record in the Middle East came to light. His application to the SAAF successful, he joined No. 62 Air School at Bloemfontein.

Bloemfontein, 254 miles from Johannesburg, was capital of the Orange Free State. Not a large city, its ground plan was based on the American rectilinear pattern – miles of streets in ordered parallel lines with distinguished public buildings of brick and local sandstone grouped around the central Hoffman Square.[8] It was a staid, sober town with a strong civic sense of order – a perfect setting for Heath to re-invent himself. From this point, both his career and his personal life improved with extraordinary speed. Within eight weeks of landing in South Africa he had met and married a very eligible young woman from one of Johannesburg's most respected families.

Twenty-two-year-old Elizabeth Hardcastle Rivers was the daughter of Charles and Aileen Rivers of Epping Road, Forest Town, a fashionable and leafy suburb in northern Johannesburg. Elizabeth was an attractive girl with 'sloe eyes and chestnut hair' coiffured in the Elizabethan style that was popular at the time. She had been educated in England at Roedean, the exclusive girls' school on the south coast and, like Heath, was very sporty – enjoying hockey, golf and skiing, which she had learned at a finishing school in Switzerland. She had come out as a debutante at one of the last pre-war Spring Balls and was very much part of Johannesburg's social elite.

Johannesburg in the 1940s was a city of opportunity. Only in existence since 1886 – when it had no buildings, only tents and a population of just fifteen – within sixty years it had transformed into a brash, modern metropolis of skyscrapers and neon. The reason for its vast and swift expansion was the discovery of gold. At the end of every street were golden pyramids, shining in the sunlight – dumps from the neighbouring goldmines. In a hastily built modern city of undistinguished architecture, the travel writer H. V. Morton felt that these goldmine dumps were 'what St Paul's is to London . . . a symbol of the city, its true coat of arms'.[9] Outside the city centre, what was once an arid, treeless veld was now covered with trees and houses built in a variety of styles – Spanish Colonial, Cape, Dutch and Tudor – which gave a Californian brilliance to suburbs like Forest Town. The surrounding gardens were full of flowering shrubs, pergolas, swimming pools and black servants moving noiselessly in spotless white uniforms. For Heath, Johannesburg offered an extraordinary opportunity to start a new life, with a new identity on a new continent; a golden lad in a golden land.

Heath wooed and seduced Elizabeth Rivers, but her parents disapproved of the match.[10] The couple had only just met and, besides, they knew hardly anything about him. But Heath, by now, was extremely confident of his charms with women. Elizabeth had fallen for him 'desperately' – for her, it was a 'beautiful dream'.[11] The pair eloped and on 12 February 1942 married in a small civil ceremony in Pretoria. None of her family were present. Heath married under the name of Armstrong, giving little thought, it seems, to whether this would invalidate the marriage. At the same time, he artfully extricated himself from his engagement to Peggy Dixon in England. He wrote and told her that he had been dismissed from the army, probably anticipating how she would react to the news. Peggy wrote back, breaking off their engagement, but kept her engagement ring.[12]

In Wimbledon, Heath's news from Johannesburg was met with some surprise. Shortly after the wedding, his father visited Mr Scott at the Borstal Association and told him

Neville's startling news. He was now training to be a flying instructor at the Central Flying School at Bloemfontein, had taken South African citizenship, had changed his name by deed poll and had married, all in the space of two months. Elizabeth had sent a very nice letter to her new parents-in-law in which she wrote that she hoped to visit England with 'Jimmy' to see them when the war was over. Heath also claimed that his father-in-law was interested in civil aviation, so it seemed that a career as a flyer after the war was assured. Mr Scott noted that though Mr and Mrs Heath were hurt about their son's change of name, they understood that this might have been necessary for him to make a fresh start.[13]

On 2 September 1942, Elizabeth gave birth to a baby boy, Robert Michael Cadogan Armstrong, so she may well have been pregnant at the time she and Heath were married. The naming of the child seems to have been all down to Heath who gave him the aristocratic (if bogus) 'Cadogan' where his own mother had given her sons the name 'Clevely' – Heath, with little irony, it seems, carrying on a family tradition, but without the family name. Sentimentally, he gave his son his younger brother's Christian names, reversed. In February 1943, the couple moved to Randfontein to be near No. 2 Air School where Heath was teaching trainee pilots to fly 1930s Tiger Moths. He was in his element.

> I loved it. They took me as a pupil pilot and gave me a test at once. My record for the years I was there shows I was right on top of my job. I was commissioned in March 1942, a month after I was married, and posted to the Central Flying School as an instructor. Even this period of non-operational flying instruction was enjoyable and I must have taught between 100 and 150 pupils to fly. These were the men who became part of the desert Air Force – as grand a bunch of men as there are in the world.[14]

Many of these trainee pilots were from Britain and the Empire as part of the JATS. South Africa's weather and clear skys were perfect for teaching them to fly over the broad open veld. Harold Guthrie, a pilot with the RAF, was taught to fly at Randfontein at the time Heath was teaching there. During his stay at the station, Guthrie remembered that Heath was exceedingly popular with everyone and was always an invited member of any party at which quantities of liquor were likely to be consumed. '[Heath] drank heavily and although he frequently appeared to be haggard in the morning, I have never seen him show any signs of alcoholic excess in any other way,' he recalled.[15]

Guthrie was aware that Heath was very well known in the higher social circles in Johannesburg and though he did drink excessively heavily, he always behaved in a perfectly gentlemanly manner, 'never speaking to women with anything other than complete respect'.[16] Heath and his wife often frequented the Inanda Polo Club where they would socialize with Elizabeth's old school friend and next-door neighbour, the actress Moira Lister, who was just starting her career in the theatre. Lister and her sister were both seduced by Heath's extreme good looks, wit and charm. 'Everyone,' remembered Lister, 'or all the girls at least, were vying for his favours.'[17]

For Heath, these sunny times in the heat, safety and abundance of South Africa were years of 'perfect happiness'. He was married to a beautiful young woman he loved, he had steered himself away from the dangers of his past and onto an even keel. He was a father now, with a healthy young son – and he was flying again. His life was contented and fulfilled. He even bought a dog. Only three years later, Heath remembered these times in a letter to Elizabeth with a sense of deep nostalgia:

Bloemfontein at [Central Flying School] *with that awful cold hotel – Greystones – the 'Rambles', with those enormous teas – The Bloemfontein Hotel and those early morning drives to the Aerodrome in that little open car which we both froze in so regularly – Randfontein and our house there. The chaps who used to come and stay with us – the parties we had there and at the Aerodrome . . .*[18]

It all seemed idyllic. But, as ever with Heath, his attempts to secure a golden future for himself and his family were to be thwarted by his past behaviour which, still unresolved, now came back to haunt him.

P&O, who owned the *Mooltan,* imposed a fine of £100 on anyone who absconded from troop transport. Since Heath had jumped ship at Durban, he was personally liable for the fine and had been pursued by the South African CID. They were also keen to trace him because of the money he had illegally withdrawn from Barclays Bank in Durban and the hotels he had defrauded before signing up with the SAAF. This meant that not only was his false identity exposed to the SAAF authorities, but the full extent of his past misbehaviour and dishonesty would now be known to his wife and to his in-laws. Heath had married Elizabeth under an assumed name, so the Rivers family were concerned that the marriage wasn't legal. An amendment to the marriage certificate was hastily arranged to make it valid. Heath had jumped ship without permission and was an illegal immigrant. His application to join the SAAF was almost entirely fiction and he had also lied that he had had no previous criminal convictions. Now that the full details of his court martial at Jerusalem were revealed, Heath's entire new life was held in the balance.[19]

The Immigration Authorities indicated that his continued presence in South Africa was entirely dependent on how the SAAF wanted to deal with his career of repeated deception. Due to the valuable work that he had done in training pilots at a time when the SAAF was rapidly expanding, the authorities discussed Heath's case at the highest level, even involving the director general of the service. Heath's commanding officer offered a glowing recommendation for leniency.

> He [has] carried out all his duties in the air and on the ground in a perfectly correct manner. He is keen and takes a great interest in the work he is now performing. His personal conduct has been exemplary.[20]

On 18 March, Heath himself wrote an impassioned and contrite letter from Randfontein to the director general of the Air Force in Pretoria. He outlined his commitment to the Allied cause and his usefulness as a pilot. He stressed that since joining the SAAF, he had not committed a single misdemeanour. He admitted that his former behaviour was simply due to his natural impetuosity. Desperate to make a fresh start for himself, he pleaded that if he were dismissed from the SAAF, it would ruin his life.

> *I decided to change my name and make a really serious attempt to change my character, the fact that I am now married has helped me – and my wife, who knows the whole story and has helped me – is shortly expecting a child.*
>
> *Proof that I have made this serious attempt at reformation is easily recognizable from my record during the past 15 months and by my present Commanding Officer's personal report. I can also produce the names of at least ten officers of Field Rank who would testify on my behalf.*
>
> *May I respectfully submit that my services be retained on probation. If I commit the slightest misdemeanour I shall have failed in my attempt to reform myself and then any action which may be taken will be entirely of my own manufacture. I can honestly promise that such a state of affairs will never come to pass.*

> *I have served as a fighter pilot for two years in the Royal Air Force in peace time and served with an International Fighter Squadron in Spain during the civil war. May I request that I may be retained in the SAAF on the above conditions and posted to one of the fighter squadrons on operations.*
>
> *I am convinced that if this request could be granted and a little trust placed in me by higher authority with regard to my future behaviour, I shall not fail.*[21]

There is no evidence that Heath fought in the Spanish Civil War nor did he have the opportunity to do so, given he was in the RAF when it started and at Hollesley Bay thereafter. It's doubtful, too, that Elizabeth was pregnant again, their son being only seven months old when this letter was written. But it's typical of Heath to risk lies such as these (one heroic, one sentimental) that could fairly easily be disproved. Fortunately for him, this gamble worked. Given his good record in service and apparent sincerity to reform his character, the director general of the Air Force thought he should be given another chance. He could remain in the SAAF on six months' probation on the condition that he repaid all his outstanding debts.[22] Heath's father-in-law reluctantly obliged. The Immigration Authorities would hold his deportation in abeyance. Once again, he was offered an extraordinary opportunity to rehabilitate and redeem himself.

Having successfully deflected these issues from the past, Heath might have embraced the strategy he had implemented at Hollesley Bay; to keep his head down for the duration and concentrate on training other pilots. However, on the international scene, the war was now moving in the Allies' favour. The Axis powers had surrendered in North Africa, British troops had landed on mainland Italy and the Italians had declared war on Germany. With a series of concentrated bombing raids on Germany beginning in February 1944 and the Germans heavily invested on the Eastern Front, Allied victory seemed a real possibility – a far cry from the situation when Heath had last been in England in 1940. It is at this point, Heath recognized in retrospect, that he made a fundamental mistake. Rather than settling for a safer, duller life in South Africa, he still wanted to go on active service and take part in the war.

> *One thing is certain, and it is that if I had I not left Training Command in South Africa to go on 'ops' none of this last eighteen months of hell would have occurred.*[23]

Heath's desire to fly again with the RAF was intense. He had been trying for a secondment or transfer since 1940. His objective was not to work as part of support staff or in training, but to go on operations in one of the active theatres of war. He specifically wanted to return to Fighter Command, the daring, glamorous face of the RAF. In April 1944 he achieved his long-held ambition and successfully arranged a transfer, with the RAF presumably unaware that 'J. R. C. Armstrong' was actually 'N. G. C. Heath', who had been dismissed from the service in 1937.[24] Arriving back in England, he was sent to Dunsfold Aerodrome in Surrey to join 180 Squadron, part of the 2nd Tactical Air Force.[25] The squadron flew under the motto '*suaviter in modo fortier in re*' (charming in manner, forthright in deed), perfect for the golden-haired adventurer Heath.

On 27 June, Heath called at the Borstal Association wearing the uniform of a captain in the SAAF, bearing his wings and two ribbons on his chest. He told Mr Scott that he was now based in South Cerney in Gloucestershire working on Intruder Operations. This involved fighter planes making night attacks on German fighter bases, hoping to cause disruption to reduce the heavy losses that were being suffered by Bomber Command at the time. However, whatever he told Mr Scott, Heath was not flying in Fighter Command at all, but had been training to fly bombers. This was a significant change for Heath as flying a fighter and flying a bomber demanded very different skills of their pilots and – some aviation experts would say – different personalities. Much of the bomber's work was done before they left the ground and flying over to Europe could mean flights of seven, eight or nine hours. These journeys were highly dramatic at take-off and landing, and particularly intense over the target, but outside these peaks there were long periods of boredom and fatigue. Heath had been used to flying up-to-the-minute fighter planes like the Hawker Hurricane – sports cars of the air. The Dam Busters veteran Guy Gibson likened flying a bomber to driving a bus.[26]

As well as the different technical and intellectual demands that flying fighters and bombers made on their pilots, one of the crucial differences between Bomber Command and Fighter Command was the number of fatalities they suffered. Of the 125,000 airmen who served in Bomber Command during the war according to one study, fatalities were as high as 65 per cent. Two thirds would be expected to die. These terrifying statistics would have been known to all bomber aircrew. Air Chief Marshall Arthur 'Bomber' Harris, Bomber Command's Commander-in-Chief later noted that:

These crews, shining youth on the threshold of life, lived under circumstances of intolerable strain. They were in fact – and they knew it, faced with the virtual certainty of death, probably in one of its least pleasant forms.[27]

One nineteen-year-old flight engineer, Sergeant Dennis Goodliffe, was told on arrival at his squadron: 'You're now on an operational squadron, your expectation of life is six weeks. Go back to your huts and make out your wills.'[28]

Yet, extraordinarily, even in 1944 when Bomber Command was suffering terrible losses, the supply of aircrew candidates never dwindled and the Air Ministry felt able to turn away 22.5 per cent of the volunteers who applied to join them.

Over several months of training, crew members would be taught in a particular role for which they had shown aptitude – pilots, navigators, engineers, wireless operators, air-gunners and bomb-aimers. But even in training the notion of death was never far from their minds as over 8,000 trainee aircrew died before they qualified – one seventh of fatalities that Bomber Command suffered throughout the duration of the war. These accidents in training often provided young crews with their first direct acquaintance with death, as many were still in their teens. The average age of an airman in Bomber Command was just twenty-two.

Heath was trained to fly American-made two-engined Mitchell bombers, the B-25. Having completed specialist training, pilots, navigators and bomb-aimers were given further advanced instruction before finally arriving at an Operational Training Unit where they would join the wireless operators and gunners, who had been trained elsewhere. It is at the OTUs that British trainees would meet their various counterparts from Australia and New Zealand who had been trained at the Empire Training Schools abroad. Crews were then put together in an extraordinarily unscientific process known as 'crewing up'. The requisite numbers of each aircrew category were put together in a large room or hangar and simply told to team up. Each potential aircrew member would need to make instinctive decisions, attempting to interpret a special chemistry between a group of complete strangers. Jack Currie, who reached his OTU in 1942, remembered that 'I had a strange recollection of standing in a suburban dance-hall, wondering which girls I should approach.'[29] And indeed, crewing up was a sort of mating ritual. Who would be calm, efficient, hard-working, reliable, great to have a laugh and a drink with and – most, importantly – who would be lucky? There must also have been some subliminal sense of attraction between the men who were drawn to each other. Heath was fit, good-looking and charming and it's easy to see how he would be able to attract an enthusiastic crew around him. The decisions that he and his fellow crew members had made in this casual, haphazard way were to be the most important decisions these young men would ever make, as it would dictate whether they – as a crew – would live or die.

Captain William Spurrett Fielding-Johnson was a hugely distinguished and much-admired flying ace, credited with five aerial victories in the First World War. He had been awarded the Military Cross in 1915 whilst serving with the Leicestershire Yeomanry. Following an injury in 1916 he had trained as a pilot with the RAF. In 1918 he destroyed four German fighters and a reconnaissance aircraft. He was exactly the sort of daring, heroic airman that Heath aspired to be.

Fielding-Johnson had volunteered for the RAF immediately the Second World War broke out and served as a squadron leader and aerial gunner. In 1940, at the age of forty-eight, he was the oldest rear gunner in the service and had been awarded the DFC. Having been wounded in June 1944, he was in recovery until September of that year, when he rejoined 180 Squadron as a squadron leader. He was responsible for the maintenance of aircraft armaments and assisting the commanding officer in observing the physical and mental wellbeing of the aircrews in his care.

As the Allies were forcing their way through Europe, 180 Squadron was preparing to move from RAF Dunsfold to Melsbroek in Belgium. The bulk of personnel, including ground staff, were sent to Belgium by road and sea, whilst the aircraft were flown over. Heath accompanied Fielding-Johnson with the land and sea party and this was the first time they came into each other's company. As the journey continued, Fielding-Johnson became aware of Heath's unusual behaviour, as he had 'periods of irresponsibility during off times and when he had a drink or two'. On more than one occasion, he took issue with Heath's behaviour – and despite Heath's ranking as a captain, Fielding-Johnson felt more and more that he was thoroughly unreliable. Once they had settled at the Melsbroek air station, Heath's behaviour continued to trouble him. When he had been drinking, Heath was like a completely different person; supremely arrogant, talking wildly about his past exploits and – in a most ungentlemanly manner – about his finances. Hugely knowledgeable about the pressures and strains that airmen had to cope with, Fielding-Johnson felt that Heath's behaviour was very similar to cases he had previously dealt with when a pilot's nerve had gone due to operational exhaustion or simply from the strain of flying itself. Effectively, he identified that Heath was in the throes of some sort of breakdown.[30]

In 1947, the Air Ministry commissioned a report, *Psychological Disorders in Flying Personnel of the Royal Air Force Investigated During the War 1939–45*. This study is a fascinating context in which to examine Heath's actions and behaviour at this point, exploring as it does the particular pressures that pilots suffered.

The physical fatigue of flying a heavy bomber is limited to the pilot who, as captain of the aircraft, has an added mental load. There was agreement that big men [like Heath] found these planes easier to fly than small men of slender build, and one station commander thought that there should be special selection for these heavy jobs.[31]

The report goes on to say, based on the evidence of flight crews throughout the war, that the incidence of neuroses was highest in Bomber Command, this being almost twice the incidence in Fighter Command, and that the crew members most affected were pilots of bombers. Psychologically, fighter pilots had to concern themselves solely with their own safety. Fighter planes were also both more agile and better armed than bombers. Bomber pilots had a much less manoeuverable aircraft, slower and more vulnerable to attack by enemy fighters. Crucially, bomber pilots felt responsible not just for their own lives but for the lives of the rest of their crew.

Flying for long distances, often in the dark, affected all flight crews. Fatigue and frostbite were common and lack of oxygen sometimes resulted in blackouts. It was not unusual for a pilot to suddenly wake after a period of unconsciousness in the air. A pilot staring for hours at his instrument panel might also suddenly find everything he saw upside down – normally the human eye sees objects inverted and the brain corrects this, reversing the image. All of these symptoms were brought on by changes in physical conditions during flights.[32]

The psychological neuroses exhibited by aircrew were collected under six headings: anxiety, hysteria, depression, fatigue, obsession and schizophrenia.[33] RAF neuro-psychiatrists established that the most important cause of neuroses in aircrew was, not surprisingly, fear.[34]

Many young airmen, paralysed with terror at the prospect of their own violent deaths, were equally burdened with feelings of responsibility for the carnage that they caused in the towns and cities of Germany. Frequently they would drown their fears off duty in alcoholic binges and it's alcohol that Fielding-Johnson identified as one of the causes of Heath's abnormal behaviour, if not the root of it. But it's also true that airmen had access to other stimulants that could be as addictive and damaging. RAF medical officers regularly distributed 'wakey wakey' pills to aircrew who were suffering from fatigue and who would need to keep awake for raids that could last for up to nine hours. This was the amphetamine known as Benzedrine. Officially doctors were only supposed to offer it to pilots, gunners and navigators on missions, but in practice it was readily available on RAF stations to aircrew, ground crew and even WAAFs. Airmen became accomplished at acquiring large quantities of the drug and storing it up for their own recreational use. They'd take the pills not only on operations when they needed to keep alert for several hours, but also at off-duty parties and drinking sessions. Joan Wyndham, a self-confessed addict, remembered the casual use of Benzedrine by WAAFs and aircrew: 'I really love the clear, cool feeling in my head and the edge of excitement it gives to everything you do.'[35]

Benzedrine usage was widely abused, and, like all amphetamines, highly addictive. It is the chemical base of the popular clubber's drug, MDMA (Ecstasy). The body quickly develops a tolerance of it, encouraging higher dosage. Side effects from long-term use of Benzedrine include hyperactivity, grandiosity, euphoria, increased libido, irritability, paranoia, aggression and psychosomatic disorders. The most severe symptoms of chronic amphetamine abuse can result in psychotic behaviour that can be indistinguishable from schizophrenia. Heath would certainly have had access to Benzedrine at the time and in combination with his alcoholism it might explain some of the more extreme behaviour observed by Fielding-Johnson.

Towards the end of October, 180 Squadron had made three daylight bombing attacks on the town of Venlo in Holland and were then ordered to make a fourth. Venlo had both a road and a rail bridge over the River Meuse and the Allies would make a total of thirteen attempts to destroy the bridges in order to cut off German supply lines and to block the retreat of German troops across the river. During the attacks on the bridges, from 13 October to 19 November 1944, 300 people were killed. Despite their best efforts, Allied attempts to bomb the bridges would fail and eventually retreating German troops would blow them up themselves in an effort to halt the Allied advance.

At this time, certain members of Heath's crew began to confide in Fielding-Johnson that they were not keen to go out with him at night off duty, though they would not give detailed reasons for their objections other than to say that he encouraged them to spend too much money. There were no complaints about his performance as a pilot. Fielding-Johnson took it upon himself to monitor Heath's behaviour from then on and actively encouraged other members of the crew to share with him anything that Heath might do or say which might be detrimental to their morale. This in itself was an extraordinary state of affairs as the tight fraternal bonds between bomber crews were thought to be crucial to their survival.

The fourth attack on the Venlo bridges was to take place on 29 October. Aircrews would hear after breakfast if they were due to fly that day. After the mission was announced, Heath's top turret gunner approached Fielding-Johnson and told him that he felt unfit. He didn't want to fly and had lost his nerve. This was known within the RAF as 'lack of moral fibre' (LMF), a bureaucratic euphemism for cowardice. It was recognized by senior officers that such cases had to be dealt with quickly as 'one really frightened man could affect the others around him'.[36] The threat of being branded LMF was used as 'little short of a terror tactic'[37] over all aircrew and many men carried on flying scared out of their wits because they were more frightened of being called a coward than they were of flying.

It wasn't so much the admission of fear and loss of self-respect that deterred men from going LMF, it was the awareness that they would be regarded as inadequate to the pressures of war in a country totally committed to winning the war. In this atmosphere, the man who opted out was a pariah, an insult to the national need. He was conscious of bringing shame to his family, and that most of his friends wouldn't wish to recognize him, or at best they would be embarrassed and awkward on meeting. Nobody cared about the explanations of the psychiatrists about stress-induced illness.[38]

On this occasion, as senior officer and an experienced rear gunner, Fielding-Johnson volunteered to take the gunner's place. Not only would the crew be able to take their part in the operation and the squadron could fly intact, but here was an ideal opportunity for Fielding-Johnson to watch Heath working under pressure.

The preliminary briefing took place a few hours before take-off in the briefing room hut. Some 120 members of the squadron filed into rows of chairs, having been checked in by RAF police. Cigarettes and pipes were lit immediately as the crews waited for the squadron commanding officer and the station commander. In some squadrons, a map of the target was propped on a stand, hidden by a blackout curtain to be dramatically revealed by the station intelligence officer, who generally led the briefing. In others, every available inch of the walls and desks was covered with large-scale maps and photographs – a mosaic of information about the 'target for today', for the attacks of the Venlo bridges were to be in broad daylight. The position of balloon barrages, ground defences and hostile fighter bases would be marked by blobs of purple ink. Threads stretched across the large maps to indicate the route the bombers were to take. The blinds were then drawn as an epidiascope projected large images of the target on the wall. On some stations, the padre would then say a prayer before final preparations began – and a medical officer would be on hand to distribute Benzedrine.

The squadron then headed to the mess for their pre-operation meal, usually bacon and eggs, a luxury in days of rationing. They were then sealed off from the outside world. Phone calls to wives and girlfriends were forbidden as they waited nervously to see if the weather was favourable, chain-smoking and reading paperback books to distract themselves. It is during these long hours of waiting that Heath first began to read the adventure stories and thrillers he liked so much: Peter Cheyney's Slim Callaghan novels, John Buchan's Hannay books or James Hadley Chase's *No Orchids for Miss Blandish*, a well-thumbed copy of which seemed to be in every RAF mess. The sense of anticipation and anxiety steadily grew from the time crews were briefed until take-off. Guy Gibson felt that this period was the worst part of any bombing raid: 'Your stomach feels as though it wants to hit your backbone.'[39] Vomiting and diarrhoea were common and men were prone to fly off the handle at the slightest provocation. 'All this,' Gibson said, 'because you're frightened, scared stiff.'[40]

When it was confirmed that the weather was favourable and the sortie was on, ninety minutes before take-off the crews got ready, pulling on their parachute harnesses, fastening life preservers ('Mae Wests') or adjusting the electric tubes of their hot suits. The kit was awkward and bulky, much of it to try and combat the freezing cold they would encounter flying at such high altitudes – for every 1,000 feet they climbed, the air temperature dropped 2.5 degrees and after 8,000 feet, oxygen masks were needed.[41] They had a whistle attached to their collar to call for help if they fell into the sea, and dog tags stamped with their name and service number made of a material that could withstand the most intense furnace. Many airmen carried some sort of lucky charm around the neck, or pocketed close to the heart, a rabbit's foot, or a rosary, letter, St Christopher, coin, photograph, playing card; anything to fend off the overwhelming fear of a violent and painful death.

The final briefing took place in the crew room where the meteorological expert gave up-to-the-minute information about the weather. Provisions were handed out for the trip – a thermos flask of coffee, energy pastilles, chewing gum, raisins, chocolate.[42] They were also given an escape kit in case they fell into enemy territory. These consisted of local money, phrase sheets and compasses as well as maps of France, Germany or Belgium printed on squares of silk. These could be secreted or sewn somewhere in their uniform. As a last precaution, all crew members then emptied their pockets and were given two different coloured pouches in which to put the contents. One of these would be sent to their next of kin if they did not return. The other would be sent to clandestine girlfriends.[43]

The aircrews piled into lorries, were driven to their waiting aircraft and assisted into them by the ground crew. Last cigarettes were smoked and many crew members urinated against one of the aircraft's wheels – a final ritual to bring good luck. Heath signed the F700, accepting the aircraft from the ground crew. He declared that all was in good order and handed the form back to the ground crew who then stood down. From a training that had now become instinct, each member of the crew busied themselves, cramped in their allotted action stations. The navigator of Heath's crew – a former teacher called Freddie Silvester – laid out his chart in preparation. Despite Fielding-Johnson's seniority on the ground, in the air, the pilot was always in command of the aircraft, so Heath was very much in charge. He checked the bomb load before ordering the bomb doors to be closed. He then started the port and starboard engines which gave the aircraft electrical power so the crew could carry out the rest of their checks. The Mitchell bomber was a safe and sturdy machine, but the engines were also extremely noisy. The sound was deafening as the engines began to roar. The wireless operator tuned up his set as the engineer checked the instruments. Heath then carried out a cockpit check. The wind from the power of the engines flattened the grass around the aircraft as the ground crew removed the vast chocks. Heath taxied into position for take-off. Mitchell bombers took off in pairs. Once a flight of six was in the air, they flew into correct formation and circled until the rest of the squadron had taken off. Then the whole squadron set course for the target and headed for Holland.

As pilot, Heath's role was to get the aircraft to the target, Silvester's job as navigator was to find it. However tense the approach to the target, nothing matched the terrifying minutes of the bombing run itself. The crew would steel themselves for flak if they were picked out by enemy guns.

Once they reached the bridges at Venlo, the bomb-aimer took over. He lay face-down in the perspex nose of the aircraft, exposing the full length of his body to the flak from the enemy bursting around him. When they were above the target, he ordered the bomb doors to be opened. A blast of freezing air filled the fuselage. Checking the lens of the bomb-sight, the bomb-aimer called corrections over the intercom to Heath, who was constantly holding the aircraft steady, all the time trying to avoid enemy fire. Finally the bomb-aimer pressed the button that released the bombs, shouting, 'Bombs gone!' The aircraft would then lurch and rise abruptly by 200 to 300 feet as 10,000 lb[44] of high explosive and incendiaries dropped on the target. Heath ordered the bomb doors to be closed. Though the mission was complete, the crew were still vulnerable as they made for home.

Flak from the enemy was excessive in the whole area around the bridges and as they turned back towards Allied lines, Heath's bomber was hit by two bursts underneath the fuselage and under the port wing. From Fielding-Johnson's position in the top turret he could see that they were in danger of losing all their fuel from the port tanks in seconds. He contacted Heath over the intercom, suggesting he should 'feather' the port propeller immediately to avoid risk of fire. Heath tried but the oil pressure had already dropped. Suddenly, the port engine burst into flames. As pilot and captain of the aircraft, Heath gave the order to bale out. The rear gunner and Fielding-Johnson got away quickly through the rear escape hatch, but Silvester the navigator struggled to get his parachute on in the very confined space as flames began to engulf the aircraft. As pilot, it was Heath's responsibility to bale out last, but time was running out – he couldn't control the bomber for much longer. Seeing that Silvester needed help, he got out of the cockpit and squeezed through the cramped fuselage of the burning plane. Having secured Silvester's parachute, he helped him out of the stricken aircraft. Finally, Heath parachuted out of the plane himself. Seconds later, the Mitchell crashed to the ground, bursting into a ball of flames.

Later, when Silvester took his two weeks' survivor's leave, he told his wife about the incident, praising Heath for his heroism and quick thinking. There was no doubt in Silvester's mind; Heath had saved his life. As far as Fielding-Johnson was concerned, Heath's behaviour in the cockpit had been exemplary. He had behaved calmly and quickly, and though they had lost the aircraft, all the crew had survived. They eventually got together on the ground and made their way to an RAF station in Holland. After they arrived, they had several drinks and a meal to celebrate their escape. The crew were now eligible to be members of the Caterpillar Club, the informal organization open only to airmen who had parachuted out of a disabled aircraft, entitling them to wear a caterpillar badge on their lapels. For Heath, he was at last a member of a small elite with membership not based on background, status or money but on the demonstration of his own character.

However, after Heath had been drinking for a while, Fielding-Johnson noticed that he was displaying the abnormal behaviour that had previously concerned him. Getting drunk was recognized as a natural reaction to the strains of flying in Bomber Command as well as a unifying way for crews to celebrate survival, so it took extreme behaviour to stand out. On this occasion, Heath's behaviour was particularly marked and caused Fielding-Johnson, as senior officer, considerable embarrassment, as the crew were all visitors in another mess. Though Fielding-Johnson did not describe Heath's behaviour in detail on this occasion, the South African writer Peter Godfrey recalls a similar incident in a bar in Johannesburg during 1944.

Godfrey was meeting Duncan Burnside, the South African Labour MP, at the Shakespeare Bar in the centre of the city. Burnside was known for his great conversation and extraordinary tales. One of his favourite stories – and one which he enjoyed improvising for the entertainment of his various friends – was how he had come to lose his leg. Godfrey had heard the story several times, but the facts were always different – the Homeric telling of the tale being part of the fun. When he arrived at the bar, Burnside was with a 'pleasant soft spoken man' in a SAAF uniform, who was introduced as 'Jimmy Armstrong'. Godfrey thought that Armstrong seemed cultured and had a sense of humour. He was drinking double whiskies and Burnside was drinking South African brandy with a Pilsener chaser. More people joined them to listen to Burnside's outrageous tales, but as the afternoon wore on, Heath became very quiet. One of the newcomers then asked Burnside how he came to lose his leg and he told a ludicrous tale about an encounter with a shark off the coast of Natal. The audience were very amused, all, that is, except Heath. Suddenly, he went into a frightening – completely unprovoked – rage, calling Burnside a 'bloody liar', grabbing a beer bottle by the neck and shattering the end of it. 'I'll give you some real scars to boast about!' he shouted. Heath lunged at Burnside's face with the broken bottle but was then grabbed by a couple of the other men until he let the bottle drop.[45]

Whatever occurred in the RAF station in Holland, it was sufficiently serious that when Heath's crew returned to London, Fielding-Johnson discussed the matter with his squadron commander.

I felt obliged to do this as the peculiar moods in which I had seen [Heath] from time to time struck me as definitely abnormal as whilst in such moods he seemed to become an entirely different person and something quite different from merely a highly strung youngster who had taken a drink or two too many and this curious behaviour apart from undermining the spirit and morale of his own crew might influence other air crews.[46]

Heath would never fly for the RAF again.

CHAPTER TEN
Out of South Africa

NOVEMBER 1944 – JANUARY 1946

We shall drink on the seas and oceans,
We shall drink with growing confidence
And growing strength in the air.
We shall drink on our Island,
Whatever the cost may be;
We shall drink on the beaches,
We shall drink on the landing grounds,
We shall drink in the fields and in the streets,
We shall drink in the hills.
We shall never surrender OUR DRINK.

> Alterations to a poster of Churchill's speech,
> RAF Officers' Mess, 1944

After baling out of the Mitchell bomber following the Venlo raid, Heath took his two weeks' survivor's leave.

Handsome Brute   201

It is at this point, he later claimed, that 'the reaction occurred' when he first started to experience blackouts. One night, he woke up to find himself on the floor in a corner of his bedroom, brushing away imaginary flames and trying to pull his ripcord.

He was then admitted to the RAF hospital in Brussels on 29 November 1944 with sinus trouble, and both his *maxillary antra* (sinuses) were washed out three times. Discharged from hospital on 13 December, he returned to England and was admitted to an RAF hospital in Wroughton with *maxillary sinusitis* and *otitic barotrauma,* the blockage in the ears often felt on descending in a plane.[1] Untreated, both these conditions can be painful and lead to greater infection. Heath's mentor, Mr Scott, who was already alert to the possibility that Heath might be suffering some sort of mental illness, was to point out later that these physical conditions might be symptomatic of an underlying psychological problem.

> I think I am correct in suggesting that in the RAF sinus inflammation after considerable flying was frequently found to be the outward and visible symptoms of a neurotic state consequent on the strain of flying duties. At the time of this breakdown Heath had completed over 2,000 hours instructional flying, plus an operational spell.[2]

Just before Christmas 1944, Heath was categorized as temporarily unfit for duty and was granted twelve days' sick leave. In the New Year, he was found fit for discharge from hospital and returned to his unit in Morecambe. But the day after he was discharged, a letter from the Air Ministry to South Africa House confirmed that no further flying duties could be found for him and that his secondment with the RAF would cease before the end of January. It's unclear what the exact reason was for the Air Ministry's rejection of Heath at this point, as the war was still in process. But his spells in hospital and either formal or informal reports from Fielding-Johnson would have indicated that he was a pilot with many problems, both physical and perhaps mental. He was repatriated to South Africa, arriving there on 2 March. Rather than reporting to his unit, he went straight back to Johannesburg to see his wife and child. But his return was not the homecoming he had anticipated. As soon as he arrived, his wife told him that she wanted a divorce.

> I was absolutely shattered as we'd been extremely happy but she was adamant. I tried everything to make her change her mind and on the last evening I saw her I tried to shoot her and myself but I blacked out and became unconscious before this was accomplished.[3]

This statement was made after he was arrested in 1946 so it may have been an attempt to provide a reason (or excuse) for the murders. In an earlier statement from 1945, Heath described his return to South Africa in less detail, but still registering his extreme reaction to the notion of the divorce.

> Arriving home I discovered my wife asked me to give her a divorce, which was rather a blow and I am afraid I flew off the handle.[4]

Here he didn't mention either the blackout or the gun, but at this stage he was being tried for a series of other crimes, so presumably wouldn't have wanted to add to the trouble he was already in by mentioning them. When he sold his story to the *Sunday Pictorial*, Heath fleshed out the incident a little more:

> On my last attempt to dissuade her we stopped the car to talk. I felt my head go tight. Then it was half an hour later. I was

still in the car, in the same place, I was given to understand that I had tried to shoot my wife and myself but had collapsed. It was a blackout.[5]

Heath's return to South Africa is also discussed in an interview that his wife gave to the crime writer Peter Godfrey in 1947. She indicated that she had only once been witness to her husband's extreme behaviour – the night before he left her. 'I was lucky, I suppose. I managed to get away before things got too bad.' According to her, Heath's behaviour on this occasion was brought on by an excess of alcohol, particularly whisky:

To me there is no mystery about his various attitudes to the various women in the case. With Yvonne Symonds he must have been sober: with the others, very much the worse for drink.[6]

She agreed with Fielding-Johnson that alcohol made Heath a 'different person', a malevolent and dangerous Mr Hyde in contrast to the breezy and clubbable Dr Jekyll that she had fallen in love with. As far as the blackouts go, alcohol-induced amnesia *can* certainly result from the large amounts that Heath was known to drink, affecting the hippocampus in the brain and leading to varying degrees of memory loss. They may also have been induced by some sort of post-traumatic stress following his baling out over Venlo. That said, Heath was a fantasist and would use any excuse to try and negotiate his way out of trouble. It's also true that by the mid-1940s, film studios from Hollywood to Elstree had embraced the new science of psychoanalysis. Memory loss and blackouts dominated cinema melodramas of the time. In *Random Harvest*, Ronald Coleman forgets he is married to Greer Garson due to shell shock; in *The Seventh Veil*, Ann Todd plays a concert pianist traumatized by her Svengali (James Mason); and in *Spellbound*, Gregory Peck blocks out the memory of (accidentally) killing his brother as a child.

In 1946, Heath refused to discuss his marriage with his lawyers and psychiatrists. But several of the doctors who questioned him were convinced that the key to his breakdown and subsequent spree of murderous violence lay in his relationship with his wife – or at least in the breakdown of relations between them. The reason given for the divorce was desertion[7] and there is no suggestion from the brief interviews that Elizabeth gave at the time of the trial that Heath had been violent towards her. Indeed she went so far as to say that despite his drunkenness he was 'a big teddy bear'. It seems more likely that in his absence from South Africa, Elizabeth and the Rivers family had become aware of Heath's debts and possibly his dalliances with other women. Having raised their son alone for much of the war, and with the support of her family, she may simply have felt that she and her son were better off without him. But for Heath, the breakdown of his marriage was a shock, affecting him profoundly.

> I think my divorce broke me completely. I have never felt the same since it happened and ever since have acted in a peculiar way on occasions.[8]

With the end of the war in Europe announced in May 1945, the Allied nations celebrated the end of hostilities and the beginning of a new era. Men who had been lucky enough to survive the conflict would be returning home from all corners of the globe to their wives and families. The world was starting again with a new contract for peace. But Neville Heath had nothing. No home or wife to return to. The future looked bleak, empty and forbidding. Everything in his life – his health, his career and his marriage – had deteriorated. Despite the fact that he knew he was now absent without leave, he went on a spree, living in hotels in Cape Town, Randfontein and Durban. Perhaps he was attempting to relive memories of happier times with Elizabeth or he might simply have been indulging his depression in bars and brothels.

Heath checked into the Queen's Hotel at Sea Point, Cape Town on 14 June and introduced himself to the hotel clerk, Reginald Hoar, as Major Armstrong. He had promoted himself and had also awarded himself the DFC, the ribbon for which he wore on his chest. A week later he made a payment of £10 1s. 10d. in cash, so the hotel assumed that Armstrong was bona fide. This is exactly the assumption Heath wanted them to make. On 26 June, he cashed a cheque for £5. The next day he wrote a cheque for £20 to pay for his room. He then told Mr Hoar that he was flying to Pretoria but would be back soon. He didn't cancel the room and said he expected his wife to join him there. He left his suitcase behind, giving the impression that he'd be back shortly. In reality, he had no intention of returning. Nor did he go to Pretoria, instead making his way up the coast to Durban.[9]

On 3 July, Heath arrived at the fashionable Durban Club on the Esplanade, looking for a room. Guy Lomax, the secretary of the club, said he could be accommodated for six days. Again, Heath claimed to be a major in the SAAF and signed the register as a member of an affiliated club. Four days later, he went to the main branch of the Standard Bank of South Africa in West Street at about 10 a.m., claiming to be a Captain Gill. He wanted to cash a cheque for £15, which was duly processed by the bank manager.

It is while he was based in Durban during July that Heath claimed to have experienced another blackout. He had been to a dinner party and left in his car with a young woman he knew. He remembered nothing more until he found himself in bed back at the Durban Club. He later heard that he had violently attacked the woman, but said he had no memory of it.[10] This incident cannot be substantiated as no charge was brought against him and there is no report of the incident in the South African press at the time. Significantly, Heath only referred to these blackouts after he was arrested.

Heath left the Durban Club on 9 July, owing £37 7s. 1d., and gave his forwarding address as the Rand Club in Johannesburg, asking that the bill be sent on there. Just before he left, he cashed another cheque for £10 1s. 0d. All the cheques he signed in Cape Town and Durban bounced. He left a trail of bad debts and dud cheques throughout South Africa and it didn't take long for the various authorities to catch up with him. In the first place he was arrested by the SAAF police for being absent without leave and was told he would be facing a court martial. But before being disciplined by the military, he was handed over to the South African civilian police. In running away from the reality of his divorce, he had only brought more trouble on himself. But the debts and the divorce were not the only issues that were about to engulf him. He had left a combustive situation in England that was also threatening to catch up with him.

In September of 1944, though still apparently happily married to his wife in South Africa, Heath had got engaged.

Twenty-one-year-old Zita Williams was a respectable girl from Nottingham, the daughter of William H. Williams, an inspector of the Nottingham Co-operative Insurance Society and a chief inspector of the Nottingham City Special Constables. Zita had first met Heath, whom she knew as Jimmy Cadogan, at a dance at Steeple Claydon in Buckinghamshire, whilst she was serving with the WRNS at HMS Pembroke V and he was training at RAF Finmere, six miles away.[11] She saw a lot of him over a three-week period, during which time he proposed to her several times. As with many of the women in his life, Heath swept the impression-able Zita off her feet: 'I was told by a good many people how lucky I was to merit Jimmy's attentions.'[12]

After he had baled out in Holland, Heath took the two weeks' survivor's leave that was due to him and returned to London. It is during this leave in November that he and Zita stayed in a double room at the Pembridge Court Hotel. Like Yvonne Symonds, Zita may have felt that she was 'unoffi-cially engaged' to Heath before agreeing to sleep with him. He had told her that he had been married, but assured her that the divorce had been finalized the previous September. Their official engagement was announced in the local paper in Nottingham. All the preparations were made including the purchase of Zita's trousseau. The church was booked, the reception organized and the wedding cake ordered. Zita looked forward to a perfect wedding and a wonderful life together with her dashing and heroic pilot husband. However, in February 1945, Heath told her that they would have to postpone the wedding as he had to return to South Africa.[13] He gave her a photograph of himself saying he would be back in three weeks. She would never see him again.

Upon returning to South Africa, Heath wrote to Zita, informing her that his wife would not divorce him. This was a huge shock to her and the first indication she had that he was not in a position to marry. When Zita replied by letter, she told him that the situation was serious. Since he had left for South Africa, she had discovered that she was pregnant.[14] When he next wrote back, Heath said he wasn't getting a divorce and advised her of a reliable clinic in London where she could get an abortion. This is particularly curious as at this time Heath's wife was telling him that a divorce was *exactly* what she wanted from him. For whatever reason, Heath didn't want to marry Zita Williams. In all probability she was not the only young woman, either in England or

South Africa, to fall for Heath's extraordinary charm and to have gone through a fantasy 'engagement' in order for Heath to seduce her into bed.[15]

Zita's father immediately wanted to sue Heath for breach of promise. From what he had told Zita and her family, they had assumed him to be a man of some considerable means. Had he not told them that he was the nephew of the Hon. Edward C. G. Cadogan, KBE, of the Carlton Club in London?[16] Mr Williams' lawyers contacted the SAAF in an attempt to make Heath face up to his responsibilities, but to no avail. By this time, the authorities in South Africa had more serious issues to discuss with Heath than a jilted girl back in England.

Out of the blue, on 12 February 1946 – a year after he had left her to go back to South Africa – Zita received, given the circumstances, an extraordinary telegram from Heath saying:

> Just returned England. Staying Strand Palace. Meet me today. Telegraph by return stating time. Love, Armstrong.[17]

Zita didn't answer the telegram, nor did she go to London. Her father wrote to Heath at the Strand Palace Hotel and told him that Zita wanted nothing more to do with him.

Eleven days later, Heath would be caught in the same hotel having tied, punched and thrashed Pauline Brees. She was not to know it at the time, but Zita Williams had potentially had a narrow escape.

After Heath's arrest, Zita and her father were interviewed by the police and both were coy in their statements about her 'friendship' with him. They didn't mention that she had been engaged to him, nor did they mention the fact that she had been pregnant by him. Mr Williams was silent about his desire to sue Heath for breach of promise, perhaps stung by the social stigma that his daughter had incurred having been involved with such a man. By this time, whether she had lost the baby or had the abortion that Heath had coldly suggested, it seems that her child by Heath did not survive.

As a consequence of his treatment of Zita Williams, Heath also lost one of his greatest and most committed supporters, Mr Scott of the Borstal Association. Scott had been corresponding with Heath and his family throughout the war. Heath himself had written to Mr Scott, telling him about the relationship with Zita and the fact that she was pregnant. He also wrote that he had suggested that Zita should consult an abortionist. Scott felt that if Heath could behave so callously towards Zita and so cruelly to his own wife, then he would have nothing more to do with him. In a sad final note in Heath's borstal record, Mr Scott recorded a few last lines about Neville Heath, once his star borstal boy, now turned bad.

> A very disappointing end to what could have been an outstanding career. The war gave him his chance and the chance provided the atmosphere that proved too much for him. I fear his post-war career as a 'civvy' will come as too great a contrast to the life he has been living since 1940. It would not surprise me to hear him next in custody charged with F. P. [false pretences] or bigamy.[18]

Mr Scott was not to know that Heath was capable of much darker crimes.

On 27 July 1945, Heath sent a letter to Elizabeth – rather formal in tone and clearly meant to be referred to in future legal negotiations between them.[19] In it he stated that he would not be returning to her and that she may instigate divorce proceedings against him. In this letter he made clear that he had no interest in challenging her for the custody of their son. Three days later, he appeared at Durban Magistrates' Court charged with defrauding the Standard Bank in Durban and the Durban Club.

At his appearance at Durban he presented himself as a man who was not fully in control of his actions and he gave plausible reasons for his erratic behaviour. Estranged from his wife, he had nowhere to stay and knowing that his rank as temporary captain was not sufficiently senior for him to be accommodated at the Durban Club, where they only took senior officers, he pretended to be a major. He was unable to collect his pay from the SAAF because he was absent without leave and without any money, he couldn't pay his hotel bills.

> When I returned home I found my home was not a happy one so I decided to leave my home. Since I left home I have had this misfortune. I was boarded back from Holland with sinus trouble. I have had medical attention. It is still giving me trouble. I had this domestic trouble. I took it badly and lost my head ... the normal person does not lose his head or get shot up.[20]

The magistrates at Durban found Heath guilty of fraud on both charges and he was given two sentences of hard labour or a fine. But sympathetic to the war-damaged officer before them, the court suspended both sentences for two years on the condition that he repaid the debts and didn't commit similar offences within that period. Elizabeth arrived at the courthouse and paid Heath's debts, so at this point, it seems that relations between him and his wife were at the least civil. Immediately he was released from the magistrates' court, he was once again arrested by the SAAF police on several counts, for being absent without leave, for masquerading as a major and for wearing the ribbons of both the DFC and – a new addition – the OBE.

At the beginning of August, Heath's lawyer sent a cheque to the Queen's Hotel at Seapoint, repaying the debts that he had incurred. But the legal process had already been set in motion and the hotel explained that the matter was out of their hands – but that Heath could come and collect his suitcase if he liked.[21] The debt to the Queen's Hotel must also have been covered by Elizabeth's family, so relations between them and Heath were still amicable. But shortly afterwards, Heath advised his lawyers that despite what he had agreed in July with Elizabeth and her family, he had changed his mind about his relations with his son. Though he was happy for Elizabeth to remain sole guardian of the child for the time being, he was not prepared to give up rights in the child 'for all time'. He stipulated that the reason for this was that he was sure that his wife would marry again and that he might not approve of her choice of husband as a suitable stepfather for his child – an extraordinarily unreasonable rider given his own extremely dubious career and criminal record.[22] This gambit may have been inspired by Heath's attempt to secure his own position by exploiting the Rivers family's desire to protect the child's future.

Elizabeth's mother, who Heath had little respect for – later accusing the family of dominating their daughter – then became involved in the proceedings. From the incomplete correspondence between Heath's solicitors and those who represented the Rivers, it seems that Heath eventually agreed to sign away all his rights in his child's future and upbringing if the family would stand his bail money and pay off his debts.[23] Despite Heath's later avowed love for his son, he used him at this point as a bargaining tool.[24]

At the end of August Heath appeared at Randfontein and was found guilty on another charge of fraud. Now that he had agreed to give up any say in his son's future, Elizabeth's family paid the debt and the £20 bail money. Heath was ordered to return to the court for sentencing in February 1946. He was released only to be sent to Cape Town to face the fraud charges in relation to the Queen's Hotel debts and was due to appear before the magistrates on 6 September.

Heath was under pressure from all sides. His marriage was over and he had effectively sold the rights to a relationship with his son. He had faced a litany of charges and fines from all parts of the Union and his military career looked set to collapse as he faced his third court martial in less than a decade. In England he had lied to his parents, alienated his most fervent supporters, detonated his relationship with his sometime fiancée and might even be facing a lawsuit from her father for breach of promise. His finances, his career and his personal relationships were all in free fall.

And yet, his next step was to turn a bad situation into, potentially, a disastrous one.

While awaiting his court martial hearing, Heath was held at the Youngsfield Army Base in Cape Town. He was billeted in a room next to Flight Lieutenant Chapman of the RAF.[25] On 5 September, the day before the court hearing concerning the Queen's Hotel debts, Heath accompanied Chapman and a Major Erick Donnelly of the SAAF on a trip into Cape Town, travelling there in a pick-up truck. Major Donnelly was also based at Youngsfield but was about to go on leave, so needed some money from his bank.[26] He came out of the bank with about £50 in cash, which he kept in a roll in his trouser pocket. The three men returned to Youngsfield and bought each other drinks in the mess of 62 Air School. As the bar closed early, they bought a bottle of brandy and a bottle of gin to drink in the lounge. Donnelly suggested that they go into town to a nightclub, but Chapman wasn't keen. Heath said he didn't want to go without Chapman and the idea was dropped. After five or six drinks, Chapman decided to go to bed and left

Donnelly and Heath in the lounge alone together, this being about 11.30 p.m. When he left, Chapman felt that Heath seemed merry but that Donnelly was getting drunk. The two men continued drinking and then left together for Donnelly's room where they had more drinks. By the end of the evening, Donnelly was so drunk that he fell over, so Heath helped him undress and put him to bed. Heath went back to his own room, which was in the same corridor as Donnelly and Chapman's.

In the early hours of the morning, Donnelly woke and checked his trousers, which were normally hanging from the peg behind the door. But when he looked, the wad of cash had gone. He went into Chapman's room, woke him up and told him he had been robbed. The next morning, he reported the matter to the military police.

That day, unaware of the drama back at Youngsfield, Heath appeared in the Cape Town Magistrates' Court and pleaded guilty to the charges of fraud. He submitted the letter from the Queen's Hotel saying that his debts had been paid by his family. Again, he made a plausible defence, claiming that the frauds he had committed were done at a time when his 'mind was disordered', highlighting the incident at Venlo and the state of his marriage as extenuating circumstances.

Due to this one month of folly I lost a certain amount of army rank and due to being absent without leave, I'm likely to lose quite a lot more …

I was at that time absent without leave and it was impossible to draw my pay. The divorce proceedings have already started. My wife was drawing half my salary. My mind did not seem to be working properly. I was fully aware of what I was doing.[27]

It's significant that Heath drew attention to this awareness of his actions – in conjunction with a feeling that his mind was not working as it should – ten months before the death of Margery Gardner. The issue was not commented on in any of his civil court appearances or at his court martial.

He was once again given a suspended sentence of two years. However, as soon as he left the courtroom, he was cautioned and searched by the RAF police. They wanted to question him about the £50 that had been stolen from Major Donnelly the night before. Heath agreed to be searched – and was found to have only £14 on him in cash.

However, given that Heath had a long history of dishonesty and fraud, the military police immediately began to watch his movements. At 9 a.m. on the 7 September, he sent a registered letter to himself at the base at Roberts Heights in Pretoria where he had been staying. He then sent *another* letter at about 5 p.m. The RAF police contacted the Post Office and asked them to intercept the letters at Pretoria.[28] One of the letters was intercepted and found to contain notes in cash. Heath was arrested by the South African Civil Police and questioned. Cornered, rather than admitting his actions, Heath decided to front it out and told the police an impossibly and unbelievably complicated story.

He claimed that £50 had been cabled to him from England and that he had cashed it at the Post Office in order to pay the fines he thought he might be given by the Cape Town magistrates on 6 September. As he was given no fines, he found he had a large amount of cash on him. On the night of the robbery, he had heard Major Donnelly through the wall between his and Chapman's room, wondering where his money had gone. He decided to say nothing as if there were any enquiry made, he felt sure that he would be the one to 'get it in the neck'.[29] He set about trying to get rid of his money as quickly as possible. The military police did not believe Heath's story.[30] He was arrested and sent to Wynberg civil prison. But despite the extraordinary evidence against him, when he appeared in court Heath was yet again given the benefit of the doubt and found not guilty.[31]

As far as Elizabeth and the Rivers family were concerned, the divorce between her and Heath was finally granted in the Witwatersrand Division of the Supreme Court on 23 October 1945. Heath wrote a letter to Elizabeth telling her that he would never contact her again. Having brought an end to the marriage, the Rivers wanted to draw a line under Elizabeth's relationship with Heath so that she could start a new life with her young son. Mr Friedman, the family solicitor, contacted the SAAF, outlining Heath's various crimes and misdemeanours – including his breach of promise to Zita Williams which Elizabeth and her family were now aware of – and pointing out that he had often claimed that he had no intention of staying in South Africa after the end of the war. Friedman requested that the military authorities encourage the Commissoner for Immigration and Asiatic Affairs to deport Heath as soon as the court martial proceedings were over. The family wanted Heath out of South Africa, and out of their lives, for good.[32]

At the beginning of December, Heath appeared before the court martial at Pretoria. There were eleven different charges including wearing military decorations without authority, conduct prejudicial to good order and military discipline and for being absent without leave. Ten of the offences related to his activities during July 1945.[33] Though he was not convicted of all the charges, he was found guilty of most of them. For the third time, he was sentenced to be dismissed from the service.[34]

Heath was placed in police detention and this time refused bail, pending arrangements for his deportation from South Africa as an undesirable alien. Even his departure caused a minor diplomatic spat. Given that he was an illegal immigrant, the Department of External Affairs in Pretoria suggested to the Office of the High Commissioner for the United

Kingdom that they should make arrangements for Heath's removal at their own expense. This was met with disdain from the British High Commission in Cape Town.

> It seems to us a bit hard that we should be expected to arrange and pay for the deportation of this man when the Union Defence Authorities deliberately kept him on in spite of knowing his previous history.[35]

It is not recorded who eventually footed the bill.

Heath sailed from Cape Town on the SS *Sumaria* on 17 January 1946, returning to England a changed man, sadder if not necessarily wiser. One night on the passage home, he found himself wandering around the boat deck of the *Sumaria* in his dressing gown, with no idea how he came to be there. He had lost his wife and forfeited his relationship with his son. He had no home, no job, no income and no prospects. The war was over. There was nothing to fight for. Endless civilian days lay ahead. Heath was just one of millions of men returning home in this period, trading a life of risk and adventure for a future of staid sobriety. Many would struggle to make the change, missing the camaraderie, excitement and danger of war. The *New Statesman* worried specifically about men – just like Heath – returning from the RAF:

> What are all these young airmen, with their highly specialized training, their terrific sense of adventure and their complete lack of earning power, going to do in postwar England?[36]

His only option was to return to Wimbledon – shame-faced and exhausted – a man of nearly thirty living with his mother.

CHAPTER ELEVEN
Thursday 20 June 1946

[He] walked home from Moorgate Station across the ruins.
Pausing at the bastion of the Wall near St Giles's, he looked
across at the horrid waste, for horrid he felt it to be; he hated
mess and smashed things; the squalor of ruin sickened him;
like Flaubert, he was aware of an irremediable barbarism
coming up out of the earth, and of filth flung against the
ivory tower. It was a symbol of loathsome things, war,
destruction, savagery …

Rose Macaulay, *The World My Wilderness*, 1950

To British servicemen returning home from the war,
London in 1946 presented a much-changed face; half
familiar, yet wrecked, ravaged and ruined.

Throughout hostilities, the city had experienced 1,224
bomb alerts – about one every thirty-six hours. It had been

raided 354 times by piloted aircraft and from 1944 was
targeted day and night by nearly 3,000 pilotless bombs, the
deadly V1 and V2s. A total of 28,890 Londoners had been
killed and another 50,000 injured. Many shops, businesses
and domestic dwellings were eradicated – 100,000 houses
had to be demolished. An estimated 1,650,000 sustained
some sort of damage.[1]

The worst losses had been in the City of London. Out of
the total of 460 acres of built-up land, 164 acres had been
destroyed. Eighteen churches were beyond repair, including
fourteen designed by Christopher Wren.[2] Ten had been
razed to the ground in a single night. Austin Friars, the Dutch
church that dated from 1253, had been a light Gothic building and was now little more than 'a rubbish heap'. St Giles
Cripplegate, which Rose Macaulay wrote of – where
Cromwell married and Milton was buried – was now a ruin.
The statue of Milton outside the church had been completely
blown off its pedestal. St Clement Danes in the Strand had
been decimated. St Mary-le-Bow was reduced to a shell, her
font destroyed and her famous bells irreparably cracked.

> [The churches of London] had suffered a disgusting change,
> a metamorphosis at first stupefying. How could these dear
> interiors, panelled, symmetrically murky, personal, redolent
> of the eighteenth century, filled with ornaments and busts,
> urns, tablets, organ cases, carved swags, pulpits and galleries,
> pews, hassocks, and hymn books, have been turned into dead
> bonfires, enclosed by windowless and roofless lengths of wall,
> with pillars like rotten teeth thrusting up from heaps of ash?[3]

Even the colour of the city had changed, whether it was
Victorian granite, modern concrete or even the 'tweed-
textured' walls of earlier buildings; all had been scorched umber.

Seventeen of the city's Company Halls – including the

medieval Merchant Tailors' Hall – were flattened; six others were badly damaged.[4] The Inns of Court had suffered several times including the Middle Temple Hall, which had hosted the first production of *Twelfth Night*, Shakespeare's bitter-sweet comedy of love and loss. The Guildhall, once the setting for major trials such as that of Lady Jane Grey and Thomas Cranmer, had been burned to the ground in 1940, just as it had been in the Great Fire of 1666. Though still operational, the Old Bailey had been hit twice and the Royal Courts of Justice several times. Hundreds of London's historic buildings had come under attack and now lay half-wounded or annihilated. The Tower of London, St Thomas' Hospital, County Hall, Lambeth Palace, Holland House, Buckingham Palace, the offices of *The Times* and the Tate Gallery had all been damaged in the Blitz. The British Museum had lost ten of its galleries and 150,000 books. Madame Tussaud's suffered a direct hit on the night of 9–10 September 1940 resulting in the loss of 295 male heads and 57 female heads. Only two occupants of the museum survived completely unscathed; Paul, the museum's white cat, was found safe after the bombing clinging to the figure of Dr Crippen, the only waxwork not to suffer any damage at all. Directly the war had finished, the figure of Hitler was moved from the gallery of contemporary politicians and placed in the Chamber of Horrors.[5]

Whitehall, the centre of government, had been frequently bombed. Montague House, the offices of the Ministry of Labour, had been hit on fourteen occasions, the Ministry of Health was hit thirteen times and the Foreign Office, ten. The Palace of Westminster itself had also been shattered. It had taken at least twelve hits in one night in May 1941 when an incendiary bomb had set the House of Commons on fire whilst another hit the roof of Westminster Hall – steeped in British history, having stood since 1097. As firefighters could not save both, all efforts had been focused on saving the more ancient building. The Commons Chamber was left to burn and was not rebuilt until 1950. The clock tower that housed Big Ben also suffered. The glass from the south dial of the clock face was blown out, but its mechanism was not affected and it continued to keep accurate time.

There was complete devastation around St Paul's Cathedral and a wide area extending north from the river towards Cripplegate and what is now the Barbican. Despite several attacks and severe damage, St Paul's miraculously survived:

> The Cathedral had become in these later years more than ever a symbol of the unconquerable spirit that has sustained the fight ... None who saw will ever forget their emotions on the night when London was burning and the dome seemed to ride the sea of fire like a great ship lifting above smoke and flame the inviolable ensign of the golden cross.[6]

Pawson and Leaf's opposite the cathedral, where Heath had spent his only successful tenure in civilian employment, was still standing, but had also been damaged by bombing. Further west in Oxford Street, the John Lewis store where he had worked for less than a fortnight in 1938 was completely obliterated. Bombs had also reached the suburbs, including Pinner and Kenton in north London and Wimbledon in the south-west of the city. Number 21 Merton Hall Road, though never directly hit, had been 'badly shaken by bombs'. Bramham Gardens in Earls Court had three houses which were beyond repair, one on the corner where the gardens met Bolton Gardens, the others to the right of number 24 where Margery Gardner rented a flat.[7]

Once cleared, the bombsites had been quickly utilized as car parks or colonized as playgrounds by children newly returned from evacuation in the country. These gaps, open spaces and derelict sites were soon taken over by several types of opportunistic weeds and wild flowers that started to sprout up across the city, enlivening the ruins and rubble. Some 126 different species flourished in the freshly created nooks and crannies; groundsel, coltsfoot, Oxford ragwort and the rose-bay willow herb. London rocket had flourished in the ruins of the Great Fire after 1666 and had only made a reappearance when the new city wildernesses first started to appear in 1940.[8]

In the centre of town, Trafalgar Square, a memorial to a more ancient war, suffered little, though one of Landseer's lions was damaged. A paw had to be replaced and in 1946, there was still a gaping wound in its stomach.[9]

On 12 February 1946, a week after arriving back in England, Heath checked into the Strand Palace Hotel. It is at this point that he contacted Zita Williams again, the girl that he had jilted and rejected the year before, suggesting they meet at the hotel, with Heath presumably hoping for a casual sexual reunion. Zita didn't respond to Heath's telegram and left it to her father to tell him to stop bothering her.

Eleven days later, Heath was asked to leave the same hotel after the incident with Pauline Brees.[10]

Later that month, the South African authorities notified Wimbledon CID that Heath had – incredibly, given his record – applied for various decorations that he had been specifically refused by the SAAF. He had applied for the 1939–45 Star, the European Air Crew Star, the Italy Star, the France and Germany Medal and the British Defence Medal.[11]

His application for these awards alerted Wimbledon police to his return and his various previous convictions involving fraud and false pretences. On the evening of 20 March, he was drinking at the Alexandra on Wimbledon Hill, kitted out in the uniform of a lieutenant colonel in the SAAF. He was noted by a local police officer, Detective Bilyard, who approached him and asked his name. Heath replied that his name was 'Armstong'. At 9.15 p.m. Bilyard arrested Heath for wearing a uniform that he was not entitled to, as well as wearing decorations that he had not been awarded, including the DFC.[12] He appeared at Wimbledon Magistrates' Court on 5 April and the case made the local paper: 'Masquerade of Ex-Public School Boy'. Heath pleaded guilty to both charges, but claimed that he had not been wearing the uniform or the medals in order for financial gain, but to help him get a job. Once again, the magistrates treated him leniently, fining him £5 for both charges, saying, 'We are ignoring anything that happened before you went into the South African Air Force because we want to try and help you.'

Heath then seems to have made a determined effort to plan his future. Throughout April and May he wrote to several air companies enquiring about work as a commerical pilot and his address book contained a long list of the various air companies he had applied to.[13]

On 12 April Heath wrote to the London School of Air Navigation asking for details of a 'B' licence flying course. This qualified a pilot to fly passenger and commercial cargo planes, as distinct from an 'A' licence which only qualified a pilot to fly solo or with a military crew, so he was certainly imagining a future as a commerical pilot. If he couldn't fly with the RAF, at least he could put the flying experience he had accumulated over the past ten years to some fruitful use. His father agreed to finance him until he passed his examinations and had become established as a civil pilot. Between February and June of that year, Mr Heath gave his son nearly £200, a substantial amount of money at the time, £42 of which he paid in fees for the flying course. At the same time Heath was 'liberally supplied with money, so that he should not have any worries whilst he was studying for his examinations'.

Originally given £2 a week spending money by his father, more often than not he was given £6.

Twenty-eight-year-old Ralph Fisher had left the RAF in November and, like Heath, was keen to work as a commercial pilot. He and Heath met as pupils at the London School of Air Navigation on 24 April when they registered for the five-week course. They both joined the Luton Flying Club and would each hire planes at £3 10s. an hour as they had to complete a certain number of hours' flying in order to qualify for their 'B' licences. At the same time they socialized together at weekends, with Fisher finding Heath a likeable, clubbable character, though he was 'inclined to brag and [Fisher] didn't believe all he said'. Fisher also noted that Heath drank 'freely' and that he didn't associate with one particular woman. He was to continue to remain on friendly terms with Heath throughout his trial and beyond.[14]

On Friday 26 April, Bessie Heath had a visit from a young woman she had never met before. The woman, about thirty years old, asked if Mr Armstrong was at home? Mrs Heath said that she didn't know of anyone by that name and then realized that the woman must mean her son, Neville. 'Oh, yes, his name is not Armstrong, it is Heath, but he is known as Armstrong in the RAF,' she said. Mrs Heath invited the young woman into the house. The woman introduced herself as Muriel Silvester, the widow of Flight Lieutenant Freddie Silvester. Freddie had been stationed in Belgium towards the end of 1944. When he had come home on survivor's leave in November 1944, her husband had told her that his plane had been gunned down over Venlo. He had struggled to get his parachute on and the pilot, Jimmy Armstrong, had raced down the burning plane to help him. Later, Freddie returned to Belgium to join a fresh crew, but, sadly, in February 1945 he had been killed. Muriel was very anxious to meet some of her husband's friends in the RAF and Armstrong in particular.

Mrs Heath invited Muriel to stay for tea; she was sure that Neville would be home soon. The two women talked about their experiences during the war, Mrs Heath telling her that even in Wimbledon their house had been affected by the bombing. Time wore on, Mrs Heath explaining that her son must be studying late at the Air School or flying at Luton as he was studying for his civilian pilot's licence. At 6 p.m., Muriel left Merton Hall Road disappointed not to have met Heath. She had so wanted to thank him personally for saving her husband's life.[15]

It is while he was flying at Luton that Heath met a young woman called Jill Harris. She was twenty years old and worked as a shorthand typist at Skefco, the ball-bearing works in the town, living just round the corner from the factory with her parents. She and Heath first met at the Royal Hotel in Luton on Saturday 11 May. He was standing at the bar with Ralph Fisher and two other girls, one of whom Jill knew by sight. Whilst she was waiting to be served, Heath asked if he could buy her a drink. She refused as she was with friends and was buying a round. During the chatter at the bar she overheard Heath say that he was going back to London the following day. That night, she saw Heath again at a fairground. He smiled and waved at her.

The next day, Jill was meeting a girlfriend at the Royal Hotel and was surprised to find Heath still there, accompanied by Ralph Fisher again. Heath said, '*Now* I can get you a drink?' So he bought one for her and her friend. Heath and Fisher invited the two girls to the Luton Flying Club that afternoon. How would they like a spin in the air? Heath took Jill up in a plane for about an hour and Fisher did the same with Jill's friend. They stayed at the club until about 10 p.m. Afterwards, Heath took Jill home and said goodnight on the doorstep. 'Beyond kissing [her] goodnight nothing happened. Heath behaved like a gentleman.'[16]

On Monday morning, Jill received a phone call from Heath at her office, saying that he had left his gloves with her. Later that day she met him at the main entrance of the factory to return them. She was delighted when he greeted her with some flowers. He said he was going back to London but would be back in Luton the following weekend. Though she was looking forward to seeing him he didn't arrive that weekend and only returned to Luton the following week.

On Tuesday 14 May, Heath and Fisher both took the Air Ministry flying test for their 'B' licence. But at the end of the third week of the course, Heath suddenly wrote saying he was ill in bed with flu and asked for some instruction books to be sent to him. The books were posted, but Heath never returned to the school. When he next saw Fisher, he said that he had taken his 'B' licence test on 5 June and had passed it.

According to his mother, Heath took more examinations between 7 and 11 June and this weekend was clearly a period of great anxiety and pressure for him. All his efforts and energy were focused on passing these examinations. At the same time, the whole country was gearing up for the celebrations for 'V' Day. This was going to be the party to end all parties.

Heath phoned Jill at her office in Luton on Friday 7 June and arranged to send a car to her home at lunchtime to take her to the Royal Hotel. Jill was in a celebratory mood as all employees at the ball-bearing factory had been given a share of a £10,000 'V' Day bonus in that week's pay packet. It's unclear from her later statement to the police whether she had sex with Heath that lunchtime, or simply had lunch with him. She met him again that evening and gleaned that he had been married before. He even showed her a photograph of Elizabeth. She assumed that since his divorce he had been dating a number of girlfriends.

The next day, Saturday 8 June, was 'V' Day itself. Heath called at Jill's home impressively dressed in the uniform of a major in the SAAF. They had lunch with her parents and then he took her to the Flying Club again. That evening they called at several pubs and after 10 p.m. they went back to the Red Lion where Heath was staying. After the manageress called 'time', Heath continued to try and order more drinks for himself and Jill. But the wily manageress thought that Heath's intention was to get Jill drunk and then take her up to his room. She saw to it that this didn't happen.[17] Heath was annoyed, so they left the hotel and went to a local park, Pope's Meadow, where despite Luton's austerity 'V' Day plans there was a £500 firework display. After watching the fireworks, they walked further into the park.

That night an incident took place between Heath and Jill. One paragraph of her statement remains classified[18] but seems to indicate either an attempted rape or some sort of sexual assault. After the incident, Heath walked Jill home in silence and left her outside her parents' house. She phoned him the next day, but didn't actually see him. She saw him at a dance on Monday 10 June, but he didn't speak to her. She was disappointed as he struck her as a 'very charming type of person until that evening in the park'.

Heath returned home and continued studying. He went to Luton again to take his second Navigation Test on Tuesday 11 June. Spooner records that on this day, Heath brought another young woman to a Marylebone hotel that he had also met in Luton and spent the night with her. They didn't have sex as the woman was menstruating at the time and according to her, Heath was not resentful.[19]

At around this time, Heath also ran into Moira Lister, his ex-wife's schoolfriend and neighbour, who had by then left South Africa and become a successful ingenue on the London and Stratford stages. She had recently secured a season with

Kay Hammond and John Clements' company at the St James's Theatre. Meeting by chance at the exclusive Milroy Club, Heath asked Moira to join him for a drink. When she asked how Elizabeth was, he told her that she had been killed in a car crash on the Pretoria Road. Moira was shocked by the tragic death of her friend but also bowled over by Heath and his 'ice-blue eyes':

> I can distinctly remember my reaction was, 'Well, you are so attractive and now a widower with a beautiful little boy – I wouldn't mind marrying you!'[20]

Heath took her contact details in his address book and said he would take her out to dinner one evening. Some weeks later when they met at the Bagatelle restaurant, Moira thought him 'charming, gay [with] absolutely nothing salacious about him'. He behaved 'impeccably' throughout the evening, drove her home and kissed her on both cheeks before saying goodnight. When she later heard about the murders, Moira couldn't believe that Heath was responsible.

> I still found it impossible to equate the savage abnormal sex murders he had done with the charming man who had taken me out on the town.[21]

The week following 'V' Day, Heath received some news that was to devastate him and might well have been the trigger for the events that would lead him to kill.

He was told that the fact that he had been previously dismissed from the RAF would make him ineligible for a 'B' licence. Though he had passed his exams and practical tests, he would not be able to receive his licence. Consequently, he would never be able to fly as a commerical pilot. All of his plans for the future, the efforts he had put into his examinations and the money his father had lent him had come to nothing. Desperate, he wrote another of his impassioned letters to the Minister of Civil Aviation begging, as ever, for one more chance:

> *Should the licence be witheld it will mean utter ruin for myself and those dependent upon me, as I have staked everything on this one chance. Issuing or witholding the licence means the difference between a decent future or a future of poverty, misery and the continued payment for misdeeds of the past. Your decision, sir, will give me the one last chance I need to make good. This licence literally means everything to me. It means the chance to regain my self-respect and give my child a decent start in life. I can only prove my words by actions, but should this chance be given me I would pledge my word that I will commit no misdemeanour, however slight, in the future, and I should be everlastingly grateful ... I have paid the penalty demanded by law for my misdeeds, which can hardly be described as criminal. Stupid and foolish, yes, but I submit that it would not be just should I have to suffer for the remainder of my life.*[22]

The letter was typical of Heath – outlining his extenuating circumstances, promising not to misbehave, claiming to be foolish but not bad. But there was no reply from the Air Ministry. Neville Heath, the golden-haired flyboy was finally brought to earth. This time he was grounded – for good.

On Saturday 15 June, Heath was drinking at the City Club in Raquet Court, Fleet Street where he met Harry Ashbrook,[23] a journalist for the *Daily Mirror* and the *Daily Mail*. They had been introduced by a mutual business acquaintance. Heath said that he had recently been demobilized and was now arranging to fly planes abroad. He had mentioned that he was planning to fly to Copenhagen the next week to discuss the purchase of some planes with the Flying Club there. By coincidence, Ashbrook was also planning to travel to Copenhagen and was about to sort out his passage with Transport Command. Heath suggested that he could probably get Ashbrook there quicker and cheaper. He would need to hire a Procter plane from an air company that he knew well from his student days, Marshall's of Cambridge. Heath showed Ashbrook a copy of that week's issue of *Flight* magazine, which had an advertisement for Marshall's in the small ads section. The flight would cost £25 return, which Ashbrook thought was very reasonable.[24]

Heath mentioned that he had married but then divorced. He was now married again and his wife was living with her mother in Nottingham. Ashbrook noted Heath's caterpillar badge – he seemed a trustworthy, reliable character. But the whole negotiation was, of course, bogus, as Heath knew that he wouldn't be able to fly at all without a 'B' licence.

That evening, Heath met a young Wren who had only recently been demobilized at a dance in Chelsea.

Her name was Yvonnne Symonds.

On Sunday 16 June, Heath was at Merton Hall Road in the morning and went out to lunch with Yvonne at about 12.30 p.m., then spent the night with her at the Pembridge Court Hotel. After he had waved Yvonne off on the Worthing train from Paddington Station on Monday evening, Bessie Heath was sure that her son was in the kitchen at Merton Hall Road when she and her husband went to bed at 10.30 p.m. On Tuesday, she believed that he left the house about 8.30 a.m. to go and take the second part of his examination and to organize his passport for the flight to Copenhagen. This trip to Copenhagen he also mentioned to the staff at the Pembridge Court Hotel. He did not return to Merton Hall Road on Tuesday night.[25]

Heath rang his mother on Wednesday morning and said, 'I think I'll just nip smartly home and collect my laundry.' He returned to Wimbledon, having been to the Air Ministry, and told his mother that he had passed his 'B' licence. This must have been an extraordinary relief to Bessie Heath, as she knew that getting the 'B' licence represented hope for her son's future – a job, security, independence. It was only later that she discovered that this was a lie.

People have said that in not telling me his application had been refused, Neville was just betraying those traits of cunning and deceit with which his character has been blackened. That is not true. He lied because he did not want to hurt me by telling me of his failure.[26]

Following his rejection by the Ministry of Civil Aviation, Heath's parents' feelings were very much in his mind as they 'had sacrificed a great deal to give [him] this chance'.[27] He told his mother that he was going to the Air Ministry that afternoon to get his 'B' licence and his passport and was then going to pick up a Proctor plane which he was going to fly to Copenhagen. He had lunch and packed his suitcase. He was dressed in a grey double-breasted pin-striped suit that had been made in South Africa, with a cream shirt, brown suede shoes and a dark brown trilby. His brother Mick hailed a taxi for him from Wimbledon Station at about 2.30 p.m.

On the doorstep, for the last time in his life, he kissed his mother goodbye.

At Victoria the next morning, after having spent the Wednesday night at the Pembridge Court Hotel, Heath met Harry Ashbrook at the Grosvenor Hotel that joined the station platform and told him that he planned to pick up the plane from Cambridge on Friday. He would then fly to

Elstree from where they would expect to fly to the continent on Saturday or Sunday, if customs formalities could be completed. Ashbrook noticed that Heath carried his flying helmet and goggles. It was sunny in the early part of the day, so Heath wore a pair of RAF-issue sunglasses. At lunchtime, they went to the Cock Tavern in Fleet Street, which was famous for its good food. Here they bumped into an acquaintance of Ashbrook's, Leslie Terry. Terry, a restaurant owner, was also a petty criminal as well as a drinking companion of the journalist Gerald Byrne. He had sixteen convictions for shop-breaking, receiving stolen goods, larceny and for living on immoral earnings. In August 1946, he was also to receive a three-year sentence for the manslaughter of a woman.[28] Terry was typical of the shady characters that peopled the pubs and clubs of Heath's drink-orientated night-time world. Heath wondered if Terry would do him a favour and lend Ashbrook some money?[29] Ashbrook needed to borrow £50 in all, £25 to pay Heath for the trip to Copenhagen, as well as another £5 that Heath wanted to borrow and £20 for Ashbrook himself. Terry phoned the nearby Barclays Bank in Fleet Street and arranged to cash a cheque for £50. He collected this at 4 p.m. and went back to the City Club where he gave the cash to Ashbrook. Heath was given his £30 and said he was going directly to Cambridge. He would contact Ashbrook when he returned on Friday. Ashbrook left. Heath immediately called for drinks at the bar.[30]

That day Terry had pulled off a big business deal and was in the mood to celebrate. Heath had something to celebrate, too, with £30 burning a hole in his pocket. When the pubs closed, Heath and Terry went to Anne's Club to continue drinking until it was opening time again at 5 p.m. They carried on drinking at the various ancient pubs along Fleet Street between the Law Courts and the decimated area around St Paul's: the Falstaff, the Cheshire

Cheese and the Cock Tavern. Heath drank beer steadily, though 'apart from a slight flush he showed no signs of drunkenness'. At around 7 p.m., the pubs in the area started to run out of beer – Heath's favoured drink. In order to carry on drinking, Terry suggested that they should drive over in his car to one of Heath's locals in Knightsbridge where, Heath said, they could get all the ale they wanted.

When they arrived in Knightsbridge at about 7.30 p.m., Terry drove past the Trevor Arms and suggested that they stop there for a drink. Once inside the pub, Heath introduced him to some RAF officers that he knew and they got into a round, Heath and the other officers drinking beer, Terry drinking whisky. After four rounds of drinks, Heath left the others and went to join a girl he recognized at the bar, Margery Gardner.

> I had not arranged to meet her ... Margery was only a casual acquaintance. In the last two or three weeks I had seen her several times in the Nag's Head. Sometimes I saw her too at clubs I belonged to. Her friends seemed to be a very queer set – a bit 'arty'.[31]

Leslie Terry had noticed that Margery had been on her own at the bar for a while, so as it was his round, he offered to buy her a drink. Heath then introduced them. They remained together for about an hour, then Margery said she'd like to eat. Heath asked Terry if he would like to join them, but Terry said he had an errand to sort first, but where would they be later? Leaving the pub, Heath told Terry that he and Margery would be dining just down the road at the Normandie Hotel. Terry got into his car, but as he was driving, realized that he'd been drinking too much – they had, after all, been drinking solidly for seven hours – so he decided to go home.

Consequently, Heath and Margery dined together alone. They then went for last orders at the Panama Club. Heath realized he'd left his flying helmet at the Normandie, but would go back for it the next day.

It was after midnight when we left the Panama, taking a taxi to Notting Hill Gate. Margery Gardner was still with me when we reached the hotel, but I don't remember asking her to stay. The last thing I can recall is going to one of the rooms at Pembridge Court Hotel – number four – undressing and getting into bed. There were two beds, and Margery Gardner was in the one farthest from the window. I put out the light. I am not certain whether I remember waking when the light went on again. But that was my first thought – the light was on. I was sitting on the floor of the room. Of what had happened in that period I had no recollection. But I saw the result. There was the body of a woman on the bed.

I had no idea what to do. There were stains of blood on me, so I bathed in the bathroom on the next floor, going back to the bedroom to shave and dress. I was confused in mind but it would be wrong to say that I was panicky. I noticed particularly how steady my hand was when I was holding the razor. Packing a suitcase, I went by taxi to the Normandie Hotel, where I had left my flying helmet the night before and from there to Victoria. It was too early for breakfast but I got some coffee. My instinct then was to go away, anywhere. It was not flight exactly, for already I found it hard to connect myself with the sight I had just seen in the bedroom. Everything seemed like a dream or a nightmare. I wanted to get away where things were light and bright and different. So I went to Brighton.

I felt ill. After having some breakfast on the front I was better and went for a walk round the town. It was just an aimless stroll round places I used to know and eventually it took me back to the railway station. Then I phoned Yvonne Symonds. I had known her in London as a very attractive girl and I think she recently took a degree as Master of Arts. We had lunch together that day and the next; I spent the night at an hotel on the front.

By this time I wasn't thinking much about Pembridge Court. It was not a sudden shutting off of consciousness about it. All there was to remember was the wakening on the floor. It did not seem to be me in any way except that I had seen it. So I could still lunch and laugh and enjoy the company of friends, as I did at the Blue Peter at Angmering. An old friend whom I met at Worthing suggested spending an evening there and I took Yvonne. We met several RAF types who were known to me.

Next day I found my name staring from the pages of the papers. I thought more about it then.

I was not afraid but I wanted to get out of Worthing.[32]

Whilst Heath was awaiting trial, Leslie Terry was keen to benefit from his very brief association with the most wanted man in the country – selling his own story to the press and negotiating a deal for Heath himself. He lamented the fact that he had suggested that they should go looking for more alcohol once the pubs had run dry in the West End. '[Heath] certainly wouldn't have met [Margery] on that fatal night if we hadn't set off, at my suggestion, in search of beer,'[33] he said.

By the time Margery had met Heath at the Trevor Arms, Leslie Terry estimated that Heath had already drunk twenty-four pints of beer.

Heath and Margery had then gone on drinking for another four hours.

CHAPTER TWELVE
Rogue Male

22 JUNE – 7 JULY 1946

I suddenly feel I can't *stand* anything any more – the boredom – hopelessness. I miss the war ... I need excitement, I
need things crashing against me, violence; the quiet will
kill me.

Elizabeth Taylor, *A Wreath of Roses*, 1949

At 3.47 a.m. on Saturday 22 June a telegraphic message
was expressed to all police divisions in England and
Wales stating that Neville George Clevely Heath also known
as James Robert Cadogan Armstrong was wanted for interview. 'He is particularly fond of the company of women and
is a frequenter of drinking clubs and bars.' The police were
also keen to trace the taxi driver who had picked up Heath
and Margery outside the Panama Club and driven them to
the Pembridge Court Hotel and they asked the press for help

in trying to trace him. Every cab rank in London was checked by the police.

At the same time, detectives kept a special watch on 21 Merton Hall Road in case Heath tried to contact his parents. They were also given a warrant from the Home Office to intercept any letters or telegrams that were sent to the house.[1] All hotel managers and boarding-house keepers in the London area were asked to keep a look-out for a man answering Heath's description, particularly anyone carrying a flying helmet or wearing RAF sunglasses. Across the capital, railway stations, bus and coach depots were under police surveillance. Because of Heath's flying abilities and his familiarity with airfields, Scotland Yard worried that Heath might have already flown abroad.

Journalists started to follow leads in the Chelsea and West End drinking dens frequented by Margery and Heath. A picture of the two protagonists quickly began to be consolidated in tabloid form – the handsome ex-RAF playboy and the bohemian artist/extra. These early stories printed in newspapers over the weekend were to dictate how Margery in particular was depicted throughout the hunt for Heath and his subsequent trial: 'Bound Film Extra Murdered in Hotel'; 'Police Watch House in Film Extra's Mystery Death'. Margery was presented very much as a Chandler-style vamp with the words 'film extra' or 'bohemian' used euphemistically for a woman of easy morals. Though Margery may only have worked as a film extra a few times and very much as a last resort, this image stuck.

Having read the *Daily Mail* that Saturday morning, in Sheffield, the Wheat family solicitor Ralph Macro Wilson rang the local police at 10 a.m. and told them that he thought that the murder victim was the daughter of a client of his.[2] The police immediately rang Reg Spooner at his office in Hammersmith and he advised the Sheffield police to interview the Wheat family as soon as possible.[3]

Margery's younger brother Gilbert was working at the time as a teacher at St Anselm's School in Bakewell, but he travelled to Sheffield to accompany his mother to the police station that Saturday evening. They were joined by Macro Wilson, who was not only their solicitor but also a trusted family friend and godfather to Margery's daughter. Mrs Wheat was extremely distressed and throughout the interview she was anxious not to discuss the more bohemian aspects of Margery's life, but Macro Wilson encouraged her to be as frank as possible. Gilbert also supported his mother through the gruelling three hours of intimate questioning.

Marjorie's on-off lover Peter Tilley Bailey and her husband Peter Gardner[4] were also interviewed by the police that Saturday. Like many of Margery's associates, as Spooner was discovering, both had criminal records[5] – and both had alibis. Gardner's record made reference to his unstable psychological state, which was confirmed by Mrs Wheat. Margery had frequently spoken or written of her husband's 'mental' behaviour. He told the police that he and Margery had split amicably because of her drinking but that they had never really argued. They continued to meet casually and he would occasionally (he claimed) lend her money. Much of what he said was at odds with Margery's letters to her mother and Mrs Wheat's recollections of what Margery had said about their dysfunctional relationship. Peter's statement reads very much as if he was attempting to distance himself from Margery; according to him they got on very well, there were no arguments between them, she did not associate with other men, and *she* had a drink problem, not him. In reality Peter was later to die of cirrhosis of the liver caused by his alcoholism. Many of Margery's associates confirmed that they had never seen her drunk.[6] Peter was very clear that he had a secure alibi for the night of her murder – drinking with friends in a pub. He was also aware that Margery had recently been associating with Peter Tilley Bailey.

Curiously, when asked by the police to identify her body, Margery's husband refused. Whether this is because he couldn't bear to see the body of the woman he once loved, or whether he felt a sense of guilt is difficult to judge. Gilbert Wheat and Mr Macro Wilson volunteered to go to London to identify Margery if necessary. Ultimately this duty fell to Macro Wilson, who would identify the body at 3 p.m. on Wednesday 26 June at Hammersmith Mortuary in Fulham Palace Road.[7]

Harold Harter, the taxi driver, also saw the story in a newspaper and came forward for questioning. He retraced his journey with the police from the Panama Club to the Pembridge Court Hotel. Several other witnesses from the Panama Club, including Margery's friends Joyce Frost and Iris Humphrey, as well as the staff at the Panama Club were also inteviewed. Staff and guests at the Pembridge Court Hotel also gave statements.

A clearer picture was beginning to emerge of the hours leading up to Margery's death. Heath had signed his own name in the hotel and Panama Club registers, there were dozens of witnesses to the fact that he and Margery had spent all evening together and the taxi driver seemed to confirm that Heath was the last person to be seen with Margery alive.

On Monday, after reading the description of Heath in that morning's newspapers, George Girdwood at the Ocean Hotel in Worthing went round the corner to the hotel annexe. When he knocked on the door of Heath's room on the first floor, there was no reply. Opening the door, Girdwood saw that though some of his belongings were still there, Heath and his suitcase had gone. Girdwood immediately rang Worthing police.[8]

At 9.10 a.m., Detective Inspector Eagle arrived at the hotel. Girdwood showed him the newspaper with the

description of Heath. He had arrived on Friday and left the
day before without paying his bill. He had not been seen
since 9 a.m. on Sunday morning when he had been taken a
cup of tea and said at the time that he would not require
breakfast. Eagle found Heath's signature in the hotel register
and asked if he could look at his room. As well as the five
newspapers from the previous Saturday, Heath had left some
clothes including his corduroy trousers, his suede shoes and
some magazines. Screwed up in the waste paper basket he
found a yellow ticket dated 20 June 1946 with 'Lt. Col.
Heath and Friends' written on it. This was the entry slip to
the Panama Club that Heath had used to sign Margery in on
the previous Wednesday.[9]

Further questioning Girdwood and his staff, the police
learned that Heath had been accompanied by a young woman
and that later on Sunday, they had received a telephone call
asking for Colonel Heath to ring Swandean 906. This local
telephone number was checked and found to be that of Major
J. C. Symonds of 'Strathmore' on Warren Road. Two police
officers went to the house and met Mrs Symonds who seemed
very reluctant to give any information except to say that her
husband had gone to London that morning to see his solicitors,
Pontifex, Pitt & Coy in St Andrew Street, Holborn. This
information was relayed to Spooner, who rang the solicitors
and requested that Major Symonds come to the police station
for questioning. Symonds was duly interviewed at Notting
Hill and outlined his daughter's brief relationship with Heath,
giving the police the information Heath had discussed with
Yvonne about his connection with the murder. At the same
time, DI Eagle made arrangements for Mrs Symonds and her
daughter to visit the police station at Worthing.

At the annexe, Eagle noted that the bed sheets were marked
with bloodstains. Under the sheet on the right-hand side of the
bed he found three iron nails.[10] The reason for the presence of

these nails was never established. Yvonne had already lost her virginity to Heath the week before, so it's unlikely that there would have been hymenal bleeding during intercourse.[11] If Heath had succeeded in persuading her into any sort of extreme sex, Yvonne was subsequently unwilling to admit to it. At all times, Yvonne stated that Heath treated her with great gentleness and care. Yet the presence of the nails under the sheets does suggest a malign intent on Heath's behalf.[12]

At 3 p.m. Yvonne arrived at Worthing Police Station with her mother and made a statement regarding her association with Heath, focusing on the conversation they had at the Blue Peter Club about the Notting Hill murder. Yvonne also brought with her the two shirts that Heath had given her to wash. Any evidential value that the shirts might have revealed had now been washed and ironed out of them. The shirts and the other evidence from Heath's room was then sent to Spooner in London. Yvonne mentioned that Heath had two suitcases, one of which he had left at Worthing Central Station. When the police investigated the left luggage there, the other suitcase had gone. Yvonne was then sent away by her parents for a holiday with some friends. A police watch was put on the Symonds' house in case Heath tried to contact her.

A man answering Heath's description carrying a suitcase had been seen at Worthing Station at about 11.15 a.m. on Sunday morning, enquiring where he could get a taxi. He didn't state his intended destination, nor did he succeed in getting a cab. Further enquiries at the bus office and the railway station drew a blank as both were exceptionally busy that weekend. Heath had disappeared into the crowds.

The hunt for Heath now intensified along the south coast, focusing on Brighton and Hove, which Heath knew well. Aware that Heath would quickly spend his way through the £30 he had taken from Harry Ashbrook, messages were sent to all police stations along the south coast to report any attempt to borrow money or sell clothing or jewellery and particularly to investigate any complaints from young and attractive women.

Spooner now made use of Heath's address book that they had recovered from his room in Merton Hall Road. The book contained nearly 400 names and addresses throughout London and the provinces, all in Heath's handwriting. Most of these were women. Spooner thought it possible that Heath had made contact with one or other of the women in the address book, so he issued a circular letter to various police forces around the country to question all of Heath's associates. These included his former fiancées, Peggy Dixon and Zita Williams. Drawing a blank on the south coast, enquiries were made throughout the country – in Bedford, Portsmouth, Leeds, Jersey, Bristol, Bath, Luton, Manchester, Cornwall, Worcester and Wales. At its peak, 40,000 officers throughout the UK were working on the case. Many of the names and phone numbers led nowhere, with some women claiming not to have known Heath at all, or if they had, that they had only met him casually at a dance or in a pub. The police's job was made more difficult as many of the women were now married and not keen to discuss their wartime pasts. Added to this, several potential witnesses had been killed in the Blitz or on active service. Many of the addresses had been bombed and were now derelict, leaving no trace of their former tenants. At one point, police were rumoured to be watching 150 women across the country and the *Daily Mirror* correspondent claimed that the police were waiting for Heath to contact one of them.

In the end one of these women – and we are convinced that a woman is hiding him – will give us a clue to his where-abouts. Yesterday [a *Mirror* journalist] talked to a dozen women in the London area who have been friends with the 'Don

Juan' Heath ... all were under observation by the police ... None would say a bad word against him. To an attractive brunette to whom Heath proposed marriage only twelve months ago [he] showed a photograph. 'The darling,' she said. 'I still would love him always.'[13]

The knotted handkerchief marked 'L. Kearns' that had bound Margery Gardner's feet was sent to the forensic laboratory at Hendon, but despite a countrywide search the owner of the handkerchief was never traced, though a second-hand car dealer called L. Kearns was known to frequent the Nag's Head in Knightsbridge, one of Heath's locals. What had appeared at first to be a significant clue proved to be a red herring in what was becoming an increasingly frustrating and elusive investigation. The press scrutinized every development of the search, further inflating public fears that an extraordinarily dangerous killer remained at large.

With Spooner's investigation focused on Worthing, but with no real idea where Heath was, the police in London then received an unexpected lead.

Superintendent Tom Barratt had been mentioned in several of the newspaper reports over the weekend. On Monday morning he received a letter at Scotland Yard. Opening it, Barratt was stunned to find that it was a letter from Heath himself.

22nd June 1946

Sir,
I feel it to be my duty to inform you of certain facts in connection with the death of Mrs Gardner at Notting Hill Gate. I booked in at the hotel last Sunday, but not with Mrs Gardner, whom I met for the first time during the week. I had drinks with her on Friday

evening, and whilst I was with her she met an acquaintance with whom she was obliged to sleep. The reasons, as I understand them, were mainly financial.

It was then that Mrs Gardner asked if she could use my hotel room until two o'clock and intimated that if I returned after that, I might spend the remainder of the night with her. I gave her my keys and told her to leave the hotel door open. It must have been almost 3 a.m. when I returned to the hotel and found her in the condition of which you are aware. I realized that I was in an invidious position, and rather than notify the police, I packed my belongings and left.

Since then I have been in several minds whether to come forward or not, but in view of the circumstances I have been afraid to. I can give you a description of the man. He was aged approx. 30, dark hair (black), with a small moustache. Height about 5' 9" slim build. His name was Jack and I gathered that he was a friend of Mrs Gardner's of some long standing. The personal column of the 'Daily Telegraph' will find me, but at the moment I have assumed another name. I should like to come forward and help, but I cannot face the music of a fraud charge which will obviously be preferred against me if I should do so. I have the instrument with which Mrs Gardner was beaten and am forwarding this to you to-day. You will find my fingerprints on it, but you should also find others as well.

N. G. C. Heath[14]

The fraud charge that Heath mentioned here is probably related to the £30 that he had taken from Harry Ashbrook in payment for the trip to Copenhagen. The whip that Heath promised to forward never arrived. Heath deliberately implicated 'Jack' who was either a figment of his imagination, or he had given a description of the army officer whom Heath knew Margery had arranged to meet on the night she was killed.

The letter was also full of basic errors (Heath met Margery on Thursday, not Friday) and was at odds with the story he had told Yvonne Symonds in Angmering in which Heath said that he had arranged for his friend to use his room at the Pembridge Court Hotel in order to entertain a prostitute. In the letter, it is Margery that Heath had supposedly been discussing the hotel room with. Perhaps with hindsight Heath had realized that he had been seen drinking, talking and dancing with her throughout Thursday night. He also suggested that Margery was a prostitute – an idea that the press picked up and continued to hint at. The alternative story that appeared less frequently was that Margery was 'sweet and refined with haunting eyes and rich black hair'. But somehow this version of the story did not appeal to the press, who were nurturing the case as that summer's media sensation.

As he continued to elude the police, Scotland Yard began to receive dozens of 'dud' 999 calls with sightings of Heath from Worthing to Wales, from Birmingham to Bognor.[15] Spooner called midnight talks to work through the mounting number of clues and leads.[16] Letters from members of the public, many scrawled and anonymous, suggested motives for the murder – for instance that Heath was at the centre of a white slave ring, seducing and exploiting defenceless young women. In the golden age of Agatha Christie, hundreds of armchair sleuths claimed sightings of Heath all over the country.

> On Wednesday evening June 26th, in a 'bus' queue in the Strand at about 6 p.m. (outside Woolworth's) was a man who answered the description given in the newspapers ... the man wore dark glasses which he took off on the bus ... but the moral of this story is that if there were a picture of the man published, the writer of this letter might have known at once whether it was the wanted man or not.[17]

This concern about the lack of a photograph of Heath arose early in the investigation and was later proved to be valid.

During the night of 27 June a two-and-a-half-ton 'Dodge' truck was stolen from Rochester and found abandoned in Worthing the next day. The truck had been loaded with rolls of tarred paper but they had all been removed when it was found. In the cabin was a carton containing twenty-four jars of Brylcreem, a camera and twenty-four rolls of Kodak film. On the box of Brylcreem was a message:

> *The police thought they had got me but I am to clever for you, don't you agree. I warn you there is going to be another murder before very long you see.*

> *J. Heath.*

> *P.S. The silly police have got to hurry if they want me.*

Though the handwriting was neat, the spelling ('to clever') didn't indicate a grammar-school education like Heath's. DI Eagle in Worthing passed the information to Spooner at Notting Hill but the clue turned out to be a red herring. It was clear that the longer Heath was at large, the more intense was the speculation about the possibility of him committing another violent murder.[18]

One newspaper, adding fuel to the fire, speculated that Heath might be carrying a gun.[19]

As well as questioning Heath's acquaintances, the police continued to investigate Margery Gardner's life and background. Her diary had been studied and copied and officers began to interview her friends and associates. It is at this point that the investigation into her death took a complex turn.

One witness, Trevethan Frampton, had known Margery

for about six months. They were both regulars at the same bars and clubs. In his interview with the police, Frampton gave an insight into Margery's character which offered an alternative interpretation of the circumstances surrounding her death.

> On occasions Mrs Gardner told me that she liked people to be rough when making love to her and also that her husband was invariably rough with her. From this I gathered that she was a masochistic. I am not very interested in this subject and never questioned her on it. I did discover though that she enjoyed the sensation of being at a man's mercy.[20]

If Margery had left the Panama Club with Heath knowing what his sexual tastes were, had she allowed herself to be tied by him in order to be beaten, just as Pauline Brees had at the Strand Palace Hotel? Another witness who claimed to know Margery well, a Mrs Smith, also attributed masochistic tendencies to her, but Spooner thought Mrs Smith was 'a borderline mental case'[21] and that her statement was questionable.

Nearly seventy years on, the complexities of masochistic behaviour are better understood and the subject is less covert than it was in the mid-1940s. High-street chains like Ann Summers sell a vast array of whips, handcuffs and ties aimed at the female consumer and intended for the mutual exploration of sexual dominance and submission. Though extreme, none of the injuries that Margery had suffered would have killed her, but Heath would only have needed to hold her face down into the pillow for as little as thirty seconds in order to suffocate her. Keith Simpson confirmed that Margery's face seemed to have been washed after she had died. Might this have resulted from Heath attempting to revive her by splashing water on her face from the washbasin in the corner of the room? Were the police looking at a sexual tryst that had got out of hand? And was this, therefore, a case of manslaughter rather than murder?

By the end of the first week of July, the investigation had been going on for sixteen days and despite several sightings, Heath had apparently disappeared. Maybe he was abroad by now or one of his women friends was hiding him somewhere in England? The police had drawn a blank.

On the evening of Saturday 7 July, Reg Spooner received a telephone call that was to accelerate the investigation, but was also to take it in an unexpected and harrowing direction. He was told that a man was being held at Bournemouth Police Station who was believed to be Neville Heath. This was the call that Spooner had been waiting for. He told the police in Bournemouth to keep the suspect at the station at any cost. He would be there as soon as possible.

Spooner instructed Detective Sergeant Frampton to fill a police car with petrol at Lambeth garage. Fuel still being rationed, Frampton drew three five-unit petrol coupons for the journey there and back.[22] At 10.40 p.m. Spooner and Shelley Symes climbed into the back of the Wolseley and raced the hundred miles down to Bournemouth.

PART THREE

Group Captain Rupert Robert Brook

CHAPTER THIRTEEN
Bournemouth

23 JUNE 1946

My learned friend quoted the great detective [Arthur Conan Doyle's Sherlock Holmes] who said that the curious thing about the dog in the night was that the dog did nothing in the night. Another great detective [G. K. Chesterton's Father Brown], known to my learned friend and possibly to you, once asked, 'Where does a wise man hide a pebble?' And the answer was, 'On a beach.' What better way of removing yourself from immediate notice at any rate, than to go and stay at a seaside place in the holiday season, taking on an identity and character which is not your own, and mingling with the seaside crowds, behaving as an hotel guest and an apparently ordinary person?

Mr E. Anthony Hawke, Counsel for the Crown[1]

Bournemouth is one of the few English towns one can safely call 'her'.

John Betjeman, *First and Last Loves*, 1952

The contemporary view of Bournemouth is very much of a place where one goes to die; a quiet place with a slower pace. But this polite and ordered town stretching towards the coast conceals a darker nature, perhaps even more sinister given the sharp contrast between its sunny, holiday face and the shadows haunting the villas and gardens that John Betjeman observed in the early 1950s. It is curious to find, for instance, that Mary Shelley, the creator of *Frankenstein* is buried in St Peter's Church in Bournemouth, along with her husband's heart, brought back from Italy after his death.[2] Robert Louis Stevenson settled in Bournemouth and in 1886 wrote one of his most famous novels here – the definitive tale of the dualities of the human personality, *The Strange Case of Dr Jekyll and Mr Hyde*[3] – strange though it may have seemed at the time that this polite English seaside resort should inspire such a tale of corruption and horror. It is also in Bournemouth – or Sandbourne as it is known in Hardy's Wessex – that Tess kills her caddish seducer Alec D'Uberville at a 'stylish lodging house' called 'The Herons' ('Tis all lodging houses here'),[4] and where Mrs Brooks the landlady first notices D'Uberville's blood 'drip, drip, drip' through the ceiling until the stain resembles 'a gigantic ace of hearts'.[5]

The position of Bournemouth, about 100 miles south-west of London, and its coastal situation had proved crucial to the town's fortunes during the war. At the outbreak of hostilities the town had been quickly prepared for invasion. In 1940, Bournemouth and Boscombe piers had been closed, blown up and stripped of their planking to prevent enemy landings.[6] The sea front itself was closed to all but the military and the beach, now a minefield, bristled with barbed wire.

Army vehicles had been positioned along the cliff tops to prevent possible invasion. Pillboxes, static water tanks and air raid shelters had been built throughout the town. All beach huts were removed and placed in their owners' gardens for the duration. Anti-aircraft guns were positioned on the flat roofs of the beachside cafes which once had swarmed with holiday crowds.[7]

Because of its peacetime occupation as a holiday resort, Bournemouth also had a unique resource to offer the war effort: accommodation. The town boasted hundreds of hotels from five star luxury to basic bed and board. As well as becoming a reception area for evacuees, many businesses and government offices from London including the Ministries of Agriculture and Education, the Home Office and the Board of Trade were transferred to Bournemouth and established in the main hotels. Consequently the town was flooded with hundreds of civil servants, all of whom needed to be accommodated as well.[8]

As the war progressed, the section of the coast both to the east and west of Bournemouth pier became crucial, not only as a defensive position, but as a practice area for military strategy. In February 1944, Studland Bay had been the scene of live ammunition beach rehearsals in preparation for the Normandy landings, supervised by Eisenhower and Field Marshall Montgomery. Nearby Poole Harbour was the departure point for many of the ships participating in D-Day itself. Thousands of service personnel from the Allied nations began to flood into the town in order to take part in these practice operations. At the same time, battle-weary survivors from the various theatres of war had been sent to Bournemouth on leave to recuperate.[9] Americans, Canadians, Czechs and – after D-Day – French servicemen were all billeted in Bournemouth's requisitioned hotels and guesthouses. By 1944 an Area Defence ban was in force creating an exclusion zone within ten miles of the coast and very few civilians were allowed within it. Bournemouth had become a garrison town.[10]

The large number of service personnel may well be one of the reasons that Bournemouth was bombed about fifty times throughout the war. It was targeted by 2,271 bombs, including incendiaries. Some 219 people were killed, 176 injured and 75 premises were completely destroyed. One of the most destructive raids took place on the night of 15–16 November 1940 when 53 people were killed and 2,321 properties were damaged. It is in this raid that Robert Louis Stevenson's house, 'Skerryvore', at the top of Alum Chine had been hit and damaged. Despite a public campaign to try and preserve it as a building of historic interest, the house was demolished the following year and by 1946 nothing of it remained.[11]

The most damaging attack on Bournemouth was a daring daylight 'hit and run' raid on Sunday 23 May 1943, when bombs were dropped in ten districts by Focke-Wulf 190s (known by the RAF as the 'butcher bird') and Messerschmitt 109s. These aircraft carried 500-kg high-explosive bombs and were light enough to fly above wave height, making them undetectable by British radar. Consequently, the town was not in a state of alert nor ready to defend itself when it prepared for lunch that Sunday. The Luftwaffe aircraft could fly so closely to their targets that survivors from the raid remember being able to look directly into the German pilots' faces.[12]

Among 3,481 buildings damaged in the raid, the Central and Metropole hotels were both destroyed. Beales' department store was completely demolished following a direct hit. Fortunately, this being Sunday, the shop was closed, but the hotel bars were busy with servicemen having drinks before lunch. In the Metropole Hotel alone seventy-seven people were killed. The attack took place exactly one week after the infamous 'Dam Busters' raid on the Mohne and Eder dams in Germany led by Guy Gibson and it may have been a revenge attack with the Metropole Hotel as a specific target, it being a Royal Canadian Air Force reception centre as well as a billet for Canadian, Australian and American personnel.

By the summer of 1946, many of the servicemen and women had left Bournemouth and a concerted effort was made to get the town ready to embrace its former identity as a holiday destination. German prisoners of war were assigned to remove barbed wire and landmines from the beach. The Russell-Cotes Art Gallery started to collect pictures that had been removed for safety from the various manor houses, rectories and churches to which they had been taken when war was declared. But the coastline around Bournemouth had deteriorated more than any other resort, due to heavy tides and coastal winds. The beach had almost disappeared leaving only a narrow strip of sand, so a great deal of intense work had to be done for the expected crowds in the summer. A gangplank was hastily laid across the skeleton of the derelict pier in order to give access to pleasure boats, but it was not to be fully restored until 1950.[13] Many buildings and hotels were still requisitioned by the military. The Royal Bath Hotel remained as the WAAF officers' mess until September 1946. The Burley Court Hotel had only recently been vacated by the Canadian Air Force in March, as had the High Cliff Hotel on the West Cliff.

The Tollard Royal Hotel was also situated on Bournemouth's West Cliff, just west of the pier and up an inclined slope from the promenade and the town's central gardens that lead down to the beach. The building remains – inevitably seaside apartments now – still commanding forty miles of uninterrupted views across the Channel. Slightly removed from the entertainments of central Bournemouth, the building continues to feel select, a little superior, perched above the town and facing the sea. Built in 1901, the Tollard Royal remained in use as an hotel until 1956 when it was divided into flats. But even today many of the original hotel features survive – the Art Deco fireplaces, mahogany doors with cut-glass panels, the grand internal staircase and even the revolving doors in the lobby.

The hotel had been requisitioned during the war as a leave centre for US service personnel but had been vacated in November 1945. After a period of refurbishment, it had reopened for guests in June and was keen to take advantage of the first post-war holiday season. It had been repainted inside and maintenance work that had been curtailed during the war had now begun again – some particularly urgent work being carried out on the roof that had been going on since March. The Tollard Royal was a smart hotel with 100 guest rooms, each having either a private bathroom or a sink with hot and cold running water. A Vita Glass Sun Lounge was 'flooded every evening and on dull days with health-giving Ultra Violet Rays'.[14] The hotel boasted two lifts, billiards, an American Bar and dances twice a week. Terms for the cheapest rooms were 5½ guineas a week – the tariff in guineas rather than pounds suggesting that the Tollard Royal was a select establishment, a cut above the rest, for the most discerning clientele.

On Sunday 23 June, a tall, bronzed South African with a military gait arrived as a chance visitor at the hotel. Violet Lay the receptionist signed him in at about 3 p.m.[15] He told her he would like accommodation for a week. His arrival was noteworthy only in that he was the sole guest to check in that day. He was allotted Room 71 on the first floor and gave his name as Group Captain Rupert Robert Brook.

The name might have raised a certain curiosity at the hotel. Rupert Brooke was the celebrated soldier poet who had died in 1915 on his way to Gallipoli. A classically educated Rugby and Cambridge man, he was distinguished by heart-stoppingly handsome features that had almost eclipsed his poetry in the mythology that developed after his death. W. B. Yeats thought him 'the handsomest young man in England'.[16] Brooke's poems were heartfelt, sentimental and patriotic. He effectively wrote his own epitaph with his most famous poem, *The Soldier*, which articulated patriotic sentiments that had become fashionable again in the war that had just ended.

Brooke had been a frequent visitor to Bournemouth before the Great War and a plaque on a house in Littledown Road commemorated the fact: 'Here Rupert Brooke 1888–1915 discovered poetry.' What a coincidence that the newly arrived group captain – as heroic and handsome as the poet – should also share his name.

Brook carried with him a single suitcase so was apparently not intending to stay in Bournemouth very long. Though he signed the hotel register, he failed to add the date of his arrival, nor did he surrender his ration book.

Like so many women before her, Miss Lay the receptionist had been seduced by the charms of the handsome group captain. He was quite the ladykiller.

CHAPTER FOURTEEN
Miss Waring

23–29 JUNE 1946

VERDICT ON BOURNEMOUTH

Two girls both of Birmingham commented: 'Been here a fortnight, nice for a rest, too little to do, queues for everything, should be more attractions on the beach and more to do on rainy nights, doubt whether local paper will print our views.' Four girls between 20 and 22 ... None had been here before. All commented: 'Days very full, nights very dull.' Thought Pavilion booking system 'rotten'.

Considered there should be more amusements on the beach and said: 'Bournemouth is too classy for a really good time.'

Bournemouth Times, 16 August 1946

The newly arrived 'Bobbie' Brook was popular with the guests at the hotel, many of whom had recently been demobilized and were taking their first family holiday since being called up. He was equally popular with the hotel staff and spent much of his time ingratiating himself with them, talking about their mutual wartime experiences and about his career as a pilot. Ivor Relf had only recently been appointed as joint manager of the Tollard Royal and had been a former RAF officer himself.[1] Brook's engaging RAF manner, knowledge of aircraft and acquaintanceship with mutual air force colleagues convinced Relf that Brook was 'very definitely what he purported to be, that is a retired group captain in the Royal Air Force'.[2] Brook claimed he was to fly in a forthcoming air exhibition at Shoreham, but this was dependent on the weather. He obtained up-to-date weather reports with ease from various aerodromes including the meteorological station at Dunstable. Whenever he phoned for these reports, Brook used either the telephone in the dining room or the one at the reception desk. Consequently these conversations could always be (and may have been intended to be) overheard. So convincing was Brook in playing the role of the clubbable RAF gent that the staff trusted him absolutely. He was never given a bill for the full fourteen days he stayed at the hotel.

Arthur White, the head night porter, was charmed by the affable group captain, who often chatted to him about flying. White gathered that Brook was from Johannesburg and was now employed in Britain by the Auster Aircraft Company in Leicester. He thought that Brook had a 'wonderful personality and was a great hit with the ladies'.[3] Throughout Brook's stay at the hotel, White and another night porter, Frederick Wilkinson, noted that beyond several sports shirts and two or three pullovers, Brook had few clothes – no hat and no coat. He always wore the same pair of grey striped flannel trousers, a brown sports jacket and the same pair of brown shoes. On about 1 July, Brook asked Wilkinson to press his trousers, as they were the only pair he had.[4]

Peter Rylatt from Haywards Heath was an army captain who had served in South East Asia Command and had also arrived in Bournemouth on demobilization leave on 22 June, staying at the Burley Court Hotel.[5] He was thirty-one years old, 5 feet 10 inches, clean-shaven and had a complexion which a fellow guest observed had 'a yellowish tinge about it consistent with prolonged service in the Far East'.[6] He had mousey, brilliantined hair slightly receding at the temples and always wore dark horn-rimmed spectacles. His speech was 'rather quiet and low', the very opposite of the good-looking and gregarious Group Captain Brook, and yet the two men very quickly became firm friends.

Rylatt met Brook at lunchtime on Monday 24 June at the Royal Bath Hotel, which was still being used by the WAAF as an officers' mess. Brook explained that he was the chief test pilot for Auster's in Leicestershire and was down in Bournemouth to take part in the aerial exhibition at Shoreham. This was to take place on Saturday 29 June, but Brook claimed that he had come down a week earlier than he ought to have done, leaving him at a loose end.

Brook got on with Rylatt famously, to such an extent that he invited his new friend to lunch that day at the Tollard Royal. Rylatt gathered that this was Brook's first trip to Bournemouth, so together, they agreed to do some exploring. After lunch the two men walked along the cliff top to the right of the hotel and then went down the zigzag path to the promenade. The freshly sanded beach and newly reinstated beach huts were full of families taking advantage of the good weather. The pair walked towards Poole, passing Bournemouth's famous chines to their right. 'Chines' are deep, narrow, wooded ravines descending down to the sea. The word is peculiar to Dorset and the Isle of Wight, chines being very much a feature of this stretch of the English coast. Walking west from the hotel towards Poole, there was Durley

Chine, Middle Chine and Alum Chine – all in the Bournemouth area. At the head of Alum Chine were the ruins of Stevenson's house, 'Skerryvore'. Brook and Rylatt walked across the boundary into Poole and stopped by Branksome Towers' private beach and threw stones into the sea. Behind them was the most secluded of the chines, Branksome Dene Chine, known locally as a place for lovers' meetings. The two men then headed back towards Bournemouth Pier, the excursion to the chines and back having taken about an hour.

Over the six days that they were acquainted, Rylatt and Brook chatted about many subjects. Brook often told stories about his time as a pilot during the war. Rylatt commented on the unusual scarf that Brook wore around his neck. It was made of silk with a map of France and Germany printed on it. Brook explained that it was an 'escape map' carried on RAF operations and sewn into the shoulder of flying kit. During their various talks, Rylatt expressed great interest in the national hunt for Neville Heath, the man who was wanted in connection with the murder in Notting Hill. The case was in the papers every day – leads, sightings and speculation about his whereabouts. Brook told Rylatt that he actually knew Heath quite well and that he 'wasn't a bad sort of chap'. Rylatt later remembered that they discussed the case every day that they were together.

That Monday afternoon, after sitting in deck chairs in the sun for a while, Brook and Rylatt went to the Bournemouth Pavilion – an entertainment complex at the heart of the town, opposite the pier. When it had opened in 1929 the Pavilion was heralded as the 'biggest municipal enterprise ever created for the entertainment of the public'. It had a theatre, a concert hall and dining rooms such as the Lucullus Restaurant offering a bargain 3s. theatre supper. The ballroom was decorated in the Art Deco style and every day hosted tea dances between

4 p.m. and 6 p.m. for 1s. (tea included). Though Brook and Rylatt danced with various young women, neither took interest in any one girl in particular. The two men didn't join anybody's table, nor did they invite any ladies to join theirs. Rylatt had an engagement that evening, so they left the Pavilion at about 5.30 p.m. Knowing Brook was staying in Bournemouth alone, Rylatt asked if he would like to come on a trip to Wimborne the following evening. He had been invited to a cocktail party and was sure his hostess wouldn't mind if he brought a friend along. Brook said he'd be delighted to join him. Rylatt went back to his hotel and Brook returned to the Tollard Royal.

The next day, Brook met several other guests who were staying at the hotel, including Mrs Winifred Parfitt and her husband who were visiting for the week from Castle Cary. Brook introduced himself, telling the Parfitts that he was the nephew of Sir Alexander Cadogan, the permanent under-secretary at the Foreign Office. He also made the acquaintance of Major Phillips and his wife Gladys who were visiting from Llandaff in Wales. Chatting to Mrs Phillips, Brook mentioned that he had left the RAF in December and was now working for Auster's.

About midday on Tuesday 25 June, Brook met Peter Rylatt at the Tollard Royal. They went next door to the Highcliff Hotel where they had a drink in the cocktail bar. Here they met four 'rather working-class' girls from Wolverhampton and arranged to meet two of them after lunch at the tea dance down at the Pavilion. The two men lunched together at the Tollard Royal and then Rylatt waited in the lounge whilst Brook changed from his sports jacket and flannels into a double-breasted, pin-striped suit ready for their trip to Wimborne that evening. Rylatt was the only person to see Brook wear this suit and despite efforts by the police to trace it later, it disappeared. At some point between

26 June and 3 July, Brook must have sold or pawned it. The two men then went down to the Pavilion and met the girls they had seen earlier. Rylatt made a date to meet one of them the next day. Brook wasn't interested in either of them.[7]

At about 4.55 p.m., they then went back to the Burley Court Hotel, so that Rylatt could change for the party in Wimborne and then took a taxi to 'Moorings', the country home of a Mrs Comyns who was entertaining about twenty people for cocktails and dinner. Again the topic of the hunt for the Notting Hill murderer was hotly discussed over the martinis and gin slings. Rylatt got on particularly well with a Major Holford of the 12th Hussars and his wife, so he and Brook arranged to meet the Holfords for dinner in Bournemouth later that week. They took a taxi back to the Tollard Royal at about a quarter to midnight – Rylatt kept the taxi waiting as he had a nightcap with Brook before he took the taxi on to his own hotel, running up a fare of £2.

Earlier that day another new guest had arrived at the Tollard Royal. Peggy Waring was an attractive 37-year-old divorcée from London, a student of psychology and philosophy. She had come to the Tollard Royal to stay with a friend of hers, Anouska Symon. Peggy had only intended to stay for a couple of days but found herself staying much longer. That night, in the bar at the Tollard Royal Hotel, she met Group Captain Rupert Brook. He was to have a profound effect on her – and she on him.[8]

He told me his name was Rupert Robert Cadogan Brook. I was introduced to Brook by some acquaintances of Mrs Symon, Wing Commander and Mrs Wilkes. Wing Commander Wilkes said he had known Brook in the RAF where Brook had been a group captain. Brook himself told me that he had been demobilized from the RAF and was then a test pilot at the Auster Aeroplane Company.[9]

Both Peggy Waring and Peter Rylatt's statements are crucial in attempting to gauge Brook's state of mind during his stay in Bournemouth yet neither of their statements was discussed at the trial and neither of them was called as a witness. From their subsequent relationship, it is clear that Peggy Waring had a great influence over Brook, but in the extraordinary game of cat and mouse that developed between them in Bournemouth, what were his intentions towards her? Was he genuinely romantically fixated on her or was he grooming her for some darker purpose?

The next morning, Peter Rylatt was playing tennis with Wing Commander Wilkes and saw Brook at about 12.30. Brook claimed he'd had a heavy night and stayed up drinking until 2.30 a.m. Rylatt went to the Highcliff Hotel to meet the girls from Wolverhampton they had danced with the day before, but Brook said he wasn't keen to do so. Rylatt then lunched with him at the Tollard Royal. On each occasion they dined together at the hotel, Brook added it to his bill, telling the waiter, 'Put it on my crime sheet, will you?' Rylatt left him talking in the lounge with Wing Commander and Mrs Wilkes, Anouska Symon and Peggy Waring. From this point on, Peggy found Brook increasingly in her company, to an obsessive degree.

[He] attached himself to me, so much so that we were together most of the time. He drank excessively. On the day after my arrival he asked me to marry him. I refused and he then asked me to have an affair with him. This I also flatly refused but each day he pressed me to allow him to come to my room or me to his room. This I would not allow but my sympathies were aroused for him, particularly when he told me his wife had left him for another man in South Africa. As a consequence of this I decided to stay on and try and help him, and this is the reason I altered my original plan. I talked to him of my religious beliefs and my belief in the goodness of people to such an extent that he ceased drinking to excess although he called me a 'bloody fool' and said I should think of myself more and not so much about other people. He still persisted in trying to have an affair with me and wanting to marry me.[10]

That day another significant change took place; Brook changed rooms. According to hotel records, this move was in order to suit the management, as Room 71 had already been booked.[11] Brook himself, despite later speculation to the contrary, did not make a request for this change in order to have a room with a gas fire, which might imply that at this point he was contemplating suicide. His new (and cheaper) room, number 81, was situated on the second floor to the west of the building and faced West Hill Road, looking out over the main entrance of the hotel and in the direction of the Bournemouth chines.

Peggy Waring's arrival had certainly altered Brook's behaviour and was beginning to have an effect on his friendship with Peter Rylatt. Brook and Rylatt lunched together again on Thursday at the Tollard Royal and Brook complained that he'd had a champagne party the night before until 3 a.m. and was still feeling the worse for it. Rylatt had arranged to meet the Holfords that evening whom they had met in Wimborne. Perhaps in an attempt to clear Brook's head, they walked along the promenade, past the private beach by Branksome Towers, with Branksome Dene Chine to their right – a stroll of about a mile. Rylatt was already feeling peeved with Brook as he had not offered to contribute anything towards the taxi fare from Wimborne. He had often seen Brook pay in cash for rounds of drinks and cigarettes and he invariably over-tipped the waiters, so money didn't seem to be a problem.[12] They walked on to the next chine, passed through the stone defence blocks in the car park and walked up the Chine Road, ending up on the main street at Sandbanks. They then returned to their respective hotels.

Later that afternoon, Brook rang Rylatt and said he was feeling ill and asked if he could be excused that evening's party. Rylatt told him that this would be extremely awkward and very embarrassing. Two young ladies had been invited specifically to entertain them. He insisted that Brook attend the party whether he felt sick or not. Brook refused. Exasperated and angry, Rylatt told Brook how difficult the evening would be without him. Brook didn't appear to care.

The next day, when they met outside the hotel, Peter Rylatt was still annoyed. The dinner party had been a failure, just as he had expected. Reluctantly, Rylatt had an awkward drink with Brook, Peggy Waring and Anouska Symon in the lounge, but refused the offer of lunch. At some point he commented that Brook's escape map scarf looked rather dirty. Peggy agreed that it could do with a wash. Relations between them still frosty, Rylatt wished Brook goodbye as he would be returning to London the next morning on the 8.20 a.m. train. He left Brook alone with Peggy in the hotel lounge.

With Peter Rylatt gone, over the next twenty-four hours, Brook's relationship with Peggy developed an unsettling intensity, with Brook apparently struggling to control himself in Peggy's presence.

I should say he was abnormal, inasmuch that when he even kissed me quite normally, his passions seemed to be so roused that he was compelled to become rough with me and then to control himself, he would immediately leave me. On other occasions when he has held my hand, I could tell the effect it had on him, because he would thrust it away from him.

Brook told Peggy that he was flying in the air display that Saturday and was eager for her to watch him, though she had already made it clear that she wanted to return to London. He was so keen, even desperate, for her to stay that he offered to pay her expenses at the hotel, but she refused. Though she had only intended to stay in Bournemouth for two days, she reluctantly promised that she would extend her stay, watch the air display and then go home immediately afterwards on the late train on Saturday night.

At about 8.30 on Saturday morning, her last day in Bournemouth, Peggy was dressing in her room when Brook whistled up to her from the garden. She waved at him. He went and stood on the opposite side of the road and pointed to the writing room of the hotel, meaning he would wait for her there. She joined him about an hour later. For the next hour Brook phoned to the meteorological station at Shoreham to see if it was possible to take a light aircraft up that day. Finally he told Peggy that it was too windy to fly – a great disappointment as he had been talking about the air exhibition ever since he had arrived in Bournemouth.

They were then joined by Lieutenant Colonel Tutt from Thurnham who was having a break in Bournemouth following the recent death of his mother.[13] The three chatted in the writing room until 12.30 p.m. when Peggy excused herself. She wanted to go for a walk, but promised to come back in time for lunch with Brook. But his insistent, obsessive behaviour was troubling her. At about 1.10 p.m. she telephoned him at the hotel and said that she wouldn't be coming back to lunch after all. Brook fired questions down the phone, wanting to know where she was, why she'd gone out alone, and where she was going. Peggy was vague and said – quite honestly – that she just wanted to be on her own. In fact, her afternoon couldn't have been more uneventful. She visited the Russell-Cotes Museum, just east of the pier, and took some notes about its celebrated collection of Victoriana. She returned to the hotel later that afternoon. Brook had apparently gone out with Colonel Tutt, so Peggy went up to her room. She was soon joined by Anouska Symon, who pleaded with her to change her mind about leaving Bournemouth that night as Brook seemed so distressed at the thought of her going. But Peggy had had enough of the constant strain of his intense and demanding behaviour. He was just too needy and jealous without reason. She broke down in tears.[14]

A few moments later, Brook himself knocked on Peggy's door and said he wanted to speak to her, so Mrs Symon left, leaving Peggy alone with Brook. He seemed very distressed and perspiration was pouring down his face. He asked Peggy where she'd been and said he couldn't be doing with being given cryptic messages. Peggy said that she had been to the museum. He said he didn't believe her. Exasperated, Peggy was in despair. Brook then begged her to stay on in Bournemouth. Once again she told him that she wouldn't sleep with him and she wouldn't marry him either, but she would like to be his friend. At this point she held out her hand to him and asked him to sit next to her. She wanted him to know that she cared about him. But this proximity to her just seemed to exacerbate his extraordinary behaviour. 'He seemed terribly distressed at the thought of being so near me and he shook his head violently and his face was contorted, at what I took to be emotion,' she later stated.

Brook then left the room telling her that she should rest and that he'd wait for her downstairs. Again, Peggy burst into tears, full of pity for Brook, but also feeling pushed to breaking point herself.

After about an hour, Peggy pulled herself together and went downstairs to join Brook and Colonel Tutt for tea. They then went for a walk, returning to the hotel in time for dinner. They sat in the lounge afterwards until Colonel Tutt left Brook and Peggy alone in the drawing room. This was the first time she had been alone with him since his extraordinary outburst that afternoon and Brook proceeded again to plead with her not to leave that night, doing so for another forty-five minutes. But by 11.00 p.m., Peggy was adamant. She was going for the 11.30 p.m. train as she had planned. Her luggage was packed and she was ready to go. Just as she was about to leave, he said to her: 'You have won yourself a magnificent victory. I only hope you congratulate yourself on Monday.'[15]

Leaving him behind, Peggy felt only 'pity and tenderness' for Brook. As a student of psychology, she cannot have hoped for a better subject to study at close quarters. The well-intentioned aim of her relationship with him had been simply 'to try and help him to believe in people'.[16]

After she returned to London, Peggy wrote Brook two letters, later to be found in his jacket pocket. He telephoned her at home in St John's Wood on Sunday and Monday, saying that he would be coming to see her in London on Tuesday 2 July; he did not arrive. Her steadfast refusal to give in to Brook's relentless demands may well have won her more than a 'magnificent victory' – it may even have saved her life.

CHAPTER FIFTEEN
Miss Marshall

3–4 JULY 1946

MURDER IN LONDON'S PARKS!

After a spate of gloomily psychological murder dramas, it is a pleasant change to turn to *Wanted for Murder*, a new British thriller which has been built around a case of schizophrenia or dual personality, a straightforward thriller abounding in hearty chills and thrills. Eric Portman gets one of the juiciest roles in his career as a pleasant-mannered gentleman who quite frequently strangles unwitting young ladies. This, believe it or not, is due to a streak of sadism inherited from his grandfather, who was the finest public hangman of his day. His crimes take place in and around the familiar spots of London, the police eventually catching up with him in Hyde Park.

Film section, *Harrow Observer*, 13 June 1946

Twenty-one-year-old Doreen Marshall had served as a Wren during the war and was discharged from the service on Thursday 27 June. After a recent bout of measles and 'flu, her father suggested a holiday in Bournemouth; the sun and coastal breeze would do her good. The family had visited the town before, so it would be familiar to her. On Wednesday 26 June, Doreen and her father had bought two first-class return tickets from the Polytechnic Tours Office in Regent Street, each costing £1 13s. 2d.[1] Doreen's mother, Grace, wanted Doreen's older sister to accompany her on the trip, but for some reason, at the last minute, Joan had decided not to go. But with an independent spirit and a WRNS training behind her, Doreen was happy to holiday alone. Doreen herself sent a letter to the Norfolk Hotel in Bournemouth, making a booking for ten days from the Friday of that week. She arranged to return home on 8 July.

Just before leaving for Bournemouth, Doreen was at home spending the evening with her mother. The murder of Margery Gardner had been front-page news for days and the search for Neville Heath continued to dominate the papers. Mrs Marshall remembered:

> I was reading details of the Margery Gardner case in the *Daily Mail* and mentioned something about it to [Doreen]. Doreen was sitting opposite me and snatched the paper out of my hand saying, 'Don't read such things, Mummie.' She scanned the headlines before putting the paper down but didn't read Heath's description or the text of the story.[2]

This seemingly casual, apparently insignificant moment was to prove fatal. The newspapers, though permitted to publish a description of Heath, were forbidden to print any photographs of him. By the time the police had changed their minds and given a directive for photographs of Heath to be published, Doreen's own young life would have been brought to an end in an orgy of horrific, terrifying violence.

Like many men of his generation, Charles Marshall had seen the full horror of the Great War having fought in the front line at the Battle of the Somme – his feet giving him acute pain for much of his later life as a result of trench foot.[3] A salesman by profession, he had married Grace Merritt in 1913 – both of them having been raised in Hackney. After the war, they had two daughters, Joan Grace, born in Harrow in 1921, and Doreen Margaret, who was born in Ealing in 1924. Mr Marshall had a close relationship with both of his daughters, but a particularly strong bond with his older daughter, Joan. Joan's surviving daughter remembers Charles as a lovely, gentle man, in contrast to his wife who came across as rather stern, the inevitable impact perhaps of the loss of her daughter.

Joan Marshall had married Charles Cruickshanks of the Royal Navy Reserve just after Christmas, 1941 and as he was on active service she lived with her family for the duration of the war. The Marshalls had moved into a semi-detached house in Kenton Road in the newly built suburb of Kenton in 1930. Kenton had been developed to take advantage of the tube expansion into Metroland with the intention of attracting middle-income commuters just like Charles Marshall, now the director of his own company. The Marshalls' house, 'Kenilworth', was typical of the period; bay-fronted with an Ideal boiler for hot water, a Radiation gas cooker, three bedrooms, a bathroom and separate toilet. For thousands of families, houses like 'Kenilworth' were an achievable dream of modern comfort and convenience – all for an affordable £800.

In early 1943, like thousands of other young women, Doreen had followed her older sister into the Women's

Royal Naval Service ('Join the WRNS – and free a man for the fleet!'). Joan had worked at the admiralty decoding messages. Only seventeen, Doreen started two weeks' intensive training at the WRNS training depot in Mill Hill. All 'on shore' naval bases or 'stone frigates' were named after Royal Navy vessels and though it may have sounded grand, intimidating even, 'HMS Pembroke III' was, in reality, a disused cancer hospital. As a probationer, Doreen had been put through both medical and written tests in order to establish a suitable division for her experience and aptitude. In her first weeks, she was taught about the backbone of the service: discipline, routine and tradition. The Royal Navy was dominated by traditions and rules evolved over many centuries. These traditions, of course, had been evolved by and for the exclusively male intake who made up the 'Senior Service'. Women had briefly been able to join the service in 1917 but this initiative had been disbanded two years later. A further attempt to create a Women's Royal Naval Reserve had been mooted in the mid-1930s but after due consideration by the Special Sub-Committee of Imperial Defence, it was 'deemed not desirable'.[4] It had taken the darkening events in Europe in the late 1930s for the admiralty to accept that the need for a Women's Naval Reserve was pressing. Effectively, Doreen had joined a new and innovative organization of women that would have an impact not just on each Wren individually, but on a generation of young women who felt that being part of the WRNS in some way emancipated them from pre-war strictures and conventions.

The WRNS exposed young women like Doreen and Joan Marshall to a way of life a world away from their suburban backgrounds. They had to learn a completely different vocabulary relating their new, unfamiliar world to naval lore; a room was a 'cabin', the dining room was the 'mess' and the floor the 'deck'. All work was divided into 'watches' with 'divisions' held in the Assembly Hall and Holy Communion in a small chapel every day.[5] Crucially Wrens were forced to engage with other classes of women that they had never had the opportunity to meet before. For the first time in her sheltered middle-class upbringing, Doreen came face to face with women from a range of different backgrounds. For Doreen, her time in the WRNS was defining – the job, like the war, having spanned her adult life. She spent her career in the WRNS serving at various sites around the London area, mostly at accounting bases like HMS Pembroke III and HMS Westcliff. Much of her work was clerical, covering everything from submarines to post-hostilities planning and by 1946 she was working in Whitehall with senior figures in the admiralty at HMS President I.

Both Joan and Doreen's duties with the WRNS were very much office-based jobs with little chance of action. Ironically, the nearest they came to danger was at home in Kenton. At 8.10 a.m. on 28 June 1944, the peace of a typical English summer morning had been devastated by a violent explosion that engulfed the entire neighbourhood.

> Without any warning there was a colossal compression and explosion immediately followed by all kinds of crashes, bangs, screams, sounds of breaking glass and God knows what else.

The neighbourhood had been targeted by a V1 bomb – the deadly 'doodlebug'. Seconds after the blast, Newton Myers, a twelve-year-old schoolboy who lived at 5 Kenton Gardens, emerged from his family's Anderson raid shelter in the garden to witness a world in chaos:

> I clambered out of bed and through the door of the shelter, out through the back room door into what was left of our

hall. There was dust everywhere ... and there were other yells, shouts and screams coming from other places. At this moment my father appeared staggering down the stairs which were still relatively intact. His face was a mask of blood and he was shouting 'this is the end, this is the end' over and over again. As we met at the bottom of the stairs he picked me up and rushed out into the front garden with me in his arms. Then he put me down and I rushed back into the house. I went into what was left of the front room. The mantelpiece had come away from the wall and was lying horizontal across the sofa. The bay window was halfway out into the garden. When I looked out and to the right all I could see were what appeared to be the roofs of our neighbours' houses. The only problem was that they were at ground level with no houses underneath them. Dust was everywhere, there were still screams and moans coming from the buried, dying and injured ... Before long the rescue teams arrived and started the grisly task of recovering the bodies. I was unlucky enough to see one of my friends' sisters on a stretcher under a blanket being carried past me towards the ambulance. As the stretcher-bearer passed me, a doctor pulled back the blanket, I had the unpleasant sight of someone who had been completely flattened. Not a pretty sight ... This whole incident had a disastrous effect on my nerves. Up until now I had borne the bombing with typical British phlegm. However now I begged my father to take me out of London. I was panic stricken and absolutely terrified.[6]

Thirteen people were killed in the attack. The most severe damage was suffered by Kenton Gardens, but the whole area was reduced to rubble. Though their house was hit, Charles and Grace Marshall and their daughters were relieved to have escaped with their lives, Grace having often despaired during air raid warnings as Joan always refused to use the Anderson shelter in the garden. Significantly, though, Doreen did not escape the incident completely unscathed. From that morning onwards, a shock of grey began to appear in the dark curls of her hair, just above her right temple. This was very distinctive in such a young woman – a continuous reminder to her and everyone she met of the unspoken but continuing effects of the Blitz.

With 'Kenilworth' uninhabitable, the Marshalls moved four miles further to the northwest and rented a half-timbered, semi-detached house in Woodhall Drive, Pinner. The house had been built in the early 1930s, very much in the stockbroker Tudor style beloved by John Betjeman. In a conservation area today, it remains a hymn to Metroland – parquet floors and Bakelite door handles, manicured lawns, sculpted privet hedges and quiet avenues surrounding a village green; all the elements of comfortable pre-war middle-class life.

Living the first months of peace in the suburban comfort of Pinner, the Marshalls were well aware that they were very lucky to have survived the war with the family intact. A photograph taken in the garden at Woodhall Drive shows a happy, relaxed family group, the horrors of the war behind them – no inkling of the terrible tragedy ahead.

On Friday morning of 28 June, Charles Marshall drove Doreen to Waterloo Station and saw her off on the 9.30 train to Bournemouth.[7] Given the huge holiday crowds mixing with recently demobbed servicemen swarming around the station, Doreen and her father may not have even noticed Faulkner's, the busy hairdressing shop on the station concourse. The Waterloo branch was ably managed by a Mr William Heath but that day he was not at work, having pressing family issues to deal with at home.

Settling into her first-class carriage, Doreen checked her luggage, which consisted of two suitcases and her black suede clutch-style handbag. In the bag she kept a small pigskin notecase, four or five pounds in cash, her driver's licence, about sixty clothing coupons and the return half of her railway ticket. She also carried with her a key for the house in Woodhall Drive, keys to the suitcases, a lipstick, a comb and a couple of family photographs. She powdered her face with a blue and gold enamel powder compact, oblong in shape containing rouge, powder and a space for cigarettes. Though there was a crack across the mirror of the compact, Doreen kept it as she'd been given it by her sister Joan.[8] She also carried a small silver penknife in her bag, with a matching fountain pen. She had won them as a schoolgirl at an ice-skating competition at Wembley. The pen was inscribed with her name.[9]

Arriving at Bournemouth Station, Doreen took a taxi to the Norfolk Hotel on Richmond Hill. The hotel, one of the oldest in Bournemouth, was the only one not to have been requisitioned during the war years, so preserved a rather select reputation. The building still operates as an hotel today, opposite the Art Deco offices of the *Bournemouth Echo*, which had been built in 1932. Doreen was booked into Room 94 by the receptionist, Elsie Jones. She confirmed that she would be staying for ten days, as her letter had indicated. She signed the registration form and was shown to her room.[10]

That evening Doreen telephoned her father to say that she had had a comfortable journey and had arrived safely. She also had a chat on the phone with her sister and mentioned that she had talked to another guest at the hotel, an American antique dealer by the name of George Wisecarver.[11] Doreen phoned home again on Sunday and told her father that she was all right, but feeling a bit lonely, so she was looking through some books in her room.[12] Talking to her sister on the telephone, she mentioned that Mr Wisecarver had invited her on a trip to Exeter, but she didn't want to go. She rang home again on Tuesday 2 July and spoke to her mother. She also sent letters to her father and sister which arrived in Pinner on Tuesday and Wednesday morning, but in these letters – her last – she didn't refer to anybody she had met since she arrived in Bournemouth. She did write that 'unless I speak to somebody shortly I shall scream'.

For a young woman alone, there was plenty of entertainment for Doreen to occupy herself with at the local cinemas that week. The Electric in Bournemouth was showing the new Gene Tierney picture, *Leave Her to Heaven*. *The Blue Dahlia* at the Odeon starred Alan Ladd and Veronica Lake and the Astoria at Boscombe was showing Rex Harrison and Lilli Palmer in *The Rake's Progress*. But it was too hot to sit in a dark cinema during the day, as the weather that week was glorious.

> Summer came into its own yesterday [2 July] with a heat-wave which, though ideal for holidaymakers, left some office workers somewhat prostrate. Sea bathers increased in number at lunchtime by Bournemouth folk going down for a pre-prandial dip – for some, their first bathe of the summer. The temperature rose between 3 and 4 p.m. to 80 degrees, the highest recorded so far this year.[13]

On the morning of Wednesday 3 July, Doreen took a walk on the promenade, packed with families at the height of the holiday season. But having been in Bournemouth for nearly a week on her own, she was now feeling isolated, bored and lonely. In her mind she had already decided that she would return home early. She would take the train back to Waterloo tomorrow. Wednesday would be her last day in Bournemouth.

That morning, whilst stopping to watch a Punch and Judy show on the promenade, Doreen was delighted to meet an engaging young man – tall, tanned, blond and handsome with startlingly blue eyes made even more remarkable by the backdrop of the sea and the cloudless blue sky above the beach. She felt at ease with him and after several days of feeling rather sorry for herself, she was glad of his company. He introduced himself as Group Captain Rupert Brook – but she must call him 'Bobbie' or 'Bob'. He was extremely charming, a real gentleman. He recalled his meeting with Doreen some days later.

> I was on the promenade on Westcliff when I saw two young ladies walking along the front. One was a casual acquaintance I had met at a dance at the Pavilion during the latter part of the preceding week. (Her Christian name was Peggy but I was unaware of her surname.) Although I was not formally introduced to the other young lady I gathered her name was 'Doo' or something similar. The girl Peggy left after half an hour and I walked along the promenade with the other girl I now know to be Miss Marshall. I invited her to have tea in the afternoon and she accepted.[14]

Despite later attempts by the Bournemouth police to trace 'Peggy', she was never found. In all probability she never existed and is one of several phantom figures that Brook conjured in his various statements. Doreen had been very open with her family that she was lonely in Bournemouth and mentioned all of the few acquaintances she had made, so it seems unlikely that she wouldn't mention befriending another young woman if she had, indeed, met one. Brook may have been attempting to suggest that his first meeting with Doreen was more socially correct – an introduction through a mutual acquaintance than the rather casual pick-up that it was. The name 'Peggy' may have been inspired by his recent acquaintanceship with Peggy Waring who had only returned to London on the preceding Saturday. It seems much more plausible – and more consistent with his usual behaviour – that he noticed Doreen was alone and introduced himself. She might have stood out particularly to him because of the distinctive shock of grey hair above her right temple.

> I met her along the promenade about 2.45 p.m. and after a short stroll we went to the Tollard Royal Hotel for tea. It was about 3.45 p.m. The conversation was fairly general. She said she had served in the WRNS and mentioned she had been ill and was in Bournemouth to recuperate.[15]

Since the departure of Peggy Waring and Peter Rylatt, Brook had spent a considerable amount of time with some other guests at the Tollard Royal, Mr and Mrs Heinz Abisch, a German couple who lived on the Finchley Road in London. Brook would join them for drinks before lunch and dinner and for coffee after meals. That afternoon, Abisch and his wife returned to the hotel for tea where Brook was already sitting in the lounge with Doreen. Mr Abisch was amused to see Brook with yet another girl. He had had several mild flirtations with girls in the hotel – and Peggy Waring from whom Brook had seemed inseparable had only recently returned to London. Abisch smiled knowingly at him. At this point, Brook excused himself from Doreen and went over to buy a newspaper from the porter, passing Abisch. As he did so, he turned to Abisch and said 'in quite a nasty tone', 'I'll soon wipe that smile off your face.'[16] Brook then returned to tea with Doreen in the lounge and Mr and Mrs Abisch left the hotel. After tea, Brook suggested that they meet again that evening for dinner. With no other plans and nobody to answer to, Doreen said she'd be delighted. She left the Tollard Royal at 5.45 and returned to the Norfolk Hotel to dress for dinner.

Neville Heath as a child, with his mother, Bessie, *c.*1918.

Vikings House, Rutlish School, October 1933.
Heath is in the second row, seventh from the left.

Neville Heath in his mid-teens and already a young man about town, *c.*1930.

Heath aged twenty in his RAF uniform, in the garden at Merton Hall Road, 1936.

Heath's wife, Elizabeth, and their son, Robert, Johannesburg, 1944.

19 Squadron at RAF Duxford, 1936. Heath is fourth from the left in the second row. Johnny Kent is standing second from the right. Squadron Leader J. W. Turton-Jones is seated, centre.

American Mitchell Mark II Bombers of 180 Squadron prepare for take-off from Melsbroek, Belgium, for a daylight attack on the bridges at Venlo in Holland, October 1944.

S 18049. STRAND PALACE HOTEL. FOYER - VIEW OF BUREAU & ENTRANCE TO WINTER GARDEN

The art deco foyer of the Strand Palace Hotel, designed by Oliver P. Bernard.

Celebrations in Trafalgar Square on 'V' Day, 8 June 1946. 'This beats everything – the Coronation, the Jubilee and any of the cup finals.'

Yvonne Symonds hurries to avoid press photographers, summer 1946.

Exterior of the former Pembridge Court Hotel, 34 Pembridge Gardens, 2012.

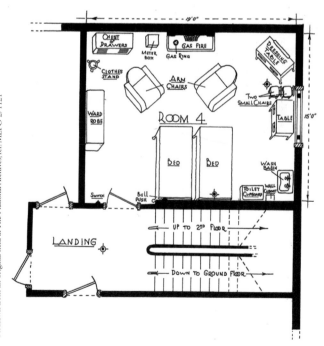

Police plan of Room 4 at the Pembridge Court Hotel.

The young Margery Wheat, mid-1930s.

Margery Gardner's identity card photograph, c.1940.

The Tollard Royal Hotel, West Cliff, Bournemouth.

Advertisement for the Tollard Royal Hotel, for its
first season since the end of the war, summer 1946.

Doreen Marshall, her father, mother and sister, Joan Cruickshanks, in the garden at Woodhall Drive, summer 1946.

Bomb damage in Kenton Road, the Marshalls' former home, 28 June 1944.

Doreen Margaret Marshall.

© Mirrorpix

Detective Constable George Suter.

© Getty Images

Divisional Detective Inspector
Reginald Spooner (right)
with an unnamed assistant.

© Getty Images

Police photographers take pictures of the scene of the crime,
Branksome Dene Chine, July 1946.

Violet Van Der Elst is arrested among the crowds gathered outside Pentonville Prison on the morning of Heath's execution, 16 October 1946.

A woman reads the notice of Heath's execution outside Pentonville, 16 October 1946.

Heath's waxwork at Madame Tussaud's in London, wearing a copy of the tweed jacket he wore to the pre-trial hearings at West London Magistrates' court.

Heath's effigy is groomed in the Chamber of Horrors at Madame Tussaud's, at some point in the 1960s. Here he wears a copy of the pinstripe suit he wore at his trial.

BOURNEMOUTH DAILY ECHO, Tuesday, July 9, 1946.

BOURNEMOUTH
Daily Echo

FINAL

REGISTERED AT THE GENERAL POST OFFICE AS A NEWSPAPER

THREE HALF-PENCE

No. 14119   TUESDAY, JULY 9, 1946

MURDER REVEALED BY CHINE DISCOVERY

BODY OF YOUNG WOMAN FOUND IN LONELY WOOD

Signs of a Struggle

EXAMINATION BY EXPERTS TO-DAY

No Possibility Of Bakers Striking
—Food Minister

SOLDIERS UNLOAD AT SOUTHAMPTON DOCKS

Strikers Expected Back At Work On Thursday

Big Four May Wind Up Talks By Thursday

A Bournemouth newspaper headline reporting the murder of Doreen Marshall, 9 July 1946.

The cover of Sydney Brock's book, *The Life and Death of Neville Heath*, published in 1947. It promised a 'Sensational-Sadistic-Romantic-True Story'.

Heath returning from West London Magistrates' Court, August 1946.

Just before 7 p.m., Doreen went to the desk at the Norfolk Hotel and asked James Newland, the porter, to call her a taxi as she was going to the Tollard Royal for dinner. Newland rang Autax, a local cab firm. The car soon arrived and Newland saw Doreen into it.[17] After a few minutes, when the car arrived at the Tollard Royal, Doreen got out and paid the driver, Sydney Bush. He remembered a distinctive glass fob watch she wore on the lapel of her lemon-coloured coat. She gave him no instructions to be collected later.[18]

The events of the evening preceding Doreen Marshall's death read like the scenario for an Agatha Christie play; the lounge of a Bournemouth hotel, an assembly of witnesses, including a retired major and his refined lady wife (Mrs Gladys Davy Phillips). Even the weather was suitably dramatic, as the evening was dominated by a violent thunderstorm with vivid lightning and heavy rain. It began with Doreen's arrival at the hotel, as she had arranged with Brook that afternoon. Brook recalled her entrance:

At appoximately 7.15, I was standing outside the hotel and saw her approaching on foot.[19] I entered the hotel, went to my room to get some tobacco and came downstairs again just as she was entering the lounge. We dined at 8.15, sat talking in the lounge afterwards and then moved into the writing room. The conversation was again general but she told me she was considering cutting short her holiday and returning home in a day or two. She mentioned an American staying in her hotel and told me he had taken her for car rides in the country. She also mentioned an invitation to go with him to Exeter but I gathered although she did not actually say so, she did not intend to go. Another American was mentioned – I believe his name was Pat – to whom I believe she had unofficially become engaged some while before.[20]

Brook deliberately suggested that Doreen may have had other boyfriends and that, as a single girl on holiday and away from home, she had made the most of her freedom. Though a plausible story – Bournemouth was still full of American servicemen waiting to be repatriated – there's no evidence that Doreen had met any other men at all, let alone become engaged to one. Wisecarver, her American acquaintance, was a respectable antiques dealer and had already left the country. Doreen was also known by her family to be a 'quiet girl who didn't have boyfriends'.

Doreen had dressed smartly and stylishly for dinner. Under her distinctive fleecy lemon box coat she wore a plain black silk frock with matching black sandals. She was also wearing silk stockings and a pair of cultured pearl earrings matching her Ciro pearl necklace. On one of her fingers she had a three stone diamond ring, set in platinum, which was a twenty-first birthday present from her parents. Under her arm she carried her black suede handbag. She used her blue compact to powder her nose. As she did so, Brook noted that it was cracked. Doreen explained that she was clumsy: 'I'm always breaking things.'

Heinz Abisch and his wife returned to the hotel and went in to dinner at about 7.30 p.m. Shortly afterwards, Brook came into the dining room with Doreen and they sat two tables away. The dinner menu that evening offered a choice of two soups, trout or roast duck, cauliflower and cream sauce with boiled new potatoes. This was followed by raspberry ice or pear trifle. Brook ordered a magnum of champagne, though Doreen drank little.[21]

After dinner, he escorted Doreen into the lounge, where the Abisches were already settled. He took one of the armchairs and Doreen sat opposite on a sofa. Winifred Parfitt came into the lounge at about 8.30 p.m. to take her coffee after dinner and Brook introduced her to Doreen. He explained that Doreen was an old friend and that he had not seen her for some time, but had bumped into her on the sea front that morning. Doreen didn't contradict this statement, and she may well have felt it was less awkward to comply with Brook's social white lie. Brook also told Mrs Parfitt that Doreen had served in the WRNS. Mrs Parfitt had also been in service in the admiralty during the war so she and Doreen had a great deal in common to chat about.

Sitting only three or four yards away from them, Abisch overheard Brook call Doreen 'darling', and watched as she was introduced to Mrs Parfitt. Eavesdropping, he heard that Doreen was staying at the Norfolk Hotel, she was from Pinner and 'would be going home the next day'. Mrs Abisch was sitting on a sofa to the right of Brook, when he suddenly turned to her and said, 'Pull that skirt down. It makes me mad.' Both Mr and Mrs Abisch were puzzled by Brook's remark, as Mrs Abisch's skirt had not ridden up sufficiently to justify it.[22] Brook and Doreen were served glasses of port on the house by Wilkinson the night porter, but Doreen refused hers, saying she had had enough to drink. Brook drank both glasses. Mrs Parfitt noticed that Doreen had only one drink – a gin and orange – during the whole evening, but Brook had had several, mostly beer in pints. To Mrs Parfitt, Brook seemed 'in a very cheery mood – not drunk – just cheery.' According to the hotel rules, drinks served outside the dining room should be paid for when ordered, but Mr Parfitt recalled that Brook told the waiter, 'I haven't got a bean on me today. I meant to go to the bank this morning. Put it down, old chap, on my crime sheet.'[23]

As the summer evening turned to night, the weather began to change. After the intense heat of the day, a storm was on its way, rumbling from a distance at first, but by 10.45 it had developed into a dramatic electrical storm, with lightning cracking across the vast dark sky in front of the hotel.[24]

Brook then suggested that they might listen to some dance music, so he, Doreen and Mrs Parfitt moved from the lounge to the writing room where there was a portable radio. That night John Reynders and his orchestra were broadcasting on the BBC Light Programme from 10.30 p.m. As the wireless played dance music, Doreen chatted some more with Mrs Parfitt, telling her that she had been ill and had come to Bournemouth to recuperate. Mrs Parfitt did think that Doreen looked rather pale. Finding her sympathetic, Doreen confided that she had been rather lonely in Bournemouth and her stay had not been particularly happy. She complained that she was not feeling well and that she felt dizzy. She supposed it was because she was feeling very tired. She may actually have been feeling unwell as her sister later confirmed that Doreen was expecting her period. She asked Mrs Parfitt to persuade Brook to take her back to the Norfolk Hotel.[25]

At about 10.45 p.m., Doreen visited the ladies' cloakroom. While she was out of the room, Mrs Parfitt told Brook that she thought Doreen wanted to go home, but he was flippant – it was far too early. Mrs Parfitt then followed Doreen to the ladies' as she thought she might be ill. When she got to the cloakroom, Mrs Parfitt wasn't sure if Doreen had been sick in the lavatory, but she was powdering her nose from her blue compact and refreshing her lips with her American lipstick. She seemed to be getting a little brighter after they went back to the writing room. The wireless was now playing music by Billy Ternent and his dance orchestra, accompanied by Ruth Howard and Gerry Fitzgerald.[26]

Between 11.15 and 11.45 p.m., the party listening to the radio were joined by Major and Mrs Phillips, who had been out for the evening. Brook introduced them both to Doreen. Mrs Phillips felt that Brook seemed rather the worse for drink as when she refused to have a drink with him, he became annoyed with her.[27] She noted that Doreen seemed sober and looked pale. Mrs Parfitt left to go to bed shortly after the Phillips' came in. Before retiring she asked Mrs Phillips if she would see about getting Doreen home, as she was clearly tired. Mrs Parfitt wished everybody 'goodnight' and told Doreen that she hoped they would meet again. Outside, it had started to rain. For some reason, Mrs Parfitt slept badly that night. When she woke abruptly from a fitful sleep, she could still hear the rain.

Shortly before midnight, Doreen asked Major Phillips if he would order a taxi for her as she wanted to go home. Mrs Phillips noticed that Doreen made this request 'in a rather appealing kind of way, touching his hand when he was about to depart for the taxi'. Major Phillips ordered a taxi from the night porter and then he and his wife retired to bed. Doreen would be back at her hotel within five minutes.

At some point during the evening Brook had said, done or suggested something that unsettled Doreen. Several witnesses commented on how pale and tired she looked, to such an extent that she was keen to go back to her hotel. Had he pressurized her to come up to his room, as he had done with Peggy Waring? Or had he gone even further? Brook had already been very open with Peter Rylatt about his acquaintanceship with the murderer, Neville Heath. Had Brook said something to frighten Doreen?

A minute or two after Major and Mrs Phillips retired to bed, Brook came out of the writing room and asked Arthur White, the night porter, if he had ordered a taxi.

'No, sir. I was just going to order it,' said White.

'Cancel it,' Brook told him. 'The young lady will order it later.'[28]

Brook went back into the writing room to join Doreen.

The midnight chimes of Big Ben played on the wireless, followed by the national anthem. There would be no more dance music that night. Brook and Doreen left the writing room and went towards the doors that opened onto West Hill Road. Doreen collected her lemon-coloured coat from Arthur White's porter's box. He noticed that the coat had a label with a foreign name on the inside. The door had been locked, as usual, at 11 p.m., so Frederick Wilkinson unlocked it to let them out.

'I'll be back in half an hour,' Brook said to Wilkinson.

Doreen stopped to correct him. 'No – he'll be back in a *quarter* of an hour.'[29]

She didn't want the night porter – or indeed Brook – to get the wrong idea. Wilkinson let the couple out. As he closed the door on them, he noticed that Doreen put her arm around Brook's waist – comfortable, romantic, trusting.[30] They went out of the front door and turned left, walking towards the cliff top. The storm had ended and the rain had stopped. But it would not be the last of the bad weather that night.

They disappeared from view, walking into the dark.

CHAPTER SIXTEEN
The Tollard Royal Hotel

4–6 JULY 1946

LIGHTNING – THUNDER – HAIL – RAGING WIND
'Mixed-Grill' Tempest Over Wide English Area
One of the worst storms for many years – with terrific thunderclaps, brilliant lightning flashes, hail, rain and wind that sometimes reached hurricane force – swept South-East England in the night as a climax to the heat wave of the past few days ... almost tropical violence and the lightning continued for hours ... The Air Ministry described the wind which rose at 1 a.m. as a freak one. It went from calm to 38 mph and gradually died down to calm again. Tremendous squalls of hail lashed Hastings. Many holidaymakers and residents were awakened and remained up. After dying away, the storm returned with increased violence and remained until nearly dawn.

Bournemouth Echo, 4 July 1946

Between 4 and 4.30 a.m. on the morning of Thursday 4 July, Frederick Wilkinson the night porter was doing his rounds at the Tollard Royal Hotel. He had noticed that Group Captain Brook hadn't returned from escorting his guest back to her hotel and assumed that he had succeeded in romancing her, either at the Norfolk Hotel or on the way to it.[1]

During his stay at the hotel, Wilkinson felt he had got to know Group Captain Brook very well. Every night Brook would chat to him before he went to bed. The previous night was the first time during Brook's stay that they hadn't had their usual talk. Wilkinson quietly opened the door of Room 81 to find that it was already daylight, though the curtains were drawn. Brook was sound asleep in bed. He noticed that Brook had not left his shoes to be cleaned. As a rule, if he didn't leave his shoes downstairs to be cleaned he would leave them outside the door. Again, this was the first night that Captain Brook had not done so.[2]

The chambermaid, Alice Hemmingway, looked after half the rooms on the second floor of the Tollard Royal, including Room 81. Her daily duties were to clean the rooms, make the beds and to take guests their early-morning tea at 7 a.m. Just after this time on this Thursday morning, Mrs Hemmingway took a cup of tea to Brook's room to find him still asleep with the bedclothes drawn right up to his nose. Mrs Hemmingway apologized for being late. Brook asked what the time was and Mrs Hemmingway told him it was about ten past seven. She opened the curtains and, remembering last night's electrical storm, chatted about the weather before leaving the room.[3]

Frederick Wilkinson then returned to the room, taking in Brook's three daily newspapers. He was still sleeping and the tea which Mrs Hemmingway had taken up earlier was untouched. Wilkinson warned Brook that his tea would get cold and offered him the newspapers.

'Here's your papers, sir.'

'Ah! I done [tricked] you last night,' Brook said.

'How did you come in? Not by the front door.'[4]

He did not give an answer. But Wilkinson remembered the ladder just outside the bedroom window that was being used by the builders working on the roof. Given that he knew all the ground-floor windows and the front door had been locked, Wilkinson assumed that the only way Brook could have accessed his room was via the ladder. Added to this, a day or two before, Brook had teased Wilkinson, saying, 'I will get in one night without you knowing.' Clearly, this is what he had done. Whilst in the bedroom, Wilkinson noticed Brook's shoes near the bed. Round them, about half to one inch up the side, was a ridge of sand. From this, Wilkinson surmised that Brook had not taken Miss Marshall straight back to the Norfolk Hotel the night before, but had diverted their walk along the beach.

At 10 a.m. Mrs Hemmingway knocked on Brook's door but received no reply, so she entered the room to find him still in bed, and still well covered up. 'Can't drag yourself out this morning, sir?' she asked. He asked her to bring him some coffee, which she obtained from the second head waiter in the still room. He wondered if Brook had a fat head as he had ordered a bottle of champagne for dinner the night before?[5] Mrs Hemmingway took the coffee to Room 81. Later that morning, she knocked on the door again, keen to clean the room. Brook was in his dressing gown standing over the washstand, scrubbing his hands. He didn't look round, nor did he say anything. She apologized for intruding and left the room. At about half past twelve, Mrs Hemmingway had just finished lunch and passed Brook on the landing near his room. He asked her if she could bring him a piece of brown paper. She got some used wrapping from the pantry and took it to him. When she did so she felt that 'he was deliberately keeping his face away from [her]'.[6]

When Brook had finally vacated the room, Mrs Hemmingway went to clean it. In the fireplace was a fitted gas fire. The hearth had only recently been painted since the hotel had reopened in June. She then noticed a burn mark on the new paintwork. The mark was round and fairly large, about 10 or 12 inches across, but there was no debris or ash from whatever had been burnt. She was certain it had not been there the day before. She got some Vim to try and clean the mark off, but there was still a faint stain when she had finished. The mark wouldn't scrub away.

Mrs Hemmingway then swept the hearth and turned back the carpet. Underneath the carpet she found some sand and dirt. She prided herself on her work and was sure it hadn't been there yesterday. Somebody had swept the hearth without turning the carpet back, so the dirt had gone under it. She also noticed that the sink seemed grubbier than usual.

At about this time, Ellen Bayliss, a housekeeper at the Tollard Royal, found that one of the lavatories on the third floor was blocked with what she thought was a ball of paper. She tried to clear it by flushing, but was unable to get rid of it. She called the hotel carpenter, who dislodged the blockage with a plunger, but he felt that the obstruction was 'something hard and clean'.[7] The lavatory was on the floor above Brook, but the stairs leading up to it were directly opposite his room.

Having solved the problem, Mrs Bayliss was on her way downstairs when she saw Brook on the first floor close to the ladies' lavatories. His appearance made a vivid impression on her; his hair was disturbed, his manner agitated and he looked, according to her rather melodramatic description, like a 'hunted animal'.[8] Though manhole covers were later raised and the lavatory cisterns inspected, nothing significant was later brought to light, but it seems clear that on Thursday morning, Brook was keen to dispose of something. This was confirmed by Major Phillips, who at some point that morning was going to the garage on West Hill Road. He saw Brook carrying a brown paper parcel about 12' by 5' by 3', but didn't speak to him.[9]

At the Norfolk Hotel that morning, the last breakfast had been served and the head waiter noticed that Miss Marshall from Room 94 had not come down for her usual 9 a.m. breakfast. He phoned her room but there was no reply. The housekeeper confirmed that her bed had not been slept in but all her things were still in her room. She also had £20 locked in the hotel safe.

At the Tollard Royal, Heinz Abisch and his wife had gone for a walk after breakfast to Sandbanks, returning to the hotel in time for lunch. They were chatting about their walk when Brook asked which route they had gone. Abisch told him that they had walked along the cliffs and then through Branksome Chine. Brook commented that he 'didn't know you could walk so far'.[10]

Later that day Major Phillips asked if Brook had got the taxi he ordered for him last night? Brook said that he had walked Miss Marshall home and then walked back to the hotel. On the way back he had been caught in a heavy rainstorm and had got very wet.

That evening, at about 7.15 p.m., Robert Cook from East London was sitting in the gardens in Bournemouth town centre in front of Bobby's department store and the Lyons Tea Room. He was on holiday in Bournemouth with his wife and child. As he was sitting, a man approached him and asked if he would like to buy a new book of clothing coupons? When Cook refused, the man walked away, but after about 100 yards, he turned back, arousing Cook's suspicions.

The man was tall, blond and handsome with very blue eyes.[11]

Soon after he started his 8 p.m. shift that evening, Arthur White, the head night porter of the Tollard Royal, ran into Group Captain Brook.

'Do you know another way into the hotel?' Brook asked.

'Yes,' said White. 'But the way I know was locked. How did you get in last night?'

'I got up the ladder and got into my room that way. I thought I'd pull your leg.'[12]

Brook then joined Mr Abisch, Mrs Parfitt and Major Phillips in the lounge after dinner. Brook reminisced about his experiences during the war. He talked of the time he was station commander on an airfield in Belgium when the Germans made their last big raid on 1 January 1945, damaging eighty-eight British aircraft. The talk then turned to politics, Abisch noting that Brook was very conservative in his opinions. Brook then spent the rest of the evening with another young woman in the lounge before retiring to bed. White had noticed that Group Captain Brook always went to bed very late, drinking and chatting into the small hours, but on this occasion he retired unusually early. On his way up the stairs, he stopped to speak to White.

'Will you give my shoes an extra shine tonight?'

'We always do, sir.'

'Yes, I know, but I have been in sea-water in them.'

Brook left his shoes outside his door for cleaning. There was no longer a ridge of sand on them.[13]

Next morning, Friday 5 July, Brook went to H. J. Tuson's, a pawnshop in central Bournemouth. He was keen to pawn a ladies' three-stone diamond ring. The pledge was taken by the shop manager, Henry Burles. Brook gave his name as Mr Brook of Loxley Road, SW19.[14] When Mr Burles asked for the street number of the house, Brook said that it didn't matter as there were only two houses in the road. Burles gave Brook a loan of £5 in exchange for the ring.[15]

Around the same time that morning, Frank McInnes, the proprietor of the Norfolk Hotel, reported to the Bournemouth police that one of his guests, a Miss Doreen Marshall, had not been seen since the evening of 3 July. She had disappeared, leaving all her clothing and possessions, as well as some money in the hotel safe. Mr McInnes had been away for a short while so that he was not aware of Miss Marshall's disappearance until that lunchtime. He rang Detective Constable Suter at Bournemouth Police Station. Suter then rang Doreen's parents in Pinner informing them that their daughter was missing.

Later that day, Mrs Phillips had returned from the shops when she bumped into Brook at the hotel.

'What have you been up to?' Brook asked.

'Well, I've been shopping a bit and then went into the bank.'

'Funnily enough, I've been to the bank myself.'

And, indeed, Mrs Phillips had noticed that Brook paid for some drinks earlier that day with cash – £3 to £4 in notes – rather than putting them on his bill, as he usually did. It was then that Mrs Phillips commented on Brook's new shirt.

'Lovely new shirt, Captain Brook.'

'No, no. This is an old shirt.'

'But it looks perfectly new.'

'I assure you it's an old one.'

The new shirt stood out to Mrs Phillips, as on all other occasions Brook had worn a buff-coloured sports shirt.

'And what about your friend, Miss Marshall? Did she arrive home safely on Wednesday night?'

Brook didn't answer and Mrs Phillips didn't press the point. She then commented on the unusual scarf Brook was wearing around his neck. She hadn't seen him wear it before.

'What a funny scarf. May I see it?'

Brook took the scarf off and showed it to her — a thin silk square with a map printed on it — the 'escape scarf'. It was then that Mrs Phillips noticed that Brook had something on his neck, just below his right ear — three scratches: one long scratch and a couple of smaller ones. She made no comment.[16]

On Friday evening the manager of the Tollard Royal, Ivor Relf, took a telephone call from Mr McInnes, the manager of the Norfolk Hotel. McInnes explained that he believed that a lady — who had subsequently gone missing — had dined at the Tollard Royal on the previous Wednesday night. Relf told him he'd make enquiries and would ring him back. He consulted the head waiter's meal book and noticed that there had been two 'chance' diners that evening for dinner, but at this point he didn't connect Group Captain Brook's guest with the missing lady from the Norfolk Hotel. Brook had introduced Doreen to Relf as an old friend and hadn't mentioned where she was staying.

Late that evening, Doreen's father telephoned the Tollard Royal himself. Doreen had been missing since Wednesday when she had gone to dinner at the Tollard Royal. She had not phoned home, nor had she left any messages, so her family were extremely concerned. It just wasn't like her. Relf promised to investigate further. It's only then that he thought of Captain Brook's young guest in the fleecy yellow coat. He resolved to talk to Brook about the missing girl the next time he saw him.

The next day was Saturday and Relf saw Brook standing by himself in the dining room drinking coffee. Relf asked him if the guest he had entertained on Wednesday night was from Pinner and if she had been staying at the Norfolk Hotel? Brook replied, jocularly, 'Oh no, I have known that lady for a long while, and she certainly does not come from Pinner.'[17]

Relf suggested that Brook should contact the Bournemouth

police as the matter had become very serious. He had had a phone call from the manager at the Norfolk Hotel, and from the young lady's father who was terribly worried.

At 11.15 a.m. Detective Sergeant Stanley Pack was on duty when he had a call at Bournemouth Police Station from Bob Brook.

'I am speaking from the Tollard Royal Hotel. I understand a young lady is missing from the Norfolk Hotel. Can I speak to the officer in charge of the case?'[18]

Pack told him he'd need to speak to DC Suter who was not available at that moment but asked if he could take a message. Brook said, 'No it doesn't matter. I have a little information which may be of assistance. If you can tell me when the officer will be in, I will ring again.'[19]

At about 3 p.m., Brook joined Mrs Phillips and some acquaintances down at the beach. About a quarter of an hour later, he said he had to make a telephone call. He walked away in the direction of Poole. Half an hour later, DC Suter answered the telephone and spoke to Brook, who explained he was a guest at the Tollard Royal Hotel. Brook understood that Suter had been making enquiries about a young lady who had come to dinner at the Tollard Royal and said he might be able to help. Brook said that he was currently at Alum Chine enjoying the sun and wondered if Suter would like to join him? Suter declined and suggested that Brook come to the station at 5.30 p.m. that evening.

At around 4 p.m. Brook called into Freed's, a second-hand jewellers in the Triangle at the heart of the town. He wondered if they bought watches as he had one to sell. Brook showed Harry Berkoff, the manager, a lady's glass and metal fob watch. It was a quality piece – a Swiss movement with fifteen jewels. Brook wanted £5 for it, but Berkoff thought that was too expensive. He offered Brook £2. 20s. Clearly keen to sell it, Brook said, 'If you could make it a little bit more you can have it.' Berkoff eventually bought the watch for £3.[20] Brook returned to the party on the beach, having been away from them for about an hour. Brook then went with Mrs Phillips' party back to the Tollard Royal for tea. After tea, he left the hotel, heading for the police station on Madeira Road. He was dressed as usual in his sports jacket and was wearing his RAF sunglasses. This would be his last walk as a free man.

That afternoon, a short distance away from where Mrs Phillips' party had been on the beach, a group of schoolboys from the Russell Cotes Nautical School were walking along the cliffs from Bournemouth to Alum Chine. Whilst they were climbing, one of the boys, eleven-year-old Clive Miles, noticed something at the bottom of the cliffs, about seventy-five yards east of the entrance to the chine behind some beach huts.[21] When the boys climbed down to the beach, Clive went and picked up the object he'd seen behind a beach hut.

It was Doreen Marshall's black suede handbag.

CHAPTER SEVENTEEN
Detective Constable Suter

6 JULY 1946

It was the policeman's nose, I suppose, but it just didn't tie up.
The little bell was ringing.

George Suter, *Bournemouth Echo*, 5 November 1980

Sometime after 5.30 p.m., it was still bright and sunny and the temperature still in the low seventies when Brook arrived at Bournemouth Police Station, a 1930s brick-built building, fronted by a low stone wall.

At the reception desk he introduced himself to Detective Constable Suter.[1] At the age of forty, Suter was tall, bald, square-jawed and broadly built. As a police officer, he had been in a reserved occupation during the war, but had volunteered for the Rifle Brigade in the winter of 1943–4. In February 1945 he had been at the crossing of the Rhine and was amongst the first troops to liberate Belsen. Though he never discussed his experiences with his family, they were aware that he had witnessed scenes of great horror during his time in the army. After the German surrender, his unit was based on the Danish border until he was demobbed in early 1946, at which point he went back to his pre-war occupation with Bournemouth police.[2] He had been back behind his desk at Madeira Road for a matter of weeks, mostly preoccupied with a spate of hotel burglaries that had taken place over the summer, before he became involved in the enquiry into the disappearance of Doreen Marshall.[3]

When Brook arrived, Suter showed him into the enquiry office on the ground floor of the station. Suter was puzzled from the start of the interview with Group Captain Brook. Brook wasn't wearing a tie, but had his shirt buttoned to the top, hardly in keeping with the dress of an RAF officer. Suter would have thought he'd wear a tie or at least a cravat. 'His dress did not tally with his station in life,'[4] he later stated. Also, granted the weather was still bakingly hot outside, but it did seem odd that throughout their conversation, Brook continued to wear his RAF-issue sunglasses.[5]

'I'm Brook from the Tollard Royal Hotel. Are you Suter?'

'Yes, sir. Now, I have been making enquiries about a young lady who was at dinner at the Tollard Royal Hotel on Wednesday evening.'

'Yes, I had a young lady to dinner with me on Wednesday evening.'

'Probably this was the same person about whom I've been making enquiries. Could you take a look at this photograph?'

Suter showed Brook a photograph of Doreen Marshall.

'That's her,' Brook said. 'Beyond a shadow of a doubt. She has a lock of grey hair here.' Brook indicated his own right temple. 'You can just see it in the photo.'

At that moment, there was some interruption in the office,

so Suter invited Brook upstairs into the sergeants' office where it was quieter. Suter asked Brook to carry on with his story.

'Will you tell me all about it from the beginning?'

'Yes. I met her on the beach on the Wednesday afternoon.[6] She was then with another girl named Peggy and I had previously met Peggy at the Pavilion. I gained the impression that it was a fresh acquaintanceship between the two girls. I asked Doreen to dinner at the Tollard Royal Hotel on Wednesday evening and she accepted. At about midnight – or just before – she said she was going home and she said she would walk. We sat on the front for a bit, then walked to the sea side of the gardens – near the Pavilion. Doreen said she would be busy for a few days but would ring me on Sunday and would be going back to London on Monday. She didn't want to go any further and she walked back to her hotel. That would be about 1 a.m. She did say she would be going back to London earlier and that she had been ill and felt a bit browned off. She told me about an American friend, that she went to Poole with him and for a ride to the country in a car and that he wanted her to go to Exeter with him but she did not want to go.'

'What was she wearing?'

'A yellow swagger coat, either black or dark blue frock. Carrying a handbag and wearing a string of pearls. She used a blue powder compact. With a cracked mirror. She told me she was always breaking things. The light streak in her hair was very noticeable.'

Brook had been upfront and honest and seemed to have nothing more to say, let alone anything to hide, so Suter wound up the interview.

'By the way, sir, I have not taken your full name or address.'

'Rupert Robert Brook, Thurmaston Aerodrome, Leicester.'

At this point, an extraordinary twist of fate began to draw Brook further into the hands of the police. As Suter's interview with Brook was ending, a clerk came up from the enquiry office and interrupted the conversation.

'Excuse me, sir,' he said, addressing Suter. 'There is a Mr Marshall downstairs waiting to see you.'

'That will be the young lady's father,' said Suter, who turned to Brook. 'May I contact you at the hotel if I need any further information, sir?'

'Yes – at any time.'

Suter led Brook downstairs to the enquiry office where they were met by Doreen's father. He was also accompanied by Joan, the missing girl's sister. Aside from Doreen's shock of grey hair, the two young women looked incredibly alike, dark-haired and petite. Suter had already met Mr Marshall and his daughter in the investigation of her disappearance and now introduced them to Brook.

'This gentleman had dinner with your daughter on Wednesday night.'

Brook repeated the story that he had already told Suter. Then, turning to Doreen's father, Brook assured him that he shouldn't worry about her.

'Doreen told me she would be busy for a few days. I wasn't expecting her to ring until Sunday. If there's any other way I can help?'

Mr Marshall thanked Brook for his concern. Brook went on.

'In all probability, she's with her American friend.'

But this reassurance didn't calm Marshall's worries. She wasn't the sort of girl to go off without telling anybody with a man she had only just met. Mr Marshall noticed that throughout the conversation, Brook didn't take his eyes off his daughter, Joan. Mr Marshall thought that Brook had a 'sickening conceit' and increasingly felt that this man was responsible for his daughter's disappearance.[7] Joan also had an instinctive feeling that Brook was involved. He had said he left Doreen at the Winter Garden near the Pavilion. It was after midnight and her hotel was only a few hundred yards from where he claimed they parted. Joan asked him directly, 'Why didn't you see her home?' Brook simply shrugged his shoulders. Joan had a dreadful sick feeling that her sister was dead and that the superficially charming man in the dark glasses had killed her.[8]

As Brook was talking to the Marshalls, Suter had the opportunity to scrutinize his handsome features at close quarters. Had his demeanour changed when he was brought face to face with Doreen's family – and particularly the girl's sister? Suter began to feel a growing sense of recognition about Brook's face. He had seen it somewhere before – recently. He recalled a photograph of a wanted man in the *Police Gazette*, pinned on the noticeboard upstairs in the CID office. Was there a similarity, or were his eyes playing tricks? Excusing himself from Mr Marshall and his daughter, Suter took Brook to one side.

'I think you must have a double, sir.'

'Oh really?'

'Yes. We have a photo of a chap who is wanted and you are not unlike him. Come up and have a look at the photo.'

Apparently bemused, Brook followed Suter upstairs to the CID office where Detective Sergeant Leslie Johnson was sitting behind his desk.[9] Johnson also noticed that Brook continued wearing his sunglasses. It was now about 5.45 p.m. Suter pointed to the noticeboard and showed Brook the *Police Gazette* photo of Neville Heath, wanted in connection with the murder of Margery Gardner at Notting Hill.

'You must admit there is a striking resemblance,' suggested Suter. 'Is that you?'

'Good Lord, no,' said Brook. 'I agree, it is *like* me.'

He turned decisively and walked out of the office. Suter followed him, but not before deliberately dropping his notes from his interview with Brook on the floor. With nothing said between them, DC Johnson picked up the notes[10] and immediately got on the phone in an attempt to contact Notting Hill police.[11] Suter and Brook returned downstairs to Doreen's father and sister where Brook jokingly said something about his similarity to the portrait. Everyone laughed.

At that point a uniformed officer joined Suter and told him he was wanted on the telephone. Upstairs DS Johnson told Suter that he had called Notting Hill Police Station in order to verify some details about Brook and to ask for a detailed description of Neville Heath. But with only an instinctive suspicion that Brook was not all he claimed to be, Suter had no reason to detain him. There was no evidence that Doreen Marshall's disappearance was sinister. Many young women disappeared for a couple of days at holiday resorts for their own reasons and then turned up again quite safe. Brook had also come to the police station of his own free will – extremely unusual in the case of a murderer on the run. All this put Suter in a quandary as he was now under pressure from his senior officer Inspector Gates to let Brook go. The group captain was clearly a gentleman and 'a gentleman's word should be accepted'.[12] But Suter was convinced the man was Heath and was prepared to stake his job on it. He went back downstairs where Brook was still in conversation with Mr Marshall and his daughter. After asking Mr Marshall where he could contact him, Suter wished the Marshalls goodbye and remained with Brook.

By this time, Brook had manouevred himself back outside the police station, leaning casually against the low front wall in the late afternoon sun, his eyes still shaded by his sunglasses. Freedom was imminent. Desperate to keep hold of him, Suter kept Brook talking about the wonderful weather, holidays and what his stay was like at the Tollard Royal. Shortly afterwards, they were joined by DS Johnson, who also entered into the conversation. Together, Suter and Johnson were determined not to let Brook go.

'I am a detective sergeant,' said Johnson. 'What do you say your full name is?'

'Brook. Group Captain Rupert Robert Brook. Why?'

'You answer the description of a man called Clevely Heath who is wanted for interrogation regarding a recent murder in London.'

'I know, he has said so,' said Brook, indicating Suter. 'Look, do you think I would come here if I was that man?'

'I don't know. You might. Have you any documents to substantiate your name to be Brook?'

'No,' said Brook, 'but I have at the hotel. Can we go there and I'll show you? I've got my "A" pilot's licence, identity card and letters.'

'No, for the time being I must ask you to remain here whilst enquiries are made. Firstly, what are you doing in Bournemouth?'

'I am here on holiday.'

'Where do you come from?'

'Leicester. Thurmaston Aerodrome. I'm stationed there, but you won't find anyone there on a Saturday.'

'Can you give me the name of anyone at Leicester who can vouch for you?'

'Yes,' said Brook. 'Any amount.'

'Who is your immediate chief up there?' Johnson was taking notes.

'Mr Walters, the chief test pilot for Austers.'

'I wonder if you would come back into the station, sir, whilst enquiries are being made?'[13]

Brook assumed an exasperated umbrage.

'Well, this is the last time I shall come to the police to give any assistance. By the way,' asked Brook, 'am I under arrest?'

'No,' replied Johnson, 'not at this stage.'

'That's all right then,' said Brook. 'By the way, when you are satisfied that I am not this man "Heath", will you give me a chit that I can show, if I am stopped again?'

'Yes, if you wish, and so soon as we are satisfied that you are not Heath.'

Brook, Suter and Johnson went back into the police station to the sergeants' office where Suter sat down with Brook. He kept the conversation to their wartime experiences – always bonding chat for men of their age at the time. Meanwhile, Johnson telephoned Scotland Yard again and was put through directly to Reg Spooner at his office in Hammersmith. Spooner outlined Heath's description and said he would verify Brook's story about his background in Leicester, but on no account must they let him leave the police station. Whilst waiting for Scotland Yard to get back to them, Johnson observed Brook sitting with Suter, chatting about the war. As he was watching, Brook dropped his pipe on the floor. As he bent to pick it up, Johnson noticed that Brook had an inch-long scratch on the right side of his neck showing half an inch and running parallel with the collar of his shirt. It was not fresh but had a thin scab for the whole length. Little by little the officers' instincts were feeling more and more justified. They now needed to play a waiting game as the Metropolitan Police verified that 'Brook' was the man they were looking for.

Brook's patience was now wearing thin and he said that he wanted to leave. Suter and Johnson referred him to their senior officer, Detective Inspector Gates. At about 6.35 p.m., Gates told Brook that he would need to be searched.[14]

'I understand that your name is Brook. Have you any means of identification with you?'

'No, I have nothing on me. But I have at the hotel. I have told your officers all about myself. My name is Rupert Robert Brook and I'm known at the Devonshire Club in London. I live in Leicester and have a banking account at the Westminster Bank there. Look, I admit that there is a resemblance to

Clevely Heath. I have seen the police notice, but I am not this man, Heath.'

Gates searched him. All he had in his possession was four £1 notes, 3s. 6d. in silver, two three-penny pieces, a pipe and tobacco pouch, some Churchman cigarettes, a box of Swan matches, five-pence halfpenny in copper, a handkerchief and his sunglasses.[15]

Brook asked if he could go back to the hotel and then come back to the station. Gates told him that enquiries were being made at the hotel by the police and he was being detained. Brook then said that he was feeling cold. Could somebody pick up his jacket for him? He had left it with the porter at the hotel, Harry Brown.

Gates arrived at the Tollard Royal at about 7 p.m. and sought out the porter. He handed Gates Brook's brown sports jacket. Searching the pockets of the jacket, Gates came across what was to become some crucial – and damning – evidence. In the right-hand pocket of the jacket he found one half of a first-class return railway ticket (number 10130), valid for travel from Bournemouth back to Waterloo, issued on 28 June 1946 – the day that Doreen Marshall had travelled alone to Bournemouth. There was also a 4d. railway cloakroom ticket (number 0800) issued at Bournemouth West Railway Station on 23 June – the day that Brook had arrived in Bournemouth.[16]

Just before 9 p.m., Gates arrived at Bournemouth West Station and interviewed William Gillingham, the chief clerk. Gates submitted the cloakroom ticket and took possession of a leather suitcase. Opening it, there was a soft hat, a mackintosh, a leather luggage-label holder bearing the name of 'Heath', and most significantly, a leather riding whip with a distinctive diamond-weave pattern – stained with blood.

There was now absolutely no doubt. They were holding Neville Heath, the most wanted man in the country.

* * *

Back at Bournemouth Police Station, DS Johnson received a
call from Scotland Yard. It was exactly the information he
had suspected. Nobody had ever heard of Group Captain
Brook at Thurmaston. His entire story was false. Spooner
told Johnson to detain Brook at any cost. He wanted them to
go to the Tollard Royal and search Brook's room for anything
that might confirm his identity, but that there should be no
further searches in order to preserve any evidence. Johnson
returned to Brook, who was still talking with Suter.

'Enquiries have been made from the particulars you have
supplied about yourself and I am satisfied that they are false.
You are *not* known at Leicester to the Auster aircraft company.
No person by the name of Brook as test pilot is known to
them. Nor do they know a Mr Walters. You will be detained
pending further enquiries as to your identity since I believe
you to be the man, Clevely Heath. Is that your name?'

'Well, I am not Heath,' said Brook.

Johnson replied, 'Would you care to furnish any further
particulars regarding your identity? You can if you wish. If
you still maintain you are not Heath, someone will shortly be
able to come to this station and confirm that.'

'I do not want to give any other particulars. If someone is
coming down here who knows this man Heath, that will be
sufficient proof. Surely it's no criminal offence to give false
particulars of identity?'

'Yes it is. If false particulars are entered into an hotel registration book.'

'How do you know that I have? Have you been up there?'
'Yes.'[17]

Stumped by the cold, hard facts, Brook made no further
comment. At 9.15 p.m., Gates arrived back at the police
station and approached Brook, who was with DS Johnson.

'From my enquiries I am satisfied that you are Neville
George Clevely Heath. Wanted for interview by the

Metropolitan Police in connection with the murder of Margery Gardner during the night of the 20 June 1946. You will be detained until officers arrive from London.'

Heath simply replied, 'Oh. All right.'

Johnson now began to enter Brook's details onto the charge sheet and asked Gates what name he should write. 'Should I enter the name of Brook?'

Gates advised, 'He *says* his name is Rupert Robert Brook, use that unless he prefers his proper name.'

Johnson asked what name the suspect himself would prefer to be entered on the charge sheet?

'Oh. Heath. Neville George Clevely-Heath. The surname should be hyphenated.'

At 10 p.m. Johnson took Heath's trousers to check for evidence and gave him a substitute pair. Gates then presented Heath with the return half of Doreen's railway ticket.

'This ticket was in your jacket pocket. Can you tell me how you became possessed of it?'

Thinking quickly, he said, 'I found it in the lounge at the Tollard Royal Hotel.'

'When and where?'

'On a seat in the lounge on Thursday last.'[18]

It was a plausible answer – he'd admitted he had sat with Doreen in the lounge on Wednesday and she might have simply dropped the ticket from her handbag.

At about 10.30 p.m., Gates asked him whether he would be able to make a statement regarding Doreen Marshall's disappearance. Heath replied that he would. In some contrast to his earlier off-hand attitude, he started writing this statement with great care at 11.50 p.m. and was still writing and examining his statement when Spooner's car arrived at Bournemouth at 1.30 a.m. the next morning.

Leaving him to finish the statement, Spooner and Symes were greeted by several members of the Bournemouth police including Gates, Suter and Johnson. They were handed the suitcase which Gates had recovered from the railway station. Examining it, Spooner found three leather luggage labels with the names *Capt N. G. C. Heath, Major N. G. C. Heath* and *Captain J. R. C. Armstrong*. The latter had *N. G. C. Heath London* written on the reverse.[19] As well as the blood-stained whip, there was a blue woollen scarf with traces of blood and nasal slime as well as a blue neckerchief, also blood-stained – both of which had been used for tying.[20]

Spooner and Symes went directly to the Tollard Royal and searched Room 81, going through all Heath's belongings. Significant among his possessions were his flying helmet and an escape scarf that had been used as a tie. Some khaki webbing straps with no obvious purpose were also found. Spooner and Symes also recovered an extraordinary number of handkerchiefs – forty-nine in all. Most of these were womens' and bore traces of lipstick.[21] Many were mono-grammed. In the middle drawer of the dressing table, Spooner discovered a handkerchief that had been tied into a knot and had recently been cut with a knife – on it were traces of blood and soil, as if it had been dragged across the ground. This bore the letters A. R. M., the first three letters of Neville Heath's South African alias, Armstrong. Also in this drawer were two pieces of string that had been freshly cut.[22]

At 3 a.m. DS Johnson met Spooner in the CID office and gave him Heath's jacket. From the left-hand pocket, Spooner recovered some things that hadn't been noticed before – a caterpillar badge and a single artificial pearl, as if from a ladies' necklace.[23] Once Heath's statement about the disappearance of Doreen Marshall had been completed, at 5.20 a.m., Reg Spooner finally came face to face with the man who had filled his days and sleepless nights since 21 June.

'You are Heath?'

'Yes.'

'I am investigating the murder of Margery Gardner in your room at the Pembridge Court Hotel on the night of the 20–21 June last. I think you are in a position to give me some information about it.'

'Yes, I will make a statement after I have had some sleep. I was there but I am not admitting I did it.'

Heath was allowed to sleep until 8 a.m. They were then driven back to London, with Heath sitting in the back of the Wolseley between Spooner and Symes, speaking very little and occasionally dozing. When he did speak, Heath addressed Symes, the more junior officer to whom he was handcuffed. He never spoke directly to Spooner. Arriving in Notting Hill at 11.25 that morning, Spooner reminded Heath that he had said he would make a statement about the murder of Margery Gardner. Heath said he was willing to make a statement, but wanted time to think the matter over. At 3 p.m., Spooner challenged Heath with the letter he had sent to Scotland Yard.

'Did you write this letter to Superintendent Barratt?'

'Yes.'

'In it you refer to the instrument used on the woman Margery Gardner and you say you are forwarding it to the Yard. Did you do so?'

'No.'

'Where is it?'

'It's in one of my cases. I'll get it later on.'

'I will get it for you so you can see if it is the one you mean.'

'There's no need, it is the one.'

Spooner fetched the whip and presented it to Heath.

'That's it.'

'Do you wish to continue with your statement?'

'I am still thinking about it and I'm tired.'

Spooner left, returning later that evening. He wanted

Heath to account for his movements during the night of 20–21 June, but after co-operating for a while, Heath said he realized the gravity of his position. He didn't want to say more until he had taken legal advice after he had been charged – and he was certain now that he would be charged. Spooner left him at 8 p.m. Throughout the day, Shelley Symes had been taking notes of everything Heath had said. Heath looked through this statement repeatedly, paragraph by paragraph. Finally he signed it.

At 12.30 on Monday morning, Heath was led into the billiards room at Notting Hill Police Station by Inspector James Stone and placed in an identity parade with eleven other men of similar age, height and build. He was allowed to take any position and chose to stand sixth from the right. Spooner and Symes were also present, as observers only.

Harold Harter, the taxi driver, was asked to take a good look at all the men, and then to touch the man he had picked up with Margery Gardner outside the Panama Club.[24] Without hesitation, Harter went straight to Heath and touched him on the chest with his right hand. Stone asked if he had any doubt, but Harter was clear: 'That is the man.' Harter was then escorted out of the building. Stone asked if Heath would like to change his position before the next witness arrived, but Heath just shook his head. Solomon Josephs, the receptionist of the Panama Club, was brought into the billiards room and again, Stone asked him to touch the person that he recognized in connection with the case. Again, with no hesitation, Josephs walked directly to Heath and touched him on the chest. Immediately after Heath had been positively identified by Harter and Josephs, Spooner approached him again.

'You know who I am. I am now going to charge you with murdering Margery Aimee Brownell Gardner at the Pembridge Court Hotel during the night of Thursday to Friday, 20 to 21 June 1946.'

Spooner then cautioned him. Heath simply said, 'I have nothing to say at the moment.'[25]

At West London Magistrates' Court, the matrimonial court that was in session that afternoon was cancelled and the courtroom opened to the public. Crowds were already gathered around the court building when Heath arrived in a police car, handcuffed to Shelley Symes and smoking a pipe. He appeared before Paul Bennett, and was charged with the murder of Margery Gardner. He was remanded until 23 July. Asked if he required legal aid, he refused, saying, 'I think I can manage it, sir.'[26] After the hearing he fumbled for his pipe and puffed on it composedly as he was driven through the crowds back to Brixton Prison.

Early that evening, Reg Spooner sat down to write to his wife and daughter. They were currently away on the aborted family holiday that he had promised they would take together when he was demobilized.

> *At last success has come in this job and only two hours ago I charged Heath with the murder of Margery Gardner. I have just returned from the police court after seeing him remanded. It has all been a tiresome and worrying business and what with the sudden dash to Bournemouth for him and other things my last night's sleep was the first since Friday night. Anyway, I daresay you have read about it all in the press. There is still an immense amount of work to be done in it, but at least we have the satisfaction of having got Heath – and there is more in it than is generally known although this morning's papers were making inferences. The job has done me quite a bit of good and I am getting congratulations from high and low.*
>
> *The press say it is one of the best stories for years.*[27]

With Heath under arrest, it was clear that the disappearance of Doreen Marshall was now a murder enquiry. Bournemouth police announced that they were not looking for anybody else in connection with the case. With no admission from Heath and Metropolitan Police enquiries focused on the murder in Notting Hill, they concentrated on searching the sea-front cliffs west of the Tollard Royal Hotel and the wooded chines leading down to the beach. Digby, Scotland Yard's famous bloodhound, was also engaged 'in the greatest hunt which the world-famed organization has ever known in its history'. But even Digby failed to sniff out any leads and gave up the chase, withdrawing 'in shame' to his home near Winchester.

> 'For the first time, I whipped him,' said his dispirited mistress, Miss Nina Elms, who, however, hopes that Digby will re-establish his fame as England's most foremost bloodhound.[28]

In London, wary of compromising the case against Heath, newspapers implied a connection between his arrest and Doreen's disappearance without actually stating it, with stories appearing side by side on the front page. But five days after she had last been seen, the whereabouts of Doreen Marshall's body eluded the police. With Heath now suspected to be a double murderer, the story of the blood-lust killer ignited the public's imagination and fuelled their hungry desire for sensational details of the case. But even the most hardened followers of the story cannot have been prepared for the shocking revelations soon to come.

CHAPTER EIGHTEEN
Branksome Dene Chine

7–8 JULY 1946

We generally describe the most repulsive examples of man's cruelty as brutal or bestial. Implying by these adjectives that such behaviour is characteristic of less highly developed animals than ourselves. In truth, however, the extremes of 'brutal' behaviour are confined to man; and there is no parallel in nature to our savage treatment of each other.

Anthony Storr, *Human Aggression*, 1968

Kathleen Evans was a cake-maker who lived with her parents in Pinewood Road, one of the well-to-do avenues at the top of Branksome Dene Chine.[1]

At about midday on Sunday 7 July, she took her dog for a run through the chine, aiming as usual for the beach. She entered the ravine through the Pinewood Road entrance, then adorned with an exotic Dragons' Teeth Gate, and walked half way down the main drive. She then branched over to the left, going down the steep steps into the chine itself. The ravine was densely covered with large pine trees and an undergrowth thick with rhododendron bushes, furze, bracken, heather and grass.

The spaniel then ran a long way ahead of her until she lost sight of him, but eventually she caught him up at a sandy cliff to the left. Miss Evans called the dog to her and carried on along the footpath towards the beach, coming to a spot with some bushes to the right and a hole in the ground to her left. The pathway began to narrow and it was at this point that Miss Evans noticed what she thought, at first, to be a swarm of bees buzzing around a bush of rhododendrons. Looking closer, she saw that the swarm of insects were not bees at all; they were flies.

Thinking that there must be 'something objectionable' in the bushes, she hurried on past, but noticed what seemed to be a dead fir bough propped against the bushes to her right. She thought no more about it.

However, on Monday morning, Miss Evans read the newspapers, which were full of Doreen Marshall, the 'girl in the dinner gown' who had 'vanished in the dark'. That evening, Miss Evans told her father about the swarm of flies she had seen in the chine the day before and asked if he would go with her to investigate.

Kathleen retraced her steps into the sloping ravine. The flies were still buzzing around the rhododendrons and Mr Evans peered into the bushes. Looking to the left, he couldn't see anything, but on the right he saw what appeared to be some clothing. Most distinctly he saw part of a yellow coat – just as had been described in the newspapers. Mr Evans and his daughter went to the telephone box at the mouth of the chine and called the police.

Given that Branksome Dene Chine was just outside

Bournemouth but within the Poole boundary, officers from both stations were sent to the chine, led by Detective Sergeant Bishop of the Dorset Constabulary, based at Poole Police Station. Approaching the chine from the beach, concrete steps led to a sandy footpath up the centre of the ravine. To the west was a refreshment pavilion with a hard road leading up to Pine Wood Road, north-west of the chine. The footpath led up the side of the valley to wicket gates at Cassel Avenue at the north end of the chine. Bishop entered from the promenade entrance, guided by Miss Evans and her father; together they walked about 150 yards up the central path from the sea. Bishop was led to what appeared to be a natural alcove, about 22 feet wide, enclosed on three sides by rhododendron bushes. A fir bough and some branches had been deliberately placed in front of the alcove. Hidden behind them, under the spur of rhododendrons forming the east side of the alcove, Bishop could clearly see a body.[2]

As it was now 8.40 p.m. and the light was already beginning to fade, Bishop decided to leave the body where it was until the next morning. The chine was closed to the public and a police guard was maintained throughout the night.

The next morning, several officers including Bishop visited the chine with Dr Crichton McGaffey, a pathologist from Somerset who practised in Taunton. Drawing back the fir bough and cutting away parts of the bush, the body was exposed to full view. The sight that met the police's eyes was so shocking that some officers vomited.

Doreen Marshall's body was in a grotesque position and had been horrifically mutilated. She was naked apart from her right shoe, lying on her left side with her head thrust forward. Her right arm was extended over her head and her left arm underneath her body. Her right leg was twisted over her left. A week since she had been killed, dried black blood covered her body, now crawling with thousands of maggots which had eaten deep into her wounds.

The body was to the right of the natural alcove formed by the rhododendrons. On the left, about seventeen feet away from the body, were two bloodstains twenty-six inches apart. This appeared to be the scene of the crime itself, just next to the pathway that led through the chine to Pinewood Road. Outside the bushes there were two similar bloodstains, also twenty-six inches apart, as if the body had been moved there, before Heath decided to further conceal the body beneath the rhododendrons. Near these bloodstains, Bishop recovered twenty-seven pearl beads that had been torn from a necklace. These were to match the single pearl that Spooner had discovered in Heath's jacket pocket.

By the stains under the bushes he found a stocking ripped in two. Near the body was the left shoe and fifteen feet away from it, Bishop found a handkerchief. Piled on Doreen's body were her clothes – her black evening gown had been pulled inside-out and her lemon-coloured swagger coat had been placed on top with the lining showing. A brassiere was on Doreen's shoulder. Underneath the coat was a corset belt, a sanitary towel and a pair of cami-knickers which had been torn. Another stocking was found in the bushes, about seven feet above the ground. Further towards the beach, Bishop came across a blue powder compact, the mirror slightly cracked – the gift from Doreen's sister.

The police continued to investigate the chine for clues, using axes and machetes to cut back the dense vegetation in the growing summer heat. Many officers were veterans of the Burma campaign and the work recalled their days in the steaming jungle.[3] Thirty yards from the body, the police recovered what they presumed to be another gruesome clue – a bunch of human hair. It had been permed, so had clearly come from a woman's head, and there was a substantial amount of it, perhaps three-quarters of a woman's head of hair. Some had been cut and some had been violently pulled out. Sent to Scotland Yard, the hair would not match Doreen Marshall's, leading the police to suspect that there may be another body hidden somewhere in the chine. Could this be the remains of 'Peggy', the girl Heath had mentioned in his statement, but who had so far not been traced? Press reports would ghoulishly hint that another woman's body lay in the chine – and that she had been scalped.[4]

As early as 7.30 a.m., holiday-makers, 'the majority of them women', in shorts, swimwear and sunhats crowded around the police cordon on the beach in the hope of glimpsing some of the horrors that rumours indicated had taken place in the chine. Children with buckets and spades also wandered up to the chine to see what the fuss was about. Later that morning, when Doreen's body was removed, the crowds lost interest in the murder scene and went back to sunbathing, eating ice-cream or making sand-castles on the beach.

Doreen's body was taken to Poole where her father identified her in the mortuary there. At 2.30, Crichton McGaffey proceeded with the post-mortem in the presence of Constable Bishop. The injuries that Doreen had sustained before and after her death indicated a frenzied sex attack of shocking brutality. Though she had fought bravely for her life, at only 5 feet 3 inches and with a small frame, she had been over-powered by Heath's powerful physique.

Doreen's throat had been savagely cut just above the larynx right to the back of her neck. The left carotid artery was completely severed, but the knife – the size of a fair-sized pocket knife – had been stopped by the spinal column. A second cut just above the first was not so deep and stopped short at the midline of the girl's throat. Both these cuts were inflicted whilst Doreen was still alive and had resulted in her

bleeding to death. But there was a catalogue of other terrible
injuries that had been caused both before and after her death
that revealed an appalling level of violence.[5]

There were a number of bruises to the back of Doreen's
head and her left temple, as well as some abrasions to her
right cheekbone, as if she had been battered about the head
and punched in the face. She had been gagged and bound.
There were nail imprints and bruising around both wrists
where they had been tightly tied together. Her fingers had a
series of V-shaped cuts that indicated that she had fought
desparately to fend off a knife attack by grabbing hold of the
blade. These wounds cut right down to the bone.

Above the soft parts of the larynx where the knife later cut
through, there was a swelling that had been caused by pressure from a soft instrument, such as the penis. In all probability, like Yvonne Symonds, Doreen had been a virgin, but
Heath had extended her none of the sensitivity that Yvonne
had been fortunate enough to receive. There was a bruise on
the right shoulder and an area of redness above and below the
left collarbone, denoting some pressure, probably from
Heath's knee. Some of her ribs had been broken and splin-
tered, puncturing her left lung. These injuries might have
resulted from Doreen being forcefully pinned to the ground
and her squirming under Heath's considerable weight of 171 lb
as he raped her, undoing the gag in order to force himself
into her mouth, pinning her down with his knee.

There was a large area of abrasion of the skin between the
two shoulder blades. On the left side of the back, below the
shoulder blades there were horizontal abrasions and corresponding abrasions at the back of the left arm. These were
possibly due to Doreen being dragged across the ground,
naked, whilst still alive.

Having dragged her further into the undergrowth, he then
released her hands, cutting the handkerchief at this point with

the knife – possibly with the intention of forcing her to do further sexual acts under duress.

At the back of the neck were two stricture marks. These were horizontal, about an inch apart, as if an attempt had been made to strangle her, possibly with the webbing straps or lengths of freshly cut string that had been found in Heath's possession. Doreen had suffered all of these injuries before Heath had slashed her throat and killed her. The final moments of her life in a dark and lonely woodland by the beach must have been terrifying.

After she had been killed, Doreen's body had been subjected to a series of mutilations of animal savagery. The right nipple had been bitten off. There was a deep cut extending diagonally across the right breast below the nipple, sloping down towards the middle. A second cut above the nipple joined the first cut below. There were similar injuries to the left breast, the left nipple having been savaged and torn until it was hanging off. Most shocking of all was a long deep cut running vertically up the front of the body, starting below the genitals from the inner thigh upwards. The blade had reached deep into the muscle one and a half inches from the surface of the skin. The cut extended up to a line joining the nipples. This long cut was done in four brutal strokes with Heath positioned by Doreen's left shoulder. There were also injuries to the genitals. The vagina and anus had been perforated and the skin between them had been torn to a depth of three inches from the surface. These injuries had been made by a rough instrument – possibly a branch – with extreme brutality.

The police puzzled how Heath had managed to persuade a sensible, respectable girl like Doreen to such an isolated spot in order to carry out his intentions. At the Tollard Royal, Doreen had been very clear that she wanted to go straight home, but somehow Heath had succeeded in coaxing her to walk down the zigzag path in front of the hotel and down to the beach. The lights of the pier – and safety – were only a minute away to the east. But Heath persuaded Doreen to walk a mile in the opposite direction from her hotel towards the Bournemouth chines. It is clear from Yvonne Symonds' statements that Heath was extremely persuasive (she recalled that he 'over-persuaded' her to sleep with him) and he may well have resorted to this tried-and-tested strategy, suggesting to Doreen that they get married. This impulsive romantic suggestion in the middle of the summer night may have convinced Doreen to accompany Heath towards Branksome Dene Chine – an area he knew from his walks with Peter Rylatt. The chines nearer to Bournemouth and closer to the Tollard Royal were more developed and less suitable for lovers' meetings. Having failed to persuade Doreen to go up to his room at the hotel (as he had failed to do with Peggy Waring), Heath's objective may well have been to seduce Doreen in the chine. Having walked her along the beach, he then suggested that they go into the chine. In doing so he had either lied that it was a shortcut back to Bournemouth or he had already succeeded in persuading her to have sex with him.[6] Even today in daylight the chine feels dark and isolated – in the middle of the night it must have seemed extremely forbidding to Doreen, but she had her air force pilot to protect her.

Most of her clothes were later found undamaged, so either she removed them herself or Heath had done so. As with Pauline Brees at the Strand Palace Hotel, he might have battered Doreen about the head to stun her, then stripped her, pulling her dress inside-out as he did so, ripping her cami-knickers and discarding the sanitary towel. He had then stripped himself naked. He bound her hands tightly, probably with the handkerchief that Spooner had found in the dressing-table drawer of Heath's hotel room. At the same time he had gagged her in order to prevent her calling for help.[7] He then dragged her further into the dense under-growth of the alcove and further away from any possibility of escape.

Having killed Doreen and mutilated her body, Heath then set about trying to hide it. Nearby a match was found; it seems Heath may have smoked after he killed her, reflecting on what he had done. Not satisfied with his first concealment of the body, Heath then moved it seventeen feet to the east of the alcove. Before doing this he took the diamond ring from her finger and the fob watch from her coat. He then covered her body with her clothes and concealed it with branches of pine and rhododendron.

After the murder, Heath was covered in blood. Still naked, he bathed himself in the sea to wash the blood away, perhaps drying himself with his shirt and underwear, which he would later try to burn in the grate of his room at the hotel. At this point he may have dropped the murder weapon in the sea, as it was never recovered. He then picked up Doreen's handbag and hurried from the chine, leaving behind him the handkerchief that he had gagged her with. Fifty yards towards the beach he opened the bag to search it, discarding the blue powder compact, possibly because he saw that it was cracked and worthless. He proceeded along the promenade as far as Alum Chine. Here he took out Doreen's pigskin wallet containing her money and clothing coupons, her fountain pen and penknife. Pocketing these, he threw the handbag over the beach huts where it was later discovered by the schoolboy.[8]

By the time he had reached the foot of the zigzag path leading up to the Tollard Royal Hotel, he had second thoughts about keeping Doreen's possessions, so he dropped the penknife. He then climbed up the ladder outside his room and went to bed where he was discovered at 4.30 in the morning sleeping deeply as if he had nothing to disturb his dreams.

What had triggered Heath's murderous frenzy in Branksome Dene Chine that night? Not every sexual relationship he had with women ended in sadistic violence. He had slept with Yvonne Symonds *after* the death of Margery Gardner and she claimed he only ever treated her gently. He had been drinking on the night he killed Doreen – brandy and a magnum of champagne – but nowhere near as much as he had on the night he killed Margery Gardner. Heath's own version of events, like his version of the events of 20 June, offer no clue to the inspiration for the attack.

> I have no recollection of going anywhere near Branksome Chine. The next thing I recall is lighting a cigarette. As I was flicking the match away I saw blood on my hands. I knew I had left the hotel with Doreen Marshall. But I did not know where she was or what had happened. Something dreadful, I was sure. I was at the lower end of the promenade, on the soft sand. I stood still and tried to think what to do. I had her watch and some other things in my possession. How late it was I did not know. But everything was quiet. I must have walked towards the hotel. Looking up at a window with a light in it I saw a woman standing there in her nightdress. I had washed my hands with seawater but I did not feel like talking to anyone, even the companionable porter. So I climbed a ladder to get into my room by the window. Again I felt the cold and calculating feeling I had felt while shaving at Notting Hill Gate.[9]

The police in London were now considering if the death of Margery Gardner could be explained as a drunken sexual tryst gone wrong. If this was not the case, then her death seemed completely without motive. But how to explain this second, even more brutal murder, committed when Heath knew he was wanted all over the country?

> If you had read such things in fiction you would throw the book aside, would you not, and said, 'That is impossible. It does not happen. If a man has once committed a crime like this he does not go straight off and commit another crime of a similar and even more awful character at a time when he knows that the police are hunting for him, when he has seen his name in the paper day after day.'[10]

Why had Heath killed Doreen when he had spent all afternoon and all evening with her in front of dozens of witnesses?

Almost immediately her death was reported, the *Daily Mirror* suggested that Heath did have a very clear motive in killing Doreen.[11] Had he deliberately sought out a victim as a potential defence for the murder of Margery Gardner? The extraordinary brutality of the second murder could establish him as mentally unbalanced and enable him to make a plea of 'guilty but insane' at his trial. Had he consciously set out to butcher Doreen Marshall – conjuring images of Jack the Ripper – in order to save himself from the gallows?

Throughout his life, even from his early childhood, Heath had committed a series of crimes and misdemeanours that he had succeeded in getting away with unpunished. He was given the benefit of the doubt on countless occasions by his parents, the police, magistrates and senior officers, all of whom had been seduced by his infectious charm, his good manners and his handsome face.

Was the killing of Doreen Marshall the biggest gamble of Heath's life – an audacious attempt to get away, this time, with murder?

PART FOUR

The Twisting of Another Rope

CHAPTER NINETEEN

3923

9 JULY – 23 SEPTEMBER 1946

Brixton Prison

9th July 1946

My dear Mother,

I cannot express how I feel about the sorrow and misery which I must have caused you all. For my own part I don't care what happens. I have never really cared since I lost Elizabeth and Rob. I got interested in life again a few months ago but that was quickly squashed by the fact that having made a few slips the Air Ministry refused to let me forge ahead again and refused to grant me my 'B' licence. I'd worked damned hard for that licence and was disappointed by their decision.

Newspaper reports are all very inaccurate and quite amusing. The one of my arrest was priceless. I was supposed to be in the Botanical

Gardens sniffing the roses — like Ferdinand the bull. Actually I walked into the police station to see them quite voluntary on a very different matter and they almost didn't recognize me.

They've kept all my money and clothes at the police station with the usual rash promise that they'll be sent on later. I'd be grateful if you could send me some cigarettes and tobacco and matches and some money to buy a few things. I'm in the hospital here which is quite comfortable. Had the offer of legal aid from the court but refused it. I've no intention of accepting charity and I've no intention of paying for any counsel.

I'm prepared to give an exclusive story to any one newspaper in return for their briefing counsel on my behalf and paying me a certain amount of money. Such a course of action would enable me to pay all my debts and it is the only manner in which I'll accept any legal aid so don't employ a solicitor on my behalf. The newspapers print anything and everything so one of them might just as well have an authentic version. If you can enquire whether the 'Mail' is at all interested. I would be pleased should they accept my offer. I shall be prepared to make a statement to Det Insptr Spooner of the Yard and to a representative of the newspaper at the same time. I feel Spooner will be pleased to have the statement as there is an awful lot he doesn't know. I think I know where the missing link is too so they may like to know something about it. But if the newspapers wish to write me up they may as well pay for the privilege. I want £500 and legal aid. That sum will just about clear all my debts. I've no objection to Insp Spooner being informed of this by you. He'll be at Notting Hill Gate Police Station I expect. Don't worry too much about me it isn't really worth it. Concentrate on keeping Mick on the straight and narrow. Please don't come to see me — I know you'll hate it.

All my love as ever,
Yours truly,
Nen[1]

Heath, now Prisoner Number 3923, sent this letter to his mother the day after Doreen Marshall's mutilated body was found in Bournemouth. As Heath's letters were being intercepted by the Home Office, Spooner was subsequently sent to visit him in Brixton Prison, accompanied by Shelley Symes. Heath had made no admission about the murders and Spooner was keen to hear what he had to say.

When Spooner arrived he met, for the first time, Heath's newly appointed solicitor, Isaac Near of Raymond, Near & Co., a firm based in Holborn. Near had been recommended to Heath by one of his flying colleagues, most probably Ralph Fisher. He had been practising as a solicitor since 1932 and had bought the firm Raymond's in 1936. In 1939 he had been called up to the Royal Navy Volunteer Reserve and thereafter found it a strain keeping the practice afloat, particularly after 1944 when his offices in Warwick Court had been destroyed by enemy action. Near proved to be a reliable and trustworthy ally throughout the trial and beyond. A rogue very much cut from the same cloth as Heath, in 1951 he would be struck off for 'conduct unbecoming a solicitor', having embezzled some of his clients' money.[2]

When Spooner was taken to the interview room to meet him, Heath affected surprise.[3] He said he hadn't asked to see Spooner at all. Spooner emphasized that the only reason he had come to Brixton was because Heath had specifically suggested that he wanted to talk to him. Heath demanded to know where Spooner had got this information from, but Spooner told him he wasn't at liberty to say – given that Heath's letters were being vetted and censored, with copies of everything he wrote and received sent to the Home Office and the prison authorities. Heath refused to discuss the matter further and Spooner left Brixton bemused.

The letter also caused anxiety amongst the prison authorities and the Home Office.[4] Heath was not allowed to sell his

life story and it had already been explained to him that legal
aid was available if he needed it. This Heath refused to accept.
In the end his legal fees were met by his family, with the help
of the money he eventually secured for selling his story to the
press. Almost as soon as he arrived at Brixton he was contacted
by Leslie Terry, whom he barely knew, having only met him
on the day of Margery Gardner's death. Terry visited Heath
several times and volunteered to find somebody to pay for his
defence, but Heath was well aware that Terry would need
something in return; his life story to sell to the newspapers.

> *I don't care two hoots whether I'm defended or not, but I am prepared*
> *to give any newspaper the full facts in exchange for certain*
> *payment . . . if they agree to my terms they can have anything from*
> *me that I can give them. If they don't, well I couldn't care less . . .*
> *I'm not prepared to argue or bargain, I'm much too tired . . . I*
> *honestly don't give a damn what happens to me. I have faced death*
> *too often in the past six years to worry about it. Anyway, I've noth-*
> *ing left to live for since I lost my wife and child.*[5]

Heath wanted £400 for his story – and no haggling. The
police were aware of Terry's criminal background ('a most
undesirable person')[6] and observed his negotiations with
Heath carefully. Heath said he particularly wanted the money
to pay back his outstanding debts to his father.

On 16 July, on narrowly lined war standard paper he wrote
two pages, outlining his life story, the blackouts he had
suffered in South Africa and the breakdown of his marriage.[7]
The document was clearly intended for publication. But
when Near visited Heath in prison to collect the document,
it was confiscated by the warder. Near then challenged the
Home Office to return the document as he argued that it was
essential for Heath's defence. Theobald Mathew, the Director
of Public Prosecutions, advised the governor at Brixton that

they couldn't very well withhold the document, but that
Heath and his legal team must be warned that it was not to be
published.[8] In the end, a deal was brokered by Leslie Terry
for Heath's story to appear in the *Sunday Pictorial*, as Heath's
favoured option, the *Daily Mail*, weren't interested.[9] Though
he never made a full statement, he managed to tell much of
his story in a series of letters to Terry and his other friends.
These letters formed the basis for the story that appeared in
the *Sunday Pictorial* over three weekends after the trial was
over. The document Heath wrote in prison was to surface
again at a contentious point during the trial itself.

As a prisoner on remand, Heath was presumed innocent
until proven guilty, so was allowed certain privileges. As well
as his legal team, he was allowed visits from his family and
friends and met them in a room 12 feet square, but always
supervised by warders. Generally he got on very well with
the staff at the prison and called the governor 'the boss', just
as if he were back in an RAF mess. He was lodged in the
prison hospital on a ward he shared with ten other prisoners.
His day began at 7.30 with breakfast served in a mess room
next to the ward. He was then shaved by the prison barber,
inmates not being allowed to shave themselves with cut-
throat razors. Afterwards he took an hour of exercise in the
flower-bordered hospital grounds. He could send and receive
censored letters[10] and corresponded with dozens of his friends
and family as well as with his solicitor.[11] The letters are generally upbeat, full of RAF slang, banter and self-deprecating
humour, not at all the tone of a man whose life was in jeopardy. He received one letter from Doreen Marshall's parents
in Pinner, but didn't respond to it.[12] He was also able to keep
in touch with life in the outside world with an allowance of
two newspapers a day, which he hungrily scanned for articles
about himself. He was also an avid reader of novels and magazines – society glossies and flying journals that were sent in by

friends like Ralph Fisher and Leslie Terry.[13] He particularly requested copies of *Esquire*, *Life*, *Tatler* and the *Illustrated London News*. Though the prison library was good, he thought many of the books were too serious or American, 'which grates a bit'. He preferred one-shilling paperback novels: 'light stuff', adventure stories, mysteries and thrillers. Any books he was sent from friends were vetted by the prison chaplain. All but one of the books he requested – with titles like *Bring the Bride a Shroud* and *Call the Lady Indiscreet* – were banned. Mostly he chain-smoked, smoking 200 cigarettes (Players, Churchman or Players No. 3) and half a pound of tobacco a week. Time went by very slowly for him at Brixton and in many of his letters his primary complaint was boredom: he was 'browned off with inactivity ... It's all this waiting that is so depressing. And wearing prison clothes doesn't do one's morale much good.'[14]

But the mundane routine at Brixton was broken up by his various appearances at West London Magistrates' Court. He appeared five times throughout July and August, travelling to and from Brixton in a Black Maria. Throughout the hearings, Heath said nothing but doodled on prison notepaper as he heard the events in Notting Hill and Bournemouth described. At his appearance on 29 July Heath was formally charged by Detective Sergeant Bishop from Poole of the murder of Doreen Marshall. He said, 'Nothing to say.' On 13 August, witnesses were called from both Bournemouth and Notting Hill, including Charles Marshall. One by one, Doreen's possessions were handed around the police court. Heath looked on as his defence counsel held up the penknife and showed it to Doreen's father.

'Are you sure about this knife?' he asked.

'Yes. Certain,' replied Mr Marshall.

'Why are you so sure?'

Mr Marshall explained to the bench, 'I know it so well. It

was a prize for ice-skating. She had a fountain pen to match it. Her name was inscribed on the fountain pen, but not on the knife. I am quite sure that knife is the one.'[15]

There was a moment's silence. Mr Marshall and the man who had murdered his daughter stared at each other for a second across the court. The last time they had met was at Bournemouth Police Station when Heath had reassured Mr Marshall that there was nothing to worry about, that his daughter would be found safe and well. Heath dropped his gaze quickly and shuffled uneasily on the fixed seat.

At these preliminary hearings only the case for the prosecution was heard with Heath reserving his defence. This meant that all the shocking details of the two crimes were now public knowledge and reported feverishly in the press, months before Heath would appear at the Old Bailey to offer his defence. Unable to publish the most graphic details of the killings, most of the reporters on the press bench laid down their pencils and stared ahead of them in stunned silence. Heath carried on doodling.[16]

At every appearance at the police court, large crowds queued for hours in order to get a glimpse of him.

As with so many crimes of violence, especially where the coarser and darker aspects of the sex-motive are concerned, the court-rooms were thronged with onlookers, mostly women, many of them 'teen-agers'. Outside the Police Court were mobs of eager sensationalists, elbowing and jostling, and some standing on walls, or tops of air-raid shelters: a trenchant manifestation of modern times and manners.[17]

Extra police were drafted in order to deal with the crowds. When a police officer refused admission to one woman, she began to cry and shouted, 'I must see Heath. I have come all the way from Golders Green!'[18]

During Heath's appearances at West London Magistrates' Court, Bernard Tussaud, the great-great-grandson of the wax museum's founder, spent three weeks observing Heath in the dock. As neither photography nor sketching was permitted in the court, he had to draw Heath's image after each court hearing from memory. The wax figure would take six weeks to make. If Heath were found not guilty or reprieved, the figure would be melted down and the wax used again.

As he prepared for his trial at the Old Bailey, Heath was very keen to get a 'decent suit'. He sent magazine cuttings of the suits he liked and took his own measurements as he wanted it to be a good fit. In the end, friends bought him an off-the-peg suit for £20 with a grey chalk stripe and some new underwear – all with Heath's clothing coupons.

Isaac Near then instructed the esteemed defence KC, J. D. Casswell, to defend Heath. Sixty-year-old Casswell had been born and raised in Wimbledon, not far from the home of the Heath family, and had come to prominence professionally in 1913 in the case of negligence brought against the Oceanic Steam Navigation Company (the parent company of the White Star Line) by relatives of several passengers who had perished on the *Titanic*. The jury found the captain to be negligent and each of the relatives received £100 compensation. Casswell then saw action in France during the First World War, but was invalided out of the army in 1917 with an eye condition. He had defended several high-profile murder defendants – forty by the end of his career – only five of whom were subsequently executed. In 1935 he had defended Percy Stoner in the murder of Francis Rattenbury in Bournemouth. Stoner was reprieved following an appeal. Perhaps most famously in 1944, he had defended Elizabeth Marina Jones, the eighteen-year-old waitress who had accompanied US Army deserter Karl Hulten on a spree of violence culminating in the murder of a taxi driver on the

Great West Road. The case became known as the Cleft Chin Murder – a sensation at the time and the story that provoked George Orwell to write his essay, *Decline of the English Murder*. Though Hulten was executed Casswell managed to secure a reprieve for Jones. She was released from prison in 1954.[19]

Casswell was known for his charm, imperturbability and doggedness and had some of the rhetorical gifts of Marshall Hall, 'the great defender', with perhaps an even better knowledge of the law. Before taking the brief, Casswell discussed the case with an eminent psychologist colleague who declared on the basic facts that Heath was 'mad as a hatter from a doctor's point of view'. But Casswell worried from the start, that though this might be true in medical terms, he was not sure that it could be proved that Heath was as mad as a hatter in the terms of the law. This astute comment was to prove true and the sole debate at Heath's trial was focused on this issue.

When Casswell was shown into the interview room at Brixton to meet his client for the first time, he immediately mistook the man he was presented with for a member of the prison staff, thinking to himself, 'What good-looking chaps they're recruiting as warders these days.' Casswell thought Heath a 'good-looking young man with a splendid physique and an attractive and charming manner ... he certainly looked the opposite of the popular image of a sexual maniac.'[20] After Casswell had introduced himself, Heath's first question was directly to the point.

'Why shouldn't I plead guilty?'

'You've a father and mother and brother, all alive. Do you want it said that a man in his right mind could commit two such brutal crimes?'

Heath reflected for a moment.

'All right,' he said. 'Put me down as Not Guilty, old boy.'[21]

Casswell felt from this first meeting that Heath was

indifferent to whether he lived or died. Whatever the press speculated, Casswell dismissed any suggestion that Heath had murdered Doreen Marshall deliberately in order to try and secure a life sentence in Broadmoor. If anything, Heath seemed to have a death wish and his half-hearted attempts to engage with a medical enquiry Casswell felt were purely for the benefit of Heath's family.

At the same time, the Director of Public Prosecution was instructing the case for the Crown. Anthony Hawke, a 51-year-old senior Treasury counsel and veteran of several murder trials, was appointed as leading counsel for the prosecution. Under the terms of English law, Heath could only be tried for one indictment at a time. It was up to the prosecution to decide which murder he would be tried for first. In discussion with Theobald Mathew, Hawke felt that there was more chance of getting a conviction if Heath were tried for the murder of Margery Gardner. The murder of Doreen Marshall looked like the savageries of a lunatic and might give the defence the opportunity to plead insanity.

During his time on remand, as Casswell and Hawke prepared their cases, Heath was questioned by several medical officers, including Dr William Henry de Bargue Hubert, who was to be called on behalf of the defence. Dr Hubert Young, the senior medical officer at Wormwood Scrubs and Dr Hugh Grierson, the senior medical officer at Brixton were to be called as expert witnesses for the prosecution.

Dr Young had various meetings with Heath whom he found very polite and personable, being particularly proud of his flying career and claiming that he had a 'fighter pilot temperament'. He was completely unwilling to discuss the charges. He didn't dispute the facts and didn't see how he possibly could. He said that he had originally decided to give himself up to the police, hence the letter to Barratt about sending in the riding whip, but then changed his mind. When he was arrested he had at first intended to plead guilty and though Casswell had persuaded him not to, he told Dr Young that he was still unsure if it was the right decision. He admitted that for some time before the murders, 'he had been conscious of an impulse to react in a certain way in his sexual relationships'.[22] He wouldn't divulge to Dr Young what this impulse was due to, but said he had tried to explain it to Dr Hubert in strict confidence after they had been talking for three hours. Young felt that the reason for Heath's unwillingness to discuss the crimes had something to do with his marriage.[23]

Dr Grierson from Brixton had interviewed Bessie Heath who admitted that her son was highly strung as a boy but that he was a kind, not a cruel person, fond of children and animals. She thought he had been particularly upset in the RAF after seeing an airman have his head cut off by a propeller. In her opinion, her son wasn't insane but she thought that 'his brain must have gone'.[24]

Heath told Dr Grierson that he didn't want to talk about the charge and denied any abnormal state of mind at the time of the murders, adding – as he had done with Dr Young – that he could, if he so wished, give an account of all his actions but he didn't wish to do so. He didn't explain why he was unwilling to discuss it, either. Though he seemed unemotional it was evident to Grierson that Heath kept his feelings under strict control. He denied any abnormality in his sex life or of ever having performed any unnatural sex acts. When Grierson specifically questioned him about any sadistic impulses, in spite of the evidence of the two killings, Heath denied that he ever had any. This was supported when Reg Spooner interviewed many of the women that Heath had slept with, none of whom 'spoke of perverse conduct'. Mr Friedman, Heath's wife's solicitor, also confirmed that as far as Elizabeth knew, Heath had never shown 'any sexual or

violent tendencies'.[25] When asked about the incident in the
Strand Palace Hotel with Pauline Brees and her claim that he
had said 'I hate women', Heath had nothing to say. Grierson
felt that he was continually on his guard, even about matters
not directly concerned with the charge. When Grierson
attempted to discuss Heath's sexual relations with his wife
and whether this might have had an influence on his later
conduct, Heath was particularly unforthcoming.

Throughout his time on remand, the issue of his wife and
child in South Africa played heavily on his mind. 'I'd rather
not defend the charge at all than have them undergo any
publicity,' he wrote in one letter. 'Look at it logically, and
you'll see that any publicity of this nature will ruin the
child's life.'[26]

He took a keen interest in how the case was reported in
the South African press and even threatened to take legal
action against those that he felt misreported the story.
Following his appearances in the police court, Elizabeth and
her son were soon pursued by the press in Johannesburg.
Journalists began phoning her home in Forest Town twenty-
four hours a day in the hope of getting an exclusive story.

> I am tired of living this haunted existence. I am tired of
> dodging photographers and being tracked down by report-
> ers; tired of offers to sell my life story. I am a normal person
> who has done nothing to merit notoriety. What happened
> in my life was something over which I had no control. I had
> only two months of married life, so there really is nothing
> for me to tell. Ninety per cent of our marriage and divorce
> we were apart.[27]

Elizabeth and her son left Johannesburg with her new fiancé
to a secret address 'somewhere in the heart of the big game
country near the Portuguese Mozambique border',[28] where

they would stay until the furore surrounding the trial had died down.

In the heaviest Old Bailey calendar for years, Heath's trial was announced as Case No. 72[29] and was scheduled to take place in the week beginning 23 September. It was expected to last four days.

One of the witnesses called on behalf of the defence was William Spurrett Fielding-Johnson, Heath's former squadron leader. His testimony, recorded by Isaac Near, discussed the breakdown Heath had in 1944. But Fielding-Johnson was never to appear at the Old Bailey. Days before he was to give evidence, he had a heart attack. He was rushed to hospital and though he survived, his evidence was never heard.

The trial would continue without it.

CHAPTER TWENTY
Mrs Armstrong

14 SEPTEMBER 1946

Number 3923 Name N. Heath

Brixton Prison

Mrs Elizabeth Armstrong
15, Epping Road,
Forest Town
Johannesburg
Transvaal
South Africa

Elizabeth, my dear,
I said that I would never write to you again, but under the circum-stances I hope you will read this last letter.

I cannot explain what has happened — you will undoubtedly

*know as much as I do about it – and the South African newspapers
have printed many (untrue) reports and covered themselves with the
word 'alleged'.*

*In the face of the evidence I cannot deny these two offences, but to
me it still seems fantastically unbelievable. By the time you get this
letter it will all be over and I do sincerely hope that I am awarded the
maximum sentence.*

*It was originally my intention of forwarding no defence, but now
it has been impressed upon me that I should tell the true story for my
family's sake, if nothing else. I am assisted by the finest counsel
obtainable in the country.*

*I am certain in my mind what the sentence will be, but my object
in offering a defence against the charges is not to get a lighter sentence
– I should hate that – but to make it abundantly clear, for the sake
of the few people for whom I have a deep regard, that I did not set
out to cold bloodedly commit two vile murders. That I am responsible, I shall never deny and I'm quite prepared to pay the piper.*

*A letter or word from you whilst I have been here, would have
meant more than anything else to me, but I can quite understand
your point of view in not writing.*

*I have reason to believe that the current opinion in Johannesburg
is that I deserted you and then blackmailed your father into a
divorce for sums varying from £2,000 upwards. All of this as you
well know is complete and absolute nonsense and I shall never
believe that <u>you</u> started this vile rumour. I have my own views as
to the source, but have asked my solicitors, through their
Johannesburg agents, to make a thorough enquiry. I, personally,
can find a great deal of ironic humour in the report, when I think
of those days when I begged you not to leave me. One thing is
certain, and it is that had I not left Training Command in South
Africa to go on 'ops' none of this last eighteen months of hell would
have occurred. Anyway, what is done is done and nothing can
repair the harm now. I blame nobody except myself.*

Liz, my dear, do you remember the last time I saw Rob? I don't think you ever realized – or will ever realize, just what that moment meant to me. I always had some hope that you would not go through with the divorce and that you would return to me. On that day I must have realized that you were so completely under your family's domination, that nothing would change your mind or alter your decision. From that time onwards, nothing was clear to me and I could view nothing in its true perspective. Hate, animosity, revenge, a hundred and one feelings completely alien to my real self consumed my entire being. Life without you and Robby was just empty. Now, thank God, it is almost over. Since we parted, I know I've laughed a lot and been on parties etc, but the whole time there was that terrible feeling of hollow mockery in the background which made my entire existence miserably unbearable.

Always, across my mind, there has been a vision of you, or a blurred picture of Robby playing so happily in the garden with the dogs and then that frightening feeling of emptiness and frustration when I realized I should never see either of you again.

Life for me during the last eighteen months has been plain hell and I shall be glad when it's over.

Now, at last, I can look back upon those years of perfect happiness with you. Bloemfontein at [Central Flying School] *with that awful cold hotel – Greystones – the 'Rambles', with those enormous teas – The Bloemfontein Hotel and those early morning drives to the Aerodrome in that little open car which we both froze in so regularly – Randfontein and our house there. The chaps who used to come and stay with us – the parties we had there and at the Aerodrome – The way you cried the night before you first went to Yvonne Kotze's to meet the other officers' wives – the day we were invaded by all those puppies and chose Baron – all these memories and countless others are indelibly printed upon my mind and will stay with me whatever happens.*

Lastly let me say this, very simply but sincerely. You are the only person with whom I have ever been in love – I still am, and shall remain so until the end. Nothing can change that. It is just an established fact which in recent months has given rise to a great deal of wishful thinking, but even now, that very simple fact, has given me a sense of happiness, and it is just about the one thing nobody can take away. That is the reason why, although pressed to do so by several doctors, I have never discussed you or our marriage in any way.

Goodbye now, my dear, and I wish you the very best of luck and all the happiness in the world.

I'll end this letter with the familiar style which may help to bring back a few of those memories for you.

With all my love, darling, always,
Forever your own,

Jimmy

Should your mother commandeer this letter I ask her to pass it on without comment, with respect for my last wishes, if nothing else.[1]

CHAPTER TWENTY-ONE
The Old Bailey

24–26 SEPTEMBER 1946

Nowadays the thrill has gone out of most murder trials ...
The normal cut and thrust of advocacy takes on an added
significance when one knows that a man's life is at stake.

J. D. Casswell, *A Lance for Liberty*, 1961

In spite of warnings from the police that all-night queues
were banned, crowds gathered outside the Old Bailey at
8 p.m. on the evening of Monday 23 September in order to
get a chance of sitting in one of the thirty seats in the public
gallery of Court No. 1 the next day.[1] Many brought blankets
to keep out the autumnal chill and slept outside the building
overnight. One smartly dressed woman from Bristol refused
to give her name to the press: 'I wouldn't want my friends to
know I was doing such a silly thing.'[2] Extra police were on
duty overnight to deal with the anticipated crowds for the

opening day of the trial. The next morning, a young couple, both students at London University, successfully secured seats in the gallery of the oak-panelled and glass-roofed court-room. Once settled in their seats the girl took out twelve rounds of toast, marmalade, a knife and a teapot from a shop-ping basket. The young man took the teapot, pushing his way through the crowds and asked a court usher, 'Can I get some boiling water in the building?'[3]

At 10.32 a.m., Heath made his appearance into the glass-panelled dock, smartly dressed in his new chalk-stripe grey suit, a shirt, pullover, brown suede shoes and his RAF tie – a new white handkerchief in his breast pocket. His blond hair was pomaded and his nails were said to have been manicured for the occasion.

The judge, Mr Justice Morris, wore a grey wig and scarlet robe finished with a black sash. He sat in a chair to the left of the Sword of State which pointed upwards on the wall behind him. Morris was fifty years old and this was his first big murder trial, having only been appointed as a high court judge the previous December.[4] A Welshman by birth, he had been educated at the Liverpool Institute and Cambridge. During the First World War he had served as an officer in the Royal Welsh Fusiliers and had been awarded the Military Cross for bravery.[5] When he spoke, he had a soft, 'almost apologetic' voice.[6] The jury of ten men and two women – Rosemary Tyndale-Briscoe and Emma Selling – were then sworn in.

Given the extremity of the evidence in the case and the dramatic countrywide hunt for Heath, the three-day trial was very considered – as if deliberately distanced from the violent and emotive material. In meticulous longhand, 'which slowed the pace of the proceeding almost to dullness',[7] Mr Justice Morris took precise notes of the evidence. One newspaper reported that 'only the facts – the bruised, slashed, beaten, suffocated body of the girl – defied the scrupulous under-statement of the presentation'.[8] On this first day, Anthony Hawke opened with one of the shortest speeches on record for a major trial. For thirty minutes, Hawke addressed the court conversationally, as if he was 'leaning over a garden fence explaining how to bud a rose'. He was precise, quiet and clear, quickly establishing that he intended to dismiss any possible defence of 'partial insanity'.

Hawke then called the witnesses for the prosecution, including several police officers who had investigated the Notting Hill murder. Harold Harter, Solomon Joseph and Dr Keith Simpson were also called. Tension mounted in the courtroom on only a couple of occasions – when the leather riding whip was held aloft by the court usher and again when a grimy pillowcase, spotted with dried blood, was presented to the jury. The dramatic highlight of the day was the appear-ance of Yvonne Symonds, who had come to court accompa-nied by her father. She wore a dark pin-striped suit and close-fitting multi-coloured hat, carrying with her a brown leather handbag. When she was called, there was a sudden hush in the courtroom.[9] Anthony Hawke said he would have liked to spare her the ordeal of reliving her experiences with Heath so publicly, but her evidence was crucial to the case. Throughout the questioning, she spoke with long pauses between her muted replies. Concerned that she might be feeling unwell, Mr Justice Morris gallantly offered her a chair and a glass of water.[10] She looked at Heath only once. 'You have met this man, here?' Hawke asked her, with a gesture towards the dock. Yvonne raised her eyes to the man whom she had introduced to her parents as her future husband. 'Yes,' she murmured and turned her head away.[11]

After being cross-examined, Yvonne was released from the courtroom. She didn't give any interviews to the press, though a couple of snatched photographs of her were taken.

Her family left their home in Warren Road in 1947. Yvonne left the country, not wanting her association with Heath to colour the rest of her life. She settled abroad and never returned to England again.

The first day of the trial ended with Detective Inspector Gates of Bournemouth police telling of the discovery of Heath's suitcase at Bournemouth West Station and how he told Heath that he was to be detained for the murder of Margery Gardner. He confirmed Heath's casual, careless answer, 'Oh, all right.'

On Wednesday 25 September, Casswell opened the case for the defence. He began by telling the jury that a few days earlier he had received an anonymous letter from a woman who had noted that three 'gentlemen' (she had stressed the inverted commas) were prepared to defend 'that inhuman monster Heath'. She placed Casswell and the defence team in the same category as Hitler and hoped that their consciences would haunt them for the rest of their lives. Casswell discussed the letter because he wanted to draw attention to the fact that despite the many 'unusual, disgusting [and] morbid details' of the case that had been discussed in the press at great length and in great detail, Heath was entitled to a defence and was entitled to be tried on the evidence put before the jury and not what they had read in the newspapers.[12] Many of the jurors, if not all of them, would already have read of the details of both murders in the newspapers in the preceding two months and must surely have already formed precon-ceived ideas about the case.

> Why have the press taken such an interest in [this case]? They have taken an interest in it because they think it will appeal to the public who are their readers. Why then have the public taken such an interest in this case? Why? Is not it because two

terrible and apparently motiveless crimes have been committed by the same man within the short space of a fortnight?
Not a man, you know, who is unintelligent, but a man who
has seen a good deal of the world, a man who has been
commissioned three times. That is the sort of man with
whom you have to deal; and yet you find that within the
short space of a fortnight, these two astonishing and apparently motiveless crimes have been committed by him ... Is it
not almost unimaginable?[13]

Casswell explained to the jury that he would not be calling
Heath to give evidence, as they would not believe a word he
said. He was concerned that Heath might seem too intelligent and that he seemed so composed that the jury would
never believe that he could be the victim of a mental disease.

Casswell's personal view was that Heath had committed
both murders as the result of an irresistible sexually inspired
impulse to kill, but he could not concede that in court, as to
do so would have automatically taken Heath out of the
protection of the M'Naghten[14] rules, the statute that was to
dominate the debate at the trial.

In 1843 Daniel M'Naghten had attempted to assassinate
the prime minister, Sir Robert Peel, but by mistake, shot
dead Peel's secretary, Edward Drummond. M'Naghten was
clearly mentally unstable, but was his mental condition such
that he was not responsible in law for his actions? Lord Chief
Justice Tindal directed the jury that if M'Naghten was in
such a mental state as to have been incapable of knowing the
difference between right and wrong, then he was not culpable for his actions. Guided by Tindal, the jury brought a
verdict of 'Not Guilty'. As there was no provision for mentally
ill criminals, such as Broadmoor, in this period, M'Naghten
was released.

The notion of a murderer being set free caused a public

outcry, so the House of Lords asked a panel of judges what they felt about the Lord Chief Justice's directive. In essence the judges agreed that in order to establish a defence on the ground of insanity it must be proved that at the time of the act, the accused was labouring under such a defect of reason that he did not know the nature and quality of the act he was doing, or if he *did* know it, he did not know what he was doing was wrong. Despite advances in the study of psychology since the turn of the century, the M'Naghten Rules remained the statute by which all insanity cases were assessed.

Casswell was to call only four witnesses. Usually the defence would be at pains to prevent the jury from hearing about any other crimes relating to the accused, but in a departure from normal practice, Casswell referred to Heath's chequered history in some detail – his thefts, frauds and court martials as well as introducing the details of the murder of Doreen Marshall. Casswell stated that the case for the defence was that of 'partial insanity' and suggested that in view of the fact that the injuries inflicted on the second victim were far more severe than those inflicted on Margery Gardner, Heath's was a case of 'progressive mania'. He tried to make clear that there would be no inconsistency in the jury finding that the charming and self-possessed young man in the dock was capable of insane behaviour at the time of the two murders when normal restraints had given way. He called Dr Crichton McGaffey to discuss the nature of the injuries to Doreen Marshall and requested that the jury examine the distressing scene-of-crime photographs: 'Rather unpleasant, I'm afraid.'

Casswell also called Frederick Wilkinson, the night porter from the Tollard Royal, to indicate how normally Heath had behaved after committing the murder, climbing into bed and falling asleep. The onus was on the defence to prove that Heath was insane, rather than for the prosecution to prove that he was not. Though he felt that his case was weak as far as the law went, Casswell believed that he might be able to persuade the jury of Heath's partial insanity, if their star medical witness could convince them from the witness box.

Dr William Henry de Bargue Hubert was a major author-ity in the world of psychiatric medicine and seemed an extremely credible witness. It was to be on his evidence that the case for the defence – and Heath's life – would rest. In discussion with Casswell in preparation for the trial, Hubert said that he was prepared to say that Heath ought to have been diagnosed as a mental defective from an early age and that at the time of the murders he probably knew what he was doing, but was so mentally abnormal that he didn't know that what he was doing was wrong. From 1934 to 1939 Dr Hubert had worked as psychotherapist at Wormwood Scrubs and had collaborated with the respected Dr Norwood East in a psychological study of the prevention of crime for the Home Office in 1938.[15] Hubert was also the assistant psychia-trist to St Thomas' Hospital for Children and had previously been psychotherapist at Feltham Prison and Broadmoor. During the war, he had served in the army as a specialist in psychological medicine and latterly as adviser in psychiatry to the Middle East with the rank of lieutenant colonel. He seemed the ideal expert witness and was certainly more expe-rienced and better respected than the two doctors that the prosecution were to call.

However, what was not known at the time was that Hubert was a drug addict. This affliction was to prove disastrous. When he arrived at the Old Bailey that day, Hubert told Casswell that he had been involved in a taxi accident, so was in an extremely nervous state. But shortly afterwards, having taken the drugs to which he was addicted, Hubert appeared confident, happy and on 'a cloud of drug-induced euphoria'. He was then ready to enter the witness box.

Initially questioned by Casswell, Hubert stated that he had interviewed Heath several times and that he was, in his view, certifiably insane. Throughout his evidence, which was to last an hour and thirty-three minutes, Hubert was hesitant in manner and paused frequently, 'sometimes for quite a long time', already giving the jury the impression that he was unsure of his own opinion. But it was his confused and inconsistent performance under cross-examination that Casswell thought 'quite ghastly'.

Anthony Hawke, with his 'customary bland courtesy and softly spoken voice', dramatically undermined Hubert's testimony with biting irony, alerting the jury to the weaknesses in Hubert's testimony by the repeated use of the killer phrase 'with great respect'.

'I take it from your evidence that at the time Heath murdered Margery Gardner he knew that he was doing something that was wrong?'

'No.'

'May I take it that he knew what he was doing?'

'Yes.'

'That he knew that he had bound and tied a young woman lying on a bed?'

'Yes.'

'That he knew when he inflicted seventeen lashes on her with a thong that he was inflicting seventeen lashes with a thong?'

'Yes.'

'He knew all those things?'

'Yes.'

'But he did not know that they were wrong?'

'He knew the consequences.'

'I did not ask that, you know, with great respect.'

'He did not consider it wrong, no.'

'*Did not consider* is not the question I asked, with great respect. I asked you whether he knew.'

'No.'[16]

Hubert argued that Heath felt that his sadism was an expression of his sexuality and that he therefore felt it right to practise it.

'Are you saying, with your responsibility, standing there, that a person in that frame of mind is free from criminal responsibility if what he does causes grievous bodily harm or death?'

'At the time, yes.'

'His criminal responsibility does not arise at a particular time. I asked whether, with your responsibility, you say that a perverted sadist who knows perfectly well what he is doing when he satisfies his perverted instinct is free from criminal responsibility because he finds the necessity to satisfy it?'

'My answer is "yes", because on questioning sexual perverts they appear to show no regret or remorse quite frequently.'

'Would it be your view that a person who finds it convenient at the moment to forge a cheque in order to free himself from financial responsibility is entitled to say that he thought it was right, and therefore he is free from the responsibility of what he does?'

'He may think so, yes.'

'Do you say that the person who has been proved to commit forgery for the purpose of improving his financial stability is entitled to claim insanity within the M'Naghten Rules as a defence?'

'I think he does it because he has no strong sense of right and wrong at all.'

'With great respect, Dr Hubert, I did not ask you what *he* thought. I asked you whether *you* thought he was entitled to claim exemption from responsibility on the ground of insanity?'

'Yes, I do.'[17]

Hubert had fallen straight into the trap that Hawke had carefully laid for him. He had forgotten that he was supposed to be arguing that Heath didn't know what he was doing was wrong. In the end he had admitted that Heath could just not help himself, the doctrine of 'irresistible impulse' that was completely unacceptable in law. This point was not lost on Heath himself. Throughout the trial he had been sending notes to Casswell (twenty-two in all), observations and questions about the witnesses. At this point he sent a note to Casswell via the court usher:

> It may be of interest to know that in my discussions with Hubert, *I* have never suggested that I should be excused or that I told him I felt I should because of insanity. This evidence is Hubert's opinion – not what I have suggested he say on my behalf.[18]

Hubert had posited an indiscriminate licence to commit crime. If the criminal thought his acts were right – however modest or extreme – then they must be so. Years later, in his memoirs, Casswell detected a note of special pleading in Hubert's testimony. In seeking to justify Heath's behaviour in this way, perhaps he was attempting to exonerate himself for his own sins? Less than a year after the trial, Hubert was found dead in the bathroom of his house in Old Church Street in Chelsea. He had taken a lethal cocktail of barbituric acid and chloral hydrate. Whether his suicide was related to his performance at Heath's trial was never confirmed.

Under further cross-examination, Hubert suggested that Heath might be suffering from 'moral deficiency' or 'moral insanity'. The prosecution was quick to pick him up on this. Was he saying that Heath was a 'moral defective'? Hawke was keen to push this line of questioning as he was about to bring up a point of law. In the Mental Deficiency Act of 1927, a 'moral defective' must have exhibited criminal propensities before the age of eighteen. Asked if Hubert knew of any evidence from Heath's youth in which he had displayed vicious or criminal traits, Hubert said he had none. Hawke concluded that in that case, Heath could not possibly be a moral defective as outlined in the law. Outmanoeuvred, Hubert was stumped, admitting, 'It is difficult to prove.'[19]

Casswell was relying on Hubert to introduce evidence from Heath's past that might have relevance to the indictment. If Hubert raised the incident with Pauline Brees at the Strand Palace Hotel, the jury could be made aware that Heath had previously practised consensual sado-masochistic sex with no serious consequences. By doing so, he might also have raised the issue that the incident with Margery Gardner might have been consensual, too. When Hawke asked Hubert if he had any evidence that Heath had exhibited any cruelty in the past, Hubert said that there was.

'What evidence?' asked Hawke.

'That similar acts without such consequences have occurred before, yes.'

'When?'

'At different dates in the past.'

'Could you give me them?'

'No.'[20]

Though he was certainly aware of the incident at the Strand Palace Hotel, Hubert seemed to have forgotten all about it. After re-examining him, Casswell declared that that was the case for the defence. Anthony Hawke then called two medical witnesses in answer to Hubert's testimony. Dr Grierson and Dr Young were both respected in their field as senior prison medical officers at Brixton and Wormwood Scrubs respectively, but neither had the qualifications and clinical experience that Dr Hubert had and neither were specialists in psychiatric medicine. But with the destruction of Dr Hubert's testimony by the prosection, far from being debated, proved or disproved, the issue of Heath's insanity was barely even discussed.

On the third day of the trial, there were few witnesses left to question. As it appeared that a verdict would be expected later that day, Heath chose not to wear his RAF tie 'at the last "knockings"' – as if wearing it whilst the death sentence was passed would in some way be an insult to the service. At the beginning of the day, Rosemary Tyndale-Biscoe, one of the two female jurors, submitted three questions that she felt had not been raised so far. The questions were very perceptive and give the only indication we have (the jury's discussion process being completely private) of the debate that took place within the jury room. None of the issues raised by these questions had been touched on in the trial. Was Heath financially embarrassed? Had he been drinking on the night of the two murders? And, crucially, was there anything in Heath's present mental condition that might have affected his brain recently?[21]

The questions were perfunctorily dealt with, Mr Justice Morris attaching little importance to them. But each of these issues was extremely relevant to Heath's behaviour in the days before the murders. With no money he had conjured the scheme to fly Harry Ashbrook over to Copenhagen – a journey he surely had no hope of making. He then proceeded to drink his way through his £30 fee until he was paralytically drunk. Each of these steps surely indicated that Heath had reached the end of the line. He didn't care what happened to him. He had developed psychological problems throughout the war years, exacerbated by baling out of his plane over Venlo and brought to the fore by his divorce. Fielding-Johnson's evidence had

not been heard;[22] consequently there was no probing investigation of Heath's past and how it might have had an impact
on his actions.

Cross-examining Dr Grierson, Casswell suggested that he
had failed to secure Heath's trust when interviewing him
and that as a consequence, Heath had held back his true
feelings. He suggested that Heath might have felt distrustful
because he was aware that a document headed 'Confidential
and Medical' had been confiscated by the prison authorities
– the document he had written about his past life which
referred to various losses of memory and the incident at the
Strand Palace Hotel. Casswell may well have been trying to
introduce the contents of the document as evidence, but
when Grierson was presented with it, he said he'd never
seen it before and simply handed it back. Warning Casswell
as politely as possible, Justice Morris made clear that he was
not permitted to submit any new evidence as the defence
had already rested their case. Consequently, the incident
with Pauline Brees at the Strand Palace Hotel was completely
lost on the jury in a series of cryptic references and Heath's
claim to losses of memory and blackouts was never aired in
court at all.

In his closing speech, for the first time, Casswell touched,
almost in passing, on the issue that might have been one of
the root causes of Heath's violent behaviour – his experiences
during the war.

> He is one of thousands of young men who has taken his life
> in his hands and risked one of the most painful of deaths, by
> burning, on your behalf and mine. You may think that the
> life which has been led by a young airman is just the sort of
> life that might bring to the surface a defect of reasoning which
> had been hitherto hidden in his life. That is the only reason I
> refer to that. The human frame was not built to fly in

machines and be fired at. The human frame and human people have had to put up with shocks and risks and dangers which were unknown up to the present generation ... The human frame and the human mind were not intended to meet with such awful shocks as they have had to meet with in the past few years, and it may be that they have not yet evolved such an immunity as to leave them normal after they have gone through those sorts of experiences. You may yourselves come to the conclusion that that kind of experience may have something to do with the outburst, the admitted outbursts, of sadism in this man after the war was over.[23]

In his closing speech for the prosecution, Anthony Hawke recognized that, to judge from Heath's actions, what he had done – how he had behaved before and after his crimes – *seemed* mad.

No one suggests that this is a normal person with whom we are dealing. I'd venture, most respectfully, to say that it might be entirely a wrong way to approach this case by saying, 'Oh, well, anyhow, nobody in his sober sense would do a thing like this. After all, the man must be mad. Let us forget all about what the doctors have been saying and what these men in wigs and gowns have been saying to us. Let us forget all that special pleading and just say, as common-sense people, that nobody but a maniac would behave like this man.' Members of the jury, with great respect, that is not the way to approach this.[24]

Madness – whether it was a moral or medical state – was not synonymous with insanity, which was a legal and not a clinical term. He reminded the jury that they were to establish whether Heath was responsible for his own actions purely in terms of the law. This was further stressed by Mr Justice

Morris in his summing up. Speaking for ninety-nine minutes with simplicity and charm of manner, Morris guided the jury, weaving a clear path through the intricate evidence. His view was very plain: despite the confused and confusing semantic debate between the defence and prosecution about partial insanity, moral insanity, moral deficiency or moral degeneracy, the legal position was clear; the laws of insanity were not to be used as a 'get out of jail free' card.

> Strong sexual instinct is not in itself insanity; a mere love of bloodshed or mere recklessness are not in themselves insanity; an inability to resist temptation is not of itself insanity; equally, the satisfaction of some perverted impulse is not, without more, to be excused on the ground of insanity. The plea of insanity cannot be permitted to become the easy or the vague explanation of some conduct which is shocking merely because it is also startling. The law of insanity is not to become the sole refuge of those who cannot challenge a charge which is brought to them.[25]

After Morris's summing up, at 4.35 p.m. the jury retired. Heath was taken down to the tiny cell below the dock and waited, reading the scrawled messages that murderers of the past decade had written on the walls. Very much a betting man, having listened to the summing up, he made his odds 'thirty to one'. Casswell went home to Wimbledon, leaving his junior Mr Jessel to take the verdict, a commonly exercised privilege of leading counsel once their main duties were over. However, the press, quick to manufacture a story out of very little, claimed that Casswell had collapsed from the strain of the trial.[26] This he dismissed as 'absolute nonsense'.[27]

At exactly 5.34, with less than an hour of deliberation following this complex trial, the jury filed back into their box. The autumn afternoon was getting dark, so the electric lights were switched on.[28] Heath hurried up from the cells, snapped to attention and for the first time in the trial, lifted his head to look up. The silence in the courtroom was intense and for half a minute there was no sound.[29] Standing straight and firm, his hands clasped behind his back with the 'slightest twitch of the mouth',[30] Heath waited to hear his fate, his chest rising and falling. Two police officers stood either side of him in the dock as the judge and then the jury filed back into the courtroom. The clerk asked the jury, 'Members of the jury, are you agreed on your verdict?' The foreman, dressed in morning coat and hard white collar,[31] stood up and answered in a loud voice, 'We are.'

'Do you find the prisoner, Neville George Clevely Heath, guilty or not guilty of the murder of Margery Aimee Brownell Gardner?'

Another pause. The foreman cleared his throat and answered in a voice which reached every corner of the court-room, 'Guilty.' There was no recommendation to mercy. The death sentence was passed and Heath was asked by Morris if he had anything to say. The garrulous airman had rarely had such an attentive audience. With all eyes on him, here was his opportunity to leave the trial with a flourish. All his life he had sought the limelight, a matinee idol at the centre of his own drama. But now there was no protestation of his innocence, no admission of guilt, no remorse or apology. Faced with death, words failed him. His only response to Morris's question, a suitably nihilistic, empty: 'Nothing.'

He left the court at 5.41, the gamble for his life rolled and lost in seven short minutes.[32]

Maggie Blunt was in her mid-thirties, a university-educated publicity assistant reluctantly working for a metals company near Slough. That night, she wrote in her Mass Observation Diary how ordinary people like her responded to the news of

Heath's sentence, not with confident cheers, but with an anxious ambivalence.

> So Heath has been sentenced to death. I have been following this case in the press all agog and aghast. The news of his death sentence came a long way down on the BBC bulletin tonight and I found Mrs S waiting for it, as I was. I wonder how many other people were doing the same.
>
> I can't see that it makes much difference whether he was 'insane' or not. He was obviously dangerously abnormal and had committed shocking crimes. N was arguing about it when she was here – that you couldn't condemn a man who was mentally imbalanced. This is a case that will be remembered and discussed in the far future when more is known of psychology.
>
> Where does one draw the line for a person being responsible for his own actions?[33]

CHAPTER TWENTY-TWO
Wednesday 16 October 1946

If ever there were a criminal quite obviously mad, such a one is Heath. It does not take a knowledge of psychiatry or long pondering the hair-splitting of expert witnesses to reach that conclusion. Not merely the circumstances of the crime, but the conduct of the murderer before and after it admit of no other answer. If that behaviour is not mad, then the word has no plain commonsense meaning.

A barrister, *Daily Worker*, 28 September 1946

This weather is quite amazing, don't you think? For, although the days are quite cold the pleasant sunshine reminds one of any country except England. I've no doubt, though, that the fog and rain will not be far off now.

Heath in a letter to his mother,
13 October 1946[1]

Taken to Pentonville in a Black Maria, Heath was introduced to the prison governor, Mr Lawton, and the
medical officer, Dr Liddell, who asked if he would like some
medication to help him get over the ordeal of the death
sentence. But Heath was indifferent. He was taken to a cubi-
cle and made to remove his smart civilian clothes and given
the special uniform reserved for men convicted of murder – a
rough grey suit, devoid of buttons or anything that might
enable him to do himself an injury. He was now registered
as Prisoner No. 2059 and shown to Condemned Cell No. 2.
No. 1 was already being occupied by Arthur Boyce, who had
been convicted of the murder of his fiancée, Elizabeth
McLindon, the housekeeper to the exiled King of Greece.
Whilst much of the country was celebrating that summer,
Boyce had shot her at the king's Chester Square home on
'V' Day, 8 June.[2]

Most convicted murderers remained in a state of complete
collapse for anything up to forty-eight hours after the death
sentence was passed upon them, but as soon as he left the Old
Bailey Heath began to chat casually with the warders on the
'death watch'. Traditionally, three Sundays would have to
pass before the execution was carried out – which would be
the week of 13 October. Under the Criminal Lunatics Act of
1884 the home secretary had the power to appoint two
doctors to examine a prisoner under sentence of death. The
time allowed for lodging an appeal was fourteen days after the
trial. But after discussion with Casswell and Near, Heath
decided against it, but did allow the medical enquiry to go
ahead, though he didn't expect it to make any difference.

> *I am not optimistic about the result, neither am I unduly anxious,
> for in my opinion, the possible alternative may well prove far worse
> than the present situation.*[3]

The fact that he refused to appeal and was to take little interest in the medical enquiry that might save his life was at odds with the assumptions printed in some newspapers that the death of Doreen Marshall was an extraordinary bid by Heath to prove that he was insane and thereby escape the gallows. Casswell thought this 'wholly unwarranted by the facts'.[4] Immediately the death sentence had been passed Heath was reconciled to it.

> *I have very little to say I'm afraid, except that I think I would rather have things this way than spend the remainder of my life behind bars. Even now it all seems like a bad dream and except for what I've read and heard I know extraordinarily little about the whole affair. God alone knows what must have happened but it is certain that I am responsible legally and therefore must pay the penalty.*[5]

During the trial, as the defence had effectively admitted that Heath was responsible for the murders, there was no necessity to fully debate the crimes and the motivation behind them. He was certain to be convicted and his only hope of escaping execution was Dr Hubert's testimony that had gone so disastrously wrong. The fact that Heath wasn't tried for the second murder also meant that many witnesses were not called and their testimony never examined. Effectively the jury had only heard a part of the story. It seemed the function of the trial was not to reveal the truth but to get a conviction. Even Heath himself claimed to have no knowledge about the motivation behind what Casswell had repeatedly called these 'motiveless' crimes.

> *Morally* [Heath wrote] *I don't feel I am guilty because I could never have set out to commit two such vile deeds in cold blood. I don't expect anyone to believe my story – except a few friends who have*

> *been terribly understanding – but without going into any details I*
> *want you to know that it wasn't the 'real me' who was the author of*
> *these acts.*[6]

For Margery and Doreen's families, there was no explanation, no sense of closure. Other than the knowledge that Heath was to pay for his acts with his life, there was to be no satisfaction for them, nor was the public's curiosity about the case sated either.

Now that Heath was under sentence of death, the press were able to print any of the stories they had collected about him, whether they were true or not; a condemned man would not survive long enough to pursue a libel suit. Details of the case were embroidered or guessed at, including the particularly unpleasant detail that Heath had stuck empty cigarette packets in Doreen Marshall's wounds (he hadn't), the feeling being, perhaps, that Heath was such an inhuman monster that he must be capable of any depravity – as if the two murders he was responsible for were not, in themselves, horrific enough. The press hinted that Heath might have been guilty of other murders and sexual assaults. But as the trial was being prepared, Spooner had already investigated any unsolved crimes that Heath might have been responsible for. A member of the public had alerted the police to the fact that Heath might have killed Vera Page, a ten-year-old girl who had been found raped and strangled in west London, a mile away from her home.[7] Spooner also investigated the death of nineteen-year-old Louisa Steele from Blackheath who had been found strangled, raped and mutilated. Both murders had taken place in 1931 when Heath would have been fifteen, but nothing was found to connect him to either murder. On 26 October 1944 Florrie Porter, a 33-year-old nurse, had been murdered near RAF Finmere, where Heath had been stationed when he was seconded to the RAF. There was some similarity between the injuries sustained by both Florrie Porter and Doreen Marshall. But Spooner, scrupulously fair as ever, ascertained that Heath could not possibly have been involved in the death of Florrie Porter as he was on operations in Belgium at the time.[8] Despite rumours and assumptions in the press in Britain and South Africa, there is no evidence that Heath was involved in any other murders or assaults.[9]

The press also became bolder in their references to Margery Gardner's character and lifestyle. Somehow Trevethan Frampton's claim that Margery liked to be dominated by men reached the newspapers, which hinted at it when the trial was over. There was an increasing presumption by the press (and possibly by the police) that Margery was in some way culpable for her own death, that having known Heath's tastes, she had put herself in danger. Throughout the reporting of the trial, both victims were discussed in Hollywood style clichés – Margery Gardner cast as the vampish femme fatale and Doreen Marshall the innocent virgin – as if women could only conform to one of two extremes. Certainly, Margery had been promiscuous but it was Frampton – a man she had only known for six months – who assumed that she was 'masochistic', rather than Margery herself telling him that this was the case. When Spooner questioned Margery's friends and lovers, including her husband, they all agreed that Margery 'possessed no such trait'.[10] Peter Tilley Bailey, who had known Margery intimately in the six months preceding her death, confirmed that 'she has never shown any abnormal tendencies to me'.[11] Assuming that she had such tendencies certainly made the circumstances of her death more comprehensible (a sexual tryst gone wrong) and provided a further salacious development for the press to exploit. But was it actually true?

Given that Heath stated several times that he would rather

hang than spend the rest of his life in Broadmoor, he cannot have planned the murder of Doreen Marshall as a ploy to avoid the gallows. But if that was not the motivation for her murder, how could it be explained?

Having failed to establish what the motives for the two murders were at the trial, there was much speculation in the press as to what they might actually be. But a series of errors, inaccuracies and mistakes quoted at the trial and in the newspapers began to obscure this issue in a cloak of confusion.

Early in Spooner's investigation in June, both Leonard Luff and Thomas Paul of the Strand Palace Hotel were shown photographs of Margery Gardner and identified her as the woman Heath had been with at the hotel in February.[12] This, of course, was not true. It is clear that the woman at the Strand Palace who had submitted to Heath was definitely Pauline Brees. But she was not called as a witness at the trial and her evidence was never heard. Once Luff and Paul had made their mistaken identification, the story began to appear in the press, repeated as fact – that Margery Gardner had spent the night with Heath before and had escaped a beating.[13] In this scenario, she would *definitely* have known the danger she might be in and therefore must have knowingly succumbed to him at the Pembridge Court Hotel.

When Pauline Brees was finally interviewed by Spooner on 27 July and it became clear that Margery was *not* involved in the Strand Palace incident, stories suddenly appeared indicating that there were *two* similar incidents in *two* different hotels which *might* have taken place in March. Or was it May? These errors were repeated at the trial itself and even resurfaced in the memoirs of Josh Casswell and Keith Simpson.[14]

In reality, there was no evidence from any witness or in any police file that Margery had ever spent a previous night with Heath. Placing her at the Strand Palace Hotel was a mistake. Heath had only recently begun to patronize the same pubs and clubs that Margery did, possibly only a week or two before they met on the night he killed her; she didn't even know his surname. Consequently, despite what was reported in the press and then repeated in books and articles about the case ever since,[15] Margery may have had no idea at all what Heath's sexual tastes were when she agreed to go back with him to Notting Hill. In all probability, all that Margery might have expected at the Pembridge Court Hotel was straightforward intercourse with Heath. If this is the case – and taking into account the witness statements which have recently become available – a much clearer motivation for both murders becomes apparent and both crimes can be explained more simply and more plausibly.

Heath had lost everything; his wife, his home, his son, his career. Rejected from the Air Ministry, he stated several times that he had nothing left to live for. On the day of Margery Gardner's death, he was given £30 by Harry Ashbrook that he knew he wouldn't be able to pay back. Nor would he be able to supply the service that he had said he could – the trip to Copenhagen – as he had failed his 'B' licence. He had also lied to his mother that he had received the licence, which she would very soon find was not true. On 20 June, he wasn't even thinking a day ahead and proceeded to drink to great excess – a fact completely ignored at the trial.

Whilst seconded to the RAF, Heath's behaviour had been so extreme that he was never allowed to fly again and his senior officer, well versed in psychological problems in pilots, identified that he was suffering a breakdown. Following this he seems to have suffered some sort of post-traumatic reaction after he baled out over Venlo.

At the same time, Heath also admitted that he had been conscious of an impulse to 'react in a certain way' in his sexual relationships. Having lost all power and control in every other aspect of his life, was he now able to feel in control solely during intercourse?

Margery Gardner, like Pauline Brees, had certainly consented to sleep with Heath. She undressed and removed her earrings. But it may only have been at this point that Heath made it clear that he wanted some sort of extreme or sadistic sex with her. He might have assumed that Margery would consent, given her bohemian reputation. But had he been wrong-footed when Margery reacted in exactly the way that Pauline Brees said she had done? Had Margery rejected him? The incident at the Strand Palace Hotel was not discussed at the trial, but in their investigations, both police and psychiatrists fixed on Heath's comment to Pauline – 'I hate women' – as if it were an indication of Heath's misogyny. But what was more telling was his subsequent comment to Pauline: *'I'll make you do exactly what I want you to do.'*[16]

Could Margery, drunk as she was, have refused to submit to the more extreme acts that Heath desired, just as had occurred at the Strand Palace Hotel? Drunk, fuelled by rejection and sexually aroused, had he then knocked Margery unconscious (the bruises on her cheek), lost all control and gone beserk?

In his relationship with Peggy Waring, she noticed that Heath exhibited physical symptoms at the thought of rejection ('He seemed very distressed and perspiration was running down his face ... His passions seemed so roused that he was compelled to become rough with me and then to control himself he would immediately leave me').[17] He had also shown these extreme physical reactions years before when he was confronted with the fact that the RAF did not want to take him ('He displayed unnatural excitement and loss of self-control. His eyes were wild, his whole body shook with emotion and he could not sit down).[18]

It's intriguing that these displays occurred when Heath

was unable to pursue the two great passions of his life, sex and flight.

Having killed Margery, in the cold light of the next morning, he was appalled at what he had done and what he was capable of. He went to Worthing and met Yvonne Symonds, sleeping with her on more than one occasion, but didn't harm her.[19]

When he wined and dined Doreen Marshall, just as he had done with Yvonne Symonds, had he 'over-persuaded' her to go up to bed with him? Hence Doreen's increasing anxiety during the evening and her desire to go home. Having failed to seduce her at the Tollard Royal, perhaps Heath had hoped to do so on the way back to her hotel. In order to secure her trust, he might have suggested they get engaged (just as he had done with Yvonne) as they walked towards Branksome Dene Chine.

By the time they reached the chine, Doreen might have agreed to have sex with him[20] or he may have suggested that the route through the chine offered a shortcut back to central Bournemouth. After having persuaded her into the isolated chine in the pitch dark, again, it may only have been at this point that Heath revealed his intentions and Doreen, like Margery, rejected his suggestion of extreme sex acts. Again, he knocked her unconscious (the bruises on the cheek), stripped and bound her – his desire merging with rage once more.

Both women were beaten in the face, both were tied and gagged, both had their nipples bitten and both their bodies were savaged by terrible genital injuries. So both murders may have been inspired by a similar chain of events rather than being the two very different scenarios they have hitherto been regarded as. This outline of events follows Spooner's thinking at the time:

> It might be assumed that Heath has resorted to violence and
> sadistic acts where his advances have been repudiated and so
> resulted in his use of physical force which accentuated his
> perversity.[21]

As is clear from Heath's whole life and career, he was very
much a creature of habit. He'd commit a crime and then
attempt to salve it with a letter. He would do wrong, then
run away before rationally thinking about the consequences.
He would propose to a girl solely in order to get her into bed.
His life was a fabric of repeated patterns and much of the time
he would be condemned to make the same mistakes and
never learn from his experiences. With the statements of
Pauline Brees and Peggy Waring, it's now possible to see the
pattern in two murders that have previously seemed to be
related but inexplicable acts; both women brutally murdered
by a man whose charm and good looks had fostered an arrogance and conceit that baulked at the idea of any woman –
whether vamp or virgin – telling him 'no'.

In the condemned cell at Pentonville, Heath was only
allowed ordinary prison food and none of the special treatment he had been afforded on remand. Asking why he was
only allowed to eat with a spoon and not allowed a knife
and fork, it was explained to him that from now on all his
food would be cut up for him by the warders. He was no
longer allowed to receive tobacco, though every day, due
to an archaic ruling, he had an allowance of tobacco and a
pint of beer. He was no longer allowed to be sent books,
magazines or newspapers from outside and was reliant on
the 'awfully good' prison library. Despite not having access
to newspapers, he was still concerned about how his story
was being presented, having been informed of this in letters
from home ('I see no reason why the press should be

permitted to print quite blatant lies').[22] Unlike his stay at Brixton, the time at Pentonville seemed to pass 'very pleasantly', playing chess and card games. He read *The Thirty-Nine Steps* twice; the story of a man on the run accused of murder, desperately trying to prove he is innocent.

The sentence initiated a new wave of stories in the press relating to the case, including great concern about the police's holding back of Heath's photograph from the public. Several headlines appeared on the subject: 'Ban on Picture Cost Life of My Doreen',[23] 'The Heath Picture: the Facts'[24] and 'Doreen Marshall; Should She Be Alive Today?'[25]

The picture had been embargoed by the police for twelve days whilst Heath had been at large and only released on 30 July when he was already in custody. It had not been issued to the press who were warned that any publication of the photograph would 'seriously prejudice' Heath's trial. But Doreen's father could only see that the ban on the picture had allowed a killer on the loose to kill again.

> We fully appreciate that publication of the picture of a man wanted for questioning might embarrass the police if he was afterwards found innocent. But in this case because normal procedure was followed it has cost my daughter's life. I am sure she would have recognized Heath from pictures she would have seen in the newspapers we take, but for the Scotland Yard request that newspapers should not print this picture.[26]

Doreen's mother concurred, recalling the night when Doreen had grabbed the *Daily Mail* from her and told her not to read about the Notting Hill murder.

> If there had been a picture of Heath she would have seen it automatically and the chances are she would have recognized

him later. Even if she felt she could not read such details a picture might have caught her mind and made all the difference.[27]

On Thursday 10 October, Norman Bower, MP for Harrow West, challenged the home secretary in the House of Commons about the embargoed photograph. Mr Chuter Ede took the opportunity to rebuff the question once and for all. Whatever the Marshall family felt, the police had followed the correct procedure.

> The circumstances of the murder of Mrs Gardner did not afford any reason to suppose that her assailant would commit a second murder, and I am satisfied that the police were right in asking that the press should not take a course which might have prejudiced the due course of justice.[28]

As well as recriminations against the police, there was also a certain uneasiness from some quarters about the death sentence. Several newspapers ran comparisons between Heath's case and that of Ronald True – another ex-airman who had been tried and convicted of murder in 1922 under the M'Naghten Rules.[29] True's appeal failed, but the home secretary had intervened and the sentence of death commuted to life in a psychiatric hospital. True was still living in Broadmoor in 1946 and would remain there until his death in 1954. Given the similarities between the two cases, some commentators felt that Heath should be sent to Broadmoor rather than sentenced to death.[30]

On 7 October, as a contribution to the medical review, Heath's solicitor sent a copy of Fielding-Johnson's statement to the home secretary together with a letter from Bessie Heath outlining the difficulty of Heath's birth and the fact that her uncle had been sent to a mental institution. Heath also suggested to his mother that she tell Near about the 'Johnstone' episode when he was at school (possibly a reference to the incident with 'Jeanette') as well as 'several other events of a similar nature which you may be able to recall'. Heath was not keen to pursue it, but told his mother it was 'entirely up to you'.[31]

The medical enquiry had been automatically put in process by the Home Office. This was headed by Dr Hopwood, the superintendent of Broadmoor, and Dr Norwood East who was president of the Psychiatric Section of the Royal Society of Medicine, lecturer on crime and insanity at the Maudsley Hospital and co-author of *The Psychological Treatment of Crime*, which he had written with Dr William Henry Hubert. The doctors visited Heath at Pentonville on the afternoon of 9 October. Heath himself didn't see the point: 'My bet is that they are quite happy wth their present verdict and I'll lay you five to one that they don't alter it.'[32]

Hopwood and East consulted a broad variety of experts including the governor at Pentonville, the chaplain, Reverend G. W. Cleavely and Dr Liddell the medical officer, as well as Dr Grierson, Dr F. H. Taylor from Brixton and Dr Young from Wormwood Scrubs. They also interviewed the six warders who had supervised Heath twenty-four hours a day since his conviction. They had two prolonged interviews with Heath himself and studied the case documents. Again Heath said he had little memory of what had taken place at the time of the two murders. The doctors felt that this was not due to any sort of mental disease or defect. They thought that it may be that the details of the crimes were so horrific that Heath had effectively shut them out of his consciousness. Hopwood and East saw no reason to stop the execution on medical grounds.[33]

On the same day as the medical review, Rosemary Tyndale-Biscoe, one of the two female jurors at the trial, wrote a letter to the home secretary, Mr Chuter Ede, enclosing a petition voicing the concerns of several members of the jury who had served on the trial with her. She suggested, 'You might give consideration to the law of Insanity 1843, to bring it more up to date with regard to modern knowledge and conditions. We found the responsibility of finding the verdict extremely hard. May I please add my petition for the future abolition of the death penalty?'[34]

On 11 October, Chuter Ede wrote in green ink across Heath's file, 'The law must take its course.'[35] This was telegrammed to Mr Lawton, the governor at Pentonville, who then informed Heath that Mr Ede would not intervene with the process of the law; he would be executed at 9 a.m. on Wednesday 16 October.

Reading of the results of the medical enquiry in the newspapers, Mrs Tyndale-Biscoe wrote to Chuter Ede again, further outlining her concerns, not just about Heath's case, but highlighting how the law in its present form was unable to properly assess cases which focused on psychiatric issues.

> *I now read in the public press that Heath is not to be reprieved. In my view the law urgently requires review in the light of modern psychological science, and as a juror carefully following the trial and medical evidence and also the discussion by the jury after it and before verdict, I feel Heath's case comes within the category of cases requiring such review.*
>
> *Though as the law now stands it was no doubt my duty to concur in the verdict, I feel and I believe there is a widespread feeling among the public, that reconsideration of the law is overdue and meanwhile this man should be reprieved pending such reconsideration.*[36]

The letter was acknowledged, but the sentiment ignored. Mrs Tyndale-Biscoe then sent an anonymous letter to Heath in Pentonville. 'Whether under the regulations he will ever see it, I do not know. But I shall go on praying for him.'[37]

The days before the execution were filled with almost ritualistic preparation, much of it behind the scenes, with the public as well as Heath unaware of the process. On 14 October, a messenger from the Home Office left Whitehall with a small box containing a rope specially made for executions by John Edginton & Sons in the Old Kent Road. The rope was signed for by the governor of Pentonville, Mr Lawton, and then kept in a safe until 4 p.m. on the afternoon before the execution. Two ropes were always supplied, a new one and a used one. Most hangmen favoured the used ropes as there was less stretch in them and this resulted in a more accurate drop.

Heath's solicitor drew up his will, with two of the 'deathwatch' guards acting as witnesses. In a letter to his father, Heath particularly requested that after he died, he wanted any remaining money to be given to his brother to help get his 'A' licence. Like his brother, Mick Heath had recently failed his matriculation exams and Heath felt that the focus on him must have been the reason. His beloved caterpillar badge, which would be forwarded with his effects from the police, he left to his mother. Despite pressure from them, he persisted in refusing to see either of his parents before he died.

> *I want my mother to remember me as she last saw me outside. I do not want her to see me as a man condemned to death for murder. I hope she will always remember me as the son she knew some years ago, and will forget the situation in which I now find myself.*[38]

Albert Pierrepoint, the hangman and his assistant, Harry Kirk, also arrived at 4 p.m. the day before the execution. This time of arrival had been designated in the days when hangmen would get drunk the night before the execution and either made mistakes in their work or didn't turn up. Pierrepoint had served as an executioner since 1931, his father and his uncles having served in the same role; it was almost a family business. From the mid-1940s Pierrepoint would become something of a celebrity. As well as executing several British murderers – including Evans, Christie, Haigh, Derek Bentley and Ruth Ellis – he also executed over 200 Nazi war criminals in the autumn of 1946.

Pierrepoint was given Heath's statistics, but also looked through the 'Judas Hole' in the door of the condemend cell, so that he could assess Heath's physique. The execution shed was just next door, a small room painted green with trapdoors set in the floor. These trapdoors had two hinged leaves that were bolted on the underside. To one side of the doors was a lever; when this was released, the bolts were drawn back and the trapdoor opened. A cotter pin acted as a security device to prevent the lever being pushed by accident. A set of stairs to the side of the execution chamber connected it to the pit below.

Pierrepoint tested the equipment, using a sandbag to calculate the drop using the 'Home Office Table of Drops'. He adjusted the length of the drop tailored to Heath's weight and stature. The sack was left overnight to stretch the rope.

That evening, Violet Van Der Elst arrived at Merton Hall Road in her cream and black Rolls-Royce and told Bessie Heath, 'I've come to make a last effort to save your boy.' Mrs Van Der Elst was the daughter of a coalman but had become a successful businesswoman by developing Shavex, the first brush-less shaving cream, amassing a huge personal fortune in the process. As well as standing three times, unsuccessfully, as a Labour MP, she was a vehement opponent of capital punishment and had campaigned against the death penalty for years. After talking to Heath's parents she drove to the Home Office and insisted on speaking to the home secretary. When she was told this was not possible, she left him a note outlining the incident at Venlo and the difficulty of Heath's birth. She also stated that his parents did not appear at the trial as Heath had told them that if they did, he would plead guilty.[39]

Isaac Near tried one last time to persuade Heath to see his parents before he died, but he was adamant. He didn't want to see them because he didn't want to break down at this stage. Near felt that Heath didn't seem worried by the prospect of his own death and was resigned to his fate.[40] A gambler to the last, he spent his last hours playing poker with the guards for imaginary stakes, as he wasn't allowed any money.[41] After Near left him for the last time that night, Heath sent him a note to thank him for his professionalism and his friendship.

I don't know what time they open where I'm going, but I hope the beer is better than it is here.[42]

Next morning, Pierrepoint was woken at 6.30 by the warder who shared his quarters and checked that the rope was in the correct position at the right height for Heath, 5 feet 11 inches. The sandbag was put in the corner of the pit, where there was also a stretcher to be used after the execution was completed. Pierrepoint drew a 'T' in chalk to mark where Heath's shoes would be aligned. He edged out the cotter pin so that it was only just in place – this would only save a fraction of a second, but it all helped to make the job faster. Throughout all their preparations, Pierrepoint and Kirk barely spoke, and if they did, only in a whisper, as Heath was in the condemned cell next door, unaware that the execution chamber had been right next to him since he had arrived in

Pentonville. The door was hidden behind a wardrobe. Pierrepoint took great pride in his professionalism and attention to detail:

> [The] job had to go to a perfect rhythm, with full understanding all round, as silently and well timed as a team of commandos hijacking a German general from his own HQ. That is craftsmanship.[43]

Pierrepoint and Kirk then went for a breakast of bacon and eggs.

That morning there was a crowd of 3,000 people outside Pentonville, mostly women 'with shopping baskets and children in prams'. There were also eighteen press photographers. Extra police had been arranged to deal with the expected crowds. The 100-yard drive between the main road and the prison was cordoned off by the police. At 8.55 a.m. Mrs Van der Elst arrived in her Rolls-Royce. Dressed in mourning clothes, she distributed handbills urging the abolition of the death penalty. Headed 'The Fresh Evidence', Mrs Van Der Elst's leaflets claimed that Heath was not responsible for his actions. She had visited Mrs Heath the previous evening and had been told that when he was born, Heath's brain was 'terribly injured' and that his parents thought he would not survive. Mrs Van Der Elst claimed that 'this man was a possessed madman and should have been sent to Broadmoor'.[44] The leaflets were snatched by the crowd and flung high in the air, falling 'like a snowstorm' on the crowd which swarmed around her car. The car in conjunction with the crowd then started to cause a traffic jam, so a police inspector, Thomas James, told Mrs Van Der Elst that she was causing an obstruction and must move on.[45]

In the condemned cell, unaware of the commotion outside,

Heath had risen early and was permitted to dress in the new grey, chalk-striped suit that he had worn for his trial. The prison around him continued its normal routine and the other prisoners carried on with their regular tasks, the prison authorities doing their utmost for the execution to take place as discreetly as possible. Prisoners normally occupied near the execution shed were given additional exercise in a yard remote from it. The prison clock was disconnected for the hour of nine.[46]

Just before 9 a.m., Pierrepoint and Kirk waited outside the condemned cell with Harold Gedge, the deputy under-sherriff, Mr Lawton the governor, two senior prison officers and the prison chaplain, Reverend Cleavely. Seconds before 9 a.m., the door was opened quickly and Pierrepoint went straight up to Heath, putting his hands behind his back and strapping his wrists as another door in the cell was opened to the execution chamber for the first time. On this occasion Pierrepoint used a special strap made of pliant pale calf-leather that he only used about a dozen times when 'I had a more than formal interest in this particular execution'.[47] He told Heath, 'Follow me.'

Heath walked seven paces into the execution chamber with the noose straight ahead of him. The two prison officers gently stopped him on the 'T' marked on the trapdoors so that his feet were positioned across the division between them. As Harry Kirk tied Heath's legs with the ankle strap, Pierrepoint looked him in the face, eye to eye, 'that last look'.[48] Pulling the white cap from his breast pocket he drew it over Heath's head. He then reached for the noose, pulling it over the cap. The noose was not knotted, but the rope ran through a metal eye. In seconds, Pierrepoint tightened the noose to his right, pulled a rubber washer along the rope to hold it and darted to his left, pulling out the cotter pin with one hand and pulling the lever with the other. There was a snap as the falling doors opened and Heath's body dropped into the pit. His neck was thrown back and his spinal column was severed instantaneously.

His body hung lifeless, swinging to stillness. Pierrepoint estimated that the average time it took from entering the condemned cell to pulling the lever was twelve seconds. But he had done it in seven.

The notice of execution with declarations from Harold Gedge the deputy under-sherriff and Dr Liddell was posted outside the prison gates at 9.25 a.m. Mrs Van Der Elst turned to a police officer near her and shouted, 'You swine. I remember you. You do your damnedest. Why did they hang that young man? You do not care a damn.'

She was charged with obstruction to boos and jeers from the crowd. Police officers forced her back in the car, one officer stepping on the running board and directing her chauffeur to Caledonian Road Police Station to be formally charged. At the station she was asked if she had any other witness to call on her behalf, to which she replied, 'Yes, my chauffeur.' Asked the chauffer's name she couldn't remember. After some time, she said, 'Jackson.' She was charged £2 for obstructing a public highway. She emphatically denied that she had sworn at a police officer.

Twenty minutes after he was hanged, Madame Tussaud's opened and Heath's wax figure was already on display in the Chamber of Horrors. The figure was dressed in sports jacket and flannels, similar to the ones he had worn at the police court hearings, but Bernard Tussaud, an ex-RAF serviceman himself during the First World War, would not permit the model of Heath to wear the RAF tie that Heath himself had worn in court for the first two days of the trial. A blue and white striped tie was found from the stocks at the museum.[49] When the museum opened its doors that morning, Heath's body was still hanging within the precincts of Pentonville Prison.[50]

The body was left hanging for over an hour. There was no reason for this last ignominy, it was a directive left over from the time when bodies were publicly exposed on a gibbet. This practice was not to be outlawed until 1949. Pierrepoint himself 'had no heart for it', nor did he approve of having to measure Heath's body after death, carefully logging in the official register the dimensions of the distortion of his body. With the spinal cord now severed, Heath's neck had stretched by two inches.[51] After the allotted time, Pierrepoint returned to the execution hut.

> I stared at the flesh I had stilled. I had further duties to perform, but no longer as executioner. I had been nearest to this man in death and I prepared him for burial. As he hung I stripped him. Piece by piece I removed his clothes. It was not callous, but the best rough dignity I could give him, as he swung to the touch, still hooded in the noose. He yielded his garments without the resistance of limbs ... In London there was always a post-mortem, and he had to be stripped entirely and placed on a mortuary stretcher. But in common courtesy I tied his empty shirt around his hips. [Harry Kirk] had fixed the tackle up above. I passed a rope under the armpits of my charge, and the body was hauled up a few feet. Standing on the scaffold with the body now drooping, I removed the noose and the cap, and took his head between my hands, inclining it from side to side to assure myself that the break had been clean. Then I went below and [Kirk] lowered the rope. A dead man, being taken down from execution is a uniquely broken body whether he is a criminal or Christ, and I received this flesh, leaning helplessly into my arms, with the linen round his loins, gently with

the reverence I thought due to the shell of any man who has sinned and suffered.[52]

At 11.45 that morning an inquest was held within the walls of the prison chaired by the St Pancras coroner, Dr Bentley Purchase. Ten jurors were sworn in. James Liddell, the medical officer, stated that Heath's death by judicial execution had been instantaneous, his neck severed between the second and third vertebrae.[53] After a short consultation with his fellow jurors, the foreman then requested if they might view the body. Even in death people were curious to look at him, to see if they could read any clue in his handsome features to the horrors he had committed. Repelled by this request, Dr Bentley Purchase informed the jury that this would not be necessary.[54]

Thorough to the last, in the final act of their relationship of hunter and quarry, Heath's body was identified by Reg Spooner. He was then buried in an unmarked grave within the precincts of the prison with no ceremony.

At lunchtime, Spooner met Pierrepoint in a bar near Leicester Square.[55] After a few drinks, Spooner turned to him and asked, 'How did he go?' Pierrepoint was quite startled. Ever the professional, Spooner had never asked before (and would never ask again) what had happened during the last moments on the gallows. Pierrepoint said that Heath had faced death bravely with no fuss. He had walked calmly to the scaffold, like a pilot facing what he himself might have called a 'one-way Op'.

When the governor asked if he had any last request – perhaps a shot of whisky – Heath said that he would like one. As Mr Lawton turned to organize it, Heath, a player to the last, added, 'While you're about it, sir, you might make that a double.'[56]

CHAPTER TWENTY-THREE
Mrs Heath

THE *PEOPLE*, 29 OCTOBER 1946

I had a son called Neville, but he was not the man who was responsible for two brutal murders. I have read that my boy was a fiend, cold-blooded and calculating. I have heard him described as a monster. I do not believe it.

He did murder, I know that. He himself knew that he committed both crimes although he could never understand how he had come to do so. To him, everything connected with those poor girls was hazy, their deaths occurred while he was mentally 'blacked-out'. I am absolutely convinced that the Neville Heath who committed those awful crimes was a different man from the handsome, laughing son of mine who used to carry me off to the pictures or tease me gaily about my new dress.

The last time I saw him was in Brixton prison when he was awaiting trial. I still cannot believe that was the same boy. To me, my Neville was the joking young man, always ready for a prank, who was yet in deadly earnest about getting his 'B' licence to fly a plane. His failure to get the licence helped to turn his brain – of that I am convinced. Up to that moment he may well have been wild and he may have made foolish mistakes, but he would not have wilfully harmed anyone.

He rang me up that Wednesday afternoon, I remember. 'I think I'll just nip smartly home and collect my laundry,' he said. And he told me he had won his 'B' licence. People have said that in not telling me his application had been refused, Neville was just betraying those traits of cunning and deceit with which his character has been blackened. That is not true. He lied because he did not want to hurt me by telling me of his failure. And, on the doorstep, he kissed me goodbye.

He was always like that – kind and considerate to both his father and me. I remember once, when he was about twelve, his father was in hospital undergoing an operation. I took Neville to the cinema to keep his mind off the matter, because I could see that he was unusually upset and obviously worrying. Suddenly, in the middle of the film, he burst out crying and I had to take him home. He had been worrying over his dad and keeping that worry to himself until it was too great for him to bear any longer.

As a child, he was as normal as any other small boy ... full of fun and ready to play a childish prank. He would do 'stunts' on his bicycle and he was wrapped up in sport. The mile record he set up at his school has still not been broken.

Yet, despite his natural dare-devilry, he was a wonderfully kind youngster. Never once did he forget a birthday and always I could be sure that he would turn up with some little present, bought from his own pocket money, which he knew I particularly wanted.

I never carried a glass mirror in my handbag and Neville

as a schoolboy knew this. On my birthday he presented me
with a steel mirror contained in a leather case. 'There you
are, Mum. You won't be afraid of breaking that.' Even
when he was in prison awaiting trial he remembered my
birthday and sent me a telegram. He also wired on his
father's birthday.

It has been said that as a small boy he was cruel to animals
and that he once attacked a little girl so badly with a ruler that
she had to be taken home in a taxi cab. Frankly I do not
know of this incident and neither does his headmaster, who
has nothing but good to say of him. Surely I, his mother,
would have heard of this, if it had happened.

When he was about eight, he longed for a puppy. One day
I bought him Doodle, a mongrel, for half a crown. He came
rushing in from school that day. 'Mum, did you get me that
puppy?' he asked excitedly. I can still see his blue eyes alight
with anticipation as he flung his schoolbooks aside and tore
up to me. I had the puppy hidden under a pile of mending in
my lap and told him that I had not been able to buy it. His
whole face fell ... until the puppy wriggled out and he
picked it up and cuddled it in his face.

I do agree with certain statements about my boy and those
are in his attitude towards pain and fear. He would not show
fear and though he hated the mere thought of inflicting pain
– either mental or physical – on others, he was not afraid of
it for himself. One day he came home from school with his
wrist bandaged. When I asked him what was wrong, he
replied airily: 'Oh, just put my wrist out a bit, that's all.' Then
he ate an enormous lunch and went off without even
mentioning that he had a broken wrist and was going to
hospital to have it set. He was always like that – cool and
contemptuous of his own feelings, and considerate towards
others. Once, I remember Mick, his young brother – who
adores him still – excitedly demonstrating a rugby tackle on

Neville who was then about sixteen and pretty hefty. The pair fell in a heap on the drawing-room floor. Neville was up in a flash and almost in tears because he thought that Mick, in tackling him, had hurt himself. The death of little Carol, the brother between Mick and himself, affected Neville considerably. He was only about six at the time, but I remember how grief-stricken he was. When Mick was born, he was delighted because he now had a young brother to look after.

My son did wrong in the eyes of the world, but the world also did him much wrong. He adored his young wife and baby son, and was deeply affected when they parted. Though his school record was not brilliant, he worked hard when he had to and his friends have never ceased to speak well of him. Even his days at borstal were coloured by happy memories because there he was loved and respected by all. The fact that he returned during the war to speak to the boys has been mentioned as an example of his arrogance. That is ridiculous – not only was he invited to speak but the governor during his time wrote to me only this month to say how much he appreciated Neville's help at Hollesley Bay.

It was his wish to die, knowing the only alternative was to be confined and watched over for the rest of his life. And both his father and I are still proud of him because we know that he died bravely and, to the end, tried every way to spare us suffering. In one of his last letters he wrote, 'As I see it, this last journey is just one more Op. This time it's destination unknown and Method of Travel Uncertain.' Those are the things I remember about my son – the good things that every mother remembers.

Everyone was more than kind to us in our trouble. I have nothing but praise for the kindness shown to me by both the police and the prison authorities. Our friends stood by us. We have received hundreds of letters expressing sympathy from complete strangers, and people in the district whom I hardly knew have crossed the road to tell me how they believed in Neville.

In the Bible we learn that Christ cast out devils and I believe that at the time my son did those awful deeds, he was, in the true sense of the phrase, possessed by a devil. I can only hope and pray that soon the psychiatrists will have learned how to do as Christ did – and cast out devils from other unfortunate young men.

Mrs Bessie Heath[1]

AFTERWORD

The return of the soldier is a potent myth.

    In 1946, many men returning to Britain from the various war-scarred parts of the globe had been changed by what they had witnessed and what they had done. At the same time many of the homes and families that they had idealized in their dreams throughout years of separation and suffering were now no longer intact; everything was in a state of flux, everything changed. Added to this, the whole concept of Churchillian 'victory at all costs' was tempered by revelations of genocide, mass rape, starvation, torture and the deadly power of a devastating new bomb.

    Approximately 60 million people were killed in the Second World War[1] and at least as many who survived were bruised and shattered by it, servicemen and women, their spouses and their children. Many lived with the legacy of this trauma for years to come – and some continue to do so, though their number now dwindles year on year.

To date, the story of Neville Heath has been the preserve of sensational and often lurid true-crime anthologies. It has been consigned to history as a sex crime, in the tradition of Jack the Ripper and paving the way for Haigh, Christie and later horrors. But examined in the context in which they happened, perhaps the murders are uniquely a product of their time and place – not a simple tabloid tale of sex and sadism, but a much more complex story of class, aspiration and damage; of damaged individuals in a damaged world. In this light, Heath might also be counted as a casualty of historical forces beyond his control – shaped, defined and broken by his experiences in the war that had just ended. In turn, Margery Gardner and Doreen Marshall became further casualties, in Heath's hands, of the early days of peace.

After the death of her mother, Margery Gardner's daughter Melody had been formally adopted by her grandmother in Sheffield and given her mother's maiden name, in order to protect her from the extraordinary interest that the case elicited at the time. Mrs Wheat was also determined that Melody's errant father should have nothing to do with her upbringing. Two weeks after Heath was executed, Peter Gardner married Kathleen Wyard. But this marriage was to be short-lived; Peter died from cirrhosis of the liver on 1 May 1947, the inevitable outcome of his alcoholism.[2]

As a young girl, Melody accepted that she was an orphan like many children of her generation who had lost parents during the war. She and her grandmother lived together in Sheffield at Oakholme Road, with her uncle Gilbert visiting in the holidays from the various schools where he was teaching. But as she grew to maturity, Melody became more and more curious about her mother and began to ask her grandmother questions. Why was her name different, for instance, than her mother's that was carved on her gravestone in the local cemetery? Mrs Wheat and Gilbert, with the best of intentions, tried to protect young Melody from the truth for as long as possible. They had done their best to put Margery's death behind them, never giving interviews and never discussing it at home. Eventually, having been repeatedly pestered by Melody, Mrs Wheat broke down in tears and told her the story of her mother's tragic death. Now that she knew, Mrs Wheat hoped that that would be the end of the matter. But Melody was by then a curious adolescent and desperate to find out more about the mother she barely remembered, but missed intensely.

In 1960, Melody was sixteen years old. One weekend she was staying with a school friend in Sussex and the two young women decided to go to London to see the sights. Arriving at Victoria Station, Melody happened to be browsing the railway bookstall and picked up a book with a garish cover, *London After Dark* by Fabian of the Yard, full of salacious crimes of sex and murder. Flicking through the book, she read, for the first time, the story of her mother's death in graphic details gleaned from police gossip and tabloid news-papers, much of it inaccurate:

> It was known to police observers on the West End scene that Marjorie [*sic*] Gardner was by no means unacquainted with such brutal and humiliating activities. Something went amiss, and Heath carried his indulgences too far. Marjorie Gardner died of haemorrhage, stabbed internally with the haft of a hunting whip.[3]

The girl was devastated. Not just by the extraordinary brutal-ity of her mother's death, but to read of her in this context stunned her to the very core. This was not the image of her dearly missed mother that she had imagined so often. Still in shock, her friend suggested that they carry on and look at the sights – Buckingham Palace, Trafalgar Square, Harrods, Madame Tussaud's. It might take Melody's mind off things.

At Madame Tussaud's, the girls entered the Chamber of Horrors, and whether she knew she was actively seeking him out there or not, Melody came face to face with the wax figure of Neville Heath, the man who had murdered her mother. She stared into his blank blue eyes. For Melody, the whole experience was deeply traumatic and one from which it would take her years to recover.

Returning home from the weekend, Melody went upstairs alone and locked herself in the bathroom. She filled the bath, feeling that all she wanted to do was slip under the water, relieve herself of this extraordinary, heart-aching pain and die.[4]

After Doreen Marshall's death, relations between her family were never the same again. Grace Marshall couldn't forgive her surviving daughter Joan for not accompanying Doreen down to Bournemouth that summer. Worse still, Joan couldn't forgive herself. She divorced her husband Charles in 1947 but went on to marry again in 1948 to a divorcé from Harrow, Reginald Adams, the father of three young sons. In 1954, she was delighted to have a child of her own, a girl she named Julia. But now a frail and nervous woman, Joan suffered from anxiety for the rest of her life. Throughout Julia's childhood, Joan stifled her daughter – always checking on her, making sure she was safe. As Julia grew into her teens during the sixties, her mother's controlling behaviour seemed suffocating. The world was rapidly changing and yet her mother wanted to keep her cossetted from it, wrapped in maternal cotton wool. It was only in her twenties that Joan revealed to Julia that the reason that she worried about her so intensely was that her sister had been murdered years before.[5]

Charles and Grace Marshall moved out of Woodhall Road,

with all its terrible memories, to a house in Stanmore. Grace died in 1967 and her husband in 1973. They were both cremated at Breakspear Crematorium in Ruislip. Tragically, Joan lived with the self-imposed burden of responsibility for Doreen's death for the rest of her life, over half a century. She died in Wycombe General Hospital on 14 August 1998.

Doreen is the only member of the family to rest in Pinner Cemetery. The grave, no longer tended, has weathered and declined over the decades. At the head of the grave there is a small bird-bath with a little stone bird, set there to encourage sparrows to drink from it, chosen perhaps by Doreen's parents wishing their daughter some company. At the foot of the grave, an inscription quotes the American poet, James Whitcomb Riley, from a poem perhaps read at Doreen's funeral, 'She Is Just Away'.

In 2012, the grave was registered by the Commonwealth War Graves Commission and will be tended by them if it falls further into disrepair.

In 1954, Reg Spooner had served thirty years in the police force with a series of celebrated convictions behind him, but none better remembered than his arrest of Neville Heath. That year he was appointed head of the Flying Squad and became one of the most recognized officers in the force. In 1958 he was appointed deputy commander. But after years of chain smoking, he was diagnosed with lung cancer in 1962. Knowing he was dying, Spooner carried on working as best he could. A former Scotland Yard colleague of Spooner's said that 'everyone knew that his work was his whole life. He had no other real interests. Retiring him because of ill health would have hastened his end.'[6]

Spooner finally died at St Thomas' Hospital just before midnight on 18 September 1963. When the night sister telephoned his wife to give her the news, she gently asked if they might have the cornea of his eyes to give sight to a blind

person. 'Oh, yes,' said Myra, 'Reg would have liked that.'
More than one thousand police officers of all ranks attended
his funeral.[7]

According to his wife, Spooner always talked with great
sympathy about the ordeal that Heath's family had experienced during and after the trial. As his brother had wished,
Mick Heath joined the RAF in January 1947 but found his
time in the service uncomfortable as corporals in primary
training would ask, 'Any relation to Neville?' as soon as
they heard his name. On a trip to Blackpool, he also went
to a wax museum and found himself staring at a figure of his
brother standing amongst a collection of ghouls in the
Chamber of Horrors. At night, when his RAF colleagues
went off to meet girls, Mick stayed behind in the barracks,
worried that he too might have inherited some element of
madness that had affected his brother.[8] He was discharged
from the RAF in 1949. In 1955, he married Irene Lovejoy,
a widow, some years older than him. William Heath died of
heart disease in 1956. Subsequently, Mick, his wife and his
mother moved back to Ilford together where Mick worked
as a telecommunications engineer. In 1982 Bessie Heath
died at the Mayflower Hospital in Billericay at the age of
ninety-one. Mick died of cancer two years later at St Bart's
Hospital in Smithfield.

In South Africa, Elizabeth Armstrong rebuilt her life,
taking a job as a dentist's receptionist and planning her
marriage to her fiancé. Following Heath's execution, she
expressed no bitterness towards him for she felt that 'there
[was] so much good in him'.[9]

> He came into my life and went out again, leaving me slightly
> bewildered. It seems like a beautiful dream that turned
> suddenly into a ghastly nightmare. I loved him desperately
> when I ran away and married him against my parents' wishes.

> But at all costs little Robert must never know the truth. Every photograph I had of Neville I have destroyed. Every letter I have burned ... I pray that all the tragedy of the past may be buried in the passing of time.[10]

In 1947, Elizabeth married a young widower with two young children of his own. He had a distinguished war service and had spent three years in a prison camp in Germany having been captured at Tobruk. Together he and Elizabeth put the past behind them and never discussed her former husband. They enjoyed a long and happy marriage until Elizabeth's death in 1990. Her son by Heath went on to have a successful career and a happy marriage with children and grandchildren of his own, the horrors of 1946 a dim, distant memory; a world away in a different country, another century.

In 1939, when Gilbert Wheat was going off to war, he discussed with his mother all his hopes for the future if he were fortunate enough to return: to marry, to settle down and (he was very specific about this) to have four children.

After the end of the war and the subsequent loss of his sister, Gilbert committed himself to life as a schoolmaster and went on to run his own school. He was a kindly, inspirational figure who combined an irreverent disrespect for petty rules with strong, traditional values. His mother, Mrs Wheat, died in 1963 and his niece Melody married an army officer some years later. With no wife or children of his own, when she was later widowed, Gilbert took Melody and her children into his home and they remained a close-knit family for many years. In the absence of his sister Margery, Gilbert selflessly committed himself to help raise Melody's four children, fulfilling his own prophecy of a generation before. He died in 2010 at the age of ninety-three.

* * *

Despite the brutality and violence that dominates the story of Neville Heath, it is the seemingly insignificant details that seem most profoundly to articulate the sense of loss, that break through the patina of sixty-odd years to pierce our hearts: a leopardette coat, a powder compact with a cracked mirror, a caterpillar badge.

Fragile, precious and fraught with danger, 'life depends on a silken thread'.

Sean O'Connor
London, 2013

APPENDIX
Heath's Last Letters

Tuesday, 15th October 1946

My dear Dad,
Very many thanks indeed for your letter.

I saw Near yesterday afternoon and understand that he told you the news [about the failure of the medical review]. *He also tried very hard to persuade me to see you. With regard to this, I know you'll understand how I feel about it and I think it far better if we just make a clean break without farewells etc. I've always hated being seen off on journeys and this I regard as just another journey, to somewhere I don't know and by a method of transport that I don't understand. To my very limited intelligence it is nothing more than that — just another 'op' — and like all 'ops' it may prove to be quite exciting.*

I'm taking with me many pleasant memories of a very crowded thirty years. Into my crowded hours I have crammed much. A lot I regret bitterly and a lot I am thankful for – but probably the outstanding thing of all is the unselfish love and loyalty of my parents. You, who have both suffered so much, have been splendid and I can only say – thanks!

I have instructed Near to send you £60 which is for Mick. You know what I want him to do with it if it is possible. The thought that I can make that possible and the knowledge that you will carry out my wishes will make me very happy and satisfied.

I have made a new will today leaving everything to Mick with you as Trustee. This is just in case any one decides to prove an old will of mine in South Africa.

Near has my instructions and a note of authority as well, so he will not prove this will unless the other one is produced.

Any money that mother has of mine will of course, go to Mick, and my personal effects from here will be sent to you and you will hand them to him. There should be about £10 from here. I think mother has about £30 so he should have a little more than £100. I don't know much about law, but I've instructed Near to send that money off now, before my death, as a gift.

One other thing, and this I am most sincere and firm about. I was painted as black as the Ace of Spades in court and you will possibly get several accounts rendered you by smart Alecs who hope to get them paid by your kind-heartedness.

You are not, in any way, and have never been responsible for any of my debts. Apart from this money which I am giving away now, I shall not leave a halfpenny. You will please not pay any outstanding accounts of mine. Once again – you are not responsible for my debts.

Well, I think that is about all, except to thank you both from the very bottom of my heart for all you've done for me and to thank you for giving me all the golden opportunities that I have so shamelessly wasted.

The very best of luck to you always, and don't let Mick make my mistakes. Goodbye and bless you both.

Always yours,

Neville

Pentonville Prison

Tuesday, 15th October 1946

My dearest Mother,

You now know the news so there is very little for me to say. One thing I feel certain of is that Near did all in his power to get the verdict altered. The sentence, I don't give a damn about. I've written to Dad and shall write to Mick. Everything has been said, but I'd like you to know how terribly grateful I am for your never-failing love, loyalty and devotion. It has always been of such a quality that no other parents could hope to equal.

Both you and Dad are unique in the way of parents and to me your honesty, simplicity, faith and sheer guts stand out like a brilliant star. My only regret at leaving this world is that I have been so damned unworthy of you both.

I'm not religious – I never have been and I'm not going to start now (at least I'm no hypocrite) – but if there is any God, and I know you believe in that sort of thing, you both deserve all the love He can bestow on you.

Let Mick profit by my mistakes. Help him to get airborne and make a success of it. If there is anything he wants to know Ralph will help him. His address is First Officer Fisher, BOAC, Central Flying School, Aldermaston, Nr Reading, Wilts.

I've nothing else to say except cheerio and thanks for all you've done for me.

In spite of Near's pleadings, I have decided not to see either of you. Please understand won't you? My thoughts are with you and you have all my love always.

Let's carry this thing through to the end with the quiet dignity that we've shown all through.

Goodbye and bless you darling Mother,
Always yours,

Nen

Pentonville Prison

Tuesday, 15th October 1946

My dear Mick,
Just a short note to let you know for the last time that your writing is abominable and your spelling even worse.

I won't be seeing you again but perhaps in the days to come you'll feel a friendly Gremlin ease your aircraft out of a sticky position. You may recognise the touch.

You'll shortly be going into a damn good service. Your future is up to you. Don't make the mistakes that I've made. If you get any urges in the wrong direction just say to yourself 'Christ, I've seen the result of those' and open your throttles and go round again. You know what I mean.

Use King's Regulations and Air Council instructions as your Bible and stick to it. If you do that you won't come unstuck. I'm more qualified to give advice than anyone else I know because I've learned all the lessons — and how! Now you take advantage of them. Ralph will always help you, never be too shy to ask him, so will any other Air Force pilot who knew me. You'll find Air Force friendships mean something and they're not easily broken.

Get your 'A' licence and go ahead. You can do great things, it's in you and it's up to you to do something to make Mother and Dad proud of you. By doing that, you'll be helping me as well.

Cheerio Mick and very many happy landings. Don't you bloody well let me down or I'll haunt you, and I've a feeling I can be a most unpleasant ghost.

Ever yours,

Nen

Pentonville Prison

Tuesday evening, 15th October 1946

My Dearest Mother,
First of all very many thanks for your cable and also for Mick's. I've written several letters to my friends and one more to Elizabeth, but I'd like the last to be written to you. I can't say more than I said in my previous letter but I meant it wholeheartedly.

I shall probably stay up reading tonight because I'd like to see the dawn again. So much in my memory is associated with the dawn – early morning patrols and coming home from night clubs. Well, it wasn't really a bad life while it lasted, and I've lots to think about.

Please don't mourn my going – I should hate it – and don't wear any black. I really mean that. Just wear your gayest colours and refer to me quite normally – that is the easiest way to forget.

So now I'll leave you. Cheerio, my dear, and very many thanks for everything.

All my love is with you both always.
Forever yours,

Nen[1]

ACKNOWLEDGEMENTS

I would like to thank the staff at the libraries and archives around the United Kingdom and in South Africa who have assisted me in my research. I am particularly indebted to the staff at The National Archives in Kew who have responded with patience and diligence to my many requests to have the various files relating to the case made available to study for the first time.

I am grateful to the London Metropolitan Archives, the London Library, the British Library, the British Newspaper Library at Colindale, the staff at the Archives of the Imperial War Museum, the RAF Museum at Hendon, the Museum of Wimbledon, Melvyn Foster at the Association of Wrens, Charlotte Burford and Julia Collins at Madame Tussaud's, Professor John Moxham at King's College Hospital, Martin Hayes at Worthing Library, Jonathan Oates at Ealing Library, the Lincolnshire County Archives, the Nottinghamshire County Archives, the Sheffield Local History Library, the *Sheffield Telegraph*, the *Harrow Observer* and the *Bournemouth Echo*. Peter Kazmierczak at Bournemouth Library provided guidance and provided photographs from the local history archive. Hazel Ogilvie was particularly helpful at the Local History Library in Harrow, researching the movements of the Marshall family during the war. Matthew Piggott at Surrey History Centre helped to investigate the archives of Rutlish School. I'm grateful to Graham W. Mills, a governor at Rutlish and the current headmaster, Mr A. Williamson, for allowing me access to the school archive. Peter Elliot at the RAF Museum in Hendon very kindly read and advised about the RAF sections.

In South Africa, I am indebted to Anne Clarkson, who accessed a large volume of new material relating to Heath's marriage and his tenure with the South African Air Force in the archives held in Johannesburg, Pretoria and Cape Town.

For access to the remaining evidence from the case at the Crime Museum – including Heath's suitcase, his 'escape scarf' and whip – I am indebted to Paul Bickley and Camilla O'Hare at New Scotland Yard. Crime historian and researcher, Keith Skinner, has been extremely helpful and encouraging as well as being a mine of information and contacts. He has generously shared his own documents and research about the case from his archive.

Donald Thomas, who wrote the last major study of Heath twenty-five years ago, shared his insights into the case and his memories of the period. Dr Paul Addison, Juliet Gardiner, Roger Hollinghurst, Alwyn Liddell, Matthew Lloyd, Don Minterne, Tim McInerny, David Pirie, Martin Ridgwell, Geoff Sherratt and René Weis all offered help and advice at various stages in the inception and writing of this book, for which I'm very grateful.

Despite the horrific nature of Heath's story, several people have welcomed me with great enthusiasm to the many buildings where significant events took place. Early on in my research, Jay and Lucy Dowle invited me to visit them at the Heaths' former home at Merton Hall Road, as did Julie Williams, who allowed me to visit the Marshall family home in Pinner. Liliya Guzheva, Jamison Firestone and Robert Field generously allowed me to visit the scene of the crime at the former Pembridge Court Hotel. In Bournemouth, Nick the caretaker at Tollard Court, allowed me to spend time in the former Tollard Royal Hotel where many of the interiors in the public spaces of the building have remained unchanged. I was also welcomed to the Norfolk Royale Hotel (the former Norfolk Hotel) by the current manager, Simon Scarborough. I'd like to thank Matt Evans who accompanied me on a trip to Bournemouth to visit the scene of the crime at Branksome Dene Chine. David McRae, the manager of the Strand Palace Hotel, showed me Room 506, which still remains, as well as providing photographs from the hotel archive.

Michael Suter kindly shared memories of his father with me. Julia Young, the niece of Doreen Marshall, has been hugely generous with her recollections of Doreen's parents and her sister, Joan. I am indebted to the remaining members of Neville Heath's family who, despite their reluctance to explore a difficult area of their family history, agreed to meet me to discuss it.

Jackie Malton has offered support, insight and practical help from the start of this venture for which I am very grateful. I'm also indebted to Sarah Waters for her help and advice. My agent, Judith Murray, has championed this book since she read my first tentative pages and I am grateful for her encouragement and support throughout. Mike Jones at Simon & Schuster enthusiastically embraced the idea and I have been greatly supported by Jo Whitford and Lindsay Davies who have worked with me on the text.

Rob Haywood has been patient, supportive and encouraging throughout the gestation and realization of this book for which I'm hugely grateful.

My greatest debt, though, is to Melody Gardner, who has not spoken publicly about her family history for nearly seventy years. Despite the painful material, Melody has embraced the revelations I have put before her with extraordinary fortitude and open-mindedness. She has offered unique insights into three generations of Sheffield women: her redoubtable grandmother, Betty Wheat, her mother Margery Gardner and, indeed, her own life. She has encouraged the writing of this book, whilst always retaining distance from it. For me, enabling Melody to read her mother's story from original documents, rather than filtered through biased and erroneous newspaper reports, has been a great privilege. I hope she feels that her mother's tragic story has been told honestly, fairly and – at last – with understanding and compassion.

FURTHER READING

Original documents relating to the investigation and trial held at the National Archives (TNA):

HO 144/22871
HO 144/22872
DPP 1/1522
DPP 1/1524
CRIM 1/1806
MEPO 3/2664
MEPO 3/2728
P COM 9/700

In South Africa, the files relating to Heath are held at the Cape Archives and Record Service and the National Archives Repository in Pretoria, as well as at the Offices of the Master of the High Court in Cape Town and Pretoria.

Books about Heath or which discuss the case:

Brock, Sydney, The Life and Death of Neville Heath, Modern Fiction Ltd, 1947

Byrne, Gerald, Borstal Boy: The Uncensored Story of Neville Heath, Gerald Byrne, Headline, 1946

Critchley, Macdonald (ed.), The Trial of Neville George Clevely Heath, Notable British Trials series, William Hodge, 1951

Hill, Paull, Portrait of a Sadist, Neville Spearman, 1960

Selwyn, Francis, Rotten to the Core: The Life and Death of Neville Heath, Routledge, 1988

Adamson, Iain, The Great Detective: A Life of Deputy Commander Reginald Spooner of Scotland Yard, Frederick Muller Ltd, 1966

Bennett, Benjamin, Why Did They Do It?, Howard B. Timmins, Cape Town, 1954

Bixley, William, The Guilty and the Innocent, Souvenir Press, 1957

Casswell, J. D., A Lance for Liberty, Harrap, 1961

Fabian, Robert, London After Dark, The Naldrett Press, 1954

Hoskins, Percy, The Sound of Murder, John Long, 1973

Morland, Nigel, Hangman's Clutch, Werner Laurie, 1954

Phillips, Conrad, Murderer's Moon, Being Studies of Heath, Haigh, Christie and Chesney, Associated Booksellers, 1956

Pierrepoint, Albert, Executioner: Pierrepoint, Harrap, 1974

Playfair, Giles, and Sington, Derrick, Crime, Punishment and Cure, Secker & Warburg, 1965

Playfair, Giles, and Sington, Derrick, The Offenders: Society and the Atrocious Crime, The Windmill Press, 1957

Root, Neil, Frenzy! Heath, Haigh and Christie: The First Great Tabloid Murderers, Preface Publishing, 2011

Simpson, Keith, Forty Years of Murder: An Autobiography, Harrap, 1978

Thomas, Donald, Hanged in Error?, Robert Hale, 1994

Webb, Duncan, Crime Is My Business, Frederick Muller, 1953

Britain at war (and after):

Allport, Alan, *Demobbed: Coming Home After the Second World War*, Yale, 2010

Beaton, Cecil, and Pope-Hennessy, James, *History Under Fire: 52 Photographs of Air Raid Damage to London Buildings, 1940–41*, B. T. Batsford, 1941

Beevor, Antony, *The Second World War*, Weidenfeld & Nicolson, 2012

Bigland, Eileen, *The Story of the WRNS*, Nicholson & Watson, 1946

Calder, Angus, *The People's War: Britain 1939–45*, Jonathan Cape, 1969

Costello, John, *Love, Sex and War*, Collins, 1985

Drummond, John D., *Blue for a Girl: The Story of the WRNS*, W. H. Allen, 1960

Edington, M. A., *Bournemouth and the Second World War*, Bournemouth Local Studies Publications, 1999

Faviell, Frances, *A Chelsea Concerto*, Cassell, 1959

Fussell, Paul, *Wartime: Understanding and Behaviour in the Second World War*, Oxford, 1989

Gardiner, Juliet, *The Blitz: The British Under Attack*, Harper Press, 2010

Gardiner, Juliet, *Wartime 1939–1945*, Headline, 2004

Garfield, Simon, *Our Hidden Lives*, Ebury Press, 2004

Hodgson, Vere, *Few Eggs and No Oranges*, Dennis Dobson, 1976

Kent, William (ed.), *An Encyclopaedia of London*, J. M. Dent & Sons Ltd, 1951

Kent, William, *The Lost Treasures of London*, Phoenix House Limited, 1947

Kershaw, Robert, *Never Surrender: Lost Voices of a Generation at War*, Hodder & Stoughton, 2009

Kynaston, David, *Austerity Britain 1945–51*, Bloomsbury, 2007

Lloyd George, David, *War Memoirs*, Ivor Nicolson & Watson, 1934

Lofthouse, Alistair, *Then and Now: The Sheffield Blitz, Operation Crucible*, ALD Design and Print, 2001

London Evening News, *Hitler Passed This Way: 170 Pictures from the London Evening News*, 1945

Longmate, Norman, *How We Lived Then: A History of Everyday Life During the Second World War*, Arrow Books, 1973

Malin, A. M., *The Villager at War: A Diary of Home Front Pinner 1939–1945*, The Pinner Association, 1995

Marley, David (ed.), *The Daily Telegraph Story of the War*, Hodder & Stoughton, 1944

Mathews, L. W., *Chelsea Old Church 1941–1950*, Buckenham & Son, 1957

Nicholson, Virginia, *Millions Like Us: Women's Lives in War and Peace, 1939–1949*, Viking, 2011

Plastow, Norman, *Safe as Houses: Wimbledon at War 1939–1945*, The Wimbledon Society, 2010

Price, Alfred, *Blitz on Britain: The Bomber Attacks on the United Kingdom 1939–1945*, Ian Allan Ltd, 1976

Priestley, J.B., *Britain Under Fire*, Country Life, 1941

Richards, E. M., *The Bombed Buildings of Britain*, The Architectural Press, 1947

Scott, Peggy, *British Women in War*, Hutchinson & Co, 1940

Turner, Barry, and Rennell, Tony, *When Daddy Came Home: How Family Life Changed Forever in 1945*, Pimlico, 1996

Waller, Maureen, *London 1945: Life in the Debris of War*, John Murray, 2004

Wyndham, Joan, *Love Is Blue: A Wartime Diary*, Heinemann, 1986

Ziegler, Philip, *London at War 1939–1945*, Pimlico, 2002

Zweiniger-Bargielowska, Ina, *Austerity in Britain: Rationing, Controls and Consumption 1939–1955*, Oxford, 2002

The Royal Air Force:

Beaton, Cecil, *Winged Squadrons*, Hutchinson, 1942

Bishop, Patrick, *Bomber Boys: Fighting Back 1940–1945*, Harper Perennial, 2008

Bishop, Patrick, *Fighter Boys: Saving Britain 1940*, Harper Perennial, 2004

Clark, Denis, *Tail End Charlie*, Lutterworth Press, 1946

Dahl, Roald, *Over to You: Ten Stories of Flyers and Flying*, Hamish Hamilton, 1945

David, Dennis 'Hurricane', *My Autobiography*, Grub Street, 2000

Falconer, Jonathan, *RAF Bomber Crewman*, Shire Publications, 2011

Francis, Martin, *The Flyer: British Culture and the Royal Air Force, 1939–1945*, Oxford University Press, 2008

Hastings, Max, *Bomber Command*, Michael Joseph, 1979

Kent, Gp. Capt. J. A., *One of the Few*, William Kimber & Co, 1971

Minterne, Don, *The History of 73 Squadron, Part 2: July 1937 to August 1939*, Tutor, 2000

Nichol, John, and Rennell, Tony, *Tail End Charlies: The Last Battles of the Bomber War 1944–45*, Viking, 2004

Simpson, William, *I Burned My Fingers*, Putnam, 1955

Wells, Mark K., *Courage and Air Warfare: The Allied Aircrew Experience in the Second World War*, Frank Cass, 2000

Wilson, Kevin, *Men of Air: The Doomed Youth of Bomber Command*, Phoenix, 2008

General:

Aulier, Dan, *Hitchcock's Secret Notebooks*, Bloomsbury, 1999

Behan, Brendan, *Borstal Boy*, Hutchinson & Co, 1958

Benton, Charlotte, Benton, Tim, and Wood, Ghislaine (eds), *Art Deco 1910–1939*, V&A Publications, 2003

Bournemouth, Ward Lock Red Guide, Nineteenth Edition, *c.*1950

Brock, Colin, *Rutlish School: The First Hundred Years*, Rutlish School, 1995

Brooke, Rupert, *Collected Poems*, Sidgwick & Jackson, 1918

Browne, Douglas G., and Tullet, E. V., *Bernard Spilsbury: His Life and Cases*, Harrap, 1951

Bryant, Margot, *As We Were: South Africa 1939–41*, Keartland Publishers, Johannesburg, 1974

Carswell, Donald, *The Trial of Ronald True*, Notable British Trials series, William Hodge, 1924

Cave, Herbert, *Practical Exercises in Spoken English*, Harrap, 1930

Chapman, Pauline, *Madame Tussaud's Chamber of Horrors*, Constable, 1984

Cooper, Artemis, *Cairo in the War 1939–45*, Hamish Hamilton, 1992

Coward, Noël, *Middle East Diary*, William Heinemann Ltd, 1944

Coward, Noël, ed by Payn, Graham and Morley, Sheridan, *The Noël Coward Diaries*, Weidenfeld & Nicolson, 1982

Crisp, Quentin, *The Naked Civil Servant*, Jonathan Cape, 1968

Eddleston, John J., *The Encyclopaedia of Executions*, John Blake, 2002

Farndale, Nigel, *Haw-Haw: The Tragedy of William and Margaret Joyce*, Macmillan 2005

Gibson, Ian, *The English Vice: Beating, Sex and Shame in Victorian England and After*, Duckworth, 1978

Gibson, Perla Siedle, *Durban's Lady in White: An Autobiography*, Aedificamus Press, 1991

Gunby, Norman, *A Potted History of Ilford*, published privately by the author, 1997

Hardy, Thomas, *Tess of the D'Urbervilles*, Osgood, McIlvaine & Co, 1895

Hollis, Christopher, *The Homicide Act*, Victor Gollancz, 1964

Honeycombe, Gordon, *Murders of the Black Museum*, John Blake, 2009

Inwood, Stephen, *A History of London*, Macmillan, 1998

Jones, Nigel, *Rupert Brooke: Life, Death and Myth*, Richard Cohen Books, 1999

Kerridge, Ronald, and Standing, Michael, *Worthing*, Black Horse Books, 2001

Lister, Moira, *The Very Merry Moira*, Hodder & Stoughton, 1969

Macaulay, Rose, *The World My Wilderness*, Collins, 1950

Morton, H.V., *In Search of South Africa*, Methuen & Co, 1948

Orwell, George, *The Collected Essays, Journalism and Letters of George Orwell*, Secker & Warburg, 1961

Orwell, George, *Inside the Whale and Other Essays*, Victor Gollancz, 1940

Procter, Harry, *The Street of Disillusion*, Revel Barker Publishing, 2010 (first published by Allan Wingate in 1958)

Read, Simon, *In the Dark: The True Story of the Blackout Ripper*, Berkley Books, New York, 2006

Reader's Digest, *Illustrated History of South Africa: The Real Story*, Reader's Digest Publishing, 1988

Scott, Sir Harold, *Scotland Yard*, Andre Deutsche, 1954

Spoto, Donald, *The Dark Side of Genius: The Life of Alfred Hitchcock*, Plexus, 1983

Walker, Eric A., *A History of Southern Africa*, Longmans Green, 1957

Weis, René, *Criminal Justice: The True Story of Edith Thompson*, Hamish Hamilton, 1988

Weisbord, M., and Simmonds, M., *The Valour and the Horror: The Untold Story of Canadians in the Second World War*, HarperCollins, 1991

Wells, A. W., *South Africa: A Planned Tour of the Country Today*, J. M. Dent & Sons, 1947

Wheat, Gilbert, *The Wheats of Sheffield*, B. A. Hathaway Press, 1996

Worthing, Ward Lock Red Guide, Eighth Edition (Revised), 1939–40

Young, Filson (ed.), *The Trial of Frederick Bywaters and Edith Thompson*, Notable British Trials, second edition 1951

Studies in Psychopathy:

Baron-Cohen, Simon, *Zero Degrees of Empathy: A New Theory of Human Cruelty*, Allen Lane, 2011

Cleckley, Hervey M., *The Mask of Sanity*, Plume Books, 1982

Hare, Robert D., *Without Conscience: The Disturbing World of the Psychopaths Amongst Us*, The Guildford Press, 1993

Hibbert, Christopher, *The Roots of Evil: A Social History of Crime and Punishment*, Weidenfeld & Nicolson, 1963

Ronson, Jon, *The Psychopath Test: A Journey Through the Madness Industry*, Picador, 2011

Storr, Anthony, *Human Aggression*, Pelican Books, 1970

Fiction inspired by Heath:

Hamilton, Patrick, *Mr Stimpson and Mr Gorse*, Constable, 1953

Hamilton, Patrick, *Unknown Assailant*, Constable, 1955

Hamilton, Patrick, *The West Pier*, Constable, 1951

La Berne, Arthur, *Goodbye Piccadilly, Farwell Leicester Square*, W. H. Allen, 1966

Mallanson, Todd, *Ladykiller*, Weidenfeld & Nicolson, 1980

Taylor, Elizabeth, *A Wreath of Roses*, Peter Davies, 1949

ENDNOTES

Foreword

1. *Daily Mail*, 28 September 1946.
2. *News of the World*, 29 September 1946.
3. From Detective Inspector George Henry Gates' statement quoted in Critchley (ed.), op. cit., p. 106.
4. *People*, 15 September 1946. The paper also added that the interest of the international press 'pales into insignificance before the morbid curiosity of women'.
5. *Daily Express*, 27 September 1945.
6. *News Chronicle*, 10 July 1945, p. 2.
7. In his Victory broadcast on 13 May 1945, Churchill thanked all the services for the part they had played in securing victory. There was, however, no mention of Bomber Command. Bomber Harris campaigned for the rest of his life

to have their achievements and sacrifices recognized. Harris commented that 'the bomber drops things on people and people don't like things being dropped on them, and the fighter shoots at the bomber who drops things. Therefore he is popular whereas the bomber is unpopular. It's as easy as that' (Bishop, *Fighter Boys*, p. xxxii). Only after years of campaigning has a monument to Bomber Command been unveiled in London in 2012, but the controversy continues.

8. Martin, *The Flyer*, p. 152.
9. *Holiday Camp* (1947) directed by Ken Annakin, produced by Sydney Box.
10. The *New Statesman and Nation* expressed little surprise at the increase in violent crimes perpetrated by ex-servicemen: 'They've been trained in lawlessness, ordered to behave like thugs and decorated for doing it ... what do you expect?', 12 January 1946.
11. Byrne, *Borstal Boy*.
12. Brock, *The Life and Death of Neville Heath*.
13. Letter from James Hodge to Sir Theobald Mathew, Director of Public Prosecutions, 18 May 1951, TNA DPP 2/1522.
14. Taylor, *A Wreath of Roses*, 1949.
15. Early in *The West Pier*, the young psychopath Ralph Gorse ties a schoolgirl to a garden roller on a cricket pitch with a skipping rope, a reference perhaps to the incident reported in the press that Heath had beaten a girl so violently with a ruler that she had to be sent home. Gorse's malevolent adventures continue in *Mr Stimpson and Mr Gorse*. The last book, *Unknown Assailant*, ends with Gorse terrorizing a young woman and tying her up: 'He liked to tie women up in order to get the impression that they were at his mercy, and he also liked to be tied up by women and to feel that he was at theirs' (*Unknown Assailant*, Chapter 15, p. 130).
16. Morland, op. cit., p. 17.
17. Aulier, *Hitchcock's Secret Notebooks*, p. 544.

18. Spoto, *The Dark Side of Genius: The Life of Alfred Hitchcock*, p. 496. In Hitchcock's version Heath would be gay, obsessed with muscle magazines and, at one point, caught masturbating in bed by his mother – a classic Hitchcock anti-hero cut from the same cloth as Norman Bates.

19. According to Fast, Hitchcock said, 'I've just seen Antonioni's *Blow Up!* These Italian directors are a century ahead of me in terms of technique! What have I been doing all this time?' (Spoto, op. cit., p. 496).

20. The 1971 *Frenzy* was based on Arthur La Bern's *Goodbye Piccadilly, Farewell Leicester Square*. The novel is suffused with references to Heath. Though set in the 1960s, it focuses on a penniless, divorced and disillusioned pilot, Dick Blamey DSO, DFC and Bar, falsely accused of murder in an alien London – cleaner but duller than its heyday in the war years. 'This, he thought, is not the heart of London. It's the anus' (p. 27). Hitchcock goes even further in emphasizing the references to Heath in the script. At one point Hetty Porter (Billie Whitelaw) directly quotes a line that Heath had mentioned to Yvonne Symonds: 'He must have been a sexual maniac.'

21. UK Homicide Act (1957) Chapter 2, Part 1 (section 2: 'Persons Suffering from Diminished Responsibility'). Quoted in Hollis, *The Homicide Act*.

22. Orwell, 'Decline of the English Murder' in *Collected Essays Volume IV: In Front of Your Nose 1945–50*, p. 100, originally printed in *Tribune*, 15 February 1946.

23. Later, *The Sunday Mirror*.

24. Orwell, 'Raffles and Miss Blandish', *Collected Essays*, p. 247.

25. *Daily Mail*, 28 September 1946.

26. The National Archives of the UK (TNA): Detective Superintendent H. Lovell Dorset Constabulary, 18 July 1946, MEPO 3/2728.

27. Byrne, op. cit., p. 144.

28. Bixley, *The Guilty and the Innocent*, p. 112.

Prologue

1. The outline of the events at the Strand Palace Hotel is taken
   from three witness statements opened to the public for the
   first time in 2011 in a file held at the National Archives
   (TNA), DPP 2/1522. These are the statements of William
   Luff (22 June 1946), Thomas Paul (24 June 1946) and Pauline
   Miriam Brees (27 July 1946). Significantly, Pauline Brees'
   statement was taken a month after that of the two members
   of staff of the Strand Palace. Pauline was the widow of
   Squadron Leader Alec Brees, DFC, who had been killed in a
   flying accident on 23 August 1945.

2. Benton, Benton and Wood (eds.), *Art Deco 1910–1939*, pp.
   217, 239. Bernard had a huge influence on the 'look' of
   inter-war London in terms of interior design. Having originally worked as a stage designer in Britain and the United
   States, as well as designing the interiors for the Strand Palace
   Hotel, he also designed the Cumberland Hotel, the Regent
   Palace Hotel and the Lyons Corner Houses throughout the
   1920s and thirties.

3. Ibid., p. 238.

4. See Allport, *Demobbed*.

5. Thomas Paul says Armstrong was wearing underpants; Luff
   remembered him as being 'completely nude'. In his subsequent attacks on women, Heath also seems to have been
   naked. Paul claimed that Pauline was tied with 'a pair of
   braces or a tie' and Luff remembered a belt. Pauline herself
   recalls a handkerchief being used to bind her, which is more
   consistent with Heath's later behaviour.

6. Many newspapers and books further embellished this moment,
   claiming that Heath was unable to stop beating Pauline when
   Luff and Paul entered the room. The *News of the World*, 29
   September 1946, stated: 'Heath stood over her in maniacal

frenzy and had to be forcibly restrained while [she] was set free.' In *Crime, Punishment and Cure*, Giles Playfair and Derrick Sington suggest that 'the hotel detectives ... had to restrain Heath forcibly' (p. 78). There is no evidence for this manic behaviour in Luff, Paul or Brees' statements.

7. In his statement on 19 July 1946, TNA HO 144/22871, having interviewed her personally, Spooner wrote that Miss Brees 'appeared of the prostitute class' but later revised his opinion in his overview of the case on 2 October referring to her as 'a respectable young woman'.

8. Pauline Brees, 27 July 1946, TNA DPP 2/1522.

9. No professional production was playing at the theatre at the time as it played host to performances by students from RADA.

10. Dialogue quoted from Pauline Brees, 27 July 1946, TNA DPP 2/1522.

11. Critchley (ed.), *The Trial of Neville George Clevely Heath*, p. 169.

Chapter 1

1. From Clement Attlee's election victory speech 26 July 1945, quoted in Kynaston, *Austerity Britain 1945–51*, p. 76.

2. Entry for Thursday 26 July 1945, Coward, *The Noël Coward Diaries*, p. 36.

3. Kynaston, op. cit., p. 116.

4. *Evening Standard,* 7 June 1946.

5. Ibid.

6. All quotes *News of the World*, 9 June 1946.

7. Imperial War Museum Film Archive, MGH 214, V Day, 8 June 1946.

8. Mass Observation reports quoted in Kynaston, op. cit.,p. 115.

9. *Bournemouth Daily Echo*, 19 June 1946.

10. For details of the progress and challenges of rationing, see

Calder, *The People's War*, pp. 276–79 and 404–408, and Longmate, *How We Lived Then*, pp. 140–55.

11. Quoted in Allport, *Demobbed*, p. 119.
12. Frank Luff, Imperial War Museum Archive: No. 27267.
13. Kynaston, op. cit., p. 118.
14. *Daily Mail*, 1 June 1946.
15. *Daily Express*, 24 June 1946.

Chapter 2

1. *Daily Mirror*, 25 September 1946.
2. Nicholson, *Millions Like Us*, p. 144. Years later Christian Lamb called her memoirs *I Only Joined for the Hat* (Bene Factum Publishing, 2007).
3. Drummond, *Blue for a Girl*, p. 57.
4. Though 'jewellery, handbags, umbrellas and coloured finger-nails are not uniform. Make-up, if worn, must not be obvious.' Drummond, op. cit., p. 57.
5. Drummond, op. cit., p. 151.
6. Bigland, *The Story of the WRNS*, p. 183.
7. Yvonne Symonds' evidence at the trial is available in Critchley (ed.), *The Trial of Neville George Clevely Heath*. A handwritten document taken from her statement at Worthing Police Station on 24 June 1946 and her testimony at the Police Court on 20 July 1946 are held in TNA CRIM 1/1806.
8. Wyndham, *Love Is Blue*, p. 10.
9. Crisp, *The Naked Civil Servant*, p. 96. Crisp remembered discussing the attractions of men in uniform with Margery Gardner in the window seat of a cafe in the Kings Road and commented waspishly, 'I should have guessed that she was a born murderee. She used to wear a leopardette coat.'
10. See Francis, *The Flyer*, p. 21.
11. Simpson, *I Burned My Fingers*, pp. 115–116.

12. 'Character of Witnesses', 24 July 1946, TNA MEPO 3/2728.

13. Re. Panama Club, including club rules and layout, see Solomon Joseph, 28 June 1946, TNA DPP 2/1522. Heath had become a member under the name of Armstrong on 20 February 1946 and claimed to be living at the RAF Club in Piccadilly.

14. Edward Louis Barton, 1 July 1946, TNA DPP 2/1522.

15. *News of the World*, 29 September 1946.

16. Nicholson, op. cit., p. 104.

17. Wyndham, op. cit., p. 103.

18. Elizabeth Wyatt, 29 June 1946, TNA DPP 2/1522.

19. Barbara Osborne, 21 June 1946, TNA DPP 2/1522.

20. Ward Lock Red Guide, *Worthing*, p. 22.

21. Ibid., p. 4.

22. *Worthing Herald*, 5 July 1946.

23. Heath himself had little time for the pictures. 'The cinema is mainly a place to go when you want to sit down.' Dr Young's handwritten report, 6 December 1946, TNA P COM 9/700.

24. *Daily Telegraph*, 21 June 1946.

25. George Girdwood, 25 June 1946, TNA DPP 2/1522.

26. The building – complete with nautical frontage – remains and is now a Cornish pasty shop.

27. Angus Bruce, undated, TNA MEPO 3/2728.

28. John Charters Symonds, 24 June 1946, TNA DPP 2/1522.

29. There is no further trace of Yvonne Symonds in UK archives after 1947. When Major Symonds died in 1977, Yvonne's two children were living in Belgium, so she may have moved abroad to join her mother's family after Heath's trial.

30. The site of the Blue Peter Club still exists on the beach at Angmering, now occupied by an Italian restaurant.

31. This dialogue is taken from Yvonne Symonds' statement at Worthing Police Station, the evidence she gave at West

London Police Court and her testimony at the Old Bailey, TNA CRIM 1/1806.

32. Barratt was actually a superintendent.
33. *People*, 23 June 1946.
34. George Girdwood, 25 June 1946, TNA DPP 2/1522.
35. Yvonne Symonds, 24 June 1946, TNA CRIM 1/1806.
36. Percy Alexander Eagle, Worthing, TNA MEPO 3/2728.

Chapter 3

1. Margery's boyfriend at the time was Peter Tilley Bailey.
2. Typescript of both letters, TNA MEPO 3/2728.
3. Quoted in Adamson, *The Great Detective*, p. 162.
4. Reginald Spooner's report, 18 July 1946, TNA HO 144/ 22871.
5. 'Character of Witnesses', 24 July 1946, TNA MEPO 3/2728.
6. '"Borrowed" Car Chased Round Hyde Park', *Evening Standard*, 27 September 1945.
7. Ibid.
8. Ibid.
9. Elizabeth Helen Wheat, 22 June 1946, TNA MEPO 3/2728.
10. Wheat, *The Wheats of Sheffield*, p. 249.
11. Ibid.
12. Ibid., p. 250.
13. Letter from Margery Wheat to her parents, 15 March 1936, collection of Melody Gardner.
14. Elizabeth Helen Wheat, 22 June 1946, TNA MEPO 3/2728.
15. Letter from Margery Gardner to Mrs Wheat, undated (probably 1940), collection of Melody Gardner.
16. Lofthouse, *Then and Now, passim*.
17. Mathews, *Chelsea Old Church 1941–1950*, pp. 7–9.
18. 'Grantham Hotel Theft', *Grantham Journal*, 16 January 1942.
19. Ibid.
20. Elizabeth Helen Wheat, 22 June 1946, TNA MEPO 3/2728.

21. Author interview with Melody Gardner, 4 October 2011.
22. Marley (ed.), *The Daily Telegraph Story of the War*, p. 84.
23. The name V1 is an abbreviation of *Vergeltungswaffe Eins* or 'Revenge Weapon Number One'.
24. Gardiner, *Wartime*, p. 549.
25. Calder, *The People's War*, pp. 559–60.
26. Faviell, *A Chelsea Concerto*, p. 135.
27. 'Robot Plane Hits Nurse's Home: Children are Trapped', *Evening Standard*, 17 June 1946.
28. Letter from Margery Gardner to Mrs Wheat, 27 July 1945, collection of Melody Gardner.
29. Kynaston, *Austerity Britain*, p. 197.
30. Ralph Macro Wilson, 24 June 1946, MEPO 3/2728.
31. Letter from Margery Gardner to Mrs Wheat, 27 July 1945.
32. Daniel Hamilton Shields, undated, TNA MEPO 3/2728.
33. Ruth Wright and Mrs Hambrook, 25 June 1946, TNA MEPO 3/2728.
34. Wheat, *The Wheats of Sheffield*, p. 251.
35. Elizabeth Helen Wheat, TNA MEPO 3/2728.
36. Peter Tilley Bailey, 25 June 1946, TNA DPP 2/1522.
37. Further statement of Iris Humphrey, TNA DPP 2/1522.
38. Joyce Frost, 22 June 1946, TNA DPP 2/1522.
39. *A Streetcar Named Desire* premiered in New York in December 1947.

Chapter 4

1. Peter Alan Gardner, 22 June 1946, TNA DPP 2/1522.
2. Further statement of Joyce Frost, 30 June 1946, TNA DPP 2/1522.
3. Ibid.
4. Ibid.
5. Ibid.

6. Peter Tilley Bailey, 22 June 1946 and 25 June 1946, TNA DPP 2/1522. Tilley Bailey said he couldn't remember if this was Tuesday or Wednesday.

7. List of Exhibits Sheet 5, taken from 24 Bramham Gardens SW5 21 June 1946, TNA DPP 2/1522.

8. Joyce Frost's two statements, TNA DPP 2/1522.

9. List of Exhibits Appendix 2, found on armchair in Room 4, Pembridge Court Hotel, 21 June 1946. Property of Margery Gardner. TNA DPP 2/1522.

10. Gynomin advertisement – 'an approved method of family planning', *British Medical Journal*, 27 October 1951.

11. Eva Eileen Cole, 1 July 1946, TNA DPP 2/1522.

12. Mary Catherine Hardie, 26 June 1946, TNA DPP 2/1522. Catherine also stated that she had never met or heard of Margery before, so may not have been aware of the status of her relationship with Peter Tilley Bailey. As Margery perhaps suspected, Tilley Bailey would spend the night with Catherine Hardie at his flat in Coliseum Terrace.

13. Ronald Anthony Edward Birch, 25 June 1946, TNA DPP 2/1522.

14. Iris Humphrey, 22 June 1946, TNA DPP 2/1522.

15. Further statement of Iris Humphrey, TNA DPP 2/1522.

16. Phyllis Mary Brown, 28 June 1946, TNA DPP 2/1522.

17. Harold Harter, 22 June 1946 and further statement of Harold Harter, 27 June 1946, DPP 2/1522.

18. Some newspapers in the UK and abroad (e.g. *Cape Times*, 1 July 1946) reported that Margery left in Harter's taxi singing, 'I've got a date with my sweetie.' There is no evidence of this from any of the many witnesses who were present at the entrance to the club.

19. *Daily Express*, 25 June 1946.

Chapter 5

1. Adamson, *The Great Detective*, p. 161.
2. Ibid., p. 45.
3. Ibid., p. 57.
4. One of Spooner's superior officers, quoted in Adamson, op. cit., p. 274, claimed that Spooner 'was ridiculous with money ... it flowed through his fingers when he was in a public house. His one fault was that he drank too much.'
5. Adamson, op. cit., p. 116.
6. Ibid., p. 120.
7. '[Spooner] did not appreciate wildness and profusion even in his garden (his flowers were planted in rows, each tied to a stick whether it was necessary or not), and one day, after examining the luxuriant but straggly growth of a peony that Myra's sister Kathleen had given them, and which he had cut and trimmed without effect, he came into the kitchen and told Myra, 'You know, that kind of bush is an embarrassment in my garden.' Adamson, op. cit., p. 275.
8. Ibid, p. 124.
9. See Farndale, *Haw-Haw*.
10. Adamson, op. cit., p. 129.
11. Ibid., p. 159.
12. Quoted in Adamson, op. cit., p. 282.

Chapter 6

1. Rhoda Spooner, 25 June 1946, TNA DPP 2/1522.
2. Further statement of Barbara Osborne, 24 June 1946, TNA DPP 2/1522.
3. Further statement of Elizabeth Wyatt, 16 July 1946, TNA DPP 2/1522.
4. Alice Wyatt, 24 June 1946, TNA DPP 2/1522.
5. Frederick Averill, 2 July 1946, TNA HO 144/22871.

6. Reginald Spooner, 18 July 1946, TNA HO 144/22871.

7. Simpson, *Forty Years of Murder*, p. 126. Simpson's assistant, Jean Scott-Dunn, who was later to become his wife, was 'located under a hairdryer in Knightsbridge' when she was called by the police to attend at the Pembridge Court Hotel.

8. Finger and palm prints are available of Margery Gardner and the hotel staff, as well as photographs of fingerprints on the sink and door handle, TNA MEPO 3/2664.

9. Reginald Spooner's report, 18 July 1946, TNA HO 144/22871, and his review of the case on 2 October 1946, HO 144/22782.

10. Elizabeth Wyatt, TNA DPP 2/1522.

11. Barbara Osborne, TNA DPP 2/1522.

12. Further statement of Alice Wyatt, 18 June 1946, TNA DPP 2/1522.

13. Elsie Mary Ellen Thomas, 23 June 1946, TNA MEPO 3/2728.

14. Procter, *The Street of Disillusion*, p. 111.

15. According to Spooner's overview of the case on 2 October 1946, Heath told his parents that his wife had left him for another man thus 'breaking up' his life, TNA HO 144/22872.

16. Reginald Spooner, 22 June 1946, TNA DPP 2/1522.

17. Reginald Spooner, 1 July 1946, TNA MEPO 3/2728. The list of names, addresses and telephone numbers from Heath's address book are also held in MEPO 3/2728.

18. Reginald Spooner's report, 18 July 1946, TNA HO 144/22871.

19. Dr Keith Simpson, TNA DPP2/1522. Simpson was also to claim in *Forty Years of Murder* that Margery was a masochist: 'she liked being bound and gagged' (p. 127). Despite there being little evidence for this, Simpson quotes Casswell's erroneous assumption in his own autobiography of 1961 that 'a month before her death [Margery] had been in another hotel bedroom and had only been saved from possible murder

by the extremely timely intervention of an hotel detective. She had been heavily thrashed, and Heath was standing over her in an almost fiendish fashion.' This is fully discussed in Chapter 22.

20. Simpson, *Forty Years of Murder*, p. 124.
21. 'Confidential Memo to all News Editors', TNA MEPO 3/2728.

Chapter 7

1. 'Offensive Started in Belgium', *Evening Standard*, 7 June 1917.
2. Lloyd George, *War Memoirs,* Volume IV, p. 2110.
3. 'Great Battle Over Thames', *Evening Standard*, 6 June 1917.
4. Parents' report to the court, 8 July 1938, TNA P COM 9/700.
5. Letter from William Heath to Neville Heath, 5 October 1946, TNA HO 144/22871.
6. Letter from Bessie Heath to Isaac Near, 6 October 1946, TNA HO 144/22872.
7. Letter from William Heath to Neville Heath, 5 October 1946, TNA HO 144/22872.
8. Gerald Byrne suggests that the Heaths were descended from James Heath (1757–1834), the celebrated engraver to the court of George III. This is not correct, as the Heaths are actually descended from James Heath (1787–1868) of Rumbolds Whyke in Sussex, a much more humble ancestor.
9. See Gunby, *A Potted History of Ilford*, pp. 88–9.
10. Title of a 1924 book about the case by E. M. Delafield.
11. For further details of this case, see Weis, *Criminal Justice*.
12. See Percy Clevely's testimony in Young (ed.), *The Trial of Frederick Bywaters and Edith Thompson*, p. 18.
13. Weis, op. cit., p. xxix.

14. *People*, 29 October 1946.

15. From handwritten notes by Dr Young, senior medical officer at Wormwood Scrubs, following a 55-minute interview with Heath on 6 September 1946, TNA P COM 9/700.

16. Letter from Bessie Heath to Isaac Near, 6 October 1946, TNA HO 144/22872.

17. Report of Dr Young, senior medical officer at Wormwood Scrubs, 17 September 1946, TNA HO 144/22871.

18. See electoral registers for Merton 1932–1946, Merton Public Library.

19. Rutlish School Prospectus, 1933, Rutlish School Archives, Surrey History Centre.

20. Other than Heath, Rutlish's most famous old boy is former prime minister, John Major (1954–9). Foreword, Brock, *Rutlish School*.

21. 'A Tribute to E. A. A. Varnish' by A. J. Doig (1970), reprinted in Brock, op. cit.

22. Conference notes between inspectors from the Board of Education and the School Governors, 10 March 1933, Rutlish School Archives.

23. Brock, op. cit., p. 15.

24. 'The First Rutlish School Song' (1916), words: John Oxenham, music: James Edward Jones, quoted in Brock, op. cit.

25. See Brock, op. cit., p. 124.

26. Rutlish School Prospectus, 1933, p. 14.

27. Gibson, *The English Vice*, p. 38.

28. *Chums Annual*, Vol. 50, 1927–8, p. 94.

29. 'Boys' Weeklies' in Orwell, *Inside the Whale and Other Essays*, p. 91.

30. Ibid., p. 95.

31. Ibid., p. 100.

32. Arthur Jones quoted in Brock, op. cit., p. 85.

33. Rutlish Archive.

34. Brock, op. cit., p. 86. See also Cave, *Practical Exercises in Spoken English*, p. 3: 'The final aim of all speech-training must be to open the eyes of students to their own deficiencies, and to encourage them to speak clearly, accurately and attractively.'

35. Conference notes between inspectors from the Board of Education and the school governors, 10 March 1933, Rutlish School Archives, p. 2.

36. In his report to the court on Heath, 5 July 1938, Varnish wrote: 'No special aptitude. Good athletics ... always a bit unsteady, easily influenced and exerted an upsetting influence on others. Boisterous. Lacked steady concentration on particular work for any length of time. Inclined to exaggerate to the point of lying but believing in himself.' TNA P COM 9/700.

37. Casswell, *A Lance for Liberty*, p. 242.

38. 'The Son I Knew', Bessie Heath, *People*, 29 October 1946. The full text of this interview is given in Chapter 23.

39. Byrne, *Borstal Boy*, p. 14.

40. Byrne, op. cit., p. 16.

41. Playfair and Sington, *The Offenders*, pp. 42–4.

42. Byrne does not identify 'Jeanette's' father, but later mentions that Heath was advised by Evelyn Walkden (1893–1970), the trade unionist and later MP for Doncaster. Playfair and Sington claim that their source was a 'former Conservative MP', but Walkden was Labour. Given that it's unlikely for Heath to have known more than one MP who lived locally and that Walkden had a daughter (Vera) the same age as Heath, it's possible that 'Jeanette' was Vera Walkden. She was questioned by the police at the time of the murders but stated that she had not seen Heath for years.

43. Heath came closest to discussing sexual matters with Dr Young in their meeting on 10 September 1946. Young recorded that Heath 'denies any homosexual experience. Denies masturbation or attempts by others to masturbate

him. Says that he had no knowledge of sex until the age of eighteen – when pressed if he did not have some insight into it at puberty he denies it and says he does not think so – a frequent reply to many questions put to him.' TNA P COM 9/700.

44. 'Antecedents of Neville George Clevely Heath alias James Robert Cadogan Armstrong' compiled by Spooner, 20 August 1946. TNA MEPO 3/2728.

45. Pawson & Leaf's report to the court, 4 July 1938, TNA P COM 9/700.

46. *News of the World*, 29 September 1946.

47. 'I Cannot Believe I Did It', *Sunday Pictorial*, 29 September 1946.

48. Ibid.

49. Bishop, *Fighter Boys*, p. 45.

50. Ibid., p. 45.

51. Ibid., p. 46.

52. Ibid., p. 51.

53. *Biggles: The Camels Are Coming* by W. E. Johns, quoted in Bishop, op. cit. p. 52.

54. Beaton, *Winged Squadrons*, p. 45.

55. David, *My Autobiography*, p. 12.

56. Bishop, *Fighter Boys*, p. 59.

57. Ibid., p. 61.

58. Ibid.

59. Ibid., p. 60.

60. Ibid., p. 60: 'Flying fighters required a particular softness of touch. Horsemen, yachtsmen and pianists, the prevailing wisdom held, made the best fighter pilots.'

61. Ibid., p. 62.

62. Quoted in Byrne, op. cit., p. 18, though no source is given.

63. Capt. Allen MacNeil Dyson-Perrins, 16 July 1946, TNA MEPO 3/2728.

64. Letter re. Pilot Officer N. G. C. Heath No. 79 (Fighter)

Squadron, 3 August 1937, TNA AIR 43/10 RAF Courts Martial Book.

65. 'RAF Officer Not Guilty of Desertion', *Evening Standard*, 20 August 1937.

66. Ibid.

67. Minterne, *The History of 73 Squadron*, p. 23.

68. Kent, *One of the Few*, p. 45.

69. *Evening Standard*, 20 August 1937.

70. Ibid.

71. Ibid.

72. *Daily Mirror*, 21 August 1937.

73. Arlene Blakely, 27 April 1938, MEPO 3/2728.

74. *Daily Mirror*, 12 November 1937.

75. Ibid.

76. Heath's father then started a new job, managing Faulkner's, a hairdressing shop on the station concourse at Waterloo. This was one of a chain of hairdressing shops situated at various London railway stations which also sold locks, clothes and hosiery – last-minute purchases before taking the train.

77. *Daily Mirror*, 12 November 1937.

78. Probation officer's report, 6 July 1938, TNA P COM 9/700: 'Average intelligence and ability. Good general conduct apart from boyish pranks.'

79. Ibid.

80. Mrs Archdall, 24 March 1938, TNA MEPO 3/2728.

81. Letter from Leicestershire Constabulary to New Scotland Yard, 1 April 1938, TNA MEPO 3/2728.

82. Heath's parents' report to the Court. 8 July 1938, TNA P COM 9/700.

83. Metropolitan Police letter, 9 April 1938, MEPO 3/2728.

84. Brock, *The Life and Death of Neville Heath*, p. 110–11.

85. Handwritten note by Heath, 8 April 1938, TNA MEPO 3/2728.

86. Bulman was the name of an instructor who had taught Heath to fly at Leicester in 1935.

87. From a report of lady visitor I. W. Davies, 16 June 1938, TNA P COM 9/700.

88. Chaplain's remarks (Arthur Casey), 15 June 1938, TNA P COM 9/700.

89. Letter from Heath to the editor of the *Daily Mirror*, 15 June 1938, TNA P COM 9/700.

90. *Evening Standard*, 12 July 1938.

Chapter 8

1. Letter from Heath to C. A. Joyce, 8 October 1946, TNA HO 144/22872.

2. *Guardian*, 18 October 2002.

3. Byrne, *Borstal Boy*, p. 25.

4. Behan, *Borstal Boy*, p. 206.

5. Behan, op. cit., p. 211.

6. Letter from Heath to C. A. Joyce, 8 October 1946, TNA HO 144/22872.

7. Byrne, op. cit., pp. 25–7.

8. Heath's physical statistics at Hollesley Bay are in his borstal record, TNA P COM 9/700.

9. Byrne, op. cit., p. 25.

10. From the printed statement that Neville Chamberlain waved as he stepped off the plane on 30 September 1938.

11. Housemaster's report, 20 April 1939, TNA P COM 9/700.

12. Behan, op. cit., p. 219.

13. Ibid.

14. Anderson shelters were mass-produced, costing the government £5 each. They were issued to 1.5 million families in 1939 and to over 2 million by April 1940 when steel shortages brought an end to production. See Inwood, *A History of London*, p. 777.

15. 27 April 1939.

16. Housemaster's report, 19 July 1939, TNA P COM 9/700.

17. Confidential report by Mr Scott, Director of the Borstal Association, 23 August 1946, P COM 9/700.

18. Letter from Neville Heath to Mr Scott, 15 September 1946, TNA P COM 9/700.

19. Peggy Dixon, 9 July 1946, TNA MEPO 3/2728.

20. Confidential report by Mr Scott, Director of the Borstal Association, 23 August 1946, P COM 9/700.

21. Ibid., re. a letter from Heath, 17 July 1940.

22. *Sunday Pictorial*, 29 September 1946.

23. Norbert Thomas Gaffrey, undated, MEPO 3/2728.

24. This story of Heath's part in the raid on Fort Rutbah was told in the *Sunday Pictorial*, 29 September 1946: 'Every officer of the RASC who tried to take part in the war at this stage was classified as unsuitable – but they'd never let one leave the organisation.'

25. Hill, *Portrait of a Sadist*.

26. Coward, *Middle East Diary*, entry for 15 August 1943, p. 49.

27. Cooper, *Cairo in the War, 1939–1945*.

28. Robert Lees, 'Venereal Diseases in the Armed Forces Overseas (2)', *British Journal of Venereal Diseases 22* (1946), p. 163.

29. Imperial War Musuem Documents 286, private papers of G. C. Tylee.

30. Hill, op, cit., p. 78.

31. Ibid., p. 85.

32. Ibid., p. 18.

33. The rand was introduced in 1961.

34. Morton, *In Search of South Africa*, p. 209.

35. Wells, *South Africa*, p. 251.

36. One of the great and lasting images of South Africa during the war was the middle-aged soprano Perla Siedle Gibson, Durban's 'Lady in White'. Mrs Gibson stood at the docks,

singing rousing and patriotic songs to troop ships as they
left Durban Harbour. She sang throughout the war – popular
songs, anthems and sentimental ballads. For many troops,
she was an iconic maternal figure who represented the
warm welcome and emotional farewell they received from the
people of South Africa. (See Gibson, *Durban's Lady in White*.)

37. Walker, *A History of Southern Africa*, p. 251.

Chapter 9

1. Smuts' influence within the Allies was so strong that a plan was
   mooted in 1940 – and supported by George VI – that if
   Churchill were to die unexpectedly, Smuts would take his place.
2. Reader's Digest, *Illustrated History of South Africa*, p. 347.
3. Ibid., p. 352.
4. Bryant, *As We Were*, p. 82.
5. Ibid., p. 83.
6. Documentation Centre of the South African National
   Defence Force and Service Record World War 2, Pretoria,
   DSCO 5892.
7. DSCO 5906.
8. Morton, *In Search of South* Africa, p. 239.
9. Ibid., p. 300.
10. Elizabeth was a member of the Hardcastle Rivers family and
    not the Pitt Rivers family as was incorrectly reported in the
    British press at the time of the murders.
11. 'Heath's Ex-wife Tells of Runaway Romance', *News of the World*, 29 September 1946.
12. Peggy Dixon, 9 July 1946, TNA MEPO 3/2828.
13. Mr Scott's report, based on a letter from Heath, 5 March
    1943, TNA P COM 9/700.
14. *Sunday Pictorial*, 29 September 1946.
15. Harold Vincent Guthrie, undated, TNA MEPO 3/2728.
16. Ibid.

17. Lister, *The Very Merry Moira*, pp. 82–3.
18. Letter from Heath to Elizabeth Armstrong, 14 September 1946, TNA HO 144/22872.
19. DSCO 5941-2.
20. Letter from Heath's commanding officer to the director of Air Personnel, 8 December 1943, DSCO 5952.
21. Handwritten letter from Heath to the director of Air Personnel and Org. Pretoria, 18 March 1943, DSCO 5944.
22. Letter from C. J. Jooste, adjutant general, 19 April 1943, and another on 21 December 1943, confirming retention of Heath's services, DSCO 5951.
23. Letter from Heath to Elizabeth Armstrong, 14 September 1946, TNA HO 144/22872.
24. The fact that Heath had a different name and date of birth on his official documents will have helped this subterfuge.
25. Heath was seconded from the SAAF on 23 May 1944 and originally attached to No. 3 AFU South Cerney near Cirencester and the satellite station of Bibury until 15 August 1944. He was then posted to No. 13 OTU at Finmere until 29 September. On 4 October he joined 180 Squadron and was posted to Belgium, TNA MEPO 3/2728.
26. Quoted in Bishop, *Bomber Boys*, p. xl.
27. Ibid., p. xxxviii.
28. Wilson, *Men of Air*, preface.
29. Quoted in Bishop, op. cit., p. 61.
30. Fielding Johnson's statement was taken by Heath's solicitors some time before the trial but is undated, HO 144/22872.
31. Air Ministry, *Psychological Disorders in Flying Personnel of the Royal Air Force, Investigated During the War, 1939–45*, compiled by Group Captain CP Symonds and Squadron Leader Dennis Williams, London HMSO, 1947.
32. Beaton, *Winged Squadrons*, p. 39.
33. No category was allowed for psychopathic personality. This omission is highlighted in the report. Possibly in the light of

Heath's trial, it was considered that such statistics might be misinterpreted – presumably by the press – and that the psychopathic state would probably develop symptoms under one of the other headings anyway.

34. Air Ministry, *Psychological Disorders in Flying Personnel*: 'Even the most seasoned pilot may show that loss of confidence which, unless immediately treated, will end in a frank anxiety state. Suddenly, for some reason not obvious to the outsider, some minor accident, private worries, or even the awakening of a too lively imagination, may liberate a series of repressions.'

35. Wyndham, *Love Is Blue*, p. 188. Seventy-two million Benzedrine tablets were officially issued to the British military during the Second World War. See *On Speed: The many lives of amphetamines*, Nicolas Rasmussen, New York University Press, 2008, p. 71.

36. Quoted in Wells, *Courage and Air Warfare*, p. 200.

37. Nichol and Rennell, *Tail End Charlies*, p. 158.

38. Ibid., p. 158.

39. Bishop, op. cit., p. 160.

40. Ibid., p. 161.

41. Kershaw, *Never Surrender*, p. 277.

42. Beaton, op. cit., p. 31.

43. Bishop, op. cit., p. 163.

44. Kershaw, op. cit., p. 281.

45. Peter Godfrey in 'How I Met Neville Heath', quoted in *Master Detective* magazine, September 1990.

46. William Spurrett Fielding-Johnson, TNA HO 144/ 22872.

Chapter 10

1. 'Antecedent History of Neville George Clevely Heath alias James Robert Cadogan Armstrong' compiled by Spooner, 21 August 1946,TNA MEPO 3/2728.

2. Confidential report by Mr Scott, director of the Borstal Association, 23 August 1946, P COM 9/700.

3. Handwritten life story by Heath,TNA P COM 9/700.

4. From Heath's defence at Durban Magistrates' Court, 19 July 1945,TNA DSCO 5972.

5. *Sunday Pictorial*, 5 October 1946.

6. Elizabeth Armstrong in 'How I Met Neville Heath' by Peter Godfrey, quoted in *Master Detective* magazine, September 1990.

7. Desertion is quoted in the Armstrongs' divorce petition, 7 September 1945, National Archives Repository, Pretoria, 8044.

8. *Sunday Pictorial*, 29 September 1946.

9. See DSCO 5969, Magistrates' Court Documents.

10. *Sunday Pictorial*, 5 October 1946.

11. The relationship is also confirmed in a letter on 19 April 1945 from Mr Williams' solicitors in Nottingham, Browne, Jacobson & Hallam, to Captain Steele, the administration officer at South Africa House in Trafalgar Square, DSCO 5955.

12. Zita Williams, 6 July 1946,TNA MEPO 3/2728.

13. Letter from Browne, Jacobson & Hallam to Hayman, Godfrey & Sanderson, solicitors, 30 August 1945, Johannesburg, DSCO 6015.

14. 'Owing to the circumstances in which our client is placed, it is imperative that she should know the full position ...' DSCO 5955.

15. In a letter from E. V. H Mickdal to the South African Commissioner of Police, Witwatersrand Division, it was claimed that 'Armstrong was engaged or was about to become

engaged to a young lady in Durban, but on her hearing that he was a married man the engagement fell through. It is believed that the young lady concerned is a daughter of one of the Natal sugar magnates.' 27 July 1944 in TNA MEPO 3/2728.

16. Sir Edward Cecil George Cadogan (1880–1962) had been knighted in 1939 and had served in the RAF in the war.

17. Zita Williams, 6 July 1946, TNA MEPO 3/2728.

18. Mr Scott's report, quoting his own entry into the Borstal Association Official Record on 20 August 1945, p. 4. He ends: 'I can only suggest that there may be reasons for investigating the possibility of Heath being a schizophrenic type.' 23 August 1946, P COM 9/700.

19. Letter from Heath to Elizabeth Armstrong, 27 July 1945, National Archives Repository, Pretoria, 8029.

20. 31 July 1945, DSCO 5962/3.

21. Letter from L. Botha, director of the Queen's Hotel to Neville Heath, 11 August 1945, DSCO 5967.

22. Letter from Heath at the SAAF base in Roberts Heights, Pretoria, to Messrs Hayman, Godfrey & Sanderson in Johannesburg, 9 August 1945, National Archives Repository (NAR), Pretoria, 8035.

23. Letter from Heath to Messrs Hayman, Godfrey & Sanderson, 1 September 1945: 'Dear Sir, I am advising you that I have forwarded, signed, to Mrs Rivers, the document which hitherto I have declined to sign. This should enable my wife to obtain what she wants without difficulty ... Could you obtain consent from Mrs Rivers to renew the bail should the case be remanded for a further period ...' NAR, 8038.

24. On 30 August 1945 in the Supreme Court, Heath officially gave up his rights to his son: 'I furthermore declare that I consent to and have no objection to and Order being made by the above named Honourable Court depriving me of all

such rights of guardianship in respect of such minor child, and granting such rights to my wife . . .' NAR 8041.

25. Flight Lt. Chapman, DSCO 6005-6.

26. Major Donnelly, DSCO 6003-4.

27. Neville Heath, DSCO 5972.

28. Telex to intercept Heath's letters, 31 August 1945, DSCO 5974.

29. Heath's defence quoted in Chaplin's statement, DSCO 5976.

30. Flying Officer James Bainbridge Chaplin RAF, 7 September 1945, DSCO 5975.

31. In his letter of 15 November 1945 to the adjutant general, H. B. Wakefield, the Rivers' family solicitor Mr Friedman had also looked over the recent charges against Heath and concluded that 'quite frankly, he was extremely fortunate not to be found guilty, and it seems that he was given the benefit of the doubt in this case', DSCO 6012.

32. Charles Friedman, 27 July 1946, TNA MEPO 3/2728.

33. The court martial took place on 4 December, DSCO 6023.

34. Document issuing court martial, 13 December 1945, DSCO 6020.

35. See letter from E. E. Crowe at the Office of the High Commissioner for the United Kingdom, Cape Town, 16 February 1946, TNA MEPO 3/2728.

36. *New Statesman and Nation*, 27 October 1945, pp. 277–8.

Chapter 11

1. Kent (ed.), *An Encyclopaedia of London*, p. 42.

2. For a detailed inventory of the damaged buildings of London, see Kent, op. cit.

3. Beaton and Pope-Hennessy, *History Under Fire*, p. 45.

4. See Kent, *The Lost Treasures of London*, and Richards, *The Bombed Buildings of Britain*.

5. Chapman, *Madame Tussaud's Chamber of Horrors*, p. 215.
6. *The Times*, quoted in Kent, *The Lost Treasures of London*, p. 33.
7. See *The London County Council Bomb Damage Maps 1939–1945* edited by Ann Saunders with an introduction by Robin Woolven, London Topographical Society and London Metropolitan Archives, 2005.
8. R. S. R. Fitter, *London's Natural History* (1945), quoted in Inwood, *A History of London*, p. 810.
9. Kent, *The Lost Treasures of London*, p. 120.
10. See Prologue, p. 1–7.
11. Letter from South African Commission for the United Kingdom to Inspector Riggs, Wimbledon CID, 27 February 1946, MEPO 3/2728.
12. Metropolitan Police Enquiry Officers' Records, Royal Air Force, Bush House, Kingsway, 25 March 1946, TNA MEPO 3/2728.
13. After his arrest, Spooner had Heath's two log books examined under an ultraviolet lamp at Scotland Yard. This revealed numerous alterations in the records, claiming many more missions than Heath had, in fact, accomplished. These alterations had been done extremely skilfully, but the fingerprint bureau photographed the alteration on the first page of one of the log books, and this clearly showed the name J. R. C. Armstrong beneath that of N. G. C. Heath. These changes had all been effected by the use of chemicals. The most plausible explanation for the alteration of the log books is that during April and May, he was negotiating with various air-transport firms for employment as a pilot. Clearly his references would need to be in his own name if he was to avoid any enquiry into his SAAF connections, which had resulted in his being deported. See 'Antecedent History' compiled by Spooner, MEPO 3/2728. Photocopies of doctored log book entries are in TNA HO 144/22871.

14. Ralph Fisher, 26 June 1946, TNA MEPO 3/2728.

15. Muriel Frances Silvester, 5 August 1946, TNA MEPO 3/2728.

16. Jill Rosemary Harris, 23 June 1946, TNA MEPO 3/2728.

17. DS Cains' interview with the manageress of the Red Lion Hotel and various individuals at the Luton Flying Club, Luton Borough Police, 23 June 1946, TNA MEPO 3/2728.

18. Until 2028.

19. See 'Antecedents of Neville George Clevely Heath alias James Robert Cadogan Armstrong', compiled by Spooner, TNA MEPO 3/2728.

20. Lister, *The Very Merry Moira*, pp. 82–3. Lister claimed to have dated Heath between the murders of Margery Gardner and Doreen Marshall: 'The only thing that may have saved me is that I am blonde and both girls were brunettes.' This was repeated in many of Lister's obituaries when she died in 2007. Though she may well have dated him, it cannot have occurred as she suggests (i.e. in the days between the two murders), as Heath was on the run along the south coast after the murder of Margery Gardner.

21. Ibid.

22. Quoted in Byrne, *Borstal Boy*, p. 48.

23. Harry Ashbrook, 23 June 1946, TNA DPP 2/1522.

24. Heath had actually been discussing the purchase of some planes with an Arthur Coombes from Reading. Coombes had been convicted of nine air-traffic offences as well as charges for false pretences in 1939. He and Heath had discussed buying planes that cost between £695 and £5,500, even the cheapest of which was well beyond Heath's means, TNA MEPO 3/2728.

25. Reginald Spooner, 22 June 1946, TNA DPP 2/1522.

26. *People*, 29 October 1946.

27. *Sunday Pictorial*, 29 September 1946.

28. This was later quashed on appeal.

29. Leslie Terry, 25 June 1946, TNA DPP 2/1522.

30. 'Character of Witnesses', TNA MEPO 3/2728. Terry was known to be identical with Leslie Turkington, CRO No. 4888/25.

31. 'I Found Blood on My Hands', *Sunday Pictorial*, 13 October 1946.

32. Ibid.

33. *Sunday Pictorial*, 23 October 1946.

Chapter 12

1. Letter to R. Morgan at the Home Office requesting to intercept the post, 3 July 1946, TNA MEPO 3/2728.

2. Chief Inspector G. Carmill, 24 June 1946, TNA MEPO 3/2728.

3. Mr Macro Wilson also identified Margery from the contact sheet of photos that had appeared in the *Daily Express* on 24 June 1946, TNA MEPO 3/2728 60B.

4. Peter Alan Gardner, 22 June 1946, TNA DPP 2/1522.

5. 'Character of Witnesses', 24 July 1946, TNA MEPO 3/2728.

6. See e.g. Ronald Anthony Birch, 22 June 1946, TNA DPP 2/1522: 'I regarded her as a particularly quiet girl and have never seen her the worse for drink.'

7. Ralph Macro Wilson, 26 June 1946, TNA MEPO 3/2728.

8. Percy Alexander Eagle, 1 July 1946, TNA MEPO 3/2728.

9. Reginald Spooner, 25 June 1946, TNA MEPO 3/2728.

10. Lawrence Kelly, 15 July 1946, TNA DPP 2/1522.

11. Statement of DI Percy Alexander Eagle, items recovered from the Ocean Hotel Annex: '3 nails found under the sheet on the right hand side of the bed. 1 bed sheet covering the mattress on the bed, the sheet bearing marks of excrement on the right hand side and what appeared to be bloodstains on the left hand side' (DPP 2/1522). On 4 July, perhaps due to the evidence of blood and the presence of the nails, Spooner noted that 'although up to now [Miss Symonds] has not

admitted that any incident took place, I feel certain that it did' (MEPO 3/2728).

12. List of property taken by Detective Inspector Eagle from the Ocean Hotel Annex, Worthing, and Miss Yvonne Symonds, on Monday 26 June 1946, and handed to Sergeant Kelly, Notting Hill Police Station, the same day, TNA MEPO 3/2728.

13. *Daily Mirror*, 29 June 1946.

14. The letter was posted on 22 June 1946 and received at Scotland Yard on 24 June 1946, TNA DPP 2/1522.

15. *Evening News*, 3 July 1946.

16. *News Chronicle*, 26 June 1946.

17. Anonymous typed letter to the superintendent, Criminal Investigation Department, New Scotland Yard, 1 July 1946. The letter began: 'Why does not Scotland Yard publish a good photograph of the man ("Lt-Col") HEATH in the daily newspapers? If the public knew what he looked like it might save you chasing up false clues. On the other hand it might help to trace him' (TNA MEPO 3/2728).

18. Percy Alexander Eagle, 1 July 1946, TNA MEPO 3/2728.

19. *Daily Mirror*, 27 June 1946.

20. Trevethan Frampton, 22 June 1946, TNA DPP 2/1522.

21. Reginald Spooner's report, 19 July 1946 TNA HO 144 22872.

22. Re. the police petrol coupons, DS Frampton, 8 July 1946, TNA MEPO 3/2728.

Chapter 13

1. Closing speech for the prosecution in Critchley (ed.), *The Trial of Neville George Clevely Heath*, p. 210.

2. Ward Lock Red Guide, *Bournemouth*, p. 34.

3. Ibid.

4. Hardy, *Tess of the D'Urbervilles*, p. 491.

5. Ibid., p. 498.

6. Ward Lock Red Guide, *Bournemouth*, p. 41.

7. See Edington, *Bournemouth and the Second World War*, p. 105

8. Ibid.

9. The Americans dubbed Bournemouth without (apparently) irony, 'the Miami of Britain'.

10. *Bournemouth Echo*, 29 March 1944.

11. *Bournemouth Echo*, 10 June 1946.

12. *Bournemouth Times*, 8 December 1944.

13. *Sphere*, 7 September 1948.

14. Tollard Royal advertisement in *Bournemouth, Britain's All Season Resort: The Official Guide*, published by Bournemouth Corporation, 1946.

15. Violet Ruth Lay, 14 July 1946, MEPO 3/2728.

16. Jones, *Rupert Brooke*, pp. 110, 304.

Chapter 14

1. Ivor Arthur Relf, 23 July 1946, TNA MEPO 3/2728.

2. Ivor Arthur Relf, 10 July 1946, TNA DPP 2/1524.

3. Arthur James White, 10 July 1946, TNA DPP 2/1524.

4. Frederick Charles Wilkinson, 10 July 1946, TNA DPP 2/1524.

5. Charles Peter Rylatt, 15 July 1946, TNA DPP 2/1524.

6. Bernard Harold Tutt, 12 July 1946, TNA DPP 2/1524.

7. In her autobiography, *Stepping into the Spotlight: The ITMA Years* (Arrow, 1976), the Scots actress Molly Weir claimed that Heath tried to pick her up one afternoon in the restaurant at Bobby's Department Store in Bournemouth. 'The most noticeable thing about him were his eyes – blue and shining and full of a curious excitement' (p. 70). He asked her not to return to London that night but to stay with him in Bournemouth. Weir claims that this meeting took place just after 5 p.m. on Wednesday 3 July and that she, therefore, had had a narrow escape. If this is true (though it may be that Weir met Heath on another day) Heath must have met her

between having tea with Doreen Marshall at the Tollard Royal and having dinner with her there.
8. The two statements from Peggy (Margaret Clare) Waring are held in TNA MEPO 3/2728.
9. Peggy Waring's first statement, 7 July 1946, TNA MEPO 3/2728.
10. Ibid.
11. Ivor Arthur Relf, 23 July 1946, TNA DPP 2/1522.
12. Though Frederick Wilkinson the night porter had noted that Brook 'did not appear to have a lot of money. The only thing he paid for in cash was for after dinner drinks in the lounge. The rest of his expenses would be embodied in his bill.' Frederick Charles Wilkinson, 10 July 1946, TNA DPP 2 /1524.
13. Bernard Harold Tutt, 12 July 1946, TNA DPP2/1524.
14. The events of Saturday are all from Peggy Waring's second statement, 13 July 1946, TNA MEPO 3/2728.
15. Ibid.
16. Ibid.

Chapter 15

1. Alexander John Brough, 11 July 1946, TNA DPP 2/1524. Brough suggests that tickets No. 1012 and 1013 were purchased together by the same person, implying that at this point Joan was going to accompany her sister to Bournemouth.
2. *Daily Mirror*, 27 September 1946.
3. Email to the author from Julia Young concerning her maternal grandfather, Charles Marshall, 11 March 2012.
4. Bigland, *The Story of the WRNS*, p. 20.
5. Drummond, *Blue for a Girl*, p. 45. As Doreen had learned, even office routine and correspondence was different from civil practice. 'W.R.N.S officers must know that "Dear Sir" is not the mode of address in the Navy, neither is the

personal pronoun permissible. Instead, "It is requested that . . ."' Scott, *British Women in War*, p. 23.

6. See *The People's War* BBC website, www.bbc.co.uk/history/ ww2peopleswar/stories/48/a1153748.shtml

7. Charles Marshall, 13 August 1946, TNA DPP 2/1524.

8. Joan Cruickshanks, 10 July 1946, TNA DPP 2/1524.

9. Charles Marshall, 13 August 1946, TNA DPP 2/1524.

10. Elsie Isobel Jones, 10 July 1946, TNA DPP 2/1524.

11. George Wisecarver, 13 July 1946, TNA MEPO 3/2728.

12. Charles Marshall, 9 July 1946, TNA DPP 2/1524.

13. *Bournemouth Echo*, 3 July 1946.

14. Heath's statement, 2.45 a.m., 7 July 1946, witnessed by Detective Inspector George Gates. This statement was commenced at 11.50 p.m. on 6 July 1946, MEPO 3/2728.

15. Ibid.

16. Heinz Abisch, 13 July 1946, TNA DPP 2/1524.

17. James William Newland, 7 July 1946, TNA DPP 2/1524.

18. Sydney Walter Bush, 7 July 1946, TNA DPP 2/1524.

19. She actually arrived by taxi.

20. Heath's statement, exhibit 14, TNA DPP 2/1524.

21. Ivor Arthur Relf , 10 July 1946, TNA DPP 2/1524.

22. Heinz Abisch, 13 July 1946, TNA DPP 2/1524.

23. Detective Superintendent Lovell's report to the chief consta-ble of Dorset, Major L. W. Peel Yates, 18 July 1946, TNA DPP 2/1524.

24. Arthur Charles Marsh, 12 July 1946, TNA DPP 2/1524.

25. Winifred Marjorie Parfitt, 11 July 1946, TNA DPP 2/1524.

26. *Radio Times* Vol. 91, No. 1187, 28 June 1946.

27. Gladys Davy Phillips, 13 August 1946, TNA DPP 2/1524.

28. Arthur White, 6 August 1946, TNA DPP 2/1524.

29. Frederick Charles Wilkinson, 10 July 1946, TNA DPP 2/1524.

30. Ibid.

Chapter 16

1. Frederick Charles Wilkinson, 6 August 1946, DPP 2/1524.
2. Frederick Charles Wilkinson, 10 July 1946, DPP 2/1524.
3. Alice Hemmingway, 10 July 1946, DPP 2/1524.
4. Frederick Charles Wilkinson, 6 August 1946, DPP 2/1524.
5. Karl John Hambitzer, 12 July 1946, TNA DPP 2/1524.
6. Alice Hemmingway, 10 July 1946, TNA DPP 2/1524.
7. Harry Taylor, 11 July 1946, TNA DPP 2/1524.
8. Ellen Janie Bayliss, 10 July 1946, TNA DPP 2/1524.
9. Alfred Jesse Phillips, 12 July 1946, TNA DPP 2/1524.
10. Heinz Abisch, 13 July 1946, TNA DPP 2/1524.
11. Robert Donald Cook, 10 July 1946, TNA MEPO 3/2728.
12. Arthur White, 10 July 1946, TNA DPP 2/1524.
13. Ibid.
14. The address of Heath's former fiancée, Peggy Dixon.
15. Henry Walter Burles, 6 August 1946, TNA DPP 2/1524.
16. Gladys Davy Phillips, 13 August 1946, TNA DPP 2/1524.
17. Ivor Arthur Relf, 6 August 1946, TNA DPP 2/1524.
18. Stanley Lionel Pack, 13 July 1946, TNA DPP 2/1524.
19. Ibid.
20. Harry Berkoff, 6 Aug 1946, TNA DPP 2/1524.
21. Clive Eugene Miles, TNA CRIM 1/1806.

Chapter 17

1. George Robert Suter, 13 July 1946, TNA DPP 2/1524.
2. Email to the author from Michael Suter, 30 May 2012.
3. George Robert Suter, 3 July 1946, TNA MEPO 3/2728.
4. *Bournemouth Echo*, 5 November 1980.
5. This conversation is taken from Suter's witness statement.
6. Heath later said he was mistaken and that they had met in the morning.
7. *Daily Express*, 9 July 1946.

8. Ibid.
9. Leslie Ewart Johnson, undated, TNA DPP 2/1522, DPP 2/1524.
10. Leslie Ewart Johnson, undated, TNA MEPO 3/2728.
11. Initially he spoke to DI Wilfred Daws.
12. Email to the author from Michael Suter, 30 May 2012.
13. Leslie Ewart Johnson, TNA DPP 2/1524.
14. George Henry Gates, TNA MEPO 3/2728.
15. List of Exhibits Sheet 9 On Person – Heath. Removed by Bournemouth Police on 6 July 1946, TNA DPP 2/1522.
16. List of Exhibits Sheet 10, in jacket found hanging on clothes peg in Lounge, Tollard Royal Hotel, Bournemouth. Taken possession of by Divisional Detective Inspector Spooner on 7 July 1946, TNA DPP 2/1522.
17. Leslie Ewart Johnson, TNA DPP 2/1524.
18. George Henry Gates, TNA DPP 2/1524.
19. TNA DPP 2/1522.
20. The forensic laboratory in Hendon later confirmed that hairs on the scarf were from Margery Gardner's head and that this scarf had been used to gag her, possibly contributing to her suffocation.
21. Particulars of handkerchiefs traced to Heath's possession, 31 August 1946, TNA HO 144/22781.
22. Metropolitan Police Laboratory, Hendon, 11 July 1946, TNA MEPO 3/2728.
23. See Reginald Spooner's statement, 17 July 1946, TNA MEPO 3/2728.
24. Further statement of Harold Harter, 8 July 1946, TNA DPP 2/1522.
25. Reginald Spooner, 29 July 1946, TNA DPP 2/1522.
26. *Daily Mail*, 9 July 1946.
27. Adamson, *The Great Detective*, p. 177.
28. Newsprint clipping translated from Swedish: 'Record Bloodhound at Fault in Hunt for Lust Murderer', MEPO 3/2728.

Chapter 18

1. Kathleen Evans, 9 July 1946, TNA DPP 2/1524.
2. Francis George Bishop, 13 August 1946, TNA DPP 2/1524.
3. *News Chronicle*, 10 July 1946.
4. *Daily Mail*, 12 July 1946.
5. The description of the crime scene is in Detective Sergeant Bishop's and Crichton McGaffey's statements. McGaffey also includes his post-mortem report, TNA CRIM 1/1806. He first examined the body at the scene at 11 a.m. and the post-mortem was conducted at Poole at 2.30 p.m.
6. This seems unlikely as she would have been self-conscious of the sanitary towel she was wearing in anticipation of her period.
7. Bishop found this handkerchief that had probably been used to gag Doreen 15 feet to the west of the body. Bishop's statement, TNA P COM 9/700.
8. Clive Eugene Miles' statement, TNA CRIM 1/1806.
9. *Sunday Pictorial*, 13 October 1946.
10. Critchley (ed.), *The Trial of Neville George Clevely Heath*, p. 132.
11. 'Theory of Second Murder – A Defence for the First', *Daily Mirror*, 27 September 1946.

Chapter 19

1. Letter from Heath to Bessie Heath, 9 July 1946, TNA MEPO 3/2728.
2. Archives of the Solicitors' Regulation Centre, Disciplinary Hearing, 18 May 1951.
3. See Reginald Spooner's letter to Home Office, 18 July 1946, MEPO 3/2728.
4. Letter from Home Office to New Scotland Yard, 16 July 1946, MEPO 3/2728. See also correspondence re. the letter in HO 144/22872.

5. Letter from Heath to Leslie Terry, 11 July 1946, quoted in Byrne, *Borstal Boy*, p. 80.

6. 'Character of Witnesses', TNA MEPO 3/2728. Spooner further states that 'he is unscrupulous and may even yet endeavour to turn his association with Heath on the day of the murder against us, if given the opportunity'.

7. Heath's handwritten life story, TNA P COM 9/700.

8. Handwritten by the governor of Brixton Prison, 23 July 1946, TNA HO 144/22871.

9. Terry negotiated the deal with Hugh Cudlipp, the editor of the *Sunday Pictorial*. As the government had recently lifted the controls on newspaper rationing, Cudlipp felt that the story 'could be expected to sell unlimited quantities of papers'. Byrne, *Borstal Boy*, p. 78.

10. As well as friends and family, several women he didn't know sent him letters in prison and also corresponded with his mother.

11. *Sunday Pictorial*, 11 August 1946.

12. Letter from Heath to Isaac Near, 8 October 1946, TNA HO 144/22872: 'I definitely feel that the letter from Pinner requires no answer, unless there is a repetition. Then go for it!'

13. In 'Character of Witnesses', TNA MEPO 3/2728, Spooner says '[Terry] has been a frequent visitor to Heath in HM Prison, Brixton'.

14. Letter from Heath to Leslie Terry, 19 July 1946, quoted in *Sunday Pictorial*, 29 September 1946.

15. Brock suggests that Doreen's mother had the pen engraved for her, DPP 2/1254. Brock, *The Life and Death of Neville Heath*, pp. 110–111.

16. *Daily Mirror*, 7 August 1946.

17. Critchley (ed.), *The Trial of Neville George Clevely Heath*, p. 32.

18. *Daily Herald*, 25 September 1946.

19. See Casswell, *A Lance for Liberty*, pp. 197–222.

20. Casswell, op. cit., p. 242.

21. Ibid., p. 248.
22. Dr Young, 17 September 1946, TNA HO 144/22872.
23. Ibid.
24. Dr Grierson's assessment, 16 September 1946, TNA HO 144/22872.
25. See 'Antecedents of Neville George Clevely Heath alias James Robert Cadogan Armstrong', compiled by Spooner, TNA MEPO 3/2728.
26. Letter from Heath to Leslie Terry, 15 July 1946, quoted in Byrne, *Borstal Boy*, p. 84.
27. *News of the World*, 6 October 1946.
28. Ibid.
29. *Daily Express*, *Daily Mail*, 10 September 1946.

Chapter 20

1. Letter from Heath to Elizabeth Armstrong, 14 September 1946, TNA HO 144/22872.

Chapter 21

1. *Daily Mail*, 24 September 1946.
2. *Daily Herald*, 25 September 1946.
3. Ibid.
4. *Sunday Dispatch*, 22 September 1946.
5. 'Welsh Judge to Try Heath', *Western Mail*, 21 August 1946.
6. *Daily Mail*, 25 September 1946.
7. Ibid.
8. Ibid.
9. Ibid.
10. *News Chronicle*, 25 September 1946.
11. *Daily Mirror*, 25 September 1946.
12. Critchley (ed.), *The Trial of Neville George Clevely Heath*, p. 128.
13. Critchley, op. cit., p. 132.

14. Pronounced 'McNaughten'.
15. *Psychological Treatment of Criminals*, HMSO, 1938.
16. Critchley, op. cit., pp. 147–8.
17. Ibid.
18. Casswell, op. cit., p. 249.
19. Critchley, op. cit., p. 155.
20. Ibid., p. 150.
21. Questions to the jury, handwritten in pencil, 29 September 1946, TNA CRIM 1/1806.
22. Letter from Isaac Near to the Home Office, 7 October 1946, TNA HO 144/22872: 'Unfortunately, very shortly before the said trial, the witness in question sustained so severe a heart attack that he had to be removed to a hospital.'
23. Critchley, op. cit., pp. 187–8.
24. Ibid., p. 213.
25. Ibid., p. 218.
26. *Daily Graphic*, 27 September 1946.
27. Casswell, op. cit., p. 255.
28. *Daily Herald*, 27 September 1946.
29. *News Chronicle*, 27 September 1946.
30. *Daily Herald*, 27 September 1946.
31. Ibid.
32. Ibid.
33. Quoted in Garfield, *Our Hidden Lives*, pp. 284–5.

Chapter 22

1. TNA HO 144/22872.
2. *Sunday Express*, 20 September 1946.
3. Letter from Heath to Isaac Near, 2 October 1946, TNA P COM 9/700.
4. Casswell, *A Lance for Liberty*, p. 249.
5. Letter from Heath to Bessie Heath, 29 September 1946, TNA HO 144/22872.

6. Ibid.
7. For the investigation into the murder of Vera Page, see TNA MEPO 3/1671.
8. Florrie Porter is discussed in TNA MEPO 3/2728.
9. In a recent discussion of the case, Neil Root claims that 'the police files on Neville Heath ... have never been de-classified'. In actuality most of the Heath archives have been available for public study for some years. This author success-fully had the majority of the material in DPP 1/1522 and DPP 1/1524 released in 2011. Root also claims that the files were withheld because of 'an unconnected murder that remains unsolved'. The National Archives have restricted some information in the files but this is only in relation to the privacy of third parties. Contrary to Root's suggestion, there is no evidence that Heath was responsible (or even suspected) of any other murders than those of Margery Gardner and Doreen Marshall.
10. Reginald Spooner's report, 19 July 1946, TNA HO 144 22872.
11. Peter Tilley Bailey, 25 June 1946, TNA DPP 2/1522.
12. Further statement of Leonard William Luff, 26 June 1946, TNA DPP 2/1522: 'I have been shewn [*sic*] six photographs by Detective Sergeant Swarbrick. The woman in the large photograph and the woman on the seat with the child [i.e. the photograph of Margery Gardner and her daughter Melody] certainly appear to me to be identical with the woman I saw in Room 506 as described in my earlier state-ment [i.e. Pauline Brees].'
13. 'Hotel Detective Says – Margery Gardner Had One Escape', *News of the World*, 29 September 1946.
14. Casswell, op. cit., p. 239: 'It is almost certain that a month before her death [Margery] had been with Heath to another hotel bedroom and had only been saved then from possible murder by the timely intervention of an hotel detective.' As

has been outlined in the text and notes, this was definitely Pauline Brees and not Margery Gardner.

15. As recently as 2011, Neil Root suggests that Margery had dated Heath previously and that she 'probably knows it is going to be another wild night out, followed by extreme sex, which both of them enjoy'. There is no evidence for these assumptions (indeed, the contrary if Margery's friends, lovers and her husband are to be believed). Root is solely reliant on secondary sources with no original research and repeats many of the errors and questionable assumptions which have accumulated around the case over the preceding sixty-five years.

16. Pauline Brees, 27 July 1946, TNA DPP 2/1522.

17. Peggy Waring's second statement, 13 July 1946, TNA MEPO 3/2728.

18. Confidential report by Mr Scott, Director of the Borstal Association, 23 August 1946, P COM 9/700

19. Though he may have attempted to use the three nails on her – or himself.

20. This may be unlikely, as she knew she was expecting her period, as confirmed by her sister.

21. Reginald Spooner's report, 2 October 1946, TNA HO 144 22872.

22. Letter from Heath to Near, 2 October 1945, TNA P COM 9/700.

23. *Daily Mirror*, 27 September 1946.

24. *Daily Express*, 27 September 1946.

25. G. F. Nash of St John's Crescent SW9 wrote to the Home Secretary on 30 July 1946, asking 'If a description of this man and his mental condition had been widely and emphatically publicised in all probability the second murder would not have been committed. Why was it not? Because you think you know what's good for us?' TNA MEPO 3/2728.

26. *Daily Mirror*, 27 September 1946.

27. Ibid.
28. Quoted from Hansard, TNA HO 144/22872.
29. 'Heath Appeal Move Likely This Week', *Sunday Dispatch*, 29 September 1946.
30. Like Heath, True was educated at a grammar school and in the First World War had joined the Royal Flying Corps. In 1922 he murdered a prostitute, Olive Young. He then pawned her jewellery. At his trial, the prosecution relied on the M'Naghten Rules to prove that True was not insane in the eyes of the law. He was sentenced to death. The case was rejected on appeal, but the Home Secretary intervened and True was re-examined by three psychiatrists who all declared that he was insane. (See Carswell, Donald, *The Trial of Ronald True*, William Hodge, 1925.)
31. Letter from Heath to Bessie Heath, 30 September 1946, TNA HO 144/22872.
32. Letter from Heath to Isaac Near, 9 October 1946, TNA HO 144 22871.
33. Letter from Drs Norwood East and Hopwood to HM Prison Pentonville, 11 October 1946, TNA HO 144/22872.
34. Letter from Rosemary Tyndale-Biscoe to James Chuter Ede, 9 October 1946, TNA HO 144/22872.
35. 11 October 1946, TNA HO 144/22872.
36. Letter from Rosemary Tyndale-Biscoe to James Chuter Ede, 14 October 1946, TNA HO 144/22872.
37. *Sunday Despatch*, 13 October 1946.
38. *News of the World*, 6 October 1946.
39. Handwritten note by Mrs Van der Elst and message taken by a secretary at the Home Office after Mrs Van der Elst's visit, 15 October 1946, TNA HO 144/22872.
40. *Daily Telegraph*, 15 October 1946.
41. *Daily Mirror*, 15 October 1946.
42. Letter from Heath to Isaac Near, 14 October 1946, TNA HO 144/22872.

43. Pierrepoint, *Executioner: Pierrepoint*, p. 127.
44. *Bournemouth Echo*, 16 October 1946.
45. See 'Mrs Van Der Elst Fined', *Star*, 16 October 1946, and 'Heath Hanged: Crowd Mob Mrs Van Der Elst', *Evening News*, 16 October 1946.
46. Pentonville Prison directive from the governor, 2 October 1946, TNA P COM 9/700.
47. As well as Heath, Pierrepoint used this special strap on Haigh and Josef Kramer, the 'Beast of Belsen'.
48. Pierrepoint, op. cit., p. 129.
49. Chapman, *Madame Tussaud's Chamber of Horrors*, p. 222.
50. On the day of Heath's execution, Madame Tussaud's opened at 9.20 a.m. in order for the public to view the newest addition to the Chamber of Horrors. Though having had several changes of clothes in the interim, in 2013, the wax figure of Heath is still on display at Madame Tussaud's in London, standing beside George Joseph Smith and Dr Crippen.
51. Prison Medical Report, TNA P COM 9/700.
52. Pierrepoint, op. cit., pp. 129–30. Pierrepoint's description here is not specifically relating to Heath, but to an anonymous prisoner, but in recording it, Pierrepoint was attempting to describe a 'typical' execution as processed by him.
53. Prison Medical Report, TNA P COM 9/700.
54. Declaration of the Sheriff and Heath's death certificate signed by Dr Liddell, TNA HO 144/22872.
55. Adamson, *The Great Detective*, p. 179.
56. The fact that Heath had a double whisky just before he died is confirmed in the prison hospital records. There are several variants of Heath's last words including, '*Under the circumstances*, you might make that a double', TNA P COM 9/700.

Chapter 23

1. Between his arrest and execution, Heath's parents received hundreds of letters of sympathy from strangers. These prompted Bessie Heath to give this interview with Barry Halton, a reporter for the *People*. Mrs Heath did not accept payment for the interview: 'I could not make money out of my boy,' she told Gerald Byrne (Byrne, *Borstal Boy*, p. 79). At her request, a donation was made to the Royal Air Force Benevolent Fund.

Afterword

1. Beevor, *The Second World War*, p. 1.
2. Peter's widow, Kathleen, went on to commit suicide on 26 August 1961, taking an overdose of sleeping tablets.
3. Fabian, *London After Dark*, p. 59.
4. Author interview with Melody Gardner, 24 October 2011.
5. Author interview with Julia Young, 19 October 2011.
6. Adamson, *The Great Detective*, p. 280.
7. Ibid., p. 282.
8. Ibid., p. 179.
9. *News of the World*, 29 September 1946.
10. Ibid.

Appendix

1. All in TNA PCOM 9/700.

INDEX

(Page numbers in *italic* indicate photographs and captions)

Abisch, Heinz, xxiii
Abisch, Mr and Mrs, 280, 282, 283, 291, 292
Acid Bath Murderer, xviii
Adams, Reginald, 391
Aeroplane, 41
Air Force Girl, 24
Air Ministry, 52, 127, 135, 156, 177, 187, 189, 201, 230, 287, 367
alcohol consumption, 17–18, 97
Amazon Rooms, 166–7, 168
American Psycho (Ellis), x
Anderson shelters, 154, 274, 275–6
Anglo-American loan, 19–20
Anglo-Iraqi War, 161–2
Ann Summers, 246
Annakin, Ken, xii
Anne's Club, 231
Anning, DS Frederick, 93

Anschluss, 88
apartheid, 174–5
Archdall, Maud, 139–40
Armstrong, Elizabeth, xxiii
Armstrong, Elizabeth Hardcastle (wife), 178–82, 202–4, 207, 225, 227, 327, 337–9, 340–3, 393–4, 400, *458*
Armstrong, Lt James Robert Cadogan ('Jimmy'), 3–7, 35, 95, 173–99, 198, 223, 235, 308
Armstrong, Robert Michael Cadogan (son), xxiii, 180, 181, 184, 211, 327, 338–9, *458*
art scene, 50–1
Ashbrook, Harry, xxii, 228–9, 231, 240, 243, 355, 367
Atlee, Clement, 12
ATS, 21

Auster Aircraft Company, 259, 262, 263, 302, 306
austerity Britain, x
Austerity Britain (Kynaston), 19
Autax, 281
Auxiliary Territorial Service (ATS), *see* ATS
Averill, Frederick, 92–3
Aviation Club, 132

Bailey, Peter Tilley, *see* Tilley Bailey, Peter, 237
Baillie-Stewart, Norman, 88, 89, 147
Banham, A. J., 140
Barker, Walter (uncle), 145
Barratt, Supt Thomas, xxiii, 38, 93, 242, 309, 336
Battersea General Hospital, 73
Battle of Britain, 130
Bayliss, Ellen, 290
BBC, 87, 284
Beaton, Cecil, 127
Beau Geste, 162
Behan, Brendan, 150, 151, 153–4, 155
Bennett, Peter, 311
Bentley, Derek, 376
Bergman, Ingrid, 31
Berka, 165, 169
Berkeley Restaurant, 4
Berkoff, Harry, 295–6
Bernard, Oliver P., 2, *460*
Betjeman, John, 252, 276
B57, 86
Biggles, 126–7, 157, 160
Bilmar, James R., 140
Bilyard, Detective, 221
Birch, Ronald, 74
Bishop, DS Francis, xxiii, 315
Bishop, Patrick, 126
Bixley, William, xix–xx
black market, 19, 47, 175–6

Blackout Ripper, xviii
Blakely, Alan, 130
Blakely, Arlene, 130, 137, 140
Blakely, Grace, 130
Bligh, Jasmine, 12
Blitz (1940–41), 14, 15, 52–3, 71, 217–21, 241, *465*
Bloemfontein Hotel, 342
Blue Cockatoo, 51
Blue Dahlia, The, 31
Blue Peter Club, 35, 37, 234, 240
Blunt, Maggie, 359
Boer War, 174
Borstal, 149–56
Borstal Association, 155, 179, 185, 209
Borstal Boy, 150
Borstal Boy (Behan), 150
Borstal Boy (Byrne), xiii, 121, 150
Bournemouth Daily Echo, 277, 287, 297, *470*
Bournemouth Police, xxiii, 247, 293, 295, 297–312, 332, 347
Bournemouth Times, 258
Bourton House, 56
Bow Cinema Murder, 84
Bower, Norman, 372
Bowlly, Al, 25
Boyce, Arthur, 362
Boy's Own, 118, 125, 157
'Boys' Weeklies' (Orwell), 119
Brees, Pauline Miriam, xxii, 1–7, 75, 246, 320, 338, 356, 366, 368, 370
Brevet Club, 4
Brides in the Bath murders, 110
British Army, 13
British Civilian Services, 13
British Expeditionary Force (BEF), 62
British Museum, 219
Brixton, HMP, 327, 329–37, 336, 340, 383

Broadmoor, 336, 349, 372, 373, 378

Brock, Sydney, xiii, 96, 141–2, *470*

Brook, Gp Capt. Rupert Robert, 288–96, 298–312

Brook, Gp Capt. Rupert Robert ('Bobbie'), 256–7, 278–86

Brooke, Rupert, 256–7

brothels, 165–70, 205

Brown, Harry, 305

Brownell, Elizabeth, *see* Wheat, Elizabeth

Bruce, Angus, 34–5, 39

Bryan, Gertrude, 19

Buchan, John, 194

Buckingham Palace, 14, 15, 22, 391

Buller Barracks, 158

Bulman, James, 145

Bulman, Sgt, 127

Burles, Henry Walter, 292–3

Burley Court Hotel, 255, 260, 263

Burnside, Duncan, 198–9

Burt, Leonard, 86

Bush, Sydney, 281

Butlins, xiii

buzz bombs, 55

Byrne, Gerald, xiii, 121, 123, 150, 231

Bywaters, Frederick, xvi, xix, 108–10

Cadogan, Edward C. G., 208

Cadogan, Jimmy, 206

Cadogan, Sir Alexander, 262

Cain, James M., 31

Cambridge Police, 131

Cambridge University, 36, 120, 177

Cape Town Magistrates' Court, 213

Carlton Club, 208

Carter, Nick, 80

Casement, Roger, 110

Casswell, J. D., KC, xxiv, 120, 334–7, 344, 347–60 *passim*, 362–3, 366

Caterpillar Club, 23, 198

Cave, Herbert, 120

Central Flying School, Bloemfontein, 180

Central One ('Murder Squad'), 84, 85

Chamberlain, Neville, 153, 154

Chancery Lane Post Office, 140

Chapman, Flt Lt, 212–13

Charles, Mr Justice, xi

Chase, James Hadley, xvii, 194

Chelsea Old Church, 53

Chelsea School of Art, 50, 51

Cheshire Cheese, 231–2

Chesterton, G. K., 251

Cheyney, Peter, 194

Christie, Agatha, x, 244, 281

Christie, John, x, xviii, xix, 376, 389

Chums, 118–19

Churchill, Winston, xii, 11, 12, 15, 18, 161, 200, 388

City Club, 228

Claridges, 2

Cleavely, Rev. G. W., 373, 379

Cleft Chin Murder, 335

Cleft Chin Murder (1944), xvi

Clements, John, 227

Clevely, Bessie, *see* Heath, Bessie

Clevely, Percy (uncle), 109–10

Clevely, William, 105

Cock Tavern, 232

Cole, Eva, 72

Como, Perry, 25

Comyns, Mrs, 263

Conan Doyle, Arthur, 251

Condemned Cell No. 2, 362, 370

Connaught Hotel, 62, 166

conscription, 21–2

Continental Hotel, 163

Cook, Robert, 291
Cooper's Stores, 69
Court Number One, Old Bailey, xix, 344–60
Coward, Noël, 12, 163
Criminal Investigations Department (CID), 82–3, 93, 137–8, 221, 301
  Heath's letter to, 142–4
  South African, 182
Criminal Lunatics Act (1884), 362
Criminal Records Office, 96, 145
Crippen, Dr Hawley Harvey, xvi, xix, 110, 219
Crisp, Quentin, 24, 46
Critchley, Macdonald, xiv
Criterion Theatre, 109
Cromwell, Oliver, 218
Cruickshanks, Charles, 272
Cruickshanks, Joan Grace (née Marshall), xxi, 271, 272–4, 300–1, 316, 391, 392, *465*
Cummins, Gordon, xviii
Currie, Jack, 187

D-Day, 22, 253
Daily Express, 16–17, 41, 127
Daily Mail, 41, 96, 228, 236, 271, 331, 371
Daily Mirror, 41, 136, 138, 147, 228, 241, 323
Daily Telegraph, 32, 41, 152
Daily Worker, 361
Dale, F. V., 138, 139, 142
death penalty, 88, 89, 110, 111, 355, 372, 375–6
Debden Aerodrome, 134, 135
'Decline of the English Murder' (Orwell), xvi, 335
demob, x, xxiii, 2, 16–17, 21, 34–5, 62, 89, 228, 229, 258–9, 260, 263, 276, 298, 311, 407
Denvers, J. R., 140

desertion, 47
Desford, RAF, 127
Devonshire Club, 304
Digby (dog), 312
Dixon, Peggy, 158–9, 179, 241
Dog and Fox, 158
Donaldson, J., 140
Donaldson, Sir Gerald, 148
Donnelly, Maj. Erick, 212, 213
doodlebugs, 55
Dorset Constabulary, xviii, xxiii, 315
Downing Street, 153
Driscoll, DS, 145
drug-taking, 191–2, 349
Drummond, Edward, 348
Dudley, Lord, 137–8, 147
Dunkirk, 62
Dunsfold, RAF, 185, 188
Durban Club, 205–6, 210
Duxford, RAF, 129–30, 131, 132, *458*

Eagle, DI, 238–9, 245
East, Dr Norwood, 349, 373
East Ham Echo, 110
ecstasy (MDMA), 191
Ede, Chuter, 372, 374
Edgware Police, 145
Edward VIII, 117, 137
Elizabeth (friend), 122
Elizabeth, Princess, 14
Elizabeth, Queen, 14, 22
Ellis, Bret Easton, x
Ellis, Ruth, 376
Elms, Nina, 312
Elst, Violet Van Der, 376, 378, 380, *468*
Empire News, 121
Empire Training Schools, 187
English Vice, The (Gibson), 118
escort services, 141
Eton, 119, 120

Evans, Kathleen, 313–15
Evans, Timothy, 376
Evening Standard, 104, 136

Fabian of the Yard, 390
Falstaff, 4, 231
Fast, Howard, xv
Faulkner's, 97
Faviell, Frances, 56
Fear Walks Behind, 31
Feltham, HMP, 349
Ferdinand, Archduke, 48
Ferguson, Mrs Horace, 141
'financial Dunkirk', 19
Fielding-Johnson, Capt. William
    Spurrett, xxii , 188–98, 202,
    339, 355–6, 372
Fighter Boys (Bishop), 126
Film Guild, 57
Finmere, RAF, 206, 364
First and Last Loves (Betjeman), 252
First World War, 18, 23, 36, 82,
    104–5, 106–7, 117, 126, 257,
    334, 380
Fisher, Ralph, xxii, 223, 224–5, 332
flagellation, 118–19
Flare Path, 173
Flight, 41, 132, 229
Flyer, The (Francis), xii
Flying Visit, A, 24
Flying Wild, 24
food crisis, 16–18
Foster, Barry, xv
Frampton, Trevethan, xxii, 72,
    245–6, 247, 365
Francis, Martin, xii
Freed's, 295
Frenzy, xiv, xv
Freud, Sigmund, 118
Friedman, Mr (solicitor), 215, 337
Frost, Joyce, xxii, 64, 66, 68–70,
    238

Gaffrey, Norbert, 160–1
Gainsborough Studios, 141
Gardner, Margery Aimee Brownell
    ('Margy') (née Wheat),
    xxi, xxii, 20, 40, 41, 43–65,
    66–78, 220, 232–4, 301, 354,
    364, 365, *463*
  artistic skills of, 46, 49, 69
  birth of, 48, 49
  body of, discovered, 92–6
  brother visits in London, 63
  coming of age of, 50
  Daniel meets, 53
  daughter's still-birth, 52
  death of, 45, 78, 92–3, 95, 100,
    214, 235–47, 271, 307,
    309, 322–3, 336, 350, 359,
    366–8, 369, 372, 389–90
  education of, 49, 50–1
  evacuation of, 56
  Film Guild membership, 57
  financial situation, 61, 69, 70, 71–2
  homosexual friends of, 46
  ill health of, 57, 69
  Jimmy's relationship with, 67,
    69, 72–7
  'Julie' novel of, 77–8
  Ken's relationship with, 67
  kindergarten attended by, 49
  letters to Miss Talbot, 56–7
  letters to mother, 43–5, 46,
    59–60, 64
  marriage of, 45, 51, 53, 57–60
  Melody's premature birth, 54–6
  miscarriage suffered by, 63
  Moseley's relationship with,
    49–50
  mother's visits to, 63
  as 'Mrs Heath', 90–1, 95
  at Pembridge Court Hotel, 76–7,
    90–100, 235–6
  Peter Gardner's relationship
    with, 60–2

Peter Tilley Bailey's
　　relationship with, 63–4,
　　67–8, 73–4
police question, 47, 48
post-mortem of, 97–9
Ruth meets, 60–1
Gardner, Melody Ann, xxi, 56, 71,
　　389–90, 394
　birth of, 54–5
Gardner, Peter, xxi, 389
　birth of, 51
　Margery meets, 51
　Margery meets and marries, 53
　marriage of, 53, 57–60
　mental ill-health of, 53, 54
　stealing offences committed by,
　　53–4
　V Day party of, 66
Gates, DI George, xxiii, 304, 305,
　　307
gay men, 24, 46
Gedge, Harold, 379, 380
Gem, The, 118, 119, 126
George V, 132
George VI, 14
Gezira Sporting Club, 163–4
Gibson, Guy ('Dam Buster'), 126,
　　186, 194
Gibson, Ian, 118
Gilbert, Frederick, 19
Gillingham, William, 305
Girdwood, George, 33, 238–9
Godfrey, Peter, 198
Goodliffe, Sgt Dennis, 186
Gorse, Ralph (fictional character),
　　xiv
Gorse Trilogy (Hamilton), xiv
Grantham Quarter Sessions, 53
Grantham, RAF, 53
Grasshopper, HMS, 22
Great Expectations (Dickens), 131
Great Fire of London (1666), 219
Great War, *see* First World War

Great Western Hotel,
　　Southampton, 22
Grey, Lady Jane, 219
Grierson, Dr Hugh, xxiv, 336, 337,
　　338, 354, 356, 373
Guthrie, Harold, 181

H. J. Tuson's, 292
Haigh, John George, xviii, xix,
　　376, 389
Hambrook, Mrs (landlady), 61, 62
Hamilton, Patrick, x, xiv
Hammond, Kay, 227
Hangman's Clutch (Morland), ix
Hangover Square (Hamilton), x
Hannay books, 194
Hardie, Catherine, 73, 74, 75
Hardy, Thomas, 103, 252
Harris, ACM Arthur ('Bomber'),
　　186
Harris, Jill, xxii, 224–6
Harrow, 177
Harrow Observer, 270
Harter, Harold, xxii, 75–7, 99, 235,
　　238, 310, 346
Haw-Haw, Lord, xix, 87, 88
Hawke, E. Anthony, xxiv, 251,
　　336, 346, 350–1, 353, 354,
　　357
Haymarket Club, 35
Hearts of Oak Assurance
　　Company, 82
Heath, Bessie (née Clevely)
　　(mother), xxi, 97, 105, 109,
　　111–14, 121, 146, 159, 180,
　　223–4, 225, 229–30, 327, 361,
　　372–3, 376–7, 383–7, 397,
　　398–9, 400, *456*
　death of, 393
　marriage of, 106
Heath, Carol William Clevely
　　(brother), 111–12, 386
Heath, Lady, 36

Heath, Lt Col. 'Jimmy', 23–8, 90, 95–6
  'engagement' of, 26, 27, 30, 35
  Margery's relationship with, 67, 69, 72–7
  Yvonne engaged to, 36–7
Heath, Michael ('Mick') (brother), xxi, 112, 115, 230, 385–6, 397, 399
  birth of, 114
  death of, 393
  RAF career of, 393
Heath, Neville George Clevely, 6–7, 46, 96, 121, 363–4, *471*
  aliases of, 140; *see also* Armstrong, Capt. James Robert Cadogan; Brook, Gp Capt. Rupert Robert; Bulman, James; Cadogan, Jimmy; Dudley, Lord; Heath, Lt Col. 'Jimmy'; Selway, Capt.
  aristocratic identity created by, 137–8
  Arlene engaged to, 130, 137, 140
  arrest of, xi, 208, 214–15, 337
  associates of, xxii
  'B' licence sought by, 222–3, 225, 227–8, 230, 327, 367, 384
  Baillie-Stewart admired by, 88
  birth of, 103–4, 105
  books on, xiii–xiv, xiv, 120–1, 122
  in Borstal, 149–72
  Boy's Own attitude of, 118, 125, 157
  brother's death affects, 112, 386
  charming and charismatic nature of, xii, xx, 26, 141
  childhood of, 111–15, 384–5, *456*
  collective memory of, ix–x

court-martials of, 132, 134–6, 147, 169–71, 182, 206, 212–15 *passim*, 349
CV conjured up by, 114
death sentence handed down to, 360, 372
deportation of, 215–16, 217, 221
desertion charges against, 134–6
disappearing acts of, 133
education of, 113–21, 123–4, 385, *457*
Elizabeth divorces, 203–4, 213, 215, 225
Elizabeth marries, 178–80, 182
execution of, 377–9, 382, 393, *468*
film based on, xiv–xv
financial situation of, 132–4, 136–7, 139–40, 162–3, 168–9, 182, 204–6, 212, 222–3, 231
flight training of, 128–9
front-page news concerning, 40
guilty verdict of, 359
illegal-alien status of, 176, 182–4
Jeanette assaulted by, 122–3, 373
Jill meets, 224
'Jimmy' name adopted by, 180
joins SAAF, 177–8, 222
leaves RAF for good, 199
letters from, 142–4, 147–8, 149, 157–8, 160, 177, 181–4, 202–3, 209–10, 228, 233–4, 242–3, 245, 281, 327–8, 329, 332, 336, 340–3, 361, 396–400
life story of, 330–1
media frenzy surrounding, xv
memory loss of, 203–4, 205–6, 373, 383
mother's thoughts on, 383–7
'Nen' nickname of, 114, 328, 399, 400

novels and magazines requested
by, 331–2
in Palestine, *see main entry*
Peggy Dixon engaged to, 159,
179
Peggy Waring refuses marriage
proposals from, 264, 265,
268, 269
petty thieving and fraud of,
138–9, 144–6, 163, 182,
210–14, 243, 349
pilot training given by, 180, 186
playboy nature of, 80, 159
police hunt for, 99, 235–47, 261,
263, 271–2, 301–5, 306–7,
371
prison letters of, xix
as Prisoner No. 2059, 362
on probation, 138–9, 142, 146
psychological state of, xv, xvi,
105–6, 118, 124, 187–8,
187–201, 335, 346, 349–50,
355, 360, 367, 373–4
public fascination with, x, xiii,
xiv, xvii
RAF career of, x, xi, xii, 125–
44, 155–6, 158, 159, 178,
458
RAF tie of, 134, 345, 355, 380
RASC career of, 158–9
returns to England, 185–6
SAAF career of, 177–8, 182–3
sanity/insanity of, xv, xvi
Scott's correspondence with, 209
sex life of, x, xi, xiii
social-mobility ambitions of, 120
in South Africa, 170–2, 173–99
South African citizenship taken
by, 180
statement given by, 307, 308–10,
317, 328, 331
studio photographs of, 111
takes survivor's leave, 200–1

trial of, xiii, xv–xvi, 41, 339,
344–60, *469*
war decorations applied for, 221
wartime bravery of, 196–8
waxwork of, 380, *469*
in Wormwood Scrubs Boys'
Prison, 146, 147, 149
Yvonne meets, 229
Yvonne's virginity taken by, 29,
37, 41
Heath, William (father), xxi, 97,
105, 111–14, 124, 146, 159,
179, 180, 276, 377, 396, 398
death of, 393
marriage of, 106
Hemmingway, Alice, xxiii,
288–90
Hendon Aerodrome, 125
Hendon Police Training College,
38, 93, 242
Hendon, RAF, 401, 402
Henegan, Dr, 93
Herald, 41
Hertzog, James, 173
Heston Aerodrome, 153
H4, 162
Hickman, DI, 137–8
High Cliff Hotel, 255, 262
Hill, Paul, 163, 167, 168, 170, 172
Hitchcock, Alfred, xiv–xv
Hitler, Adolf, 219
Hoar, Reginald, 205
Hoard, Dudley, 84
Hodge, James, xiii, xiv
Hole in the Wall, 84
Holiday Camp, xii–xiii
Hollesley Bay, 149–72
Hollis, Dick, 34, 35
Holy Cross Convent School, 113–14
Home Office, xvii
Homicide Act (1957), xv
Hopwood, Dr (superintendent), 373
Horler, Sydney, 31

Hornung, E. W., xvii
Horse Guards' Parade, 14
Howard (friend), 122, 123
Hubert, Dr William, xxiv
Hubert, Dr William Henry de
    Bargue, 336, 337, 349–50,
    352–5, 363, 373
Hulten, Karl, xvi, 334, 334–5
Human Aggression (Storr), 313
Humphrey, Iris, xxii, 74–5, 75, 238
Humphreys, Travers, 110

Ilford Recorder, 110
Imperial War Museum (IWM),
    165, 401
Inanda Club, 171, 181
Inns of Court, 219
IRA, 150
Iris Products, 43, 44

Jack the Ripper, xviii, 323, 389
Jackson (chauffeur), 380
James, DI Thomas, 378
Jeanette (friend), 122–3, 373
Jeffries, Richard C., 140
Jessel, Mr (solicitor), 357
Joan (waitress), 25
John Lewis, Heath works at, 142,
    144
Johns, Capt. W. E., 126
Johnson, Amy, 126
Johnson, DS Leslie, xxiii, 301,
    302–4, 306, 308
Joint Air Training Scheme (JATS),
    177, 181
Jones, Elizabeth Marina, xvi, 334
Jones, Elsie, 277
Josephs, Solomon, xxii, 24, 25, 346
Joyce, Cyril A., 149, 151, 155
Joyce, William, *see* Haw-Haw, Lord
Jude the Obscure (Hardy), 103
'Julie' novel, 77–8

Kaleidoscope, xiv
Kearns, L., 99, 242
Kelly, Dr, 43, 44, 69
'Ken' (Margery's boyfriend), 67
'Kenilworth', 272, 276
Kent, Johnny, 134, *458*
Kerby, Fl. Off., 134
Keynes, John Maynard, 19
Killer Inside Me, The (Thompson),
    x
Kirk, Harry, 375, 377–9, 381
Knightsbridge Barracks, 66
Krafft-Ebing, Richard von, 118
Kynaston, David, 19

Ladd, Alan, 31, 278
Lake, Veronica, 31, 278
Lance for Liberty, A (Casswell),
    344
Lawrence, Gertrude, 22
Lawton, Mr (prison governor),
    362, 374, 379, 382
Lay, Violet, 256, 257
Le Mee Power, John, xxii, 74, 75
Lee, Norman, 31
Levy, Benn, xiv
Liddell, Dr James, 362, 373, 380,
    382
Life and Death of Neville Heath, The
    (Brock), xiii, *470*
Lindbergh, Charles, 126
Lister, Moira, xxiii, 181, 226–7
Lomax, Guy, 205
London After Dark (Fabian of the
    Yard), 390
London School of Air Navigation,
    222, 223
Lord Nelson, 60, 62, 63
Lordship Lane School, 81–2
Lovell, DS, xviii
Lowell, George E., 127
Luff, Leonard William, xxii, 1,
    3–4, 366

Luftwaffe, xii
Luton Flying Club, 223, 224, 226

MCA, xv
Macaulay, Rose, 217, 218
McFarlane, Mr (housemaster), 153, 155
McGaffey, Dr Crichton, xxiv, 315, 349
McInnes, Frank, 293, 294
McLindon, Elizabeth, 362
Macro Wilson, Ralph, xxi, 58, 236, 238
MacRobertson Air Race, 132
Madame Tussaud's, 219, 380–1, 391, 393, *469*
Maden, John, x–xi
Magnet, The, 118, 119, 126
Man No Woman Could Resist, The (Brock), *see The Life and Death of Neville Heath*
Manor House School, 49
Margaret, Princess, 14
Marples Hotel, 52
Marshal Soult, HMS, 21–2
Marshall, Charles, xxi, 272, 275, 276, 278, 294, 295, 300, 302, 317, 331–3, 391, *465*
Marshall, Doreen Margaret, xxi, 270–86, 331, 364, 365, 369, *465*, *466*
    death of, 316–23, 329, 332, 336, 349, 366, 389, 391, 392, *470*
    disappearance of, 291, 293, 296, 298–311, 314
    post-mortem of, 315–17
Marshall, Grace, xxi, 275, 331, 371, 391–2, *465*
Marshall, Joan Grace, *see* Cruickshanks, Joan Grace
Mary, Queen, 132
Masters, Percy, 144–5
Mathew, Theobald, 330

Maudsley, Dr, 109–10
Maudsley Hospital, 373
Maxted, Stanley, 15
Maybrick, Mrs, xvi
MDMA (ecstasy), 191
media and press coverage, xv, xvi–xvii, 13
Mediterranean Expeditionary Force (MEF), 159, 160
Men Only, 41
Mental Deficiency Act (1927), 354
Merchant Tailors' Hall, 219
Metropole Hotel, 254–5
Metropolitan Police ('Met'), xvii, xxiii, 6, 38, 46, 304, 312
Midsummer Day (1946), 20
MI5, 85, 87
Mildenhall, RAF, 132, 133–4
Miles, Clive, 296
Military Service Act (1916), 105
Military Training Act (1939), 154
Millions Like Us (Nicholson), 26
Mills & Boon, xiii
Milmo, H. L. B., 135
Milroy Club, 227
M'Naghten, Daniel, 348
M'Naghten Rules (1843), xv, 348, 349, 352, 372
The Modern Boy, 126
Molotov–Ribbentrop Pact, 156
Molyneux, Edward Henry, 22
Mooltan, SS, 163, 169, 170, 172, 182
Moore, Henry, 51
Moors Murderers, x
Morland, Nigel, ix, xiv
Morning Post, 134
Morris, Mr Justice, xxiv, 345, 346, 355–9
Morton, H. V., 179
Moseley (Margery's boyfriend), 49–50, 51
Moss Bros., 145

Munich Agreement, 153
'Murders' (game), 122
Mussolini, Benito, 160

Nag's Head, 26, 67, 69, 71, 72, 242
Naked Civil Servant, The, 24
National Archives, xvii–xviii
National Coal Board (NCB), 18
National Gallery, 14
National Service Act (1939), 156
National Service Act (1941), 21
nationalization, 18
Natural History Museum, 24, 70
Near, Isaac Elliston, xviii–xix,
    xxiv, 329, 339, 362, 373, 377
necktie murderer, xv
necrophilia, xviii
Nelson's Column, 14
New Scotland Yard, *see* Scotland
    Yard
New Statesman, 216
Newland, James, 281
Newman, Myra, *see* Spooner, Myra
News Chronicle, xii
News of the World (*NOTW*), 15
News of the World (*NOTW*), xvi
Nicholson, Virginia, 26
No Orchids for Miss Blandish
    (Chase), xvii, 194
Norfolk Hotel, 271, 277, 280, 281,
    283, 291, 294, 295
Norland Training Centre, 83
Normandie Hotel, 73, 233
Notable British Trials, xiii
Notting Hill Police, 40, 79, 92, 93,
    96, 233, 239, 245, 302, 309,
    310, 312, 322, 328, 332
Nottingham Petty Sessions, 138
Nottingham Police, 137–8
No. 2 Air School, 180
No. 62 Air School, 178
Nuremberg Trials, xviii

Observer, 152
Ocean Hotel, 32, 33, 35, 40, 41, 238
Oceanic Steam Navigation
    Company, 334
Oddenino's, 4
Odeon, Worthing, 31
O'Dowd, Desmond, 67, 68
Offenders, The (Playfair, Sington),
    122
Officer Cadet Training Unit, 159
'Officer in the Tower', 88, 147
Official Secrets Act, 88
Old Bailey, xi, xix, xxiv, 110, 146,
    219, 333, 334, 339, 344–60,
    362
  Heath's first time at, 148, 149
Oldham, Christian, 22
Olympic Games (1948), 12
Operational Training Units
    (OTUs), 187
orgies, 165
Orwell, George, ix, xvi, 119, 335
Osborne, Barbara, xxii, 29, 91–2
Overseas Club, 23, 25, 26, 27
Overture Repertory Players, 31
Oxford University, 120

Packenham Pub, 68
Page, Vera, 364
Palace Cinema, 84
Palestine, xviii, 124, 159–63, 168,
    168–9, 171
  Heath's arrest in, 162
  Heath's repatriation from, 169
Panama Club, xxii, 24–5, 73–6,
    233, 238, 239, 246, 310
Parfitt, Winifred, xxiii, 262,
    282–3, 284, 292
Paul, Thomas, xxii, 1, 3, 366
Pawson and Leaf, 124, 146, 220
Paxton's Head, 68, 69
PC 475 'J', *see* Spooner, DI
    Reginald

Pearl Harbor, 176

Peel, Sir Robert, 348

peep shows, 165

Pembridge Court Hotel, xxii, 27–8, 62, 90–100, 207, 229, 230, 234, 235, 238, 310, 367, *462*
murder at, 37–9

Pentonville, HMP, 362, 370, 373, 374, 378, 381, 396, 398, 399, 400, *468*

People, xi, 39

People's Day of Victory, 174–5

Perrins, Allen Dyson, 131

Phillips, Gladys Davy, xxiii, 262, 281, 284–5, 293–6

Phillips, Maj., 262, 284, 285, 291

Phyllis (waitress), 25, 75

Pierrepoint, Albert, 85, 375, 376, 377–9, 381–2

'pint-sized Romeos', 24

Pittard, Dora, 109

Playfair, Giles, 122, 123

P&O, 169, 182

Police Gazette, 99

poker, 28, 38

Police Gazette, 301

pornography, xiii, 85, 167

Porter, Florrie, 364, 365

Portman, Eric, 270

Portrait of a Sadist (Hill), 163, 167, 170

post-war anxiety, xi, xiii, xviii, 2–3, 12, 17–19

post-war crime, 46–7, 89

post-war immigration, 107

post-war morality, 47, 58, 61, 64

post-war sexual awakening, 24, 26–7, 58

Postman Always Rings Twice, The, 31

Power, John Le Mee, *see* Le Mee Power, John

Practical Exercises in Spoken English (Cave), 120

Price, Dennis, xii

Private Lives, 22

Procter, Harry, 96

Prophylactic Ablution Centre (PAC), 166

prostitution, 3, 4, 37, 46, 130, 165–7

Psycho, xiv

Psychological Disorders in Flying Personnel of the Royal Air Force Investigated During the War 1939–45, 189–90

Psychological Treatment of Crime, The (Hubert, East), 373

Purchase, Dr Bentley, 382

Queen Elizabeth, 86

Queen's Hotel, 205, 211, 212, 213

Radio Hamburg, 88–9

RAF Advanced Training Squadron, 129

RAF Police, 193, 214

RAF Training School, 127

'Raffles and Miss Blandish' (Orwell), ix, xvii

Rake's Progress, The, 103, 140, 278

Random Harvest, 203

rationing, 16–18, 47, 164, 175–6

Rattenbury, Alma, xix

Rattenbury, Francis, 334

Rattigan, Terence, x, 173

red-light district, 165–7

Red Lion Hotel, 53

Regent's Park Open-Air Theatre, 14

Relf, Ivor, xxiii, 259, 294–5

Renaissance Club, 72

rent boys, 165, 244

Rentoul, Sir Gervais, 47

Richards, Ceri, 51

Rigg, Tia, xi

Riley, James Whitcomb, 392

Ritz, 23

Rivers, Aileen (mother-in-law), 178, 211

Rivers, Charles (father-in-law), 178

Rivers, Elizabeth Hardcastle (wife), *see* Armstrong, Elizabeth Hardcastle

Rivoli, Worthing, 31

Roberts, William, 51

Rodean, 178

romantic novels, xiii, 24, *470*

Room 4, Pembridge Court Hotel, 38, 90–100, *462*

Room 506, Strand Palace Hotel, 1, 3, 5–6

Royal Aero Club, 132

Royal Air Force Air Display, 126

Royal Air Force (RAF), x–xii, 4, 13, 15, 20, 35, 39, 52, 53, 69, 73, 125–7, 142, 168–9, 177, 181, 259, *459*

   Bomber Command, xii, 186–7, 190, 198

   Fighter Command, 126, 130, 185–6, 190

   Heath dismissed from, 136–7, 138

   Heath's attempts to rejoin, 155–6, 157, 161, 185

   'Mae Wests', 194

   neuro-psychiatrists, 190–3

   Peter discharged from, 54

   psychological report commissioned by, 189–90

Royal Army Service Corps (RASC), 36, 158, 160

Royal Bath Hotel, 255, 260

Royal Canadian Air Force (RCAF), 255

Royal Courts of Justice, 219

Royal Drawing Society (RDS), 49

Royal Flying Corps, 104

Royal Hospital Infirmary, 53

Royal Hotel, 224, 225

Royal Naval Air Service (RNAS), 104

Royal Navy (RN), 13, 156

Royal Navy Volunteer Reserve (RNVR), 329

Royal Society of Medicine, 373

Royal Sussex Hotel, 144, 145

Russell-Cotes Museum, 255, 267

Russell Cotes Nautical School, 296

Rutbah, Fort, 162

Rutlish Cadet Corps, 117

Rutlish School, 115–21, 157, *457*

Rylatt, Peter, xxiii, 260–6, 280, 285

SAAF Police, 206

sadism, ix, xvi, xvii, xx, xxiii, 41, 98, 118–19, 120–1, 163, 167, 170, 270, 322, 337, 352, 357, 365, 368, 369, 370, 389, *470*

St Anselm's School, 237

St Clement Danes, 218

St George's Hospital, 56

St Giles Cripplegate, 218

St James's Palace, 14, 117

St Jim's, 119

St Mary Abbot's Hospital, 54, 56, 63

St Mary-le-Bow, 218

St Paul's Cathedral, 14, 179, 218, 220, 231

St Paul's Church, 124

St Peter's Church, 252

St Thomas's Hospital, 219, 349, 392

Sams, Fred, 152

Sandhurst, 88

Savoy Hotel, 5

Savoy Theatre, 5

Scoley, Lavinia, 115

Scotland Yard, xxiii, 40, 41, 82, 84, 96, 99, 142, 244, 304, 312, 317, 390, 392

Scott-Dunn, Jean, 93
Scott, Mr (Borstal head), 155, 157,
        159, 161, 179–80, 185–6, 209
Second World War, ix, x–xii, xi,
        xiii, xvi, xviii, 1–3, 2, 5,
        11–12, 14, 15, 16–17, 21–2,
        30–1, 45, 52–5, 104, 117, 125,
        153, *465*
    Bournemouth during, 253–5
    deaths caused by, 388
    end of, 217–21
    Normandy, 253
    Normandy landings, 55
    North African Campaign, 184–5
    outbreak of, 85, 88, 156–7, 175,
        188
    POWs, 169, 170
    Scapa Flow sabotage, 86
    sex trade during, 165
Secret Service, 85–9
Seddon, Frederick Henry, xvi, xix,
        110
Selway, Capt., 176–7
Seventh Veil, The, 203
sex and psychopathy, xiv
sexuality, xi, xiii
Shaw, Bernard, 171
She Wouldn't Say Yes and *Cornered*,
        31
Sheffield School of Art, 49
Sheffield Police, 236
Sheffield University, 48
Shelley, Mary, 252
Shepheard's Hotel, 163–4
Shepherd's, 4
Sherwood Inn, 137
Shields, Daniel Hamilton, Margery
        meets, 60, 61
Ship Hotel, 34
Shrapnel, HMS, 22
Silvester, Flt Lt Freddie, 194,
        195–7, 223
Silvester, Muriel, 223–4

Simpson, Dr Keith, xxiv, 93, 94–5,
        97–9, 346, 366
Simpson, William, 24
Sington, Derrick, 122, 123
Skardon, William, 87–8
Slim Callaghan novels, 194
Smith, George Joseph, 110
Smith, Mrs (witness), 246
Smuts, Jan, 174
Soldier, The (Brooke), 257
SOS Agency, 141
South African Air Force (SAAF),
        3, 4, 23, 28, 35, 36, 95, 177–8,
        182–3, 208, 210, 215
    Heath as Armstrong joins,
        177–8, 222
South African Civil Police, 214
Spanish Civil War, 184
Spellbound, 32, 204
Spilsbury, Sir Bernard, 93
spivs, emergence of, 19
split personality, 252, 270
Spooner, Alfred, 81
Spooner, Blanche, 81, 82
Spooner, DI Reginald, 93–9, 105,
        113, 226, 304, 306–11, 320,
        329, 337, 364–6, 369, 382,
        467
    death of, 392–3
    Flying Squad promotion of, 392
    hunts Heath, 236–47
    memo issued by, 99–100
    retirement of, 392
Spooner, DI Reginald ('Reg'),
        xxiii, 46, 79–89, 93
    as 'Britain's greatest detective',
        89
    career of, 82–5
    education of, 81–2
    first murder case, 84
    Intelligence Corps commission,
        86–9
    joins police, 82

Spooner, DI Reginald ('Reg') –
  continued
  lifestyle of, 85
  memoirs of, 80
  MI5 secondment, 85–6, 87
  Myra marries, 83
  Myra meets, 80
Spooner, Jabez, 80, 81
Spooner, Jean, 83, 85
Spooner, Myra (née Newman), 80,
  85, 86, 88, 393
  as Norland Nanny, 83
  Reg marries, 83
Spooner, Reginald, 6
Spooner, Rhoda, xxii, 29, 90–1
Spooner, Rodney, 81
Steele, Louisa, 364
Stone, DI James, 310
Stoner, George Percy, xix, 334
Storr, Anthony, 313
Strand Palace Hotel, xxii, 1–4,
  5–6, 221, 246, 320, 356, 366,
  368, *460*
*Strange Case of Dr Jekyll and Mr
  Hyde, The* (Stevenson), 252
Suez Canal, 160
Sumaria, SS, 216
Sunday Pictorial, xvi, 202, 331
Suter, DC George, xxiii, 293, 295,
  297–312, *467*
Symes, DI Shelley, xxiii, 79, 93,
  93–4, 97, 307–11
Symon, Anouska, 263, 264, 266,
  268
Symonds, Gertrude (née Werther),
  xxi, 35, 37, 40, 239
Symonds, Maj. John Charters
  ('Jack'), xxi, 35–7, 40, 239
Symonds, Yvonne Marie, xxi,
  21–42, 73, 207, 234, 240, 244,
  318, 320, 346, 369, *461*
  birth of, 36
  'engagment' of, 26, 27, 30, 35

Heath meets, 23, 229
'Jimmy' officially engaged to,
  36–7
lucky escape of, 41–2
as 'Mrs Heath', 27–9, 90–1
at Pembridge Court Hotel, 27–9,
  95
virginity of, 25, 29, 37, 41
in Worthing, 32–4
WRNS joined by, 21–3

Talbot, Miss (matron), 56
Taylor, Dr F. H., 373
Taylor, Elizabeth, xiv, 235
Ternent, Billy, 284
Territorial Army (TA), 62, 117,
  124, 128
terrorist attacks (1939), 150
Terry, Leslie, xxii, 231, 232, 234,
  330, 331
Thirty-Nine Steps, The (Buchan),
  370
Thomas, Donald, 168
Thomas, Mrs (hotel guest), 95–6
Thompson, Avis, 108
Thompson, Edith, xvi, xix, 108–11
Thompson, Jim, x
Thompson, Percy, 108–10
Tiddles (Peter's girlfriend), 59, 63
Tierney, Gene, 278
Tilley Bailey, Peter, xxii, 47, 63,
  67, 73–4, 75, 76, 365
  jailing of, 48
Times, 11, 219
Tindal, Lord Chief Justice, 348,
  349
Titanic, RMS, 311
Tollard Royal Hotel, xxiii, 255–6,
  259–69 *passim*, 280, 287–96,
  298, 299, 302, 305, 307, 308,
  312, 319, 321, 369, *464*
Torch Club, 73
Tower of London, 14

Trevor Arms, 66, 72, 73, 232, 234
True, Ronald, 372
tubercular meningitis, 111–12
Turf Club, 165
Turner, Lana, 31
Turton Jones, Squ. Ldr J. W., 132, *458*
Tussaud, Bernard, 380
Tutt, Lt Col., 267, 268–9
TV broadcasting, launch of, 12–13
Twelfth Night, 219
Tylee, Graham, 165, 166
Tyndale-Biscoe, Rosemary, 355, 373–4

Uncensored Life of Neville Heath, The (Byrne), *see Borstal Boy*
Uncle Tom's Cabin (Stowe), 118
Union Defence Forces (UDF), 174, 176
Uxbridge, RAF, 129

'V' Day, 12–16, 20, 31, 66, 225–6, 227, 362, *460*
VAD Nurses, 169
Varnish, Edward, 115–17, 120, 124, 146
VE Day, 2, 11, 58
Victoria and Albert Museum ('V&A'), 2, 70
Victory Celebration Party, 66
Vogue, 74
V1 attacks, 55, 56

WAAF, 21, 23–4, 154, 191, 255, 260
Wagh el Birket ('the Berka'), 165, 169
Walters, Mr (test pilot), 302, 306
War Office, 159
Ward Lock Guide, 30
Waring, Peggy, xxiii, 258–69, 278–9, 285, 368, 370

Wartime Economy Standard, 17
Wavell, Gen., 161
Welfare State, xii, 12
Wellgarth Nursery, 56, 57
Wellington Wendy, 24
Werther, Gertrude, *see* Symonds, Gertrude
West London Magistrates' Court, 47–8, 332, 334, *469*, *471*
Westminster Abbey, 14
Wheat, Elizabeth ('Betty') (née Brownell), xxi, 43, 46, 48, 49–50, 52, 57, 237, 389, 390, 394
Wheat, Gilbert, xxi, 46, 51, 52, 54–5, 62, 237, 389, 390, 394
Wheat, John Bristowe, 48
Wheat, Margery Aimee, *see* Gardner, Margery Aimee Brownell
Wheat, Robin, 49
whippings, 118–19
White, Arthur, xxiii, 259, 285, 292
Whitechapel Murders, xviii
Whiting, Margaret, 25
Wilde, Oscar, 110
Wilkes, Wg Cdr, 263, 264
Wilkinson, Frederick, 259, 286, 288–9, 349
Wilkinson, Frederick Charles, xxiii
Williams, Tennessee, 65
Williams, Tom, 16
Williams, William H., 206, 208
Williams, Zita, xxii, 95, 206–8, 215, 221, 241
Wimbledon Police, 221
Wimbledon School of Art, 115
Winchester, 119
Winged Love, 24
'wingless wonders', 24
Wisecarver, George, 277
Women's Auxiliary Air Force (WAAF), *see* WAAF

Women's Royal Naval Service, *see*
   WRNS
World My Wilderness, The
   (Macaulay), 217
Wormwood Scrubs, HMP, 86, 146,
   147, 149, 336, 349, 373
Worthing, films shown in, 31–2
Worthing Golf Club, 35
Worthing Herald, 31
Worthing Pier, 31
Wren, Christopher, 218
Wright, Ruth, 60
WRNS, xxi, 21–2, 25, 90–1, 154,
   206, 271, 272–3, 280, 283

reunion dinner (1946), 23
W7, 169
Wyard, Kathleen, 389
Wyatt, Alice, xxii, 27, 92
Wyatt, Elizabeth, xxii, 27, 28, 29,
   90, 92
Wyatt, Henry, 27
Wyndham, Joan, 23, 27, 191

Yeats, W. B., 257
Young, Dr Hubert, xxiv, 336, 337,
   354, 373
Youngsfield Army Base, 212